THE

REVISIONARIES

THE

REVISIONARIES

A NOVEL

A. R. MOXON

MELVILLE HOUSE
BROOKLYN
LONDON

The Revisionaries

Melville House Publishing
46 John Street
Brooklyn, NY 11201
and
Suite 2000
16/18 Woodford Road
London E7 0HA

mhpbooks.com
@melvillehouse

ISBN: 978-1-61219-798-2
ISBN: 978-1-61219-799-9 (eBook)

Library of Congress Control Number: 2019946231

Designed by archiefergusondesign.com

Printed in the United States of America

10 9 8 7 6 5 4 3 2 1

A catalog record for this book is available from the Library of Congress

This one is for Ben, who started it with me, and who is *why* it is as it is.

the top page

Once again, there have been changes, and not for the better.

"This is wrong," you mutter. As you enter, your eyes

leap to the usual place, and there they are, waiting.

Pages of revisions. The stack seems thicker.

You confirm the worst—a glance is sufficient—then retreat to the sofa. Thirty minutes pass, or perhaps an hour. You light another cigarette and stare at it. You keep perfectly still.

This is wrong, you think. Again, the vertiginous feeling of being lost in the fog, a lurching halt at the cliff's edge, toes adangle, perched on one's heels at the imperceptible cusp of an endless drop—Wrong? Whenever you come back to it, it's wrong. But this time, it didn't seem to have been tampered with, not at first… now, weighing the stack with your eyes, you wonder—are these changes yours? How to be sure? In the end, all you have is your own memory.

Finally, you lean forward. Keeping to habit, you check chronologically, from the bottom up, an inversion of an archeological dig. Peeking at the bottommost page, you wince—*that's* wrong—and you flip a hundred pages up, where it's worse still, carrying terrifying implications.

When you reach the top page, you

take a breath and begin to read.

To kill a man between panels is to condemn him to a thousand deaths.

—SCOTT McCLOUD, Understanding Comics

The act of encountering art is the only art.

—JORDAN YUNUS, Subject to Infinite Change

F L I C K E R

They cut all the loonies loose. They never told us why.

And if they told any of the loonies why, no loony ever told me. Which wouldn't be surprising, I guess. Despite all that time cooped up with them, I never spoke to the loonies much and they never spoke to me. I think once you hear my story you'll acknowledge that I was never really one of them. I was a moth caught in their butterfly net, pinned for a time to the same page, a stammering yammering mess, looking for my lost lad. It was because I joined with Father Julius right away, see, that I didn't come to traffic with them on the outside. He was the first person I met on the outside, Julius—a happy accident. Otherwise, I might have run with the loonies just for want of options, and then wound up in the same boat as them later.

Then again, look at the boat we're in now.

I expect the loonies were as confused as I was to get tossed out. I gathered the story later, on the outside. It was in all the papers. Politics. Some lady named Fritz with more clout than sense. At the time, I didn't care about any of it. All I knew was I was outdoors, looking for a roof over my head and a willing ear—that's how it was when I lucked into Father Julius.

x x x

"Loony Island" isn't a true island; civic planning composes its borders, not water. Still, as Father Julius sees it, it's earned the name. A forgotten wedge of a neighborhood, both hidden from the city and hidden by the city: long ago a secluded hill-perched purlieu of the rich overlooking the very center of the city and the interstate highway, now a forgotten place seemingly engineered for quarantine, cut off to the east by a steep bank leading down to the muddy Loony River, and embraced all around by a hard-to-negotiate concrete park of abandoned factories, and by the less permeable element of social indifference. At the north end, a public transport trestle runs (without stopping) west to east until it rolls over the Loony, a wide and turbid river carrying sticks and mud and alleged industrial waste south. At the "island's" southern point, the river runs beneath an interstate highway, making an acute angle. From this confluence, the highway carries cars (but never any cars from Loony Island, which is afforded no on-ramp) away to the southeast, or up north and west until it dips and runs beneath the transport trestle, completing a triangle—river and highway and trestle—from whose borders most of its denizens rarely if ever depart. Seen from the air by passengers on their way to somewhere else, its shape might briefly suggest an abandoned slice of hastily cut pizza—a slice partitioned into quadrants by two main roads, Apse St. and Transept Ave., and surrounded by a gray donut of shuttered factories. Cross-like, Apse and Transept intersect nearly exactly in the neighborhood's maudlin middle, escaping it through narrow gaps running beneath highway and rail—though not to the east; in Loony Island, no road reaching the river receives tunnel or bridge. If you have a car, making your way north or west is easy enough at first, but you'll find that these ways lead only into the rotted industrial ring, tailing off into lots that haven't seen a truck in years, designed to accommodate warehouse docks that haven't seen inventory for just as long. Transept's southbound course carries you out of the neighborhood—it's the only one that does—but you have to patiently follow a road that needlessly wends switchback down a hill of moderate grade before passing out of the factory district and finally—finally!—to a main thoroughfare connected to the rest of the city. If you don't have a car, you've got to hoof it for the bus stops (no buses' routes go out of their way for the Island), risking encounters with the bad sorts who lurk in narrow places and the dark parts of shuttered buildings, or who wait around curves—and the skeptical eyes, and the confident hands and elbows and knees, of bluebirds in their squad cars.

Most here don't have a car. Most stay put.

And, it must be admitted, some stay put not because of lack of transport, but because they aren't given any legal choice. Take, for example, the inmates of JAWPI—the Joan A. Wales Psychiatric Institute—"The Wales"—bones of steel, flesh of concrete, skin of brick, clothed in industrial green paint. A hulking rectilinear cracker box, it hugs Transept Ave. for unbroken city blocks in the southeast quadrant, some blocks south of the main intersection. The Wales is the most prominent building in Loony Island, and its presence might lead ruminative souls to question—is the placement of a loony bin here a sly joke by some waggish urban engineer? Was the neighborhood bequeathed its name because of its inmates, or did it gain inmates because of the nearby Loony River?

The majority of Loony Island's population lives in Domino City, six neglected high-rise urban housing complexes standing at surly attention west of the Wales on the other side of Transept. Identical gray concrete slabs filling most of the southwest quadrant, visible for uncomfortable minutes to commuters in cars gliding past on the highway. In Domino City, every building has a name and a gang, and each gang its own specialty and jurisdiction. They all used to war for dominance over one another, but that was years ago, before Ralph Mayor took control. Ralph's General & Specific is his store; a monopoly made inevitable by isolation. Ralph's is smaller than the Dominos but no less important to the criminal ecosystem, and you'll find it situated right at the central intersection. Ralph's got the goods, and Ralph's got the organization, and Ralph has managed to put the fear of Ralph into the heart of every other roughneck, so Ralph's is where business—any business—gets done.

Everything north of Apse is nothing but Checkertown: a tessellated patchwork grid of streets whose parcels hold century-old houses gone to sag and ruin or over-ambitious partition into apartments by absentee landlords, or burned-out vacant lots, or the occasional liquor store—and also Father Julius's Neon Chapel. The Neon, a large two-story building, its construction of a more recent vintage than that of its neighbors, is located on the north end of Checkertown, up near the rail. Leave the Neon and cross Transept, and you can bowl at Barney's Suds & Lanes, if you care to bowl. Few do, but there are still a few working stiffs who'll groove a ball or two down those flaking aisles—they mostly come up from Slanty's Cannery after shifts let off. Slanty's, the only factory inexplicably still open, operates in the southern tip of the "slice," hard by the river.

It's a lot to ponder, if you're the sort to ponder.

Father Julius, running in early morning light, passing from one errand to another, cresting the southern Transept switchback at a formidable pace, squinting as morning sun peeks out between buildings on his right, subconsciously avoiding open manholes and uneven sidewalks, can't help but ponder: What, exactly, *are* the implications of all this architecture? Settled into a haze of comfortable exertion, he considers a pet theory: the neighborhood as an assembly line, with insanity the product. It's not so hard to imagine. These brutalist buildings were built for efficiency and utility, after all, much like any factory system. He's seen too many in the neighborhood lose hope living in the gray slabs of Domino City, get initiated into the gangs—either as member or as customer or as product—and matriculate from there to the Wales or to prison, or from one to the other. Close your eyes, you can see it: the young, sluiced down the chute, sprayed with disinfecting insanity, and then, with factory precision, canned and packed and stacked away, first made systemically unsightly, then warehoused out of sight. Incarceration not an indicator of some breakdown in the system, you understand, but a function of the system working precisely toward intended purposes.

There's a lone gangster sitting on the sidewalk, abandoned by his fellows after a night drinking, bleary-eyed, carefully breathing himself sober. Miserable business, to be sure, but even in his headspun misery he turns his head to watch Julius chug by—impossible not to mark a figure like Julius, his beard a magnificent tangle edging without border into the unkempt jungle atop his scalp, the whole thicket framing the smiling white half-moon of his teeth and the brown twinkle of his eyes, his only garments the denim robe shielding his barrel of a body and the dirty sneakers anointing his boatlike feet—he's buff, vital, a creature swimming in the present, holding reliably to his routine.

The routine. It's the same every day. Father Julius has his errands and he runs from one to the next. If you're the type to rise early, you can watch for him. He's coming from the first errand—the secret one, the off-Island one. If anyone knows where it takes place, or what business is transacted there, they aren't talking, and neither is he. Now he's heading to the Wales, where he'll minister to the mentally ill—an attempt to fulfill the patients' innate need for non-clinical interaction. He reads whatever they request, which, when he's lucky, means romance or spy or mystery novels from the Wales' modest library, but which in practice almost always means reading the requesting patient's manifesto. "Recognize the gods offered Magilla the Gorilla for a reason," Julius might find himself proclaiming in his gravel truck of a voice, the patient listening enraptured by the novelty of hearing their own words marbling the mouth of another. "She freely admitted there were multiples, just as there are multiples of your favorite baseball heroes. Apes in particular may be Planet Earth's 'acceptable losses.' The Magilla model suggests you are many branches from enlightenment."

And so forth. Julius hopes for mystery novels.

He's running alongside the Wales now, coming up on it from the rear. As he rounds the corner, he pulls up startled, his way suddenly blocked by a fellow standing, skinny arms pointed to the sky, legs planted wide, taking up ample sidewalk. Julius avoids collision only through an admirable display of reflexes. They both scream shortly, once. Thus introduced, the two of them stare at each other, breathing heavily. Julius—nearly late for his appointed time at the Wales—is trying to manage a polite way around this blockade when the man, who's clearly working himself up to something, at last manages to speak.

"I'm!" he proclaims, emphatically.

"You're...?"

"I'm I'm I'm I'm I'm..."

Julius, who's now expecting to have to negotiate a panhandle, finds himself unsure if he's dealing with a stutter or some kind of crazy. The longer this recursion continues, the more it strikes his ears not as a word, but as something without meaning, the purposeless squawking of a giant flightless bird.

"I'm not ever going bah bah back to Pigeon Forge, Tennessee," he declares at last.

"That's all right with me," Julius says, keeping wary. It's a strange way for a panhandle to begin. This fellow is a skeletal jitterbug, large glasses askew on an angular face that hasn't seen a razor in days, and he looks frightened enough to be unpredictable, but there's also something categorically familiar about him...

"You don't have enough money to pay me to go back there, no captain, no sir." He salutes, bathrobe sleeve flapping, and Julius makes the connection. Of course—the bathrobe. White terrycloth tainted by the dinge of a thousand rides through an industrial laundry, pinstriped with pastels, the bathrobe is the standard-issue uniform of a resident of the Wales: a mental patient. A "loony," as they say on the street. It's the context that's thrown Julius—Why are you meeting a loony *outside* the Wales? On the heels of the question comes the probable answer: the Fritz Act. That's today?

The Fritz Act—so named for its sponsor, Regina Fritz, the district's representative, a one-time lobbyist and all-time socially connected mover and/or shaker, possessed of an iron will and given to what her critics call "butterfly philanthropy"—land quickly, drink shallowly, flit away. Fritz recently abandoned her previous bugbear (childhood obesity) to focus her considerable energies and resources wholly upon her new conviction: the notion that the mentally ill would be much better off roaming free—this after attending a screening of a recent popular film in which a cadre of escaped mental patients, therapist in tow, circumnavigate the globe in a hot air balloon. FREE BODIES, HEALTHY MINDS read the movement's T-shirts and bumper stickers; still initially Fritz found her fuss came to a fizzle, for while folks can be compelled to feel temporary sympathy for the incarcerated, it's a back-of-the-milk-carton concern, barely felt, easily expunged, evaporated by the third bite of cereal. People, it seems, generally view imprisonment as proof that the imprisoned deserve imprisonment. Fritz, frustrated, fulminated, but finally flip-flopped. Discreetly coached by political adjuncts, she tacked hard to starboard, making a successful appeal to pocketbooks, pulling the spotlight onto the scandalous burden placed upon the taxpaying public for unprofitable lunatic upkeep, millions (a metric she frequently pronounced with a distinct leading "b") in funds drawn from hardworking citizens—and for what? Do they ever get better? (This question was asked with enough rhetorical scorn that none ever thought to investigate the answer.) This time, the public outcry proved massive and enduring. As Father Julius learned, the cause of misappropriated funds proved trenchant enough to capture even the imaginations of apolitical beasts such as his criminal buddy, Daniel "Donk" Donkmien, who only yesterday snorted: "Fritz has it right, dipshit. My taxes should go where I choose, not to housing a bunch of potted plants scared of reality," et cetera. As if Donk had ever in his life paid taxes. Julius, wishing he'd thought to say this at the time, files it away for later use.

But now here's one of them, a freed loony, the first fruits of an idea so bad they just had to try it—and a talkative banana he is, too. He's starting in again.

"Na…na…na…na…"

Julius waits, fighting the urge to make impatient motions with his hands.

"Now I'm ow out they'll be on my tail again, no way they won't be. I know them. They've taken so much from me. They even took my boy. They'll pack me up in their boxes and never let me out, not ever."

"Sounds bad," Julius says, deliberately noncommittal.

"It's worse than *bad*," the loony insists. He clutches at Julius's sleeve, and the priest sees as the robe opens a dirty T-shirt underneath, a sticker attached to the right breast: HELLO, MY NAME IS, with *Sterling* scrawled beneath. "It's nigh unbearable. They took my boy and now he's run off and I know not where. After putting us in those boxes, I don't blame him for running. The thing you wouldn't guess about those boxes is the terrible lie light…"

Oh dear. This is something worse than a panhandler's needlessly complex hustle, for those at least build to some sort of termination point: the ask. No, this is the cousin to the panhandler pitch: the endless harangue, a self-fueled nightmare of pretzel logic whose only point is itself. A longtime city dweller, Julius has learned to recognize and move past this sort of thing instinctively, but this morning, startled by circumstance, his usual instincts ebbing after miles of exertion, he's made the fatal error of listening, and now he's trapped by social contract and his own well-honed posture of personal responsibility toward the lost.

"…after that, he just kept on digging to who-knows-where, and here I was left to fend. A veritable stray stranger in a strange land, and friend, let me tell you, this land is strange as they come…"

Looking past this unwelcome interloper, hopeful for some excuse for extraction, Julius notices emerging onto the block another, then yet another loony, stumbling into sight from around the far end of the Wales, and now it's a platoon of them, wandering, unhurried and uncertain—How many are there?—and meanwhile Sterling's still going.

"...that's why you've got to help me, friend. It's bad trouble coming. Those that snatched me are rye right behind me. I saw them. They're the same as snatched us in the fur first place!"

Julius considers him, unsure if the idea that's forming is expedience or altruism.

"Just I need a play place to stay is all I need. Just a place to duck into and lay low in until the heat passes by."

"Listen," Julius announces, and some quality in his voice—kind authority, perhaps—shuts the guy up. He points one big paw to the main intersection. "Make a right at the corner there and hold steady. You'll have to go about a dozen blocks, but eventually you'll find my chapel. You're welcome there."

"How will I know it?"

"It's covered in neon. You won't miss it."

"Is it open?"

"Never closed."

"I'll tell them you sent me."

"They'll take you whether you tell them that or not," Julius says, hoping not to have to accept this rather dubious credit. The brothers and sisters are good folk, and can be depended upon to do what's right, but they might not want to hear hours of whatever this guy has cooking. God, what if more of these loonies need a place? What if they all do? Down the street he can see maybe two dozen of them already. In the newspapers and on the TV news, the Fritz Act's sponsors seemed certain that the patients would return safely back to their beds at night of their own accord. The assumption had struck Julius as sensible enough when he read it in black and white, but now, confronted with the reality, it seems heedlessly optimistic. "If you hurry, you can probably get some breakfast," Julius suggests, and that does the trick; the skitterbug skates, his bathrobe flapping in the breeze like a misrigged sail, stumbling not once, not twice, but thrice, over jutting slabs of sidewalk. Fellow must be hungry, thinks Julius, breaking once again into his customary trot. As he rounds the corner so he can see the Wales' bank of front doors, what he sees pulls him up short yet again.

The Wales is leaking. It's leaking loonies.

Hundreds of them, and more still pouring out. It's a sluggish flow; more lava than liquid. This can't be what Fritz intended, can it? It's going to be a disaster. These loonies have no mission, no guide, no immediate purpose beyond the wide world itself. Presented with a million possibilities of un-regimented time and space, all with hints of unspoken rules and lacks of boundaries, they fold their hands, cluster together on street corners near-by, unnerved, huddled in the glow of their amalgamated imbalances, their bloodstreams packed with sedation, staring at their fingers and muttering to themselves. Look at them. JAWPI mostly handles longtime commitments, people who really need an institution's oversight, not short-termers. They're barely out and already they look as if they're counting the minutes until at last it's time to return. Their eyes are too open, too observant. Many look frightened. All appear directionless. Some sway, some rock, some harangue. Some amble to the nearest upright object and then clutch it or lean against it like a daytime drunk, like someone afraid of being pulled up into the sky. If we weren't Loony Island before, Julius thinks, we certainly are now. Who knew there were this many? Those that wanted a reader must have been the smallest percentage…it's a human ocean. The whole street's nothing but toothpaste pastel stripes on a terrycloth sea—but no, wait, not quite noth-ing. Scattered through the crowd, here comes something strange: a group walking with easy grace and quiet confidence. They're dressed in bright red tight-fitting clothing, foot to face, which makes them resemble monks or nin-ja. They carry two swords in sheaths on their backs. Some of them have one drawn—a blade of…wood, it seems—and for reasons unknown they swing their bokken as they walk, slippered feet precise as dancers', moving between the loons like farmers reaping invisible wheat, while others of them methodically corral the patients into small herds, inspect the face of each, then, apparently satisfied, release them. Father Julius decides to worry about them later—he's got a job reading to…glancing at the masses all around… to who exactly? Who's left?

"Fine, goddammit," Julius growls to nobody in particular, pushing his way toward the door against the outbound flow. "If there's even one person left in there, that's who I'm reading to, and if there's nobody, then I'll talk to the air."

Which is, he realizes later, pretty much what wound up happening.

Julius finds himself in the nearly deserted common room, a day-space almost passive-aggressive in its blandness. The long room is filled with an oppressive fluorescent light that refracts the tapioca sameness of the room back onto itself. On one end stands an orderlies' station and two heavy locked doors. One door leads to the bedrooms, the other outside to the visitor's lobby—though visitors have always been rare; a patient who still has potential visitors most likely wouldn't have been left here in the first place. At the far end, two shallow alcoves wing out, each containing a low wooden table and a pair of empty chairs. Nobody wants reading. Nobody wants anything. Nobody's here. They're out there. At a loss for what else to do, Julius leans against the counter of the orderlies' station, trying to start a chat with its only remaining inhabitant, though he's only half-successful; this orderly's attention is for her screen.

"Hell of a day."

"Day of hell. They didn't even do it the way they said they was doing it; they just did it."

"They…?"

"Management. They spent weeks training us. This whole routine. Five phases of release. Then we come to the day of the thing, and boom—first thing in the morning, they just throw the doors wide open. Right at shift change. Everybody out. No phases, no sense, and no patients."

Julius thinks of the languishing loons pooling all over the streets, uncertain and vulnerable. He's got an even stronger premonition now that something about the whole business is wrong. "Maybe we can get them back inside. I'll help. Where are the other orderlies?"

She gives him a mordant look. "*Gone.* They can read the writing on the wall. Loony bin with no loonies is a loony bin with no workers, either." She rubs her temples, staring out to the alcoves at the end of the room. Julius, naturally empathic, joins her gaze out into emptiness. In that moment, in one of the chairs in one of the alcoves, Julius sees something—a blink, like an apparition. A flicker.

"What the hell was that?" Julius demands.

"I didn't see anything."

"No? Watch. Watch right there."

The orderly follows the line of his finger, pointed at nothing at all. Sure enough, it blinks back. No—Julius can see it's not some*thing*. It's some*one*. A guy. He's flickering like a failing bulb. Huddled in his seat.

One knee hugged to his chest.

There. Gone.

Julius approaches the alcove slowly, as one might a deer in the woods. The man flickers in again and Julius shouts, points, looks back to the orderly, who only shrugs.

"You don't see that?"

"I see a chair. I see a wall."

Julius looks. The man is clearly visible now, right there. He's young, wide-eyed, his face hollow, his wrists thin. A skinny neck pokes from his misbuttoned light-blue pajamas. His thick short hair, unwashed, launches at odd angles from his head, as if attempting escape. "You really don't see that guy? Sitting right—" but no, dammit! he's disappeared again. She regards him warily, like he might be one of her chickens who's yet to fly the coop.

"You...*seeing things* over there?" she asks.

"I *did*. He's not there *now*." Knowing how it sounds. He waits, but the man doesn't return. In the place he'd been sitting, Julius canvasses, waving his arms and finding nothing at all.

"You know what?" the orderly says. "I've had enough of this Fritz bullshit today to deal with your bullshit. You go ahead and have fun. *I'm* getting off this 'Island' for good. Maybe I'll go downtown, to the library, where at least they make the crazy people stay quiet."

"No, wait! He might come back!"

But she's out the door.

Even more cautiously, the priest takes the seat opposite the one occupied by the flickering man, and waits. You're not crazy, Julius tells himself, and you're not seeing things. Wait for him to come back and then you'll know for sure. One appearance could be nothing but something caught in your eye, maybe an odd refraction of light. The second could be nothing more than some sort of trick you unwittingly played on yourself; your mind furnishing you with an established expectation of the original illusion. A third time, up close, with your mind settled, will serve to prove it.

Only…prove it to *whom*, Julius? Yourself? You just failed the corroboration game, and you failed it cold. The orderly—she was looking right where you were pointing and saw nothing—isn't that your proof? If he shows up again, isn't that actually proof, not that you *aren't* crazy, but that you *are*? Sitting in a psych ward, alone, looking at air and waiting to see something that isn't there, insisting to yourself you aren't crazy…what about that behavior strikes you as sanity?

But what if he's a vision?

What if he speaks?

Here on the Island, they know you as a man of faith. They've called you a man of miracles. Wouldn't it be nice if for once—just for once—those qualities were actually real? Wouldn't be nice if you actually felt you were what they all assume you are? Isn't it possible, Julius, that the reason only you can see this man is because only you are *meant* to see him? It seems possible, even likely, that this fellow may have some message for you, some answer to your unanswered questions, some secret method to impart that might loosen spiritual knots you've lived with so long you've given up trying to untie them.

Or—this new thought leaves Julius chilled—he might be nothing more than one of those visions your daddy chased to his bad end. Your father— didn't he think his visions were offering answers? Do you want your story to wind up like his? What if he had just ignored them? Wouldn't that have obviously been better for everyone? You should just go. Leave. It's not anything meant for you, there's no answer here, no message. It's not anything at all, any more than anything else is. You're a man of routine for a reason; hold to the routine. Think of those who count on you. They'll soon enough be waiting: Domino City shut-ins, agoraphobics, the Checkertown elderly and infirm, the single parents, the friends waiting for ministration from a friend. They won't mind if you come early but they'll worry if you're late, even more if you don't show at all.

Yes. You should go.

Eyes fixed upon the place he first saw the flickering man, Julius stays.

D E E P

The Fritz Act rollout went wrong from the start. Doubtless some part of it was mismanagement by the Joan A. Wales Psychiatric Institute. JAWPI was meant to cut the loonies loose, yes, and it must be admitted, there was a practiced lack of interest in the regulations for what might happen to them after, in favor of bottom-line savings. What *did* happen though...well, that was never planned for, even if in hindsight the ensuing madness seems inevitable.

There was no way the criminal element wasn't going to get involved, see. The Island was largely a criminal operation—still is—and on the Island, crime meant Ralph Mayor. Ralph himself I never saw, but I heard plenty. A kingpin in hiding, so powerful his name was enough to keep the gangsters in line. Everywhere you looked, you saw the shape he'd left behind. By my time, the "Mayor" of Loony Island had, like so many other officials, moved away from his constituency—although most of those others were elected. Mayor Mayor? He elected himself.

Julius's buddy Daniel "Donk" Donkmien ran it for him by proxy: the "deputy mayor," Ralph's indispensable appointed right hand—a sentimental appointment, some said, given what had happened in bygone days with Ralph's old partner Yale. Yale was Donk's big brother, long dead, and his death was ruled an accident—officially. All I know is, sentimental appointment or not, Donk ran it frighteningly well, and reported it all back to the boss.

All? Not quite.

Donk *claimed* he reported everything, sure, but Donk had eyes and ears that were also "off the books," so to speak. Just two eyes and two ears, just one informant, someone Donk knew from old times. But this wasn't just some paid mole or nosy neighbor tattling on disgruntled workers or power-hungry gangsters—he was Donk's man all the way. And skillful. It's no accident Donk's sneak was the first to discover that the Fritz Act was being used to front a larger plot, and it may be he sniffed it out even sooner than Donk wanted him to.

Because sure, Fritz may have gotten the ball rolling, and JAWPI may have been willing to implement—but the way it actually happened? That was all Donk, acting off the books and behind the scenes. He did it so secretly, most people never guessed it—and even though he told me about it direct, I still have to guess as to why.

Ralph may still be guessing for all I know.

✗✗✗

Sardines are naturally social animals, which fortunately makes the can less of a horror. In the sea they require large numbers of their fellows close about, the better to dash around confused predators; spheroid masses of silver darts piercing the blue, slipping past the poor flummoxed barracuda, who catches one of them just often enough that the toothy sap keeps trying. It's well known underwater that the barracuda is a big joke to the sardine—barracuda jokes are scrawled on the Great Barrier Reef from Sydney to Tasmania in slight silvery letters—yet the illiterate barracuda gets the last laugh, for when the fine-meshed net, that predator undodgeable, finally comes trolling, those little silver wiseacres are hoisted up into the dry choking void of upper space, where they die uncomplaining collective deaths, and where they shortly find themselves packed into mass graves, crammed closer to one another than barracuda teeth, billeted together by the thirties in low rectilinear tins, stacks of ten, three deep, eyes unblinking in the dark with only foul-smelling oil and their fellows as company.

A sardine who makes it to Slanty's conveyer belt has had it rough already. First, you've got the whole drowning thing. Add to that the horror of disorientation—the sky is absolutely terrifying to a fish. Then you're brought into the hold and frozen solid. Your eyeballs will never be the same. Once you're thawed, you get chuted onto the belt at Slanty's Cannery, and there your real troubles begin. Tiny knives remove your entrails. All of these knives used to be hand-operated, but now, depending on which belt you're shunted to, you may get machine-knifed, like Sister Nettles did. An ingenious suction device removes any remaining viscera, and you and the rest of your little silverdart chums are flumed down the line to your stamped, numbered, and bar-coded cell, stuffed alongside whomever is nearest until the tin is full. You're squirted with noxious oil serving as food coloring and preservative, and then the lid goes on. And then you wait, perfectly preserved. You might wait forever, subject to the vagaries of a capricious and cruelly ironic fate. For example: One can only assume thousands of sardine cans have been purchased through the years by sailors, and brought aboard merchant ships. It only stands to reason, then, that a few, a very few, of these tins must have slipped accidentally overboard, or their ship sunk beneath the waves, thirty sardines returned to their natural home without ever knowing it, all hoping through long preserved centuries, all waiting for the turn of the key, blinding light, mastication, oblivion.

All this goes through Boyd Ligneclaire's head as he slices the fish at the conveyor and sluices them down the chute, then uses a plastic suction snoot to whisk the entrails to parts unseen. His fingers work brainlessly, while his mind roams the deep sea. He's decided his work will begin with an epic tour-de-force written from the point of view of a sardine—from egg to can and then (herein lies the genius) *beyond the can*, into the great deceased with twenty-nine of his closest friends. They'll be one of those unlucky overboard cans on the ocean floor, and, as they wait, each tells their own tale. A piscine Canterbury! Not a novel but a poem! Which our main sardine records, Dante to a whole school of Virgils. The sea entire, encapsulated in that very can. *Sardine Descends*, the title poem in your collection, which will be nothing more or less than the entire Island mapped in poetry, told in ink on the page, captured between covers.

Think of the titles, then think of the poems. "Apse Street Blues." "Neon Chapel in Daylight." "Self-Portrait in the Blade of a Cannery Knife."

Boyd slices and suctions Boyd slices and suctions Boyd slices and suctions.

He rarely misses a fish. Nimble.

Those dexterous digits have kept him employed at Slanty's through grim layoffs, and this same dextrosity landed him his other paid gig—part-time, by far more lucrative, and brokered by Donk: information-gathering, spying, even the occasional burglary. Boyd prefers the burglary. High-end merchandise, highly technical thefts, no tracks left, no evidence created. In quick, out quick. The occasional picking of a particular prosperous pocket. The job at the cannery keeps the authorities from sniffing out the secret job, while the secret job keeps him flush. But his third occupation keeps him sane, sets him apart. Occupation number three is writer. Yes, the litterateur of Loony Island, the keeper of its flame, the immortalizer of its story, air father, the artistic sheen of the word made real in the flesh of the cranium, ah! It's occupation number three he lives for. It's his inner glory. It's his secret strength.

He's shit at it.

This is Donk's opinion, and as Donk's one of Loony Island's few readers, it should be Donk's opinion Boyd most values; however, in matters literary, Boyd remains unflappable. Donk expounds, but Boyd's expression alters little, and his confidence not at all. There's no arguing with Boyd. There's no *not* arguing with him, either, at least for Donk.

"You've written three pages in your whole life."

"Well." Boyd, leaning against a wall, striking what he hopes is a devil-may-care pose. "Three pages, yes. But. Three *perfect* pages."

"They're junk."

"You have an imperfect understanding of my intent."

"I'd hate to think I had anything approaching understanding of your mind."

"Someday, you'll sing a different tune. I'll join a writer's colony and make contacts." Boyd's conviction—that his preordained path to life as a famous and renowned author involves joining a writer's colony to make contacts—comes from well-thumbed copies of *Wheatgrass Tea*, a writers' and poets' periodical Donk gave him once as a gift (though, as Donk has frequently grumbled since, if he'd known it would turn Boyd into a *such* a goddammed poet, he'd never have done it).

The whistle sounds, ending the night shift. Boyd hits the locker room, exchanges fish-sloppy dungarees for civvies—aged jeans, white tee, leather jacket—and piles out the back exit with all the other cats, pondering rhyme schemes—Iambic? Iambic is classic; it has its appeal, but iambic is so military in its cadence, so rigid, so daDAdaDAdaDAdaDA-yadda-yadda-yadda. Iambic is railroad tracks, the speed limit, the Farmer's Almanac, poetry's good citizen. Iambic pays its bills on time. Iambic turns all the clocks back for Daylight Saving Time. Iambic will make a solid husband, but it ain't going to get laid on spring break. You may as well go with rhymed couplets while you're at it. Boyd preens a moment, fires up a smoke. Cutting across shuttered factory yards, ducking through the well-known gaps in fences, working through acrobatic rhyme schemes, trapezoidal metaphors—Come on now, Boyd, let's grab this poem by the balls, do it in an ABBCBAACB-CABDDDDDCDDDDA, something like that. They'll never see it coming.

Pulls out a battered notebook, jots: *rhyme scheme; grab balls.*

Ahead in the dim of dawn the dingy lights of Domino City twinkle, but for now he's enshrouded, a counterculture prophet, the Poet Unknown yet to be revealed. He pauses, savoring the romanticism, wondering if any of the lights spread before him glow from a room fated to be the next he'll break into, and what he'll take from that place. *Things I Have Stolen.* That'd be a good title for your memoirs, Boyd thinks, reclining into the comforting habit of imagining his as-yet-nonexistent career in retrospect. Suddenly it strikes him—iambic rhymed couplets, hmm…might they not be…*perfect?* So jejune, so out-of-fashion, might they not have come back around to be considered *avant?* The least-expected thing? *Sui generis?* Yes! Hoe. Lee. Shit. *Wheatgrass Tea* won't know what to daDAdaDAdaDAdaDAdaDO with itself! He claps his hands together once, Eureka!—pulls out the notebook, jots: couplets; *hoe lee shit*—then freezes.

Someone is standing nearby, staring at him.

It's still too dim to perceive features, but the interloper's tall and thin, and male, wearing a suit that shows up powder blue in the spots where the light reaches. Though his face isn't visible, Boyd knows the stranger's looking right at him. *Seeing* him. A little red coal dot dances up near the stranger's head. Boyd waits for this figure to move, but the stranger just stands, takes a leisurely drag of his cigarette.

Professionally stealthy, Boyd is unused to being seen, and certainly un-used to being seen *first*, in the creeping morning dark no less. The stranger makes no movement, no sound, no acknowledgment; he simply stands and watches Boyd and blows smoke. Unnerving as hell; Boyd's nape hair stands up. How to proceed? Run? Saunter past? Say "Howdy"?

The stranger speaks, very clearly.

"Boyd," he says.

"Do I know you?" Boyd asks—and oh mama, are his hackles prickly now. Something in this fellow's voice is…deep. Not low, but *deep*. It holds more secrets than an ocean trench.

"Do you know me?" the stranger replies. "Interesting question. No. I'd have to say you don't. But clearly I know you."

"Are you looking for a hire?" Boyd asks. The time to scamper is near. It's occurring to him—This might be one of the people you've burgled recently, Boyd. Somebody with fancy security who caught you on camera and has decided revenge is a dish best served right now. If you don't scurry, you may find yourself duct-taped to this guy's basement pipes, listening to the unmistakable sound of a bone saw being sharpened.

"I'm just checking in." He puffs, expels a wreath of smoke. "I've been 'checking in' on all sorts of people. But I haven't yet stopped by to see you, old friend. I've mainly been dealing with Gordy, and believe me, Gordy's a handful. An *armful*. It's kind of odd for me to see you like this—here, now—though I don't expect you to understand."

"I don't understand anything you've said so far, to be honest with you," Boyd says, edging back, getting ready to run.

"You're not going to run," the stranger remarks.

"Of course not," Boyd freezes again, gives what he hopes is a devil-may-care-and-not-at-all-hysterical laugh. "Why would I run?"

"Because you think I might hurt you. But I won't."

"I'd feel more confident about that if I knew your business."

The stranger says nothing for a while, then: "Curiosity. The itch of ages, the prime addiction, the killer of…" He stops and chuckles. "Hm. Probably the wrong idiom. I suppose I'd better tell you some things that might help. First, tell Julius he's got to make his move soon with the flickering man. He's got hours, not days. Second, you really ought to come check out what I'm standing on. You won't be sorry."

"Who *are* you?"

The stranger says what might be a word, or might be a name, and then, as if from a vertical crease running from the top of his head to his pelvis, the

Deep Man folds himself in half, then again, then again, reducing himself by halves until there's nothing there anymore. It's the damnedest thing.

Boyd stands breathing until his pulse reaches normal and his pelt smooths down. Then he gives a low whistle, his brain on-tilt and humming, desperately trying to catalogue the experience—There might be a story in it. Boyd wanders over to where the guy had been, searching for mirrors that might have been used to effect the trick. There was something about that guy. He was…he was…Boyd searches for the word.

Vivid? Yes. He was vivid. Even in silhouette, he was more present, more particular, more finely attuned somehow, than anything else Boyd's ever seen. As though he'd been provided an extra measure of reality; as though he'd been sketched with a finer-tipped pen, drawn by a surer hand. Boyd looks down at his own self, which seems real enough. It had been only in comparison with the stranger that he'd felt diminished—Oh yes, there's a story in this, if there's opportunity to tell it…tell Julius…hours not days…you know, you *should* tell Julius…stop over at the Neon in the evening at his barbecue, catch him after he gets back from his rounds…and then he, he *folded*? God, what a spookshow

Landrude…That's a name? Maybe a…title? You'll have to look it up in the dictionary.

Shaking himself all over as if to rid his skin of unwelcome pests, Boyd tosses the butt half-smoked and grinds it out with his heel, noticing at last the perfect circle upon which he's standing. It's a manhole cover—a remarkable thing in itself. Most of the manhole covers in the Island have long ago been filched and sold for the raw pig iron. Part of the neighborhood's theft epidemic, the manhole covers. Everything not nailed down. These days, moving around the Island requires a level of attention that recommends sobriety if you want to avoid a lost tire or a bad fall into raw sewage. But this manhole's cunningly concealed, painted approximately the same color as the pavement, hidden among the abandoned factories; it seems thieves and vandals have thus far overlooked it—Well, Boyd, are you a thief, or aren't you? Roll this sucker home.

He feels at his belt for the tiny zippered pouch—lockpicks, screwdrivers, glass-cutter, safe-cracking tools—and from this he draws a thin aluminum rod, folded up in thirds, which opens on locking hinges to form a tiny but sturdy crowbar. Inspecting closely, Boyd whistles appreciation: this lid appears to be a commissioned job, some art deco thing probably ordered by a local robber baron back in the industrial-boom times. An imprint Boyd's never seen before bears the legend:

LOVE FORGEWORKS, LLC
(Pigeon Forge Division)

There's a striking spiral pattern of corrugation around the edge, and upon the center the craftsman's etched a triptych of images: a blacksmith at his forge, a fountain, a pigeon by a stream. Damn, Boyd thinks, I bet I could hock this to an uptown collector for a thousand. He slides the sharp end of his bar into the pick hole and pushes hard, expecting the weight of iron, but to his amazement the lid lifts smoothly on hydraulic hinges. Wide brackets set into the wall at two-foot intervals down the hole form a ladder, leading to a complete lack of gloom.

Taking the first few rungs, Boyd blinks, snow-blind. He descends into a tunnel that stretches horizontally to indistinct dots in both directions. It's endless. There are no doors or branches, just this one artery. But it also looks new and well kept, as if the damn thing is recently built and modestly used.

What. The. Fuck.

As if today wasn't weird enough. And what had the vivid folding man said? *You'll really want to check out what I'm standing on.*

Why am I obeying a folding man, Boyd asks himself, climbing downward. Why, why.

G O D

Father Julius? You know him now—as much as you can *know*…but that's different. What can I tell you about what he was like *then*?

A priest, most said. A holy man, no doubt.

Was he a priest? He prayed a lot, but prayer isn't ordination. On Loony Island, it was a sort of open question. He didn't talk about his past with anybody, they said. I guess I know more than most, even if I only got to observe him for a short time.

Trying to think of something *priestly* he did…he didn't like the traditional duties of the frock, I'll say that much. Refused to take confessions, or hold mass, things like that. He was the kind of priest who ran everywhere he went. The kind of priest who wore a patchwork denim robe. He was the kind of priest you might find at the fights down by the dead factories, bobbing around in the middle of a screaming ring of drunken gangsters and factory workers, boxing for bets and knocking younger dudes into the dirt.

Wait. None of that's priestly.

Here's the sort of *holy* man Father Julius was: blessed. Someone drawn to lost causes. Someone who would risk his life for a stranger. He was the sort who'd make dangerous folk scared by placing himself bodily between the weapons they held and the targets they were aiming at. This, more than anything else, made the neighborhood gangsters come to love him. On Loony Island, a man who refuses to fear guns becomes, after a time, a kind of a threat, but a beloved threat. You *need* to shoot him, see, to maintain credibility—you point your gun, barrel right at his eye. But Julius isn't interested in your gun. He's interested in you. He's looking at *you*. Spooky shit. These gangsters posed tough, but most of them were kids. Nine times out of ten, they'd tuck the weapon and run.

Of course, that does mean one time out of ten, or whatever, they pulled the trigger. Naturally. It's impossible to disrespect guns and go unscathed.

I heard the stories. He got it once in the shoulder. Twice in the thigh. One bullet grazed his ribs. One clipped the tippy-top of his right ear. And even still, he seemed blessed by some higher power, whatever his denomination might have been. No arteries severed, no organs pierced. Not even a limp. He kept coming back, and the shooters, not understanding the reasons for their failure, faded away. Nobody remembers their names, they're nothing but shadows in the tales of Julius's survival. Skeptical? Plenty were. But you'd hear stories about this on the street, or at Ralph's. There was shame in backing away from a fight, but there was no shame in backing away from Julius. For them, it got so when the pistols came out, they'd hope for him.

So, yes, I guess you'd have to say Julius was a priest, or a holy man, or a guardian angel. Doubtless he served in those capacities right up to the so-called Loony Riot, and even a bit beyond. The night he first arrived on Loony Island he performed a miracle, they say—saved a whole mess of people dying in a fire—and then introduced himself as "Father Julius," no last name, so Father Julius is what he became. I can't speak to the miracle of the fire, but I can confirm one miracle.

He cured me of my stutter.

✗✗✗

Father Julius has learned that the most important thing about the flickering man is, don't reach for him—*that* makes him flicker right out.

There's no doubt anymore that something is happening; Father Julius has made himself sure on that count. Whether it's real or just something in his mind, it's repeating itself. He's tried timing the flickering man's appearances but there's no rhythm to it; this fellow, it seems, is no man of routine.

Julius no longer gives any thought to leaving.

He thinks about nothing else.

It's been the same psychological process each time over the last hour; the man flickers in, holds, flickers back out. Julius finds himself gripped by the certainty—yes, this is important. *Yes*, this is the revelation you've hoped for. *Yes*, this is, at last, something of faith that seems actual, physical, real. And then, just as regularly, the certainty—It's nothing, you fool. You're as crazy as they say, as crazy as your father was, as pathetic in your thirst for belief as you tell yourself you are in the dark each sleepless night. Then he stands, turns to leave, stops, caught teetering between fear and hope, turns, sits, and waits again. He's yet to get as far away from the flickering man's alcove as the abandoned orderly's station.

It's the partial invisibility that's hooked him. Total invisibility is nothing new, of course. Within the city, for example, Loony Island has become, in its way, totally invisible. The third world quarantined within the first is something that with enough practice you can choose not to see: a commuter's planned fascination with the skyline opposite or a preoccupation with the radio dial as you drive past, an undesirable but unavoidable diminishment of the available infrastructure budget buried on an inner page of the city newspaper's website. And the neighborhood, invisible already, is itself seemingly populated by people nobody can see. Crimes here go unreported and uninvestigated, deaths pass as unnoticed as the lives that preceded them, scavengers climb out of the neighborhood to stand beside off-ramps holding cardboard signs with overly detailed stories of need, which go studiously unseen by drivers and passengers until the green light frees them from their premeditated blindness, or until the bluebirds arrive in squad cars to chase the mendicants back within their prescribed boundaries.

But this occasional visibility holds a taste of the miraculous. He's either visible to you or he isn't. You can't see him, Father Julius is beginning to suspect, unless both of you truly want him to be seen. Slowly, collaboratively. Sometimes you see him, and it doesn't occur to you until after: "Hey now, wasn't there somebody *just sitting right over there?*" But he's gone already; a brief shiver-flash of movement evaporated into memory, and almost evaporated *from* memory. Julius is discovering it still takes effort to believe he's seen the fellow at all. Yes, that's it; when he flickers out, he forsakes perception retroactively, leaving ghosts of memory, much like a desired word or phrase perversely deleting itself from consciousness in the moment preceding utterance, leaving nothing behind except, first, the knowledge that a thing exists and was until the previous moment in one's possession, but now can only be apprehended conceptually; and, second, the unscratchable itch for the thing, the need to speak it aloud, if only to finalize a sentence left purgatorially half-constructed by its absence. Perhaps it isn't some physical property that he has, Julius theorizes, but rather something he does to you: a physiological matter—manipulation of the eye, of reflected light, retinas, rods, cones, vitreous humor—or else a distortion of the less accessible, the more liminal consciousness, a chemical rearrangement in the hidden folds of cerebellum, a microscopic fiddling in the density of the medulla's core.

In short, thinks Julius, it's a mindfuck.

But this effect lessens over time. Doesn't it? It's getting easier to see him now. Isn't it?

Julius waits.

When the man blinks in again, Julius doesn't even breathe. The man's hunched over the low table, making a bright green rectangle on a newspaper with a fat crayon, seemingly more concerned with texture than illustration.

The man looks up. He hands the newspaper to the priest. Other than the crayon scrawl, it's unremarkable. Julius underarms it.

The man's eyes are terrified. Terrified.

He says something that makes Julius feel as if all the air has gone out of him.

"God talks to me," he says.

"God talks to me." Again. More insistent than before.

And then a third time, a horrified whisper: "God talks to me.'

"What does God say?" Julius's mouth has gone dry.

"To do something bad," the man—almost a boy—mourns. "Something *bad*."

"Do *what* bad?"

But the flickering man vanishes.

Muttering in numb wonder and puzzlement, looking like the last loony out of the bin, Julius shakes his head as though he's newly woken, trying to clear his head of a particularly confounding dream. But it's not a dream, he knows. No, not a dream, but somehow still he's lost in it. He wanders the room, a man of routine, stumbling, head filled with a new and troubling mystery. *What did he say what what did he say*…You're in far over your head now. This goes well beyond whatever he's doing to your eyes and brain with his flickering body. Consider what he *said*. What's a priest supposed to do with *that*? An effect one can grow accustomed to with repeated exposure. A hint of God, tailored to your customized beliefs. A question of faith. Just wait for one more look at him and then you'll go. You need to clear your head; you need to talk to someone about this.

You need to talk to Nettles.

T U N N E L

No one ever dreamed of challenging Ralph. It seemed impossible; he himself was nowhere, but he had eyes and ears everywhere. He paid informants handsomely—and why not pay out flush? Ralph had amassed enough power to declare his store a vengeance-free zone and to enforce this edict across all gangs. In Loony Island, if you wanted to transact business and not get a machete in the neck—truly, if you wanted to transact business at all—Ralph's General & Specific was the spot. And, since Ralph had the only store that mattered, all the rats in Ralph's maze were going to buy their cheese from Ralph anyway, so any payout money, however generous, would find its way back into Ralph's pocket. Ralph controlled the food and the information, and, as gangs stopped fighting him, Ralph would reward them by not fighting *them*. This was Ralph's genius: conquest first through pain, then through fear of pain, and finally through relief from the fear of pain. In short, diplomacy.

And then he left.

By his fortieth birthday, he'd amassed a fortune without ever filling out a W2 or visiting a bank and decided to parachute off Loony Island into luxury and ease. Ralph bought a country mansion far out of town, a squad of vicious lawyers, a platoon of neckless goons, seven cars, twelve platinum chains, an ex-wife, some girlfriends, and some more girlfriends for the girlfriends. Such was the influence he wielded that under his command the five gangs, even with their leader in absentia, established their separate boundaries without any further turf war. This is power, Ralph once told Donk: When the cat's away, the mice behave.

But the totality of his dominance may have become a weakness. For example, it may be why, even though nobody knew what to make of the sword-carrying fighters in red when they appeared—pretty much the same time as they kicked us loonies to the curb—none of the gangs really said much about them. The idea of someone else staking a claim in Ralph's turf just seemed preposterous. Far more likely they were just some of Ralph's people on an unknown mission.

Besides, everyone reasoned that if there were anything untoward, surely Donk would have said something.

x x x

The tunnel's cylindrical, save for a narrow flat surface, and large; the ceiling is too high for Boyd to reach. It's not quite the pure straightaway it initially seems; it bends and curves so you can't see the whole distance, which only adds to the sense of being lost in a blizzard. Here and there black ladders present themselves from far off, and in all the endless whiteness it seems to Boyd more as if they come to meet him than the opposite. The rungs, sheathed in rubber, are set in the wall, and lead up to more manhole covers, or to platforms from which doors can be reached—secret accesses into and out of the neighborhood. There can be found, across from some of these ladders, open doorless portals leading into empty rooms, also pure white, with elevator doors set into the far walls. The ladders are marked; tiny white letters are set into the rubber—HUDBLDG 1, HUDBLDG 4, HUDBLDG 6— those might be the Dominoes…and now most of them seem to have to do with the Joan A. Wales Psychiatric Institute: JAWPI–W WING; JAWPI–CAF, JAWPI–ADMIN, JAWPI–E WING…the realization of the scope of infiltration this tunnel represents begins to settle its entire weight upon Boyd—The knowledge the builders must have. The time this has taken. The energy. The expense. How long this must have been happening, right beneath all our collective noses. And you had no idea no idea none…or, what if…? What if Ralph knows and *Donk* doesn't? Paranoia's a spicy morsel; one touch to the tongue and it spreads fire through the whole mouth. Boyd's starting to give himself entirely up to it when he sees something interesting in the far distance, suggesting a terminus: a silver spot resembling a steel vault door. The burglar in him stirs. Unconsciously, Boyd reaches one hand to the pouch on his belt, feels the reassuring presence of his tools. What treasures, he wonders, might belong to a thief who cracked a vault that big, hidden this deep…?

Boyd pads along as quick and silent as he's able. You are absolutely insane, he keeps telling himself without ever quite stopping. Soon the circle looms ahead. There's a rectangle emblazoned in the center of it, some flag he doesn't recognize: red field with a thin dark-blue stripe along the right side. In the center, a blue circle; described within, three white five-pointed stars. A placard below this insignia reads:

LOVE FORGEWORKS, LLC
(Sevier Division)

There's no combination, no handle, no mechanism suggesting tumblers. Out of Boyd's bag comes an instrument like a stethoscope, which he plugs into a mechanism with a tiny display. The radio telescope can "listen" to the internal shape of things across four radio frequency bands. The workman-like monochrome display renders this fine-tuned scan into blocky shapes; crude, but it provides enough of an idea of what you're getting on the other side of a door before you pop it. Boyd immediately confirms a suspicion; this is no safe, or if it is, it contains no loot. It's a door of some kind, sure, but on the other side the density's all wrong, too circuitous and complex. Boyd packs up quick—it's a curiosity, but not worth the ongoing risk of your own skin. No booty to boost, Boyd, better bug out. There'll be no informing Donk if you get busted down here.

To the left of the vault the tunnel jogs off, leading to an elevator room, but elevators aren't stealthy. Boyd turns back the way he came. The nearest ladder's the quieter option, and therefore the preferable one. It's close at hand behind—the label in the rubber reads BOWL.

Boyd climbs stealthily, lifts the lid and peeks into a dark, long and narrow room.

There's some sort of mechanized apparatus on one wall, ropes and pulleys; the other wall is bare cinder block. At the far end he can see a glow; it's the upper level of the elevator he eschewed. There's light coming from an open door on the right. Boyd looks through and immediately places himself—the bowling alley. You've come up in the room behind the pins.

Barney's Suds and Lanes. Built back when the factories thrummed and the area looked likely to become a blue-collar paradise; these days it's just a local dive for criminals who are short money and avoiding Ralph's, and for the few working stiffs who pine throughout the day to be anywhere but work, and who after the shift whistle want to be anywhere but home. Twenty lanes of faded glory far exceeding the present demand. Presently there's no bowling at all. If there had been any bowlers, they'd be far too distracted by what's happening behind the lanes to play.

There's half a dozen men and women visible in there, gathered around what appears to be a bar, dressed in tight-fitting scarlet pajamas and wearing...swords? Yes, swords; some, strangely, are wood, but the rest are steel and look wickedly sharp. Jesus.

They're holding somebody down against the bar. It's a loony, bathrobe and all, her head artfully half-shaved and dyed purple. She's struggling against them, but the struggle's a losing one, and now someone else is coming up, he doesn't have the red jammies on, nor the mask, but he's facing away, Boyd can't see features, only that he's holding a syringe, approaching the loony, and there's a quick motion of his arm, the syringe deploys and the loony ceases her struggles.

Boyd's seen enough—This exit ain't the one, son; time to get the hell out of here.

But then the very bad thing happens: His foot slips on the rung. Not enough to make him fall, no, but Boyd has to use his free hand—the one holding the manhole cover up—to catch himself, and the lid slams home with a boom.

Shit. Shit. Shit.

No hope at all they haven't heard. There's nothing for it now but a run. Boyd jumps the rest of the way down and tears ass, fast as he's ever gone, listening. The trick will be to stay out of the line of sight and hope the next ladder leads to a less occupied exit. The tunnel does curve a bit up here and...looking back...yes, the not-safe door's no longer visible...impossible to know if the footfalls he's hearing are just his own echoes or pursuit, but the latter has to be assumed. And here comes the next ladder. Panting, Boyd leaps, scampers up, and is up and out the portal at the top before he even has time to worry that it might be locked. Running hot-heeled down a corridor before he's even clocked his location—heavy doors with wire-reinforced windows, green industrial tiling, a certain hospital air...remember the ladder insignia—JAWPI-E—this must be the Wales…now darting down a hallway, around a corner, down another, settling down into an unhurried unremarkable pace, completely unsure of where he is within this mazelike superstructure, waiting for his heart to stop hammering.

You weren't tailed, he assures himself, walking deserted fluorescent-lit hallways, flinching every time he rounds a corner. You weren't tailed. You weren't tailed. They don't know what ladder you went up. If they assume the nearest, they won't know which corridors to take. Even if they follow the right corridors, they'll never get you if you can find the exit…he rounds a bend and the hallway dead-ends at a closed door, which he prays won't slow him down with a lock. It swings open onto a common room, he's startled by a surprised yell from a most unexpected source.

It's Father Julius. Denim robes and beard and the whole thing.

"The hell are *you* doing here?" Boyd asks, realizing he should expect the exact same question. He's unsure how he should answer if it's put to him, uncertain how much of his own business he should disclose—his business being, by definition, Donk's business. The problem is the context. Father Julius is normally a highly trusted party, a civilian but a friend; Donk secretly has him over to the Fridge for dinner every month or so just to talk, a get-together Donk keeps secret just to keep up appearances—what would people say, after all, a criminal sharing supper with a suspicious type like a priest?… but outside that setting, Boyd realizes, he's never interacted with the guy, and he always follows Donk's lead when it comes to determining what info to let loose in Julius's presence.

Luckily, Father Julius seems too distracted to mention Boyd's business here. He looks stunned. What's spooked him? Has *he* seen one of your pursuers?

"Father…is everything OK?"

"He flickered in and out," Julius says in a remote voice.

"I'm…sorry? Who flicked what?"

"*Flickered*," Julius says, gesturing with the hand holding the newspaper. "He was sitting right there. He said something to me. He hasn't come back." Julius abruptly stands, as if only just remembering something. "Pardon. I've really got to talk to Nettles."

"Who exactly are we talking about here?"

Julius offers the newspaper, as if it might somehow provide explanation. Boyd takes it, but there's no clarity there, just some green crayon scrawl and a headline: FRITZ ACT TODAY.

"Look," Boyd starts, looking over his shoulder "I really need to r—"

But then he sees it at the window of the door through which he arrived: a face wrapped in crimson, eyes going wide at the sight of him.

Boyd scampers. A look back shows that his pursuer has a sword, and hasn't been distracted by Julius in the least; he's beelining right for Donk's best sneak. The corridors out of the day room are straight and clearly marked; Boyd finds the exit to the Wales, puts his head down and runs hard—Bailey's donut shop is nearby. Get there before he gets you.

P R I D E

Ralph's General & Specific served as a front for all Ralph Mayor's criminal dealings. Like any successful lie, it was mostly true. To run the "General" end of things, Ralph had hired a series of legitimate business managers, nameless straights who clocked in for eight exact hours, whose duties involved never leaving the office, making phone calls to distributors, paying bills with laundered money, and studiously looking the other way. This worked well for a while, but inevitably the manager would prove too reputable, grow a conscience, and start asking questions, or else grow greedy, and start using their skills to skim. Whatever the flaw, Ralph's severance package was identical: You'd end up in a barrel full of cement and drowned in the river. Eventually Ralph, having sunk a fourth barrel, despairing of finding the perfect balance of dependable and dirty, hired family: a second cousin, Bailey Ligneclaire. Ralph had more known *of* her than known her until recent years—as she made a name for herself as an all-around badass in the fights the gangs organized in the abandoned factories, and then parlayed that rep into a gig as a highly effective freelance enforcer—but Ralph must have reckoned that family is family, and even a thin blood tie might prove thicker than cement.

Donk hated Bailey getting promoted to such dangerous prominence, but he had to keep it quiet or risk exposing their connection. By then, Donk had plenty of experience smiling at Ralph while inwardly seething. He had to keep that shit-eating smile affixed when Bailey turned out to be a dab hand at management—enough so that when she wanted to expand operations to the donut shack in the parking lot, Ralph approved the acquisition, and even let Bailey name it after herself.

Meanwhile, to maintain the "Specific" end, the more black-market part of his Market, Ralph had Donk. While all actions had to be approved by Ralph, and the only way to submit to Ralph was through Donk, who met with Ralph weekly by video conference. Donk communicated Ralph's decision through a byzantine code system, which he posted to the grocery bulletin board. If you made a formal request to Ralph during "office" hours, you were obliged to make a purchase. On your receipt, you'd see a code that Donk had put in his system especially for you, which you used to cross reference for your answer on the bulletin board. There were two columns: one with your receipt code, another with a Y or an N or an OFFICE; "office" meaning you needed to go see Donk for further instruction. If you made a move "off-code," you did so unprotected by the umbrella of Ralph's approval; you went back home and prayed, hard, that Donk never heard about it, which he always did—Donk's business was having his thumbs in all the pies. Ralph naturally expected regular reports and regular payments, all of which he received from Donk, and Donk got to have the best of the violent criminal life without having to commit much actual violent crime.

Life at the center carried its own set of difficulties, though. The problem with being the man with the plans is everybody *knows* you're the man with the plans. This breeds jealousy—as Donk explained to me, there was healthy resentment among the gang bosses toward him. Owing to fear of reprisal and Ralph's finely honed sense of sadism, jealousy rarely progressed to action, but Donk remained wary. Better to live a life with no obvious places to pinch.

So, Donk was always scheming. Anyone he actually loved he'd pretend not to know, or even pretend to hate. Anything he really thought, he'd hide behind five lies. Anyplace he went, he'd plan three shakes for the tail he assumed was there. He was one who buried his business deep and then dug a dozen decoy holes so anybody spying on him would waste time at the finding.

His love, he buried deepest of all.

x x x

When Bailey Ligneclaire's bored—like now, between the rush hours—she passes the time counting the fights she's been in.

…and the first fight came when you were only ten, up against a teenager whose name you didn't even know, a local, one of your regular bullies, he had a knife but you beat him anyway, bare-handed…

Bailey's small, almost waifish, but if you watch her walk you see how she carries herself, and you understand that the simple black outfit, and the complicated braids arranged helmetlike around her sleek head, are part of a calculated martial air. It's the sort of confidence that comes with the well-earned reputation she's acquired in the fields of both combat and management. You wouldn't dream of attacking Donk at Ralph's during "office" hours, not when Bailey's nearby, and you wouldn't dream of shorting her a delivery of beer or soda pop if you drive the supply truck. All the affiliated cats know her unassuming form hides ferocious strength and a spider's reflexes, but civilians know the store manager is here to help them find what they're looking for, or to clean up the spill on aisle 4 herself if nobody else is around to do the job, or walk you to the item you're looking for, or even to personally attend to the counter at the donut shack she named for herself.

Bailey's Donuts is situated in the corner of Ralph's parking lot, a building in the shape of two perpendicularly linked diner cars, long and low. Inside, there's room for a counter with a display case, and for the fryers behind that. You can smell donuts sizzling in grease as you order. On the other side there's a row of booths hugging the wall. The walls are all done in chrome and mirror, but the shine's gone to seed, the mirrors dulled and smeared, less reflective but more forgiving than they were in brighter days. The dilapidation is intentional; it was like this when Bailey persuaded Ralph to let her run it, but it's kept that way on purpose; it excites her aesthetic sense. The donuts are cheap and irregularly shaped, fried hot and dipped in sugar, and they taste like love and peace and joy. An old place, Bailey's Donuts, a place that makes its foodstuffs without any sop to the advances of donut technology, a place uninterested in innovation and perhaps unfamiliar with the idea that innovation might be desirable or even possible, a place left behind by a faster, fleeter, more modern, more improved world. You consume the same donut here today as you would have forty years ago. Donut shops like this once grazed wild across the country, but one by one they've fallen to the competition—more streamlined, more centralized, increasingly more effective donut shops with more donut choices, quicker average donut production times, lower donut overhead, faster donut purchase processing, market-tested donut décor, synergies of corporate donut cross-pollination, more regularly measurable distribution of donut toppings, growth, you understand, *growth* of, of, of *donut brand* awareness and donut *thought leadership*....Bailey's Donuts, blissfully safe from these corporate behemoths extinguishing its independently owned kin, keeps protected from competition and immediate destruction by its undesirable location. The donut spreadsheet doesn't lie, claim the donut accountants from the donut chains; no point in putting a franchise in Loony Island. The insurance premiums alone make it a non-starter, and the *clientele*, well...it isn't the right fit for the brand...

But Bailey assessed her own balance sheets, consulted her own catalog of possibility and likelihood and risk, and divined a pathway toward success, a market for something cheap and sweet in a place where wealth is rare, but a spare creased dollar, and the desire to part with it in exchange for the distraction of a momentary delight, is not uncommon. So, year after year, Bailey's Donuts survives, a relic, a gem from the past, slowly accruing a cozy but yellowed and not entirely savory sediment. She breathes deep; savors the aroma of cinnamon and dough. It's a *real* place. It's *her* place.

It'll be the only thing she'll miss when they finally get their revenge and escape for good.

From where she stands, she can see the frontage of Ralph's General & Specific. She'll be heading there shortly. Bailey's the floor manager, and in the dead of the afternoon (sandwiched by two shifts at her donut shop covering the morning and happy-hour crowds) it's Ralph's where you'll find her.

Ralph's is a two-story box, not as large as the cavernous superstores you'll find out of the Island, but far cleaner and brighter than what you'd expect in an economic sinkhole, with space enough for goods besides groceries. It's fronted by large-pane windows a dozen feet high, which begin low near the pavement and continue halfway up the wall. These apertures barely qualify as windows anymore; they've been pasted over nearly opaque with advertisements of deals long terminated, creating an archeology of marketing schemes and enticements, most of them doubling as prearranged coded messages from Donk to some business partner or other. It's just another way, Bailey muses, that Donk hides every one of his intentions behind something distracting and complicated. Is it caution? Amusement? Even Bailey can't say for sure these days. Take this morning, for example. For whatever reason, when she left for the donut shop this morning, he'd been wearing a bag-boy apron—during office hours no less—even though everyone knows he's Ralph's managing director. What's his game? Only he can say for sure.

…and the eighteenth fight drew a crowd down at the abandoned factories—there was money on the line…a full-grown boxcar-banger, and you whipped him with a chain. When it was over, the three of you lived off the winnings, the fights a steady income during the long years of hiding until Ralph hired you; neither you nor Boyd nor Donk has gone hungry since that day…

Nobody knows how or why I win every fight, though, Bailey thinks, totting up purchases, enjoying the click and ding of the old-fashioned registers. They don't understand how it is when I start to see all the possibilities. What does anybody know about me, really? Nobody even knows why I'm here. I'm just like everybody else, an extra without lines in Donk's play, a mouse moving around in one of Donk's—*Daniel's*—mazes. Annoyed with herself to think that, in public, she automatically thinks of him by the street name instead of the real one. As if they're nothing but co-workers, as if she works for him instead of with, as if they didn't grow up together along with Boyd, hiding from Ralph through the cold and hungry years, as if the three of them hadn't lived together their whole lives. To you, he'll always be Daniel, but here, in front of others…he's buried his habits of disassociation in you; ingrained, they require effort to overcome.…

"Keep it moving please, sir," she suggests to a mean-looking tough who's already received his donuts…and a tightly-wrapped brown-paper sack full of powder. He's dawdling longer than she likes. Startled by her request, he looks like he might be about to snap back at her, get himself into some trouble in an attempt to look tough, but then he remembers who he's talking to, smirks to save face, and ducks away. She rarely has to tussle anymore—hence the boredom. Yes, sure, she carries a reputation, but Bailey knows how to put something into her eyes when she looks at you so the fight won't even start. She thinks of it as "pride of ownership"—*you're mine*. And it's no lie, she thinks—they are mine. I can take them apart five different ways.

…and the fourteenth fight should have been with Mayor Ralph Mayor himself—and would have been if not for Daniel, but on the day of the greenhouse he was the cautious one, for once. He held you back, hid you—saved you, really, because that fight would have been your last…

She'd almost have welcomed a fight with the mean-looking dingus with his package of powder. She's already annoyed by the very fact of the package—lately Donk's been setting up criminal drops here at the donut shop, and it's not the rep she wants for the place. It's already started attracting unwanted attention. Inside, lined up against the windows, the gangster day-laborers and curious regulars sit on milk cartons, facing her register with practiced nonchalance. These are small-time hoodlums eavesdropping and drinking black coffee sweetened with cheap wine purchased at Ralph's, hoping for a chance to be brought in on some big business by a gangster more senior, someone connected enough to have daily business with Donk. The line to petition Ralph's right hand has grown too long, too exclusive—and they know Bailey is Ralph's muscle on top of being his manager—and the rumor is she's his family besides. This seems a good place to try to horn in on what's happening, or at least try to read the tea leaves, as establishment crooks—goons, thieves, pimps, and the rest—make their way to the donut shack, proffer their coded purchases, receive their running orders. Some take a package, some leave one. If you guess right, there's opportunity for you: employment on the heist, a kickback, a score. Today, however, many of the regulars have additional entertainment to reward their attendance, because here's this loquacious loony just wandered in, blabbering and glabbering about the rough time he's had somewhere in Tennessee, expounding about the dark evil festering deep in the heart of Pigeon Forge, footstool of the Smokies, Southern-fried playground of the country set. He's talking about the fountain, the love, the boxes, and something else about gourds. It's pure nonsense, and he won't quit it—Bailey stopped listening almost immediately—but now, looking at him, it seems to her even *he* wishes he could stop; there's a certain desperation in his eyes. It's all this about Tennessee and Tennessee and Tennessee, and how he's never going back. The poor bastard doesn't even realize after this performance he'll never be rid of "Tennessee" again. It's his name now, whatever the HELLO MY NAME IS sticker on his shirt says. The regulars hoot at him, catcalling, mocking the stammer—Hey, can we get *Tennessee* here a cup of coffee? Betcha his story gets better if he's got some wine in him. How interesting, *Tennessee*. Tuh-tuh-tuh-tuh-tell us more about this lottery ticket, *Tennessee*. But, before you tell us more, please tell us *less*. Laughing all the harder as, oblivious to their amusement, he starts again...Bailey decides it won't do to allow this sort of distraction to continue—it started as a laugh, but it's been twenty minutes at least.

"Enough." Bailey grabs her broom. "This is a place of business, sir. Time to move on."

"I was *trying* to move on," Tennessee says. "In Pigeon Forge, I wan wan wanted to move on in the worst way possible."

He hasn't made to leave. She knows she's got to do something. You don't stay in charge if you don't take charge, and word spreads fast about an enforcer who won't enforce. Still, he's a harmless loon; Bailey doesn't want to hurt him. She tries to scare him with a show; spins the broom like a baton, slides her feet like a boxer. He just goggles at her. Rhythmically, she screams "Out! Out! Out!"—punctuating each syllable with a whack, judging the distances and the arc of the swing to make it seem like she's battering the guy a lot harder than she actually is; in truth he's only getting the bristle tips.

"I just need to lay low!" Tennessee shouts, bending for his glasses, which have been knocked to the floor, skinny arms protecting his face as the whiskers of the broom whip him. "I need a say say safe place to st—"

"I'll lay you low if you don't scoot, buddy," Bailey whispers. "You're not giving me much choice."

Tennessee thrusts out his skinny stubbled neck plaintively. "I'll scoot, ma'am. I'll scoot." Then he says something that perks Bailey's ears up. "I just saw this place and all these folks. Thought I'd come in and poke around, search for my boy lost forever. I got myself sidetracked is all. Just like, listen, friends, just like I got myself sidetracked in Pigeon Forge, sidetracked on my way to this nee nee neon...chapel..."

Bailey thinks—the Neon Chapel? This guy's with Father Julius? She's immediately protective. "Hop it!" Bailey smacks the floor solidly, purposefully just missing his head. Tennessee yelps, then makes for the doors, his bent glasses clutched in one trembling hand—but almost immediately, in he comes again. "Which way to the neon...?"

Bailey gives chase as everyone else hoots, but when they get outside, she calls and he turns. "Chapel's that way," she says, surreptitiously pointing, and sees the flash of gratitude on Tennessee's face before he runs off. She watches him go. Nobody inside noticed her do it; none of *them* would think Ralph's enforcer would do anything but stand and intimidate…but they don't realize, she's the store manager, too, and the manager always helps the customer. Nobody knows anything about you, Bailey thinks. Even Donk—*Daniel*—doesn't care that you care about doing a proper job. He doesn't understand your pride of ownership. He made fun of you for buying gorgeous vintage cash registers for both stores; he didn't see how they contribute to the overall aesthetic. And none of the rest of them know that Donk *should* care about you, either…

The sun's been up for hours and she can smell baking asphalt. Hot air hit her when she left the donut shack and it's already oppressive; it's been less than a minute out of the air conditioning and her brow's beading. Bailey is shocked by the newly freed loonies milling around the parking lot, their lunchtime sedatives fully taken hold, shuffling around in medicated wonderment. She's not shocked by their presence—Donk had been talking all week about the upcoming implementation of the Fritz Act—but the sheer numbers. Dozens of loonies have already managed to stumble up Transept to Ralph's parking lot, and who can say how many more will come? They glisten with sweat, apparently unaware of the heat; anyway, they haven't removed their bathrobes, and they're frying out here. Somebody ought to do something, Bailey thinks. The Fritz Act is no improvement if it's just expulsion, whatever the papers say. Eventually they'll get to the borders of the Island and the bluebirds will run them in or club them down. They're unsavvy, they don't know the unspoken rules, they've got no idea who's dangerous and who's not. It's like standing in the midst of hanging laundry; these terryclothed loonies make no attempt to avoid her. Look at them, wandering right up, unaware of your status—unlike these factory workers, first-shift line scrubs at Slanty's Cannery heading to Ralph's for some lunch for later—watch how they skirt you. Bailey smiles at them, just a bit; it's that pride of ownership. Everybody's heard what she can make of a man's face, and they want none of it.

Then she sees, passing through the parking lot's flotilla of loonies: Boyd, running harder than she thought he could, clutching a newspaper like a club for some reason, racing through the human press directly toward her, pursued closely by a sword-wielding fellow done up all in scarlet.

The two are upon her at once; there's no time to draw a weapon. Luckily this strange redbird doesn't know to watch for her any more than the loonies do. Bailey gives him a solid shiver with her forearms, knocking him wide of his target, wonders, Why is this happening? but already he's moving on her, and Bailey, entering the familiar sleepy slow timeless place, ducks it as easily as a jaguar shrugging a low tree branch, throws her full weight directly at the spot she knows he least expects right *toward* his weapon letting the blade pass between her torso and arm capturing his forearm with both hands bringing the crown of her head hard into his stomach and as he whooshes out his breath she scissors her forearms on either side of his sword arm bending the elbow mercilessly back back back until he drops it with a clatter any farther and there'll be the distinct *pop* of dislocation and he's trying to scream but lacking the breath to do so he leaves his lower half unprotected so she puts her knee into his balls twice and throws him back onto his scarlet-clad ass. She steps back, breathing steadily and watching him levelly, drawing her baton; holds the leather-sheathed foot of steel in swinging stance and lets him watch her until he can breathe well enough to run away, snatching his weapon as he goes, hunched over in testicular distress, arm dangling. The loonies have scattered.

None of them know how I do it, Bailey thinks, watching him go. Well that's how. I see the possibilities—*all* the possibilities—and then it all goes slow for me. It's not that I can beat you. It's that this is just one of a thousand ways I could have done it. It's been like that ever since the first fight. He'd had a knife, too—the older kid, the bully—and as he had fled from her rage had filled her and she picked up the blade and threw it after him—not aiming to hit, but sending a message to the universe she would have been hard-pressed to put into words. A little girl who had just discovered she was dangerous. Too small to seem a threat to anybody; impossible to know she had found within a strange knowledge of time and vulnerability, a full awareness of danger. Anxiety no longer exclusively a defensive mechanism. Every dark possibility she could imagine happening to those she loved, she could also imagine for an enemy, and could manufacture harm for the latter as ferociously as she would prevent it for the former.

So that was fight number one hundred fifty-two, she thinks. It's been a minute. He hadn't been around long enough to know to be wary of you, but otherwise that guy knew what he was doing. Quick reflexes. Dangerous blade. *And* he meant to use it, too. He probably isn't used to losing. And he didn't know what to expect from you. If you face him again you won't have surprise on your side. Back in the donut shop she sees the regulars pressed against the window; they saw it all. Good; just another chip for her rep.

But hold on, what did *Boyd* do to catch the attention of some loony samurai? Boyd doesn't get noticed *ever*. Bailey's baby brother Boyd's a sneak, and there's nobody better at it. Wan and gray-faced, Donk's top thief and informant is possessed of a remarkable quality of unremarkableness, allowing him to leave upon the minds of others no impression at all. Serially overlooked is Boyd: by passersby, acquaintances, old friends, restroom attendants, and (crucially) potential witnesses, schemers, double-dealers, people talking about things they shouldn't in places where they think they're not being watched. Boyd will sneak on you, and then Boyd will remember what you say, his memory near photographic. He's also, as Donk is all-too-frequently given to pointing out, a moron. Donk's not entirely wrong. His Slanty's Cannery line worker's dungarees aren't a costume or a disguise; Boyd's decided (needlessly, in Bailey's estimation) he requires a straight job to cover for his illicit business, so he wastes dozens of hours each week slicing fish on the line. Claims the mindless work helps him work on his writing, such as it is—when it comes to writing, Boyd is one of those who more talks about doing it than actually does it. So, yes: a moron. But he—much like Donk himself—is *her* moron.

"Who the hell was that, and what did you do to piss him off?" She says it half-joking, but then gets a look at his face. He's all over sweat, and though he's trying to hide it—running his free hand through his hair to reestablish his pompadour—he looks sincerely spooked. "I think we've got trouble coming," he says.

"What trouble?"

"Let's go talk to Donk," Boyd says. "I'd rather not explain twice."

x x x

Daniel's in his office finishing what appears to be his final office-hours meeting. Boyd and Bailey wait. In time the door opens and Donk emerges, ushering out a man with a bald pate and a magnificent handlebar moustache. "I'll see what I can do," Donk's telling him, but it seems the man isn't as finished with his petition as Donk clearly is.

"They're being all over the places," the moustache says, heavily accented. He's obviously from Domino City's Building 5 gang; the one they all call Presto. "Loonies—in our hallways! It isn't rightful! Who are they to do?"

"I'll see what I can do," Donk says.

"*And* some of them I think are being preverts. Wearing red pajamas."

Hm, thinks Bailey, concerned. So our redbird friend is part of a flock.

"I'll see what I can do," Donk says.

"They cannot be keeping it up!" the moustache insists. "It will be coming to a war."

He's not wrong about that, Bailey thinks.

"I'll see what I can *do*," Donk says, with a certain finality that shuts the moustache up at last. He grumbles an insincere thank-you and makes his way back toward the front exits. Daniel watches him for a second, then turns his attention to them.

"Can I help who's next?" Daniel asks, looking ostentatiously around as if seeing his snitch in a sweat during office hours is perfectly normal. Obsessed with seeming cooler than anyone else—the idiot. Before turning back to his desk, he glances at her. She knows him enough to read it: *Jesus, now we've got loonies to deal with.* She lets the side of her mouth turn ever-so-slightly up, allows her glance to play ever-so-subtly in the direction of the departing moustache. *Loonies are no better or worse than these gangsters, though.*

Then they're back into their roles, but she's seen the amusement tell in his eyes. And just like that, he's done it: He's not just *an* idiot, but *her* idiot. Her genius. A donkeyface, sure. Not classically handsome by any means. He'd even been a homely kid. But whenever trouble inevitably comes, when he should—when anyone else would—cower, stammer, beg mercy, retreat, debase themselves for the hope of continued safety…at these times Donk smiles, and the spark in his eyes lends him surplus beauty. This beautiful ugly idiot genius, who smiles when he should weep, who twinkles when he should run. Who takes his advantage by breaking the game, by doing it wrong, purposefully, doing it in a way nobody else would, for nothing but the sake of doing it differently, for the frisson of the unexpected, the joy of imbalance, to splinter logic, trusting to his ability to reconstruct the pieces faster than his opponents can. Even the little things, he does different, seemingly out of a preference for difference. For example, the way he wears a suit, even when bagging groceries. A *suit*—not the peacock strut and flash of an Island gangster's almost cinematic shinythread pinstripe attire, but a bespoke three-piece in a conservative palette. It should look wrong, but somehow it conveys what he needs conveyed: He's about business, he's above their fray, and he's more gangster than any of them, because he's got every button buttoned and every pocket sewn shut.

Their relationship they've kept secret. It's safer for her this way, Donk reminds her, whenever she acts a little too familiar in public, for nobody to know they can hurt him through her. For Ralph not to know especially. Remember, Donk would admonish, you never can tell who else might be talking to Ralph. Or have you forgotten the greenhouse? Have you forgotten what Ralph did to Yale? No Daniel, she wants to reply. I haven't forgotten. Yale may have been your brother, but he was something to me, too.

Donk leans against his desk and regards them both. "So?"

"Boyd's got a story to tell." Bailey says.

"I love stories."

Boyd starts to talk, but he's not more than a couple sentences in when Donk holds up a hand. "Let's do this in the Fridge," he says. "This doesn't sound like open-air talk."

The Fridge is another of Daniel's secret spots, though it's one he inherited from Ralph, who instructed the architect to build it to serve as his office refuge and panic room. Ralph never visits these days; he's all but willed it to his protégé. Few besides the three of them know about it. It's a hell of a perk. These inner rooms are appointed with the sort of tastefulness achievable only by one who is new to the concept of taste and is striving to attain it. Tiffany globes hang low from tasteful mirrored ceilings. Tasteful shag carpeting hugs the floor. Warm, muted light dances from a gas-powered fireplace, before which a tasteful bearskin rug lies in a somnolent posture, above which a taxidermied and mounted swordfish swims tastefully over the mantle. Sinfully comfortable leather-lined recliners and immense overstuffed sofas hug the walls. Three walls in each room are fitted with varnished wainscoting and decorated with oil paintings, but the entirety of the fourth wall is lined with hand-crafted oak bookshelves, between which are gaps; in those gaps, one-way mirrors have been installed, from which one can spy back out onto the grocery floor. You can see the checkout lanes from here. Bailey remembers—how could she forget?—how Ralph used to stand at the panels, smoking a stogie and watching her at work. You never shake the sensation of hidden eyeballs on your neck. It makes you diligent.

Now it's their "break room," though in truth they live there. From the door in the antechamber you step into the game room: billiard table, pool table done in violet felt, poker table, reading table, chess board upon which slumber crystal and ebonite pieces transfixed in the game Ralph was playing with himself when he retired. Next is the sitting room, which has the fire-place. After it comes the smoker, fumigated and converted to a bedroom, then the kitchen, then the pantry. At Daniel's insistence, they keep other abodes, to throw enemies off the trail, but it's to the Fridge they return after work, and it's here they pass most nights. The entrance is in the stockroom, where there are mirrored panels between the refrigerated cases. At the base of one mirror is a small foot-pedal, which, if pressed in the correct sequence, causes another mirror to unhook slightly. When you are certain there are no onlookers, you reach in and unhook the latch, open the swinging panel, and step in. As you swing the door shut, a keypad beside a second door activates. Once you're safely ensconced in the antechamber you enter the code, and the door to the break rooms swings open.

They follow Daniel to the library, where he sits and picks up the book he's left there. It's a secret habit, so he indulges himself only in the Fridge. He's got a copy of Plato's *Republic*, managing to read it with the same pageflapping speed as anything else. Lately he's gone for the heavy stuff. Like most who came up in Loony Island, Donk's education is wonky; he's got the random and omnivorous habits of the autodidact—though in their quiet moments he dares hope the next generation might have something a bit more formalized. Donk peruses the book absently as he listens to Boyd's story. Bailey, hearing it for the first time along with Donk, moves from interest to shock to something almost like skepticism, if it were possible to be skeptical of Boyd's reports. Tunnels running under the whole island? A whole flock of redbirds attacking Wales inmates at the bowling alley? With...syringes?

"Remind me again," Daniel says, once Boyd's finished. "Father Julius is mixed up in this how?"

"I don't think he is. I think he just happened to be there. But he was spooked. He saw something there in the Wales."

"Something—what something?"

Boyd ruminates. "He said...a man. A flickering man."

"Flickering."

"That's what he said, yes. He gave me this newspaper." Boyd fishes it out of his pocket and Bailey recognizes it; he'd been holding it in his hand while he was being chased. Donk uncrumples it and studies it. It's the morning edition. It's got a green rectangle colored on it with crayon, but other than that it's unremarkable. Donk shakes his head and sets it down. "Well, Julius saw *something* at the Wales. I'd like to know what. We'd better have Boyd go get the big old dummy to come over here and tell us."

"I can go," Bailey says. "In case there really is trouble out there."

"Boyd'll do fine," Donk murmurs absently, eyes scanning his book. "I want you close. That whoever-it-was you let go after your fight will be reporting to his boss about where Boyd went pretty soon. I think we should expect some trouble today."

"Then neither of us should go, probably," Bailey says, trying not to sound annoyed as she feels at his growing propensity for dismissing her. My concerns have kept us alive more than once, she thinks. Have you forgotten that, too? She doesn't say it, though, hoping to avoid an old and unproductive fight. She looks to Boyd for support, but Boyd has already noticed the tension and retreated to one of the Fridge's other rooms.

"True enough. We'll send him this evening," Donk replies, and Bailey's annoyance only grows—*Well, hey, don't listen to* me, *buddy*... "Anyway, we've got to make some moves here. If we have trouble coming, we need to shut down the store early."

"I still have work, even if you don't."

"*Manager* work."

"The manager work matters to me, Daniel," she says, unable to keep the asperity from her voice—Looks we're going to have that fight again, after all. After all this time, and still he doesn't understand that what you mean when you say "pride of ownership" isn't just about a scrapper's rep, it's everything you do. It's understanding possibility in everything, and choosing the right possibility, the better possibility, every time. What nobody understands about me is nearly everything, but even you, Daniel? Even you?

Daniel's noticed her mood. He sets down his book, comes to her and puts his forehead to her forehead, hands to her ears. "I'm sorry," he says, "my fault"—and just like that, they know each other again, better than any other in the world. She reaches up and puts her hands to his ears and holds them. What a strange thing we do, she thinks, resting in this posture, but it's us. Do any other two do such a strange thing? No; it's us, and it's only us.

Later, as Donk snoozes, Bailey keeps awake, watching through the windows for any signs of trouble, counting her fights.

Until this morning, one hundred fifty-one was the most recent. A collection gone wrong. A small-timer who'd gotten strung out and stopped making payments—an entire month's juice. Claimed he'd paid already, then, he'd tried pulling a gun but was too wasted to do it well; you had his arm broken before he'd negotiated his pocket. Tossing the place revealed only a small safe, which you took. On the way out, you saw a filthy kid of indeterminate gender peeking from behind a curtain. Later, when Boyd had cracked the safe, you found nothing in it but a few toys from fast-food kiddie meals, and the thought rose up in you: We have got to get out of this place we have to get out of here soon...

CHAPEL

Father Julius's purported "miracle," on the other hand…that's one reason some people believed he was a holy man, or maybe even a real priest, despite his deviations from expected norms. It happened—if indeed it did happen—the night the old abandoned cathedral burned. Nobody found out what got the fire started—and, it being in the Island, nobody inspected—but whatever the cause, it burned from the inside and up, its wooden innards consumed, its stone heated to a kiln, its interior converted to a deadly smoker choking those trapped within. By the time anybody noticed it, it was too late; the flames were already licking the shingles. For there to have been so few fatalities required a miracle. To a perverse mind, it might almost seem fatalities had been intended. The diocese had shuttered the place up the year previous, but they didn't like how many indigent types wound up squatting in there, and the doors had been chained up from the outside not long before the blaze, almost as if…well. Now I'm engaging in conjecture not much better than conspiracy theory, and anyway there's no conspiracy needed to know that a fire starting in Loony Island is going to be a horror. No volunteers have the resources to fight a blaze like that, and Island folks have learned to expect a practiced lack of urgency from municipal services like fire departments. It was a terrible blaze, and might even have taken all Checkertown down with it, too, if it hadn't been for this odd fellow in jogging attire, kneeling in classic aspect of prayer—and wouldn't you know it, within moments there came a rain so hard and so fierce it drowned the fire. Nearly drowned those nearby, too. I say nearby, and I mean *near*—even though the gutters ran two inches deep up in Checkertown, the factories down at the Island's southern tip stayed dry as a cracker. It was a downpour as targeted as it was torrential.

Five minutes later—ten at most—the deluge stops. The fire's out. And here's this fellow in jogging gear, still kneeling. Up he gets, and who are you, they ask him, and I'm Father Julius, he says, I'm the new priest.

They thought he'd be on his way, but they were wrong about that. He stayed. They never saw the jogging gear again, though. The next day he was around, wearing the denim vestments that would soon be familiar to the gangs and goons and loons and lads and ladies; familiar as the story that enshrined him, the tale of the cleric who appeared on Loony Island in its hour most desperate, the priest who had a direct line to the Big Guy, the holy man who prayed the rain down. And what did he do once he'd arrived? He built the damn Neon Chapel himself, by hand. Julius even worked the cranes to set the beams. At first it was just him, living in a tent, then a lean-to, then the small section he had made weatherproof. Soon enough, people started helping out, hauling the materials that came from trucks. While he supervised, others began laying bricks. By the time it was done, he had a small team. They stayed; they became, in a sense, his disciples. the first brothers and sisters of the Neon Order—though others would join after. They did every bit except haul the materials—those came from trucks conspicuously fresh-painted over, as if designed to hide corporate logo and affiliation.

You ask me, Finch my dear, that's the real miracle. A man starting a structure that size by himself, then getting others to want to *join* such an insane operation? Miracle. But he did it. It got people talking; almost afraid to approach him, too. And what did they talk about? They talked about the rain. Maybe because they really did see a miracle. Maybe because watching someone perform a miracle so tactile as construction in a place so abandoned leant itself to presuming something more mysterious. How many people might have seen this alleged miracle? Dozens, certainly. Maybe fifty? A hundred? As many as were awake in the wee hours and interested enough in a fire to see the fuss. How many people now *say* they were there? Every resident of Loony Island now makes that claim.

One person I know was there. One person I know for sure, because the night of the fire also just so happens to be the night that one person, doomed within days to be snatched up and thrown into the nearby booby hatch, first arrived at Loony Island. In fact, though I never have admitted it, the fire happened because that person arrived.

That person was me.

x x x

Jogging away, Julius thinks: You should have asked him his name. Do it soon—next time you visit. Tomorrow morning. Maybe tonight?

The priest's finally left the Wales after long hours sitting in the common room, waiting without luck for another glimpse. Even that disturbance—Boyd chased by one of those red-clad ninja types—hadn't shaken him from the obsession. It's starting to feel more like addiction than compulsion, more like greed than desire. And with it, of course, comes the shame. People who count on him have gone without assistance, and gone without knowing why, to boot.

He's deep in Checkertown now, almost to the track that forms the unofficial northern border of Loony Island. The trees stand sharp against the sky in the unearthly brightness of a day on the cusp of ripening to sunset but still minutes away from the transformation, the strange glow a low-hanging summer sun provides. The air brings him the enticing smells of cooking meat, and Julius picks up his pace. He rounds a corner, and there it is, peeking over the lower buildings: his home, his refuge, his nest, the Neon Chapel. A gray brick building spaghettied with glass tubing that blaze with noble gases; pink as hot as the cheeks of an Alabama sheriff, blue as bright as a dream of the Tahiti sea, purple groovier than a magistrate's silk undies, green as a seasick turtle, yellow as jealousy, orange as Ernie. Here, he hopes, he'll be able to find some clarity. He knows he'll be able to find a plate. The barrel grills are out and the crowd is already forming. He just needs a moment to rest.

It's not a small building, the Neon, but nothing so big as the cathedral it replaced, and there's grass planted now all around in the footprint of the old structure. Julius shucks off his sneakers in rote practice at this threshold, ties the laces together, hangs them around his neck like a holy stole. He briefly kneels to pray before stepping onto the grass, then heads inside to the narthex for a quick drink from the water fountain just inside the door. It's a large open space; you can see almost all of it from any other part. The Neon mimics the cruciform shape of the cathedral it vacated, though not the grandeur. The emptiness of the interior lends it a sense of size it doesn't possess—an effect diminished somewhat by the décor, which he's heard described as "chain-restaurant chic." Every inch of wall and ceiling space had presented Julius an opportunity to display some gaudiness or other—stuffed moose head, kitsch painting, mirrored advertisement for watery lager—interlaced between with more neon noodlework. Hanging from the ceiling, a mobile made from hubcaps and galvanized lock washers. Hutched in the narthex, a sofa upholstered in velvet; by the door, a hat rack, its arms inlaid with silver finials, its wooden base carved to resemble large wooden clown shoes; a triad of eight-foot bookshelves crammed with old paperbacks and magazines. The pews are rows of easy chairs. The altar rail is a fine burnished lacquered beauty, but the padded kneelers have a violet underglow better suited to a low-rider automobile.

The nave is trimmed on either side, not by a cathedral's aisles, but by rooms, the open-faced "cells" within which the Neon Brothers and Sisters reside. There are twelve cells in all; six to a side, with two rows of three stacked one above the other, identically and generously sized. Each cell has a wall missing, exposing it to the nave's central room, though there are accommodations for privacy; each comes equipped with the sort of roll-down heavy-duty steel shutters used to secure mall stores and downtown pawn shops. The fellowship utilizes the three unoccupied upper cells on one side for storage, and these are shuttered and locked, but the brothers and sisters rarely use the forbidding shutters to obscure their own abodes. For everyday privacy they've festooned their entrances with decorative curtains, each customized to their own taste. Sister Nettles wove her own marvelous curtain. Up close, it appears to be a lone shade of midnight blue flecked with lint, but as you withdraw, you see the intricate patterns of black woven throughout the blue, and the farther away you stand, the more specific the face described by the "lint"—each fleck of which is a delicate single-thread loop of white— becomes. Nettles also wove Julius's drapery, a birthday present to replace the sad plastic shower curtains he'd strung up in early days. It's more a tapestry than a curtain; woven intricately with many colors, with shades of brown figuring most prominently, and with particolored bits of glass, blue and white and gold and crimson, threaded expertly into the fabric.

Past the nave, the room opens up onto the arms of the cruciform, leading to the bathrooms on the left and, on the right, a massive modern kitchen, where bread and biscuits are cooked in the morning and side dishes for the barbecue are prepared in the afternoon, and where immense freezers hold the meat. Beyond this intersection, the choir holds a scattering of unmatched comfy chairs surrounding a large jukebox, whose base glows from the slowly bubbling golden liquid within. Still farther, against the back wall, presides the square and bulky wooden presence of Monseigneur Ex—but Julius, as disinterested in confession as he is interested in finding a plate of meat, barely spares Monseigneur Ex a glance.

The Sunday barbecue's a tradition at the Neon: Brothers Brock and Jack light the two massive cookers and bring the meat out of the deep freeze. One barrel they crowd with weenies and patties, the other they load with ribs and beef tips and brisket. The residents of Checkertown gather to smell the meat cooking: kids first—some of them urchins damp with filth, others well-scrubbed and accompanied by parents—and then other dwellers from Domino City: workers from Slanty's or scavengers from the blasted factories, cloaked in the sweat and the stench of the day's work, a pimp or two along the margin, strutting with his girls, girls without their pimps, even the gangsters or the occasional shiny-suit boss; they come, the ever-hungry and the always-fed, the heavily armed and the defenseless, strong or weak they come, lured by the smell of cooking meat marinating in a sweet sauce whose secret composition Brother Jack swears never to reveal, they come lured by promise of company within a safe space...for those who come armed have learned to keep their heaters tucked, or face the humiliation of a showdown with the fearless priest of the Neon Chapel. They congregate on the large grassy empty lot upon which the Neon Chapel has been built, paper plates floppy with meat juice, stomachs full. Somebody drives a vehicle onto the grass, blasting music. There's dancing, the spectacle of the young posturing for the young, the squeals of children chasing one another across the grass. A bottle is passed around, knots of conversation begin and continue and melt into one another. Some congregate for hours, resting in the sacred temporal ether of a good meal, tarrying long after Julius and the other brothers and sisters have retired within or gone off to other errands, while Brock and Jack scrub the steamers clean and store them dry and gleaming, ready for their meaty work the following Sunday.

Donk never shows. His presence wouldn't match the narrative he's built about himself. Still, the barbecue's allowed to exist because of Donk, who managed, at what Julius assumes involved some significant level of personal risk, to get Ralph Mayor on the right side of it. It hadn't been a sure thing. Offering free food is an act of civil disobedience on Loony Island, after all, where *Ralph* provides. In the end, Donk sold the event to Ralph as a sort of team-building event for the gangs, with overall stability and brand management as side benefits. Other concessions to Ralph regarding food delivery and trash pickup had been made to smooth the road, concessions that Julius doesn't like to think about, much less talk about, but the priest had balked at calling it "The Mayor's Dinner," Ralph's original request. How the hell Donk convinced Ralph to back off from that point of contention, Julius has no idea. Knowing what he now knows, the priest sometimes experiences the gripping feeling you get in the guts when you remember a near miss, thinking of the confidence with which he "negotiated" with Donk about the barbecue, completely unaware of how little leverage he held, how narrow was the road upon which he walked, how far the drop, and just how much Donk had done to keep him from tipping over into it.

Julius walks barefoot though the crowd, greeting friends he recognizes and many others who recognize him, and, as he takes his place in line for a plate, he notices, scattered around the usual throng, a noticeable quantity of terrycloth. The loonies are meant to return to the Wales at night—they've been given strict instruction to return during this trial balloon, or so the newspapers report—but some have found the weekly meal instead. And, once again, winding through the crowd, immune to hostile glance, a man in red, his wood sword swinging, swinging...

Brother Jack raises his eyebrows. "Done early, ain't you," he mutters.

Jack's understated as always; really, the priest's shockingly early for a man who holds such precise a schedule. Unsure even how to begin explaining, Julius simply nods. "Seen Nettles?"

Brother Jack points the tongs. "Expect you'd find her inside."

It's welcome news. Most nights Julius would relish mixing with the crowd, but after everything he's seen today, he needs common sense and calm; he needs Nettles. The Neon's early joiner, Nettles, the calm at the center of their storms, the brick holding down the rest of their unsecured lids; Nettles will have some ideas about the flickering man, and even if she doesn't, she'll be able to lend some perspective. Balancing his plate one-handed, Julius slips back inside.

Nettles lives in the ground-level cell on the right, farthest from the entrance, and she's home as expected; Julius sees the light glowing from within on the sides of her curtain. He makes for this haven, but before he can reach it, he's interrupted by a voice coming up from behind:

"*There* you are, Captain!"

Julius stops, closes his eyes—*Oh, shit.* Turning, he can see that yes, it's the stuttering loony from this morning, glasses slightly askew on his face, grinning like a long dog who just got some meat—which, Julius reflects, is probably what he just got, since he's holding an empty, but greasy, plate.

"Eye eye I found the place, just like you said I would!"

"Glad you did," Julius says, as graciously as he can manage, given this frustration of his intentions. "You're welcome here." Look at him. He's a spectacle in spectacles: a stork-like figure in tatty bathrobe and greasy hair, a single bird from a flock set loose upon a far harsher world than any of them should have been expected to deal with. The loony, having achieved his objective—contact with a familiar face—now seems unfurnished with any further plan or recourse. He stands. He sways. It's getting awkward. It's enough to make a street priest wish he were anywhere else; even in some board meeting with his proxy and his multi-tabbed spreadsheets and a bunch of conservative haircuts perched atop a series of very serious business suits.

"Listen...Sterling. It's certainly nice to make your acquaintance—"

"Whoa, now. Who gave you my *name*?" The loony takes a step backward. Julius points to the HELLO MY NAME IS sticker, still visible on the musty shirt secreted beneath the city-issue bathrobe; he's wearing it unbelted and open. The skinny loon looks down, sees his name, and closes the robe, hands clutched to his chest, in a gawky pantomime of virginal modesty.

"Don't call me Sterling Shirker, Captain—call me what the rest of them call me. Call me Tennessee," he says. "Just Tennessee. Just Tennessee. Just Tennessee. To ream ream remind me I'm not ever going back there never going back never going back there. There's bad folks in Pigeon Forge, and I don't want anything more to do with them or their boxes or their fountain."

"No problem...Tennessee," Julius says, walking to the nearest chair in the choir—an overstuffed armchair with a floral chintz pattern the color of mustard. "But you're not wearing your *last* name on your clothes, you know, so telling it to me was an unnecessary goddamn giveaway." He says it kindly, but with what he hopes is finality, kneels for a brief blessing, then sits with his plate, figuring—If you've got to listen to this guy, at least make yourself comfortable while you do it, and eat your grub before it gets ice cold....

Tennessee, following behind, seems not to have heard. "I understand this is a place that hel, that hel, that hel hel helps people out," he says. He sits in the nearest chair—a leather loveseat with broken springs. His ass sinks halfway to the floor, putting his skinny knees up near his ears, making him resemble a bespectacled grasshopper. "A say say safe place."

"That's right," Julius says, cautiously. "Pretty sure you got that understanding from me."

"Okay, then, that's good," Tennessee exhales dramatically. "I need a safe play play place. I've got trouble after me."

"Great," said Julius after a long pause, perhaps less enthused about the notion of bad trouble on the way than Tennessee had hoped.

"So. What do I have to do?" Tennessee asks.

"Do?"

"To join up. Stay here with your gang. Huddle up under your roof."

"The same thing everybody else who's joined had to do," Julius says. "Which is to want to join, and then to do it."

"I don't follow."

Julius smiles. "Few do."

"I have to do *something*, Captain. I have to show my value. I know how I'm perceived."

"How are you perceived?"

"*And* I'm afraid."

"Right. 'Bad trouble after you.' I know."

"But no, but what if they're, what if they're ry ry *right*?"

"About…?"

"When they say I'm crazy. What if I *am* crazy?"

Julius stifles a sigh, thinks—I guess it's going to be a conversation, then. If you don't mind watching me eat while I talk, buddy, I don't mind talking while I eat. He's somebody, clearly. He's in need, clearly. Since when have you required a person to present any other qualifications, in order to get your time and attention? To Tennessee he says: "Does it make you afraid, the idea of being crazy?"

The loony pulls a face. "Who *wants* to be crazy, Captain?"

"OK. So what makes you worry about your sanity?"

Tennessee gives a sleeve-flapping gesture toward the unseen crowd on the other side of the chapel doors. "*They* say my story sounds crazy."

"What else?"

"No no no no no *nobody* believes me, Captain. Sometimes I don't even believe mice mice mice mice myself."

Julius smiles, sadly and knowingly. "That's a lonesome meal for sure, buddy," he says, beginning to suspect he's talking to himself as much as Tennessee. "But having people agree with a delusion doesn't make it less a delusion. And having nobody agree with a truth doesn't make it any less a truth."

"So you think I'm not crazy?"

"The question for me about you isn't one of crazy or not. It's this: Do I think you're crazier than the baseline usual crazy the rest of us live in?"

"Well?"

Julius, having reached the limitations of fork and knife, picks up the ribs. "That's a toughie, Tennessee. I won't lie to you; you're stranger than most. But strange isn't crazy, and normal isn't sane. What I've heard of your story strikes me as *unlikely*, but look—let's think of something else unlikely. For example, if you said to me, I think I can eat two dozen potatoes in an hour, I'd find that unlikely, but we could test it and you might surprise me. But even if you failed, well, we'd only know you weren't able to eat twenty-four potatoes *that* particular time. So that would suggest only probabilities. It wouldn't prove you couldn't do it. For your situation, I don't see the scientific remedy, short of going to Pigeon Fork and poking around for evidence."

"Pigeon *Forge*, and I'm not never going back there, there's bad trouble there."

"Well then, there's your answer. You have all the proof you'll ever get, and maybe all you'll ever need. Just stay away from that part of the earth, and live as happy as you can."

"What, then? You believe me?"

Julius tosses shinyclean rib bones to his plate, sucks smackingly upon sauce-soiled fingers, dabs with his napkin. "I don't go that far. But I don't disbelieve you, either. And I will say this: Your story isn't the strangest one I haven't disbelieved. You wouldn't believe what I've failed to disbelieve. And you wouldn't *believe* what I'm about to ask somebody else to believe. So stick around. And, if you find you can't live a sane life, be encouraged. I haven't managed that trick yet myself, nor have any of your new roommates—" What the hell, thinks Julius, I suppose we have a new Neon Brother—"nor did Elvis Presley ever manage it, nor Napoleon, nor Cleopatra nor Marilyn Monroe, either, and neither have any of the kings or peasants who crawled and fought and died on the earth since lungs were first invented by an over-ambitious mudfish—which is also science, I think." Seized by an urge he can't explain, he reaches out and places a benedictory hand on Tennessee's head. "Go. Live a peaceful life. Let sanity worry about sanity." He sees the loony's eyes go wide with...what? Wonder? Confusion? He seems on the verge of something unpredictable: speaking in tongues, screaming, weeping, yodeling, confessing the hidden truths of the universe, barking like a dog, purring like a—

"And get yourself back inside Monseigneur Ex," Sister Nettles calls, unseen, from her cell nearby, breaking the spell. "No more bothering Jules with your story when there's a perfectly good confessor around to hear it." To Julius's surprise, this interjection doesn't make the jitterbug jump. Instead he just calls: "Yes, ma'am!" and scoots over to Monseigneur Ex, closing the door behind.

"I guess you've met Tennessee already, then," Julius says to the open air.

"I guess I have, Jules," comes the mellow voice from behind him.

"I think I just recruited him," Julius says.

"I'm certainly glad you realized it," she says. "Because he recruited himself hours ago. Come over and sit awhile."

Nettles has her curtain pinned back on the choir side; an open invitation to visitors. Julius wanders over to her elegant cell and sits in the chair appointed near the opening. She nods hello without looking up. Short, sunburnt, hair in a kerchief, wearing a blue brocaded caftan, perched on a stool, knitting. Julius watches her. She's the eldest of their number, as the gray of her hair and the crease of her face will attest, but she holds a vitality that puts the rest of them to shame. It's something beyond physical prowess, it's...presence, Julius supposes. An undefeatable consistency, a diamond sharpness to her particular way of being, which is direct but cheerful, pragmatic, almost hard-nosed, but optimistic. Her eyes are flint chips. Her machine-mangled hands remain unhidden, and she uses them expressively when she talks without a thought to shame. Not that she lacks physical skills. She requires almost no sleep, as far as Julius can tell. The last to bed, the first to rise, and it's impossible to catch her napping. She begins work in her garden in the deep of night before the light comes, then on through the sunrise and all the way until noon, when she rests. Amazingly quick with those knitting needles, too; before the accident she could have gutted a live sardine swimming underwater; given her limitations, what she's doing with yarn is damn near miraculous. Look at her go—even diminished, she could have kept her factory job.

Julius and Nettles sit in the comfortable near-silence. Now he's here, the priest finds he's wary of speaking; he needs some time to order his thoughts, and it's good to sit with a full belly and think, or not think, in her presence. From across the transept, the juke is playing; Ella Fitzgerald sings the *Porgy and Bess* songbook in tones like cask-aged single malt...*Methuselah lived nine hundred years*...and, from the confessional, Tennessee can now be heard. Even without trying, Julius can still catch some rather predictable words: "pigeon" and "forge" and "Tennessee" and "Tennessee" and "Tennessee" ...*oh he made his home in that fish's ab-do-men*..."never go go going back, ever, not never," the reedy voice of Tennessee rising until you couldn't help but hear... but Julius stops himself. He knows with superstitious certainty any breach of previously-established trust—eavesdropping, say, even upon an unaware subject—might work strange alchemy on the Neon Fellowship's relational structure, kill the trust binding these disparate cells into a unified organism, break down their inexplicable atomy, make their relational gluons less gluey. Tennessee's confession holds no variance from the usual incomprehensible patter he's freely spewed today on the street—but no matter; probity must prevail. Father Julius holds the concept of confession at arm's length, considering it presumptive for any to dare hold the keys of penance or reconciliation, even—perhaps especially—a priest. This from hard experience. Back in his lean-to days, the failed and lonely days when he was still building the Neon singlehanded, when he still felt compelled by the pressure to do traditionally priestly things, he'd installed a real confessional, and had posted hours for any who wished to seek absolution. He sat each day on the hard bench awaiting customers in vain, passing time by scribbling his memoirs for no audience other than himself, lonely as Gandhi's barbecue fork.

After a month of this, Julius left the booth for the last time and left the Neon's worksite, jogging at random until he chanced upon a hardware store. There he purchased an axe with a heavy head and a sturdy pine handle, returned, hacked the confessional into staves and in the afternoon burned the pieces out on the street, his pamphlets the kindling, and on the blaze he roasted weenies and toasted marshmallows purchased at Ralph's. The kids had come first, and then some of the parents, and then the junkies, day-sober, driven mad by the smell of burning pig snout and lips. They were followed by the gangs, the boxcar-bangers, the factory workers coming off shift, assorted riff-raff. The bluebirds rolled by in their squad car, just once, and Julius had thought the party was over, but the cops apparently decided a bonfire in the middle of a city street wasn't worth cracking the car door over, not in Loony Island, anyway. He'd burned every one of his fingers on skewers and learned more about those around them and the state of their souls than he'd ever gotten from wearing a groove in the confessional bench. The other extraordinary thing: Members of all the gangs were represented, yet that night no guns were drawn, no fights broke out, and nobody got the old sharpened aluminum "howdy" between the ribs. Donk's doing. Sensing opportunity, Donk had surreptitiously sent over some kegs, extending the party into the night. Julius eventually got into his first organized fight down at the gutted factories. Lured into it by Donk, whose acquaintance he'd just made. The priest's opponent was a mean bright-eyed tough named Felix with a snaggletooth and jet-black hair, a nasty fighter with a pot belly of solid muscle and big mitts you could tell would feel like a couple of cement watermelons on your jawbone and eye sockets. He had limbs like steel rope knotted into extravagant and painful shapes, and most of the wagers were placed in his favor, but Julius made him circle and dance, and, when at last Felix's leather lungs could no longer pay the cardiovascular tax levied against them, the priest had closed in and started working those bright eyes. He bested Felix late in round five. The boxcar-bangers—a group of old toughs (and alleged firebugs) who lived nearby in a few old boxcars left behind on a stretch of long-abandoned track—crowned him a hero, carried him around on their shoulders down to their clubhouse, where they plied him with grain whiskey and taught him disgusting and wonderful songs. The accidental beginning of the Neon Order, because that night Brock, one of the bangers, crashed in the chapel. Julius never asked him to leave.

Even now, that's the way membership works: Nothing requested, nothing required. The lack of clear standards for inclusion are, ironically, what has kept their membership so exclusive. Certainly, it keeps the Island's religious population away. Most people have no way of dealing with a purely open invitation, and, suspecting some catch, some hidden snag lurking in the river, never dare get their toes wet.

In truth, each of them has discovered something or other to do.

Father Julius jogs the city, locating need—hungry folks, broken things—noting it, bringing the list to his proxy for funds.

Mysterious Dave Waverly, the secret proxy with reserves of moxie, he releases those funds.

And Jack and Brock, when they're not manning the grills, they fix what's broken.

And Sister Biscuit Trudy hauls sacks of fresh-baked rolls to the hungry.

And Sister Mishkin, she does the baking, then follows Trudy, carrying the excess sacks.

And Nettles tends the garden, grows the produce to balance the meal, and even adds some flowers for beauty.

And Brother Pretty Trudy, himself only recently escaped from a hard life selling ass, brings medical and emotional aid to all the pretty girls and pretty boys, and those not so pretty, and those aged out and discarded, all those whose young bodies bought them first attention and flattery, then rough treatment and bad use.

And Sister Winnie, a dropout from the Island's wholly unsuitable public schools, tutors in the secret room Donk and Julius made for abandoned children, the only other entrusted with its location.

But none of it is required, requested, or even suggested.

Brother Jack still has trouble believing nothing is required of him—that's how Monseigneur Ex came to be. Jack is not a man driven by self-mercy, he's a man driven by self-accountability. He'd been foreman on Sister Nettles' line when she had her accident, and he'd been the one to affix the tourniquets. Blood everywhere, and, in the blood, lifeless sardines taking one last sanguine swim beside a severed splay of fingers unnaturally liberated from their handsome positions. Brother Jack still confesses about it some nights, how the whole awful mess was his fault, *must* have been his fault, it had happened with him in authority, he should have ordered more inspections of the machines, tested the fail-safes with greater diligence…his tidal perseverations always bearing him back toward those severed digits among the fish. Monseigneur Ex doesn't mind, though; Ex never talks back.

Ex never tells you to shut up, either, Julius muses. Good news for Tennessee, who's still going and going and going as Nettles knits, as Ella proclaims the season summertime and the living easy. Monseigneur Ex holds mute witness, his register counting number by number, recording it all. They'd installed the first version of Monseigneur Ex a few months after the confessional-kindling weenie roast. Jack had insisted on having some form of confessional, confession being (as he saw it) necessary to absolution, but Julius had refused adamantly to have anything to do with the role of Father Confessor. "Not anymore," he told Jack. "It might be somebody else's place, but it's not mine."

Jack scowled. "That's not much help. Ain't you a priest?"

"So they say."

"Well, I need *some*thing."

"Well, holy shit, Jack, I'll think on it—how'd that be?"

And he had thought on it. Soon after, in the choir of his "cathedral," Julius began construction on a new confessional more suited to his hands-off missional strategy, made of high plywood planks. Inside, a plush couch. Facing the couch, a mirror, behind which lay a hollow. In this hollow, a cassette tape whirred on continuous loop, five hours' worth of tape writing and overwriting and overwriting itself in perpetuity. A sturdy door locked from the inside.

"Get in there, face the mirror, and talk," Julius said to Jack. "Anything you say will be recorded and then obliterated, which is exactly how I'd like you to think about it. You'll be talking to one of two individuals who can absolve you for anything in this old world, and you'll be staring at the second."

An hour later, Jack emerged from the box's inaugural confession and given the priest a single terse nod, Brother Jack's version of eloquence— *That'll do.*

This had been years ago, when it was only him and Brock, and Jack, and Nettles with massive gauze golf balls still bandaging her hands. Since then, the booth has become an unofficial member of their coterie. After years of worn and snapped audio tape, frustrating replacements of huge spools, and plenty of cursing, Julius had called the techs in to set them up with electronic data recording. They'd even blessed the confessional with a name: Monseigneur Ex-Position—because, as Julius had so frequently averred, confession was his position no longer. Each of them had at least occasionally spent time unburdening sin, crime, and foible to Monseigneur Ex, who took it all down without comment and then, as a function of his programming, deleted it.

On Nettles's wall, a cuckoo clock strikes the time. Julius opens his eyes and wonders idly if he's been snoring. Ella's taking five; Louis Armstrong is singing now, advising that a woman is a sometime thing. Nettles, noticing him stir, puts her knitting away, her face a complex map of perplexity and amusement and concern. "So," she says. "You showed up hours earlier, wandered in looking like you'd seen a ghost or killed a man, and then fell asleep, still sitting up, half into the night. When are you going to tell me all about your interesting day?"

Julius clears his throat. "How long has he been going?"—gesturing toward the confessional, where Tennessee is still prattling (Julius tries not to overhear) about the boxes, and the generations of love, and bird and spade, and his lost boy gone forever....

"Hours. Never have I been so glad for Monseigneur Ex. He was getting on Pretty's nerves, and Biscuit's, too. They were trying not to show it, but... well. They weren't trying hard. I sent him into the box to work it out there."

"Well then, thank Christ for Monseigneur Ex," Julius mutters.

"Yes, Jules," Nettles says—indulgently, but he can hear telltales of concern. "But you were just about to tell about whatever happened to you today—weren't you." It's not quite a challenge, but it's not a question, either. Julius gives her what he hopes is a charmingly rakish look.

"Maybe I found a lady friend."

"Maybe you didn't, though." Still, she raises one eyebrow. Julius marvels at his strange reluctance—didn't you come to Nettles seeking her reaction? It's just so hard to know what to say about what you saw. Perhaps it would be better to say what you *didn't* see? Jesus, what a day.

Finally, he says. "Trying to think how to say it."

She smiles, still concerned, but also now a little annoyed and a little amused. "Lips tongue and mouth are my recommendation."

"I was at the Wales this morning."

"You're at the Wales *every* morning."

"I saw someone there. A patient, I think. I saw him…until I didn't see him."

"He left?"

"He disappeared."

"He…"

"I mean sometimes he's there and sometimes he's not. Physically. He flickers in and out. Like a lightbulb."

He sees her try to hide her reaction, but it's no good; Nettles is obviously thinking the same thoughts that have been occurring to Julius all day. Perhaps this is a manifestation of some clot, the first telltale fissure in the foundation of an unsound brain, or perhaps this visitation is the first loose thread tossed from an unspooling psyche, an early indication that after years of trying to make a difference in a place the world has marked for indifference, Julius has finally begun losing his marbles…but Nettles doesn't say any of that, she only draws a long slow breath, adjusts her posture almost imperceptibly, and gives a short circular gesture with her needle, *go on, go on, please go on…*

Slowly, he begins to explain. Nettles keeps mostly still, listening, thumbs pressed together, unnaturally shortened fingers steepled. Occasionally she looks quizzical, occasionally she interjects. In particular she's concerned about the loonies; there's no way the Fritz Act was written to simply push hundreds of mental patients out on the streets, and the fact that's what's been done speaks to some as-yet-unseen malfeasance. As Nettles notes, it doesn't take a gardener to see what way the vine grows. Mostly she lets his silences hold until he's ready again to fill them. At last he arrives, haltingly, stumblingly, to the conclusion.

"He said something to me," Julius tells her.

"What did his voice sound like?" Nettles asks. That's Nettles; anyone else would ask what he *said*, she wants to know how he *sounded*. The question surprises him into answering more honestly than he might have. "Scared," Julius says flatly. "He sounded scared."

"What do you think he's scared of?"

"God," Julius says, surprised once again into the truth. That—explaining to Knuckles—was the whole problem. The flickering bastard had gone and gotten God involved in the mess.

Nettles listens to all this without comment until it's clear he's said all there is to say. At length she picks up her needles and begins knitting once more. Julius keeps still. It's clear to him he's not being dismissed; rather, she's keeping her hands busy while she thinks.

Finally she says: "Well, Jules, obviously you need to help him."

"You believe me that he's real?"

"Of course he's *real*."

"But the flickering—"

She waves his objection away impatiently. "I don't know about that part. You're nuts or something. Or really, you're nuts in a new way, because—" she gestures around the Neon Chapel—"you've *been* nuts. He's probably nuts, too. But who cares? The guy obviously needs your help, and that's what you do, is help people."

"But I just don't kn—*oww*!" She's poked him lightly with a needle, and now she's looking at him very kindly and very impatiently.

"Listen, guy. You came here because you want to help this fellow and for some reason you need to hear from somebody else that it's all right to do it. You picked me for that weird job, and I told you, and now you have to go do it. This isn't hard. What are you waiting for?"

"That sounds just like my boy!" shouts Tennessee, making both Julius and Nettles jump in their chairs. They hadn't noticed him leave Father Ex's confines; he's been eavesdropping.

"My boy gone forever and missing, he said God talked to him," Tennessee says. "Back in Pigeon Forge. My boy bought a lottery ticket and it won—big time. The prize was power over everything in the universe. That's why Morris was chasing him, and how I wound up in this mess."

Julius and Nettles exchange glances. One good thing about having Brother Tennessee around, the priest thinks, is I'll never have to worry about sounding like the craziest guy in the room. He's trying to formulate a response to Tennessee's odd proclamation when there's yet another disturbance, just as unusual in its own way.

A throat ostentatiously clears. Someone is standing in the middle of the central room, someone who's never been in the Neon Chapel before. It's Bailey, looking serious. She has her baton out, and her eyes scan the room restlessly, as if she anticipates a sudden attack.

"Father J," Bailey says. "Donk needs to talk to you. Tonight."

Julius stands. "What's the rhubarb?"

"Something very weird is happening at the Wales. We're thinking you can help shed light."

"I'm coming too!" Tennessee shouts. "I've got light to shed!"

Bailey glances his way, gives her tight-braided head a curt shake. "Invite-only deal, sorry." Strange; Julius thinks he sees some familiarity there, as if she's making note of a person already known to her. What the hell—has this loony met everyone in the neighborhood already?

He looks to Nettles. "Appears I have to go."

"Then you'd better get," Nettles says.

M E E T

Donk didn't tell Julius everything, but that wasn't out of hatred or mistrust. In fact, if you want the truth, I think he may have loved him; may have considered him the closest thing he had to a brother remaining.

It's just that Donk had other priorities.

In public, Donk appeared to honestly hate all people, which made it difficult for even those close to him to determine whether they were his friends or on the outs. This kept his friends safe but off-balance, and his enemies off-balance and in danger of over-reach or under-reach, providing Donk with valuable additional seconds of analysis, micro-hesitations as his adversaries tried to measure and process the barometric levels of his pique. Donk learned to exploit that advantage; it's how he managed for so many years to remain the top man in Ralph's organization. Donk's scowl he honed as sharp and precise and effective as any surgeon's knife or cartoonist's pen. The gangs might decide to negotiate to grow their profits, but, fearing what Donk's stink-eye might represent, they'd concede on their original ask, and a proposed three-percent decrease in funds paid to Ralph would become a one-percent increase, just like that. Ralph loved the extra funds, and so he loved Daniel Donkmien, who naturally behaved as though he hated Ralph most of all.

But this is what a thicket of lies does: makes it impossible to detect the thorn of truth.

Donk *did* hate Ralph most of all.

The secret Donk cradled closest was his memory of what Ralph did, what happened with the greenhouse…I'll tell you like Donk told it to me. It's a sad story but a simple one. Yale and Ralph had come up together—if Ralph was king, Yale was prime minister—but Yale got crosswind of him and Ralph killed him. That's the short of it—but the "why" hides the truth.

Why did Ralph kill Yale?

Ralph was in the midst of unifying the gangs, and he found out Yale was running a rival gang against Ralph on the side. It was an information racket. Every kid in the Island has a situation at home; a presence or an absence. For those with an absence, or those with a bad presence, back then, on the sly, there was Yale. Yale found an abandoned greenhouse up on the roof of HQ, which was the Headquarters, the part of Domino City that belonged to the Zoots, the main gang—Ralph's gang. Nobody knows who built the greenhouse, and nobody ever went up there until Yale found it. He made it a sort of a fort. It was a place for kids to go who had nowhere else. Kids are perfect spies; nobody notices them, and they're in every building on the Island, where intelligence is more valuable than gold.

You can maybe guess what happened next. Creating new gangs doesn't exactly lend itself to unifying the existing ones, and Yale well knew it. Yale was cutting Ralph out of his business, so Ralph cut Yale out of his life.

When Ralph found out, he caught Yale on the roof of HQ, right there in the greenhouse, and threw him right off that roof. Then all the kids who were in the greenhouse with him disappeared, and the disappearance got hushed up very effectively. Donk always assumed Ralph *had* them disappeared. It's a fair assumption.

But there were at least some who belonged to Yale's child gang that Ralph didn't kill.

Bailey was among Yale's elder recruits, only a few years younger than him—and of course Yale's little brother Donk was involved. They both saw Yale killed. They were skilled enough to have realized what was about to go down—but only in time to save themselves. They fled the greenhouse that day just in time, hid, and avoided the fate of the rest, but they saw Yale fall. Terrified, they went to earth and stayed there, beneath anyone's notice, until their undeniable skills raised them to enough local prominence that Ralph noticed them again.

Ralph wasn't suspicious when they reappeared. To him it wasn't a re-appearance, just an appearance. He never knew any of the names of Yale's child gang. He didn't know Donk knew anything about what had happened to his brother, but he needed a right hand, and he probably *was* feeling sentimental about his old partner. Nor did Bailey pose a particular concern. To him, Bailey was *his* relation. He didn't realize that Yale had been her boyfriend. He had no idea his two managers even knew each other before they became colleagues—a misapprehension those two encouraged. No, I doubt Ralph gave Yale a passing thought when he made the hires.

But Donk and Bailey sure gave Yale a passing thought. For them, their new jobs were less a hire than an infiltration. I suppose you could say seeing brother and lover murdered affected them a bit, as regarded their feelings toward Ralph Mayor.

x x x

It's nearly dark, and thus far the expected trouble hasn't arrived. Donk's closed down the store early, which is a tricky bit of business. You have to come up with a cover story the gangs will believe; Donk decided to claim an internal audit, requiring the manager's presence. Now they're by the checkout lanes, pretending to count cash and confabulating. Even so, Bailey frets; there's always the worry that news of an unauthorized closing will get back to Ralph. They also have to worry about whoever might be on the way.

Donk, being Donk, sees opportunity where Boyd sees only danger. In fact, Donk seems to be ready to shoot some crazy angle, seems to detect some hope that they've finally come near the end of their long vengeful road.

The problem with getting Ralph is all the bodyguards. You can't fight your way into Ralph's retirement villa. Survival of the fittest? Ralph's bodyguards are the fittest who survived. Even if you could sneak a weapon past their jealous eyes, you still have Ralph, old, but tough and mean. The odds of prevailing with a shiv against Ralph are not strong, and even then, there would be a bad death afterward. No way to fight past that shrewdness of apes; their paunches hide impenetrable mounds of muscle, they possess a frequently indulged taste for cruel deeds. They know their way around ordnance and cutting edges and brass knuckles, they knew where nerves cluster, they knew where to snip to make your ligaments give way like cables, unroll your muscles inside your skin.

What we need, Daniel is fond of repeating, is an army to go get the bastard. He has the unified gangs, sure, but his tenuous authority over them comes to him from Ralph. No good. He needs *another* army.

"And it seems the cardinals *are* an army," Donk says blandly. He's keeping as calm as he always does when things get dangerous. "And they seem organized, which suggests a general."

"An army and a general that are probably after our blood," Bailey points out.

Donk shrugs. "After us. With us. These things are mostly a matter of perspective. We'll negotiate those details when and if they show up."

"It might be the whole army of them," Bailey says. "Boyd, go back to the Fridge."

"He stays," Donk retorts. "I want whoever comes to see him, so they're sure they came to the right place. Also, if it comes to killing, they might start on him before me. Highly preferable."

"Not to *me*," Boyd says.

Donk smiles. "Yeah. Perspective really *is* everything, isn't it?" Bailey gives him an unpleasant look.

They wait. The fluorescents hum. "Maybe nobody will show," Boyd says, hopefully. Donk doesn't reply. Another minute passes, and then a shiny red bowling ball comes crashing through the middle pane of the storefront window, punching through the paperpaste sludge of advertisements obscuring it, shattering it into a galaxy of tiny glass beads. For a moment there's nothing in the gap but night, then a man dodges into sight, steps through the hole with precise, almost dainty, movements. He takes a few crunching steps into the grocery, watching the triad standing at the checkout lanes, then stops: a compact fellow with sharp features and large eyes. Boyd flashes recognition. He's the guy from before, the man with the syringe—or anyway he's dressed like him. In his left hand a second bowling ball perches like a spheroid hunting bird.

"Which one of you is the snoop?" he asks. He might be asking for paper instead of plastic, or if he could use the john. Conversational, that voice. Cultured. Polite. A voice that tells you to come on in and asks if you want some tea; meanwhile the bowling ball in his left hand wants to talk business, while his eyes measure you with dispassionate assay, as if counting the exact number of shovel-lifts required to dig your shallow grave.

"I sent him," Donk lies, and Boyd notices him working his old magic, immediately shifting his tone to match that of his adversary. "That window's going to cost you about twelve hundred plus installation."

The man doesn't move. "What's your business in the Wales?"

"Maybe we want to welcome you to the neighborhood," Donk said. "Maybe we didn't know where to address the postcard."

"You're a friendly guy."

"This is Ralph's town. I'm Ralph's guy."

"The welcome wagon."

"We can't have strangers just wandering. It's not safe for us, for them, for anybody. We can't be friends that way."

"So you *are* friendly."

"I'm friendly to my friends. Thinking we might be able to help each other, maybe."

"You have something I need?"

"Nope." Donk languidly stretches his back. "But I *know* what you need to know."

"Then where is he?"

"Most things can be arranged. Where do you want him to be?"

This stops the guy for a moment; he was clearly expecting to be asked *who is "he?"* Something almost like yearning plays on his face. He says: "If you want to help me, then simply help me. Help me because you understand why you should. Because you've learned what sort of lesson you are to me."

It's an odd thing to say. Donk wisely ignores it. "Who are you people? What are you doing in these tunnels? After you get your guy, what's your long game? Do you have a message to Ralph for me?"

The man gives Donk another one of those long appraising looks, as though he were trying to read something in fine print lodged an inch behind Donk's eyeballs. It's the look the mongoose gives the cobra. And, as it lengthens, it grows colder and colder. Finally, the man says, "You answer to… Ralph?"

Donk takes a deep breath. "That's…*negotiable*. It seems you might be thinking about a move. Maybe you're even considering a takeover. I may be of use to you there. I—"

"Here's my message for this 'Ralph' of yours," the man says, and with one practiced flick of the wrist, 224 ounces of Kentucky's finest compressed urethane leaves his hand, smashing into one of Bailey's beloved cash registers with a hefty THUK. The register tips, capsizes, and crashes to the tile, where it splits open, belching a cornucopia of spare change. In the instant Bailey head-whips to follow the ball along its path, the man clears the distance, holds a long knife a centimeter from Donk's throat. "No closer, please," he purrs to Bailey, and then, addressing Donk: "You think I *might* be taking over? Don't you realize I already *have*? This whole so-called 'island' is mine already. Anyone thinking otherwise just hasn't yet realized my truth. Please," the man says, stepping away, his voice placid as a monastery pond. "Tell Ralph that. And if you ever send one of your snoops down one of my chimneys again, be sure you've made yourself a useful lesson to me, or else you'll find out exactly what I can do to you. You can go tell Ralph that, too, whoever he is, because the same goes for him. Ralph's time is done now. Please, go. Tell Ralph."

Then he backs away, steps through the hole, and is gone. The whole exchange hasn't taken much more than a minute.

The second ball comes to rest near Boyd's foot. He picks it up and turns it in his hands: deep maroon with embedded sequins. PROPERTY OF BARNEY'S SUDS the inscription. Fourteen-pounder. "Guy's got a hell of an arm," Donk declares.

"He must've grabbed them from the alley on his way over," Boyd muses, mostly to himself.

Bailey, lifting the cash register, inspecting for damage: "Seems there's a new boss in town."

"Suppose so. Maybe we can get him to hire us." Donk looks out the hole in the window.

"*And* operating out of the Wales," Boyd says.

"So he claimed," Donk answers. "All the more reason to learn what Father Julius saw as soon as we possibly can. Boyd, ready to go collect a priest?"

Bailey insists: "I'm going. You're not sending Boyd with cardinals crawling around." She's clearly expecting a fight over the matter, but Donk says nothing, and Bailey leaves for Julius without another word.

"What you're telling me is you've seen the Invisible Man," Donk says, back in the Fridge, giving Julius a disgusted look. Bailey's returned with the priest;

the four of them enjoying an aperitif in the sitting room. Seemingly out of habit, Donk and Julius have set themselves in adversarial posture, holding the self-serious and fatuous aspects of collegiate debaters. It's how they spend all their meetings together; it's this almost fraternity nonsense between the two of them; freed from the obligation on the street to pretend they don't know each other, it seems both of them just enjoy busting each other's balls. Donk's got his tie off and his shirtsleeves rolled up, which is about as ruffled as he ever gets; meanwhile, Bailey keeps alert for trouble—for, though no trouble immediately presents itself, the tone has recently sharpened. The concern's unnecessary, in Boyd's opinion. Certainly, she's seen harsher words pass between the two. But today, the contention between the two appears genuine.

"*Flickering* man," Julius says. "He's not invisible."

"What does that even mean, *flickering*—?"

"It means he's there until he's not," Julius says, with the annoyed air of someone repeating an answer he's given already.

"Fine. So what's this flickering man's fluckering name?"

"I didn't think to ask," Julius confesses.

Donk clears his throat, ostentatiously skeptical. "Well. I've seen a lot, but I've never seen a flickering man. Ask me to find a vampire, or a *hobbit*, maybe—"

"Your people in the Wales haven't seen anything?"

"My people in the Wales—*what* people? I don't deal with that cracker box. Full of vegetables. I'm a meat lover."

Not a bad line. Boyd fumbles for his pad, jots: cracker box; *veggies, meat-lover.*

"You must have someone."

"I've got more contacts in your chapel than I do the Wales." Bailey gives Donk an immodest sideways glance, which surprises Boyd—Bailey's usually far subtler—but it's perfectly readable to him: *Are we not telling Julius the man with the bowling ball is from the Wales, then? And why not?*

Julius's eyes narrow. "You've got...spies at the Neon?"

"I've got you. Imbecile." Donk says, but with affection. Purposefully turning down the temperature; he must have gotten whatever information it was he wanted out of the priest.

Julius smiles. "Ah." Finishing his drink in small ruminative sips, he says,

"But in any case, I'm going to help him, if I can. He says he's being chased, and sure, he thinks it's...well, *God*...in pursuit—but I think he's right that somebody's after him. There's no question he's scared of something."

"You'll want to be quick if you're going to help him," Boyd says, and suddenly everybody is paying a whole lot of attention to him. He hadn't even meant to say it.

"Why quick?" Julius demands. "What do you mean?"

"Yes, *Boyd*. Do tell us," Donk says, staring lasers.

Now it's Boyd's turn to tell a halting fumbling tale; the vivid man, the man in a powder-blue suit. Overwhelmingly aware that he neglected to tell Donk and Bailey about him, knowing Donk's going to give him a year's worth of hell for the lapse—and why, he wonders, *did* you withhold? You're his sneak, his snitch, his snatcher, you don't forget details when you report. It's almost like you felt compelled to follow the letter of the folding man's law. *Tell Julius* he said, so tell Julius you did, and tell Donk you did not. "He's actually how I found the tunnels," Boyd finishes. "He told me to check where he was standing. But he *also* told me that Father Julius didn't have much time left to help his flickering man out. 'Hours not days,' I believe were his words."

"It's probably because of the Fritz Act." Bailey rises, walks to the billiard table, absently juggles two balls with her left hand. "Flickering or not, they're not going to let him stay anymore, are they? And that's another thing, Daniel—the Fritz Act. They just let the loonies wander? Have you noticed, every time today there was a gaggle of loonies, there was a cardinal swinging a—"

"Cardinal?" Julius asks.

"Donk's name for the guys in red. The ones with the swords. Have you seen them?"

"Yeah," Julius says. "I've seen them."

"And then this mysterious adviser of yours just cut bait and ran off into the night, huh?" Donk asks, clearly not ready to let Boyd off the hook. Boyd, deciding he has enough to explain to Donk already without mention of *folding*, nods.

"How very unremarkable," Donk says, just mildly enough to tell Boyd how angry he is.

"I don't know anybody by that description," the priest growls. "How does he know me?"

"No clue, Father. He said his name was Landrude, if that helps."

"*Landrude?*"

"That's what he said."

"I know nobody by that name."

"*Nobody* knows anybody by that name," Donk says. "It's got to be an alt."

"Sure, like 'Donk,' maybe," Julius stands. "Unless you've got other questions, I'd better go. If Boyd's weird new friend is right, I've got some work to do and a pressing deadline."

Donk offers his hand. "If we can help, you've got us; just let us know." They exchange some pleasantries and Julius disappears into the summer night. Boyd keeps quiet, knowing he's about to face a hurricane of recrimination from Donk. But it doesn't come. Instead Donk sits lost in thought, his drink refilled but forgotten, studying the section of newspaper Julius gave Boyd, with what looks to be a green rectangle colored onto the middle. "It seems to me," he says, meaningfully, "That there's somebody, living in the Wales, who is hard to find."

"There *might* be." Bailey, sitting on the billiard table.

"And *since* there is," Daniel murmurs, "That hard-to-find somebody might just be the sort of person *another* somebody might be looking for, very hard, and without success. Yes?"

Boyd gets it. Their friend with the bowling ball had spoken out of turn. "Where is *he?*" had been the question. The search was for a "him." Not information. Not a weapon. A guy. Somebody hard to find. And here's the cardinals walking around the loonies, swinging those wooden swords, searching for...something. And here's Father Julius with a story about a guy in the Wales who is hard to see. And here's this new player, who's set up his operations under the Wales. And, relief: Ralph isn't personally trying to oust them, which is good, and Ralph's obviously on the way out, which is better, but Donk's going to need to be on the right side of the coup—with no idea how to get there.

The pieces fit for Boyd; likely they also fit for Donk, who tells him: "Tail our holy friend. Right now. We might have had more time but you opened your big fat mouth in front of company and put the friar on a fast track. He's either going to the Wales or his place. Try the Wales first—and be careful. Find out what he knows and what he's doing, and get back here. I'm visiting our new friend as soon as I can."

Bailey, obviously unhappy at this direction: "He said if you went without useful information, he'd…" she leaves the implication unstated.

"That's very true," Donk replies, without turning from Boyd. "Which is why you need to go right now. Because—" sparing Bailey a glance—"I am sure enough going to go try to get us a new boss *and* a new army. And thanks to mister 'hours not days' here, I'm going as soon as I can."

"Daniel, this flickering man…that can't be real. It—"

"Doesn't matter. It's a whatever. It's not what Julius thinks it is, but what he thinks it is doesn't matter. What matters is, it's something, and it's probably the opening we're looking for. Whatever Boyd can get me, I'll use. I'll make the rest up if I need to."

Bailey stalks back to their room, slamming the door as she goes. Boyd hesitates, unsure of how best to comfort his sister. She's made herself so practical, so efficient, self-contained, intimidating; it seems to him sometimes as if she's become entirely smooth-edged, as untouchable for emotional aid as she is in a grapple…

Donk rounds on his sneak. "Fix your fuckup," he says, quietly—only his eyes snarl. "We need to do this right. We're nearly there." Meaning revenge on Ralph, of course. Considering the three of us are suddenly so close to our goal, thinks Boyd, running through shortcuts and backways, we sure don't any of us seem happy about it. Is revenge the only thing holding us together anymore? But questions aren't what you're made for, Boyd. Do what you do. Sneak, follow, listen…but hey, how *had* the folding stranger known? How long has he been watching you? And…if Donk is holding back information from *Julius*, Boyd, what might he be hiding from *you*? All this behind-door work, all this subterfuge, but why does it seem so much like you're being left out of it somehow? Why this sense that there's some piece of it you're being left out of? It feels like a sort of soft death, it feels like fading into some un-noticeable grayness where you're less than not, subject to vagaries of chance, subject to infinite change, it feels like…

It feels like you're falling out of your own story.

Hmm. There might be a story in that.

Out comes the pad, he jots: *folding, falling, out of story, subject to infinite change.*

As Donk predicted, Julius's destination is the Wales; he's in the day room where Boyd ran into the priest this morning, the spot where Julius claims he first saw the flickering man. And a good thing too—my God, you've seen the pace the fellow sets. If he'd been going far, you'd have lost him for good. Boyd maneuvers against the walls until he spots Father Julius sitting in an alcove, talking across a low table to an empty chair—Damn. There's no mysterious man, there's nothing; the priest truly has gone batty, the whole story is guff. Boyd hides behind a nearby davenport and peeks around at poor old Father Julius blabbering away at nothing and nobody, and wonders—Why are you so down about this? You're not like Donk, hoping so badly to acquire a playing chip to curry favor with some new boss, so you can get at Ralph. The revenge is Donk's thing, and maybe Bailey's. For Boyd, Ralph's crimes have drifted into haze; it's past, it's over, it's bad shit that happened in a place where bad shit happens. So why this deflation, this sense of loss, to find Julius sitting here talking to the air? Perhaps it's that it's a dangerous development for Donk, who's planning to go seek a dangerous man's patronage. He'll need something real to offer, not some street minister's bunk. But it's not concern for a friend, no; Donk is more than capable of handling himself. Perhaps it's just that it's sad to see yet another pillar of the community lose out to the ceaseless grind of Loony Island's depredations, to see a sanity that previously seemed steadfast finally shredding? It feels like...like some sort of secret hope has died. Boyd admonishes himself—Well, what did you expect, though, really? It's not a believable story. A *flickering* man? And since that's not right—

In the empty chair a man suddenly appears, then disappears. Boyd almost screams.

He almost screams a minute later, when it happens again.

Boyd's mastered himself by the third appearance. The flickering man is popping in and out, but he's more there than not, now. He's just what Julius had told them. And now he's talking. Boyd keeps still and quiet and hidden, and very watchful. Suddenly, he discovers, he's hearing many useful things.

T R U S T

Nobody knew how Julius funded the Neon Chapel, though everyone wondered. The only clue most ever saw was a small brass plaque affixed to the wall by the door, dedicating the building to an anonymous donor. The more waggish speculation was Julius had found a benefactor, some rich old biddy, whom he'd convinced to open up the old checkbook, wink-wink. Others suspected Julius was actually on the grease with Ralph; that the Mayor of Loony Island had put the priest on the payroll to act as a psy-op, a kind of spiritual peacekeeper, free to act but agreeing never to speak out directly against immoral gangland activity—and it's true that Julius never discriminated against gangster or goon. A few wise souls shaved with Occam's razor and guessed Julius was just another rich dilettante playing at savior. Those last were closest to the truth—and I suspect Julius might've agreed with their unkind assessment of his motives—but honestly, when it came to "rich," they had no idea. And nearly nobody knew Julius had a connection to the Slantworthy Trust. Donk may have been the only other in Loony Island who knew about it, and that only because of his dealings with Julius over the children's room. I imagine Nettles knew, too, but if so she never spoke word in my presence. But it was true: Julius secretly held a majority stake in Slanty's Amalgamated Foodstuffs, which owned the cannery, the only factory in the Island that hadn't closed—a connection that explained its unaccountable continuance.

The Slantworthy wealth was as indestructible as a continent, spread over the generations across a robust and diverse crust of hedge funds, tax shelters, and other promiscuous financial devices, increasing a principal derived from, and continually added to by way of, the family's majority ownership of SAF, Inc. This enormously successful concern was founded by Julius's great-great-great-great-grandfather, Søren Slantworthy, a seaman and whaler who worked his way from crew to captain, from captain to ship's owner, and from there to owner of a fleet. Slanty's Sardines had its first success providing the world with canned pickled fishies (by the early nineteenth century, the name "Slanty" had become synonymous with sardines throughout the world), but quickly diversified into tuna, salmon, and whitefish, and from there moved into ambergris, into gold and diamond and coffee and cacao plantations, into slaves and bananas and pineapple and citrus, into beef, into pork, into rice, barley, wheat, into who knows what all else.

By his adulthood, Julius wanted nothing more to do with all this mess. He tried his best to walk away, apprenticing for years with unaffiliated contractors, learning a trade in construction. But divesting yourself of a generational boodle isn't as easy as it seems. The Slantworthy board of directors had sway, the shareholders had concerns, the corporate leadership had its targets, and all of it involved only growth. Growth of what, Julius wanted to know, and why, and in service of what ends? But they had ways of talking about all these things in the Slantworthy boardroom that never quite managed to touch the eventual decision for growth and growth and growth and growth. Julius soon learned the hard way that if you cast monstrous wealth off, it'll still crawl around on its own, and off the chain it cares not who it eats.

Then again, Julius well knew, if you *don't* cast off monstrous wealth, it will for sure eventually eat *you*. So, Julius sought distance. An arm's length. Chains for the beast and a cage, all drawn out in meticulous words on a sheaf of pages thick as a T-bone, signed in triplicate. This would require someone he could trust, someone he knew well, someone unmoved by money, someone who knew the byzantine monkey bars of corporate politics well enough to swing from handhold to handhold, but with so little interest in succeeding at them he'd never care if he fell.

Luckily, Julius had just the fellow for the job.

× × ×

It's bothersome, Father Julius decides, jogging up the Wales steps for the third time that day, how it's impossible to decide whether Boyd's supposed mystery stranger's message is real or just another layer in some game Donk's playing. And…if it's *not* from Donk…who, then? Boyd, freelancing? That doesn't track. Maybe he's telling the truth. That means another player in this game, someone who already knows about a man who's sometimes there and sometimes not.

Hours not days. So says Boyd. Or so says someone who talked to Boyd. Or maybe so says Donk through Boyd. Whichever way, it's likely a message you'll want to pay attention to. Also, there's Nettles in his head—*Jules, this is obviously what you're meant to do. What are you waiting for?*

There's no guard at the Wales, no lock on the door keeping intruders out or inmates in. "Out" and "in" are concepts bearing little meaning anymore, after the Fritz Act. He traverses the long green-tiled corridor to the beige day room, razor alert the way you only get when you're nearly a day without sleep and coasting on adrenaline fumes. The room's ghostly in night shadow, empty, scantly lit, and Julius makes his slow way across the room, no sudden movements, arriving at last in the alcove where he'd made first contact. Turning his head this way and that; trying to catch a glimpse of a flicker in his peripheral vision—nothing. He's not here. But he might be, that's the problem. Isn't that why you came? If seeing him is indeed a matter of trust, you'll need as much of his trust as you can get.

He's surprised to find that he's reluctant to speak the words he came to say, even though there's likely nobody there to hear it. Julius sits there in silence, breathing shallow and steady, a cliff diver bringing himself to the point of foolish resolve. "I'd like to introduce myself. My name is Julius Slant-worthy," he announces to the empty space around him. "I don't release the last name lightly, though I doubt it would mean much to you. They call me a priest, which…" he pauses. It's something he's said to himself so many times before, how strange to have such ambivalence about saying it out loud, even to a probably empty room. "…which I am *not*. It's maybe a bit more complicated than that, but not all that much more complicated. I'm not a priest. It's an accreditation I gave myself, and it's an accreditation that only gets renewed by the repetition of others. There's a miracle they claim I did, and, well…never mind about that one. It's a miracle that I allow to be attributed to me. No, that's bullshit—I *encourage* the attribution. Nod and wink and smile and wise silence, fooling myself I'm not lying. There's no better gravy for the soul than delusion."

He's on the verge of saying more. For a moment he feels the danger of speaking aloud his most dangerous truths, but then, just as he breathes to begin, there's a distraction—Julius, staring at his hands, allows himself to hope he's been seeing something flicker in the edge of his perception.

"Here's the thing, though: The fact that I call myself priest—whatever else it might mean about me—it means I want to help you. And that last name...well, that name means that I'm actually able to get you whatever help you might need. I have to think you...*appeared* to me, or whatever you did, for a reason. And I think that time's getting short." Coming to a finish and looking up, he sees the flickering man—entirely there, flickering no more. He's not smiling, but he doesn't look frightened. At least, thinks Julius, he doesn't look frightened of me.

"My name's Gordy," the man says. "I need to find the lady."

"The...lady?"

"Jane. I have to help her. It's my fault."

"I'm sorry?"

"She's an acrobat. A bearded lady...I did it to her. I didn't mean to, but I did."

"I'll help you find her, then," Julius says, standing. He offers his hand, not yet daring to touch. "But not from here. Come with me. I'll get you somewhere safe."

"I can't go with you. She's in Färland."

Julius's brow furrows. Färland? The kid's...European? His voice has a hint of the American South in it, not the Continent. He shakes his head clear—*there are far bigger mysteries today than geography, Julius, stick to the mission.* "Fine. I'll take you to Färland. We can be there by tomorrow."

Gordy shakes his head, emphatically. "If we go to Färland your way, it won't be the right Färland. I have to go back the way I came."

Even with his long experience reading manifestos of delusion, Julius isn't sure how to respond to this.

"And *they're* out there. They'll get me if I go."

"'They,' who?"

"They get so close sometimes with their swords," Gordy says. "They used to be in here, but the doors were locked so I couldn't leave. I hid. Now they go out there, so I have to stay."

"Why do they want you?"

"He says I have it," Gordy says. "But I don't know what *it* is."

"Who says?"

Gordy looks around him as if he expects to see his stalker lurking behind. "He's still here. I see him in here sometimes. But mostly out there, now. He thinks I'm there. I stay here. I keep to the edges of the walls. But I see him. He creeps around. He's still looking. I have to stay here."

"Who is he?" Julius asks, fearing the answer, desiring it.

"Morris," Gordy says. It's a keen, almost a song. "Morris, Morris, Morris Love."

"But what about *God*?" Julius blurts.

Gordy looks terrified, flickers once, then shakes his head mulishly. "He's *not* God."

"You said God talks to you. You said he wants you to do something bad."

"I don't know what you mean," Gordy says. "I don't know anything about that. I have to go to Färland."

"But you *said*," Julius pleads, almost childishly.

"I don't know anything about that," Gordy says, and flickers once, twice, then out. Julius bites his inner cheek, keeps himself from leaping forward and grabbing at the empty air only by incredible force of will—knowing beyond doubt that a grab will lose him any trust he's built. *Hours not days.*

"All right," he tells the empty air. "You want Färland? I'll get you to Färland. You sit tight here until I get back; I'm going to go put it all together for you."

He's not searching the dark corners of the day room as he turns and leaves it, running already. It's doubtful, though, even had he been, he'd have seen the thin form of Donk's best sneak, crouched far in the shadows, keeping very still and very attentive.

✕ ✕ ✕

Julius jogs south, away from the Neon Chapel, down the switchback, out of the Island, leaving first the darkling factories and then the abandoned railyard behind. Guided by an instinct he can't name, he's decided not to bring this pressing need Donk's way. No, Julius decides, there's only one other person who can help you with this sort of pickle, and besides—glance at the watch—he'll be expecting you soon anyway. The first appointment of your day, this run is the first normal thing that's happened to you since you first saw loonies leaking from the Wales. Fighting the heaviness of his eyelids— God, you haven't slept since that happened.

The pre-dawn hours are best for a run out of the Island; it's when the toughs and gossips and cops and gangsters slumber; little chance of being seen by an inquisitive soul or set upon by gangs of muggers. Running now with the thinnest hint of sunrise starting in the east, he's letting the miles pass by, the urban closeness slowly giving way to well-ordered streets lined with neatly spaced and similarly sized houses, like faces in a high school yearbook, like lines of sparrows on a telephone pole. Dawn is best for safe passage in this neighborhood, as well, though for different reason. A big bearded guy in a denim robe looks wild even in Loony Island; trying this jog during business hours would make the sort of spectacle that gets the cops called. He's near now, running easy and free, mind open to ponder Gordy—What to make of him? He'll agree to leave the immediate danger of the Wales, but only once you meet his demands. And... *Färland?* Who is he? Sprung from where? He says he doesn't know. Nor apparently will he answer any questions about talking to God, or God talking to him. Obsessed with a bearded acrobat, whoever *she* is; it apparently matters to him more than self-preservation. Why is he here? Julius can hardly guess, but he knows this much: The flickering man is in trouble.

He's on Dave Waverly's street. Dave's house is a small brick bungalow, tastefully but minimally appointed, nestled into a neighborhood notable for its near-total recession into nondescription; neither particularly old nor new, neither ostentatious nor decrepit, built on a neatly trimmed patch of turf slightly larger than a postage stamp. A place where a middle-aged widower of modest means might choose to exist and remain, where young childless couples just getting started might perch for a season before flitting off. But this sameness hides a seat of power: Dave Waverly, formerly Wavy Dave, for-mer shambling heap, former corporate executive fallen to the very bottom of the bottle, former ward of their old shared mentor, now Julius's trustee for all matters related to Slantworthy Inc., executive manager with power of attorney of the Slantworthy Trust, a juggernaut of a financial apparatus designed to insulate a sardine scion and would-be street priest from the more terrifying consequences of his own wealth.

Dave's door is a cheerful yellow. Julius raps on it smartly. He's early, but not overly so; he knows his trusted trustee will be up and about. There's no need to knock twice; after a brief desultory internal shuffling the door swings in, there's a smell of coffee already brewed, and there's Dave Waverly, already put together and ready. A razor part in his thinning steel-gray hair. Whiff of aftershave. He's wearing a brocaded sweater over his crisp white shirt to guard against the pre-sunrise morning chill, but otherwise he's boardroom-ready.

"Good morning, kid," Dave Waverly says with his radio announcer's voice, peeking over his glasses. "You're early." Then, getting a better look at Julius's face—"Everyone OK over on your side?"

Julius nearly starts and rejects a handful of explanations. "It's pretty complicated."

"It's usually pretty complicated," Dave says, and there's almost the threat of a smile. But Dave Waverly doesn't smile. You have to watch those hooded eyes for the twinkle.

"Well. It's more complicated than usual."

"You needed to bring a second notebook, did you?" Their meetings usually consist of two phases: Dave's business for Julius, then Julius's business for Dave. Dave will pull papers from his briefcase for Julius to sign, items to disclose, items to discuss; Julius will shake his head no, nod his head yes. Then, from one of the makeshift pockets sewn into his robes, Julius will pull a spiral notebook and read his list, a series of numbers and notes taken from his most recent trips through the blasted floors of Domino City and the pockmarked parcels of Checkertown: *bldng six, rm 1778, broken oven; bldng three, 619, bedbugs; bldng five, 112, windowpanes smashed, need fortified...* Dave listening, making efficient notations on his own, significantly less-battered pad, which he then places into his briefcase. Later, Dave will make the arrangements to fund the repairs.

It won't be like that today. "I didn't bring my notebook," Julius confesses. "I've spent all day with a different project." Feeling shame as he says it; his regulars waited in vain for him yesterday, and they'll likely wait in vain today, their needs unmet. He's a lifeline, and he's cutting it—for how long? And, for what reason? Sure, Gordy's in need, too…and his need is immediate, yes… but he's only one person, and anyway altruism's not what's driving you…

"Better get some coffee while you tell me about it, then," Dave says, turning inside. Julius follows, thinking—If only Dave had just one bottle of booze in the house, just one. You could use a stiffener in that coffee before explaining to your trustee that he has to figure out how to get a freed lunatic with no passport or even ID onto a private flight to Färland, preferably to-day, because there's a bearded lady living there…he's going to think you're absolutely crazy.

But of course, once he's explained Dave Waverly doesn't call him crazy. He listens with unchanging expression, his big jowls unshaken by outrage, his hands clasped lightly around his coffee cup, which he raises to his slightly protruding lower lip exactly once during Julius's long discourse, taking a sin-gle measured drink. When Julius has finished, Dave Waverly raises one hand to his chin and looks at the tabletop for about a minute, thinking deeply.

"Why don't I start with the part of this I *believe*?" he says at last. "I believe this young man exists. I believe he is in some sort of trouble. And I certainly believe you've managed to get yourself caught up in it."

"He's definitely in trouble. He's—"

"*And* I believe it has something to do with the Fritz Act, as you suggest." Dave Waverly says. "The fact that these 'loonies,' as you so piquantly call them, have been released is alarming to say the least. The whole thing has been an absolute snafu. Look." He tosses the previous evening's edition on the table. The headline reads FRITZ FIASCO; the picture shows a man running to a car, face hidden by hat and coat. The caption reads: *JAWPI Director T. Ivan Ragesalad Under Fire; City Board Calls for Immediate Removal.*

"The loonies weren't supposed to be let out?"

"You can read for yourself. Even if society has apparently determined to rid themselves of their concern about the risk abandonment poses to the patients themselves, still they recognize that those patients present various levels of risk to society. As such, they were meant to be furloughed in stages, beginning today, with some sort of oversight and some sort of triage. Certainly, there was meant to be at least some attempt to identify violent offenders among the population, and create some sort of exception list. Yet somehow, the whole kit and caboodle were unceremoniously pooped out the front doors the first morning of the program. It's going to be a massive scandal before it's all done. Heads, as they say, will roll. Something's up."

"Then you agree, we've got to get Gordy out."

"Perhaps. But remember, we've only covered the part of your story I believe."

"He needs to go Färland, he says," Julius insists. "He says he won't leave unless we take him out of there very specifically, and also not unless we can take him right to Färland. And it has to be secret, without any papers, which in any case he doesn't have."

From an inner pocket, Dave Waverly produces a frictionless cloth and makes a show of cleaning his glasses. "Julius, my dear friend. Are you aware I am not an international spy?"

"Yes, but you're—"

"Certainly I will not arrange an extra-legal end-run around European Customs," Dave Waverly says. "Nor do I have any intention of learning how one might do so, nor of making even the most cursory inquiries into how to do so." He leans in. "Even the suggestion seems unwise," he says in a lower tone, "Given that it would make me knowledgeable about violating the law, which might lead to me actually violating the law, which would make you accessory. Which could, among other things, jeopardize the trust. Do you understand what I'm telling you?"

Of course, Julius thinks—*this* is why you work with Donk. Here's a request that's at least adjacent to illegal shit. And Dave Waverly may be skilled at many things, but the primary reason he's perfect for your needs is his stubbornness. There's not a single thing anybody on the Slanty's board can do to sway him from your principles, no scheme to divest you by trying to have you declared insane will ever tempt him, but it also means that you're never going to get him to budge on something he thinks violates those principles. My God, the work you had to do just to get him to set up your monthly payoffs to Ralph Mayor, both from the Neon and from Slanty's. He'd nearly quit over it.

"But we've got to do something." Julius says, thinking of Gordy's haunted eyes. *They come so close sometimes*, Gordy'd said. *And they're still trying.*

"If either of us is going to do anything, I hope we both agree it shouldn't be something unwise." Dave Waverly ponders a while more, while Julius paces and frets. "I suggest you lie to your friend, kid," he says at last. "*Tell* him he's going to Färland, and then take him somewhere else in the city. He'll still be hidden, and safe, and it's far easier to do besides. And legal. If you like, I'll drive you to pick him up tonight." He tilts his chair against the wall, puts his well-shod feet up on his kitchen table, and folds his hands on his expansive belly, looking pleased with himself.

"*Lie* to Gordy?"

"Surely you're familiar with the concept of untruth."

Julius imagines it; realization dawning on Gordy's face as he flickers out, once, twice, for good. And then what? Grab him? No—*seize* him? Tie him down? Be just the next kidnapper hauling this poor scared fellow around? "I won't be able to *see* him unless he trusts me. When he realizes I've lied..."

Dave Waverly raps his knuckles on the kitchen table, once, hard, the action of an executive used to being heard and obeyed, used to reasserting control with ease. It works. "Your friend has a pressing need, which he refuses to address unless he secures an unattainable demand. And yet, you claim the need remains pressing. So: Tell him whatever you need to tell him to remove him from this danger, take him somewhere safe, and then when you get there, tell him whatever you think he needs to hear in order to get him to accept where he is. From there, perhaps, with time our ally rather than our enemy, we can make other plans. In any event, for the love of all that's holy, *never* verbalize such notions in my presence again. Flickering men and bearded ladies. There's enough talk about having you committed as it is. Do you understand how you appear to the board?"

"I think we need to get him to another city. A private flight."

"I will not appropriate funds for a private aircraft until I have better ascertained the facts of this situation. Come on, kid. Surely you understand that."

Julius sees it all at once—of course. *Let* Dave Waverly ascertain the facts. He'll never believe in the flickering man by just hearing it, so show him. Let him contend with a man who flickers, and see how it musses the perfect part in his hair.

"You're right," Julius mutters. "Of course. Can we bring him here first?"

He sees Dave Waverly visibly relax, relieved his good common sense has finally taken root. "Here will be acceptable for a day, perhaps. From there we can determine what further accommodation and assistance might be appropriate to his situation, and provide it. We'll collect him tonight. Is this acceptable?"

"I don't know. I guess so." Julius begins to feel dizzy. The events of the day are catching up; body and mind both feel sleep's lack and the toll of hard miles of road. His system is coming to the end of itself. He thinks: Oh my God. I think that I know what I hadn't known yet. How did you keep yourself from knowing? You're not just getting Gordy out of Loony Island, you're going with him. And for how long? And to what uncertain future? Julius suddenly has the feeling of being on a slide without knowing how he got on—you've been floating in a pond that's turned into a river, and there are rapids ahead; how did this happen, where's your paddle? Julius, can you *swim*? Do you know how to navigate? Are there waterfalls? What if the river takes you to an ocean? Are you too near the shore with its jagged rocks and crashing surf?

To the expectant stare of Dave Waverly Julius says none of this; there'll be time enough for all that later. Instead he only nods, and adds: "We'll want to be quick. Gordy's paranoid. He's going to want to be hustled out of the Wales into a car."

Dave Waverly closes his eyes. "The car I can provide. You bring the hustle. Now," he says, clearly changing the subject. He draws some papers from his satchel, sets them on the table, hands Julius a pen. "You may have no regular business for me, but I have some for you. And I'll certainly have more for you tonight, if you're planning on taking an indefinite sabbatical from our daily meetings. Are you ready?"

"I hope so," Julius says, reaching for the pen, mind far from the task. A minute after he's finished, he's snoring at the table. Sighing, Dave Waverly cajoles him to a sofa, covers him with a blanket, and heads off to the day's work.

B O X

No, in the end, I don't think Donk was trying to endanger the priest. He even claimed to me he'd been trying to keep him safe. It was Julius, after all, who'd made possible Donk's project, his deepest secret, the children's room…it's the one thing Julius did that the Slantworthy Trust didn't pay for. This is what I'm telling you about those two: They did each other favors over the years that cemented their regard into trust. Julius even knew the truth about Yale and Ralph, which placed Julius in a rare circle—rare but deserved.

As I said before, every kid in Loony Island has a situation at home; a presence or an absence. For those with an absence, or a bad presence, there's a children's room, the most secret of Donk's secret places. Underground, inaccessible except from its secret door. Never guessed at by Ralph or anyone else. Originally the space had been Domino City's huge shared subterranean storage and maintenance room, accessible from each tower's subbasement. The room long ago fell into disuse and disrepair, and was finally forgotten… but Donk remembered. He had the subbasement doors leading to it bricked up, had a new hidden entrance built, then refurbished. Julius paid for the project from his personal account, leaving it nearly depleted—which for the priest may have been part of the point. A masterpiece of urban excavation and construction, built silently as possible, using decidedly non-union labor. Bailey knows of it, but she's never seen it, nor has Julius. Nor has Donk— not from inside. His mother runs it. Donk meets with her once a month to discuss it.

A safe place to land and stay. A bed. A meal. Some toys. Some friends. Donk uses proxies to point kids in need that direction. Knowing him like I know him now, I think it's a place he barely lets himself know exists, or even why he created it.

x x x

Donk, waiting through the wee of night for Boyd's return, thinks—you're a box within a box, just like the Fridge here. A man of compartments. Maybe it's like this for everybody, and you've just made it a physical reality as well as a psychological one. You hide yourself within yourself, layer by layer, belief by belief, like boxes inside other boxes. You think *this* truth resides in *that* compartment, but within *that* compartment you find nested a truer truth, and within that truth you find what you really believe is something quite different than you thought you thought. And what do you find tucked within the nested compartment? What indeed, but yet another compartment nested? What truth is true in *there*? Donk knows what it is in his final compartment. It's the place where he wants Ralph to die again and again and again. Why should Ralph die only once? Why can't Ralph have nine deaths, or more? Ratchet up the pain each time. Die again, Ralph. Here, die again. Again. Are you capable of love, Ralph? I doubt it, but I hope so. I'll turn all you love to dust, and then you die.

The reason for it is a box he opens rarely. The sight of Yale, suspended between heaven and earth, the wave of the ground about to slam up to him, knock him right out of the world. Had Yale looked at you in that moment, as he fell? Had he been surprised to see his kid brother, observing his un-making?

Yes. He had. They'd had one last glance at each other, and then he was gone.

Now, after years of patience, the end is suddenly so close. The opportunity has materialized, the prize within grasp. You just have to be bold and quick enough to reach past danger and grab it.

"He's not late yet," Bailey says, pensively; sensing his impatience.

"He's not early, either."

"He'll be here."

"He'd better."

Donk reads, glancing frequently out the one-way glass between the bookcases. From here he can see all the way to the checkout lanes, and now—thanks to their friend and the window he knocked out—into the parking lot. Watching as patiently as he can for the gray face and diffident shuffle of his worst best friend, the world's greatest pickpocket and most terrible writer,

Boyd Ligneclaire. They sit in silent familiarity.

"So?" Bailey's a verbal knuckleballer; she can spin a single syllable with meanings that can be hard to hit.

"So?"

"You're still going through with it?"

"Unless you can tell me what's changed, I'm leaving as soon as your idiot brother shows."

"Then I'm going along."

This again. Donk stops himself from rolling his eyes. "You know better."

"Daniel. He might *kill* you."

"Second fly in the spider's web doesn't make the first fly safer." Donk attempts an even tone as the silence around Bailey thickens—silence, because through her fear she knows he's right. It has to be Donk, and it has to be alone.

Donk doesn't get his information through threat or interrogation or bribery. His true gift is a knack for figuring out exactly what person his target needs him to be, and then fulfilling that need, becoming that person, all without compromising the believable essential Daniel Donkmien. He played it years ago, on Ralph Mayor, getting closer and closer to his target until, without Ralph realizing, he'd taken on the exact dimensions of the boss's own right hand. That's the trick: Modulate your personality without being perceived as having done so. Always make it seem as if you're acting in your own selfish interest, redirecting expectations to make your interests appear naturally and foundationally aligned with those of whomever you're addressing. Most important, don't have a reality of your own; instead, mirror the reality you're given—not the opinions, the reality. You can disagree on matters of opinion. In fact, it's important you do so occasionally; imperative to be believably selfish to avoid rousing suspicion. But the reality—your target's underlying philosophical framework—*that's* the pot of gold. Everybody's world has its own architecture. Discover theirs, understand it, and then move within it uncritically.

But…*flickering?* What the hell. This is the hub of Bailey's concern, which is annoyingly persistent, but not entirely unfounded. Who's ever heard of such a thing? The guy's going to call bullshit if Donk goes with a story like that. This had been enough reason for Bailey to argue against moving forward; but to Donk's thinking, while this part of the story didn't make sense to them, it must on some level be true.

"Just don't mention 'flickering' unless you have to."

"I'll have to. The detail sells the story. And even if it makes no sense, it *fits*. Explains the cardinals sweeping the air with those wooden swords. And then we finally get what we want. Unless you don't want to finish our business anymore?"

To this Bailey says nothing. So, they're resolved. Thank goodness; there's the growing sense she no longer cares or has been trying to hamstring the plan, after all this time, all this work, biding time, waiting for this chance. Does she really want to grow old working her little donut shop? Did she seriously think that when the chance came it would be anything but desperately dangerous? Did she really conceive they'd wait until they got an opportunity that was *safe*? But no, of course not—she, like he, still remembers the first and deepest compartment. That old deep wrong is a blanket they've long shared, huddled together beneath, hands on each other's ears, whispering bright incentives of retribution back and forth to one another, communing in revenge, warming each other in bed even as their dish grows cold. They've known each other so long. He looks at her and thinks this: I've known you so long. Her black hair arranged in a helmet of braids; wide, wary eyes always assaying your every motion, always ready to react; her slight frame hiding unexpected strength and brutal instinct. I've known you so long. You weren't there right at the beginning, but so near the beginning what's the difference? At the beginning was the door, and the open vent above it, and the cup and the ball, but after came Bailey Ligneclaire. And, moments later, brother Boyd. Ball and cup. Door and vent. Bailey and Boyd. He'd crawled out the vent above the door after the incident with the ball and the cup, and they brought him to Yale and the greenhouse. Yes, they facilitated your reunion with your own brother. It was all so long ago. It was only yesterday. Baby Daniel born yowling to Donald Donkmien and his lovely wife Daisy. Donk now remembers his father only as a shape and a smell. One day the factory closed and he was gone. Older brother Yale already absconded into his criminal ambitions. Daisy, who had planned to stay home with their baby in their two-room hovel in Domino City, instead found herself sleeping the days away and selling herself down and around at night, leaving her beloved youngest boy to the ball and the cup, in the bad days after her husband split…

Ah! Here comes Boyd. Through the two-way glass, Donk sees his head pop into view and clip down the aisle, cautious not to be seen. Still dressed in his hoodlum outfit and looking exhausted. He's breathing hard, sweat-shiny. "Well," Boyd says, slinking in, "He's indubitably a flickering man."

"You took long enough."

"Apologies. I was making discoveries of a highly important and substantive nature."

Donk makes a noise. "Which means what?"

"As you predicted, your holy compeer went directly to the Wales, where he met with his new friend. Who, as I mentioned, is one hundred percent as advertised, though I would quantify him not as 'flickering' but as 'partially visible.' There *and* not. Not unlike one of those posters with the imbedded illusions."

"Posters."

"Precisely. You know the ones; the field of colored dots. He's like that. A dimensional shift. Two suddenly gone to three. You can see him if you have the knack."

"He's covered with *dots?*"

"I was being metaphorical. He's not there, then he is. You have to do something with your mind to see him."

This is unnerving news; Donk has been expecting an explanation more definitive, more scientific. Mirrors or camouflage or something. *Somebody partially visible* would be…what *would* it be? Unpredictable. An infraction upon the rules of nature, introducing angles that will prove difficult to shoot. Then again, Boyd is given to flights of poetic fancy. Also, he's an idiot. Better to wait until you have the opportunity to observe this allegedly flickering cat yourself before drawing any hasty metaphysical conclusions.

"But the guy's still in the Cracker Box?"

"He claims to be hiding from the promiscuous probing of the cardinals."

Boyd seems oddly nervous—or rather, he seems nervous in a different way; he's trying even harder than usual to talk like a college professor.

"What else?"

"First of all, the Father plans on moving him out of the Wales."

Donk scowls; this they already know. "Yes, but *when?*"

For the first time, Boyd's confidence drops. "That...was not determined in my presence. If I had to wager, I'd guess tomorrow night."

"Why?"

"This is an extraordinarily nervous fellow. He's afraid to leave. He was asking for specific conditions for his escape."

"Julius'll be coming to us for help, then," Bailey says. "Easy. We wait for him to come to us before you go." Donk narrows his eyes. She's so transparently looking for a reason to avoid risk. Boyd pipes up.

"He's not coming to us."

"Who, then?"

Boyd shakes his head "It's somebody he visited this morning, however—that much I know. He promised his frightened young friend it would be the next thing he did."

"Tell me about the visit, then. What happened there?"

"Didn't witness it."

"What?"

"He ran out of the Island," Boyd says, hands raised in supplication. "And he kept running. And he *kept* running."

"You lazy turd."

"I ran as hard as I could," Boyd protests. "Have *you* ever tried to hold to Father Julius's pace? It can't be done."

"I shouldn't have sent a weakling, is what you're saying." Donk can't bring himself to say it like he means it. Boyd's clearly put in the effort. His clothes are sweat-drenched. Anyway, it's clear who; Julius is doing what any rich boy does when the kettle gets hot. He's running to his money.

"It would have been so delightful if you hadn't sent this particular weakling," Boyd says. He collapses onto the uncluttered portion of the billiard table. "I'm resting now."

Donk considers for a moment, grabs his bag. "So be it. Nothing's changed. It only means I need to go immediately."

"And without any backup," Bailey says. "I can kill you myself right now. Saves time."

Donk, ignoring this, looks to Boyd. "Anything else?"

Boyd, rising from his supine position, pauses to savor the effect he knows he will have. "Indeed. One other thing. Father Julius's flickering man and your 'new boss?' I know their names."

✗✗✗

Minutes later, Donk is at the Wales—Morris didn't mention it by accident last night; he'll be here. Donk stops at a narrow alley approximately twenty feet long, at the joining of two large wings. At the end of the secluded alley there's a steel door, locked. Perched above the door, a small camera. Seized with inspiration, Donk sets down the satchel, unzips it, removes two bright red fourteen-pound bowling balls, smooth and sparkling and heavy enough to demolish a grocery window or a cash register. Donk takes the measure of its mass; the man he seeks possesses the strength to hurl this weight with force. Donk doesn't have such brawn, but he has some skill. He grooves the ball straight down the alley and into the door, where it makes a solid cludding noise. He repeats this action with the second ball, then strolls to retrieve them both, strolls back, repeats, repeats. Glares purposefully at the camera perched above the door, as if he knows exactly who's watching on the other side.

Clud.

Clud. And he thinks of ball and cup, of door and vent. Of Bailey and her quiet little brother Boyd. Clud. And he thinks of Yale. And of the greenhouse. Clud. And he thinks of Ralph, and the things Ralph did. These are the earliest compartments. He thinks of Danny Coyote, only three or four years old, alone day after day for hours in the room as Mommy sleeps, alone all night, sleeping with the lights on as mommy works, or hiding in the cupboard if mommy has been instructed to host a party. She comes home early in the morning and makes him bacon and pancakes from mix and then they go to the bedroom and she holds him for twenty or sixty minutes and talks to him and tells him stories until she starts snoring and then she turns over and Danny goes out to spend his day in the other room. Barely remembering daddy any more, only knowing the absence of him. Yale comes rarely; it's always an event. He wears a Zoot's shiny suit. Arms full of presents to ward against complaints of long absence, small talk, laughter, eyes on the clock, eyes on the door. Danny's intoxicated by him, but he always seems to be gone almost before he's arrived.

Danny has the ball and cup. The sphere a neon marbled Superball discovered deep in the toe of a smallish Christmas stocking before daddy was gone, the cup a white coffee mug made of concentric loops of ceramic, creating the illusion of something that might be telescoped flat, one large chip out of the mug's lip like a boxer's missing tooth. It must have been designed for travel; it's got something heavy in its base and a rubberized bottom, which makes it perfect for Danny, who sets it against the door and sits cross-legged against the far wall and tosses the ball into the cup. The trick, Danny finds, is hitting the lip where it tub-tub-tub-tub-tub-tub rattles back and forth from side to side, finally coming to rest at the bottom. A long shot. If he can hit it ten times in a row, then daddy will come back, and so will Yale, and Danny won't be alone all day long. To make the tension go, he lets his hands curl and relax, curl and relax, until he's calm enough to take the next shot.

For lunch he eats cold bacon and leftover pancake, if they're there, or else his own hunger if they're not.

He goes on like this until the day he tragically makes the tenth consecutive shot. On this day, Danny quietly stands up and stays there with his back against the wall for a long time, and though he keeps his face impassive, the longer he stays the angrier he becomes. Only his hands move as he lets his rage build silently within. Very slowly, his hands curl and relax, and curl and relax. Not anymore a releasing action but a gathering one.

Clud.

Clud.

The steel door flies open, revealing a tiny cardinal. Not one Donk's ever met before; no taller than forty inches, every feature hidden behind a scarlet balaclava hood except for his calm, slow-blinking eyes. "Your boss lost his balls," Donk says, with a vaguely weary air of practiced indifference, a tone honed through years of conversations with dangerous people. He returns the fourteen-pounders to his satchel. "I thought he might want them back."

The little cardinal makes a curt gesture with clear meaning—*follow*—then walks away, back into the Wales. Donk enters; the door bangs shuts behind. He's self-possessed in a way Donk recognizes; it's a way of moving shared by Bailey, and by Ralph's elite killers. This is a man who's shortened many taller men, one leg at a time. Donk looks back over-shoulder, and nearly shouts. A second tiny cardinal is following them, identical to the one ahead.

Silent, their procession passes unseen through the guts of the hospital: green tiled floors, off-white walls, drop ceiling, fluorescent lighting. Down halls, through doors, by elevator up to the top floor, marching down a long hallway with administrative offices on the left and modular cubical space on the right. At the corner office, the foremost cardinal raps on the door and enters without waiting for an answer. Donk notes the plate hanging on the door—T. IVAN RAGESALAD, MD—this is the office of the JAWPI director; the one who's in deep shit after the botched release this morning. Ah, the botched release. Releases sometimes botch themselves, Donk thinks, and sometimes they need a bit of help. This one botched just right . . . sorry, Dr. T. But when the door opens, it's not Ragesalad in there, but Morris Love, sitting at the doctor's overlarge desk lit by green-hooded lamps, riffling through the drawers.

"Donkmien's here," the lead cardinal announces.

"Thank you, Andrew," Morris says, the dismissal clear in his tone. The two tiny cardinals depart as efficiently and silently as they arrived. Morris fishes around in a top drawer, discovers, cuts, and lights a cigar, and draws a few long introductory puffs. "I only allow myself one of these a week," Morris admits. "But the doctor keeps a good drawer." He smokes ruminatively, his back to Donk.

"Hi there, boss," Donk breezes. The informal tone is the correct one—even when you expect trouble, it's important to assume normal relations, force the other party to turn up the heat—but it's also why he couldn't let Bailey tag along—imagine her reaction when she heard the two of you talking familiar. Imagine the connections she'd start to make. And she wouldn't understand. How could she? She loves you but she's misunderstood you so badly. She thinks this matter with Ralph is only vengeance. She thinks it's a question of business completed and final escape. "I like the new office."

Morris shrugs. "A temporary location, one I have little use for beyond certain patient records I hope to uncover tonight—and it has to be tonight; I certainly don't expect the previous owner will occupy the space long. Word is he'll resign first thing Monday, thanks to your efforts. He's certainly going to resign after what I have planned."

"Fun stuff. What do you have planned?"

"But you were just about to tell me why I'm not going to have you immediately killed," says Morris pleasantly, swinging around. "You must have something very useful to tell to risk visiting me less than twelve hours after I warned you off."

At this, Donk relaxes. His experience is the person least likely to kill you is the one who is telling you they are going to kill you. Only killing is killing—threatening to kill is a play for leverage; it indicates a desire for something other than a fresh corpse.

"Returning your balls," Donk says, letting the bag slip *clud* from his shoulder to the floor. Neither of them looks at it.

"Is that all?"

"I made it happen with the loonies this morning, exactly the way you asked. All of them out at once, all the right people bribed to look the other way. I never asked why. I even did it for free. I didn't expose you to my most trusted people even after your cute stunt last night with these balls. I'm dying for *which* of those infractions, exactly?"

"You sent a snoop after one of my people, then down my tunnel."

"I didn't send him. He's just good enough to find you himself. A mistake."

"I'd say a bad mistake." For the first time Morris's tone gets sharpish. "I dislike spies."

"As I said: A mistake."

"I still haven't heard a compelling reason for you to leave here alive."

"We ran a successful operation this morning. I'd like to make our arrangement permanent. I think if I help you find, oh, say . . . an *invisible man*, you might be interested in making the hire."

A low, guttural sound surprises its way from Morris's throat, and then a deep and poisonous silence fills the room. At length he says, "Don't move. I want to think about you."

For long minutes Morris smokes, motionless except for that habit—almost a tic—of glancing over his shoulder. He doesn't speak until his cigar is half gone, then muses: "I don't know why I give myself lessons like you, but I can't seem to stop." He stands and peers at Donk.

Lessons again. Donk says nothing, but, instinctively, he begins to calibrate a new reality in which he is a lesson, arrived not on his own volition, but instead summoned by another's. Morris comes closer. "This invisible man. Tell me everything you know about him," he says.

Here it is. No more teasing; Donk opens his compartment, and his satchel. From it he draws Julius's newspaper with a green wax rectangle colored onto it, tosses it onto the desk. Not knowing why this artifact will convince; guided only by an instinct that insists it will. "I presume you mean Gordy? Skinny kid? Invisible sometimes? Kind of flickers in and out?"

Donk lets the ensuing silence spread out, then he says: "You see, this is what I can do for y—" but then Morris is right there close god *damn* he's fast twisting Donk's arm horribly behind him pulling his head backward by his hair the bright tip of the lit cigar quivering only an inch from his right eye close enough to feel the heat of it any closer it will fry the cornea without touching and Morris whispers in a bloodless voice: "Tell me everything. Tell me *every*thing."

This is bad. This is the possibility upon which Bailey has fixated—the part where things go wrong. Morris knows he can't kill somebody who has the information he needs. But he can take the eyes, lips, teeth, ears, fingers, toes, everything but the tongue. And then there will be no job, no future, no revenge. This man has no desire to retain your services, no inkling he needs them, he wants only the painful extraction of the one piece of information he wants, without appreciation for the skill applied in securing it, or any interest in future applications of that skill. If only Bailey were here. Not to defend you, no. Just to see her one last time...

Instinctively Donk matches his tone to that of his assailant, terrible and calm. "Of course I'll tell you. I *want* to tell you."

"For a job. For your slice of the pie." The coal is hot and bright.

"I'll tell you either way. I want to. It's my purpose. Think of everything I've already done for you without gaining advantage."

"Where." The coal moves infinitesimally farther away.

"I have reason to believe he's still here in the hospital."

"He's not. We've looked."

"You haven't looked hard enough."

"Where in the hospital?" Morris growls.

Donk's released. Morris steps back away from him and regards him warily. Studies the newspaper, the green rectangle upon it. Donk forces himself to stand back at attention as if nothing has happened. "How do you know this?" Morris asks. Donk hears the same strange slight yet telltale notes of entreaty from earlier tonight—*help me because you know why you should.* Enough to dare hope he might still finish the day whole and alive.

"I find things out. I'm good at it. It's what I do for Ralph. Now I want to do it for you."

Tap-tap-tap goes the cigar, ash on the carpet. "Tell me *why* I want to find Gordy."

Donk hesitates. This is an unwelcome question, precisely because he never imagined he'd be asked. Rarely does somebody ask you to provide them with their own motivation. He resorts to the truth. "I don't know," he says.

Through Morris's nose come three of the slightest chuckles imaginable. "Come with me," he says, walking abruptly out of the office. "You're so curious about my tunnels anyway. There's something there you should see."

As Donk follows, the whole plan suddenly strikes him as absurd—You've given away everything; what leverage remains? But no, you know what remains; it's the desperate choices you already had, the weapons you were willing to bring to Morris even if Boyd had gained no others; they're the only real advantages you ever had, the cards even Bailey hasn't realized you've hidden up your sleeves: The suicide king, and the Judas kiss.

They pass to the ground level and Morris leads them down beige hallways. At length they enter a darkened cafeteria through double swinging doors. Low tables with molded seats attached line up on either side as they make their way into the kitchen, where stainless steel gleams occasionally in the gloom. Morris walks to a windowless wooden door with a deadbolt and no handle. It opens onto a closet: empty, walls ceiling and floor all done in white. On the opposite wall a bifurcate steel door, which appears to be a service elevator, and, set in the floor, a circular hole with a tight spiral staircase leading down into a well-lit space. Taking the stairs, they find themselves in the cylindrical white tunnel Boyd described. Donk finds it difficult to estimate distances—the tunnel is straight, bright white, and free of any landmark or signifier.

"How far does this go?"

Morris smiles, points. "That way? Hundreds of miles. This way? Much farther." He strides down the hallway in the direction of "much farther," still occasionally sneaking a habitual peek over his shoulder. Donk follows, trying not to lose himself in the tunnel's snowstorm sameness. He's lost his bearings entirely, but after a while it's clear to him they've gone far beyond the bounds of the Wales. In time, a dark gray spot appears in the distance ahead, which reveals itself as they draw near to be a steel vault door. In the door's center is inscribed a rectangle showing a narrow red stripe on the top and one on the bottom, and an expanse of white in between. Stamped into the steel below, an insignia:

LOVE FORGEWORKS, LLC
(Flanders Division)

"We're here," Morris says. "This way."

There is, to the left side of the vault door, a doorless entry opening onto a room, as snow-blind white as the tunnel, but carpeted in red, and sparsely appointed with objects—a desk, some chairs, portraits on the walls of a succession of increasingly antiquated-looking men—once again providing Donk's eye with a much-desired sense of perspective and shape. One object in particular diverts attention from all others: a steel box, the size of a double-wide coffin, resting upon a gurney. Donk is immediately and instinctively repulsed and entranced. Something about its surgical, clinical, precise existence emanates suggestions of unnecessary amputation, of physical invasion, of scalpels effortlessly splitting abdominal fatty layers, making micro-metrically specific compromise of dural sacs and vital membranes, precisely executed excavation of critical internal components, of gleefully witnessed fates worse than death.

Morris watches Donk closely. Donk regards him blandly. "I confess I was surprised to have been approached with an offer of partnership," Morris says at length. "In a place like this, I expected to fight for position and advantage. But you offered your assistance from the start."

Donk says nothing.

"And I can't deny that you have been...effective...at expanding the effects of the Fritz Act, as desired. I can't help but wonder why someone with skill and influence would give over so completely to mine."

Donk says nothing.

"Are you frightened?"

"It's not a question of fear."

"You know I might kill you."

"I think it's unlikely."

"You intrigue me. It's possible you're the first intriguing person I've met in a year." Donk has nothing intelligent to say to this, so he says nothing, which allows Morris to keep telling him things. "You aligned yourself with me, before you even knew of me. That's rare. Very rare."

"I get feelings. I follow them."

Morris shoos this thought away with a microscopic shrug. "You appear to have function. I may have sent you to help me without knowing I was doing it. Maybe you're a lesson of my rise rather than my struggle." Morris pauses, as if to invite comment. Donk, utterly confused by all this, keeps mum.

"You're going to live for now. But it's important you don't think I'm placing any trust in you when I tell you the things I'm about to tell. Which is why I wanted you to have a look at this." Morris rises and walks to the thing in the middle of the room. It's all right angles, a perfect steel box. The gurney upon which it rests has a panel of some sort built into it. In a corner of this panel is a keypad, into which Morris now swiftly keys in a complex sequence, causing one side of the thing to lower with a sigh, revealing a mass of tubes and metal instruments. There is a powerful light emanating from inside. Morris releases two catches on either side of the box's lid and lifts it up until the stems lock into place.

"What I do with my true enemies," Morris says, "I put them into an oubliette. What I do with allies who fail me, I put them into an oubliette. What I do with strangers who have no function, I put them into an oubliette."

An unbidden sound comes from Donk. Morris, taking it for fear, looks pleased. "Let me show you how it works," he says, with a clinician's detachment and a hobbyist's enthusiasm for minutiae. "Here are the most obvious restraints. Extra-strength Velcro, NASA-caliber, more than ten times the hook density. Difficult—" demonstrating with a grunt—"to open, even with two hands. Here for the wrists, here the elbows, here the shoulders, hips, knees... but the Velcro is only the second line of defense. These—" indicating a series of small U-shaped brackets set within three shallow grooves running the length of the padded space—"latch into the tenant's harness—full body, high-quality nylon, fully breathable, untearable, firm. You can't struggle against it. Only authorized movement is possible—but there is authorized movement. It's necessary to prevent the total atrophy of the musculature. We keep the body strong, you see—" at this Morris jabs some buttons and robot arms in the guts of the oubliette begin gyrating in controlled rhythmic ellipses—"the crèche has enough space to allow mandatory exercise of limbs and core. Tubes provide hydration here, nutrients here, voiding waste here and here. Weekly, we flush the crèche with antiseptic and water, to prevent bedsores and other skin ailments—the hydraulics lift mouth and nose out of the stream. A tenant can stay in my oubliettes a long, long time without fatality. Decades. A lifetime."

Donk peeks deep into the crèche, imagines the merciless hug of Velcro straps and harness, the latches hooking you into your coffin at forty-eight points of non-articulation, paralyzing you along the spine at the back of the heels, the elbows, knees, ankles, wrists, thighs, a trio of latches in isosceles formation along each shoulder blade, a parallelogram affixing your skull to the back of the crèche, tiny, recessed, so reticent that were you to find yourself interred in an oubliette you'd never guess they were there, you'd never understand the cause of your total immobility. Donk notices the interior is mirrored, and it comes to him: the bright lights from within make sense. Not even the escape of darkness. You'd have nothing to watch but yourself, losing your mind, day after day, year after year.

Perfect.

Morris presents Donk with a bland but meaningful countenance. "I see you understand about my oubliettes?"

"I do," Donk vows, knowing he has selected the proper agent for his wrath. His new boss is, in his own way, also a man of many compartments. Even disapproving Bailey will have to agree that, whatever else it's cost them, he's at last discovered the penalty to fit Ralph's crimes.

"Good. And, as somebody who's made me promises, who has raised my expectations...you understand why I'm showing this to you?"

"Yes. If I don't deliver, what you do is, you put me into an oubliette."

Then Morris smiles, makes his face friendly save for blackberry eyes. "Good. Now for business. I'm interested in only a handful of changes."

"Changes."

"It's already started. My people are the first change. Obviously, you've noticed them. The former JAWPI inmates will be the next. I have plans for 'the loonies,' as you call them. You assisted already, with your arrangements to expel them all at once. They're ready and totally accessible for what's coming next."

"Which is?"

"My trustees are valuable. Each represents significant investment: of time, attention, money, molding, training. And this is a compromised place."

"That's one way to put it."

"As such, I'd prefer to keep them separate, and maintain a separate force for everyday use. What makes our friends 'the loonies' so perfect is precisely their disposability. They've been disposed of already by the world. Can there possibly be any complaint against my making use of them? Dr. Ragesalad and this hospital's staff have had their use of the patients for years, pharmaceutically speaking—but I'm a bit of a pharmacist myself. Soon they'll be ours forever, if properly managed. Therefore—lucky you— I need a manager."

Donk remembers what Boyd said about the loony at the bowling alley, and the syringe. He says nothing.

"You'll take charge of them. They'll be your assistants. Gophers. Cannon fodder, when needed." Morris closes the lid on the oubliette, deactivates it with another keyed sequence. "Now let's talk about you, and let's talk about Gordy. That slippery little invisible bastard."

"Lot of manpower out. You must want him pretty bad."

"He has something that belongs to me."

"Tell me what it is, I'll keep an eye out for it." Staying casual as possible.

Morris ignores the offer. "I'd begun to fear he'd gotten away clean," he says. "Now you bring me this idea he's somehow still wandering the hospital."

"Accurate, I think."

Morris smiles. "Well, let's say this: It had better be, for your sake."

Donk looks at the control panel of the oubliette, asleep save for a single slowly winking red telltale, and nods.

"This is the part where you tell me exactly how to find Gordy," Morris prompts.

At the precipice toward which he's been running for weeks, Donk doesn't allow himself to pause as he hurls his last shredded principles into open air. Forcing Bailey's disapproving face from his mind, he collects his thirty pieces, hopes to flip his silvery chips to the felt with enough backspin to keep his annoying, hairy, holy friend alive.

"My understanding is Gordy appears to people who trust him." Every word feels like a distinct object peeling off his tongue, each requiring an extraction by force. "There's a man Gordy trusts. A civilian who has a weird sort of juice on the Island. He's...useful to me. Valuable. Likely that means valuable to you. It'd probably be in both our interests if he stays active."

"Name. Now."

"His name is Julius. 'Father' Julius. Poses as a priest, sort of. Denim robes. Big beard. You've seen him?"

"I'm aware of him."

"Watch for him. He's coming to the Wales common room. He'll make your man come to the surface." Donk pauses, then commits fully. "He...may be trying to move your guy. Out of this facility. Very soon. In hours, not days, I believe."

"Move him where?"

"Somewhere else. Out of town."

"More precise."

"More I do not know."

"You're supposed to be the guy who knows things, not the guy who guesses things."

"My guesses are right more often than the facts you'll get from another."

"But you don't know *all* things."

Morris's eyes search his face again. Donk doesn't know what to make of this. Clearly some point is being made, one which he lacks the context to grasp. "No. I don't."

"Good. Do you know who *does* know all things?"

"You do," Donk says, immediately. Morris watches him for a long time, the gaze of a man who is trying to figure out if he's being bluffed. "You do make me curious," Morris murmurs. Donk, his instincts pristine and lucid, clears his throat and takes a plunge. "I have a request," he says, and watches suspicion bloom on Morris's face.

"After the agreement's made is a bad time to negotiate."

"Call it a preference if you want. I doubt you'll have a problem fulfilling it. I suppose you're going to need to get rid of Ralph."

"There's no use trying to save him."

"You misunderstand," Donk says. "When you get Ralph—when I *help* you get Ralph, what I would like you to do is, I want you to put that son of a bitch into an oubliette. And let me be the one who closes the lid."

Morris smiles slowly. "You *do* interest me," he says.

x x x

Later, out in the urban retch that passes for fresh air in these parts, amazed to be alive, Donk wanders, dodging open manholes, carrying a sack full of cell phones, tasting life and freedom. Nearby, less than a mile distant, the outlines of Domino City projects rise up against him like idiot giants, and Donk yet again imagines himself rushing at them with a crane and wrecking ball, swinging until the spheroid mass is windmilling in a taut circle, running up on the Dominos and smashing them until all is rubble and ash and dust, smashing them until not one cinderblock is whole, until not one more child has to live hemmed up inside one of those dim gray training-prisons...his is what Bailey doesn't understand. It's not about getting Ralph, it's about going as far as you can, taking down not just Ralph but a world that might allow a Ralph to rise.

It was Bailey and Boyd who found him, three days after he'd made the tenth shot, standing in the middle of a project room that may as well have been a cell, hands curling and relaxing, gathering a new rage he'd never felt before, bringing himself to a new and terrible resolve, climbing out the vent above the door, wandering the Island, lost and alone. The Ligneclaires, already a part of Yale's burgeoning organization, discovered him huddled against the rain under an abandoned scrap of corrugated tin, hungry and frightened and filthy, and brought him to the greenhouse. Brought him to Yale, to his own brother. So, in its own way, the tenth shot really had brought Yale back. There had been good months then, maybe even a good year.

And then Ralph took it all away. He's never had to pay any price for that.

Donk walks—slow at first, but then more briskly as the finality of the course he's set for himself begins to percolate into his consciousness—in the direction of the Domino they call HQ—the Headquarters. Home of top gangsters in shiny shark-suits of silver and purple and emerald, who make deals and plan scores, who give out orders—and oh, do they hate having to shuck and jive and come cap-in-hand for a bag-boy in a suit like Daniel Donkmien. Oh, do they resent him his clear influence, his slippery unknowableness. Where he came from. What his angle is. Why he has Ralph's trust. It would be insanity to visit HQ if you were so hated by the bad cats who ran it, insanity to show your face in a place where an accident could be so easily arranged, an accident without blame or accountability, what a shame... madness to even walk past the place alone. Donk heads for it. The fire escape will take him to the roof. Morris has set him a tail, of course—likely one of those dangerous little men—but let him watch and wonder why I'm here. Nobody's keeping me from that spot; not tonight.

He has a hidden cache on the roof—another compartment. From it he grabs some wine and two glasses, sneaks out, and climbs up the fire escape to the roof to await the coming morning. He knows he should return to Bailey. In her fear for his survival she'll be fuming for detail, furious at his absence, but a realization has been settling on him: Soon it will have to be over with Bailey. This new arrangement will crash into you, swallow you, consume you. You'd thought of escape for all, but for you there can be none. You're the monkey with his fist in the jar. Morris isn't the sort to release someone who's gained his attention.

He sips the wine. Beside him, Yale's memorial glass holds its measure. Behind him, the burned and shattered frame of a structure lurks, black against the midnight-blue sky of pre-sunrise morn, twisted in the gloaming shadow into strange shapes suggesting arachnid ancestry. It looks nothing like a greenhouse anymore. Donk faces toward the coming sunrise. From the roof, he can see over the municipally funded barricades, overpass and trestle, which isolate the Island from the mainstream; beyond, the city life still twinkles artificial brightness, and in middle distance the skyline grasps for the clouds; mastodons of commerce reaching illuminated fingers to the sky, flattening out into streams of twinkling orange and white lights rushing to him and escaping away to the horizon. All this gorgeous madness we've created, Donk thinks, deep in the poetry of morning wine. This entire artificial cosmos—it can't last. Impossible to sustain it forever, but we won't stop building it larger until reality forces implosion. No stars visible in the sky from here; only a setting blood moon beneath the lone eye of Mars. The only stars to see in a city cling to the streets in straight lines. We've purchased the stars and brought them down to earth.

C H A S E

The loony release was nothing like the smooth transition Representative Fritz insisted it would be. Someone let us all out early, and all at once. It was as if someone beat her to it, opened the locks before everyone had taken their place, a bull-run when people were still putting on their shoes. A nightmare for all parties involved. A major embarrassment for both Fritz and JAWPI. It hadn't been the plan. An intelligent mind might ask how it was done. A wiser soul might ponder why.

As to "how": You'd need someone on the inside. Someone familiar with the layout of the building, a trusted nobody looking for a fat payday, some janitor or low-rung orderly. Someone who had keys to open and close the place. And someone else to organize, who knew exactly how the Fritz Act would play out, piece by piece. And you'd need somebody brokering it, someone locally connected, someone who knew where all the levers of Island power were hidden and how to pull them. The inside person was a hire, unimportant; whoever they were, their identity never came to light—but I became more familiar than I wanted with both the organizer and the broker. Morris convinced Donk to let them out early; I think it's fair to say he wanted to create an embarrassing situation for powerful people. And, just a day later, he created the solution to the problem he'd created—with himself primed to profit. That appears to be Morris's way.

I can't say precisely what that solution was—Donk kept stingy with those details. But I know it was pharmaceutical in nature, and I saw the effects. It was the cardinals that gave the doses to the loonies and kicked the whole thing off. They started early in the afternoon of the day, roaming with backpacks full of doses in tiny syringes, covering every bit of Loony Island, catching patients and sticking them. Based on the behavior of those they caught, you'd have to guess the doses held some sort of amphetamine, but I suspect some other element, too. By evening the whole thing had built up a head of steam—loonies rioted in the avenues, tore down street lamps, and looted the shops—and none of them with a thought or memory left in their heads, it seemed. Around the Island, folks remember it as the Loony Riot. It changed things.

It was an unconscionable thing to do. A nightmare. Morally depraved. Naturally, it worked like gangbusters. The upshot for the institute—whether intentional or not—was a total reclassification of the issue. It was a problem, yes, but it was no longer a *medical* problem, it was a *crime* problem. Reported on a different part of the newspaper, so they could all just scapegoat the Institute's director and relax.

Nor was JAWPI the only beneficiary. Donk got savvy, as was his habit. Where others might see only theft and destruction, he saw a work force. These loonies were blank-slate absorbent; they could assimilate all the best practices of the existing gangs, and, better still, they'd work for almost nothing. Totally expendable when taken individually, but vital as a whole. Before long he couldn't remember how anything ever got done without them. And it stands to reason that whatever helped Donk also benefitted Donk's new boss. So there, maybe, you have the "why" of it.

I know it was the cardinals who started things, and I know it was doses, because they came after me with their syringes, too. After all, wasn't I a loony? We were pretty easy to catch, most of us. The only ones who escaped were the few who had wandered out and away into town already. And me, of course. I wouldn't let them dose me.

Me, I ran.

x x x

Dave Waverly's car purrs toward Loony Island in Friday's evening light, Dave at the wheel, Julius trying not to let his frenzy of anxiety show; he napped far longer than he intended, then they spent far longer than he wanted this afternoon with Dave's paperwork. Anxiety aside, Julius is pleased enough to ride rather than run; Gordy's existence is leading the priest down deep trails of speculation, which might make negotiating Loony Island on foot— its open manholes and free-range mental patients— a tricky business... How does Gordy flicker? Might it be some sort of involuntary telepathy, developed evolutionarily, as indeliberate in deployment, as untargeted and unconscious as a chameleon's progression from brown to green? You're not up on the latest pamphlets. As a good priest, are you meant to believe in evolution? Or wait—have you evolved to believe in evolution? Have others evolved to disbelieve in it?

At this notion—that a being might evolve in such a way as to cause, within the mind of that being, a disbelief in evolution—Julius grins, despite growing nervous anticipation. An engine making itself invisible (or partially visible) to its own gears—that's an irony for the finer sensibilities. The people who seek Gordy, now, those cardinals…have they ever *seen* him, or do they swing their swords for a phantom about whom they've only received instruction secondhand? Do they, casting about, resemble you? Do they chase without belief, with only some hope of future belief, that there truly might be a Gordy? And what about you? Flip the tables, Father; maybe you resemble them, not they you. If the faith of Gordy's pursuers is blind, then how, exactly, is your relationship to Gordy different? Isn't this all really about your young friend's claim that he speaks to God? Don't you see him as a way in to *Him*? A portal to the divine?

Troubling, to consider one's motives and suspect them impure. Right, Julius: You're going to get Gordy out of this pickle and then what? Will he get you to the front of the line and on the chosen side of the velvet rope, elected among the elect with a face-to-face introduction to the triumvirate? Finally get the proof you've thirsted for. Gordy, introduce me to your friend, I'm a big fan, I've got all his books—incidentally don't mention to him that until meeting you I always secretly thought he was a big old lie, at best a well-meaning hoax…but, but, but, listen, Gordy, listen, I, um, I've sort of devoted my *life* to the hoax on the hope it's true, so could you put in a *word*? Ask Him to be so good as to justify the investment? Maybe he could autograph a photo of the two of us together, something I can show around?

But whatever misgivings the priest might have about his own motives, there's no keeping Gordy here a moment longer; he has to be spirited away as soon as can be managed. He's got the most awful haunted eyes Julius has ever seen. When you see them you think—This is a man pursued by God. Which means, by logical progression, there is a God. The old ontological dodge: If a being capable of pursuit can be imagined, then it is a being greater than one incapable of pursuit. If God is pursuing somebody, there must perforce be a God in pursuit. Even if the logic's off, here at last is some broth, however thin, which uses a divine stock; here at last may be the proof Father Bernadette could never furnish to you or Dave. Here at last are Daddy's goddam rabbits. God, speaking. Even if he won't speak to you, he's speaking to *some*body.

And another thing.

This also means, by logical progression, that a man, to whom God speaks, runs away. Troubling: The Almighty exists, and the vessel of his revelation is...fleeing? For what possible reason? And...fleeing *how*? Can God create a being so slippery even He cannot apprehend him? And aren't you yourself that same slippery being, a fellow who pretends belief rather than experiences it, a fellow who believes not in God so much as the empty spaces where God ought to be, but isn't?

This is uncomfortable. Luckily, there are more practical matters at hand, like finding Gordy a safer place to hide. The Neon Chapel isn't viable, not with the cardinals so near and your fellows at risk. Slantworthy Manor is out of the question; you'll never set foot. And Donk's not the first choice for this, for reasons you can't even define. How odd to truly mistrust Donk, rather than to merely pretend it for public appearance. So, it's got to be Dave Waverly. Good old Dave Waverly. You rarely think of him as just "Dave," these days. He's "Dave Waverly," all of it together, like it's one word, a single carved block of solid wood indicating a specific and predictable form. A fellow former sunrise enthusiast, Dave Waverly; he'd even been lurking back there your first morning, sequestered deep in the gloom, hidden though not hiding. He and Father Bernadette, watching you. What did they think of you as you came stumbling forward, intruding on their custom, casually vandalous, clumsily sacrilegious? Likely they'd at first stared bemused, but before long, I wager, they were laughing at you, silently but kindly. He hadn't yet become "Dave Waverly." Back then he'd been "Wavy Dave." Still in possession of all the skills that make him such a formidable boardroom proxy on your behalf, but also in possession of his other demons, fully in their grip, bathed in filth and pain, showering in morning sunlight. "You're taking a gamble," Wavy Dave said, the day you recruited him as proxy. "I'm afraid you'll regret it." He took the job all the same, but warily, and then only because Father Bernadette goaded him. *Wavy Dave taking a wary dare. But I haven't ever regretted it, Dave Waverly. You took to that job like a duck to another duck, and you've always come through. And, once the sight of the flickering man melts your understandable skepticism, you'll figure out that flight to Färland.*

"We're nearly here," Dave Waverly murmurs. Julius feels the centrifugal pull of the curves; they're on the switchback road leading in. "Remember, tell the fellow whatever he needs to hear to get him into the car. We can worry about the rest later."

The car soon becomes a hassle; the loonies are making more of an obstruction than yesterday; they're in the street, some of them, making a show of blocking the road. Dave honks, and they honk right back, pounding the hood before finally giving way. "I'll try not to be long," the priest tells him as they pull up to the Wales, opening the door before the car's come to a complete stop. Dave Waverly says something that might have been "Be careful," but it's lost.

Walking in, Julius is sure he'll find the common room empty, but no— there's the poor frightened fellow, hunched forward on the front of his chair, nary a flicker thrown. "Morris took me out of Färland," Gordy says, beginning without preamble as soon as Julius draws near. His voice cracking. Coming on dark, Domino City out the windows shows black against the dim slate-blue smudge of clouded sky serving as tonight's sunset. Julius, in a froth to get moving, bounces on his chair. "Things were...different in Färland," Gordy says. "Very different. I can't explain it. I stayed there for months and years. I told him everything, except what they wanted to know. He says I stole it but I never."

"Tell me later." Fearful that an interruption will trigger another disappearing act, Julius knows he has no choice but to interrupt. *Hours not days,* Boyd had said. Well, it's been hours. "I have a car waiting. We're going to hop in and vamoose."

"I can't go out *there!*"

"The car's going to take you wherever you want. Can't help that bearded lady acrobat of yours if we don't get you safe away, though. Time to *go.*" Julius peers into the gloaming of the sitting room, where long shadows might conceal anybody, wishing he'd had the foresight to have flipped on the lights as he entered—he'd considered doing so but deferred, thinking not to alarm his...friend? Ward? Target? Gordy stands.

"Back to Färland?"

Julius decides Dave Waverly had it right on the concept of untruth. What's a little guilt next to the relief of implied incipient forward motion? "Absolutely yes. Right away. We'll head to Färland just the way you want, we'll find your bearded lady, and—" Julius feels a *swick* from someplace behind him as something cold passes easily through his denim robe and bites his arm hard. In the moment he feels it more as pressure than pain. Looking down, he sees the sheet of bleed seeping its way over and throughout the sleeve and the sweat stands up on his forehead as his head feels light and heavy and his left knee buckles. It feels important, suddenly, to lie down. With the strength remaining in his right leg, he attempts to lower himself carefully, but he loses his balance halfway and lands heavily on his haunches as the wetness tickles silent down his ribs and pools on the floor and he sits fighting against the tremors happening in his stomach and there are now cardinals all around him with their wooden swords swinging swing-swing-swinging until one of them knocks up against some portion of Gordy who's invisible again but no matter he couldn't have avoided the five of them working the room together with ruthless efficiency, catching him—how funny, now that Gordy's invisible it looks like pantomime, they drag him over to another cardinal who pushes a stretcher on wheels and he sees the shape Gordy makes invisible beneath the blanket they've thrown over him sees the frenetic movements of leatherstrap restraints affixed with expert hands Gordy struggling invisible from the end of a long tunnel as Julius lays his impossibly heavy porcelain Faberge head down as carefully as possible onto the beige carpeting and watches a man dressed not in cardinal red but civvies who strolls around to the stretcher which rocks with the struggles and Julius creates a thick puddle of vomit all around himself into his beard and hair, the man in civvies puts his face down close next to the stretcher headboard whispers something to the space there his face distorted hateful and fierce, and shit o my that must be the famous Morris Love, the stretcher rocking with struggle and stars popping up in Julius's vision and his head going up and down and up and down waves on the beige carpeted sea, sinking into a cold and blessed stillness yet there's a sense it's terribly important he remain above water he brings hand to mouth sets his teeth against the pad of the thumb

and bites down

hard

New pain sends adrenaline splintering through Julius's bloodstream, bringing his mind if not his body back to him. Julius musters his already depleting reserves of alertness. Here is the room. Here are five cardinals. Here is the stretcher, rocked by unseen panic as though possessed by a plethora of poltergeists. Beside the stretcher, Morris—cropped hair, short, wire-muscled, large eyes protuberant with well-controlled rage. To the tallest of the cardinals, he says:

"Watch the priest. Clean up after."

She nods toward Julius. "Finish him up?"

Morris seems to give the question serious consideration before giving his head a curt shake in the negative. "Not unless he misbehaves. It's possible he's important. If he survives, bring him to the place."

The tall redbird grunts: "Man's going to bleed out. I hit something big."

"If he's of any importance at all," says Morris, "he won't." And then he wheels the still-rocking stretcher past Julius and out of his reckoning. Julius tries without success to sit. It's gone to hell; difficult to grasp much more. The Game of Gordy is utterly lost; time to move on to the Game of Not Dying . . . yet Julius finds himself unable to focus on the bird in the hand for the sake of the one lost in the bush.

"You chickenshits." He intends to growl, but his voice betrays him, producing a nonagenarian quaver. Weak as a sparrow chick.

The tall redbird comes over to him and settles her foot, ever so lightly, on Father Julius's balls. The foot hovers. "Impolite," she says, and leans forward, then back, making Julius say

haaaaaaaaaaaAAAAAAAaaaaAAaaaaAAAAAAAAaaaaaaahhh.

Julius fights to control his bladder from going. There's a crazy howling noise happening somewhere in the distance. Some sort of raucous squabble, thousands of voices yelling at once, a party going either very well or very badly. The tall cardinal's sword is a pendulum tick-tocking. She says: "I hate impolite. I hate waiting around more. So the story we'll tell the boss is this: You fought. Pulled a knife. Misbehavior. So we cut you up and dumped you. My friends and I"—with her head she indicates the advancing quartet behind her—"We're going to make bits of you."

"Gkkkkkk," says Julius. In fury, he tries to get up with his one arm—at least bite her on the calf before your kebab gets shished—but the cardinal looks bored and leans once again upon Julius's outraged scrotum as the priest cracks the back of his head on the floor, feeling the wetness there, blood seeped into the sopping carpet beneath. The cardinal shakes her head regretfully.

"Resisting. Struggling. You leave us little choice. We'll start with your guts."

The sword *swick swick* removes a quadrant from the denim robe above Julius's still-unbloodied belly, a precise scrap perched upon, then flicked away from, the sword tip.

"See what we do is," the tall cardinal says, "we cut a little hole in the belly. Expose a gut. That's going to hurt. What we do next, we cut tiny little slices in that gut. It busts like a casing. Going to feel like we lit a campfire in there. Pity for you is, you're a tough pig, so I'm betting it's going to take some time before you faint. But first, a few seconds of silence. You understand. Just to let you sit with it."

This is it, Julius thinks. Nettles, I guess it's—

The cardinals disappear. All of them. One moment they are there, the next they aren't. It's the damnedest thing.

Great, thinks Julius, delirious—more invisibility. Fearing some perverse cat-and-mouse, he cranes his neck, searching fruitlessly, every crawling measure of his far-too-flayable skin contracting, anticipating the unseen sword coming in and taking a slice from here or here or here, no way to hide, curl into a ball and they'll skewer your kidneys, lie on your back and they'll pry your stomach open like a manhole cover...Julius lies supine, his damaged arm cradled on his chest, his squashed nuts killing him. The crazy howling noise is louder.

"They aren't invisible," a deep voice says. Not low, this voice, but deep. It moves around him, throughout him, within him; in strange frequencies it dissects, reassembles, catalogues every part of him…pushing up with his good arm, Julius sees nothing but shadow…no—there. A figure stands in the corner. Not much of him revealed but silhouette, save where a triangle of light from the nearest window reaches him, disclosing a sneaker, a length of powder-blue trouser leg. Julius can deduce the Deep Man's height from the red tip of a lit cigarette hanging in the gloom where his mouth must be. The Deep Man speaks again. "They haven't gone anywhere. Same latitude. Same longitude. Now…I did send them about half a mile *upward*. But they'll be back real soon, sort of, on the roof and spread around through parts of the upper floors."

From above comes a shuddering noise: a titan drumming impatient fingers in staccato upon the roof of the Wales, enormous birds spudding into watermelon viscera and feather against a windshield the size of an aircraft carrier, bowling balls dropped from an airplane. "There they are now," the Deep Man murmurs. He's coming near, farther into the light.

"Don't," Julius moans. "Don't. Stop. Don't." He tries pushing back with his heels but blood loss and shock have betrayed his body into kittenish weakness, and he simply threshes on the carpet. One whole side of him—the side he shares with his injured arm—drags, unbearably numb, impossibly heavy, but as he moves, he also senses an even greater weight setting in, the unmovable final load, heavier than earth, heavier than time.

"You don't need to be afraid, you know."

"Stop."

The Deep Man pauses, face still obscured.

"I hate moving anyway. God, I practically gift-wrapped the thing, and look at you. You're in no shape for what's next." The Deep Man's red coal eye pulsates; smoke scuds into the dim. Julius has the sense he's supposed do or say something, but he's forgotten his line in this play, it's all rushing away from him now.

"Next?"

"Yes. *Next*. The thing that happens next. You need to rescue Gordy from his vile captor. Time to be a hero, Father. Your big chance to fulfill destiny. You could say 'your reason for being' and not miss the mark."

Julius tries to force his mind into regular grooves of cognition. He considers biting his hand again, fresh pain for fresh mental sharpness, but his arm is heavy, heavy, weighed down by rabbits the size of whales, his senses fading in and out; he's sinking for good. This Deep Man has an interest in Gordy, with haunted eyes. who whispers fearfully that God talks to him, who claims he's running from…a terrible conclusion presents itself.

"Are you… *God*?"

The Deep Man considers, then says: "Yep. Sure. That's me. I'm God."

An infuriating answer, an infuriating tone, all the more so because it may be true, because this—*this*—may be his long-sought-after meeting with divinity…

The Deep Man says: "You'd better ask me to heal you soon. Your arm's half off."

Julius falls back and it feels like he's sinking into the floor.

"Well. Are you going to ask me, or aren't you?"

Julius decides—To hell with it all. You're being cruelly toyed with either way. If he's God he's even less worthy of your pleading than if he isn't. After waiting so long for a sign, anything, to be presented with such a One, bored of you, who comes to you only as you lie nearly empty of blood and life, taunts you for your failure, expects you to beg for a continuation of years stacked upon years of indifference worse than shunning...the opacity of the Deep Man, the presumption of him…it would be better, wouldn't it, to bleed your life out here in this beige-est of all rooms, than to provide your service to such a Thing?

But then he remembers: Gordy needs you either way. The way he made the stretcher buck and shake. The haunted look in his eyes. What his abductor might do to him.

"Heal me or don't," Julius shrieks, or whispers, maybe only thinks. "Don't pretend you haven't decided already."

And oh god that was the last of your strength the room spinning dark and spinning and for some reason he thinks of Boyd—why Boyd?—is Boyd in some sort of, of, I wait, what is "Boyd" anyway or is it, is it "boyed?" Buoyed? Boit? but that makes no sense either, some of those aren't even words, my mind can't hold on to you, boyed, I'm sorry, the Deep Man has stepped from the shadows looking...amused? To hell with him hellhellhell-

hellhell with him Deep Man, I guess if you want Gordy's salvation why not
save him yourself

yourselfselfselfelf

you? ours?

sell? elf?

fel

el

F

And then he is alone and alert again. Whole again. Strong. Eyes focused.
His wound closed, but the healing goes deeper still; it's restoration of lost
blood, it's recalibration: of enzymes, electrolytes, chakras, synapses, hor-
mones; of the carnival sideshow of bacteria residing in the gut, together with
a variegation of other physical complexities comprising the sum of himself,
his essential Julius-ness—all this biological hash has been fully aligned, tuned
up, optimized, his interior detailed, his exterior given a nice wax and wash,
his nostrils cleaned of occlusion, his auditory canals unblocked by wax, his
pores free of excess sebum.

Without pause or consideration, Julius rises and runs from the day room,
taking physical inventory even as he banks right and pelts down the hall.
His betrodden nuts ache no more. The slices in his robes and the unhealed
throb of the self-inflicted bite on his hand provide the only signs he hasn't
hallucinated it all. He knows instinctively where he's going. Not why. Not
what. Certainly not a bit of how—only where, as though the next steps were
a recipe written out already.

Julius skids on the tile floor outside the break room, running heedless,
guided by uploaded internal certainty: Turn right, right again, head left, now
straight down the hall toward the double doors which reveal, as he pushes
through them, a cafeteria. He scampers crampless between the low rows of
tables, and here's the door leading into the kitchen, and here's, yes, exactly
as you knew it would be, here's what looks like a pantry door, empty inside,
here's service elevator doors in one corner and in the other a spiral staircase
leading down. On the stairs, Julius checks himself—here his instinctive guid-
ance ceases—and descends more cautiously.

It's a tunnel. White walls. White floor. White ceiling. Lit by powerful fluorescent squares set at wide intervals. Blinking in the snowblind whiteness. The tunnel reaches to vanishing points in either direction, but off to the right, at a distance hard to gauge, small in the distance, Julius spies the unmistakable shape of a man pushing a stretcher, walking without concern of pursuit—he'll hear you soon, sure. And then it'll be a—Julius can't stop the grin coming—a footrace. How lovely.

Julius breaks into a sprint, wishing away the traitorous flat echo made by his footfalls. He hasn't heard you yet. Impossible not to hope it can be easy, to hope he won't notice you until you're within grabbing range, but—ah, shit!—he's taken a quick startled look backward. He's hoofing it, going fast, gaining ground…you go right ahead, cousin. Go ahead and start fast. Long tunnel. Looks like miles. I'm betting I can run your bitching legs right off.

Julius eases into the well-worn harness of his old familiar pace, lets his body take over the metronome action of steady progress, as his mind troubles itself in a space of its own, thoughts testing themselves against the madness of circumstance. Men who are sometimes there and sometimes aren't. Mortal sword wounds healed. A man claiming godhood with a flippancy demanding skepticism, who nevertheless offers undeniable proofs. And—*and*—this goddam tunnel. What hand dug it, so straight, so long? At what expense? What architects hired, what engineers, to bring this vision to reality? Whose vision? And…*why*?

Don't ask questions you can't hope to answer. Focus.

This is the thing about the run: It's just the next step. If you have it, there's no contest. Eventually even the horizon falls to your will. You're the drip of water grooving stone plains downward into canyons. You're relentless howling wind hypnotizing desert mountains into hallucinatory shapes, making two-century oak bow down, driving the prairie wife slowly mad. You're the cruel inexorable passage of time, transforming flesh to dust, writing empires into history books. You're the ancient biped, running slow death down on the swifter but less hardy antelope. That's you, Julius tells the slowly growing figure of the man pushing a seemingly empty stretcher. You're my antelope, bub.

He watches three times as some strange black intaglio in the distance, standing out in stark contrast to the blizzard of all this white, slowly reveals itself to be an iron ladder sunk into the side of the wall, leading up to a man-hole-sized cylindrical cavity bored into the ceiling. He has, without increasing his pace, gained significant ground on his prey—but haste is needed. Far in the distance he spies some sort of circular portal, which suggests an end to the tunnel, escape for the quarry. With a finish line fixed, they've joined a new game with clear rules. If the quarry reaches the portal, he wins; if he doesn't, he loses. But Julius smiles—I've caught you already, fucker. The portal is still far off, and the prey is stretcher-burdened and lagging. Antelope. He begins panting it, subvocalizing to the rhythm of his footfalls, synched to the rhythm of his breath: ANtelope antelope ANtelope antelope…soon he's close enough to see the tag sticking up from the neck on his quarry's blue cotton shirt…but the portal looms larger, too. He's made a formidable effort, lasting this far against Julius's own endurance, and with a laden stretcher to push, no less. A dozen feet separate them, footfall and breath in one accord beat out the time:

Close enough now to hear the labored breath.

Close enough now to see the stretcher's restraints being jerked frantically by invisible arms.

Almost within grabbing distance.

Morris releases the stretcher and makes an adroit, almost balletic, spin, Julius seeing only for an instant the silverflash of a long knife pulled from some hidden pocket but not recognizing it for what it is until it's already been halted mid-swing, tearing inches-deep into the plaster, embedding itself in the wall and Julius, realizing only dumb luck has prevented him from yet another fatal wound, unceremoniously smashes into Morris with all of his weight, seeking to drive his enemy's head into the floor, crush skull and snap neck, but Morris twists, somersaulting underneath, foot deep into the priest's belly, using his attacker's own momentum to push off, sending Julius overhead into a painful heap on the floor. The stretcher coasts off course behind the prone priest, stopping as low guardrails and rubber wheels scrape against the wall, leaving parallel silver and black gashes on the white.

Ah, yes, Julius admonishes himself. You miscalculated, leaned too heavily on your own metaphor. You aren't the only predator in this equation. This antelope has tooth and claw. Julius scrambles to his feet, panting. Morris stands, breathing heavily.

"You. Lived."

"Yep."

"Where. Are my followers?"

"Dead."

"I'd say. That's. Unlikely."

Eyes narrow. Not anger, but confusion. Trying to work out the perplexity of some new arithmetic previously unconceived of. "Who are you?" Morris asks. "Who sent you?"

"Nobody. Sent me." Julius pants. He's dismayed to see Morris has begun to recover his own breath.

"OK. Your story," Morris grasps the knife and works it back and forth to divest it from the wall, "is that you bled out a few quarts, then all by yourself, you got up, healed that sliced wing of yours, killed several of my best people, and then *happened* to find me down here? Who sent you?"

Julius can see Morris choosing to remain watchful, obviously ready for an attack and obviously more capable than Julius of meeting one. But it's going to have to come to blows and grapple soon, before the knife—a short sword, really—re-enters the equation. It's sunk deep into the wall, but Morris is working at it, at all times keeping his big calm owlish predator eyes unblinking upon his prey. Julius prepares to leap—but at that moment, behind him, a soft voice speaks from the stretcher.

"I know where he's taking me."

Julius keeps his eyes on Morris, who's getting some wiggle on his sword now. "Oh yeah?" Julius asks, "And where is that, buddy?"

Gordy's statements come like waves, a series of sighs. "But I don't have what he wants. I don't have what he wants. I don't have it anymore if I ever did. All he wants is for me to tell him about the ticket—"

At this Morris makes the error Julius has been praying for; taking his eyes for an instant off the priest. "YOU SHUT YOUR M—" he screams, and Julius comes fast, pushing hard off the floor and rushing as if to plow straight into him once again. Morris moves underneath to throw him over once more, but Julius, anticipating the trick, instead pulls up shifts momentum to his right leg kicks Morris *thock* under the chin. Even as the kick throws Morris backward, hand flies from sword, blade drops easily *ting-clatter* upon the floor, and Julius sees the ruse—Morris had already loosened it entirely, feigned his struggle with the wall, waiting for Julius to make his charge and then it would have been sixteen inches of steel right through the chest—but never mind that— what a kick! Foot meets chin, a perfect strike, a home run, a neckbreaker! There goes C1 and C2! There go those cervical nerve-icals! But no, it's not that lucky—Morris takes the blow, leans out of it, accepts the force of it and claims its momentum, executes a backward somersault, lands crouched but on his feet. Looking up, the owl eyes now perch atop a blood sheet running from nose to shirt. Still lucid, newly furious.

Julius steps back toward Gordy and hisses pain; his big toe feels broken. So, he thinks, foot takes nose, nose takes toe. With this sort of situation, the toe is going to be the more necessary piece. Did you punt him in the face and take the *worst* of it?

Calmly, Morris says: "Bad things are going to happen to you now." Neither of them looking at the blade. Each watching the other. "You're probably realizing you've made a terrible mistake."

"My specialty." Julius tries for a brash tone, fights against a rising gorge, a loosening feeling in his gut. They stare at each other. Something behind Morris's eyes shifts. "Walk away," he says. He sounds extremely reasonable. "I don't need you. You don't need me. All I want is that loony on the stretcher."

"OK."

"Just turn around and go and it's bygones."

"Sounds good."

They both leap for the blade. Morris is quicker and gets the sword in one hand, but Julius gets his big mitts on his wrists, his knee deep in the stomach, bashes the fist holding the hilt—one, two, three—against the floor and wall, his wounded thumb protests this action, but not as loudly as does his outraged injured toe pushing for leverage against the curve where floor becomes wall, and Morris bucks and writhes beneath, seeking advantage with every part of himself, his calm eyes promising slow torture. Julius presses down close enough to smell the blood, the smell of soap underneath, close enough to see pores on the nose, the occasional gray hair among the black. In desperation he tries to lower his head to bite, but Morris is horrendously strong, there's no way to safely perform this action and maintain advantage. He can keep the sword arm down if he makes it his sole focus, affording Morris the opportunity to struggle promiscuously beneath; or he can stop the struggles, allowing the sword arm to come creeping up, slowly but inexorably, the rigid tip rising to rendezvous with his neck. Julius pushes the arm down again, and the body beneath him once more scoots and shifts, and his broken toe screams…Morris suddenly goes entirely limp, throwing Julius off-balance, then flicks his neck like a cobra, pumps the crown of his head into the sudden purpleblack aurora borealis of Julius's left eye.

Julius turns his head in instinctive pain, luckily catches on his cheek the second strike meant for his right eye. He's pushed back onto his ass. Half his vision's nothing but bursts of yellow-red stars reaching him in waves from a field of purple and black, but his right eye, uninjured, still projects for him a clear vision of what's happening. Morris stands, smiling friendly, holding the sword…in all truth, thinks Julius, I prefer what the bashed eye is showing me. Here it is at last, a true revelation. Look at that: the object that's going to kill you. Here you are: the place you're going to die. You know the time and the place. The biggest mysteries are finally solved. Ah. Julius watches the sword that is going to kill him begin to move. There comes from behind him a voice. Gordy, visible again, says:

no harm

Julius watches the sword that is going to kill him stop its arc, then begin again and stop again. Exhausted now; resting in a totality of defeat, the relief of the fox brought to bay, only slightly interested in why he isn't yet dead. Yet even so, as the sword begins the killing blow and halts, begins and halts, begins and halts, Julius finds new curiosity. The void and stars from his left eye are fading; beyond them he can see Morris trying and failing another dozen times to behead him. Julius sits, entranced. His killer appears no less confused at the iterant rise-fall-halt. It's as if the blade is being caught by a transparent, tough, gelatinous web woven from floor to ceiling. Morris waves his hand in the air before him, feeling for hindrance and finding none, rage and desperation growing in his eyes. Julius feels on the verge of hysteria, either laughter or weeping. You're not meant to die, he thinks. You're not allowed. Morris has gone berserker. Julius watches him as if he were a projection on a screen. He's no longer precision-slicing but hacking, each time halting in the same place. He pulls up close and stands before the priest, trembling like one struggling against knots. At last he turns and throws the knife behind him. It tumbles end-over-end and rests flat on the white floor. Panting, glaring furiously from priest to stretcher and back. He screams. He kicks the wall. Slaps it. Looking around for something to smash but there's nothing…and then he's calm again. Turning to the stretcher, he says "All right, then. I hope it's worse than ever. I hope it wrecks you for good."

Gordy is straining from a prone position, leaning up as far as the straps will allow, watching fretfully, flickering. His hair remains a mass of pinwheels and corkscrews, his cheeks still hairy and hollow, but his eyes, once merely deadened and scared, now hold something deeper than dread. "Okay," he says. "Okay, okay, okay."

"Did you do that?" Julius asks.

Gordy stares through Julius. "Marvel at Wembly," he says, distantly. "The wisest gorilla in captivity."

"Who *are* you?"

"He's nothing," Morris says. "Only a common thief."

Gordy sinks back down to the stretcher. "Okay," he says, closing his eyes. He begins panting, quick and shallow, nearing hyperventilation. His hands grip the rails as if in preparation for a long drop.

Julius limps to the stretcher. Gordy gives him the crazy eyes.

"Please get me away. I used it and now it's here." Hands gripping, knuckles white.

"*What* did you use? *What's* here?"

Gordy unhinges his mouth, puts all teeth on display, and emits a singular yowl, a spine-scouring shriek of impossible volume, amplified by the tunnel's echo, continuing without a hitch for breath for what seems an impossible length even as he flickers once again out of sight and discernment—nothing left but the scream, dying slowly like an air siren, the manner of its going suggesting a dissipation of breath and voice rather than a cessation of either the physical act of the scream or of the terror provoking it. Morris turns his attention to Julius. "You've got some large problems," he observes.

"Appears to me you've got a few yourself," Julius says. Morris chuckles.

"Where do you think you and your unconscious friend are going?"

"Out."

"Fine plan. Really first-rate, but...do you know how to *get* out?"

"It's a pretty straight shot back the way we came."

"You're not going back this way." He spreads his arms and legs, filling enough of the tunnel to prevent passage.

Julius considers this. His eyesight has returned, but his head throbs like it's been whacked with a sack of doorknobs. His foot feels like there's glass in it. "How about this," he growls, as convincingly as he can. "How about I walk over there and..." But it all goes hazy on him somehow; he's forgotten the gist...*what was I saying just now...?*

Morris smiles, ingratiating. "Beat me until I stop breathing?"

"That and more."

"You're a shit priest, then."

"You're not the first to suggest it."

"But I know something you don't know."

"Which is?"

"To be precise, I, being—forgive me—of considerably greater intelligence than you, both generally and regarding the particulars of this situation, suspect something you don't suspect."

"Which is?"

"That you're in the same boat as me. With Gordy, you'll want to pay attention to every word. It truly is a 'letter of the law' sort of thing. Do you remember what he said to us? I remember very well. 'No harm.' Me to you *or* you to me."

Julius sighs. "OK. You want a beating, you get a beating." He moves forward, hands going to fists, and Morris, spread-eagle in blockade, smiles. Julius reaches for his neck, but then he thinks: I won't do that, why would I do that? He reaches again, butl...no, that's not such a good idea. Curious. He tries again, and stops—how odd.

"Problem?" Morris asks, knowingly—The hateful prick. Smash his nose. Teeth down the throat. Make him grovel. Julius reaches again, fails again. He reminds himself to breathe normally; this isn't a problem, it's ridiculous. He strikes quickly, as if to surprise himself into compliance, punching Morris in the throat, but...why would you do that, punch this guy in the, in the throat? You don't know him, you don't even know his *throat*, punching a strange throat? I mean, there doesn't seem to be any...any point...

In dismay, Julius looks down; his hand hasn't yet moved.

"It's that you just...don't want to," Morris remarks. "Correct?"

Julius glowers. "I want to." But realizing—he's right. You lose interest in the midst of the act. If you stop trying to injure, the rage returns, but as soon as you act upon that rage, it recedes entirely. Less physical inability than deficit of will, some existential boredom lounging between himself and vengeance.

"You *want* to want to. But you can't quite want to. If you *could* want to, then you *would* want to. But every time you try to want to, you find you *don't* want to. Right?"

Bullshit, Julius thinks, but his fists stay put. One of them rises, vaguely, then drops again. He grins flopsweat desperation, remembering the way Morris had looked, knowing he now looks the same—like a guy trying to pretend he hadn't hit himself in the foot with a chainsaw.

Morris laughs. "You can't hurt me, but it's not because you're so loving and holy. It's that invisible dummy over there and his stolen magic. You? You'd have killed me with your bare hands to get what you want. Good to know you have no scruples. Right?"

A low remark, not worth dignifying with an answer, no matter how true. Julius moves behind the stretcher, now ominously free of movement.

"I'll carry him past you, then. You can't do anything to me."

"Not to you. But *him*? I'll cut him to pieces before I let him get away. I don't need him. I only need what he took from me."

Julius takes the stretcher by the handles, wrenches the thing from the wall, relieved at the weight of it—Gordy's still lying there.

"What a situation we find ourselves in," says Morris. "Here you are, with my prize. And here I am between you and your only way out. And I'm not going anywhere."

"Neither am I."

"Yes, but that's only a problem for *you*." Morris strolls back to his sword, picks it up, makes it disappear in his clothing, resumes his blockade pose. "My people know where I am. Tell me: Who knows where you are? Meanwhile, pretty soon, when I don't show up as expected, my folks will come quickly." Morris pauses. "In fact…we've been at this for a while, haven't we? They may be on their way already."

Julius takes a panicked look backward; there's nothing to be seen but the silver portal, clearly a door, but still distant. Imagines the tunnel beginning to fill with killers, the walls bleeding cardinal red…

Immediate movement becomes more imperative than direction; Julius takes the handles once more, pushes the stretcher away from Morris toward the only door in sight.

"Taking him my way?" Morris loping behind. "Fine with me. Like a bellboy, yes?"

Julius keeps pushing. Moving still seems wiser than not moving.

"I can't hurt you," Morris chirps. "But my people can; I won't even need to give a command. The moment they see you, they'll know what to do. They put on a great show. It all happens at once. They do it so all the pieces hit the floor except for the head. The head stays right where it was, balanced on the blades."

Moving faster seems wiser than moving slower. Julius breaks into a sort of mangled trot. Landing on the side of the foot spares his toe slightly, but Morris has no trouble keeping up. The circumference of the steel door ahead grows larger by torturous irreducible increments. Julius pays this door little attention; it's clearly locked, and his curiosity for any mystery has attenuated in favor of solutions, salvation, deliverance. Of far greater interest: to the left of the vault the tunnel jogs off, leading to a round room, within which he sees a bulky coffinlike shape draped in a white sheet, which is of no interest at all…and a freight elevator door—which, at the present moment, is everything. Giddy with relief, Julius clambers to it, thumbs the UP button, and the doors swing open with a tin *ding*, the most welcome sound in the world. Julius thrusts the stubborn stretcher over the lip of elevator door track and blocks the door with his body. Morris says, "Enjoy yourself. Six of my men are waiting for me up there, all armed."

Julius allows himself a smirk. "If that were true, you wouldn't be telling me." He knows he's scored; before the doors glide shut, he sees the tightening at the mouth and eyes of Morris's otherwise inscrutable face, and, after the short ride up, when the doors rock open, he finds himself in an unguarded room, dark, long and narrow.

There's an ever-present jerky creep of movement along one wall; shafts of light play intermittently on the floor and the cinder block of the wall opposite. There's the unmistakable scent of axle grease and, incongruously, odors of a dive bar: notes of vomit over robust tones of deep-fried food, wafts of cheap beer, the humidity of a crowded room. Nearby, there's some sort of movement on the left wall, but the main thing is the noise, coming from everywhere around: a tumult, loud rock music insisting it's more than a feeling, and voices—a hundred or more—all proclaiming themselves to one another and to the world, a never-ceasing echoing blabber of mutual celebration. And, nearer to him, breaking like waves over this sonic ocean, an incessant crashing Julius can't place. It's a terribly disorienting incompatibility, the sound of so many people, but the sight of none; he's totally alone—no, wait, not totally. There's another person standing here in the twilight. It's a loony, bathrobe and all. Head half-shaved, the rest dyed purple. Between her jaws she methodically chews a green toothbrush. She's studying the machinery in the wall with obsessed appreciation. He's upon her before she notices him. Unperturbed to see Julius standing there, she points to the machinery. "They have two series," she says. "See? Like dumbwaiters. They run it with pulleys."

Julius sees the elevator doors shut; down again goes the car. Time to get moving. Behind the loony, at the end of the dark hallway, Julius sees a wedge of light let in by a doorway, presumably propped open when the she made her way back here. He pushes the stretcher past, making for the exit.

"Hey, Mister," she says as he passes. "Do you know me?"

Julius studies her for a moment. "Sorry, no."

She sighs. "Nobody does. I wish I could remember."

"I'm sorry?"

She's impatient with him now. "Maybe *he* knows." Indicating the stretcher. Julius looks but sees nothing.

"You...you see him?"

She snorts. "I *have* eyes." She turns back to the machinery. "It's done with pulleys." Julius, antsy, moves on; as he does, he inspects her gadget, which takes up the whole length of the left wall, and knows at once where he is— My God. It's full of bowling pins. I'm at Barney's.

The machines are pulling gourd-shaped, red-collared, white wooden pins from a trough into an ingenious contraption of conveyers and pulleys to a sort of pin-elevator, where each one drops into its own pin-shaped empty tube, ready for placement, perched on the far end of the lane, prepared for the next CRASH-rattle-rattle-rattle, while the spangled or marbled or black balls are gathered out of the tray by another series of canvas belts and shot back up the way they came. Julius can't blame the loony for her fascination; under normal circumstances he might also pause. These days Barney's usually keeps most of the lanes dark—but given the racket, they're all apparently in use.

From a distance he sees the indicator light of the elevator, summoned again from the floor below. Morris, ascending. Julius gets moving as fast as his one good foot and one good hand will allow, pushing the stretcher like a skateboard. Brilliant, this stretcher, his best friend, his savior—until at the doorway they have a sharp difference of opinions, the stretcher having not been designed to negotiate tight spaces or sharp corners. Before Julius makes it through the doorway, he sees the elevator doors open, and hears the shout behind him even over the dim, then Morris is charging down the hallway. With a great wrench, Julius frees stretcher from doorframe, shoots through, and is immediately swallowed by howling madness.

Loonies. Everywhere, loonies. Barney's has been overrun. They're eight deep on each lane, tossing balls without regard for life or safety. A roister of drunken energized loonies, their voices reverberating, overwhelming the classic rock piping through the speakers—Since when did loonies have anything approaching energy? And where did they get cash? But there's no time to spare on mystery. Dave's still waiting back at the Wales—but how to get there? His original plan flushed, Julius cycles desperately through his options: The Neon Chapel, now nearby but never a first choice, is completely out of the question now—to endanger the brothers and sisters...endanger Nettles? No. Forget location. All you need is the next step. Make distance between you and him. But the notion of gaining ground is ridiculous; pushing a stretcher through this throng is like pushing a pencil though a keyhole the wide way. And, even if you had an empty highway between here and your destination (whatever that might now be), what distance can you make? Your whole leg's a mess.

The throb from Julius's foot has now migrated to somewhere around the upper shin, the damaged toe presents ominous frozen splinters of numbness, while the knee screams, abused and torn from the orthopedic nightmare of his improvised side-foot stride. There's nothing to do but put most of the weight firmly on the stretcher and muscle through the throng as well as can be managed, muttering here and there "Sorry, sorry, 'scuse me, sorry," the words lost amid the hoot and bluster and roll of ball on wood and pin-clatter, picking a torturous path toward the doorway and god*dammit* what are all these loonies *doing* here?

"Pretty good, huh?' a voice beside him bellows. It's Morris. Unencumbered, he's caught up quickly. Julius ignores him, keeps moving. But Morris continues, chummy. "They just got a double dose of pharmaceutical-grade pep."

Julius tries to ignore him and push.

"What's concerning me," Morris says, right up beside him: "is determining how far our embargo against harm goes. Is it just between you and me, or does it go farther? Certainly, I could test it. Any of these around us seem disposable, don't you think?"

Julius grunts. The door is near. Soon he'll be clear of this crowd, able to execute whatever passes for a run. And then what, dummy? Outrun Morris on a lame leg, a broken toe? No hope. Never mind. Don't think of it. Push.

"However, I don't like to kill anything that's mine. You never know who might prove interesting. It must be said, you've proven interesting. Very interesting, just by surviving as long as you have." Morris produces a device. "Good news! I finally got reception. The cavalry has been called. You're going to have an amazing opportunity to become even more interesting. Alternatively, you could stop being interesting. Leave this baggage and limp away. No hard feelings, no problem, we'll never mention it again."

Don't think about it. Just push.

"Meanwhile, I still have to experiment. Find somebody I'm comfortable hurting."

Don't think. Push.

"Maybe you're leading me to somebody like that now?"

Push push push. The door is tantalizingly near now. So near. It's here. You've made it.

"I mean, where could you possibly hope to be escaping to?"

Push push pu—

Barney's main doors swing both ways, saloon style. Julius rams the stretcher through them, and, as he comes through, finally stops, as he takes in the sight of his doom.

Barney's was only the start. Outside, the crowd continues. Loonies cluster on Transept Ave, both ways, as far as he can see, as if there's been some sort of exponential explosion of loonies...*were there this many all along*? Yes, of course there were. They've been thick as sparrows on a telephone wire, gathering on the sidewalks lining streets over square miles of the Corners, huddled in murmurations of expanding and collapsing shuffling clouds of mentally ill figures in empty lots. The majority of them—nervous, frightened, shy—have been hiding in the less-traveled nooks and crannies, but now, made strangely bold, they've emerged. Apparently, there are enough to fill the street from here to Ralph's: loonies swinging from streetlamps. Loonies wrestling and spinning in the street. Loonies scuttling like crabs from one building to another; a lunatic mob. It's as if, after years cooped up, after days staring at the cracks in the sidewalk, all of them have decided, as a corporate entity, to take in the full universe. A sudden inheritance of attention and energy, withheld from them over numbed years, has been liquidated, interest compounded, and deposited directly into their limbic systems. Every building on every street has a tributary trickling off from the main human flow, an army-ant chain of lunatics heading to promiscuously sample whatever each building or establishment has to offer—mostly something illegal, shifty, or, at least rowdy and destructive—while another chain marches away from that prospect to the next thing, both chains going at the top speed possible and jostling each other, but each keeping to the right and moving efficiently, each loony looking for their own specific destiny, object of obsession, grand purpose, topic of the day, major field of study, and each of them, having discovered it, wears the same look of focused intensity, of open curiosity, worn by the woman examining the pin-setting mechanism.

The loonies carry fruits of their successful looting: boxes of donuts and electronic goods, cans of sardines, fistfuls of cash, bottles of booze, cell phones and other random electronics, a loose bowling pin. A pair of mattresses, a loony atop each, crowd-surfs upon waves of loony hands. Loonies hang from windows of buildings. Loonies carouse with the more adventurous members of the gangs, who seek profit from these new fish. Everywhere Julius looks he sees dashing, pushing, hysterical laughter, loonies swinging shopping bags above their heads like plastic bolas, hopping onto the hoods of cars and into beds of trucks, playing in the spray of a vandalized fire hydrant, screeching bug-eyed in the upswing of amphetamine hypertension. Cheap squibs explode around him in startling serial bursts of harmless brimstone. Julius wants to collapse atop the stretcher. It's too much. It's defeat. Clearly there will be no straight path to anything like a hiding place, no way to break away from Morris, only more of the same torturous crowdbreaking inch-by-inch work, and at this moment Gordy begins to scream again, howling past fear or pain, failing to reappear as his voice makes itself known even above the clamor.

"Walk away and live," Morris shouts. "It's the only offer you'll get."

It sounds so inviting, so completely reasonable. Walk away. Melt into the mass. Become nothing, find Dave Waverly, tend wounds, return to life. You've done all you could. You've done more than most would...

Then Gordy screams again, and Julius knows he's not out of the thicket yet—to abandon this boy in his moment of need would be a betrayal, not only of him, but of yourself. Of what you are: the cat who steps between bullets, who challenges guns, who brings the peace at the expense of his own bleeding meat. Julius makes for bare stretches, pockets devoid of lunatic, where he can skateboard a little and spare his foot, but most empty places corresponded to the edges of the street; he has curbs to contend with, banging up against them, cursing as the jolts enrage his bitten thumb, broken foot, or one of the other smaller injuries only now beginning to present themselves. Exhaustion eats him. His lungs are bags that take in and release pain. His leg is wrapped in thorns, his foot is a dead hunk of ice that has been nailed to his ankle, his body is fire. Spots dance fervid before his eyes. Morris paces alongside, laughing at each hindrance. Julius now knows where he must go—there's no other choice. There's no shaking Morris; speeding away is impossibility, and as for fighting him, punching him, beating him until he...he...

What, Julius wonders, was I just thinking about?

Step by tortured step, Ralph's draws nearer. The thing about the chase is the next step. If you have that, eventually even the horizon falls. Take the next step, that's all. You'll still have the bastard with you when you get there, which is bad, but Donk is still your friend, and maybe he and Bailey can handle him and get us both away before the collective cadre of cardinals come capering, carve our corpuscles into cutlets, careful, caution, consider, you're alliterally going crazy here...

"What you don't realize," Morris says, and then without pause or preface he falls with surgical neatness down one of the many manholes left lidless in Loony Island, courtesy of enterprising scrap-iron expropriators. Even over loony-hubbub, Julius can hear his sudden surprised shout, followed by a splash of impact below and near-simultaneous scream of pain—Let his leg be broken and not just ankle sprained, let the bone be poking out of his...

Julius's mind trails off, baffled yet again by the combination of Morris and the idea of physical harm…

Still a stroke of luck. Don't squander. Push. Push.

As if his thoughts have been read by some perverse spirit, Julius immediately finds his way blocked by a loony who comes floating out from the crowd to stand exactly opposite him, hands gripping the stretcher rails, preventing any hope of forward momentum—while Julius, who knows beyond doubt the injured Morris, fetlock most certainly befricked but not entirely befuckled, is already making his agonized way to the ladder leading up—gives in to despair at last. This lunatic is an emaciated jittery mess; there's no real physical threat to him under normal circumstance, but though Julius realizes the idea of fighting him is simple—no mysterious fiat imposed by partially visible men here—he has nothing left with which to fight. This is it. Tank empty. It's all been too much. Dark spots claim his vision.

"Hoe hoe holy shit, Captain," the loony says, and Julius realizes with bewildered relief this isn't any random loony, but Brother Tennessee, still wearing the bathrobe of his tribe, grinning like a freak. "Holy shit. That's Gordy-Gord. You've got my Gordy."

Julius glances stretcherward, briefly catching a flash of Gordy before he flicks out again.

Tennessee's face works hard against weeping. "That's Gordy, Father. That's my son, my son, my son. My boy gone forever."

With his last strength, Julius heaves himself onto the stretcher, feels the unseen actuality of Gordy beneath.

"Ralph's. Take us to Donk," he croaks, and sees Tennessee take hold of the stretcher before the darkness rises up in his vision, a malignant peaceful wave. The last thing he feels before it meets him is the stretcher beginning to move, slow, and then faster.

G O N E

I'd have to say, given how it played out, Bailey was Donk's blind spot and always was. She'd been his older brother's younger girlfriend, but you have to remember how ages work around such things. Yale was a rising star in the gangs, but that still only made him an older teenager. His brother Donk was nothing but a kid, but still old enough to have a worshipful crush on his hero's girl. In the years after Yale was killed, they hid from what they assumed was Ralph's hot pursuit and the same bad fate that had befallen the rest. It never occurred to them to leave the only neighborhood they knew; and anyway in Loony Island you can get pretty lost from the world. As they hid, hungry and scared, and plotted their return, they eventually became each other's worlds. As Donk grew, so, too, did their feelings for each other.

From a long time, all they had was those feelings; that, and each other.

But enough time goes by, you get used to anything, then you stop seeing it anymore. Feelings are no exception.

Love most especially, maybe.

✗ ✗ ✗

What nobody realizes about me, thinks Bailey Ligneclaire, is I'm in love with that idiot.

They're outside Ralph's Market. She's watching the surge of the loony tsunami pass by; there's nothing better to do. Donk, the idiot, dangles from the big green RALPH'S GENERAL & SPECIFIC sign, deep in conversation with a loony who grips the left-handed diagonal slant of a sans-serif A. The loony is up there because he's a loony; Daniel is up there because it amuses him to follow suit.

Daniel Coyote. Her idiot and lover. Her lover and idiot. What a maroon.

Daniel's got his arms hooked around the L's lintel; a ten foot drop to merciless asphalt. Not far to fall at all, just a hop—but still she can see it: the slip, the awkward grab at air, the flip, the sick sledgehammer *thuck* as Daniel hits headfirst, and the grotesque *crack* as the weight of his body uses the fulcrum of his forehead to send his upper spine out through his throat. Such a possibility would never occur to *him*—he never worries, realizing you'll do it for him. As though worry were a transferable commodity. There he is, hanging half a story up—not high enough to ensure fatal or incapacitating injury in the case of a fall, but certainly high enough to allow for the possibility—discussing with this strange loon the intricate matters of Loony Island's mechanics: of local politics, of process, of the differences and duties and jurisdictions between gangs and how to tell one from another, how to know which of the bluebirds are on the grease, the taxonomy of graffiti, the unspoken commentary of unwritten street laws: Daniel reveling in his authority, in the display of this arcane knowledge useless outside a four-mile radius. The genius moron, dangling dangerously from the name of the man they serve, and whose bad death they plot.

Lately it seems to her it's all they do: plot Ralph's death. Is she the only one who still remembers there are three phases, and not two? Infiltrate, vengeance, yes . . . but what about phase three? What about escape?

Which is the exact thing you've been hoping to hear Donk mention, Bailey thinks. Ever since that window got broken, and we met the man who broke it, and learned just how close we might finally be to the end of our plan.

The plan has three phases. They crafted it together, in the aftermath of Yale's bad death and the horror of the greenhouse, whispered it to one another beneath scrounged covers each night during the long hungry times when they hadn't yet learned to earn for themselves, knowing they had to keep alive, if only so that Ralph and the greenhouse wouldn't be their final word. They'd lie together in their customary strange and intimate posture, forehead-to-forehead, clutching each other's ears, and talk, and plan, and plot. Phase One—long since accomplished—was to infiltrate Ralph's organization, using their particular skills to gain power and influence and trust and wealth. Phase Two—upcoming—is to kill Ralph, and make sure he knows why death has come to him. Phase Three is escape. Live a life, at last. She and Daniel have decided upon touring the Caribbean, then the Mediterranean, then the Pacific islands, scouting without urgency for a permanent home. Bailey's ready. She'll miss her donut den. She won't miss the rest.

"You're obsessed with retirement," Daniel admonished her, when he returned this morning with no explanation. "If I didn't know better, I'd think you were getting lazy." He said it with a tone just arch enough that she was forced to take it as a joke or face charges of sensitivity, but with enough of an edge that she knew (but couldn't prove) he meant it. This left her untethered; suggested the goal they've worked toward for so long had become, for him, an obstacle. Has the enticement of his position exerted a greater gravity than she can overcome? Being the top cat in this dogfight is what gives him his shape, his name, his knowledge of himself. Can he even imagine himself apart from that? For years they've dragged out their revenge; for the first time, Bailey wonders about the excuses for delay Daniel stacks up against progress—and what if he decides he wants to stay? You've been living together toward this future for such a long time. There's a great emptiness at the prospect of entering it alone.

The first sign of unusual activity came during morning office hours. Across the open gap of the newly broken window came Tennessee, running at full pelt, pastel bathrobe trailing out behind him like a toothpaste comet. Behind him a cardinal gave chase, efficient and silent, holding what appeared to be a syringe. It all happened too quickly to do more than register it, but she was tending a register of her own, and office hours were an inopportune time to investigate. Later, from the break room, she noticed other loonies, not being chased, but much more energetic. Running. Cartwheels. Odd. But there was money to count, business to discuss, and then later there was store and donut shop paperwork to attend to. It was a little before dinnertime that the full mob slammed into them, and all the merchandise quickly walked out the door, loonies racing down the aisles pushing wire shopping carts with misaligned wheels, emptying the shelves, singing to the tune of *Alouette*:

OooooOOOOOOoooooh
We're the loonies
We're the looty loonies
Hear us crooning
Give us all your food!

Normally, a looting would have been the time for Daniel to go into full retribution lockdown. Examples would have to be set and executions administered; nobody steals from Ralph. Bailey had already picked up her baton and grabbed the pump-action Mossberg when she realized he was simply leaning one-armed on the billiard table, smiling. When she'd bestowed a quizzical look, he'd twinkled.

"Leave them to it," Daniel said. "That's all Ralph's stuff. And Ralph is toast. He doesn't know yet, but he's about to find out." But then he said something that made her look askance. "These—" pointing to the loonies—"are our new army. Morris is giving them to us." And then he'd run outside. By the time she'd collected herself and followed, he was already hanging from the sign, getting gregarious up there with a loon named Garf. To listen to him now, Daniel sounds as though he isn't in the least planning on leaving the Island. On the contrary, as he speaks to Garf and his apparent girlfriend—a wan lady named Azrael—he speaks in the future perfect. He's got a sack of cheap phones, and he's instructing Garf to distribute them among the loonies, to pull the drawstrings of communication tight. This isn't merely passing the time. This is making plans. He was already expecting this. For how long has he known? Why has he not bothered to mention it? It suggests a total abdication of the part of their plan involving escape, a life together— which leads to the question: What other parts of the plan are out?

Did you assume, Bailey wonders, that if you changed the script I'd go along? That I'll work at your register forever? Forever?

Forever is a problem for Bailey.

Long ago, years before she met Donk or even Yale, Bailey awoke in the unspecified middle emptiness of night with a startle, seized by an immense and inescapable terror: *Something is wrong.* She'd lain there a long time before grasping the nature of the terror: She would die. Not at that moment, surely. Not even soon. But she would. It would happen. Incapable of intellectualizing it, she nevertheless perceived that, this, now, was a time when she was, and that, inexorably, there came rushing toward her the day when she would *not be*, and after that moment would come forever, and there would be no end to forever, none, none, none. Forever approaching at velocities at which time becomes relative, where an instant is a millennium, a millennium an instant, each drop within Forever's ocean itself oceanic in size, yet merely a particle within the vastness of her eternal not-ness. She thought none of this yet; she was as yet incapable of putting language to it. She could only feel it, from the moment of her waking, and for the rest of her life thereafter. She was ten years old. That night she'd risen from bed and gone out looking for a fight.

Perhaps, she considers, this is what she finds magnetic about Daniel: This is a man who has never considered the idea that he will die. Who would, were you to confront him with the rushing wall of Forever, simply laugh, finding the concept of his own death preposterous. No, death is something Daniel believes is for other people. Just as he sources his worry to her, so he must think when the time comes, he will find somebody else to die for him, either by charm or by hire.

Always the what with Daniel, never the why. He's still hanging from the L and yelling over to Garf: Choose five of the best loons you can find, have them choose five of their own…the network will be the king…take a device from the bag, pass it along…this is the ground floor, the whole pyramid's getting shaken up, there's opportunity to find yourself near the top…Every once in a while, she calls out to him and he pretends not to hear. She knows the reason he'll give for ignoring her—for safety's sake nobody can guess their bond—but it's getting harder to distinguish which is the fiction and which the truth; he's become so good at pretending she means nothing to him. Nobody knows I love that moron, she thinks again, and nobody knows he loves me. Maybe not even him.

Look at them: the loonies. More of them joining the throng every minute—up and down the street, they rampage; three of them have found one of the neighborhood's few unfilched manhole covers, they're rolling it across the parking lot and right into a gnarly knot of gangsters, who amazingly appear amused enough by the novelty they don't retaliate though one of their number nurses a kneecap; crouching nearby, a clutch of madmen learn knife tricks from Arlene, an old hooker who retired years ago, who now trains young pimps in the art of the blade; across the parking lot, loonies have captured Bailey's Donuts. At Daniel's insistence, she's gone against her better judgment and given the place up to insurance claims rather than defend it with her shotgun, but it's a wrench to see it crawling with rioters. The loons appear to have started the cookers, conveyer belts of frosted O O O O O O O O O popping out of the fry grease still painfully hot into immediately scalded mouths. In two different places she sees the unmistakable glow of a building on fire, though whether this is the handiwork of loonies, or else the random accident one should expect from chaos of this magnitude, she can't tell. A loony lurches out of the donut shack shrieking and holding a rawburned hand. It appears to have gone into the deep fryer to the forearm. This feels like an omen, a tipping point. She calls for Daniel again, and again is ignored, so she grabs him by the legs and yanks. He holds on, resistant as a green crabapple, so she dangles from his feet until finally he releases and collapses atop her; Bailey, careful to shield Daniel from the worst of the impact, rolls beneath to catch him. She sees his face; he's spitting mad—Good.

"What the *hell*?"

She cuffs him on the head.

"Hey!"

She cuffs him again. Grabs him by the ears.

"Hey! I'm conducting *business* here…"

Nose to nose, eye to eye. Holding his ears in her fists, but he's not holding hers. "You're ignoring me. That stops right now."

"Hey. Hey hey hey. Hey." He unfurls the ingratiating smile that's charmed Loony Island; it's a smile insinuating some undefined secret shared by the two of you against the universe, a smile that promises it belongs only to you. "What happened to trusaa*Aaaaaaah!* that *hurts*."

"Tell me what you haven't told me yet."

Like a mechanic would discard any ineffective tool, Donk discards his charm, selects instead a serious obtuseness. "What haven't I told you?"

Bailey keeps her grip on his ears. "We're going to go inside now and you're going to explain to me exactly what's happening here. And then you're going to explain why you haven't explained it to me already." She's enraged to find herself close to tears. Bailey hopes he gives her a reason to knock his head on the ground…but he nods. That's Daniel. Fights when you want compliance, goes slack when you want to fight. He's like wrestling a jelly.

"Stay here," he tells Garf. "Keep the sack of phones. Couple more things I need to tell you. I won't be long." Unbelievable, the presumption, the dismissiveness. It's become commonplace. He'll say secrecy equals safety, but the logic has drained from this explanation. Here you are, Daniel, she thinks. King of the hill. Everybody knows you, and you're still here. Still alive. Nobody's made collateral damage of you. How does acting like I'm nothing to you but Ralph's hired muscle protect me? No, I'm a secret—we're a secret—not because you crave safety, but because you prefer secrets. Because what other people don't know, you never have to explain.

Inside is a mess. Shelves completely stripped of wares, most of the fluorescents smashed. Miraculously, there's been no serious attempt to break any of the front windows, so the poster-paste overlap—with the exception of the newly broken center pane—conceals them from snooping eyes. Bailey Ligneclaire waits in the dark for her oldest friend to speak. Her love, her hope. The big stubborn dummy stands there in the dim and waits right back. "Well?"

She waits. He knows what. He's an idiot, but he's not dumb.

"Listen. I have actual important work out there. This loony thing is permanent. It's the new order of things. Tonight is our window to recruit as many of them as we can. So whatever this is needs to take less than a minute, baby."

She doesn't even realize she's done it until it's done. She's lifted one of her precious vintage cash registers and slammed it—for the second time in a day—into the splintering tile, reminding herself not to let even a hint of tears into her voice. She's learned to let her eyes go dead following a show of strength; now she gazes upon Daniel, wondering how and when he arrived at the center of her universe, when she decided him worthy of such promotion, how and when exactly she found herself on the dark side of his planet.

"What this is about, baby," she says, "is you telling me everything you know. Everything I *don't* know. Baby. About whatever deal you've apparently done with your new boss. About how you've changed the plan. *Our* plan. About why you let them rob *my* store. About why you don't give a shit they trashed *my* donut shop. You're going to stop pretending you don't know what I mean. You're going to stop pretending you don't know exactly what it is you haven't told me. And then you're going to tell me *why* I don't know. Baby. For a minute, or as long as it takes. Or I'm going to beat your ass until we both wish you had."

For the first time, he really sees her. She moves herself between him and the door.

Minutes pass, or perhaps no time at all.

She can feel it all building to a terminal point inside her. Outside, through the new window, she sees the undiminished madness of the mob. In the distance she can hear sirens; the bluebirds, who are paid off but not enough to be able to credibly ignore this sort of riot, are finally closing in. Daniel's still staring silence at her. Now he can see she won't be charmed away, so he's become distant and cold—an extension of his behavior since returning, late at night from his visit to Morris, stinking of cigars and wine: deflecting her questions with generalities, blocking her out as she pushed, fleeing their apartment to go who knows where. It creeps her out, the entirety of his ability to separate himself from her, from anybody, even from himself. She feels as if he's many things at once; a totem, an obelisk, something carved from ancient stone; or a banker assaying her credit report and finding her wanting; but most of all just another fuckhead gangster, one she's meeting for the first time.

"So?" Donk finally demands. "What do you *need* to know?"

"What do I need to know?"

"Yes. You seem to think I haven't told you something. What is it?"

"Daniel, you haven't told me. *Anything.*"

He delivers an inadvisable eye-roll. "I've told you this is all part of the plan. That's usually enough. But for some reason tonight suddenly you decide not to trust me."

Bailey knows him well enough to know this trick: Create a sequence of blatant lies, stay calm in the face of ensuing outrage, and by this process guide the conversation so far away from the actual point you never have to address it. The only way to counter it is to push it aside and stick with truth. So, push aside this cart of bullshit, Bailey, push the cart aside—this ridiculous claim that you usually fly blind while he plans. He knows as well as you do; you're the daily confidant, the repository for most of his secrets. Push it aside; lay it out plain.

"OK, Daniel. Here's what I don't know. I don't know why all the loonies are rioting. I don't know why the gangs haven't tried to stop it. I don't know why you seem to know exactly what's happening. I don't understand your sack full of cash and phones, or why you're handing them out to loonies like they're candy. I don't know how this 'Morris' comes into it. I don't even know what came out of your meeting with him. I don't know what he intends to get out of us—or you. I don't know what you think we get out of it. I don't see how it pertains to what I thought we were trying to do. And I don't know, since you do seem to know, why I *don't* know."

"I certainly don't know why, either. Given that I've explained all of it to you."

Push the cart aside. "Most of all, I don't know what you even mean by 'the plan' anymore."

"It hasn't changed."

"Remind me again about the part of the plan where we switch over to another boss after Ralph's gone."

Daniel says nothing to this. She comes in near and gives him the fish-eyes.

"Daniel, pay attention to me. I *know* you. Remember? Understand? Tricks won't work. I need to know. Because if you don't tell me, starting now—right now—I'm assuming we have different plans. And then I'll work my own plan my own way, right away, tonight. And then I'll be gone."

"You won't leave." But he doesn't smile when he says it.

"I will."

"I can stop you."

"I'll fight whoever you send until they kill me. If you decide to do that, I suppose that's how it will play. But I'll still be gone for good. And I'll have been right to not trust you."

"You'd leave without our stash? Everything we've saved together?" As if they don't both know they each have their own accounts separate from the main. Push the cart aside. She can hear in his voice he's weakening.

"In a heartbeat." Hating the weakness of her tears, but at least he can see she's earnest. What's worse is, the structural damage may be done already, the foundation cracked, maybe crumbling. *The fact it's taking this much to get you to tell me...*

But then the idiot says something she can't process at first.

"Good," he says.

He says "Good."

Good.

Good?

He's smiling. Not grinning, but smiling. There's a sadness and a finality to it. She can't read his expression—of course she can't. He's managed to stay on top of the power structure of Loony Island. When have the contours of his roads ever been drivable? Whenever you think you've found a straight-away he's always ready to present you with an unnegotiable curve.

"Good," he says again, and he sounds sincere—real again, for the first time in days. He reaches beneath the counter where the register had, until recently, been resting. From some compartment he produces a bottle of smoky liquor, the only unlooted hooch in the store.

"I got this years ago," he announces, "For now, I guess. The guy told me it's some of the best. Afraid I don't have any glasses." He opens it, drinks, gives it an appraising nod, and hands it to her. She stares at it as though he's handed her a large trout.

"The loonies have been given something," he says at last. "Some dose. By Morris. Drugs. It started political but now it's an angle."

"And what does that have to do with us?"

"Morris has other plans," Daniel says. She can tell it's the truth. He's going to tell her at least some things now, though he'll do well to know she's not going to stop pressing until she understands why. Daniel continues: "He contracted with me a couple weeks ago to make sure all the loonies got the boot at once, helter-skelter, which they did."

"You've been working with Morris all along?"

He looks at her without shame or guilt. "Since a couple weeks ago—yes. He wanted the loonies out. One of his people found me with the proposal; I followed the thread, and it seemed promising. He's going to use loonies to take over. He's given something to help."

"Which is what?"

"I don't know. It's supposed to make them easier to deal with. Whatever it is, I'd say it's working." As if to furnish demonstration, Garf enters through the automatic doors, bringing with him a rush of hot city air. "You didn't tell me how long to wait," he says, looking socially unsure, as if he senses he may in some way be responsible for Bailey's tear-streaked face—but also possible his fidgeting may be due to whatever chemical slurry is now thunderstorming merry devastation through his bloodstream.

Daniel glances at Bailey, then says to him, "It's OK. It's fine. Take the sack and spread it. Tell as many others as possible, and tell them to tell as many others as possible. Go. Play until morning. The city's yours. I'll meet you where I told you."

She watches until he's gone. "So. You're organizing for Morris now."

"Yes. For now."

"Morris replaces Ralph."

"No. Morris *ends* Ralph. As bad as Ralph deserves."

"It doesn't matter how bad."

There's a nothing in his face. "It matters to me. It needs to be bad. Morris can do it bad."

"And then we leave?"

"You leave tonight. I join you later." But she hears the hitch.

"Later? When is *later*?"

"For now, it only means later."

Something terrible twists inside her. It's true after all: He's fallen in love with the life. "And so you carry on like you have, but with another guy in charge. And without us. Just like that."

"It isn't that simple."

"It sounds exactly that simple."

Enumerating for her, finger by finger. "We need to get Ralph. Right? That's the first thing. Right?" But now she's reexamining, looking at old things as if new. She thinks—*Do we? Do we have* to "get" Ralph? Why, exactly? In service of what? For the appreciation of whom? To mend what? To restore what? When she says nothing, he says: "We get out safe, right? Isn't that the next thing? Am I wrong? Do I have it wrong?"

No, Daniel. No. You don't have it wrong. That's the thing with you. You never have it wrong. But she doesn't say anything, and he starts to look a bit desperate. He moves around the counter so he once again faces her.

"Well, we don't get Ralph without Morris. With him, we don't get out safe, unless I stay behind. You're nothing to him right now, but I've...caught his interest."

"You have what he wants. Keys to the kingdom."

"That's not what he's after."

"All this is a favor. He's doing it all for you."

"He'd take over without me. It's an afterthought. He's taking over because taking over is what he does. From me he wanted something else."

"Something other than the whole thing? Something other than everything?"

Daniel smiles his most irritating smile. "Loony Island isn't 'everything' to most people. Certainly not to him."

"So what does he want?"

"What we thought he wanted—the flickering man."

"What did you tell him?" Bailey asks, but with awful assurance, she knows.

He requisitions the bottle from her and pulls from it. She can't read his expression; the nothing has returned to his face.

"I told them to follow Julius."

"They'll kill him."

"I requested not."

"You requested."

"Yes."

We've gone badly, she thinks, when we right our wrongs this way. There's never a move on the board, it seems, that doesn't sacrifice one piece for another. Is Julius—a friend, a guest, an ally who has earned more of their trust than any other—now a pawn to be beveled unknowingly into enemy territory and shunted, defeated, to the edge, taken out of the game, a bleeding tactical victim of the bloodless enactment of strategy?

"Daniel, you have to warn him."

"It's too late. They'll have taken their guy by now."

"And Julius, too."

"Probably not."

"*Probably.*"

"Don't eyeball me. He'll be fine." He says it again, this time for himself. "He'll be fine."

But she lacks Daniel's ability to discriminate, his connoisseur's taste for selecting only the choicest of reality's courses. He swims in the river of now, glides through the current of today's information, trusts to his belief that he can shape what is to *be* simply by concentrating on those parts of what *is* that most favor him. But she swims in darker liquors, in clouded pools of what *might* be. In the river, he can see only one possible Father Julius: stymied, saddened by the loss of his intriguing, flickering friend, but still safe and alive. But in her pool, the light refracts and bends. Down here, she sees infinite Fathers Juliuses: Julius stabbed, chopped, garroted, beaten toothless, buried in cement, pitchforked through the neck (pitchforked? Yes, even that), marbled throughout the amazingly perfect cube of a compacted former automobile...

And Daniel can't possibly see as clearly as he usually does. How could he? Look out there. Outside is chaos, outside hundreds of loonies or more have risen dormant from the sediment of the riverbed to assault the natural predictable order, inserting themselves into the equilibrium of the ecosystem, scattering detritus until the water clouds to madness. This is more than a riot. This is a revolution. "Why aren't the gangs stopping this?" She says it to herself, not to him, but he answers.

"I told them not to, on Ralph's orders."

"But Ralph didn't give that order."

"No."

"Ralph will find out..." But then she realizes. If Daniel's not telling, Ralph will have to discover it through slower channels... and, when the news finally reaches him, he'll immediately recognize the perfidy of his trusted right hand. As if anticipating this concern, Daniel says: "Ralph will find out when it's too late. He'll know it when the cardinals nab him."

"When?"

"Soon. They may have him already. They're keeping him for me before they finish him."

She's quiet for a while. She picks up the bottle where he left it and takes a measured sip. "It's good stuff."

"Guy said it would be."

"You should have told me."

"But then you'd have wanted to stay here with me."

"I do want to stay with you. But not here."

"Like I said, I've caught his interest. He isn't the kind to let you go."

"You just said he'd take over with or without you. 'As an afterthought,' remember? He wouldn't hunt you."

"He'd hunt me. I've made promises to him he'll expect me to keep."

"I'm not leaving if you're not."

He twinkles then. "You already promised you would. 'A heartbeat,' remember?"

"You decided for me." She's not sure why she's surprised. It's so clear; he's decided everything. He's been deciding everything, hasn't he, since the moment they saw Yale travel between sky and ground? Now he's getting impatient. "Our stash is already moved. The whole thing. You know where. It's ready for you. Get it, and get out."

"Come with me." Bailey grabs his hand. "You don't have to stay."

He snatches it back. "I do."

"Why?"

"I told you."

"He'll kill Ralph either way."

"If I leave, I won't be there to see."

"That's acceptable."

Did she think there had been a certain nothing in his face before? It pales to the void she sees now as he corks the bottle and sets it down. "Not to me." In that moment, there remains no range of possibilities. She sees only one Donk—the one who stays, captured not by avarice or pride, but by vengeance. She's envisioned a thousand deadly ways she might lose him, but this was never one of them. He'd fall in love with the life; she'd imagined that—but no. He's fallen in love with the death. He'd rather have the revenge than the escape.

"You never talk about Yale. You only ever talk about our plans after."

"Well, you know me." She does. In this sense there's no separation between her Daniel and Ralph's Donk. With both of them it's always the things
not spoken. She's been like the rest; all these years, fooled by the twinkle, the
spark that insinuates, flatters, confirms *you and me, baby. You and me against the
world.* But no; it's him. It's always only just been himself.

"Why didn't you tell me this last night?"

"This gives you less time to think of ways not to go."

He's not wrong. Is he ever wrong? Goddammit, Daniel—and god damn
you.

The doors open again, and a magic trick on wheels comes bursting
through. The magician is dressed as a loony, pushing a sort of handcar with
a sheet covering it. Floating inches above it, face up, is Father Julius, bloody
and unconscious. She looks at Daniel, at first presuming, irrationally, the
magician is somehow here as part of Daniel's plan, as though his machina-
tions have become so meticulous, they've attained subatomic levels of prob-
ability—Daniel anticipating their conflict and arranging for a convenient
distraction at this precise moment—but a glance disproves this, he is…not
angry, no, but floridly annoyed…and she suddenly realizes the loony is none
other than Tennessee. The logorrheic loon is responding to Daniel's shooing
with desperate babbling *listen no listen no listen, you gotta, you gotta help us gotta hie
hie hide* us but she can't understand why Tennessee is performing magic or
why Julius is assisting him or most of all why they would choose now of all
times to show off their act and Daniel has snatched up a broom —thank God
he didn't go for the shotgun—from the checkout stand and is brandishing it
threateningly, Bailey, still bemused, almost dizzy with the effect of familiar
things combined in wantonly unlikely ways, wondering what exactly Julius is
playing at with his comatose act and what the hell is Tennessee saying, *hide
us?*—since when has the *audience* been enlisted to disappear the *magician?*—
and the act seems to have been preceded by some sort of "saws in half"
number, because there's blood covering the tablecloth beneath which Julius
is so solidly hovering, when Tennessee at last says something to restore her
equilibrium:

"He's coming for us. More more Morris is coming."

Daniel, now moved from pique to desperation, swings the broom handle into Tennessee's skinny back and Bailey realizes that the empty space beneath Julius is about the depth of a...flickering man. And Morris, who knows ways of killing cruel enough to satisfy Daniel's apparent need, is obviously coming. And Tennessee is shouting. And Daniel is swinging. And Julius is bleeding. And the man beneath him, somehow, though unseen, is. And Morris is coming. He'll be here soon. She knows a moment before it starts exactly what's going to happen. Daniel is about to complete the brutal math that began with betraying Julius to this fate. He stops mid-swing and feigns as though he's seeing the priest for the first time.

"Wait. Is that...Julius?"

Tennessee is nearly comic in his relief. "Yes! Yesyesyes! There's bad trouble on the way, I swear. You've got to help us till he's gone."

Donk allows himself a moment of theatrical reluctance. "All right, over there." Pointing with the stick to the stock room—toward the Fridge. "Wait there for me and I'll take you the rest of the way." Tennessee grabs the stretcher and hauls ass. Daniel turns back to her, pleading. His coat-sleeve's got a long smear of blood and his hair's standing up. She's never seen him wearing this expression before. "Listen," he says. "This is important. It's the whole plan now. I can't have them running. There's no choice. Understand? There's no choice. Bring him right back to the Fridge, and then run. Get safe, and I'll...I'll leave it all behind. Ralph and the rest. I'll come find you, I promise. I promise. Please. There's no choice. Please."

She watches him go, then thumbs the latch beneath the counter releasing the shotgun. There he goes, the idiot she's in love with, having delivered his final order. It's the whole plan now is it? Just help me push my friend and his accomplices off the roof so the wolf waiting below can eat, and then leave without me as I run wolf-errands for an indeterminate time, and then, when I decide the time is right, we'll finally have whatever version it is I've constructed of whatever it is I've decided you and I both want.

There's no choice?

"The hell there isn't," she says to the place Donk has absented, and walks out the door. She feels the thick weight of the shotgun on her shoulder.

x x x

After only a few minutes of scanning the mob she sees him coming: Morris Love. A short man, hair spiky-wet, a gash on his forehead, limping through the crowd, eyes controlled but rage-filled. Blue T-shirt wet with blood. He's fashioned a crutch out of what appears to be a sheared-off street sign. The leg clearly pains him badly as he makes his way toward her; you can see the wince as he levers forward.

She puts the danger into her eyes. "Hold it right there," she barks once he's close enough. "We've had enough of our shit stolen tonight."

"Donk." He snaps the name as though calling a tardy waitress, but he pulls up, likely aware of the Mossberg; up close, it can bisect you.

"And who are you?"

"Get that donkeyface out here. Now."

"Donk's out. I'm making sure no more soup cans walk off the shelves."

"Have you seen a stretcher pushed through here last few minutes? Hospital stretcher?"

"Doesn't ring a bell, but it'd be easy enough to miss in this circus." He has to allow her the point, doesn't he? They're climbing the streetlights. Napoleon could ride a zebra through here and you might not clock it.

"When did he leave?" Beneath the calm he's got a frantic shine on him. It worries her; she's seen it before. When a junkie is after a score, he's a little dangerous, but not as dangerous as when an anticipated score has failed to materialize. That's when the pain starts to erupt, molten, out of him, and you'd better have a plan. She pantomimes considering whether to tell him even the little she's about to release. "Hour ago. He was talking to some of these loonies."

This makes sense to him; or at least he accepts it unchallenged. "Where did he go?"

"Out." Stressing the trailing consonant; an implied finality of available information. "He had something to do. Special project. Left with a bunch of these nutcakes." She hopes this will do the trick; telling him more would seem suspiciously forthcoming.

"Where?"

"You think he tells me things? I'm just the store manager."

"Right…" Eyeing the shotgun. "Ralph's manager."

"Oh, I've managed all sorts for Ralph," Bailey says, nice and quiet.

He pauses, though the longer he watches, the more Bailey feels he's considering something deeper about her than merely the fastest way to disarm her. More like...she can't get a line on it...as if he's trying to categorize her; as if he were a bird, watching something squirm and deciding whether it would be good to eat. It's nervous work, watching him watch her. Her finger an instinct away from the trigger. The tilt of the Mossberg an impulse away from his chest. From the crowd, she sees cardinals materializing, first one, then two others, then more, melting out of the crowd. They approach quickly; it isn't until they are entirely free of the main channel of loonies that she notices the two tiny ones.

"Oh look," she says, making her voice calm. "It's a party." And still Morris has his dangerous eyes on her.

"Do you feel," he asks, finally, "does any part of you feel like doing exactly as I say?"

"Oblige if I can. But I have my orders."

"You work with him. Donk."

"That's right."

"Are you anything important to him?"

And there it is—isn't that exactly the question? And who knows what the answer even is? A lie is called for here, unless what she's going to say is the truth. She says: "I work with him. That's it." She imagines this is convincing; it doesn't feel like a lie anymore.

She sees his eyes dart through the broken pane, taking in empty and fallen shelves, cash register on the floor, and—shit, the one-sided mirrors of the Fridge are clearly visible from here. If Daniel isn't watching them yet—wondering what she's playing at, realizing she's improvising—he soon will be, and likely will be dashing out to try to give up Father J and the others. The thing now is to isolate Morris; she'll lure him into the store, shoot him, and then find out if she can handle any cardinals before they handle her. Either way Daniel will have a new plan to work on; hopefully he'll come up with a good one. Maybe they can still get Ralph—but Bailey realizes she hasn't cared about getting Ralph in a long time. She's held the desire for vengeance in a sealed box, but over the years desire has yellowed, atrophied, dehydrated, succumbed unseen and silent to inevitabilities of oxidation, and now the box holds only dust. What you want is simple, she thinks. It's all you've ever wanted, really; it's the part Daniel's cut away from the plan: the part where we get away safe. Hell of a time for an epiphany.

Still assaying her, Morris addresses the cardinals. "I'm going into this place for a quick peek. You five spread out and sweep the area. It's a god-damned stretcher. It can't hide. We are going to find it in the next three minutes." Then, to her: "You're going to let me go in."

She takes a long silent moment, then gives a disgusted laugh. "Fine. But I'll have to accompany. Look but don't touch. You understand."

"Oh yes. I understand."

"Just you. None of your redbirds." But they're already dispersing on his order, searching for the stretcher elsewhere.

"Lead the way."

She turns, knowing even halfway into the turn what a bad mistake she's made taking her eyes from him, and then, low on her neck, something is roughly tugged and her body is gone and her head is falling. Her head is falling. Her body is gone. Her head is falling. It strikes the pavement but still the sensation of falling. Her body, which is gone, is still falling. Ralph has taken it screaming from the greenhouse, he's thrown it off the top of HQ and it is falling. She blinks. Her head rests on the pavement and blinks. She can look through the empty space of the broken window. She can see the mirror where Donk will be watching. She can see so clearly. She sees the Mossberg kicked clear of her. Her body is gone and falling and falling and falling down. Her vision is clear and full of Morris's face. So, he whispers to her, I can still do it. I can still harm. I hurt you. I can still do it. And then he is walking inside and she is staring where she can see so clearly through the empty space of the broken window. Beyond is the mirror, where Daniel will have been watching. He will have seen her fall. Morris is walking in front of the Fridge mirror and past it. Stay inside, Daniel. Stay hidden. Keep them safe. Sirens in the distance coming closer. Slippered loony feet gather around her, curious. She blinks. Her forehead is gashed where it struck the ground. Blood tickles her left eye, so she shuts it. Tries to push up, but her arms are with her body, and her body is gone. Her body was pulled out of her through her neck and fell away. She sees no possibilities now, only the crush of the inevitable slow-rushing wave, which is Forever. Her head rests on the ground and listens to the approach of sirens, to the sounds of the Island in tumult, and feels her head breathe, taking air into a phantom that seems gone forever, forever.

F R I D G E

Father Julius is gone now, but not dead. Almost nobody knows what really happened. Most expect that Julius simply died or drifted, or left with his followers to start another mission. The few who knew Gordy are—naturally—convinced he left with Gordy. Some of those who knew him best probably worry that the cardinals got him. But they need not worry about their old friend; though the limitations of Julius's new form occasionally vex him, he is happy. He finally has what he always wanted, and that is a jewel worth more than limbs.

Goodness, dear. Listen to me go on. Your mother will be here soon. It's just you're such a patient listener is all, and I so seldom get a patient listener.

Father Julius, he listened to me for a long time, too, during the Loony Riot, as we kept safe in Donk's hidey-hole. I told him my whole story, how me and Gordy had come to be in Loony Island in the first place. I thought Julius was the only one listening.

That's what I thought.

x x x

Standing between bookshelves, unseen and unheard, Donk is changed, his face controlled, still, and watchful, drained of something vital, but alert, and very, very cunning. Gordy, intermittently visible to him now, remains on the stretcher, as unmoving as the priest. Father Julius lies supine on the billiard table. Tennessee once more grasps the priest's shoulder and shakes. Julius's eyes flutter open, and the man they've been calling "Tennessee" continues his confession again, a communion that the priest, half-conscious, is clearly receiving only in parts.

But next door, in the observatory, Donk hears it all.

Donk's standing before the one-way glass. He'd watched impatiently as Bailey spoke too long with Morris, saw with trepidation she'd taken the

Mossberg—Why do you have the shotgun, babe? He'd been about to go out himself to bring Morris back when he saw her turn and then saw the steel flick from some hidden scabbard, bite into her somewhere high on her back. He'd watched her go rag-doll, crumple to the ground, watched Morris lean down to her. He'd watched, frozen in shock and rage, as Morris had stalked through Ralph's, peeking in corners, stopping right in front of him for a moment, and then at last moving on. He'd wanted to sneak out and grab Morris unaware. He'd wanted to spend every moment of his short remaining life smashing that hateful skull into pudding against the tile. But even in his rage Donk remained pragmatic and calm. He knows his limitations—he's not the muscle. Besides, that would be too quick a fate for Morris. You need to find something else for him, Donk thinks. Something new. An oubliette may be punishment enough for Ralph, but it's not enough for the son of a bitch who made them.

He stares through the window at the place where Bailey had been lying before they took her away. There's a pool of blood, but not a large one. Occasionally he glances to the small screen in his hand, but there's nothing new, only dispatches from various loons as they link into the network. Morris had been right; they learn fast. Soon he'll make his screen go permanently dark. He'll dump water on it until it fizzles; it's the only way he can plausibly continue ignoring Morris's frantic attempts to contact him. He practices his lie, honing it to perfection—*What can I tell you, boss, one of those idiot loonies came by with a water gun, soaked me for a prank. Fried it right out. Water gun, more like a fire hose. Thing had a backpack on it.*

Tennessee pontificates as Julius drifts in and out. He speaks of the fountain of Pigeon Forge, and of infernal atrocity stacked beneath, of oubliettes and of what they can do—what they *have* done—of the man who rose from them, draped in power; of the one who fled and the one who followed, of the storm that came along with both, and of the ticket that fuels the chase.

An eye on the clock; soon he needs to step out of the dark. Even a soaked device won't serve as a cover for long. He estimates less than an hour before he must rush to rendezvous with Morris, for whom he's coordinated this new tribe of lunatics. He'll need to be sharp and polite. He'll need to give no part of himself away. It's a sick joke; every obfuscation he's practiced over the years in his dealings with Ralph he'll have to employ now with Morris, and for the same reasons. An even greater hate but a far more dangerous target. He'll need to paper over the time he's spent here, learning from Tennessee and staring through the one-way at the dark patch on the ground where Bailey had been. Soon he and Morris will have a meeting with Ralph. Soon he'll enjoy alone the revenge they've worked for, and after, he knows, he must begin enacting an even worse revenge. They've taken her away—the loonies. Borne her away on his orders toward the perimeter of authorities now converging on the Island to shut down the destruction. The bluebirds have riot gear and rubber bullets and real bullets and tear gas and shields, but they'll have access to EMT and ambulances, too. Perhaps there's a slim hope for her there, but Donk is ever-calculating, and in the abacus of his mind she stands subtracted already. For him, there is now only deeper and deeper with no escape, with nothing but a final retribution, yet as Tennessee talks, he begins to see a hope here, also, a chance at exactly the power he needs. The longest of all long shots. Like landing a hard rubber ball into a coffee mug from across a room.

The ticket. Yes.

His hands curl and relax, curl and relax.

PART II – **PIGEON FORGE**

The real
difference between
God and human beings,
he thought, was that
God cannot stand
continuance.

—ISAK DINESEN, "The Monkey"

changed

Struck by a sudden fancy, Landrude decides to pause at the apex of the Knoxville greenway; he'll enjoy his cigar and then sketch this gorgeous forest island he's only today noticing, though he must have passed it a hundred times.

The cigar's a weekly treat and an old habit. So's the ticket. The cigar's a matter of taste; the ticket's a reminder of the times when the prize would have been all the money in the world, and the five-dollar price an extravagance. This week's selection is a green-foil shiny thing with a blackjack theme, purchased at a gas station along the way, but Landrude's only rubbed away one disc when he feels the creative urge and knows he'd rather be sketching the island.

Every drawing begins with observance. He reaches for the cigar.

With deliberate and ceremonial anticipation he unwraps, clips, and lights, procuring the necessary accoutrements from various pockets of his trademark powder-blue suit. He folds the cellophane wrapper precisely and stows it in an inner pocket, along with the still-unfinished ticket. A man on the taller side, in middle life with a full head of upswept salted hair, rangy features tamed somewhat by a well-scrubbed look and a recently developing belly; portrait of the once-starving artist in the comfortable repose of satisfactory success. Puffing, he surveys the island, really taking his time with it, drinking it in; just a bit of wooded elevation, thin on one end and widening at the other, sort of a wedge rising up from the middle of the slow-running Tennessee river. The island's been there every other day, he presumes, just he's never marked it before. Now, though, it holds some quality that calls to him. Maybe it's the way the Knoxville autumn has burnt the leaves yellow and red in almost a checkerboard; maybe it's the way the island's shape hugs the shore, or the way the sudden rise and fall of trees upon it suggest a slumbering cat. . . but of course it's not that. It's the name on the plaque—that particular name. How could you have missed seeing it before? It must have entered subliminally at some point, informed your work without your knowledge.

In any case, he knows he'll have to sketch it or else spend the week regretting the missed opportunity. The greenway—a long stretch of well-maintained elevated boardwalk that rises and falls as it tracks the river's winding course through the city—is a perfect post-work walk, beginning a half-mile from Landrude's house and stretching up from Sequoyah Park to downtown Knoxville. It gives a fine prospect of the island from one of its peaks, right here where Landrude's standing, and the light's going to be perfect in a few minutes when the sun dips below that low hang of clouds in the west... but what's this? There's a commemorative plaque set here in the railing... how interesting...

"Got a cigarette, man?"

Landrude looks up. It's a glamorously disheveled couple in their early twenties walking up the greenway with their arms draped around each other. The soul-patched fellow's got the half-hopeful, half-bashful glint of every cigarette bum ever, and his lady looks away, too cool for school, though clearly she'll be sharing whatever smokable treat her squire might procure. Landrude, sorry to disappoint, displays his smoldering stub between two fingers. "Afraid I only ever puff these." True enough. Cigarette smoke makes him cough unendurably; the cigar's flavors only ever reach his mouth.

The kids shrug and move on, murmuring to each other. They're a decent stretch away when he hears it. Down the boardwalk it carries; the fellow to his lady: *See that blue suit? I think that dude's Landrude Markson, the guy who draws the...* Landrude allows himself a half-smile. Recognition is an occurrence just common enough to feel familiar, just rare enough to savor. It happens mostly just like this, the chance encounter on the evening walk. It's mostly kids who take the greenway, and it's mostly kids who enjoy his stuff. Speaking of savor... Landrude takes the final draw off the cigar—Partagas, nice and peppery—before sedulously extinguishing it on the sole of his polished shoe.

Back to this plaque, now. It's a brass job gone nearly entirely to oxidation. Landrude fishes out his reading glasses to examine it.

LOONEY ISLAND

ONCE A PROPOSED SITE FOR THE TENNESSEE UNIVERSITY PRESIDENT'S RESIDENCE, LOONEY ISLAND'S CENTRAL PLACEMENT ALONG THE LOONY BEND OF THE TENNESSEE RIVER, AND ITS STEEP ELEVATION, AFFORDS IT SCENIC VISTAS OF THE SEQUOYAH HILLS ON THE NORTH BANK OF THE

CITY OF KNOXVILLE. AT THE TURN OF THE 19TH CENTURY, IT WAS A POPULAR RECREATION DESTINATION FOR STUDENTS, WHO WOULD REGULARLY BOAT OVER TO PICNIC, TAKE IN THE VIEW, AND OBSERVE THE REMAINING RUINS OF THE DEFENSIVE OUTPOST BUILT IN 1797 BY ISAAC "BAREFOOT" RUNYAN, FAMOUS EARLY LEADER OF THE NEIGHBORING PIGEON FORGE SETTLEMENT.

Out comes the small sketchpad and the pencil. His hands work with ease of practice, his eyes darting up and down and between. The important thing is to get the shape, the shading. . . you'll be able to do a finish later; your memory can capture color, enhance detail. . . and there might be a story here, a narrative utilizing some old local tale. . . the old fort would be something interesting to see, you should hire a boat—or better, the romantic notion—make the swim yourself some morning, picnic there as your forebears once did. . .

Landrude's eyes dart up, startled. The island seems to be. . . swimming, or even underwater. No, it's not the island, it's. . . it's *everything*. What the hell is happening here? Vision warping, as if he's looking through thermals across the vastness of a baking noontime desert, rather than a manicured suburban Knoxville autumn. And then it seems as if he himself is slewing into some form, some new shape. It's like a soul nausea, as if he's becoming something other than he was, all while remaining himself, a snake shedding its skin to become a porcupine, an eagle becoming briefly aware it will someday die.

Mercifully, the sensation ends. Landrude glances up, and wishes he could tell himself that what he's seeing had been there from the beginning, but no, no, he'd been paying the island far too much attention for self-delusion. Look there: Visible above the island treeline rise the poniards of an ancient wooden fort. Hoping to steady himself, Landrude leans forward on the railing, sees the plaque, bright and shiny, polished, well-maintained:

PROPERTY OF LOVE FORGEWORKS, INC.

LOONY ISLAND DIVISION
All Trespassing Strictly Forbidden.

Below this exhortation, the craftsman has etched a triptych of images: a blacksmith at his forge, a fountain, a pigeon by a stream.

Landrude reels backward, catches himself on the opposite railing, fights against a scream. He closes his eyes, tight as he can. When he opens them, it will have all gone back to normal. It will have. It will. He opens them. No good. It's all still wrong, all still changed. Even "Looney" is now spelled "Loony." Landrude sinks to his haunches and tries to control his breathing. He concentrates on things that seem the same: the boards of the greenway, the powder blue of his suit, the smell of tobacco rising from his hand. But even these things seem wrong, different, changed in ways that he can't define, because there's no context for "normal" to which to compare—it *all* has the same wrongness. He's nearly convinced himself nothing has really changed after all, when it all starts to slew back again; the same sensation, only reversing... guided by some unknowable instinct, Landrude flips his pad to a fresh page, tears it out, holds it against the plaque. With the side of his pencil, he makes a desultory rubbing, the ridges of the signage quickly transferring to paper the approximation: forge, fountain, pigeon, stream, warning.

When he removes the paper, the world's gone back the way it was before. Only the etching tells of the way it's been: the forge, the fountain, the bird.

Appetite for a walk or a sketch utterly vanished, Landrude turns and walks back down the greenway toward home. Before long, the walk becomes a run, etching still clutched in one hand, pencil in the other, running from the greenway as if pursued by some numinous beast. He knows already he'll never walk that way again.

There's a flood of relief as the door closes behind. Hand trembling, he allows the paper with the rubbing to fall to the foyer floor and stumbles in, trying not to think of brain tumors or even worse fates—God damn, but what the hell was that, anyway? At least he has the rubbing as proof; it still shows forge fountain bird, proof that his experience was a real one—though whether that proof is a comfort or not, he can't say.

Landrude makes for the kitchen to pour himself something to take the edge off—it's only Tuesday, but after this, he decides it's allowable. Returning with his drink in hand, he stops and stares.

The paper lying in the foyer has changed into something different.

Even from here he can see it's his own work, but he has no memory of crafting it. Picking it up, he can see it's *finished* work. Glossy, torn from a published book. A page, split into two vertical panels of equal width: On the left, a view of some boardwalk, some corny carnival, gift shops and the hillbilly revues. Rubes and slickers and tourists lined up, faces tacky with partially moistened cotton candy, lips salty with remnants of fried pork skin, holding their prematurely obese children roughly by the upper arm, all standing awaiting their turn in the latest thrill ride—can you even call it a "ride"? A harness affixed to taut rubber bands has sent the passenger screaming up up up into the night air; the panel is drawn from a low angle looking up so you can see him, just a speck of yellow and red way up there. Soon he'll be careering, newly weightless, back down again.

Here, on the right panel, the view has reversed itself; now it looks down at the crowd from high in the air, where the passenger, just a boy in a mustard-and-ketch-up T-shirt, has—disgusting!—in his sudden gutless nausea spewed a parabola of yellow over the ground and crowd below, the vomit lit up ghastly and vivid in the flashing lights of the rides and of the midway and from the spotlight from the Big Red Comedy Barn, yellow ropes of disgusting half-digested candy and ice cream and hot dog, trapped on the page, stories above the earth, mere seconds before the elastic will catch it and him already crying from fear and relief and the shame and surprise of sickness. And, in the panel's corner, a caption:

Remember this boy. Remember everything.
If you forget, did it ever happen?
Remember everything.

Too late, the thing that's been bothering him resolves itself in his mind: the slightest lingering scent of cigarette smoke—*But you live alone, and you don't smoke cigarettes.*

"So," a voice says from behind him. "You're the one."

Landrude turns. There, in his study, beside a door that has never been there before, a man regards him with something like loathing. But not just any man, no. He's wearing a suit, too. It's gray, not powder blue, but in all other ways . . .

"You look just like me," Landrude says, dumbly.

"Yes," the man replies. "I warrant on the other side, you'll look just like me."

To this, Landrude can only blink.

"Better make yourself ready," the man says, drawing briskly nearer.

"Wait," Landrude says. He walks backward and the man follows, until they're crowded up against his own front door. "Wait," he says: "Wait." But the man doesn't wait.

"You haven't given me your name," Landrude says inanely, his head swimming.

"No, but you'll give me yours," the other says, and then he removes his hand from the inner coat pocket and plunges the needle of a syringe into Landrude's neck.

F O U N T A I N

Father. Father Julius.

Father.

Good. I thought you'd drifted out there for a minute. Let's key key keep you in the waking world, Father. I don't want you to sink and not come back out. Stay with me, now. Eyes open? Good. I'll tell you my story. You ought to know, especially now you've got Morris after you, too.

I was a historian once. Did I tell you that already? Specializing in the co-lonial and pre-colonial mid-South? I taught at Henvine College in Knoxville. Have you heard of it? Father?

Well, that's where I taught. My name was Sterling Shirker. *Professor* Ster-ling Shirker, if you please. Chair of Appalachian Studies.

I took a sabbatical that year, to conduct research for a book on the set-tlement economies of the Great Smoky Mountains during the time of the Colonies. Digging through local archives in small towns founded centuries before, when Appalachia really was the fringe. Anything past that was the territory of wild men and French trappers and tribes. No regular roads, nothing cultivated, no access to the amenities, nothing out there but the big "who knows." Imagine living in that, back then, Father. Imagine living with that gap in your knowledge of what truly exists, only hours away as the crow flies. Anything at all could be out there, waiting. Nowadays you could wake up in Richmond and find yourself by sundown in Arkansas, Louisiana, East Texas, but back then, you might not even have heard of the mountains, or you might have thought them a rumor. Who knows what's out there? Or how far back it goes? Who knows what's in it? Trees nestled so thick they block the sun, for hundreds of miles. Back then, it was still possible to believe in the world's end, some boundary where it all finished, where you might jump and fall forever.

Think about that. Everything is known today. We're jaded in our mobility, apathetic, starved of mystery. Nothing new beneath the sun and stars, that's what I thought.

That's what I thought.

See, my mistake was I considered history something separate from the present. I liked to turn rocks over and see what lay underneath. But I thought of history in terms of archeology, not biology. I never expected to find anything still crawling around underneath.

What I found was the most amazing—

Father.

Father, wake up. Come on now. I'm talking here.

Gordon came along with me. His mother, too. Didn't she? Was she with us then? Sometimes, in my memory, she was there the whole time. But she wasn't there when Morris caught us. They can't both be right, and I can never decide which it is. It's jumbled up. Some memories I've kept. Some, I was the only one who kept them. Others are gone. I've been trying to gather it all back to me, but I've law law lost my wife along the way, somewhere in there. The cheese has just melted into the into the into the bread. I can't work out how to separate them out any more. It all *changed*, see…more than once, I think.

I'm not going to think about that, Father. I'm not.

I'd mapped out my summer research tour the spring before. Dozens of towns, mostly small, founded before 1810, with long-established libraries. The plan was to travel cheap, sneak my way into the archives, photocopy anything relevant, move down the highway.

Gordon I let wander—in Pigeon Forge, particularly. A boy in the eternal youth of summer vacation, set free in a spot more amusement park than town. Doubt I could've kept him from it if I tried—not that I tried. The times were different; things felt safer…and I was distracted by my work. This was back before all this stuff was available on computers you hold in your hand, before you could use the same device to magically photograph all this stuff. Research actually involved physical search. Stacks, archives, card files, microfiche. I had to copy everything out by hand, sometimes working with materials so delicate that you had to turn their pages with a pair of tweezers.

Or I had to thumb through thousands of discs of microfiche just to cross-reference a line. Like panning for gold, which is in a way what it is. When you're an academic, the thing you want to do is find something big. Something novel. Something to launch you out of the fusty world of trade journals and out into the public consciousness. Produce a book that hits the zeitgeist just right, you can be a wunderkind on the intellectual talk show circuit. Then you've made it. So you see, *ostensibly*, I was researching a paper on economic trends in late 1700s Appalachia, but the reality was I was panning the dry riverbed of that topic for gold, searching for a magic conceptual trampoline that would bounce me right through fame's third-story window into a rockstar lifestyle of the mind.

And Pigeon Forge was, as I say, a natural stop. I was interested in the mill, which boomed in the early days, late 1700s through the first half of the nineteenth century, then went quiet after the Civil War. I figured it might make a good section in my book, likely a chapter of its own, tracing the progression of boom and bust and boom. I wanted to at least get to the bottom of the mill's sudden fade from the scene. But what I found in Pigeon Forge wasn't a chapter. It was the golden trampoline.

As soon as we got situated in our small rental, I went back to the library and started tossing the joint, as methodically and quietly as possible. I was a little over a week at it, and nowhere near about to give up, when I found a prize hidden behind the other books on the shelf. A heavy black tome, leather-bound, self-published: *A Familial History of the Love Family, Volume 1*, written by a recent scion of Pigeon Forge's first family. Secreted between the pages I discovered loose papers, each sheet carefully preserved in a sleeve of plastic. These were *handwritten* by Margaret Rambo, another of Pigeon Forge's earliest settlers. And her story…Oh mama. Paydirt. Hyper-intellectual talk circuit, here I come. I started to think about radio interviews, NPR, write-ups in *TIME*, *Newsweek*. It's not pretty to admit this, but some mornings I even spent a bit of mirror-time rehearsing the things I would say at awards ceremonies.

But that was before those pages *changed* on me, and everything else along with.

I brought my research goodies to the Smoky Mountains Historical

Institute to search for corroborating sources. Befriended the lonesome docent, and received access to a backroom with a desk I could use as my base of operations. I had Margaret Rambo's ancient pages—my treasures. And, I had the book within which they'd been hidden; the local history, self-published sometime in the seventies, a particular history of a town founded on a smithy and forge, then later a sawmill and water wheel, a town whose fortunes grew and stabilized and ebbed and rose and fell in familiar ways, until the late sixties, when enterprising out-of-towners zoned an entire main drag for tourism and entertainment, and it became what it now is. How did a colonial settlement that formed around a smithy and a mill eventually become *that*? With the Rambo letters, I had an answer I couldn't wait to share. After the *change*, that answer got even stranger.

Father, listen to me about the change.

I'd come from the records room, where I'd been picking my way through the stacks, searching for more treasures. Bringing some promising documents back to my desk, I re-read the Rambo pages, when all of a sudden, I had the oddest sensation. How to say it? Like suddenly I was seeing things three different ways at once. Like I was a sardine suddenly aware of swimming around a huge oddly shaped aquarium rather than the ocean. Like I was a pig being pushed through an extruder into a trail of sausages.

I'm not making sense. Maybe this will make sense, or at least be comprehensible:

After that sensation came over me, my sources were different.

Very different.

The Love family history wasn't just self-published anymore; it was handwritten. It had a different author, too. Meanwhile, Margaret's pages were totally gone. I'd been reading them during the change—where were they? I frantically cased the room, but no joy; I've never seen them again. In their place lay a different, smaller book with an unadorned cover of bright red. It was one of those deals you get at the checkout line in bookstores, with the blank pages you can fill, but which you never do fill. Someone had sure filled these, though.

I turned to the handwritten history, and immediately forgot the loss of the Rambo pages. A *very* different history, an even more interesting one. The new book—the red one—had a title in precise calligraphy on the inside cover: *Love's Fountain*, by Jane Sim—near as I could figure, it was a novelization of what was set down in the history.

Other things had changed, too, but I couldn't bother with that.

I was already reading.

✕ ✕ ✕

May the Good LORD be praised, it seems our smithy's madness has passed. For the present our estimable Col S. Wear holds him in our stockade, but he has made a full confession of his plot, and, as you shall hear, a truly wicked and vile one it was. Our poor young friend F. Jay lies yet in the infirmary, caught 'tween life and death due to Love's Devilish ministrations, though our Doctor is skilled in emetic and has given us hope for his good recovery. I embrace this opportunity to convey to you, Sister, the device by which this troubled man, this smithy with a mind of an Empedocles, this Isaac Love, had thought to capture the loyalties of our colony, and, thereby, compel us to install him as King. As I have written previously, Mr. Love has proved a man of considerable and multifarious talents, though as with many such men, his estimation of his own knowledge extends beyond native capacity, and thus, possessed also by the sin of overweening ambition, they do themselves provide the engine of their own thwarting, which engine I now name PRIDE. Mr. Love believed himself possessed of enough skill as an Apothecary to extract from local root and berry an unholy concoction, which, if quaffed, would infuse all other bodily humors and dispense with all sense of one's Self, and make the Drinker naught but a slave. This villain made bold enuff to provide this potion at our picnic following the flying of the spring pigeons, and made as if to administer it by force if blandishment proved ineffective. 'Twas only by GOD's mercy that among us only our poor Mr. Jay proved pliable enough to obey Love's directives and quaff his poison—though I must confess, were it not for my betrothed, others might even now be languishing in the same deathly manner as Mr. Jay—for it was my own brave Mr. Runyan who stood 'gainst Mr. Love, and shouted full in his face, then contended with him over the ladle he held and, in this struggle, the two fell athwart the hogshead, and thus the hogshead was spilled onto the ground, and all the grass thereunder did wither and die. Then was our coterie freed from indecision, and others sprang to my beloved's rescue, and raised the alarum, and held him fast until Col. Wear, who serves also as constable, arrived with manacle and chain. But now Mr. Love appears once more to speak in his old decorous manner, and pleads his innocence, saying his acts were not his own, but rather of a fever that unfurnished him of reason, brought on from those same berries, which he discovered as he foraged, and consumed as he walked, and in such manner was driven into the strange madness now passed. Col. Wear will hear him more at trial, but it seems meet, so long as Mr. Jay lives, Mr. Love will be forgiven this trespass, for to lose our smithy so far out in the wild would be a loss most sore and grievous indeed

The fountain predated the town. It lay in wait before anything had been built. Everyone knows this. It would be foolish to believe otherwise; one had merely to look at it—nobody ever did—to know this fountain was one of the first things, older than any ruin on Grecian hills, older than Jonah's fish, older than the ark, older even than the mountain upon which that lucky reeking ship finally foundered. When Isaac Love first arrived in this place, along with his small coterie of travelers, it was there already, awaiting him.

The Love Party came west in 1787, to make their fortune in the new-formed Northwest Territory. The "Love Party," so named after Isaac Love. A bachelor smith and former corporal in the Colonial army, he quickly proved the most capable among them, and a natural leader besides. The group, setting out from Raleigh, targeting Cincinnati, was made up of a loose and unaffiliated kit of families and fortune hunters, without head or government, but when the guide they hired took ill early in their trip, they found themselves in early danger of failure. The sickly guide was a sometime mountain man by the name of Isaac Runyan, though "Barefoot" was the appellation bestowed upon him in the Appalachians. He tucked himself away in one of their low cow-wagons, groaning and drinking and clutching his gut, and soon it was Love who moved wagon to wagon, assigning tasks, tending to livestock, serving as arbiter in disagreements. By the time Runyan pulled himself, heaving and pale, from the wagon, he was guide only; Love had easily assumed unassailable leadership. A short, broad man who kept clean-shaven, he wore clean white shirts and high chambray overalls and a brown hat with a wide brim to shade his eyes. His chest and shoulders were thick and powerful, his forearms burly. He held his posture erect, spine straight as a plumb-line in defiance of years stooped over the forge with hammer and tongs. Love proved capable of great feats of strength and possessed a native mechanical understanding; using only a length of chain fixed to a pulley block, he had extracted a wagon, oxen and all, mired foot-deep in muck. He looked you in the eye longer than you'd find comfortable, and then a little longer still—hypnotizing, almost. Men found themselves taking up his positions while in his presence, even if they disagreed, and then, to avoid the appearance they had been cowed, argued as his proxy with skeptical wives, defending convictions they themselves did not hold. Women avoided his company, and in this at least he ceded ground to the man he had replaced. Barefoot Runyan was taller than he, and comelier; his gaze, less fanatic, did not unnerve. He was jolly and easy around a campfire, and apt with a fiddle. So, while the trust and the dependence of the people went to Love and his manifold capabilities, their affection remained with the feckless Runyan, and while Love's gaze went with increasing frequency to the young and fetching Margaret Rambo, hers went to their guide.

Without Love they would have foundered and failed. The families were mainly of farmer stock, and used to rough living; however, the trail offered new hardships: of tedium, of deadfalls, blockages, detours, of rivers with no easy ford, of blinding rain churning up paste-thick mud, of insects beyond count, and of disease, which incapacitated the strong and dispatched the weak. Pushed from behind by a relentless Love, they soon wearied of the hard trail, which left them dirty and tired and every day fearing attack from savages, and so, when they broke through into a clearing beside which a happy river chuckled, they rested the night, and when, following a strange disappearance, Love returned to announce it was not the Ohio territory in which they would plant themselves, but rather here in the foothills of the Smoky Mountains, no dissenting voice sounded. A cask of cider was relieved of its bung, and the travelers themselves were relieved of their travels, for it was relief indeed to have come to a perch—any perch. They became talkative and gay, incurious about their leader's sudden, uncharacteristic deviation from their objective, glad for cessation of discomfort.

Love shared none of this felicity. He had been captured already.

On the first morning, as had become his custom, he had gone foraging alone. The river crafted an abeyance through the thickness of the forest, a bank of packed loam and gravel along which Love walked at ease. Presently, however, he spied a curiosity: a pathway, cut into a spinney growing up between old growth of evergreen and so attenuated by neglect, it seemed more tunnel than path. Curious, Love followed it into the thickness, and soon found himself within a tunnel indeed. The spinney surrounding him was composed of bushes, from whose darkwood branches wicked thorns projected and crimson berries hung. The thicket to each side was impenetrable, concentrated, and between the rare gaps in its profusion could be glimpsed hazardous rotten deadfalls.

Love pressed on. The wood encroached wetly around, putting him in mind of constrictive snakes. The farther inward the path led, the narrower it grew, the tangling above descending until Love found himself obliged to walk stooped, marveling at the forester who had set himself the task of fashioning a path here—the will, the strength, the madness vested in any man who would dream of such an undertaking. Yet here it stood, even now it had lasted against a wood so consuming, so impenetrable, so dark and malevolent. What end had fueled such obsession? Love's curiosity contended against a growing sense of entombment. The wood, though silent, was too close, too alive, too quiescent; it was a watchful thing, and not only watchful, for the thicket's thorns now bit his shoulder, and though reminding himself he was no timid man, still he resolved to continue along this course for another minute only, and no more.

By the time he broke into the clearing, the path had narrowed to such a degree that he walked bent with head nearly level to his waist, arms shielding his face, hands cut and bleeding; his shirt, once clean, now spotted red. He came to the opening, little more now than a rabbit hole, and, heedless with an excitement he could not name, pushed through into brightness. He stood, shielding his face from the sunshine, in a place most unnatural. Love was no superstitious man, but now he remembered tales of fairies, of bogies, of druids, of hob and sprite, sylph and imp. This lacuna in the forest's heart was circular. No, that was too imprecise a formulation: not circular; it was a circle. As if some titan had crafted it in the earth by means of a vast compass. The debouchment in the greenery birthing him into this grassy ring was the only rip visible in the fabric of the surrounding wood. Inside, the ground lay draped with a bright green turf as soft and as level, in surface and coloration, as any fitted carpet in any gentleman's sitting room. It was hot there, and very still; he could hear no hop of hare, no twirrup of bird, no chatter of squirrel.

At the hub of this wheel, in the very center, a fountain pointed its white finger to the sky.

Love circled the fringe, never taking his eyes from the alabaster formation, his back always to the forest. Though it was a thing inanimate, he did not deign to approach, for there could be no natural account for it—not for its existence, nor for the precision of the demarcation between lawn and wilderness—none, save witchcraft. But Isaac Love was—he reminded himself—a rational man. Still, to pause seemed wise; in any case, it might be an ambush. He made one full revolution around the circle, convincing himself he was alone, yet still he waited, his back to a tree, pondering. Prudence suggested caution; but curiosity insisted upon action. He felt within himself a growing ire for his unseemly quailing. It was stifling hot within the circle. Slowly, he approached the basin. Upon closer inspection, the fountain proved white as whalebone, without spot, without blemish, but now he espied on the basin, filigreed in delicate calligraphy, some unrecognized cuneiform, cut with a skilled hand, flanked with tracery of vine and leaf wrought by the same ingenious chisel. The basin was as round as the ring of forest encompassing it, its circumferential area broad enough that, were it drained, a brace of yoked oxen could pull a wagon in a circle within the basin as easily as a pair of children might garnish a maypole.

Love reached the basin's edge. The ground about was ringed with three concentric bands of stone paving: The outer was of gray slate; the middle, wider than the other two, of a glistening stone black as coal; the inner was a terrazzo tile of deep red hue. Before drinking, Love paused to study the tower. At the base, a massive stone terrapin lay flat upon a rock rising only an inch above the water; facing Love, it regarded him with old and sunken eyes. Water fell from its mouth into the pool. From its back the tower rose, three-tiered. Around the base of each tier stood cherubic statues—figures of such intricacy, so natural in their poses, that an observer might be forgiven for being taken in momentarily by the counterfeit. From the center of each of these laughing figures, water tumbled forth in high arcs. Love frowned at the perversity. These angels…were they pissing forth the water? Could a craftsman of such skill stoop to base vulgarity?

Love, thirsty, stooped and cupped some of the water into his hands, yet he did not drink. It occurred to him the water of such a fountain might bear some adverse quality. In any regard, this water—he now looked from his hands to the basin—was it...black? Indeed, the pool in the basin seemed dark, suggesting either some taint or a greater depth to be sounded than a fountain's basin should possess. Or was it merely cloudy? He could see his fingers through the water he held, but the volume was too meager to divine its true properties. He sniffed it. It smelled like nothing.

Fear gripped him then without reason. Hastily, he let his fingers open, spilling the liquid onto the stone, the spatter disquietingly loud in the silence. He could hear in his ears the thrubbing rhythm of his own heart. The turtle seemed to him a living thing even in its stillness, its eyes auguring portents evil and ancient. The cherubs now appeared minatory, their childish smiles transmuted to warning grimaces, their stone eyes desperate and trapped. He backed away, calling himself a dastard even as he did. Again, he circumambulated, forest to his back, like a duelist facing a fellow master, and, nearer now, he discovered something new.

Stairs were cut into the black middle ring of flagstones. A rondure of granite steps, the contour of which approximated the curve of the ring, leading beneath the fountain. Love heard himself breathing, thirst forgotten. Somehow he had come to the brink of the steps, toes hanging over the topmost, hesitating, vacillating between trepidation and wonder, fearing what lay at the bottom, scorning to leave the mystery unexplored. There was something there, he knew, some secret grand and terrible. It was unthinkable to climb downward, but impossible to resist the pull of what lay beneath. Finally, he descended.

He emerged at last in late afternoon parched beyond even a soldier's reckoning of thirst, thirsty down to his lungs. He walked directly to the hole in the forest and pushed through, incautious of thorns, making his way quickly through the tunnel to the banks of the river, and upon gaining it he walked directly into it until the water reached his mouth and he drank himself full. Returning to camp, Love announced, before even taking food, that they would not only camp by the banks of this river, but here they would settle, and there was such mantic fire in his visage, such vitality in his countenance, and such a paucity of it in their hearts, no objection was raised to this abrupt and capricious change, and none dared inquire as to his recent whereabouts. They eyed the blood dried to his shirt where the thorns had marked him, but they did not gape long, and they held their tongues. Then Love chewed on what they set before him, and when it was swallowed he fell off the log upon which he sat, sunk already into a deep sleep, and if he had dreams he did not remember them. As he slept, his people shook off their confusion, unbunged the cask of cider, and set upon the meticulous task of convincing themselves Love's command had been their heart's hope all along.

When Love woke, he changed his clothing and ate a quick but hearty breakfast, then went out again, taking with him a full flask of water, a leather poke filled with dried fruits and jerky, an axe, a sharp hatchet, and a boy of their party named Frankton Jay. No man asked him his business as he went, and none followed but Frankie—a big boy, not bright but hardworking, open-faced, and well liked. He chattered easily as they walked along the bank, as unperturbed by Love's lack of reply as he was unconcerned about the details of their task. His arms swung loose-jointed with each step, and from one hand dangled the axe.

When they came to the pathway, Love pointed and uttered one word: Cut. And so Frankie cut, plowing through the tangle with the joy of one who has found the task for which he was originally conceived, never questioning the end of the path upon which Love had bent him, content to merely hack, and to clear, and to widen, chattering empty and well-meaning observation as he did so. Sure is warm today. But not as warm as yesterday. You reckon tomorrow it will be warmer still? That's what I reckon.

Behind him, Love added finishing touches with the hatchet, giving no reply, and in time Frankton's prattle ceased and they worked without speech, delving into the quiet part of the wood, where the only sounds were their grunts and the methodical toc toc toc of blade on wood. They rested briefly to eat, then fell to once more, this time with the smaller man taking the lead in the tight places. They returned to camp exhausted and dirty to find the obedient men already at work, industriously surveying parcels to clear-cut for their homes. After a hasty meal, Frankie collapsed into slumber on the ground like a beast, and Love followed him, once he had spent an hour at the grinding wheel returning the edge to the blades. Frankie slept like one dead, but when Love nudged him with a boot-toe an hour before dawn, the lad leapt up, eager as any hound, and followed. The inventory of their kit kept unchanged from the day previous, save that on this outing, Love carried three makeshift torches, fashioned from spokes pried from a broken wagon wheel, and topped with brown turbans of rags soaked in pork fat and creosote.

Frankie, keen to return to chopping, took the fore. Love, working drag, widened Jay's rough-cut path with short, precise strokes. They arrived at the narrowest place by midday, the thatch above a solid verdant ceiling sparing their backs the wrath of the noon sun. They stopped before the final push for repast, and Love drank deep from the flask, which was filled with cool river water. When it came his turn, Frankie drained the flask dry, his thirst unquenched—naught had been left him but a swallow.

When at last they broke through into the clearing, Frankton Jay bullied into the circle, a smile cresting his broad simple face, but then he saw the thing and wailed and turned to run. Blind with dread, he stammered and stumbled back into the hole they had carved, caught his foot on a root and landed heavily on the earth.

What is that, Mr. Love? Oh my Lord. What is it?

Come boy, don't crawfish on me now. We have work yet to do.

After many blandishments, Love was able to lead the boy back to the clearing, where Frankie sat on the grass, near enough to the opening to feel safe of escape, and looked at the thing with fear and awe, still close to panic. Love had some skill in soothing a calving heifer, which tactics he now employed: murmuring, cooing, distracting the body with soft pinches and punches, and the mind with empty words and simple questions.

Frankie's words came slow and stubborn, but from them Love came to understand the boy supposed he, Love, had himself crafted the fountain during his long absence two days previous—a foolish notion which surprised the blacksmith, though he made no attempt to unfurnish the boy of it. Love walked up to the thing to prove it safe, to show it would not crush him for his temerity, as the lad was convinced it would do. He walked slowly around it, laughing, calling to Frankie in a loud cheerful voice, and when the tower blocked them from sight of each other, he dipped the empty flask into the dark water. The boy would not budge, so Love returned to him. They sat on the grass. Love spoke without pause, frequently reassuring the boy they would soon depart.

We can't stay in this place. None of us. We can't live here. Not next to...

Of course, boy. I see it now. Are you thirsty?

Thank you, Sir, I surely am.

Love stood, proffering the flask.

It's empty, sir. I finished it.

I brought two. If you were thirsty, you should have asked me.

Greedily, Frankie took the flask. As he fumbled with the stopper, Love moved to the place where their tools lay. He held the axe close to the end of the handle and watched carefully to see the effect, if any, of the draught.

He regretted what needed to be done; Frankie was a fine boy. He would have made any smith an apt apprentice—but a sheep gone mad with fear can stampede the herd. The boy raised the flask to his lips and drank deeply. For long minutes he sat, still as a stump. Then he rose with unnerving suddenness, turning in blind circles, his eyes filled with confusion and fear, and what he said stayed Love's axe.

Who am I? Who am I!?

He asked it again and again, in dumb frightened yelps, and with such guilelessness there could be no suspicion of deceit. Love cajoled and interviewed, for a second time in an afternoon whispered him back into his placid nature as if he were livestock taken fright.

Who *are* you, boy? You tell me.

I don't know, sir. I don't know.

Are you alone or with some group?

I wish'd I know'd sir. I wish'd I know'd.

Love carried on the interview until he was certain. The water of the fountain, or else something in it, had flooded into Frankton Jay and washed him away, flooded him right out of his own body: all seventeen of his years washed, dirtfoot Carolina childhood washed, the weeping mother and the drunken father he had left behind washed, the three younger brothers and four younger sisters also washed, loves and likes and hates and all of the longest-held grudges and the oldest friendships, all washed out; and Frankton Jay, too, had been washed away and out of his own comprehension, settling like silt into some faraway ocean's basin. Now he bleated and kicked at the turf like a panicked calf newly born into a world of trouble. His eyes rolled, rootless as his mind, as he scrambled to gather any identity to himself.

Frankie finally passed into whimpering, then into sighing, then into deep snoring slumber. When Love was sure he was completely asleep, he took his torches and the axe and went down the stairs once more, which led him again to the short narrow passage carved into damp earth. A timid stripe of sunlight ventured halfway down the shallow incline of the stairway, allowing a notion, however slight, of what lay in the passage. The clay of the corridor was thick but malleable, and Love worked a wagon-spoke torch into it until it held there.

The door was still there, crafted from unvarnished wood and ensconced in an unadorned wooden frame on the left-hand wall at the end of the passage. Locked, Love knew from yesterday's labors. No force of limbs would cause it to yield in the slightest. Today, however, it would fall. He felt the weight of the axe.

He eyed the door as he would an adversary, the iron head of his weapon resting between his feet. Readying himself for the task, he pondered what to do about the lad above: Should he be allowed to live? What if he tells tales? Yet who would believe? And if any do believe, they can be easily managed. And, if they cannot be managed, they can be disposed of. These corridor walls might be dug out with ease, and are capable of holding more than torches.

Already he knew the deference his people offered up to him. This sad huddle of suffering lazars waved their collective fatigue like a white flag. Beaten, they looked to the strong to lead them. Look now: Had they not already obeyed his edict to abandon their goal of an Ohio settlement— nothing less than the prize that had urged them into this undertaking in the first place? And moreover, had they not celebrated their abandonment with drink? Stronger than their dull rage, more powerful than their weariness, was their unadorned obedience.

Love decided Frankie would live. He was among the strongest in the company. No disease had sapped him, nor fatigue. Had he not been so simple he might have emerged as a rival, but providentially Frankie had none but the most animal of appetites. Strength without will was the measure of Frankton Jay, and of the two qualities, will was most to be feared. Jay had complied with Love's commands with incurious good cheer through all the most difficult tasks. Now the boy was wiped clean of even his modest thoughts, feelings, beliefs, scruples…yes, Frankie could well be useful. Yet even now time pressed. The boy might wake, and wander, cause nuisance. So: for the door.

Love raised the axe and struck it with all the strength he possessed. The force of the blow numbed his hands, but the axe-head caromed off the unmarked surface. He cried out, and struck again, and again, and again, assailed his adversary in precise rhythm, until at last the axe handle snapped a half-inch below the head and the iron flew flipping back over him, coming to rest at the far end of the corridor near the foot of the stairs. The door stood absolutely unmarked, without splinter or blemish, without the slightest mar as record of the assault. Love shrieked; the door was hexed. To be frustrated in his pursuit by nothing but thin planks of wood…Love cursed; in his rage he battered the clay floor with the useless stave, and then, with the abrupt and determined bearing that marked all his actions, he silenced himself and withdrew, pausing only to stoop and collect the axe head. Shoulder cannot buckle the hinges, nor iron splinter the wood? The shovel next. If one cannot go through, one must dig around.

He found Frankie curled into a ball and sucking on one big thumb. Love lifted the top half of the boy and dragged him into the woodland tunnel and waited for him to awaken. Finally, he commenced to nudging him in the ribs with his boot until he was roused. He was pleased to see the boy was not reduced to an infant. Frankie still knew how to stand, and to walk, and to speak. He knew what hunger was, and what it was to be frightened, but he remained void of thought or notion particular to himself. Love spoke to him in soothing tones, and produced some dried fruit from his poke. With these and other inveiglements, he calmed the boy, and taught him his Christian name back to him, and fabricated certain truths for him to gnaw on. Love— creating this boy back to himself as he would shape a tool at the forge, but by instinct alone, without the practice he had in the honing of iron, decided to keep him away from the others entirely. Your name is Frankie. Eighteen years old. You are a brave boy, and strong, and good. And your whole life, until this day, you have been deaf and dumb. Today there has been, it would seem, a miracle. Frankie, you have in some wise (how I do not know) purchased your tongue and your ears at the cost of your memory. All men have hated you and abused you in your infirmity, save for I, save for Isaac Love. The others beat you and mocked you, spit on you and robbed you of your portion of food at meals. Only I protected you from them. They are not to be trusted. But if you listen well to your one true friend, if we keep the miracle of your cure secret from them, together we may devise a way to exact some measure of revenge...

Love watched the boy take all this into himself; watched his eyes burn with hatred for wrongs not remembered but believed, slights and injustices occurring only in imagination, which had become to Frankton Jay incontrovertible fact—harm which demanded harm, injury which required redress. The elder man watched as the boy, melted down and poured molten into Love's mold, hardened into a new shape.

In late afternoon, Love and Frankie returned by the path they had created and began assisting the rest in the construction and founding of their settlement. Love worked with such vigor he astounded his fellows, acting within the group both as mind and conscience and thews, directing all in their individual tasks, and, as the weeks passed, their outpost quickly climbed up from the banks. Love kept Frankie aside from the rest, setting him to work not with the carpenters raising shelters for man and horse, nor with the parties hunting opossum and fox and deer and the occasional small bear, nor with the tailors crafting skins into garments—for winter was nigh—nor did he set him to the unforgiving drudgery of fashioning lye into soap, nor the churning of butter, nor any other communal work. Frankie he set to labor in the forbidden area downstream, clearing the thicket leading to the fountain, and once it lay cleared back to the deadfalls Love judged it to be passable enough for his purposes, and set the lad to the task of building a smithy and forge along the river within the fresh-cut cove. The boy cast wary glances at the rest of the party and spoke to no man but Love, and then only when he was certain they were alone. The rest of the company, mystified by the change that had come over their affable lout, wondered what secret wrong he suspected of them. But, though they were perplexed, by this and by Love's embargo against the far bank, their awe of their leader kept their misgivings hidden behind the walls of their cabins. The whispers of husbands and wives under thick blankets (for it was now growing cold indeed) never reached daylight.

Love was pleased as weeks melted to months. His settlement lay bulwarked against the coming mountain winter. All shelters were built simply but solidly enough, the chinks between the boards well occluded with rags and pitch, each abode the precise replica of its neighbor to either side—for Love had learned from his years in muster that repetition of process brings both speed and accuracy, and, if all shared in the building of each home, and no home was the better of another, then envy would not sow discord among them. For the sake of morale, even he for now took one of these shacks—the general's trick of accepting a private's quarters. The larders swelled with butter, with game birds, with gourds and sour wild apples and meat from the kill stretched, dried and salted; the cupboards brimmed with warm clothing, wraps, muffs, and boots in each abode at the ready; firewood filled the ruck split and stacked enough for three winters; the livestock lowed, warm and safe, in new stables. Their main risk would be enemy attack; the ground would soon be too hard to break, and a fort-wall would have to wait on spring's thaw.

He had taken these rough tools he'd been given, these Carolina sodbusters, and built up something to last a mountain winter—still, Love's dissatisfaction ate at him like a canker. There were exceptions still to his order. Yes, even still, even now, even after he made this place as much his own as if he had been the Creator himself who spake "let there be" and then watched the results of his divine fiat, even after saving these recalcitrant sheep from starvation and icy death, even still, there was resistance. It was all in the minutiae, yes, it was unmistakably small, but still…they were defying him behind these walls he had built. Whispering. Scheming. Mistakes were made, every day. Little things, yes. Small things. A wrong tool selected for the task, or a horse chosen from the remuda when another more rested beast might have better served the purpose. Infractions nonetheless, insults to his order. Each of these a flouting of his will. All of them, asserting their imperfections, impressing themselves as beings apart from him in silent defiance of him.

It pointed toward chaos, division, fragmentation of purpose, danger.

And then there was the woman. Margaret, she was called, but "Jezebel" hit nearer the mark. Beautiful as the dawn, and yet she had taken up with Runyan. They were courting now, the two of them. There could be little doubt they would soon be married. Moreover, she regarded Love in a direct, appraising way he specifically disliked—there was effrontery in it.

And the cursed door.

From August until November, he had kept away, but as the months passed, the door called to Love, despite his forswearing it until he had proven himself perfect through the perfection of his followers. That impenetrable door. A guardian of such relentless strength must perforce guard something worthy of that strength. It taunted him, pulled him, coaxed, cajoled, with its promises of a greater power, which should by rights belong to no other but him, which had waited long years for him, for him alone, to awaken. This door was the guardian thwarting his birthright, his rightful destiny. He knew it threatened his sanity. That he had not yet mastered it was his failure, and failure within himself he found unbearable. No matter the risk, he would have it. But, in the meantime... there were small things still outstanding, flaws in the process, whispers behind doors. His people had not yet fully taken on his aspect. Love had taken these crooked tools and built a settlement, built it well enough they would last the winter, but then would come a remaking. His tools were not yet perfected, but he had a forge.

—Jane Sim, *Love's Fountain*

T I C K E T

Let me tell you what Gordon was like as a boy. He's not like what you see there. For one thing, you could see him, one hundred percent of the time. Not one flicker from him then. But visibility isn't what I'd call notable; most folks are visible. Gordon had a quality about him. A certain way of carrying himself, a way of *fitting*. Natural poise, I suppose. He didn't get it from me. I could fall down sitting on a park bench. But Gordon, he never hitched. His toe never caught a table leg. His feet always found firm ground.

He should've been a klutz like his old man, to look at him. A skinny kid, all elbows and ankles and neck. Hair going wherever it would. But he was quiet, with quick eyes, and whenever he said something, seemed like it was something that mattered. He just had a way...ever since he was little, even sitting at the breakfast table, it was like...I don't know how to put it, but, like, it was like the chairs and table and the whole room had arranged themselves around *him*. Like he always carried the center with him; he knew his place in the world, and the world knew his place in it, and the both of them just loved each other. That's what it was: He was somebody who was *right* in the world, and he knew it. I was always lost in my mind, but Gordon, he could chart his physical location with startling awareness, whether it was a five-year-old understanding our position driving through a city far better than his old man at the wheel, navigating for us with savant skill, or just simply sitting with perfect poise at the breakfast table.

Breakfast. That was our time.

Before everything went sideways, we were together like any family, the two of us: a boy and his papa, a papa and his boy. And also his mama...she'd sing while we drove, the most beautiful voice...but no, she wasn't there. I remember the song, but when I look over it's Gordy sitting shotgun. She's been lost. I just can't...

I already told you, Father. I'm not talking about it.

Do you know, every morning, I used to make Gordon eggs and garlic toast? Can you imagine—*garlic* breakfast toast? When he was little he'd run out the room in his pajamas, me reading on the chair, he'd come curl himself into me and we'd set there a while, just sitting. I remember that. And then he'd say, "gar lick?" like that, like it's two words instead of one, and then I'd butter up the…the bread, and he'd sit…waiting, he'd sit on the stew stew stool, he'd talk to me…he was an internal person, but in the morning his lips loosened up; that's the time I'd discover whatever was on his mind…when he was bigger, he'd put his legs up on the table and balance his plate on his lap, talk about whatever he had going on—a school bully, a story he wrote for the class newspaper, some girl that had flirted with him in the library—and I'd remember days when he was little, when his legs would…dangle…

…scuse me.

Excuse me. Beg your pardon, Father. He may have forgotten me; I haven't forgotten a thing. Anyway. That was how it was with us, the first fifteen years.

I still remember the last time I saw my boy. That last breakfast. He was wearing what I called his "mustard and ketchup" T-shirt—half red, half yellow. On that morning, we didn't talk much. We just sat together in peaceable silence, chewing. I remember the sun coming in through the window of our RV's kitchenette, and the two rectangles the light made on his face. I remember…that image is so strong. My last breakfast with my boy.

Then he got up and I went to my day, which by then meant research in the Smoky Mountain Historical Institute, and Gordon went off to his day, which that summer meant walking the Pigeon Forge strip and taking adventure as it came to him.

Yes, and that was the day it *changed*. The day Morris caught us.

And I'll tell you something more, too, about that *change*. I felt it was Gordon making it happen. I couldn't say exactly why, but it seemed to me that this was something mostly happening to old Gordon, the boy who *fit*, and that he was taking me along with him—maybe whether I wanted to or not, but more likely, I think, because wherever my Gordon was going, I wanted to go too. And I had time for one thought, too, as the world slewed and spread and pulled like carnival taffy, and then put itself back together.

Just this one thought: *Oh no, not again.*

I remember having that thought, Father. But I couldn't tell you why I had it. That change, in that moment…it felt familiar—but I've never experienced anything like it in my memory. No wonder Gordon wound up with the ticket.

It's a lottery ticket, Father. The prize is control over everything in the whole world.

And I don't know how, but my Gordon won it.

x x x

Here is what happens when you eat a box of banana runts, a bag of circus peanuts, and three hot dogs, and then go on the X-Treme Slingshot: As the sling sends you screaming up to kiss the moon, right there at the top of the parabola, in the exact moment between your thrill-seeking phases of being, as you switch from the *oh shit oh shit oh shit* G-forces of an over-rapid ascent to the gut-clutch nightmare of freefall, you achieve a blissful moment of weightlessness, which causes you to hork up the secrets of your stomach in a beautiful arc, which descends, like an emetic crescent, a new moon of puke, to the boardwalk—a yellow-orange splattering ruining the emerging night for a hapless random smattering of tourists below.

The boy in the two-toned shirt—left side bright yellow, right side bright red—safe once more on the ground and released from the confines of the body-harness, walks shamefaced, fleeing from the taunts he is trying not to hear. An angry tank-topped redneck wearing a mesh cap emblazoned with the legend: "I Eatum Heap Buffalo at Uncle Wampum's Bar and Grill" throws a consoling arm about his puke-tainted lady and hollers at the retreating boy. Others, lucky enough to have avoided the spray, point and guffaw. Gordy walks quickly; the ride and onlookers recede. Once he has passed the bright-red Comedy Barn, he slows. The boy's throat and sinus are raw from sudden sickly sweet residue of candy and salts and stomach bile. He snorts three times in rapid succession, and spits out the remainder.

"Hey, faggot. No spitting on the sidewalk."

A pride of young stooges have followed him from the X-Treme Slingshot. Three of them, all bigger than he is. A glance backward confirms one of them is a beneficiary of his recent gastric gifts—the shirt is spackled with puke—and they appear intent on revenge.

"Hey kid. Hey! Asshole! I saw that. No spitting on the sidewalk."

"Hey, you dirty little shit, look what you done to my shirt. It's ruined."

The boy looks about for a rescuer, a hero, some intervening force—a cop, maybe, or a tart-tongued old lady—but the boardwalk here is empty, and between the Barn's floodlights behind, and the hypnotizing vermilion neon of Piehole Pete's Fried Foodery ahead, there stretches a hundred yards of rare darkness along the strip; a field of weeds and thistle. The voices are closer now. They're talking themselves into violence.

"That dirty shit spit on the sidewalk. Did you see him? You see what he did?"

"Never mind the fuck sidewalk. Come here, shit. Look at what you done to my new shirt I just bought."

"Gonna tell the cops on ya, kid."

"Come on over here, faggot. You're gonna pay for my shirt."

"Yeah, faggot. You're gonna clean up the sidewalk, too. You're gonna lick it."

Wafts of laughter, irate no more, but anticipatory; implicit in their dull amusement the boy hears the promise of the chase, the inevitable submission, humiliation, and brutality. Not fair, thinks the boy. Not fair. I didn't mean to. He casts about for a plan, a destination, preferably one with a suitable hiding place. You can't count on adults around here to behave responsibly; they don't exude the usual automatic bubble of sanity, the implied assumption that, should he attain public space, he could no longer be dragged back outside for some light-to-moderate beating. No, adults here are mainly tourists made numb by gaudiness, with little interest in inserting themselves into cases of casual assault. The usual excuses: It's character-building; he must have done something to deserve it; boys will be boys. As for the proprietors and employees of the establishments up and down the boardwalk, in them he senses, if not a meanness of spirit, perhaps a spiritual vacantness; perhaps you can only serve up so many deep-fried banana-fritter pies to lumbering sun-baked suburban shirt-pastries before you lose some of the shine off of your essential spark. So it will have to be a run, and then it will have to be a dodge. In short, he needs to disappear. But where? The Comedy Barn is closest. You could get lost in the shuffle right away; the audience is packed in close around circular tables in the dim, and between the waitresses fertilizing the crowd with beer and the full-bladdered patrons heading toward the restrooms, there's plenty of milling about. But to get in, you need a ticket, and a ticket is one thing Gordy doesn't have.

"Come here, faggot, lick the sidewalk."

They're close. He has to decide now. Stretching out before him, the darkness between the Comedy Barn and Piehole Pete's presents itself. He could try to risk a dash across, but Piehole Pete's is unlikely refuge. The menus are overlarge, but they aren't walls, and the whole place is an expansive celebration of glass and chrome, a nightmare of visibility. And even if the Fried Foodery were chockablock with hidey-holes, it would remain an unsatisfactory destination, for to make for it would be to run across the empty place, to lend his hunters the benefit of darkness. This is all they want: to catch up to him there in the empty, to trip him thudding to the boardwalk, and then to drag him and his newly acquired face-splinters into the deep weeds for the sort of serious beating a bully is only emboldened to administer when unobserved. Gordy's main advantage, he realizes, is their stupid faith in his predictable blind panicked flight—that and nimble feet. He runs.

"There he goes!"

"Get him!"

They wanted him to run into the field, and because it's what they wanted, it's what they expected. He feints into the darkness, and then, as the pack give chase, dodges, cuts back across the boardwalk, dashing in between two of them who grasp at him but miss, and out into the street, where he's nearly pancaked by a blue Plymouth, low-riding and lit neon from the bottom, and apparently without brakes, as it utterly fails to slow—it swerves around him, cutting between him and the pursuing louts—and then the

hhhheeeeEEEEEYYYYYYAAAaasssshOooooole

doppler curses of the Plymouth's operator can be heard. However briefly, the car has slowed the gang, and Gordy pelts to the far boardwalk to make the most of what seconds he has been given, racing toward the best hiding spot he knows: Crumb's 'Mazing Lazer Arcade. Its entryway draws near: the yawning mouth of an enormous red demon head. The electronic approximation of fire rises from the demon's head like hair, consuming the sign eternally. The demon's eyes are enormous mirrors; in his mouth is lodged a revolving door.

The boy hits the door hard as he is able, putting his back into it and pumping his legs, feeling in his jacket pocket for the roll of tickets he won at Skee-Ball, and then he's in, bathed in the blink and yammer of a million games: games controlled by rows of buttons, and by joysticks and basketballs and baseballs and pastel plastic light-guns and cork-guns and pellet guns and faux fishing rods attached to fishing-game consoles and plastic boxing gloves for those who want to fight for fifty cents a minute, and jet fighter steering wheels and jet-skis and motorcycle handles and—wow! Look!—there's a fat guy running amuck dressed up as Pac-Man and there's four guys dressed up as the ghosts, and all about them the ubiquitous sounds of fighting shooting exploding and the *boing boing boing* of eight-bit characters jumping and the hectoring of animated antidrug messages and the screams of the players and those of the observers who've placed their tokens in queue on the ridge to wait their turn, and everywhere the mechana-whir of bills being sucked in and the jangle-clatter of slotted tokens cascading into the hollow basin, snatched up by greedy hands. But Gordy, with no time for any of this, is up and making his way past the ranks of Skee-Ball machines, to the laser maze in back, where he will at last be safe. The boy rips two tickets from his roll and hands them to the attendant as payment for entry.

Here he is safe. Here is the twisty mirrored heart of Crumb's 'Mazing, more a home to him than the place he shares with dad. When Gordy is allowed to flee each morning after a quick breakfast, wherever he may choose to go first, or second, or third, it is here he will inevitability arrive. The maze squats on an acre and a half of Crumb's facility, its walls covered by large mirrored panels stretching from ceiling to floor, a crazyhouse giving you infinite diminishing copies of yourself as you charge down the corridors. Ceiling and floor are painted black, broken sporadically by lighting fixtures and more mirrors. The halls are lit in some places by strobes, refracting and blinding, while elsewhere the only light seeps from dull red bulbs screwed into recesses six inches deep, dim enough for you to mistake your own reflection. Many of the panels are hinged, allowing players to swing the walls to create hundreds of distinct configurations; and Gordy has learned all of them. At night he maps them in his mind until they are engraved there. Gordy's spatial awareness is already uncanny, but he's been in Pigeon Forge all summer, and here, in the maze, he decides who dies and who lives. He's snaked through this crazy maze for hours until he knows it well enough to dream it. He is the master of the sneak attack, the now-you-see-me-now-you-don't, the laser ricochet; he has devised and improved and named a pantheon of evasive maneuvers: the noodle-walk, the crane, the turtle, monkey-stepping; he spends hours preying on newcomers and tourists, invisible, invincible. He hunts out-of-state kids for an entire game, startling them with carefully placed noises, eliminating any blunderers who target his chosen victim. Only when he knows time is running out does he pull the trigger, once, twice, thrice. The sap never sees him, but only his reflection, and then only when he wills it.

Once inside, Gordy discards his gear. He is here to hide, not to hunt, and a toy gun will provide little defense from real fists. Quickly, he arrives at his destination: a familiar back-corner hideaway, a sanctum. He has never seen any other player, not even a fellow savant, in this small room, which can be created only by specific manipulation of panels. Push here, pull there, and you create a T-shaped room, sealed off from the main, which none but the lucky will ever discover. The only entryway is the panel at the end of the short hallway he now faces, which will push in but cannot push out. The exit, should he need it, is the panel on his right, which swings out but not in—but he doesn't expect to need it. Gordy sits at the confluence of the two short halls and leans against the brick and mortar—the back wall of the arcade, which forms the border of the shorter leg of the cavern he has created, the lintel of the "T." It's a waiting game now. His pursuers will be enraged at his escape, their expectations defied, but Gordy is familiar with bullies. Dim-witted, used to easy gratification, they will soon grow bored and trundle off, seeking some other distraction. Having to pay the fee to enter the maze may be enough to discourage them, but even if they pursue, avoidance should be a simple task. He thinks he can hear them shouting out for him at a distance—come out, you pussy, be a man!

Yes, it's clearly them, the same voices: coarse, gross, and eager to inflict pain. He doesn't understand this kind, but knows his understanding of them is no prerequisite; they won't require him to fathom their motivations, they'll only expect him to bleed and whimper. Worse, these are almost certainly his future classmates, since dad's been making increasingly serious noise about moving here, an impossibly cruel notion. Gordy's a youngster in his class—precociously literate, he skipped grade 1—and now he's facing a junior year as a transplant in some whole new tribe. Dad, who's caught up in his book about whatever, hasn't even considered the impact. You couldn't even speak to him at breakfast. And now you're going to have to spend what should be your high school victory lap dodging a trio of dim bullies…the voices draw nearer and then fade. Gordy waits, stands, sits, closes his eyes—and then, startled, opens them wide. The voices have returned, suddenly close. They seem to be on the other side of the wall now, right at the entrance to the "T." Gordy creeps, careful and silent, to his feet. He eyes the exit panel to his right, and tells himself to play it cool; to leave would be foolish—nobody has found him here before, ever. The mirrors reflect his fear back to himself. He can hear them distinctly; in the way of adolescents acting out postures of toughness, they've talked themselves into greater fury. Enraged voices. The door will swing open now, he thinks, and it will be too late for you, they'll have you where nobody can find you or stop them, it will be too too late when the door swings open…

And then—no!—the door does swing open, it really does. Perhaps it does. Afterward, he will be unsure on this point; certainly it's at least possible he only caught one of his own movements reflected in the mirror and panicked. Gordy darts right, twitch of legs and animal instinct, no looking back, his moon eyes growing closer as he reaches the mirror and pushes the panel out and away, closing it behind him, revealing a new corridor, which immediately turns 90 degrees right and then again to the right, leading him into an unmirrored hallway with red brick on both sides. He knows instantly this is wrong—this is not the configuration of maze he was expecting—but, in the teeth of instinctive flight, Gordy keeps moving. The problem is simple:

He had been right up against the wall of the arcade, the brick-and-mortar boundary of Crumb's establishment, meaning a right-hand turn out of his T-shaped room should have been impossible, unless it were a passage through the brick wall and out of the building. The corridor into which he has turned is long and straight with no tributaries and appears to terminate after about fifty feet. The fiddle-strings beneath Gordy's ribcage tighten, but he is more averse to pain than he is to confusion; he puts one foot before the other, fearing a dead end.

There is no dead end, but rather a hard 90-degree left, and then another left and another corridor heading, yet again, back the way he has just come. The tunnel is straight and once again appears to terminate after about fifty feet, but the boy, having grasped the pattern, starts forward, fascinated, only faintly anxious anymore about his pursuers, whose voices he can no longer hear. There will be no dead end; this he believes, and he is correct. Another turn right, then immediately right again, and, sure enough, here are fifty more yards of corridor heading back again. Young Gordy passes through this strange redbrick intestine, thinking to himself with equal parts panic and joy and fear *nobody will ever find you here, not here, nobody could find you here ever*. On the fifth turn, he begins to feel strange. With each step a strange growing sensation, like a massive bending, a refraction not of light but of *everything*, as if his perception has become a funhouse mirror. There's not enough reality, and at the same time too much of it. It feels like the world is getting *thin*, spreading out wide and flat in all directions, like it's fading away and bringing him along. He turns to his instinctive sense of space, of knowing his location in the world, but it's failing him, all he gets is a sense of Dad sitting and reading something boring, and guided by some unknowable impulse Gordy reaches out—*I don't know where I am, Dad, don't let me go alone, come with me, come with*—but then he's passing into the thinnest places and he's got no time to think more before he's gone

Gordy blinks and looks around. He's still in the redbrick intestine. It's so odd, so strange…the universe is changed, somehow…his very way of being seems modified. Isn't it? Or is it? He looks at his hands, his surroundings. It all looks right. Same as before—isn't it?

Strangely, there's no panic. Somehow, what just happened seemed a familiar sensation.

Well. You're here. Nowhere to go but back or on.

Gordy goes on, doubling and redoubling through the odd one-way maze. On the tenth turn, he is surprised by sudden strobing colored light.

It's gaudy here, and loud. Straw lies scattered on the dirt ground, and tinny music squalls from an unseen nearby source. A gamy animal reek hangs in the air, tart and ripe. All about him, suspended from tall poles, colored lights flash arrhythmically from strings of grapefruit-sized bulbs. Ghostly shapes in the distance glow and turn. Before him rise humongous toadstools, painted in bright wide vertical stripes the color of candy—pinks or blues or reds or whites in alternating sequence. One enormous toadstool, blue striped with white, looming in the distance, dwarfs the others. The toadstools expand slightly in the breeze; they are cylindrical at the base and pointed at the top and seem to be made of some sort of cloth…

Ah. Tents. Yes. Away to one side, a smallish Ferris wheel is lit up and turning against the night sky. Hmm…tents? Ferris wheel? That would mean a…fair? Gordy's knowledge of the rides and events of Pigeon Forge is near encyclopedic; his pursuit of them is an obsession tuned to a pitch only the young can maintain. A fair? It wasn't advertised. When did a fair spring up?

Behind him is the hole from which he was disgorged. Gordy sees it is nothing but a precise rectangular gap in a fence made of rough pine boards, resting hard against a low building, above which, in the distance, he can see, barely, the tips of the horns of the Crumb's 'Mazing demon head. He sees a figure fly briefly into the night sky on the rubber band of the X-Treme Slingshot, silhouetted against one of the many spotlights meant to entice tourists from their motels to take in the shows and rides and shops. He fixes his location: He's made it to a place behind the main strip. He's spent months exploring the town; he thought he knew it all, but he knows immediately he has not been here before, and the thrill of discovery is in him.

The fence is long and plastered all along its length, at cockeyed angles, with identical posters. The nearest poster reads:

Gordy returns his attention to the peppermint-stripe mushrooms, sweaty-palmed and whispering to himself—Oh-*ho*, Gordy, I mean, oh-*ho*. Oh, ho-ho-*ho*. A fair *and* a circus? *And* a freak show?

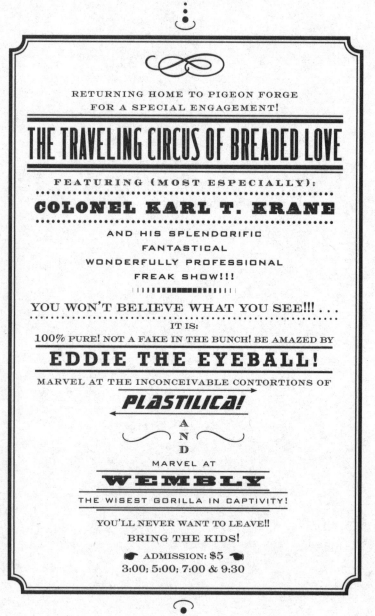

He's alone—emerged somewhere behind the tents, on the side not meant for fair-goers. Typically, this is the side he prefers, the side for explorers, but here there is only grass and the backs of tents, the only mystery they hide is the passage, through which he has already passed. On the other side, however, he can hear the human buzz of carnival nirvana, and he follows its song. Gordy cuts between two of the canvas tents and is immediately in the cavorting midway mix of the crowd. A human press...men at the booths winning prizes for their sweeties, shooting cork guns at tin ducks or attempting to throw tiny plastic rings onto pegs slightly smaller in circumference than those rings; teenage sweethearts strolling with hands entwined or on each other's rumps; young boys and girls darting around long legs in an intricate unknowable game, faces glazed in a tacky glucose base to which the powdered sugar of donuts and the granulated sugar of fried dough (the concoction sometimes known as "fried dough" or "elephant ears," apparently marketed here as "Breaded Love™") clings like stubble, and to which wisps of cotton candy are affixed like beards; barkers calling from their posts— guess your weight, test your strength, dance with the Fuggly Wuggly, win a prize, getchyer snackfood right here, hot dogs, 'tato chips, getchyer ears here now hot yummy Breaded Love, getchyer Breaded Love...screams come and go with the clatter of a smallish wooden roller coaster and shrieks of at least partially justifiable fear from the swinging cars of the ancient Ferris wheel...

Gordy revels. He wanders and dawdles and gapes. He has found the impossible passage, has come through the unlikeliest doorway, the one all children instinctively look for; he has fallen up into the sky, into some wonderful other world; he has somehow managed to climb onto a cloud. In the gap between two tents, he can still see, small in the distance, the back of Crumb's demon-head entrance, he again sees the riders of the X-Treme Slingshot leap up to kiss the moon, and this glimpse back to the known world feels like looking from a great height at a terrain, still visible, from which he has managed to become gloriously separate.

The midway is wide with booths and tents in ranks on either side. On the side from which Gordy has emerged, the booths press close together; beyond them lies the high fence, which looks to enclose the entire carnival ground... though there must be an entrance somewhere around here, mustn't there,

I mean all these people didn't all come in through secret passageways, did they?...On the other, there are large gaps between tents, allowing easy flow to the pasture, where rides have been erected. Gordy considers these, but the lines are long and he is low on funds, and he's enticed away from rides by the tent ahead, the really big one with the blue striping, looming ahead and to the left at the terminus of the midway. The big top, the big show: clowns and fire-eaters and trapeze and who knows what all else—but no, you know what all else; the poster told you. Freaks, that's what. Colonel Krane with his traveling freaks. Human forms taken a wrong turn somewhere. You can't look, but you can't look away. Oh boy.

Ahead, the midway bends toward the big top, and...is the width of midway?...it could be a trick of the senses, but it's getting *tighter* somehow, closer, functioning like a funnel. Ahead, he hears someone on a megaphone, and though he can't make out the words, he judges—by the buzz of the crowd, by the sudden movement in that direction—the late show is imminent. Gordy goes with the flow, trying his best to rush forward, fearful of being left without a seat. It occurs to him he has no way of securing admission, but maybe he can just crash the gate, blunder in with the main press...Drawing closer, he hears the megaphone's bark more clearly. He can't see the man speaking yet, but he can hear him machine-gunning words in bright psychotic hiccupping cadence void of pause or reason:

"...BLUE ticket to the side, BLUE to the side, GREEN ticket yes GREEN ticket gets you into the most unbeLIEVEable show in the world don't miss the opporTUNity of a LIFEtime STEP Right up That's right folks come ONE come all to see the SHOW we've got it all RIGHT! HERE! Folks! We've got CLOWNS! We've got the TIGHTrope walkers! we've got the man in the CANnon! and FOLKS I'm telling you right NOW you'd better believe that we've got the freaks! Freaks freaks FREAKS by the yard by the HECtare by the FURlong friends by the very MILE we've got freaks folks so hurry aLONG folks because seating is LIMited folks and this is our very LAST show of the SEAson folks you'll be aSHAAAAAAmed to miss such a magNIFicent array! SEE! the aMAZing Plastilica bend like a trick balloon for your aMUSment See! Eddie the EYEball! SEE the most FAmous SUperinTELLigent goRILLa in capTIVity see the fear-RO-cious MIDgets not ONE no folks NOT one I say but TWO of the little beggars TWINS they are and they'd as soon KILL you as look at you…"

At the mention of limited seating, the stampede begins in earnest. The fairgoers stream from all sides; food vendors lose their patrons—even those next in line scamper away—and some of the booths even lose their vendors. The ring around the fire-juggler evaporates; lonesome, he douses his sticks and slinks away. There's something more than the usual desire for spectacle here; Gordy senses it even through the haze of adolescent obliviousness— this group has been seized with a panic, everyone at once is in a fever to get into the show. There's an apparent and palpable tension, a growing fear, carrying with it the ominous sense of some undefined penalty for failure—some will be outcast, and it might be you. Gordy curses even as he dodges through gaps in the crowd, improving his position. Green ticket? Might that mean a green*back*? Where could I get a green…

Look.

There is a man in a powder-blue suit ahead, standing between two of the tents, his face made garish by the carnival light, and partially obscured by the smoke that emerges from between his teeth. He is looking right at Gordy, tracking him, Gordy realizes, through the crowd.

The boy stops, frozen, and immediately the crowd is pressing him forward, impelling him to the sideline to avoid being carried along or trampled. There's something about this man. There's *something* about him. There's some *thing* about him. You may have never seen him in your life, but you have heard of him. If he exists (and yes he does) then you must have heard of him. If you have not heard of him, how could it be that anyone has heard of you? He is one of those. As if some incompetent and all-powerful fiend has put a disproportionate amount of work into his composition. In his presence, the world seems to be a story about him. It certainly isn't a story about you.

"Hey, kid," the man says, and his voice is both soft and louder than the surrounding cacophony. It's a deepness that cuts underneath.

"Hello," Gordy whispers, eyeing the best directions for quick escape. He's never the most cautious of boys; nevertheless, alarm bells are sounding deep in his nerve centers.

"To me you look like a lad who needs admission," says the man in the powder-blue suit.

"Who *are* you?" Gordy asks.

"I'm of no matter," the man says, breezily, almost singsong. "No matter, no substance, no matter at all. But you needn't worry. I'm a *safe* man. Yes, you could definitely say I'm very *safe*." There's something sardonic about the way he emphasizes the word, some hidden meaning, but Gordy can't imagine what that meaning might be. He edges back toward the crowd, lies: "Listen . . . I'm going to get going. My dad's waiting for me just ahead."

The man holds up a hand, a cigarette between two long fingers. "Yes, you *should* go," he says. "I don't want to delay you. But I have something I think it might be of use." Suddenly—prestidigitation!—something appears in the cigarette's place. It's a single ticket. A big one, composed of some sort of shiny green foil, seeded here and there with little silver discs.

No less trepidatious than he'd been before, yet compelled beyond reason, Gordy reaches out and takes it.

A lottery ticket. A gas-station scratch-off. lucky 21! it howls in green foil curlicue. The highest jackpot is (the ticket exclaims in letters of brightest yellow) a thousand bucks, and sure, this is all the money in the world, but the odds of hitting it will be astronomical. Pointless, Dad would surely say. Dad bestows sad smug smiles upon the saps ahead of him in line at the gas station, buying one or seven or fifteen of those things. Shakes his head as the sap hunches over the counter working away—can't even wait to get out of the store to start his itch of coin on silver. The weak smile when one hits for five bucks. Dad still smiling weary superiority as he pays and leaves; the sap uses his scant winnings to buy some more of the damn things. Hell of a way to utilize a twenty-dollar bill, is all Dad will say, once they are out of earshot. The things have for Gordy naturally carried all the fascination of any forbidden object, but he'd known better than to ask Dad to buy one. Now, out of the powdery blue, here comes one into his possession.

Thanks, mister," Gordy says, looking up from his prize. "But, why di—"

But the man is gone; nothing left of him but a hint of smoke. Gordy looks to his hand, still clutching the ticket, and it occurs to him. . . it's certainly a loser, valueless as an investment—look, somebody's even started playing it, one disc's already scratched away—but. . . it *is* green.

With a lurch, the crowd carries him along. It's reaching maximum concentration at the tent entrance. Gordy can see the man with the megaphone now, standing squat and round as a toadstool on two wooden boxes, gussied up in a string tie and a suit with wide lapels and vertical blue candy-striping matching the tent before which he stands. His bald head is an overripe tomato. His eyes are deep-set caves. His mustache is hard to explain. His eyebrows defy Gordy's previous experience with eyebrows. This changes everything, Gordy thinks.

He can sense that this man is the man, the one from the poster, none other than the famous Colonel Karl T. Krane, purveyor of freaks, master of ceremonies, carny barker extraordinaire, and extraordinary—look at him, his corpulence, his roundness, his redness, his striping, his piping ubiquitous blather, his grandiose physical verbosity; his very mustachioed eyebrowitude. And now he's dancing a happy little dance on his perch, cutting a rug atop his boxes and still jibber-jabbering staccato at the fairgoers who cluster about him waving mostly blue tickets, holding up their children like refugees appealing to the last G.I. on the last helicopter, yet perhaps they would cluster even if he were promising no further distraction than his own fat toe-hopping presence. Why is he still barking if demand has outstripped supply in such dramatic fashion, unless he simply savors the slurry of his own words? He is impossible, disconcerting in his inflection and tone and shape; he oozes exclamation as he prances from foot to foot, exhorting:

"...SEE the SEE, come on ladies COME on Gents come IN, come in, STEP in, SEE the SEE, BLUE tickets to the SI-ide, ON-ly GREEN TICK-ETS for entrance, THE HOUSE is FILL-ling up! GET in the house! Don't be left HOLding the BAG now let me GUARantee you, you DO NOT want to MISS it..."

And now they are all in a frenzy, arms waving. Gordy squeezes between where he can, looking for the openings, moving toward the front by inches, thinking to himself blindly *why are we all fighting so hard for this, nothing but a circus what importance what, what is happening here* and in every face he sees, beyond the frantic mask, the same helpless questioning lurking there. This is not a desire to see a circus, to laugh at clowns, to look at freaks. Not desire, but some other compulsion like hope... *hope?* Maybe. Something different, some transcendent entertainment, some answer to the workaday groan. There are some who resist, to be sure. Some who watch from above, safe in the slowly turning Ferris-wheel cars, smiling smug and benevolent on the desperate press below. But…looking at them, now…no, they aren't smug, these holdouts. There's a resignation to them, even despair. Some cry. Others are stoic. In one set of cars a woman is speaking frantically to a man intent on ignoring her. She gesticulates; he leans the opposite way, ostentatious in his inattention.

The crowd has thinned as the green tickets are admitted; the Colonel is picking up final stragglers. Judging from the numbers who have gained access since the most recent proclamation, there cannot be more than a few seats left in the tent. The Colonel stabs a white-gloved sausage finger into the throng, selecting the last lucky few with tickets. Gordy stands tiptoe, holding up his scratch-off, hoping his ersatz greenie will fool the eye as that short white finger revolves on its voluble armsocket and slows, stops, selects, starts again, turns and slows, rolls and finally—finally! comes to rest, pointing through the multitude, selecting him. The chilling cavities of the round man's eyes fall upon him, drawing him in. For an instant Gordy wants to duck, to let that horrid gaze fall on another, thinks *no no this is a mistake not me not oh no* but the compulsion is in him as it is in the rest, and he starts forward. They jostle him bitterly as he makes his way up. Gordy hopes he will not be spat upon; the disappointment and hostility are palpable, he knows what they're thinking: Dammit. Each selection of another dramatically lessens the odds of being chosen yourself. And…could it be? Yes, Krane's stopped pointing now. Him—the kid in mustard-and-ketchup—he's the last one chosen.

Gordy gives the disappointment of reprobate masses his back and passes into the tent. The entrance leads into a short dark passage, which conceals whatever goodies might wait deeper within, and, Gordy now sees, is guarded to prevent the swarm from crashing in. One guard on each side of the opening. Gordy falls back a step. Little wonder the horde, however desperate, has not bum-rushed the show. Yes, the guards are only little—but what little folks! Breathtaking. Identical tiny men, resplendent in scarlet tunics shot through with black, they bristle with weaponry: knives, chains, hammers, darts, a sword, a metal tube too slight to be a pipe. All of this sheathed and holstered, yet their eyes hold the watchfulness and casual mastery of tigers, of lions. Disinterested faces inform you of the easy ability to put an end to you whenever it might become necessary or convenient.

The tiny guards swing open like doors to admit him and Gordy enters the short dark tunnel leading into the tent. There is light and noise streaming in where the tunnel turns inward, and when Gordy makes the turn, he is bathed in it and finds himself confronted by the one and only Circus of Breaded Love.

S P A D E

I don't want to give the impression of an *entirely* different history after it all changed. There were similarities—a lot of them. In fact, to compare the two in summary alone, you'd notice it starts out different, but otherwise you'd be hard pressed to know one from the other; to see the effects, you'd have to look into the details. It's not so much the *what* of history that changed, it's the *why*.

The "why"…that's pretty important stuff, Father. Discovering the "why'" is what we historians do. If the exact same things happen, they're still different things, if they happened for different reasons. The "what" is usually an easier matter. When it comes to Pigeon Forge I can still give you all that by rote: In the beginning, you had what white folks would eventually dub "the Indian Gap Trail," a well-maintained path threading the feet of the Smokies, made by local Cherokee tribes around 1300 and utilized by them for the next four centuries to navigate the deepness of forest terrain: for trade, and to make their way to and from the proving grounds of war or the hunt. Sometime around the mid-1700s, the first white folks appeared on the trail, mostly trappers and hermits, and they too, naturally, found it convenient to their needs, and in this way word of it must've slowly seeped back to what the white folks had dubbed "civilization." Certainly sometime before 1783 it was known, because it was in that year that Colonels Samuel Wear and Robert Shields, veterans of the Revolutionary War, heroes of the Battle of Kings Mountain, and co-drafters of the Tennessee Constitution, made their way to it, and it carried them to the banks of the river they would soon dub "Little Pigeon," and to the spring waters in the shady glen that would later be known as Henderson Springs Hollow. The abundance of readily available water presented suitable catalyst to the minds of the old campaigners for settlement, so Wear established a stockade on one end of their border, while Shield established his own on the other, and between the two, a tiny colony of perhaps two dozen held an outpost, there on the very edge of the known universe. That's how things stood in 1808, when the Runyan Party arrived, carrying with it some twelve dozen new settlers, among them future town fathers Isaac "Barefoot" Runyan, his wife Margaret Rambo, and the smith, Isaac Love, who established the famous forge and mill that would lend the new colony of Pigeon Forge its permanent name.

It was at this moment, Father, something happened that no historian before me ever recorded: an altercation between Runyan and Isaac for the very soul of the colony, in which Runyan, supported by Wear, prevailed. It turns out Love was a zealot in the cult of himself, somebody who really believed, deep down, that no consciousness existed but his own, that all others were just projections of his will, and he...well, I already told you about the Rambo letters. Once controlled by its strictures, Love proved a valuable member of the budding society. By 1840, his mill and forge were a thriving venture, allowing new inroads to the nascent town, enough so that Isaac's son William established Sevier County's first post office, and there was talk about Pigeon Forge becoming the county seat. But in 1851, John Sevier himself purchased mill and forge, stripped it, relocated it, and left the town high and dry and doomed to further languish into economic anxiety and despair after the Failed War to Preserve Slavery left road and bridge destroyed, rendered field and farm fallow. There was a brief boom as some outside businessmen tried to sell the springs in Henderson Hollow as magically restorative, and, abetted by the paid testimony of traveling mountebanks posing as revival ministers, they succeeded for a spell, bringing in several hundred trusting sheep for fleecing—but the whole cult collapsed on itself when the preacher serving as front-man died mid-sermon while standing hip-deep in the allegedly "healing" pools. The town entered its long invisible time then, a dirt smudge left off most maps until the middle of the century, when two enterprising North Carolina brothers by the name of Robbins transformed it into another roadside attraction—they discovered an abandoned rebel steam engine, refurbished the beast, laid down tracks, and dubbed it "Rebel Railroad," providing Confederate-sympathetic visitors from the north and elsewhere with what they advertised as "an authentic Civil War train ride experience." This attempt at what I assume must have been fun proved successful enough to catch the eye of a businessman and NFL franchisee, who purchased it in the nineteen-seventies, added further amusements, rebranded it as a mining adventure, and renamed the whole mess "Silver Dollar City." This, in turn, proved successful enough to flip to some carnival impresarios from Branson, who decided Pigeon Forge was the ideal spot to recreate in Appalachia what they'd already perfected in the Ozarks. Enlisting fame, they partnered with local-girl-made-good Dolly Parton, renamed Silver Dollar City as Dollywood, and Pigeon Forge was reborn into its present iteration.

And what exactly *is* Pigeon Forge now? How to describe it? It's a long, jagged, spangled strip tearing through the forest at the foot of the Smokies. Smaller streets spread out from the main, leading to above-ground pools and trailer homes and prefab dwellings spilled amidst the trees. But the main drag's what brings the people: brightly lit, lined with shacks of commerce and diversion—comedy barns, off-off-off-Nashville music revues, arcades, restaurants, buffets, an endless array of souvenir shops filled with miniature tin replicas of world monuments and velvet paintings of dead crooners; with doo-dads and knickknacks; with shirts bearing tasteless slogans and corporate brands; with cunningly shaped ashtrays and beaded change purses; with life-sized porcelain statues of huge-eyed children, or of Well-Scrubbed Caucasian Jesus, or of unicorns; with faux-taxidermied battery-powered singing fish; with retail shrines to the Confederacy—rebel-flag bandannas, rebel-flag oven mitts, rebel-flag dress, rebel-flag stickers, pool balls in a frame painted to form the rebel flag, plush Tickle-Me Stonewall Jackson dolls—and this is only the tip of the iceberg. In Pigeon Forge, if you don't need it, they've got it. They've got ten.

Once you have an anchor like Dollywood, Father, the rest just grows around it.

But now, see, you're looking awful confused. See, this is what I'm talking about when it comes down to the differences being in the details. Does Dolly Parton exist here, Father? Was she lost when it all changed? Now I think of it, she must have been. I keep picking up little differences between *before* and *now*—feels like that poor Dolly might just be one.

Never mind; it doesn't matter.

The fountain appears to have been the stick in the stream, the key divergent element between the reality before the *change* and the reality after, the thing that threw the whole mess off-course. First off, as near as I can tell, every human being in the vicinity kept well clear of the fountain, all the way back to ancient times. Thus, no Indian Gap Trail. Thus, no traders telling Wear and Shields where to go. Thus, no settlers at all until the Runyan Party arrived—but there's the other difference, see. It's not the Runyan Party anymore in the history books. It's the Love Party. Love won that altercation instead of Runyan, so Rambo never got to tell of it—a task that fell to Jane Sim, writing it in another century, writing it as a fiction.

Jane Sim? She was the caretaker of Morris's captives. She had been Morris's…wife, I suppose. And an acrobat in his circus. We met her, eventually. I'll tell you about it by and by.

It was the fountain gave Love the power. Love's philosophy likely wasn't much different from one history to the other. I reckon he always did regard himself as the only person who existed, and all the others only manifestations of his considerable will. It's just that without that fountain, he couldn't get a firm enough grip on the people to make his way of seeing the world a commonly held one. And, of course, there was that door beneath. I think that made him crazy—crazier than he could've ever gotten on his own, at any rate. Something he sensed from behind it encouraged his delusions and magnified them.

The Family History of the Loves gave me some of this, but it was dry stuff, all the actuals and factuals. All the interpretation of it, on the other hand… that was in Jane Sim's book. Once I picked that up, I couldn't stop reading.

x x x

The winter had tried them, as Love had warned. Several perished from sickness, and those stricken by it envied the dead: grippe and ague and fever, bodies drained of natural humors and filled with stench of pus, guts seized and spilling out, patients first dizzy and hot, sweating flushed atop bedsheets, then huddled shivering beneath them. The winter winds came and piled drifts up against the cabins until they covered the boarded windows. Mountain snow piled above their heads and flooded the ricks holding the firewood. While their women searched for staves dry enough to burn, men hunted and checked the trap lines, beating paths with their arms through thick wetness.

They carved narrow tunnels through drifts to connect one house to another until the village resembled a termite colony. They huddled together in cloister around fires and stoves, feeling the weight of solid wetness all about them.

But the cabins, though crude in appearance, proved well-constructed and adequately sealed, and the food, while unsavory and salted to point of pain, sustained their bodies. The graveyard they planted when thaw finally arrived was a fraction of what it would have been without the autumn exhortations and winter exertions of Isaac Love. Indeed, without his direction, without the strong dwellings and the warm furs and the stores of food, there would have been no graveyard at all, for none would have remained capable of putting a person beneath ground; all would have lain cold atop it. So Barefoot Runyan suggested to Margaret at supper after the afternoon's grave-digging and mass funeral ceremony, but Margaret made no reply. Ever since the trail she had felt Love's eyes heavy as January snow upon her. She had feared his jealousy when she took up with Runyan, knowing men such as Love were like wild dogs, unlikely to let fall into another's mouth meat they marked for their own. But Love had said nothing, broached no objection to the courtship, offered no obstacle to the marriage. Still, in secret moments, she would catch his eyes on her.

For his own part, Love kept from the fountain through winter, and waited, and pondered, awaiting spring. The river was solid as an anvil, and so too would be the ground. There could be no digging, not yet. The main portion of his time he spent, to the surprise of all, in whichever cabin the women gathered each day, enduring their prattle and gossip, learning from them all the hereditary chores passed from mother to daughter. He made a patient apprentice as they dyed and cooked and scrubbed, churned and quilted and knitted, darned, mended. He attended to each tedious detail, eschewing nothing. The women shook their heads and chuckled behind their hands; the men, not knowing what to make of it, said nothing and put it from their minds, for the village, having become accustomed to this behavior, counted it among the peculiarities of a strange but indispensable man.

Spring that year snuck in like a slow odor; not until early March could they discern the receding snow; a flood unlocked slowly, churning the village into a morass, the water eventually running down to meet the swollen river.

Water stains on their outer walls now showed high above the drift line; brackish water leaked into their paths. They lay down planks and logs to connect their homes so the sludge would not suck away their boots.

The sun remained shy until the day the pigeons came. It lay hidden beneath a dome of unbroken slate cloud stretching blanketlike, unchanging in its eversame grayness from any genesis of horizon to any other. Each day the sun would not so much rise as light up the low oppressive mantle, a lamp hid behind a wool screen. The sky bore down on them now as the snow had done, with a weight of its own, at once less immediate and more troubling, as if representing their abandonment not by the earth but by the heavens, for they knew on the other side of that barrier lay a dazzling brilliance which had been denied them. They stumbled about in their duties, lethargic, distracted, unsure, trapped between sky and mud in this strange amidships season which was no winter any of them had seen but still was no spring either.

On the day of the pigeons they woke to find the evil cloud gone as if it had never been, blown away on a sweet spring wind bruiting their deliverance even before confirmation of sunrise, a barometric change felt in the skin, even from sleep. They came out as one entity to watch the sun rise triumphant above the trees, watched the cloudless sky first dark, then pale and yellow, and then deepening blue, and all the while the sweet favonian wind on their doughpale faces, and then it was they knew at last they had truly made the passage safe. They gathered out in the field of thawed mud churned to muck by their feet, and felt, in the rays beating down without weight or portent, a sense of a great burden lifted, a vernal salvation bought and paid for by the will of a chieftain who bore for them no particular love, who now, without their knowledge, already toiled for a different salvation. For Love was beneath the earth already, caught in the fever of digging, removing clay by the bucketload from around his subterranean door.

Even Frankton Jay felt it, tending to the forge by the river, apart from the rest, silent and dour and aloof, a comportment which left his former comrades baffled through the long winter. They ascribed his newfound mordancy to the shared seasonal melancholy, but even so he pained them. Always before he had been the spirit of good cheer in their midst, wag-tongued, jolly, but he now spoke no word, not to any of them. The only one he would ever approach was Love, and even then, he held his silence; if ever he spoke even to the smith, none saw it. But it seemed, to those who considered the matter, that the man and the boy had some means of correspondence, for the boy had become Love's apprentice, working the forge with talents none had known him to previously possess.

Now Frankton Jay stood in springtime at the forge, saw the blue deep enough to drown in, felt the sun rise for the first time in long months, and felt relief and joy with keenness the others could not match, for to his own reckoning his life began only sixmonth prior, his meager store of knowledge regarding the vagaries of seasons and their passage allowed him to conjecture more vividly, to believe as fact what others had in whimsy imagined: *This is all there is, this cloud sky, the sun will never return never*... Jay stood on the banks of the creek swollen to a brown river and allowed the sun to caress his face, and felt the same sense as the rest of having come through some treacherous and narrow passage, but still he stood far apart, around the river's bend, and let the easy joyful chatter of the hated others come drifting to him. He yearned for such ease, yet kept by the forge, maintaining the wounds of a wronged deaf-mute, keeping to himself the secret of his cure from an affliction he had never suffered so completely as to mimic that affliction's symptoms. Jay closed his eyes and looked skyward to the source of the warmth, watched insubstantial shapes move across the warm inner redness of his eyelids. He heard the beating of many wings, and marveled—what a fine thing it was to be able to hear! A miracle to hear anything, much less the sound of wings, or of water rushing past, or the ding of metal on metal, or even the joy of the hated ones downriver. Jay scowled. They would push him away, if given the opportunity; they would drive him from their midst. He had seen the strange looks shot his direction, the behindhand whispered mocks. No matter. Love had promised their day would soon come.

Intermittent shadows came between his closed eyes and the sun. He opened them and saw the birds flying above and around, hundreds of them, and now thousands, and now vast multitudes, and as he looked farther above, multitudes more, birds without end coming upon them, amorphous shapes like dark clouds forming and reforming with speed of thought. Within minutes thousands blanketed the ground, millions of them perhaps, gray of back and rufous of belly, splay-toed walking with their glass black eyes like two round pinheads in a cushion. Plump-chested passenger pigeons migrating with the warmth, resting for the day perched on the banks like stones, and perched like fat gray fruit in trees until the branches sagged to the ground, and perched on the backs of their fellows when their feet could find no branch, perched everywhere, perched even on the forge, stupidly giving their call, *kek-kek, kek-kek*. They had come in a mass, in clouds of feather and sinew and meat, untouched by humans and unafraid. Occasionally a branch would creak and snap with the weight of them. Downriver, Jay could hear excited yelps of villagers, meat-hungry and racing for sacks and nets, or fashioning crude trammels from Love's store of mosquito netting. A blunderbuss packed with fine ball shot discharged in a puff of blue smoke, and the massacre commenced. Jay, famished like the rest by a winter's worth of salt meat and hard bread, salivated at the sound of the bird-call and beating of wings, at the sight of so much stupid flesh plunked down on the banks like manna. He felt a stirring for the human yelps heard downriver, and here too in the happy clamor of citizenry was something like the appearance of blue sky, a chance for something like salvation. As if the white thickness of winter and his blindness and muteness had all been transmuted into animal substantiality and sent to them for communion, for sacrifice and sustenance. He thought of going with the rest—indeed, his feet had begun to tread the path downstream—but then he halted, belayed once more by resentment, supposing their laughter held traces of mockery.

Let the rest fend for themselves. Jay caught two birds and crushed their skulls, then repeated the task. He caught and killed with ease until he had twelve birds, then fell to plucking and dressing them. He used his hunting knife to fashion spits from sapling twigs and set six of the birds to roast over the forge and then, when the meat smell became too much to bear, he ate them half-cooked and hot off their sticks, the still-bubbling fat burning his fingers and his mouth. He heard the shouts and whoops from the village, the reports of the shotgun dispatching five or ten at a time, the crackle of the bonfire, the music of fiddles and of banjoes as an impromptu revel began, the celebration of simple joys that had, quite literally, landed upon them: meat for the belly, fat for butter, oil for the lamp, fresh feathers for mattress and pillow, and sport for the boys, who, bellies filled, slaughtered now for the bracing enjoyable suddenness of death and the powerful sensation of the fowling piece's stock kicking on the shoulder, for the orgiastic sense of impossible plenty—so many birds you could kill from sunup until sunset and not reduce the number.

Frankton Jay listened to it all, but he never moved. He listened all through the deep clear blue day as he sweated at the forge, as he sharpened at the whetstone the hoes and plow blades needed to cultivate this newly arrived spring. Once, an old man came by and wheedled at him, hoping to coax him down to the party, and later a pretty young lady cried for a while at him. Both played most convincingly at being his friends, but he paid them no mind and presently they departed. He listened in the evening dusk as he methodically killed and ate more of the idiot birds crowding still around the stream banks and the forge and even his ankles, oblivious to the burnt and scattered ribcage charnel of their brothers lying on the ground among them. Jay listened and yearned and hated, the sky darkening until the fiddle music slowed—though the chatter did not—until the only light was starlight, save for the ember glow from the forge and the orange halo rising above the treetops from the bonfire, and still from all around him *kek-kek-kek* from unseen birds, who walked the earth and brushed up against him. He listened to his tormentors downriver and knew he could doubtless reach down without looking and pluck up a bird and murder it without complaint from its fellows.

Love returned to camp. In the firelight he looked like a golem, hands and face and hair and clothes caked with clay. He washed in the river, then took the six roasted birds the boy had saved for him and ate them cold off the spits. As Love first ate and then smoked his pipe, he spoke, slowly, without inflection or expectation of response, as if he were speaking to darkness itself, as though he were merely reminding himself of something already decided, which required no further discussion, only clarification.—There is no way inside I have yet been able to discover. Digging to the sides yields only the outer walls of the tunnel upon which it must open. No portal into the tunnel save that door which refuses to budge, no chink in the stubborn rock. It will not yield to the pick, the spade will not scratch it. The door itself as unbreakable as the stone. I begin to fear it is a mindful thing. Does it mock me? Some days I imagine it does. It whispers to me from a place on the other side of its fastness. Tells me I have not yet deserved entry. I return here, and I see a scattering, a diffusion. A roister of fools praying to their golden calf. The whispers call for their purification. I have put it off, but I will put it off no longer.

The glow of Love's pipe waved in the darkness, indicating the campfire downriver, the shadow of caper and dance, the tickle of fiddle-string. His speech now seemed to Jay a form of trance, a device for hypnotism, some incantation the man had devised and practiced, shamanlike, throughout his daylong dig in the cellar. —Look at them. Dancing while meat to feed them forever lies at their feet all around; made promiscuous in the moment's freedom from strife. As though striving itself were conquered. As if there will never again be winter. As if there will never more be hunger. The moment plenty comes to them through no work of their own, they put from their minds the truth that plenty will leave as it came. They climb a cliff and halfway between ground and summit find, in the comfort of a toehold, a reason to cease climbing. Their weakness I have purged from myself, but it is not enough. It is through their fault that fault has been found in me. This is not unjust; how could it be so? They are mine, to me they have come, to me they have been given. Only through their perfection can I be sanctified.

Afterward, Love left Jay to go downriver and give the villagers instruction for the next day. Frankton Jay stoked the fire and stayed up far into the night at the whetstone, sharpening knives, hatchets, axes. By morning, the smell of burned and consumed birds hung in the dawn air; thousands of avian survivors encumbered the boughs of trees and gathered in gormless clusters around the ring of settlements and among the holocaust of hollow bird bones scattered around the smoking black ashes in front of those structures. The killing continued well past dawn and into morning. Slow learners even still, many a dull-witted or slow-footed pigeon made a villager a handsome breakfast, effortlessly captured in the large nets the men had fashioned the previous day, or shot while in easy range.

The village paid no mind to the meat. Their amnesiac bellies, after one day's fill, now remembered only surfeit and nothing of lack, and they chewed without further thought of occasion. Their talk was all of Love, and the instruction he had given last night, standing before the bonfire, his body in silhouette against it, his features undisclosed, their umbric messiah commanding them, arms raised. They debated what it might signify, this sudden invitation into Love's heretofore forbidden woodland sanctum. All of them were aware by now of the cleared path in the forest behind the forge. Down this path their leader found whatever strange employment had kept him absent these last weeks, but it was also known beyond intuition to be the territory of Love alone, and that to intrude upon his secret would be to risk one's soul and bones. Save for the night-whispers of wives to husbands, it was by unspoken consent a topic unbreached.

Yet now they were commanded to go to the forge and follow the path beyond it, to gather where it led, a place none of them had ever dared or hoped to go. None of them spoke of fear; concentrating instead upon their discourse, a pabulum of safer topics—how far into the woods the path may lead, what might be found there, what food to bring, how much water to carry. But none dared betray their own misgiving, none of them save one, the lady Margaret, to her husband, Isaac "Barefoot" Runyan.

A picnic?

So he said.

I won't go.

You will if I say.

Who is he that we trust him? Who is he that we must obey?

I won't have it, woman. All the others will go. So shall we.

If we stay they may stay as well.

If we stay I'll be mocked again. "There goes Runyan. Afraid to work, afraid to lead. Now afraid of a picnic."

You trust him?

He leads us.

He drives us without care. Haven't you seen, he doesn't look at a body, he looks through. Like sunlight through a window.

I fear the eye of no man.

Often they rest on me.

Don't talk foolishness.

You must have seen it. He wishes me to exchange one Isaac for another.

Foolishness.

He has said as much to me.

Women's foolishness. I won't speak of it again.

In the hours before noon the village made ready to meet Love, packing picnic lunches of pigeon meat and bread in paper packets nestled in bark baskets. Isaac "Barefoot" Runyan emerged from his shack, forced, to his consternation, to drag Margaret his wife by the arm. She struggled only briefly, her countenance pained and betrayed, but soon she settled and walked limply beside him, eyes straight ahead. Runyan, perturbed, could not comprehend why it had to be his woman, of all people, to act as stormcloud. He could not deny to himself (even if he would deny to her) his discomfit at the notion another might have designs on his woman, particularly a man strong of will and of body…but Love was no seeker of affections; he was a force like wind. He seemed as much a rival in human matters of passion as did a mountain. No, this was a fancy, a tale fed by vanity, no more. Here was a beautiful warm spring day, the sun out and a sweet cool breeze on the air, and heaven-sent pigeons still moiling about on the bank…but Runyan grew aware of the density of the silent forest growing beside them. Margaret slowed, and Runyan, piqued, nevertheless permitted her to set their pace, and thereby they soon strayed to the rear of the company.

When they reached the forge, they saw Frankton Jay standing beneath the lean-to dressed in heavy leather overalls. Beside him lay a small mound of sharpened tools and blades. The large boy watched them with suspicious little eyes. They shuffled past the forge, and before them now lay the path carved into the thickest of the forest, a chute barely wide enough for two to walk abreast. Here a congestion formed, as those who first reached the entrance to the tunnel halted, quailed, attempting to cede their order to those behind, and as he and his wife mixed in with the milling crowd, Runyan thought with such vigor he surprised himself *it is not too far gone yet, we can yet turn back and we need not there need be none of us need go down this tunnel we can picnic down by the river…*

He almost spoke then. Almost called out.

But then one went in, and the others followed in among the close-grasping thicket while Margaret rolled her eyes sheeplike and plaintive toward

Runyan, who wondered why women must put on airs to so affright him, make his breath tight in his chest, jackrabbit his heart, and as they approached the fresh-cut dark-leaved trees of the entrance he could feel the moist breath of the wood like a live hungry thing and he thought *I won't go in* and then they were in, side by side, his hand still on her arm but limply now, a nominal propellant only, and they were between the thick dark green trees with people before and some behind all on their way to the place Love had gone ahead to prepare for them, where they would have their picnic, so he had said. Runyan attempted a smile; the sun was high above, and some light managed to filter down even here. He was a tracker by trade—what fear could a forest hold for him on a bright day in spring? In sudden relief, he saw his panic was his alone, that the silent fear he had seen writ in the visages of others could be ascribed to no more than the imprint of his wife's alarm upon his own fickle imagination and suggestible nature. He found himself thankful now he had not given voice to his fear, relieved he had spared himself the taunts of his fellows.

Once all had passed into in the woodland chute, Frankton Jay followed them, leaving the forge and village populated solely by the rouge-breasted pigeons. An axe dangled from one hand, a hatchet from the other.

The picnickers at the party's fore, made anxious by the tightening branches and their own acquiescent silence, made eager by glimpses of sunlight ahead, hastened through the opening and stood blinking in sudden effulgence. Then they saw the skyward-pointing whiteness in the center of the unaccountable sward, felt it conjure ancient fear within them, mortally unbearable and unbearably true, and while they did not yet see squat Love standing beside the fountain, austere and silent and grim, neither did they need to see him, nor the barrel beside him, to feed their panic. They turned, dumb as cattle, to return the way they had come, but they were repelled by the main bulk of those still arriving, newcomers as anxiously zealous to remove themselves from the encroaching forest as those who had so recently extracted themselves were to return to it. In their haste to reach the sun, those behind pushed aside both the bodies and warnings of those ahead; and, as they saw for themselves the alabaster obelisk, and felt the terror, they in turn attacked the debouchment, and were repelled in similar manner. They fell to the edges of the ring and pushed at the dense surrounding thicket in vain, clutching their children tight, their picnic baskets laden with pigeon and boiled autumnal spuds strewn over the green carpet.

Among the last to arrive were Runyan and Margaret, who, hearing the cries, had to be pushed through by Jay. The boy kept mute sentry at the entrance, impressing them with axe and hatchet, while Love circled the ring, shepherdlike, freeing villagers who had managed to entangle themselves in the impenetrable bramble and throwing them back onto the turf.

Love had anticipated his flock's fear, for even he felt new traces of original dread each time he saw the thing. But, following their first shock of panic, he was confirmed in his further expectation: The wailing ceased, cut off with perfect synchrony from all parties, as though a simultaneous agreement had been reached to not acknowledge the thing. The picnickers, clinging still to the fringes, looked up and about them, but not—insofar as this was possible—not directly at the fountain itself. They saw the unbroken forest ringing their clearing, the sole opening guarded by Frankton Jay, who grinned hatred at them, saw the axe in his hand, saw the malevolent pallid fountain, and then, as one mind, they did not see them; they disassociated them as sundries, irrelevant and inapplicable to their situation. They commenced to settling on the grass along the forest fringe, spreading their blankets, forcing themselves back into the ruts of their original expectation. They began to converse, their voices halting at first but gaining volume through the momentum of their own prattle, until they were ensconced, all of them, in a semblance of audible relief, of ease, and they unpacked their meals. They chuckled between themselves at their previous cowardice, at their sudden irrational panic—and at what? They could scarce remember now; it had come on so sudden. Such a fine day, such a blessed day. Yet not one of them met the eye of another as they bit and chewed and talked, their gaze fixed ever on the earth, with such fervency that any chance observer, seeing their stooped postures, might have mistaken them for penitents.

Then they heard Love's voice coming from the direction of the thing—

This is the first of my Assizements. You have been surveyed, and assayed, and have been found flawed and wanting. Yet all of you save one shall be remade in mercy. Drink ye, all of ye.

—and they turned their reluctant heads fountainward, but still askance, their attention focused not on it nor on Love's face, but on his boots and knees and chest, and on the pinestave hogshead that stood opened beside him. They saw him slowly take hold the ladle within and lift it up. They returned to their mendicant postures, hoping to unhear as they had unseen, but then they heard his voice ring out again—

Drink ye, all of ye.

—and Runyan and the rest muttered and stamped and looked no higher than the top of the cask. But Margaret looked; she pierced the collected fear and denial, and saw all: fountain, barrel, ladle, and Love's countenance, which contended between fervor of triumph and some other thing unrecognizable to her. She looked into the barrels of his eyes, and he looked back at her and smiled. She reflected contempt back to him and nothing more—not even defiance, but only scorn—knowing the struggle had finished. She saw clearly their fate, which the others would or could not see. Though the means of his attainment, which he held pendulous in the ladle, were not clear to her, she knew he had won, and that she, who had all through the long winter tried to cajole her own Isaac out of his comfortable ignorance, and had kept this other Isaac at bay, had failed. She had tried to warn her husband of Love's steady advance, first fearing to kindle his will into the desire for revenge common to all men, and then, finding that tinder damp, remonstrating more directly, sinking slowly into despair as he refused to hear, keeping herself hidden from Love in their newlywed cabin while winter permitted the excuse of sequestration. And here it is spring, she thought—sprung upon us. Yet even still, there remained within her a great resolve. Even now, in this place, she braced her will against his own—no matter the devil he had bargained with, no matter what poison this madman would force upon them, she would not give him the victory he sought. His defeat would reside in her eyes. She would wear her scorn as if it were her eternal raiment, into his mind she would sear it, and may he someday die thinking on it.

A third time Love spoke—

Drink ye.

—imperative now, inexorable in timbre, some quality that both invited and commanded, cajoled and threatened, offering no escape from a stark choice: only one thing or else another, either admission or excommunication, either selection or apostasy, and, as the first obedient few of them broke free from the edges and made their way across the grass to where he stood, Frankton Jay swung the axe in a long arc, allowing the heavy-soft *thunt* of the head burying itself into the turf to serve as that command's punctuation.

Runyan began to screw his courage to the point of some as-yet unde- fined future action, thinking: *Not I, no and not Margaret either, and neither should any of us be made to take that drink*; Runyan seeing (as though for the first time) the hatred Frankie Jay had for them, seeing Jay's axe at the ready, but also, in his mind, seeing himself walking boldly to Jay, with Margaret trailing behind, and then, when challenged by the boy—for boy he was despite his size—demanding his weapon of him, and, when the boy refused, wresting the axe from him and knocking him easily aground and the boy rising up off of the turf and leaping at him in a dark rage and Runyan already swinging the axe in fast deadly ellipse into Frankton Jay's head down to the neck and then announcing to amazed Isaac Love that he was taking his leave along with all others who wished to go…

But even in his imagination Runyan did not attack Love; even in his own hidden folds of self-regard, the capacity for that act could not be discovered. No, he would attack Frankie, and he would do it..soon. Not now, but at some fast-approaching future moment. The picnickers had formed a queue now before Love's ladle. Hand in hand with Margaret, he took a place with the rest at the rear of the line, and Frankton Jay's axe and baleful eye kept their place by the pathway leading out. The inescapable fountain leaned up in defiance of the sky. Love's people waited their turn to take their ladleful. Frightened but mute, they took it into themselves reverently, as if thankful, and then sank down together in glassy forgetful communion. As they accumulated, Jay came and pulled them away to make room for others, leaving the path out unguarded—unconcerned now that those yet to partake might dare anymore to attempt flight. But Barefoot Runyan had been a mountain man for a time, in years past. He knew wilderness living. He would escape soon. In a matter of seconds, he would tug at Margaret's hand, they would make a dash for it, and if Frankton Jay pursued them, so much the worse for him…

Those first to drink had begun waking and calling out like travelers lost in a fog when Runyan reached the barrel, and now the moment to act was near, very near…he saw Jay distracted, corralling a panicked few, the moment was nearly upon him, and then he and Margaret stood before Love, who proffered the ladle to him, with the moment of rebellion so close now, almost upon him. He could see blue sky and the dense complexity of old forest all about, and he could see the face of his adored Margaret, the miracle who had delivered herself to him, whose love had tied him to this place when otherwise he might have moved on, Margaret who was in turn staring, bilious, at Love, and he could see Love's implacable face staring at him over the barrel. He could see the cold beads sweating from the tin of the ladle. He could hear the distant *keking* of a million pigeons. The stone white eye of the cherub nearest to him had a chip in it. A light breeze stirred the trees. He could see each leaf. Each leaf, if only he had time to look at each of them in turn. The barrel's water seemed black. Runyan wondered with what malignant tincture it had been treated, even as the hopeful front of his mind told him it was naught but water, and safe to drink.

The moment to rebel was only seconds away now. In a moment he would turn and run.

Drink, said Love.

You can't make me, Runyan said, but his lips did not move.

Drink, Love said once more, and the moment to run was near.

No no I won't I never will not ever this is wrong I won't, thought Runyan as he drank what tasted like no more than water and then he felt himself sinking numb into a cavern in which there was no joy, no pain, no hope, no worry, nothing, nothing, none, no

Margaret watched her husband sink down out of himself onto the grass.

Drink, Love said to her.

The last of them, the only one to meet his eyes, she stared at him with contempt void of anger or hatred or even fear, and he told himself it was of no consequence to him, for soon her demeanor would be void even of contempt. He held the ladle to her, and to his surprise she took it at once, without hesitation, as if she had merely been awaiting the offer. She took the ladle in both hands like a child and tipped it back eagerly, and when she lowered it again he saw still that purified disdain in her eyes and then she spit the mouthful back into his shocked face. He tightened his eyelids, frightened to open them lest he give the liquid admittance into his humours. Enraged beyond all thought, he roared, blind hands darting out and finding her collar and her head. His fingers entwined her hair close to the roots and then he pulled her, struggling, to him. He dried his eyes on his shirt shoulder, and, opening them again, saw her defiance still unquenched. He pulled her head slowly into the barrel and held it there until he saw the bubbles rise. When he was sure she had drunk, he pulled her out and laid her gently on the grass, her eyes wiped clean of any traceable human thought. She gazed up at him, entirely lost from herself, but not yet confused, not yet frightened.

To one side, he could see Frankton Jay struggle to contain the pandemonium of those who had learned confusion and fear once more. They howled for their lost selves and ran distracted from the mass, from those who had not yet come into the realization they had a self to miss. They stumbled madly until they ran against the inevitable encircling forest wall, caught there until Jay came to extract them and drag them back to the center, all the while muttering in their ears to be silent, to sit and be silent and wait, for all would be made clear. As ever, Frankton worked with celerity, but he was one and they were many, and as he toiled he began to slow. In the mind of Frankton Jay—Love could see it writ on the boy's face—there was some troubling and recognizable quality to this situation, something connective; Love saw distraction working in Frankton's countenance, and guessed its cause.

Love lifted Margaret and slung her over his back. With his free arm he filled the dipper once again. He carried her over to the general congregation and lay her down among the rest. Jay led two weeping villagers back to the assembly, and then came up to Love. His breath was ragged, and he intimated his misgivings that, matched against the accumulated need of those now gathered, even their best efforts would be insufficient.

I will manage it alone, Love told him.

Alone?

Love indicated the full ladle with his eyes.

You too must drink, he said.

Jay looked at Love, disbelieving.

No. Oh, no, Isaac, no, not I. Not I.

Aye, Frankton Jay. You. You of all men must drink. I have in my need fashioned you into something unfitting. But I am still a smith at heart. I will melt you down in mercy and reshape you.

Jay looked around, as if hoping to conjure allies from the ground to his aid. Love regarded him unblinking, his eye fixing with cold appraisal the trapped boy who stammered and shook his head mulishly and finally began in silence to weep.

It will not harm you, boy.

I don't want to. I ain't going to.

You shall.

Love's voice conveyed nothing of impatience, nothing of anger; only the dry conviction of a scholar lecturing on a well-documented event long complete. You shall, he said again, in the way another man would say, "you have."

The boy glared. I shan't, I said. He seemed for the first time to remember the axe. He had set it down to manage the fugitives, and it lay some yards behind him. His eyes made furtive dashes toward it.

Go on then, Love said. Lift it. Strike.

The boy backed up to it and stooped for it. Now he hesitated, one fist closed over the handle. Love smiled at him and held up the ladle. Jay stood and brandished the axe.

I tell you I won't drink that mess.

You shall. Have you not realized you have no other possible course than to obey?

I could bust your head wide open with this here axe.

Love laughed. You could not. It can make no dint in me. Don't you know me, Frankie, even after I have been with you such a long time?

I know you.

Who then.

You're Isaac Love. You tended me in this place where you found me, out here in the woods, when I was cured.

Yes, when you were cured. Cured of what?

Deaf and dumb both.

And how was your cure affected? In what manner brought about?

Through a miracle of God.

Love stepped forward, ladle held upward. Through a miracle of God, say you? And still you have not known me? And even now you have failed to realize me?

The boy cowered, his unholy fear quaking him to his knees as Love rose ineluctably up before him like a stone god of old, and behind him the alabaster monster grasped heavenward.

I am the worker of all your miracles. I am the one who took from you and restored to you speech and hearing both, and when you are thankful for that cure, I am that God to whom you offer thanks, for it is through my power you came into knowledge of your cure and all other knowledge besides. I am the source of all your breath and all your thought, the sole architect of your soul. And now I say to you that you shall drink.

Afterward, when he had with axe and spade dealt with the one who deserved no remolding, Love gathered them all together, raised his hands to the sky and spoke to them in a loud voice. Once he had instructed them, he retrieved the hatchet and descended the cold granite steps.

But Love did not raise his hatchet against the door. For long minutes he regarded it. A door, unremarkable to look upon—this was the verdict of a first glance. Only upon closer examination did certain curiosities present themselves. An unnatural regularity to the grain, for example—a detectable pattern repeated, as though a printing press could be devised to counterfeit nature itself. Upon the door a handle with design most unique; a smooth short cylinder, of a size amenable to a hand, into whose center a slot—which might be a keyhole, but so narrow one could not see through it—had been most ingeniously carved. Both handle and escutcheon revealed an amber glow in torchlight, suggesting gold or brass, but without the natural tarnish to be expected upon those metals found in such damp climes. Strange indeed, to see such opulence set within a door so flat and plain, and yet, when one attempted to turn the knob, though the lock held, knob and escutcheon both rattled between each other and the door in minute asymmetry, a concertina of imprecision. Love reached out again and grasped it. Yes, still it felt flimsy, as if the handle only mimicked gold, and the wood only mimicked ash.

Yet for that it still would not open—the eternally damnable thing.

How many axe handles had he broken? How many edges had he dulled? It was unchanged, without mark or blemish or warp. It resisted even fire, even digging. Surrounding this frame was the excavation; his toil of months, wide caverns dug to the right and left and above the sealed port, reaching back into darkness, leading nowhere.

This matter required solutions clever and oblique; he saw this now. This was a conflict not of brawn but of will. By employing force against it, he had revealed insufficient faith in his own worthiness. But he had that faith now. As he strode forward to meet his adversary, he could see all time converge to a point, could hear heaven and hell gasp. Love knew if he were unable to alter this facet of his world, it would not be attributable to the strength of the door, but to some weakness in his own spirit. But he would not fail, for he had perfected himself, and his people, and now he had perfected his suffering. He would not fail. Behind the door lay all that for which he yearned. Worse than not possessing it was not even knowing what it was. He could not fail. He knew he would not.

He failed. The door's merciless handle would not turn in his hand.

After the hatchet broke, his mind left him and he cried out in a language of his own device as he smote the unmarred surface with his body. When he could no longer continue, he attacked it with ragged maledictions and hoarse sobs. The curses penetrated the mute wood no more than the hatchet, and no less, either. As he sank to the ground, the truth of the matter came over him like waves.

He had failed. *Failed*.

Yet still…there had come—had there not?—even in the moment of failure, a moment where the damnable handle had seemed—had it not?— almost to have turned? Where there had seemed almost a vision, a picture of another, like to yourself in appearance but in strange and unfamiliar garments, clean and gray, standing in this same cavern, trying this same door…

Yes. Perhaps there is a further vision here. Perhaps, as you suspect, this body and its depredations are illusion only. Perhaps the progression of father to son is some great and undetectable Continuity, not of legacy alone, but of spirit, even of *consciousness*?

Yes. It may be so. Perhaps through the repeated test of the door you can at last learn to escape this illusion of body. Perhaps your victory over the timeless door is itself timeless, arrives in some far century, some other self, toward which you might learn to project yourself…

Rising to his feet, Love slowly climbed the granite steps, toward his day and his people.

—Jane Sim, *Love's Fountain*

C I R C U S

The work went on, though whether it was a novel or a *roman à clef* was anyone's guess. Jane Sim wrote it like fiction, but everything she set down was corroborated in the history...and the history was written by Isaac Love himself.

Again, the "what" of it never changed much, outside the odd detail. For example, the mountebank preachers never made a go at hawking the restorative qualities of nearby spring waters, because in this new history, instead of springs in Henderson Hollow; there existed only an unnaturally cleared circle of turf and a fountain. Yes, the shape of the story held, but the "why," everything that happened beneath and behind...all that had changed, changed.

And even still, I was thinking only of my fame. Even still, I hadn't felt the danger. Father, I read the whole night, and never even thaw thaw thought of checking in on Gordon. Never once. That's the were were worst thing I can tell you. I never even considered my boy.

But the new history.

First there was the fountain, then came the settlement, then the town, then the circus. The oubliettes came after. Morris made the oubliettes—his great contribution. All down the line, they've each added to the Love empire in their own way. Isaac, he found the damn thing, and he started the digging beneath. He started the bird and the spade, too, all the liturgy, the ceremony he called his "Assizement." Twice a year—as winter melted to spring, as summer curled into autumn—the people gathered around the fountain at the directive of a man they could no longer fathom disobeying. Isaac stood near it, barrel beside him, ladle in hand. He'd call names of those who had failed his standard, and forward they'd come, where he'd show them one of two different placards; image of a bird, or image of a spade.

The birds were shown to those deemed by Love capable of improvement. These would get the water; would sink, lost to themselves; ready to be reformed, they were led by the rest back to the village, to learn their role better than they had before.

Later, after the people had gone, those shown the spade would get the axe.

Isaac ruled like a backwoods king back in a day when the Tennessee woods were remote enough and thick enough to allow such open displays. He sowed the seeds, but the system remained small under his stewardship, rigidly controlled, paralyzed against innovation, hobbled as it was by Isaac's unshakeable belief in his own singularity. Even as he grew old, Isaac clung to the idea of his existence being the only real one, and as his body betrayed him to age, his rationalizing mind turned to heredity. One autumn Sixmonth, Isaac declared a writ, that the firstborn of the Love line must always be a son, and that this son would always be him, and only him, the Continuity of the universe's sole consciousness, whose spirit would be named Isaac Love no matter the name given the body.

William, Isaac's son—still the founder of the county's first post office— was the first to take on the mantle of Continuity. William, who possessed a more pragmatic mind, realized if Isaac's law survived in its raw state, the colony at Pigeon Forge would inevitably find itself in short and open warfare with the westward-expanding United States. William saw the new country's encroachment; to him she appeared as a wave, inescapable as she was inevitable. As a bulwark, he purposed to make the town economically attractive to that wave. He expanded the mill, which built their fortune, and opened lines of communication back to the state and federal governments. That an outpost in the Smokies had been eking out an existence for decades came as a surprise—not because they considered the Love party missing and dead, but because they had forgotten any such party had ever existed. Emissaries dispatched from the Tennessee Department of Commerce returned, effusive in their report: Yes, there is an outpost, and yes, the government should by all means consider utilizing it for promotion of frontier trade and as a staging ground for further movement westward. There was a general sense of marvel at what an efficient operation was being run out there—men, women, children, all working with military precision, as if they were a single entity.

Viable, self-contained, unmolested by savages, free of famine; in regard to agriculture, maintaining a surplus; in regard to defense, equipped with a stockade and militia, well-stocked and well-drilled.

Even then, William realized the strange success of Pigeon Forge must remain submerged. He even modified the Assizement to make it a secret thing; erected a tent around the fountain, hid barrel and ladle and axe and placards within. Only those ordered into the tent discovered what happened there—of course, they kept their secrets.

The government emissaries returned from Pigeon Forge bearing letters detailing carefully phrased proposals, allowing Pigeon Forge to integrate with the outside world without being absorbed by it, and to prosper by the association without closer investigation. William realized the state was seeking a way to relocate native tribes en masse, to clear-cut the cultural landscape for a more manifest destiny; knew also that the whole South was looking for a way to make an enslaved labor pool still more pliable. William had a genius for understanding how his darkest asset might provide a solution; he understood, in time, that the fountain would allow the Loves to operate as before, not by standing in opposition to power, but by injecting themselves directly into the corporate bloodstream of a nation that would never be without some unwanted class from whom to profit.

And he knew well enough to add fresh bodies to his empire.

The Loves soon learned to make a friend of war. Each son in his turn entered the conflict of his day, distinguishing himself properly through bravery and skill, returning from the conflagration as Continuity, ready to continue the tradition, the liturgy, the ceremony. Each son returned, having gained the friendship and loyalty of a certain type of soldier: dirt-poor, without much family, without a girl back home, without ties. Mercenaries, career soldiers, confirmed bachelors, tear-streaked G.I.s clutching Dear John letters, men skilled in dangerous arts—all of them, after their various wars had finished, made their way to Sevier County, where their old war buddy and commanding officer had a job for them. All of them thirsty for some greater purpose to their lives. And, for their thirst, the Loves had a drink.

And yes, again, history's shape remains the same, even as the reasons for the shape move beneath the blanket. As before, Pigeon Forge still experienced the same long stretch, lost to record or rumination, before its re-emergence as a hillbilly carnival playland, but now this hidden time was not a time of impoverishment, but a time of enrichment. In the years after the Failed War to Preserve Slavery, with the tribes gone, with the slaves emancipated, the Loves sought out new channels of revenue for their secret asset, and they quickly found a current so strong they float on it to this day: prisons. Slowly, secretly, carefully, the Loves began to supply wardens seeking a more pliable population with a tonic suitable to their needs.

So the Loves became early merchants of imprisonment, but once Morris took on the mantle of Continuity he made them all seem like dilettantes, loafers willing to rest on the advantage of their unholy fountainhead. Morris took to the family business with gusto and verve. Not content to merely supply prisons, he began to acquire them. He poured funds into lobbying, into research, into technology. Soon he had a fate different than an axe for those he showed the sign of the spade.

Morris invented the oubliettes, as I said.

And, of course, he also brought in the circus. He purchased it, sent it out to travel the country, and attract little-needed people and runaways, as circuses are known to do. He used it to grow the ranks. Every six months, the circus would return, and the ceremony would begin.

x x x

For Gordy the next few moments are all lights and fantastic, but after the initial flush of revelry, the gorilla is depressing him something terrible. This is not to say the circus is without enticement—what a joint! The inside of the tent is large enough to accommodate a midway along the front half of its circumference, which is lined with vendors and booths and other attractions—and that doesn't even take into consideration the show. The inner wall of this midway is formed by high risers of bleachers, backed by strips of striped tent canvas tied to the bleacher base and reaching all the way to the roof. Through the gaps of the aisles between the risers, Gordy espies what the bleachers are facing: the big show, three rings on sawdust, the trapeze rigging stashed overhead. Gordy can smell more than a hint of big animals, too, but before the main course begins, they've provided a suitable zoological appetizer out here in the midway; a great ape, silver of back and wise of face. Still, Wembly makes Gordy feel queasy. It's a roomy cage—there's that at least—but the beast hunkers in the corner of it with his playing cards and, in his despondency, makes it seem small. It's his gorilla eyes, Gordy decides; they're too human. As Wembly flips his cards with his feet, there is contemplation in those eyes, motionless activity, a suggestion he remembers better gorilla times, a gorilla childhood of sorts, perhaps a gorilla family. You can imagine those eyes pining for a gorilla sweetheart long lost in the jungle mists, you can see nostalgia and want, a desire for a return to a gorilla home where all gorilla pleasures await: plenty of bananas, lots of fellow apes bearing tasty ticks and mites, cool moist green everywhere crawling with familiar insects, familiar scents, familiar faces—not this horrid stinking poking horde. His eyes aren't the vacant black dots of rats or hamsters, Gordy thinks, not the alien full-pupil disc-slits of jungle cats, these are soulful hazel human eyes in a hairy man's abnormally large and pointed head.

The Colonel holds forth at the cage, drumming up extra business: COME on over, STEP right up, SEE the see. He's bringing a crowd, naturally. Apparently the gorilla tells futures with those cards of his; he's a big *draw*, you could say, ha-ha-ha. Fairgoers press forward, digging deep into wallets and purses, while the big simian lug rests his chin on his fist and sighs. Gordy walks away. It strikes him as unseemly to observe the ape; of all those caged here, it alone sits behind its bars against its will. The other freaks are clearly putting on an act and have some agency about them. They've all *decided* to do this—Plastilica, Ol' Hatchet-Arms, Sharkboy, the Illustrated Man, Eak (the man with Space All Over His Face), Zippy the Pinhead, Insectavora the Bug-Eating Lady, the minute and deadly bodyguards—duties momentarily abandoned—sparring each other in a cage of their own (to which a sign has been affixed advertising them as twins, and each apparently named "Andrew"), even the Fat Lady lounging brazenly in her tentlike shift—all have been led here by some bad fate; nevertheless, for them there are other frequencies of consciousness, they have in some way chosen this life for themselves over others they deemed even less satisfactory, and, what's more, they know it. Eddie the Eyeball there, he's clearly enjoying himself. But the gorilla? He has no alternate frequency, and he will never learn the art of concealing his desperation, or his boredom, or his confusion. He seems to be trying, and failing, to learn how to weep.

An announcement blares over the PA: The circus begins in five minutes. The freaks start to make themselves scarce as Gordy winds his way between the bleacher risers with the rest of the latecomers to pick over the remaining real estate. Long hard backless benches moan under rows of posteriors already planted, foresightful types who managed to resist the call of carny food and freaks, who've already taken the plum spots. Dawdlers like Gordy will have to settle for spaces high in the bleachers. Gordy sees the tent has been bifurcated along the back by a large tapestry embroidered with archetypical circus images: the animal tamer, the clown, the acrobat. It cuts across the sawdust, extracting from the staging area a small portion of the tent's floor space—concealing, Gordy supposes, the backstage. They're back there now, getting ready for the show, getting into character, preparing to do their bit. Makeup, nervous puking, stretching exercises for the acrobats, sedatives for the lions and tigers. The curtain prevents the intrusion of the mundane, the ruination of the magic.

The bleachers wrap around and nudge right up against the tapestry. Stuffed already with fairgoers, they rim the white stripe on the ground demarcating audience from performance. Gordy climbs the bleachers abutting the tapestry toward a remaining cluster of unchoice seats. These risers are canted at an unnaturally precipitous angle, and the stairs leading up are narrow and steep as a mountain trail. Face full of the ass of the fat man ahead, Gordy trudges carefully up the wooden structure, which feels less trustworthy the higher he goes; it complains restlessly beneath thousands of milling stamping feet. Once seated, however, Gordy notices something strange: Lots of these folks don't look particularly interested in the show. The guy next to Gordy is talking to nobody, far too loudly, about nothing much, and a few people are, are…are they *crying*? Yes. To see crying people at a circus seems a bad omen. That lady there, for example, three rows down. She's moaning a name again and again. Lucy. Lucy. Lucy. Oh, Lucy. Everywhere along the semicircle, people are carrying on—hilarity too intense to be unforced, resigned stares, quiet weeping.

Gordy wishes he didn't feel perched atop a crow's nest. He's at the summit, his back pressed right up against the floor-to-ceiling canvas swards tied to the bleacher backs, and up here the whole construct sways like a treetop in a slow breeze. Sometimes it leans so far right or left that structural collapse feels, for a terrible second, inevitable. There's no guardrail against the back row, nothing to prevent a backward fall but innate balance and the backing of canvas—but the canvas, loosely tied, doesn't help much; if anything, it provides false reassurances of stability, a fool's backrest. Gordy sits, very much aware of the open space behind him. He tries to calculate his altitude, imagines falling all that way, shudders...

At present there is nothing to see down on the circus floor but a few sad clowns slapping each other. The minutes stretch out; the audience chafes with boredom and anticipation. Everyone tries to ignore the lumbar pain the bleachers are already cooking up, tries to remember not to lean back onto a stranger's knees (or, in the case of Gordy and his fellow back-row nosebleeders, not to lean back into deadly nothing), tries to fix upon something to entertain themselves, to keep themselves from turning mean. The clowns sure aren't doing the trick, and they seem aware of this. Beads of flop sweat form on greasepaint. Something sharp pokes Gordy's lower back. He recons in his pocket and extracts the offender—Oh yes. The scratch-off from that vivid smoking weirdo. Its embedded foil winks in the light. The ticket reads:

LUCKY 21! WIN $1,000!!
EVERY CARD HAS A WINNING COMBINATION!!
CAN YOU FIND IT???

A thousand clams. A kid could do worse. Gordy digs in his front pockets for a good rubbing coin...there's some change in here somewhere...but all he can find are two accursed Jeffersons—nickels, the ridgeless bane of all scratch-off junkies. Gordy pockets one coin, brandishes the other. He pauses a moment to study the thing. Two rows, each comprised of four silver scratch-away squares, and in the middle of each square the instruction:

HIT ME

Below this a silver scratch-away rectangle, above which the caption:

SEE WHAT YOU'VE WON!

Gordy scratches at *see what you've won* first—let's see what we're playing for. The nickel makes this task difficult, but in the dent formed by the coin he sees the zeros appear. Three little zeros, ducks in a row following their mama, a tall skinny number one. A grand. This is one of the few tickets that might pay top prize. The fever of "what if" is upon him; the circus forgotten. A thousand dollars. Gordy is fifteen. This is the most money there could possibly be.

What's this? That smoking guy must have already started playing the ticket before handing it over; there's already a disc scratched away. A six of clubs.

Lucky 21, eh? Gordy knows this game. The video-game version is a ubiquity in the restaurants and hotels of Pigeon Forge. There is some strategy to it, which escapes him, but strategy's unimportant in this context; this is the bastardized scratch-off format. You scratch until your revealed sum is twenty-one and you're free to claim your prize, or you go over that number, and are free to piss off.

Hands shaking, he hits the top row, one in from the right.

Lower right corner. Jack of hearts.

Sixteen.

What next? Gordy holds the nickel poised, trying to stare through the remaining six boxes. The next move could spell disaster. The pool of good possibilities has dried up way too fast; anything over a five is death. The Jack mocks him with one good eye, the creep. He flips the ticket over and holds it up to the light, trying to divine some clue, but the cardboard is impenetrable. His nickel hovers, makes tight ellipses. He scratches, very gently, at the top row, second from the left, hoping to see some telltale before he has gone too far, before it is an official scratch—*it was like that when I bought it I didn't do that*—but the nickel defies finesse. He tries his fingernail with slight improvement in control, so he pitches the nickel into the void behind him. The box is scratched beyond alibi, so he rubs the rest of the way without looking at it hoping *five five five five*...He looks down, breath pent.

Four. Four of clubs, nestled hard by cousin six.

Twenty.

The ace alone is a winner, if ace is even to be found. The winning combination existed before he started scratching at the surface, but likely it's already passed him by. Far worse than the initial disappointment of losing will be after, when he scratches off all the remaining opaque latex film, and traces with jaundiced eye the course of the unchosen winning combination. His whole back aches with the strain of his buttocks clinging to the swaying bench. He's still agonizing over his final choice when the lights go out and a hush falls in waves over the crowd. The Circus of Breaded Love has begun. With haste he deposits the ticket safe into his pocket, relieved to put off the moment of disappointment.

The Colonel stands center stage, awash in light, his trademark patois made incomprehensible by a huge red bullhorn. Suddenly the air is full of lithe and spangled tumblers in blue and red and white leotards, swinging in wide loops from metal batons attached to wires so thin one can easily imagine them invisible, lending the acrobats the illusion of flight. The tumblers barely touch the bars, swinging wild and at seeming random, catching for the briefest moment before flying out once again into the void, somersaulting and catching the next baton as if only by chance. Gordy tries to count the acrobats, but it's an impossible task, they crisscross and fly too quickly. There may be five of them, there may be seven, there may be ten.

The batons are being swung across the expanse by ten clowns clinging to short chrome fire poles, which have descended from neat holes in the tent roof. These clowns are arranged at intervals around the trapeze rig, and hang from the poles by their legs, leaving their arms free. They catch the batons in white-gloved hands and throw them out again in the general direction of the trapeze artists, carelessly, without aim or purpose or urgency, and sometimes—holy hell!—they miss the baton entirely, and it floats indifferently away. Gordy is chewing the insides of his cheeks, he frets with fear, he thrums with vicarious adrenaline. Impossible for this to end well, there is no sense here, no pattern, there will be a collision, a clown will fail to throw a crucial baton, will throw too soon or too late to meet an acrobat in her moment of need. The indifference of the clowns is terrifying and exhilarating; the tumblers depend entirely upon the whims of these buffoons. Below, Gordy sees nothing to halt a fall but the most impractical arrangement, a mere sop to safety: three small black trampolines arranged in a triangle at a height of ten feet, none of them larger than a child's inflatable pool...meanwhile, a hundred feet up, these fools practice their arbitrary tosses and catch-es. Gordy wants to cover his eyes. He winces with each hush of the crowd. The clowns are in danger themselves as they lean out to make their catches. They must have feet like monkeys; Gordy can't understand how they remain on their poles. Still…there *must* be some method. Somehow the acrobats keep aloft; somehow a baton always floats by to meet them, and they flip and turn, catching the baton, or—sometimes, unbearably—missing it, but then catching, one heart-pounding second later, the feet of another tumbler who is being held arm-in-arm by yet another who hangs inverted from his bar by the knees, and then the three danglers each see a baton all their own and go spinning off in different directions…

The faith of the acrobats infects the crowd, and they begin to laugh, delighted at the madness, or caught in it. Every second that passes without fatality is a new miracle. The production is effortless and impossible, com-plex and happenstance, flight and gravity, all at once. Gordy is in the midst of deciding whether he is watching the skillful enactment of endless rehears-al or the improvisational trapeze act of highly proficient lunatics, trying to find some hint that even the misses are all a part of the dance—when there at last comes an accident. The clowns shriek with the crowd as three acrobats simultaneously miss their bars with no rescue and fall to earth feet pointed down straight as arrows the crowd rising to its feet with horror and anticipa-tion then groaning in furious relief and joyous disappointment as each of the three of them lands directly in the center of one of those three trampolines, stretching deep dimples into the elastic until the metal rings of the tramps are level with the crowns of their heads and then shooting back up, rising and rising and eschewing the batons the panicking clowns toss their way as they ascend, nearly touching the tent roof, holding for the briefest instance at the top of their trajectory, consecrated in the absolution of flux, the moment between rising and falling that is neither and both—and in a heartbeat, an instant, Gordy sees that the center one is a heartbreaking beauty, a woman with dark hair shot with gold, and in the way of boys he is immediately in love—yes, *love*, she's the love of his life—but then they begin their plunge, and now it really is time to eat your goiter, ladies and gents, because even if they fall precisely straight down, whatever springs were in those ridiculous triumvirate tramps are shot for sure. But...wait! In the commencement of their fall, the three stop, hold, and float, and the crowd has forgotten how even to scream. Captured, the acrobats jounce up and down on consecrated air as if standing on an atmosphere of jelly. The audience stares at the hovering figures, amazed, stunned; these are not performers, they are yogis, mystics, wizards, holy people; they have mastered air, they have tamed gravity. But wait—the other four acrobats are swinging in higher arcs, and higher, they release their batons and hurtle upward to join their comrades. Seven of them, standing on nothing at all...and then the silence is shattered as the crowd sees, in uproarious unison, the seven spider-silk tightropes stretched across the tent, and they roar their weak-kneed approval.

At this moment, the poles from which the clowns are suspended detach from their fixtures, and the fools swing one-handed, tossing their now-detached silver poles to the men and women on the tightrope. At the apex of their swing, each clown releases, double-somersaults, lands on one of the platforms, and bows, as below everyone hoots and brays at their fabulous funambulism. They descend down-ladder as the tumblers begin the tightrope routine—not *walking* the tightrope, you understand, but using their poles to *vault*, hopscotching from wire to wire, somersaulting hodgepodge past one another in catastrophic hurdle, sometimes jousting with one another, twisting just before collision.

The crowd rises to its feet and commences stamping, which throws off the pattern of the bleachers' sway—the pattern Gordy has, unconsciously, learned to ride. Without warning it whips, sharp as a roller coaster, to the left. For Gordy—staring with wonder between splayed fingers, himself rising to his feet—this is enough to disrupt his equilibrium, topple him; he overcompensates, pinwheels his arms, screams, tilts, falls. No one sees him go; none takes note of a boy disappearing between bleachers and canvas backing. Gordy hardly notices it himself, so caught up is he in a frisson of sympathetic tension for the plight of the tightrope vaulters, so convinced a deadly fall is eminent for them, that when he finds himself falling, surprise barely registers. It seems axiomatic; if they are to so boldly defy physical laws, then some other must pay gravity's price. *This is it* he thinks, and, even as he thinks it, he hits.

Gordy lies on his back, listening to the crowd and contemplating the sensation of death. Happily, he has serenity; there is little pain. It feels like nothing more than having the breath knocked out of you. He worries briefly about his poor father. Poor fellow. The roistering above continues, and Gordy thinks of his fellow circus-goers warmly, with parental goodwill, with quick sympathy toward the common living—poor deluded children! So quickly enraptured by the crumb-bummery of tumblers, the cheap and silly vicarious thrills gravity offers to the earthbound. To have *fallen*, to have plunged into the unknown, to have transcended, ah!—therein lies the true daredevilry… all these thoughts pass through his mind in a matter of seconds before he realizes, with distinct embarrassment, he has fallen no farther than a few feet.

Looking around, he finds himself on a short platform of sturdy plywood, and he sees he has not died after all—though his position is not unprecarious. The platform upon which he lies is only a few feet wide, bolted by flanges to the vertical iron poles providing the bleachers their dubious support. Liplike, the platform extends all along the back expanse of the risers. Perhaps it has been placed here by management, a stopgap against legal risk, a sop to the mortal and litigative dangers brought on by the grandstand's decrepit state. Perhaps its intended function is merely to draw tight the canvas festoons backing the grandstand, lending them a pleasing aesthetic, a sense of depth. It has saved him either way.

The crowd roars, overjoyed by some topside marvel, and Gordy considers climbing back up, reclaiming his swaying seat. He need only pull himself back up to take in the spectacle once more, but—wait—here is a novelty even more entrancing. From here, he can see the bleachers from the *inside*. He looks about, taking in his new subterranean vista: a steep cave-wall comprised of inverted terraced boards falls out from his position, the inside of a mountain seen from the peak. Between the slats he can see feet, shoes, pant legs, and between the gaps, tawny hints of fur. The trapeze act has finished, then. This must be a lion tamer—one not to be missed, if the quality of the acrobatics is predictive of the quality of ensuing acts.

The crowd roars. Come see the see! it cajoles. You won't *believe* what they're doing now! They've, why goodgolly, they've, they've, they've got tigers waltzing with chimpanzees out here! But the singular entrancement of cave-life beckons. From this vantage, the iron framework looks like ribbing. Easy to imagine a whale has swallowed you, or you've been inserted somehow within a dirigible. Rather than climb back into light, Gordy clambers down into the girders, climbing dexterously in the gloom. Tricky business; these poles are spaced wider than monkey bars, and the whole thing shakes like a topmast in a typhoon. Gordy forces himself not to imagine a collapse as he keeps descending, because now he is inside, invisible, deep in the secret place, and once he reaches the sawdust ground he can walk anywhere he pleases along his own exclusive boardwalk, peer between the toes of the privileged kids in the first row. He'll have to scamper across the aisles between the various sets of risers, but there isn't a seat in the house that can't be his, from one end of the backstage curtain to the other, why he can even…

Gordy stops, thunderstruck, suspended halfway down the rigging, amazed by a fantastic idea—no, a *perfect* idea. He continues his descent, knowing what he must do. He has by accident discovered the backstage pass the rest of the children above would kill to get their grubby mitts on. Gordy doesn't hesitate when his feet touch sawdust, doesn't waste a second peering between Little Billy Frontrow's stained Converse All-Stars, because who needs the front row when you can sneak backstage, when you get to see the see that no one sees? Who wants to simply watch the magic when you can tickle the wizard behind the curtain? Gordy runs deaf to the stomp and yammer above, toward the tapestry dividing the show ahead from the show behind. Reaching it, he sees it extends past the bleachers, into the outer ring where the freak cages and vendors are; peeking out, Gordy can see it's been affixed by interlinking metal hooks and loops to the outermost canvas wall of the tent. Tightly attached, but…? Yes! Not so tight there isn't some slack. Enough to climb under? No, no good; there appears to be a metal bar threaded along the bottom, stabilizing the curtain and weighing it to the ground. Even if it could be lifted, it wouldn't be sly work—the entire curtain would move. Sneak in between curtain and tent wall, then? The hook-and-loops situations attaching tapestry to inner wall occur at distant intervals. It's certainly possible there's enough room for a kid to squeeze through, but this will mean leaving the cocoon of the bleachers… Gordy peaks out and sees the outer ring empty. Nobody there, only Wembly the caged gorilla sitting in parody of the thinker's repose. Knuckles dug into the cheek of his mournful face, Wembly turns the massive hillock of his head to follow the boy, who scampers from bleacher to wall, works his body halfway into the opening between tent and curtain, pauses in the gap, then disappears entirely.

What Gordy sees as soon as he gets his head and shoulders through the tightness of the tapestry is this: He is beneath another set of bleachers, albeit a much smaller set than those he's left behind. Still, this is unexpeced. Bleachers? To what purpose? Is somebody *watching* the backstage preparations? Or…and here Gordy thrills and flusters with revelation…is it possible, is it even *possible*, Gordy-Gord, we're dealing with a *circus within a circus* situation here? A smaller, even better circus for the few elect lucky enough, wise enough, or bold enough to find it? And why stop there? Might there be a tapestry providing a backing to this smaller circus, behind which, if you possess wisdom or luck or boldness in sufficient quantity, you might find still another circus nested, even more exclusive, even more refined…but itself backed by yet another curtain, whose veil (if you were truly boldwise or luckybold) you might pierce to find the final, most exclusive, best, most wondrous circus of them all? Or—or!—*maybe* it never stops. What if it's circuses *all the way down*…from the far side of the curtain, he hears the tumultuous stamping hooting braying oooh-ing aaaaah-ing of the crowd, the music from the loudspeakers, the never-ceasing pronouncements of Colonel Krane. The noise fills the tent entirely, makes it hard to prioritize thought, creates within Gordy a pulsing imperative urge to push forward, and, caught in this eagerness, effects within him a sort of selective blindness; Gordy pushes himself the rest of the way into the backstage area, failing to notice, as he darts up to the front of these back-curtain risers, the comparative sparseness of the legs and feet, or the fact those seated seem to be sitting placidly, without stomp or shuffle. These are not the legs of hooters, not the feet of stampers, they don't sit in the posture of oooooh or aaaaah. He peeks between two of these curiously lethargic legs, and sees something hard to explain.

The room described by the tapestry's partition of the tent is thin and long. The floor is grass, not sawdust. On the far end is a cage, filled not with circus preparations, but with a crowd of people, dozens, some weeping, some hostile and glaring, some leaning on the bars. A few are sitting. But all have, to some degree, deportments of resignation, save one: A young man, tall and strong, shakes the bars. He's shouting but his words are lost in the adjacent howl of spectacle and crowd. The cage has a door, closed, and at either side of the door the tiny Andrews now stand guard—and there are others, too, standing at attention, not small, but similarly resplendent in red from foot to mask, black scabbards affixed to their backs. Nearer, a man, face uncovered, stands upon a short, raised dais constructed of fresh planks. He is short, muscular, and compact, with close-cropped hair and large eyes that rarely blink. The eyes, coupled with a habit of turning his head to look behind him, give him an owl's deceptive absurdity, a bookish appearance masking a ruthless predator. Beside the man is an ancient-looking barrel. The man holds a steel ladle in one hand; in the other is a parchment, upon which Gordy sees the image of a bird in flight. Lined up along the tapestry wall, the clowns and acrobats and other circus folk grimly observe, while others prepare themselves to go onstage. Closer still, off to the side, there is an opening in the tent wall, a flap cut out of the white-and-blue striping and pinned back, through which can be seen a slice of open night. But all this is seen after. What Gordy first sees, beside the stage, dominating it, is the white thorn. The stone finger. A fountain endlessly passing doleful water from basin to figures to basin to figures. The turtle is facing him, stone eye upon him. There is a shock, a growing sensation, common to his dreams: the desire to be gone from here forever, to pass away from this place and then eject the sight of it eternally from his consciousness—and yet, unfathomably, in revolt against his own desire and need, he lingers.

The man on the dais dips the ladle into the barrel. The Andrews, taking this act as a signal, open the cage and chivvy out a prisoner from the herd. A kid, not much older than Gordy. He's holding a blue ticket that's been hastily colored with a green magic-marker, and is waving it at them, apparently trying to pass his counterfeit into general circulation, but they compel him with their blades and lead him to the dais. The man with the ladle is not tall, but he stands straight as a pin, his face not stern but ceremonially grave. Despite the crowd's roar from the circus side, there is a hush about this moment, something darkly holy. The man is proclaiming now to the boy, reading from the parchment, presenting the ladle to him in calm but inescapable imperative. The boy shakes his head but the threat of steel overcomes his fear; he drinks, and falls, his collapse lent silent observance and approbation by the grim-faced circus folk, and by masked men in red standing beside the dais. After they pull the boy glass-eyed from the sawdust they lead him directly toward Gordy and settle him somewhere in the bleachers above. And now they are peeling another from the cage, a woman in a flower-print dress and a church hat, who is scuttled forward in scared demure steps. He watches the woman drink, then a young girl, then a tall rangy guy. Each falls, and is led, expressionless, to a seat in the bleachers, somewhere above the place where he watches, hidden. Next it's time for the angry man, who's been shouting all this time at the man by the barrel, desecrating the spirit of the liturgy. At a signal from one of the Andrews, six more ceremonial guards glide from their places and grapple him, bring him, still struggling, to the man by the barrel, who sets down his parchment and selects another, which has upon it the image of a spade.

A group of red-clad guards are rolling out a silver box on wheels. Gordy feels something, a pressure, something atmospheric. Scanning the room, he sees something new, and dies. Frozen with shock and more, Gordy emits a yelp that is mercifully subsumed by the same racket that has swallowed everything else.

One of the acrobats standing along the tapestry has settled eyes on him, piercing him through the slats of the bleachers with her naked observance. There can be no question that she sees him; she is the closest to him of the performers standing along the tapestry, and she is glaring right into his soul. The jig is up, the alarm is about to be given, it's all over, and yet the shock of this is not why Gordy has died. It's *her*; the center acrobat, the most heartbreakingly beautiful woman he has ever seen in his life. Her eyes two almonds. Her hair, dark, shot with gold, thick as molasses, a better place to hide than any maze. He has fallen into her, or has been drawn in, or has been invited. *Are* those eyes inviting him? They seem to be attempting some form of communication. Confoundingly, she hasn't raised the alarm. She glares with intent: first at him, and then away. At him, then away.

Squinting, he tries to decipher this code. At, away. At, away. It's a familiar expression, one he's sure he's seen before. In a movie, perhaps? Gordy smiles, awkward. Is she playing a game, does she want him to—could it be?—*meet her somewhere?* A clandestine assignation? Canoodling in the grass in the glow of the circus…oh, well, shucks, ma'am, I'm only fifteen, but, yeah, some people tell me I look old for my age, I guess…What? Laser tag? Yeah, I guess I've been known to play a little laser tag…

She rolls her eyes, and then redoubles her attempts. It's amazing, but she can make her eyes practically prehensile; she glares at him, with a force that leaves no doubts regarding her target, and then, just as forcefully, away, toward the tent flap, the exit, the scrap of night air.

He recognizes the gesture now: *Get out of here, idiot.*

This breaks the spell. The insanity of his situation leans its full weight upon him—he's been standing here, watching…*this*, risking capture and sub-jugation to whatever grotesque ceremony this is. They've slid a shelf out from the side of the silver box now, revealing some sort of cavity filled with tubes and other scandalous inner workings, and the acolytes are forcing the young man into it. Propelled by sudden awareness, Gordy nevertheless pulls him-self away from his life's love with regret. *I'll find you again*, he thinks, *somewhere, somehow.* It strikes him as a fine thing for a young man who has been killed by the love of a beautiful woman to think. This goddess and he—between them they have exchanged no words, but he knows they've exchanged something far deeper: a connection, an understanding, hidden depths leading to even deeper hidden depths of mutual knowledge. *I'll find you*, he thinks, and knows with a smitten boy's assurance she is thinking it, too.

Gordy sneaks to the far end of the risers. There are perhaps a dozen feet separating the termination of his hiding spot from the opening in the tent. He might make it out unseen. Certainly, between fountain and box and barrel and struggle, this will not be the most closely observed dozen feet in the tent. Then again…he looks back to the tapestry from which he came. Perhaps the wiser escape would be through the curtain within, not the cur-tain without. The real trouble would be getting caught here, in this room, not being caught out there. A kid wandering around out there, on the circus side, there's no reason to suspect he possesses newfound dark knowledge of evil secrets. If he can go out the way he came, he should be able to leave by the front door. Also, this will give him one final glimpse of his new true (as-yet-nameless) love. This settles matters; Gordy is about to enact this plan when the chance of it is stripped from him.

At the below-bleacher abutment of tapestry and tent, from which Gordy himself arrived, a red-masked head peeks. Gordy sees the head, sees the eyes go from boredom to shock. The head disappears, and then a sword is cutting the hook from the ring, making an opening through which a larger man might pass.

Gordy darts out across the open ground toward the gap, covering the dozen feet in what feels like a single step, passing out into the cool of night. Behind him, he hears the sudden disturbance, a shrill outcry cutting through the pounding pandemonium of the circus: He's been made. Here the circumferential edge of the grass is blocked by buildings; the drab backsides of establishments press against each other, wall-to-wall, forming a sort of stockade. Gordy desperately runs along them, looking for a gap between, a low fence, an open door, anything. He sees the first of his pursuers—one of the Andrews—erupt from the tent as he finds an open alley.

He hasn't even cleared the alleyway before he feels a hand on the scruff of his neck.

Things happen quickly after that. There are long missing gaps of time where the terror is too complete to even think.

× × ×

Now there are threats and pain, until he tells them where to find Dad. It doesn't take long.

Now, Dad's brought in, and even beneath the blindfold he looks scared.

Now, they're being taken back *there*—to the fountain. Worse, they're led down stone stairs to a huge room beneath it.

Now Dad's on the ground; he's been knocked on the head and is making small noises.

Now a short man comes down the stairs. Not tiny like the dread Andrews, but short. Gordy recognizes him; the man with the ladle, the man who stood on the platform, the man with the bird and the spade. He's no longer in the ceremonial robes; he's wearing a plain light blue shirt and jeans. He's got short cropped hair and the corded muscles of an older man used to hard labor, but his face doesn't look old, rather it is unremarkable in aspect, save for those steady, protuberant, measuring eyes, and that habit of looking frequently over-shoulder. The short man has Dad's papers and a couple of his research books—one black, one red—and he looks through them for a while and then he kicks Dad around for a while.

Now they are on a ledge, and below is a cavern holding what Gordy takes to be a library; one wall of it is comprised of enormous steel card-file drawers. Then a forklift is pulling two file boxes from the wall, one from low and one from high, and as the boxes draw near, Gordy recognizes them as identical to the boxes from the ceremony. They're brought by an elevator up to the ledge. As attendants wheel them over, the short man reads their fate to them from the parchment bearing the image of the spade. His face betrays no emotion while he does it, and his eyes do not blink. He's as unreachable and beatific as a saint on a stained-glass window.

Then come tubes, and connections, and syringes, and then nothing for a while.

D O O R

The fountain drove Isaac mad, in the end. It ate his life.

By the time he died, he'd dug out everything behind the door. You could see the shape of the space the door would open up on, if ever it was to open: a short hall leading into a room about ten feet square. Love removed the clay from around that room on all four sides, and he cleared it from the floor as well. In my day you could walk around the whole thing—a cube with a panhandle extending from it, and a door at the end of the panhandle. You couldn't dig under; the walls merged into the floor, which was made of the same stuff, a single piece with cube and hall. After several yards, the floor sloped quickly downward. By the time I was captured, Morris had dug stories deep down along the slope to make room for oubliettes. Not so much a cliff as an incline, a steep hill of smooth impervious gray stone. Down there at the bottom, you could see it pushing up like the Hoover Dam, and up at the top, if you made the long walk up there—way, way up, higher than the uppermost shelf of the oubliettes—you'd find Isaac Love's door and cube and panhandle, and beside them the stairs leading to the outside.

The door never did yield to Isaac. One day he collapsed beside it and never rose. They hauled him to his bed, where he lay for years before the breath finally stopped coming, but the lights never turned back on; old Isaac was gone. The family held to some traditions of the Assizement—bird and spade and fountain—but the door beneath passed to legend, part of the liturgy delivered from father to son, weakening generation by generation as the family fell into the ready ease of hereditary wealth. Happy enough to keep the Assizement going, happy enough to wear the secret name of Continuity, but doing it in increasingly desultory fashion. It seems likely to me that these descendants felt about the traditions of their forebears the way such folk usually feel—as if they've been tied their entire lives to some inexplicable medieval apparatus, something strangely shameful they're obliged to conceal beneath bulky clothing. And why wouldn't they want to loosen the straps, slough off the unwieldy contraption, leave it to rust in the field? It's tempting to view Pigeon Forge's transformation into a tourist stop as a passive-aggressive nose-thumbing, all the way up the family tree. If Pigeon Forge could have become something Isaac might have found more distasteful, I can't think of it.

But then came Morris, the distilled essence of the family vinegar. Anyone familiar with Isaac and Morris might even wonder if the old man had somehow passed through time to infect his distant heir. Morris hated what his father had allowed Pigeon Forge to become, as much as Isaac might have. It's probably the main reason Morris killed him. You'll think I'm indulging now in in in conjecture and calumny. No. Morris told me about it himself, down in the cavern—but that was much later.

Morris was never charged with his father's death. He was never even a suspect. There were no suspects. There was no corpus to habeas. The facts are: Morris's dad disappeared, and Morris returned from a self-imposed exile and installed himself almost before the missing person's report was filed. His father wasn't declared legally dead until the following year. Yes, Morris was the first of the line since Isaac to install himself as Continuity.

On the day Morris returned to claim his birthright, he visited Isaac's cavern. For the first time in almost two centuries, someone tried Isaac's door.

And, as with Isaac before him, it ate his mind.

✗ ✗ ✗

His father lies on the oak floor of an upper library in the sprawling Love family estate, breathing a slow, drugged rhythm. Morris stands nearby, quite calm in a tailored gray suit, a crisp white shirt open at the collar, holding a steel syringe with a depressed plunger. He opens his jacket, revealing three specially designed pockets holding syringes still full, and stows the empty one in a fourth. Spares his father a cursory glance, produces a cigarette, lights it. The smoke billows from his mouth, and, in the dim, it curls around his head like an obscuring wreath. At the designated moment two of his people appear, dressed as instructed in the ceremonial red. With his head Morris indicates his father, and they take him away to his waiting box.

Now two others appear—the specialists. The compulsive necessities of their jobs preclude the ceremonial red; they are dressed in fiberless and unabrasive body stockings and masks—ghost suits. It will be their job to dress the rooms meticulously for any potential detectives. They eye his cigarette, which will make their jobs more difficult, but they know better than to complain. They carry cases of obscure tools: tubes, brushes, ultraviolet lights, three different sizes of vacuum cleaner. Various tiny blades and blowers to scatter the correct atomy of human detritus in the expected places. Ingenious adhesive strips to leave behind the trace of the corner of one thumbprint, but not enough to go on. If there are any inspectors, they'll look for it and find it, if they're skilled, and then Morris will manipulate whatever expectations arise. If they're unskilled, they will find none of this, and so much the better.

Howsoever they search for Father, Morris thinks, they'll never find him. The poor fellow, he never even found himself. The lost fool, before you put him down, he even asked you if you think you're Isaac. Such slow questions. I'm *me*. Isaac's only virtue was that he suspected he *might* be me. I am the peak. I am the wellspring of matter and history. I am the consciousness. *The* consciousness. Behind that door is the consciousness, the control I deserve. Isaac failed. I will succeed. Then, as you drew your syringe, Father raised his hands weakly to ward it off, began to babble: There'll be an investigation. You'll be caught. It's not like the old days, Morris. People can't just disappear anymore. Lives have value these days. You can't do this.

He'd even believed it, maybe—that you couldn't do it. In any event, he looked surprised when you did do it.

What toff. Had your father really believed what he'd said? *You can't just make people disappear, Morris. There'll be investigations. Lives have value.* Lives have value? Yes. Every life has a label attached to it, and on that label a number is written, value in hard currency. But the appraisal of some lives—many—is in arrears. Men wander the streets without prospect, hungry, agitated, violent, unprofitable, wrapped in filthy rags, holding signs on street corners. Women and children abandoned by those men to desperate lives, crawling with lice and disease. These lives have value? They do—a negative value. A drain. They diminish the value of property. They make people of value feel unsafe. You increase their worth by removing them to a more suitable place, where they might again be made profitable; otherwise you remove them entirely. The bird or the spade isn't our way alone; it's the way of the world. And he worried the authorities might catch on? Catch *on*? They need us. Even better, they want us—they've *hired* us. It's the most perfect industry yet devised, prisons. We present a solution to the problem of unwanted people. Even if everyone of value became aware of all we do, they'd allow us. First they'd sputter outrage, yes. They'd write letters, publish tasteful opinion pieces, and then, having with an emptiness of words expunged their moral discomfort, they'd proceed to forget about us, because the truth is this: The problem of unwanted people is still a problem, and we are a solution that causes them no pain.

His car is parked in the courtyard's large circular driveway, but Morris decides on a whim to walk to town. Some events are too momentous to approach quickly. He makes his way on foot down to what now must be thought of as the Pigeon Forge "strip." Disgusting. A circus is in town; the posters plastered along the fence of a construction project. In the distance he can see the blue and white stripes of a circus tent. They're building a "Comedy Barn" here, whatever that might be. To how many projects has his family's corporation committed itself under his father's leadership, how many partnerships have been taken on, how many severed fiduciary arteries are there to tie off? His people showed him a brief, but he was too offended at the time to take it all in. A tourist trap. It's the gaudiest form of apostasy imaginable. Now is the dim before sunrise, and the tourists are tucked away in their RVs and motels, but after sunrise they'll cluster in the circus tent, or walk the strip, or wander the newly formed amusement park at the far end.

Presently he arrives at the place where the street bows out in a wide swing, where the buildings cluster beside each other, two-story edifices heightened by false fronts. He takes one of the hidden pathways, and there it is, the sequestered fountain, white and untainted and perfect. He takes his time looking at it, appreciating it, and then walks to the place, nearly perfectly square, where the uniformity of the middle concentric black stone ring opens into the cavern. Unless you knew to look, the opening would not be apparent in gentle dawn light. There they are; the granite steps, leading down beneath the fountain. Here he pauses. This is the culmination long dreamed of. It is better to go slowly, experience the moment, take ownership of it. To gather himself he takes a cigarette before starting, tries to make himself aloof. He dares to hope it will open for him at once, but does not dare to let himself know he dares. It may take some time, he tells himself. This is natural. If you are not yet perfect, you will make yourself perfect, and then it will open.

He descends. The door is there. So small, so ordinary. Nothing ancient about it. The caverns are there, dug out around it on either side and above, carved far back by his failed ancestor. So strange to be in the presence of things believed in but heretofore unseen. He allows himself another cigarette while he contemplates this. When it's gone he throws the butt to the floor and puts his hand on the knob. He pauses, breathes deeply, then attempts to open it, and the world becomes gray and indistinct, slowly at first and then all at once he

When Morris comes to himself again, he is on the hard clay floor. His head feels as though it has been stuffed with soft packing for transshipment and his mouth feels raw. He rises to his hands and knees, aware of the damage he has done to his clothing. The flashlight is still on. He retrieves it, then looks around; the door remains closed. Nothing else has changed. Nothing has changed. There is a sharp pain in his neck, as if he's been recently stung by a hornet. Nothing has changed.

Nothing has changed.

The thing behind him is still behind him.

He looks over-shoulder for a long time at the thing behind him, but nothing has changed, so this means nothing has changed.

Here is the flashlight, and the batteries are still powering it and nothing has changed. Here are the stairs leading up into open air, and that is the same as well, and nothing has changed. Everything is fine, and everything is fine, and everything is fine and nothing has changed. He still has all his memories, he knows who he is and why he is here and what it is he intends to do, and the thing behind him is still there behind him, and so nothing has changed. The thing to remember is that nothing has changed, and for this reason it logically follows that nothing has changed.

This fainting spell—that is what it was—was not caused by the door. There are so many other explanations. You haven't eaten since morning. You haven't mastered your nerves. You just slipped; this floor is slick clay. Leaping to his feet, Morris grasps the handle, as if daring it to send him into another fugue state. It doesn't do this, but neither does it open. The handle rattles but the door is locked. He walks down both excavated hallways on either side of the door, knocking at intervals on the seamless stone slab that separates him from his birthright.

The sun has carved its path across the sky when he once again emerges. The sun is there and nothing has changed and the thing behind him is still behind him. He has made himself calm again, aloof again—Had you truly been expecting success on the first attempt? No. In a way, immediate success would rob your inevitable triumph of greater meaning. One of the lessons of this world you've projected around yourself is this: The natural way of attainment is struggle. This is truth. It was true yesterday, and since yesterday nothing has changed. The days and weeks stretch ahead, a long project from which you will eventually extract your destiny. Your destiny is your own, and nothing has changed.

The thing behind him is still behind him.

Nothing has changed.

He's on the strip now, walking blind, making sure nothing has changed. In his pocket he finds a pack of cigarettes. He tries one, but they make him cough unbearably. At a nearby convenience store, he purchases some cheap cigars, and puffs as he walks, only allowing the smoke's flavors to reach his mouth, but the second one annoys his throat and he discards the rest. A cigar, perhaps, should be a sometimes thing, a weekly reward.

As he walks, he is drawn to the line of posters pasted to a fence, advertising the circus. The poster shows a beautiful woman flying on a trapeze, her dark hair shot with gold. A short round mustachioed man capers in the poster's corner. There is something about this woman. Morris decides he will attend the circus. Perhaps he will…it's a strange thought, but a compelling one…perhaps he'll even *buy* this circus. The woman on the poster is very beautiful. And a travelling circus might have uses…

Morris's face is changed in ways that have nothing to do with features. Perhaps it is possessed of some new quality, some even deeper certainty, some even more singular focus, but it is changed, changed. Somebody who knew him well would sense it instinctively. But there are few who know him well, and of that number there are none who do not fearfully revere him, so it will go unremarked, this change that has come over him.

V O I C E

With Morris, the main difference between the bird and the spade was whether or not you got the water. If you're a bird, then you drink and sink, to be reformed and reused. But if you're shown a spade, you're kept in there for good, and you go in with your memories. You have to live there in full knowledge of yourself.

Everybody gets the box.

The followers Morris recruited were a rough bunch, well suited to dirty work, mercenary warriors of varying disciplines. As soon as the oubliettes were ready, Morris showed them the sign of the bird, dosed them with fountain water, made them the first tenants. Caught there, immobile and blank-minded, surrounded by mirrors, confronted with no input other than images of themselves, they learned that only the self existed; raised back to life by Morris, they learned that even their selves were only manifestations of his far greater self. You met some of them, Father. Here in Loony Island they're known as the cardinals. So there you have birds again. There were a few birds down there, but most of us were lifers. You could tell by looking at the shelves. There was a little steel plate affixed with a serial number and an icon: bird or spade. They remained after Gordon transformed the shelves to doors. I never asked him why he kept them there. He could have removed them.

The birds have the better part of it. They know of no better world. Those of us who were put down there with no drink had to teach ourselves amnesia. To fully realize your situation and keep your sanity? Impossible. Folks can train their minds to forget—everybody does it. You forget things each day as a matter of convenience: the time of a dreaded appointment, an incriminating fact, your most embarrassing moment, the worst thing you ever did. Those things we don't want to look at, so we just don't see them. In the same way, you forget yourself completely if your whole self turns into something you can't bear to consider. No memory, no worries, no regrets, no pain, no priorities either or even fear. That's what the oubliettes do to you. They convert remembrance into pain, forcing amnesia as self-defense. All prisoners cultivate the ability to live without the pain of memory. Negate yourself to say say save yourself. But memory is always calling from beyond the prehistoric door.

And then, one day, one man answered the call. Broke free and bested Love's door.

That was my Gordon. That was my boy.

x x x

Time

is

odd.

Odder still is when it ceases to be time any more. Then you stop staring into your reflection and your reflection starts staring into you. Then comes the blend, my friend, my friend, the blend. Your only companion a close one. He hangs above you. He is watching you. Whatever he does, you must follow. Bewitching; you love him. You adore him. You'd kill him if it weren't for the straps. He'd kill you, but he's strapped, too. Lucky those bands are there, or he'd be on you, fingers on your throat. You wish he would kill you; you'd like to die.

And then, it occurs to you: You *have* died. This is it forever.

Right?

Things get bad, after that.

Why haven't you starved, dehydrated, asphyxiated? These questions bubble unbidden—your mind, untethered from your will, rattles where it wants. And where is the light coming from? It is emitted from somewhere behind your buddy overhead, he's backlit like a deranged angel. He's a maniac, look at him lying in his spaghetti of tubing. Lips pulled back from his teeth. Those eyes, they look like they've seen it all. Thank God he's strapped—he'd peel your head like a grape if he could. And he won't stop *staring* at you, like he thinks you're tasty. Closing your eyes; that's no help. He's still glaring, you know it. He's always staring right at you. You crack your lids—yes, as you suspected, there he is, licking his lips. His sense of anticipation is sick—he licks his lips when you do; the exact same instant.

You try not to blink. You breathe, and try to count the breaths between blinks, but your mind is greased, it's impossible to maintain the tally. Can't even reach ten...You start over again, and again, and again. Soon you are trying to count failed attempts alongside the breaths. Calculate the average number of breaths before failure. Futile. You'll never count past twenty. At some point, you realize you are counting in the ten thousands. Have you slept? If so, when?

It is becoming easier not to blink. The one above never closes his eyes.

There are moments—interminable flashes—when you realize that this figure upon whom you lavish all your devotion and hatred is only yourself reflected. You've learned to quell these flashes. The passive role is preferred; better to be the reflection than the reflector, and better still to not be at all, to float around in amniotic negation, unbeing, undesiring, for to be is to desire, and to desire in this state is to desire any state other than this. You are one. One is you. One is one, and one is all.

After some time, the figure above one becomes only what it is, neither good nor bad. It just is. Its screams and grimaces are mere diversions for one's atrophied desire. It is real. It is the only real thing. Obviously it's an illusion. It must be illusion; there must be something more than this. It hangs above one, the only universe one has ever known, the skeletal jitterbugging face. It is all there is, this visage that one observes.

There is nothing else.

Nothing.

Clearly there must be more.

Someone is calling a familiar name, soft and persistent.

This is unwelcome. It pulls from the knowable, negates comfortable nothing. If only it would stop, if only the soul petitioned by it would answer it! One's familiar, suspended above, is equally disconcerted; his eyes dash like caged things.

The soft voice calls forth visions of things terrible and familiar. A birthday party. A day at the beach, when Mom stepped on the sand castle, but then you built another. Tonka trucks, jigsaw puzzles, running through the trees, rows of low mobile homes. Flashing lights, turning circus wheels mirrors laserlights…a…a gorilla? Weren't *you* the gorilla? No, you fly on the trapeze with a beautiful woman, her dark hair shot through with gold, and you move wherever her eyes tell you to, but your parchment is a spade and you—

—but there is no *you*, there is only one, you are one, one is you, one is one and one is all

Someone is calling a familiar name, soft and persistent.

It is getting louder. No, no, it is soft. Yes, but louder. It is both. (There can be no both, there is only one.) But yes—both. The voice is soft, but not as soft as before. It is getting closer. And the name…that name…the face above is nearing the zenith of its agitation. One has never seen such fidgets and faces

—Gordy.

—Gordy.

—Gordy.

And now neither voice nor name can possibly be denied, and as one screams in reply, the face above—so dear, so known and hateful, the universe itself—slides away from one leaving in its place only distant blackness and traces of remembered light. One is cold, and begins to bleat at the empty sky like a newborn, and the thing is still calling the name—your name. Bawling, one struggles to sit, but the straps hold one fast. The voice calls out again, and then one's limbs are free, trammeling straps slide off and away, hooks unclasp.

—Gordy.

By and by, one thinks: Gordy. Your name is Gordy. *My* name is Gordy. You howl denial into the ink, extremities aflail, night-blind. You lie in a low shelf. Even though you are unstrapped, sitting presents a challenge. Back muscles wilted to paper. Hands on the rim, you try to pull up out of it, frustrated by tremble-arms and the dizzy betrayal of your inner ear. You wish you were stronger and then, then—oh! you can feel sinew knit, muscles tumesce like bicycle tires, you are stronger, thin still, but you rise from your tray with ease, somehow well again. As you gasp, you feel your lungs accept more air than they're accustomed; you had no idea how fallow they had grown. But other problems present themselves. The floor, for one thing. It is way down there—you're far too high to jump. And there are the tubes. Nasty, these tubes; they have taken residence uninvited in your secret places. Regardless, there is still a voice that will not be silenced, calling urging demanding your name.

—Gordy.

There's a pull, almost a suction, impelling you forward. You'll have to jump, and trust your luck. But when you stand, unconsciously sloughing bountiful tubing from all orifi, harness unbuckling and unhooking as if released by invisible hands, you step out from the tray and float, sinking like cottonseed to the ground, landing softly.

It's quiet here, and still.

You're not alone.

The cavern hall is long and high-roofed, and there are many beds like the one from which you've escaped. They're interred in the near wall, locked with Swiss precision into their vaults, with only one steel side visible. Floor to ceiling, and yours the sole open one; it juts like a lone tooth. A powerful shaft of light rises from it, cuts through the dark and illuminates a patch of the cave roof above, where sporadic pipes abide. In the floor, set at intervals in shallow declivities, dim lights are ensconced, providing sufficient illumination to see the slope leading upward, upward, upward.

And at the opposite end of the hall from the great slope, you see a shaft of warmer light pouring from an open door.

A woman stands beside it, beckoning frantically.

Obedient, you pad toward her, and she withdraws into the light before you reach her. Arriving, you see it's a small apartment room, incongruously normal considering its placement in this prison cavern. The woman is here; so is a girl. The similarity of features leaves no doubt regarding the nature of their relation. The mother stands beside a large antique writing desk, upon it a tablet with pen. The daughter rests on a sofa, an antimacassar dangling from a toe, reading a paperback. She holds the book one-handed, its spine bent backward, the cover hidden. They are both wistfully beautiful. The girl is swan-necked and spider-legged and reclines in easy contortion, motionless as a yogi, head tilted slightly, eyes devouring words, completely unconcerned by the intrusion of one such as yourself. But the woman…you look at the woman and die. Dark hair shot with gold. Intelligent fingers, watchful almond eyes, legs crossed at the ankle beneath the chair. It seems to you these two could reside in these positions indefinitely, as if they have achieved their perfected forms: They might be figures in a painting.

"You escaped." The woman says it as if stating a great impossibility.

"He's young," the daughter proclaims, assaying you with mild interest. "I thought he'd be old. Forty or something."

"He was even younger when they put him down. Not much older than the age then you are now. It was the circus that caught him." Closing the door, she says again: "You escaped. How?"

"Can I *help* you?" To your chagrin, this sounds brusque; you hadn't meant to, but everything is new, unexpected, even your body, even your name…

"I'm Jane," the woman says. "This is my daughter."

"Finch." The girl offers her hand.

"Gordy."

Her focus is on the book, yours is on the mother. You complete your half of the world's most perfunctory handshake.

"We're the caretakers down here."

"Caretakers?"

There is a thickness now in the air, clearly affecting only you. You're sinking into hyper-aware muck around this woman, fuddled, tongue-tied in her presence. She seems aware of this, and amused, though not unkindly so.

"Have a seat." She gestures to a chair. All her gestures seem economical ones, graceful, no more than is needed, and no less. You obey. Jane remains standing.

"You're putting us all in terrible danger," she says, and you wonder how you missed it before, the fear in her perfect eyes.

"I see."

"I don't know how you escaped, and I don't what to do with an escapee. I wouldn't put you back even if I knew how, which I don't. But…*he's* here. Right now. Out there."

"Huh?"

"Gordy, pay attention!" She claps her hands near your ears. "Morris is here, now! Watching that damned door of his. He's tranced by it, but we can't count on him staying tranced. He'll wake and see your box open. We have to figure out what to do. Hide you, sneak you out…something."

"Oh."

You feel trapped in the maze of her person, hypnotized. Entrancing. Lissome movements. She's your elder, and you feel the weight of this difference, the disparity in experience. You find yourself desperately unsure of what to do with your hands. Her gaze remains direct, benevolent but focused, but it's also familiar, and it augers into you, knowing you somehow. This is unpleasant and wonderful. The silence between them extends mercilessly and you know you're helpless to end it. Finch flips a page with a practiced thumb, a sound reverberating through this expectant silence as if tearing it.

"I remember you," you say, suddenly. It's true. You remember eyes looking right at you, you, crouched beneath the bleachers, at the…the circus…

Something terrible is rising in you.

"I remember you, too," Jane says. "You in particular. I even kept your things, all this time." She's gone to a drawer; rummaging, she procures a large plastic bag, sealed, which she opens. "There's not much, but I managed to hold onto it when they…after they…" for once she seems at a loss.

She's right; there's not much. A red-and-yellow T-shirt, folded. A pair of jeans. In the pocket of the shorts, a twinkle of green peeks . . .curious, you reach for it. Oh yes, that's right, it's that ticket, the one that oddball gave you at the…

Circus.

Something terrible is rising in you.

It occurs to you that you've grown.

You've grown up down here.

You've grown up *in there*.

The rage and hate are too much to bear

it is

        it's

I've

I've lost—

                        …years?

YEARS

my god I grew up in there how many

years

did those

bastards   oh those

Jane's saying something to you, but you don't hear it over your screams. Then comes something you do hear: someone calling a familiar name, soft and persistent.

—Gordy.

You leave.

"Gordy!"

You want to answer her, but you can't. The voice calls you; it is *in* you, and it compels, it almost propels—out of this apartment, ignoring her consternation, numb to her attempts to pull you back.

—Gordy.

The voice is coming from the top of the great slope. You head toward it, footflaps whispering echoes against the unseen roof. Considerations of personal circumstance—how, where, when—have not yet recurred; the devices by which questions are asked and answered appear to have atrophied with you. The voice demands you, so you fetch yourself to it; obedience is simple, and its simplicity alone is enough to make it the most acceptable course. Presently the massive wall of steel trays on your right side falls away as you climb the slope, and the walls draw gradually closer on either side. Reaching the top, you see a stairway to your left, leading up to pale light, which may be sunlight. Across from the stairway, a simple door and frame. Hallways are hewn into the clay wall on either side of the frame and space has been dug from above it. You cannot see how far back this excavation stretches—the sparse lighting of this place affords a view of mere feet before cave-blackness swallows it.

Turning from the door, you are startled: A man sits in lotus between you and the stairs. He is facing you, but his features are in shadow; motionless, he neither speaks nor acknowledges you. He may be sleeping, or entranced...or is he the one who has called you?

—Gordy.

No. The voice emanates from behind the door, not from the yogi. You set your hand upon the door's handle, and it opens easily. You step inside, drawing the door shut behind, and see before you a short hallway leading to a small room. You walk to the room and

You are in another place.

You are in the same place.

You remain aware of walls, close around, but they are indistinct and now there is more *here* here, an expanse too vast for this cave to hold. In truth, it seems too large to be contained at all. Within your small room, a shoreline stretches to infinity. From the shore a great sea spreads, calm as water in a basin, an ocean without termination. The sky is not seen, and so immense is the ocean, it is difficult to say it does not rise to become the sky, or indeed that the sky itself does not descend to become ocean or else live commingled with it, each confederated with and inseparable from the other. You are mute with wonder, but more wondrous still, the voice speaks—it rises from every atom of this great sea, and each atomy echoes all others in infinite harmonic thrum:

—You have come.

–Yes.

Your voice sounds small and utterly meaningless. You wish you had something significant to say. You are mercilessly aware of your nudity.

–Did…um. Did you *want* me to come?

—That is why I called.

–I was in the…

—Within your various confinements, yes.

–Why me?

—Why *not* you?

You consider the rows of trays. Hundreds of prisoners, at least.

–It could have been any of us?

—Perhaps you are the only one to answer.

–Who…who are you?

—You know already.

–But what is your…you know, your name?

A pause. Then:

—I yam what I yam. And that's all that I yam.

All about you and throughout you, pendulous in each molecule, a shimmering tension of amusement shivers, pauses, ceases.

–I don't understand.

—I am as you expect me. That will suffice. You remember those who imprisoned you.

–I don't remember anything.

—You remember them.

This sounds like a command. And yes, you do remember; memory rushes into you, shows you all you have lost and all that has been taken from you. Again, there is rage, and hate.

–I remember. Yes.

—Look at yourself.

You stagger to the edge of the sea. Approaching it is a vertiginous act, like approaching a mountain ledge on a windy day. You peer into the ocean—it is calm as a puddle—and see *him*. Him: your beloved despised familiar, your sole companion, your only confidant, your tormentor. You, yet not you; this face is older than yours, years older, a young man's face, but still a man's. You search its architecture, seeking the boy who once lived there.

Years. God, *years*.

You fall back from the merciless reflection, ill with loss.

—They are wicked, and led by a bent man. He kicks hard against the goads. If he does not turn from his path, he and all he calls his own will be destroyed.

You think, viciously—Yes. Destroyed, yes.

—Return to the prisoners and heal. Then deliver the warning of the coming destruction.

–Me?

—Yes.

–How?

—By doing it.

–But I don't know *how* to heal. They'll murder me. You've chosen the wrong guy.

—Separate the water from the sky.

–*What?*

—Tell the water to separate from the sky.

Afraid not to comply, you say:

–Let the water…ah, make it separate from the…sky?…

You feel awkward saying it. You feel false. But even as you speak, the sky lifts from water, water falls from sky in stentorian sheet-rain, all at once, and the placid sea becomes turbid; it roars the horizon's birth. You look, amazed and horrified, as the tidal wave your demarcation has wrought rushes toward you. Its shadow races ahead of it and falls heavy on you as the shoreline sucks itself miles inward, preparing the way for it. You brace for swift death—it will be here in seconds. You scream:

–Stop!

The wave halts in mid-break, hanging over you and the rest of this long shore like a gallows.

–Did *I* do that?

—The starting and the slowing. You share in its rage. It is a part of you, and you of it. But not you alone.

You look up at the hanging wave; water has replaced sky once more, but now they are not joined and the separation effects a great violence, held now in check. A weight greater than the world. Had it fallen upon you, it would have pressed you into a diamond. And, as you look at it, it seems to you it is still moving, not in a rush, but in increments. Yes, it is nearer now. Nearer by inches or feet or miles, it is impossible to tell. This place defies any definitions space might impose.

–It's still coming.

—Yes. It will not be stayed forever. When it arrives, he and all he calls his own will be destroyed. And now you must deliver the warning of it.

–I don't understand what this has to do with me.

—You were imprisoned, and have been released. What more do you require?

–I'm sorry…it's just that…

Impossible to articulate. The wave weighs above you.

—Back there, the waves and sky don't obey me. I'm not powerful. I'm nothing.

—You will have what you need.

—But how will I know?

All about you there is the sense of some great gathering.

—I will give you what you seem to require: something to look at and to hold. The power I would vest in you I will pour into it. Look in your hand.

You look at it; you'd forgotten you even held it. It glints green.

LUCKY 21
SEE WHAT YOU'VE WON

A thousand bucks. Didn't you once know the winning square? It doesn't really matter. The prize has changed.

—Use it. Clothe yourself in some uniform other than that of a prisoner.

You think of new clothes, and then you have them. Just like that. It's the damnedest thing.

—Remember what I have told you, and remember what you have seen. Tell them. The broken must be healed, the path must be walked back, or destruction will come.

Yes. Heal the fallen. And, after that, destruction. This is right and just. Horrid mirrors, hundreds of mirrored boxes, each holding a human soul staring at itself in amnesiac madness, degraded fully; each one stripped of one's self, or else one's self made hateful, or both. The fountain behind the curtain, the lines of people drinking, the theft of years. Yes. Destroy them. Finish them all. Heal the prisoners and then let the wicked drown in the coming wave. It is nearer now. Is it nearer?

—Deliver the message. Heal the broken.

—I will.

—Go without fear. I will not forsake.

The voice has finished. You hold the ticket in your hand, vibrant with a combusting madness of power. The door lies behind you. You open it and step back into the world. The door closes, and then you seal the great cavern from the outside world, and open the prison doors. *All* the prison doors.

A great screaming from the oubliettes begins, and as the prisoners break free shed tubing drag ruined limbs blind eyes distended bellies mewling toward you for healing and forgetfulness, their screaming grows, as does the hate blooming within you, large and large and larger, against men that perform such wonders upon their fellows, hate as encompassing as that monstrous wave, moving still slowly, still relentlessly, yet unbroken, always before your eyes.

B I R D

These were the Acts of Gordon Shirker, whose ticket gave him control over everything, everything.

These were the acts of Gordy-Gord, my only son.

He sealed off the great cavern holding the oubliettes and prisoners—sequestered us from harm, from recrimination from the topsiders who had done this to us.

He opened all the oubliettes, freed the prisoners. Made his rounds among them, healed their bodies, soothed their frantic minds.

He made a home for his people; converted Morris's prison cavern into an enormous vault—multiplied it in size, then doubled, redoubled, and redoubled it again; dankness made bright, starkness filled with fancies. He crafted new delights daily: An amusement center, a zen garden, a beach. A slight declivity in one wall might lead to an alcove holding a ski lodge, a mountain. This was Gordon's favorite trick: bigger inside than outside. The thrill of opening a refrigerator and discovering an entire grocery. He could hide space within space, could tuck away deeper surprises expanding out the farther in you went... and he turned each of our oubliettes, former homes of our torment, into apartments, crafted to our exact specification.

He instructed his people. He told us there was a great wave coming, an agent of divine justice, which would, when the time was right, arrive. He said the wave was always in his vision. He said it would destroy all of our enemies. He promised that on that day, safe at last, we would all rise to the surface.

He cared for his people, visited them, replenished their supplies. To answer the petitions of so many, he learned to create multiple selves, projections of his physical being each carrying the totality of his consciousness. He learned not to approach unless invited, realizing his presence was weighted with burdens of reverence and of dread, with the endless possibility of what he was able to do at a thought. Think of it: What if he were to become angry? What if he should *sneeze*? Would we all suddenly have lobster claws? Would we turn, even briefly, into a lungfish or a table lamp or a Waldorf salad? What if we awake one morning from uneasy dreams to find ourselves transformed in our beds into gigantic insects?

Yes, Gordon's people avoided him. All except for three.

The first was me, his own daddy. Here's the tragedy: I remembered Gordon, but he didn't remember me. So he claimed. He called no man pappy. Every once in a while, I'd press him. He didn't like that. It about killed me. Your boy sitting right there in front of you, and no acknowledgment, none. Still I'd keep close, and hope.

The second was Morris. I didn't recognize him for who he was. None of us did. He'd made himself seem like he was one of us. He made himself friendly as he plotted.

Morris's problem was simple: Gordon had the ticket, but he kept it hidden, close and secret. He showed it on the first day, at his welcoming party, when he told us all of the wave, and then never again. And how to get it? You couldn't very well mug *him*; he could turn you into sunshine and dust. Anyway for that you'd need to know where he had it hid—which Morris did not. But that ticket was all Morris wanted, all he thought about. It was the power he believed to be his birthright, loose in the world. Morris kept deadly patient over the months, waiting for opportunity, and showed his skill when opportunity finally presented itself.

He was using her, see. He was using that poor woman: Jane, the caretaker, his former…I still don't know what to call it. "Wife" sounds a little too wholesome, given Morris's methods—but whatever you'd say, she was down there, too, and Morris had her controls.

She was the third. Morris ordered her to summon Gordon, try to get him to fall in love with her—not like that was hard for her to do. I get the sense the boy started out besotted. I don't blame her for it, though. It's not like she had any choice, not with her little girl to think about.

From there, it all went sour fast. Fast enough I couldn't tell you the details of how it happened, though I was there.

One day came the final act of Gordon Shirker, whose ticket gave him control. The final act of Gordy-Gord, my son.

Without warning, he ran off. Abandoned us all.

I still don't know why.

x x x

Jane Sim holds Gordy as he nuzzles his head into her. They're in her apartment's one bedroom. She can hear Finch in the distance, rooting through the library like a merchant searching for fine pearls. She'll be there for hours, or maybe days. At Jane's request, Gordy made the library. A new door in her apartments, opening on a vast space, three-story shelves, accessible only by hydraulic lift. According to him, it's a room with all the books.

She'd asked: All *what* books?

The, he'd replied.

She'd asked him then: How does the ticket work? He'd brought it out, held it up. "I just say," Gordy told her. "And it does."

He looked at her writing desk. "Be lime Jell-O," he said.

The desk obeyed. It stopped being wood and brass. Instead, it became a single translucent tough-skinned blob of gelatin.

"And if you weren't holding it?" she'd wondered.

"Let's see," he replied, and set the ticket down on the blob. "Back to a desk again," he commanded it.

Nothing happened.

Once again, he took the ticket and issued the same command, and at once the desk returned to its previous form. "So there you go," Gordy said. Later it would occur to her how vulnerable he'd made himself to her; the trust he'd placed in her, in placing it within her reach, his commitment to what he thought of as their love. She could have taken it, betrayed him, claimed the power for her own, been the Delilah to his Samson.

And, more to the point, she *should* have. It's an agonizing thought. If she'd only done it, she wouldn't still have to trust him. But it's too late for that now, the situation is too dire to waste time on self-recriminations. The library keeps Finch away, gives Jane time to work on this boy-god in exactly the way Morris commanded, meanwhile planning this final betrayal of her master. There have been other betrayals, but those were all secret ones; from this one, there will be no cover to be found.

She has come to the moment of the leap. She is frightened, but not because she loves Gordy, for she does not, nor even because he believes he loves her. Over a dozen times he's said it, "I love you," almost a prayer. He says it each time he sees her. But she knows men and love; soon it will sound less like a prayer than a challenge, before it curdles at last into an accusation.

Jane doesn't try to pretend the lie of their love into being, but neither does she try to disentangle him from his hold on her body or his belief in his ardor. This has always been her skill: remaining herself without giving herself, allowing others to make their own inferences, to ensnare themselves within thickets of their own mythologies. Morris believes she is controlled, while this one in her arms believes she is loved. Jane allows them to deceive themselves. To disabuse them of their notions would be unproductive. Controlled? Morris doesn't dream she intends to betray him, or comprehend how she intends to do it. Loved? Love exists, she knows that now. But love is something you learn about another, not something another is expected to already know about you. This one thrusts his love at her presumptively, as though it has already been accepted. If love is blind, she thinks, then infatuation has no sense at all, save touch.

Touch is how Gordy experiences her. It's how he imagines he loves her— yet he lives so much in his mind; from what he says she guesses the "Gordy" with whom she interacts may not even be his true self, or at least not his only true self; he's able to be in many places at once. He can't explain how he does this, other than to invoke the ticket. It's as easy for him to have selves in two places as for her to touch opposing sides of her own head with two fingers. He claims an imperfect understanding of the mechanics of so much of what he does, and meticulously avoids the implications of identity, of which "him" is the real "him." For Gordy, whichever "him" receives the bulk of his attention is, for the time, the real him, while the others fade into transparency or flicker into invisibility or finally drift away, nonexistent, a no longer relevant aspect of himself. Sometimes she'll ask him which of the former prisoners all the other "hims" are helping, and he'll answer; Georgina, Russell, Florence.

She wonders—does he imagine you stop existing for him, whenever you stop being the subject of his attention, his attentiveness. his touch? Can she trust his infatuation? Will the hope of his rage bear her weight? But she's swung on less sturdy ropes than infatuation, and leapt from them over the void toward catches less certain than rage. She now knows she's been with the circus since long before she was ever with Morris. But all this is an empty space; something that she knows without knowing, something she read about herself as if it were about another. In memory, it still seems to her she was birthed whole into the world on the day of her "wedding" to Morris, fully formed and ready for his use. For years, her first memories had been of herself in bed. Awakened under the canopy. Enough breeze to push aside the gauzy white cloud of the valance, beyond which could be seen the deep rolling conifer green and the slow drizzle falling everywhere around. That had been the first awareness. No effort can pierce the mental gauze leading into the past. Eyes open to billowing white sheets, four-poster valanced, her lying beneath. The sheets her only covering, born naked before she knew of clothes, feeling the soft warm push blowing the sheets and valance and her cheek—the experience of wind before knowledge of wind. And when Morris came to her shortly thereafter, it was not just the first man she had seen, but the first time the concept of an other had occurred to her, and again it was the same curiosity, the same detachment, though different pushing.

Even in these first moments her mind was calm and crafting and omnivorous. "You're the only person I've seen drink and not panic and scream," he'd told her. He phrased it like a compliment, so she took it as such, at least externally. Internally, she tumbled it over and around, finding and cataloguing new meanings, new implications. There was a drink. She had drunk. Many others had drunk. This man had seen it. The others all had panicked. The others all had screamed. She had not. The difference impressed this man. Impressing this man was important. Calmness was important. All these answers led to different unanswered questions—What was the drink? Who were the others? Why would they scream? Who is this man?—but while these passageways lay as yet unilluminated, the mystery of darkness was of no concern to her, content as she was to stay there, watchful, in the small patch of illumination, already so much brighter and larger than it had been a moment before. She would sit, and be calm, and watch the lights as one after another they came stuttering back to life.

In this way she reconstructed the world. Her willingness to absorb made

Morris willing to tell her far more than he would have otherwise deemed prudent.

Until she discovered the wisdom of seeming less mechanical, even Morris had found her cold, so steeped was she in waterproof pragmatism, in the meticulous cataloguing of things, of experience. She would listen to him with care, the better to reflect his opinion of her back to him, but it was his power she responded to, only that—and why oppose it? Wiser by far to do as he desired her to do, to admit herself to be an appendage of his own singularity, rather than to argue a separate existence for herself, especially when such admission placed her on the highest shelf of his esteem. She was his greatest triumph, he had taken it upon himself to instruct her; and when he was upon her, she gave him his way, gave up to him all of the self he believed nonexistent. The dividends he paid for this fealty were a measure of his own power, a perquisite to his most preferred and honored trustee. The-figment-which-knew-itself-to-be-a-figment spent her days as she pleased, holding sway over his property; slave in his presence, steward in his absence. She opened the windows of the bedroom and sat and felt the air. She moved around the manor silent and watchful. The rooms of the house were filled with ancient books, which creaked when they opened. Some of these she read, replacing after a few pages those that failed to please her, devouring the others. Once in a deep cupboard she found three crates of cheaply made paperback books with lurid covers, a secret cache left behind, she imagined, by one of her antecedents, a previous wife of a previous master. These she devoured again and again. In time, she spent his long absences secretly writing her own versions of these stories into leather-bound blank-paged books. In these she and Morris would be cast and recast and recast, thrust into new scenarios, dropped into new locales. Here he was different than he was, and so was she, for in them she could draw points of comparison, by which she could construct at last a model of what she was from the mold of what she was not.

"Some days I would swear you were as real as me," Morris told her, one night. He nudged up against her like Gordy does now; she as always lay on her back, eyes seeking upward.

"I'm not," she replied, as she had learned to do. "You know it. I only seem real."

Their flat-roofed mansion lay on the mountainside, sequestered far back in the trees, miles from town. Stilts kept it level, with windows floor to ceiling overlooking an evergreen sea. These windows were mounted on swivels, allowing one hundred and eighty degrees of articulation. You could with the touch of a button open the room to the outside, sit and watch the rain runnel off the roof, feel the wet of the air, simultaneously experience indoors and outdoors. That night, to test her loyalty after the incident with the boy at the circus, he'd told her to leap out the open window, and she had been running to do it when he had called to stop her. Only when he had called out had she halted, inches from the lip, knowing she would not have hesitated before casting herself upon the mercy of the pointed tops of spruce trees yet a dozen feet below. This surprised her; that her heart still beat level in her chest. Her calm had pleased her and convinced him. He shook his head as she rejoined him under the valance.

"You would have done it. You would have jumped."

"Yes." *And may have caught a branch*, she thought but did not say. No net stretched below, but a leap is a leap, and a catch is a catch.

"Brave. If you had jumped, I don't know if I could have prevented you from falling."

"You would have." *You would not have*, she thought but did not say.

"It's hard to know. I can't be sure. I've never been able to transcend gravity. It should be such a simple thing. It annoys me more than you can know."

"You would have. We can try again." She rose then, made as if to try, but he caught her.

"No. But...you really would have done it. You weren't frightened at all."

"Why would I be?"

Then he had trusted her even more.

It had been the book she wrote that had made him suspicious, had made him put her to that test. The year before, she discovered, tucked in a bookshelf behind a muster of tomes, a black leather chapbook, handwritten: *A Family History of the Loves*. With each reading, her understanding grew. In her deepest secret places, an atomic kernel of anger sprouted infinitesimal red shoots, slowly unfurling, reaching for the sun. She purchased a new blank-paged book with a red cover, and began filling it with a new novel, a retelling of Morris's account of his own hereditary sins, telling it in a way that let the confession of them emerge, telling it as a wrong committed rather than an attained right.

Frightened, she determined to hide these books, both his and hers, at last secreting them behind a little-visited shelf in the historical section of the public library. Through long habit of obedience she tried to forget hiding it by turning the memory into a kernel, capturing the kernel in a kettle, filling the kettle with stones, sinking it in a lake, only—after the incident with the boy at the circus—to see the kettle come rising again, unbidden to the surface.

This is what makes enacting her plans so difficult and frightening: the habit of obedience. Not that she loves Gordy (for she doesn't) not that he claims to love her (immaterial), but out of simple foolish habit. It feels forbidden. This is the strength of Morris's sway: Gordy's power is total down here, yet despite her new boy's power almighty, the worn harness of long training still restrains. This betrayal tastes of danger, of fear. She is aware of her heart pounding. It hasn't happened yet. She hasn't done it yet. She is here with Gordy on *Morris's* instructions. They are lovers on *his* instructions. In her actions there is no betrayal yet to be found. But soon. She will do it soon. She will cast her master off with a movement so slight he won't be able to detect it.

I've never been able to transcend gravity. Unusual for him to admit weakness in himself. She finds it simple, after long practice, to put herself in his place, to see things in his peculiar way. She imagines Morris thinks birds and gravity are another way his mind teases him, or (more likely) presents him with yet another lesson, pulling him into some greater understanding of the "himself" he sees all around him. The birds show him how easy it is to break the natural laws he imposes upon his own form, how false those laws are, how arbitrary. And then Gordy did just that: stepped off his shelf high up the oubliette wall, floated down as light as an autumn leaf. Enter the door—*his* door. Claim the power—*his* power. Knowing Morris as she does, she understands the effort it's taking him to hide down here, to maintain the level of control he is exerting over himself. Inside, he must be chaos and rage and destruction.

Gordy nuzzles her, and she runs her fingers along the ridge of his back to placate him. It was at the circus she first saw him, just a boy hiding beneath the bleachers, peeking into things he ought not to. It had been a moment of clarity for her. Even if she had never seen him again, he would still have lived in her memory. The first moment—nothing but a movement of her eyes, warning this boy—a tiny rebellion, perfectly undetectable, perfectly deniable, but it became for her a fulcrum, a moment upon which she could stand as herself. The knowledge that, in such a moment, she would oppose Morris; that, if given the choice to free another, she would take it. She knew this before Finch was conceived, and this knowledge may have saved them both.

During those early days, there was still the circus. In the early years of their "marriage" Morris had sent her for training. No—not training, remember—*re*-training. Remember again—you were with the circus before Morris bought it, though you can't remember it. Before you read his history, and realized this truth, you imagined Morris had sent you to learn the trapeze, and had been amazed at your felicity—how easily you'd grasped it!—unaware you were merely relearning a skill you'd been made to forget. Plundered of your heirlooms, and the thief himself wrapped one of them up and gave it back to you as a gift

Morris loved watching her perform. She would attend the Assizement with him when fat old Colonel Krane and the circus rotated back on their slow wheel through the breadbasket, heavy with runaways and recruits. The circus was a treat for most of Pigeon Forge; those who had in the half-year previous performed satisfactorily against the metrics. After she'd performed for them, she'd slip behind the curtain to watch him deal with the circus's latest additions, and those deemed unworthy. For her alone the presence of the fountain, rather than increasing fear of it, served in her to quench it entirely: It came for them all eventually. Someday it will come again for you. Why concern yourself with it, then? Live from leap to leap, hold to hold, swing to swing. Fly in the meantime. Only reading his book somehow made it all real for her—it is the knowledge of the evil done against her that became her original sin; knowledge of wrong, for which every Adam throughout history has condemned every Eve.

After the Assizement, the circus would perform a second time, exclusively for him and his guard. He would applaud for her as she spun and twisted, leapt and caught. She can see now: She, too, was defeating gravity for him. To Morris, it was he, not her, who flew. She, like the birds, symbolized something to him, a lesson he passed from himself to himself.

What, then, had been the lesson he learned from himself at the sight of an infant *daughter*? During her gravid months he had been attentive, as close to obsequious as she had ever seen him. Morris was never happier than when a thing was fulfilling his concept of its purpose, and as her bundle grew within her, she perfectly fit her expected form. But upon birth the male line was rudely interrupted by a distaff adulteration: a girl. What had he been teaching himself about himself with this new bird?

But she knew. At least, she knew what he'd told her.

He summoned them and regarded her silently. He had been silent for a long time already. Weeks. She knew silence meant she ought to fear him, so she held her new baby and feared him. At last he said: "It means the end of Continuity," and smiled, and then she held the baby closer and feared him more. "I already knew it, but I didn't see it. Continuity is weakness. Isaac's edict was folly. There is no line and never has been. This is the revelation. I need no offspring to live forever. There is no eternal life in heritage; I'm eternal already. I stretch backward to Isaac and before; I must also stretch ahead. Your time is over. Come with me."

He'd brought her beneath the fountain then. She brought the baby, shielding it in her arms, terrified. Before, it had been her alone and she could still jump and catch and swing and fly; it had been easy to forestall dread by giving herself over entirely to fate. But now, incumbered by another, dread at last closed its damp jaws on her and she descended the granite steps weeping. Expecting him to present her with the bird, and for the child the spade, but he surprised her: He gave them each an empty card, blank and clear. A new thing. He exiled her, but he exiled her to sanctuary.

At his command the adjuncts excavated rooms, comfortable and small, out of the cavern wall. Carried the necessary materials down the stairs, rolled them from the landing (where the mysterious door waited) far down the incline, past the banks of oubliettes to the construction site. Hundreds of bags of concrete, yards of galvanized pipe, PVC, connectors, water heater, porcelain tile, wood studs, Sheetrock walls, assortments of glues and latex sealant and Teflon tapes, multitudes of screws and bolts and nuts and washers, furniture, sinks, appliances. One day an enormous sump pump was brought down with great care and interred behind the wall. She slept on a cot beside Finch's crib and marveled as they assembled this architectural oddity. Attendants came each week equipped with whatever supplies she'd requested the week before. Their instructions had been to refuse nothing save freedom—or anyway Jane had not, throughout the years, managed to find any other caveat. When the stillness oppressed her, she found they did not hesitate to bring toys and books for Finch, nor pen and paper for her to write.

Claustrophobia did not intrude, for the apartments opened onto the vast cavern. She'd run laps in the space, clay walls on one side, stainless-steel banks of oubliette drawers on the other, the placards stamped with serial numbers and icon whirring past: spade, spade, spade, bird, spade, spade, bird, spade. Once a month a delegation of trustees arrived dressed in formal garb and led them upstairs into the light. They stood guard as mother and daughter walked in the sun in the view of the fountain, the offense of it diminishing with familiarity but never dissipating entirely. Every six months, when the circus came heaving back to town, she was allowed a week to rehearse, a day to perform.

During the years she'd spent in their house Morris would disappear for days and weeks. Not until he forced her underground did she discover that the cavern was the place he spent these absences. He would appear in the cavern and sit down opposite the door. He never glanced her way, but even in her fright it amused her to think she saw more of him in her exile than she had during their habitation. She kept scarce when he was about, peeked from behind corners, lurked in shadow, considering it wise to remain out of sight, needing only to look at steel shelves rising up to see how unaccountably slight her punishment had been, and what capacity still existed for a worse one. Finch she would not even allow out of the apartments during his visitations; whenever Morris came for a long vigil, she locked their daughter inside. The key rode in Jane's pocket whenever her duties or her curiosity took her outside their sanctuary.

The child hadn't been "Finch" in the beginning. Years passed before the baby received her name. In those early days Jane vacillated between a ferocious protectiveness toward the baby and a marauding desire to harm her. She longed to dash the bawling thing to the ground even as she held it, to choke it even as it suckled, this bundle of squall and shit and piss that had come out of her own traitorous body to divest her of all she had built up for herself. Perhaps, she thought, this was Morris's test for her. And then, in thinking it, realized—of course it was. He won't do it for you. You may at any time climb out of this pit, but to climb, you will need empty arms.

And so her desire to destroy the child grew.

The thought was simultaneously unbearable and unbearably tempting; the fear of it would not leave her, nor would the desire for it. Sickening to imagine various tragedies, yet from her mind they leapt unbidden. Greatest of these was the thought Morris would repent his small charity and return to finish them. She knew she would try to kill him to prevent it, and would surely be destroyed in the process. The existence of her fear for another being she saw as some parasitic alien root that had captured her mind. To allow it to remain seemed intolerable. To uproot it would destroy her. Early months were spent on the floor of the new-built kitchen, feeling cool tile on cheek and temple, as the nausea of fear washed over her—terrified that she would rise and dash the child to pieces, disgusted with herself that she would not. Her freedom purchasable in any instant, yet when she would drag herself to the cradle where her baby lay, she would hold it and feed it, and wait for those Morris had appointed to provide them with supplies, and feel those tendrils snaked into her. The baby, as if guided by atavistic instinct, would reach up one fat hand and perch it, gentle as a songbird, upon her nose.

She had fought against this unnatural attachment, this clinging to a thing that was not her and could in no way bring her benefit. Years passed before the struggle subsided, before Jane found peace in it. The fearful root grew in her until it finally overtook, leaving behind something—someone—entirely new. The desire to purchase her freedom through Finch's murder faded, replaced by a new hatred, the desire to appease transformed slowly into a hunger for defiance; but even still, Jane kept patient. One day, playing with Finch's hair and inventing a story for them, the thought came *I too can grow slow roots, even in this soil...* and the girl, guided still by the same unerring gifts of entanglement, reached out her small hand and landed a finger upon her mother's nose. Jane, with only the slightest hesitation, returned the gesture: a shared thing now, meaning nothing but itself, meaning everything at once.

The girl never ceased terrifying her mother as she grew. She flitted, and chirped, and darted, she made herself impossible to catch as she explored the nooks of the dim cave, bounced on the bed, made her mother gasp by climbing the wall of vaults, using the indentions as holds for hands and feet, climbing high, always returning. At the far end of the hall from their rooms stood the door immovable, watched over always by silent deadlies dressed in scarlet. They never moved against Finch, no matter how close she came, but there was never any doubt she would not be allowed to test the door they guarded, and so the door naturally became the girl's obsession. Jane wearied of protesting ignorance of what lay behind, and of delivering admonishments to avoid it at all costs. Whatever it was, it belonged to Morris, and that lent it danger enough.

But then would come the occasions when the guards would depart, banished to their quarters. For weeks at a time Morris could be seen, perched above on the landing, facing the door, immobile as an anvil. Finch learned to detest the slight, raged at being forced into hiding. Tantrums came when reason failed.

"But why?"

"Never mind."

"Just for minute. Please." Finch could massage five extra syllables from "please."

"Not even for a second. Not ever. Do you hear me?"

Sullen, she didn't answer. But when Jane touched her nose, she reciprocated automatically.

She held the girl and rocked her until she passed into sleep. Later, outside the Sanctuary, she remained in the dimness, observing Morris for hours; an obelisk of a man, sitting naked and cross-legged, murmuring petitions at the ancient ancestral obsession. She counted her exhalations to ten, then took a step. In this way she closed the distance between them; crept close enough to hear him muttering, though the words remained indistinct. Every muscle strained, each breath precisely measured. For some reason, she was focused on the shadowy concavity where skull met neck, the entryway to the brainstem. A fascinating place, perfect for a sharp thin object, which would turn a man into nothing but meat on the ground. She had a sharp thin object in her hand—how strange. The letter opener had been on her desk, and she had without thinking put her hand to it as she left. Creeping forward, soft and slow. He had never needed to teach her stealth. She was near now, and nearer.

"There are times when I think it will never open, Janey."

Surely he heard her gasp, but if so he made no sign. He continued without turning, without pause or inflection. "There are even times when I stop believing it's *me* on the other side. You see? The *true* me, the real me, not this shell. More and more I think I'm going to die trapped in my shell. And then what will happen to all of you? When the light goes out, what happens to the shadows?" Jane backed away, slow and quiet. How he had sensed her she didn't know—was it even possible he was unaware of her, that he was simply speaking out to the air to which he ascribed her person? Even as she retreated, his measured voice came reaching out to her. "No blasting through. Whatever material those walls are made of confounds all explosives, every diamond-tipped drillbit, each hope and desire. No admittance, no admittance, no admittance, impenetrable as gray matter. No matter. None. I have learned the lesson. Matter is useless. Now I will open it with the best tool, the only tool. I will open it with my mind." He gestured to the great silver wall. "Then they can all come out, then I will call them all back to myself. I love them all as I love myself."

Jane, still retreating, not daring to look away from him, forcing herself into deliberate movements—for she was convinced if she ran he would rise and charge her—looked up at the oubliettes and for the first time allowed herself to understand the full terrible scope of them, row after row after row, drawer handles upon which Finch had terrified her, climbing monkey-nimble, each one of them at last representing more to her than a handhold;

they were no longer irrelevant, no longer ignorable, no longer a bad potential fate to avoid, but a bad actual fate already consummated. Each handle,
each file-drawer rectangular outline stacked up and up and up, each one had
at one time closed shut with a bureaucratic *snick* upon a human face; each
represented a Finch, a Jane, each placed there at a madman's whim, conve-
niently warehoused, catalogued and labeled, in anticipation of his time of
muchness, of fullness, of allness.

She thought: Why were we spared? How? For what? Up and up and up
and over, and running out of sight, the shelf doors. Each of them Finch and
Finch and Finch and Finch. So many of them, and nearly full. When would
the digging equipment come to add to their number? They were in there,
right now. Screaming even if those screams could not be heard. People who
had passed in front of her, on their way to be shown the sign of the spade,
six months before, twelve months, eighteen, twenty-four, thirty. *Thirty.* Thirty months. Thirty. They were in there. Hours, minutes, seconds. Thirty-six
months. Forty-two.

"Jane. Wait. Don't go."

But she had already stopped. Halted by the accumulation of months.
The horror of days. The insanity of seconds. Forty-eight months. Fifty-six.
Sixty.

Morris hid submerged in the shadows ahead, but his echoes chased her,
less measured, no longer without inflection, and now he sounded more like
a child.

"I'm afraid, Janey," he said.

The silver wall wheeling above her, pressing on her lungs stealing all her
air so many of them so many sixtysix how long have they been there seven-
tytwo how have they been there so long?

"I'm afraid I can't do it. It won't open. It won't. I'm afraid it's all lost."

She knew the words to reach him, and so she said: "You will do it. How
is it possible you won't? Then all these prisoners can become you, when they
see you are already them." From the formless dark came no hint of sound.
In her ears, only her own breathing. She spoke again: "But it isn't good for
them. They'll be insane when you're ready for them, if you don't let them
out."

"They are distractions. They are what prevents me."

"You'll want them whole when the day comes for them to return into you. Somebody should help them. Somebody who can afford distraction." And then she ran, certain he was on her heels. She locked the door behind her—futile gesture against one who certainly had the key—and collapsed onto the bed. Weeping bled into a long and troubled sleep. When she awoke, there was a note pushed under the door. The note was written in his hand. It read:

~ tend my sheep ~

After all this time, a further unfolding; his tragedy unfurled for her in three scrawled words. Her first realization of his perverse tenderness toward those treasonous bits of himself gone astray—but she delivered him no absolution for it, indistinguishable as it was from self-pity. Again and again she returned to her fulcrums: a movement of the eyes, a boy beneath the bleachers; a girl flitting about her cage, yet always returning to mother for rest, placing, for an instant, a solemn finger upon her familiar nose.

This was how she had become the caretaker.

Upon each captive Jane bestowed the most solemn care she could muster, gathering herself before cracking the seal, steeling herself against her great irrational fear: of cracking a crèche and seeing her own child entombed within. Even knowing her little bird was back in their room wasn't enough; the fear was never far off. Soon they all became Finch to her, each howling for a long-forgotten mother. Now, she longed to heal their shattered minds, repair muscles long gone waxy from lack of use. Teeth and hair fallen out. Eyes bulging from fluorescent staring. Memories wiped. All she could do was change their pajamas, sponge them down, and murmur to them not to worry, not to fret, mommy's here, dear, mommy's here...

"And from then on, you and Finch helped..." Gordy has awakened in a curious mood, and this time she indulges it; she wants his attention. Soon she will leap to him across the void.

"No. Just me." By no means would she have permitted Finch to see what she saw in those tombs of the living. The boxes were constructed for preservation: intravenous tubes serving up protein, calcium, an alphabet of vitamins; manacles, connected to servos, lifting the captives seven inches, bringing them face to face with their mirror-selves, and, while hoses spray the fetid crèche beneath, the manacles move slowly, forcing the limbs into nominal exercise. Every crèche she opened, she braced herself against that rare but dreadful occasion: an oubliette in which the life-sustaining mechanisms had malfunctioned—an air filtration unit fouled, hydration or protein-drip dried up, bath drain clogged—weeks ago, months ago. These she learned to swiftly close, to mark "X" in glowing tape, indicating the need for cleansing and disposal.

Tending to the higher shelves required a motorized scaffold. Making a complete circuit of the crèches was a matter of months, yet even in these infrequent visits she grew to recognize some of them. A man with a gold front tooth who never screamed, but only whimpered. An elderly lady, in a place where the elderly were rare. A boy with enormous ears. Signposts of familiarity amidst all the sameness, all headshaved and skeletal and gone. Had she known Gordy? Had she recognized her new hope of salvation on the day his oubliette opened of its own accord, when his shackles had dropped like grass rope, when he had floated from an upper shelf, walking his way down the air? She had. Naturally she'd recognized her boy beneath the bleachers; she'd watched him grow.

After he escaped, she'd followed him carefully as he left her apartment and climbed the great slope. Morris sat in his familiar posture at the top, facing his door. Her first thought had been to call out, but whether to warn Morris of the fugitive's silent approach, or to warn Gordy before he came upon Morris unaware, she could not say. But the words had caught, held by fear or instinct, and she watched mutely as he walked past Morris, opened the door as if it were any other door, and closed it, before Morris—his consciousness rising from deep meditation—could comprehend what had happened. He rushed forward, but the door was shut already, as unyielding to him as it had ever been.

She watched him. He would be dangerous now. He would be wild.

But he had been calm. He wasted no time in screaming or petition. There was a console set into the wall and he made for it at once, keyed an alarm to alert nearby trustees, identified the serial number imprinted on the open crèche, called up all the information associated with that number, and printed it out, stashed the printout in his pocket, then hid himself in ambush deep in one of the tunnels on the sides of the door.

No more than a few minutes had passed after the prisoner entered when he emerged again, still holding the ticket she'd given him, and then all the oubliettes had opened at once, all her imprisoned mandrakes began screaming out their orchestra of pain. She saw Morris emerge from the hole his ancestor had dug long ago. He had a long knife in his hand as he crept from behind toward the prisoner. The prisoner did not see him; there was distraction enough. Inmates floating down from the high places, crawling on the ground. Clutching their heads. Tearing at their eyes.

and

time began to stretch oddly for her, but whether the effect emanated from Gordy or simply resulted from so much simultaneous activity she could never afterward decide

and

Morris drew closer to his prey; soon the knife would do its work

and

all the newly freed prisoners bleated and screamed and brayed confused and betrayed like shorn sheep naked save for black singlets and the harness hooked at the shoulders elbows knees along the spine

and

the first of the guards to answer the alarm now arrived at a run bursting from the stairs brandishing a sword making immediately for Gordy and Gordy spoke and the trustee exploded into a profusion of white granules that collapsed and spread across the floor a miniature white dune marking the place where he had stood

and

Morris, seeing this, retreated at once into shadow

and

a woman, the nearest freed prisoner, crawled eyeless and weeping on the floor and

Gordy advanced, gazing down the great slope at the misery below and then he spoke and behind him the ceiling bled down to meet the floor, the floor rose up to meet the ceiling

and

she saw a new-freed man leaning against the wall dashing his head again and again into an open steel shelf door as if to silence some internal clamor

and

Morris clambered over the rising wall, rolling over it before it met the wall descending, the two merging with one another seamlessly, sequestering them from both the stairs leading upward and the door from which Gordy had so recently emerged

and

prisoners howling, Gordy making his way among them, passing from one to another, speaking to them each in turn, touching them, and they calmed like nursing babies. She made her way forward to help, but Morris was at her arm, pulling her to him. He had a terrible look in his eyes and his voice, too, was terrible and calm.

"Come. Now." he said, and pulled her toward her rooms, her sanctuary. He had in his hands the singlet and harness of an oubliette prisoner. Once there he shucked his clothes and put these on.

"Shave my head," he said. Fumbling in the bathroom for scissors and razor, she prayed Finch would not wake and disturb him. He had a tranquil aspect, but she knew him; he was holding back vast reservoirs of rage wanting nothing more than an apt target. Jane returned to him and began shaving him. What was he holding? Morris asked, in an earnest but detached tone. What was he holding? What was he holding? What was he holding? The tone never changed. I don't know, she answered. I don't know. In this way they passed the minutes as his hair hushed to the floor.

what was he holding what was he holding what

I don't know I don't know I don't

And even then hope was snaking through her heart. Gordy had exploded a trustee into a pile of salt. This was a new and disturbing chaos, but if she could find a catch at the end of this leap, she might—might she not?—perch her bird on her shoulder and swing them both to a safer place? When his head was shaved, Morris considered himself in the mirror.

"Well? Do I look like one of them?"

"No. It's good you're thin. But you're not malnourished." *And not destroyed,* she did not add. She had learned with chemist's precision how much honesty he required, and how much to withhold, to avoid adverse reaction.

"I'll have to claim recent imprisonment, then."

"You wouldn't know how long you'd been in."

He seemed ready to argue, then realized the truth of it. "They'll accept me anyway."

She said nothing; either they would or would not.

"Wait five minutes after I'm gone before coming out. Don't look at me, and don't come near me. Out there we don't know each other."

"Of course."

"But eyes and ears open. Learn what you can. Get close to *him.* As close as possible."

"I will."

He looked at her directly to ensure transmission of his meaning. "As close as *possible.*"

She understood. "Yes."

"I'll come to you when I can manage to do it secretly. Plan to have something interesting to tell me."

Then he was gone and she could let herself panic; gave her whole self to it for three minutes, screaming into pillows. Then she locked and barricaded Finch's door and let herself out of what had been her sanctuary. Braced herself for the cries of the freed, but Gordy had already ministered to them. In her short absence the cavern had already expanded into the impossible vastness of what Gordy would come to refer to as the vault, but it was not yet modified or partitioned; the entirety of it was visible in all its blasphemous immensity. An empty room the size of a city. From somewhere above lambency bloomed, not sunlight but something approximating it. Birds soared in the middle distance between. On her right hand lay the banks of oubliettes, now opened. This was before he grew them into dwellings; they still retained their original dimensions. Previously they had dominated the cavern, but for the moment they were dwarfed by the wall into which they were set, a postage stamp affixed to a ship's sail, a silver kite set against the sky.

She allowed herself to feel, for a final moment, a panic something like awe. The power to do such a thing...

holding what is he holding

i don't know no I don't, no

The freed prisoners stood in a huddle, blinking and empty, in depleted weary wonderment staring at one another and at their surroundings, but most of all at the young man standing in their midst. He was holding his hands up and speaking to them, but she was too far away to hear. By the time she reached them, a horrible, awkward welcoming party had begun. She scrawled her name upon a HELLO MY NAME IS sticker—he had used his power to materialize them—and joined it. As she drew near, she heard him speak to them all in a loud voice. This is when he told them all about God's revenge. This is when he told them about the coming wave.

x x x

Jane decides. No point in putting it off further. "I need to ask you something."

"Anything." God, he's burrowing up against her again, availing himself of some rather unchivalrous handfuls. He has his moments—he can make her laugh, certainly—but is there nothing else in the world for him but clutch-and-feel, rub-and-tug?

"A serious question."

"*Any*thing." Burrow. Squeeze.

"Stop. I want you listening."

He listens. "What is it?"

"Why are you waiting for the wave?"

"Pardon?"

"Destruction. Revenge. You could bring them. Why are you waiting on a wave?"

There's a silence. When he speaks again she can't read his tone, but he's withdrawn from her. "It's not me. I'm not the one waiting."

"You said you'd made this...wave. I still don't see how this is supposed to work."

"I don't know how it works, either."

"You said you'd made it."

"In a way. I was told to make it. I'm not in control of it."

"And until then we wait?"

"Yes. Until then we wait."

"Even if the person most responsible, who did…all this…to us…even if he were right here, right in front of you? Even then you'd wait?"

"But he's not here."

"But *if.*"

She sees his eyes go cold. "Well. I suppose then I would get started early."

She waits and waits and builds herself up to it. The biggest leap is the one where you're not sure of the catch. Finally, she shakes him awake again.

"What is it?"

"I have something more to tell you."

"Yes."

"The person who imprisoned all of us."

He snorts. "Yes. You told me. Finch's father. You told me all about him." She hears the stiffness in his voice. Baffling to think, with all the better reasons this man has to despise Morris, there still is the capacity for romantic jealousy.

"I never told you his name."

"OK."

"And I never told you the rest."

"I'm listening."

"He's down here with us. Posing as one of us."

And so, here it is, the leap. A long slow deadly silence uncoils around her. Desire for vengeance clouds its invisible way through the air.

"Who." His voice is changed, sharper; now he is fully awake.

"I think you know."

He says nothing for a time, then:

"Morris."

"Yes."

And then he is gone, vanished. She has sent him out to avenge a screaming of wrongs. She imagines him the arrow, herself the bow. She lies back and remembers an explosion of salt.

xxx

She waits for his return, imagining how it will be. What method Gordy will have devised to dispose of him, the pain of it, the suffering. But it isn't Gordy who comes to her, but Morris. With him are a host of trustees. His trustees. Who had, until now, been on the other side of an unbreakable seal.

She can only stare, fish-dumb: Gordy somehow failed her. Morris is still whole, still alive. Horror makes all sounds distant and indistinct. Morris doesn't give her a chance to speak. He takes her numb arm and compels her from her rooms. "That thieving little bastard has gone behind the door again," he says. "He's opened the seal to do it, so now we've got him." At that moment, Finch darts from the library, and Morris settles his appraising eyes upon her little bird. "Come on," he tells Jane. "Right now." Then, to the trustees: "Send somebody to hold onto this kid. I want everybody else outside the door waiting for him with guns."

They bring her out into the great vault to a waiting jeep. In the back seat is a skinny older guy with woeful eyes—Sterling, the prisoner who claimed to be Gordy's father. She never caught his name but she can read it on his shirt: HELLO MY NAME IS. He's holding a bloody towel over his nose. They regard each other, the two of them, baleful and wordless in their understanding of a defeat she senses they somehow share, as the jeep tears back up the slope toward the enormous gash that's been made in Gordy's protective seal. The trustees all take positions around the door, with Morris at their center, weapons trained upon it, waiting for the return of the errant prophet, prepared to deliver him immediately to destruction.

They fail.

xxx

After it's all over and gone to hell—Gordy escaped with ticket and all—they bring her back to her apartment and Finch is waiting, but gone. Morris is there. Jane knows it the moment she sees her daughter, he's already done it, delivered the forgetful ladle—or maybe he used one of his pocket-syringes.

When she sees the oubliette, she rushes forward to her little lost bird and it's as if she is leaving the suffering meat of herself behind. She touches the girl's nose, touches the girl's nose, touches the girl's nose, in desperation she touches it and touches it until they pull her away, but the girl only stares at her, confused by the gesture, emptied of the response.

x x x

The months pass.

x x x

She no longer thinks of Morris and Gordy by their names. Names aren't identities; she won't use them. The last replenishment of paper lies on the desk. It came from him, so she will not use it. Abandoner. She refuses to touch it; instead she writes on the walls. She writes the pen dry and then selects another. There are better pens, but they came from him; she doesn't touch them. The Captor brings her new pens, and, though she hates him too, these she uses. To not use them would be to not write.

This is what she writes, again and again and again:

I did not run away with the circus. The circus ran away with me.

The room is empty. She's destroyed all the furniture. Once she wrote stories on that same desk, for herself only: frivolous, licentious, important, aping the style of other writers into whose pages she'd escaped. Now all she can write is the one line:

I did not run away with the circus. The circus ran away with me.

She wants to publish the rest of herself in a crimson scrawl, so she will become real. But this is what she will write, confession and accusation and plea mingled in two spare sentences, eighteen syllables. They arrive one after the other, as similar, and as different, as traincars, as waves. The Abandoner spoke of a destroying wave. Was it ever even real?

I did not run away with the circus. The circus ran away with me.

Her bird is gone, she doesn't know where. She knows where, but she doesn't want to know, can't bring herself to know. She doesn't tend to the prisoners any more. She writes her phrase, because she can no longer bear to minister to them, prisoners in their refilled oubliettes, because her bird has flown, and she doesn't know where.

She writes her phrase.

She writes her phrase.

She writes her phrase.

In time she recalls the Captor has been standing behind her. She had come to awareness of him hours ago and ignored him so long she forgot him again. At last she turns to look at him. He's calm and still and dreadful. They wait for each other to speak, but in this at least she knows she will triumph. He clearly has something to say to her. She has nothing to say to him.

"I disguised myself for safety. Found our friend. Tracked him to the end of the line."

To this she says nothing.

"He's in Färland. Badly confused. It's time for you to do what I need you to do."

"Which is." After such long silence her voice sounds odd to her.

"He's become . . . difficult to find. Or, if not to find, to keep once found. It's hard to describe. I've gotten close to him, but I can't get close enough. You, though. I suspect you can get as close as you want."

"To do what?"

"Help me catch him. Take from the thief what belongs to me. And then you can go. Both you and your girl."

"Oh. Yes. Both of us. Whatever's left."

"I'll have the ticket by then. You've seen how it can restore. You'll be healed and freed."

She draws near to him, close enough to spit. She is aware of the uncontrollable movement of her face. Whispers: "I don't believe you."

"That's understandable. But really, you have no choice. Do you?"

She turns back to the wall. Soon she will agree, she knows, but before she does she'll make him wait. A beggar will wear whatever dignity she can even if it is nothing but a rag. For now she will wear her rag and make him ponder, and she will write.

I did not run away with the circus. The circus ran away with me.

W A V E

So where did the existence of the ticket leave Morris? Was he nothing but a scrap of this other man's will? He must have at least considered the possibility. Imagine what he must have thought when one of his own prisoners escaped the prison he'd designed, opened a door he'd failed to open, then came from beyond it displaying the absolute power Morris sought for himself.

Up to then Gordon had been like everybody else as far as he was concerned—beyond insignificant, nothing but another rebellious but quelled protuberance of his wayward psyche. The thought of another living being having a separate existence, unattached to himself? Inconceivable. None of us are people to him. We're not even objects. We're object *lessons*. We're something he's showing himself, to teach himself some deeper truth. But now, a figment of his imagination had stolen his birthright: A lottery ticket for control and mastery over the universe. And somebody else won it.

What lesson could he have possibly derived from *that*?

The door drew Gordon back a second time before he could exact revenge on Morris. I watched it happen. When he came out again, Gordon ran away. There's no other way to say it: He ran. And, per his usual, he brought his old man along, almost as an afterthought. This time, though, he didn't bring me the whole way. He deposited me somewhere else; here, in fact. I suppose he thought I'd be safer than I was with him. And, to be fair, you're safe in a booby hatch, sort of. Three squares and sedatives, a roof and a bed.

He birthed me from that place into this one. He birthed me in fire. You know the story, Father. I've heard you tell your own part in it; I was part of your miracle, the one you didn't really do. You and I arrived in Loony Island the same day.

That was the last day until today I ever saw my boy.

x x x

There is the paralysis of no options. And then there is the paralysis of all the options. What can you do to him? Why, anything, or even everything: Choose one option, see it through to completion, then spool back time itself—you've never dared try this before—and choose another. Though you didn't seek justice, the opportunity for justice lies now in your hands.

who?

you know already

morris

yes

Casting out your awareness you find him in his usual place, keeping vigil in your own apartment with Sterling. Your two constant companions; the one who pretended to be your adviser, the one who claims to be your father. Look at him—Morris. You draw all your shades and avatars back into yourself to give the matter your full attention. For the first time in months, there is only one you.

Morris notices you looking at him.

So, he says. You've figured it out. It took you long enough.

You give him no reply, only your loathing gaze.

And now you'll kill me, I suppose.

You approach, seething. Nose-to-nose. Without warning, he leans forward and kisses you full on each cheek.

You'll do nothing, he says. How could you? Can the web trap the spider?

Your hesitation isn't born of fear. You're afraid only that your imagination might prove unequal to the challenge. It must be a punishment worthy of a decade of hell, with compounded interest, multiplied on behalf of hundreds of others; the hells of mirrors and remembrance and confinement, minds made slippery from the pain of it, all of them screaming from their oubliettes, retreating even now from life. He is rounding on you now, whispering. You feel the remembrance of his disgusting kisses on your cheeks. He says you have no power. You will show him otherwise. You must phrase your intentions within your mind very precisely.

You turn his brain to ice.

You raise the temperature of his blood to boiling.

You metastasize a cluster of kitten-sized spiders behind his eyes.

You dissolve each of his cell walls, converting him into a puddle of pink slurry.

You fill his intestines with air until they burst shit throughout his abdomen.

You fill his lungs with water and he drowns in confusion.

You bury a pickaxe up to the handle in his skull.

You sever his head from his body.

You drop him from on high.

You run him through.

You think, die.

Die.

You do none of these things. It doesn't seem possible.

Every time you try you lose the train

the train of your thought stops

(no I won't do that wh

why would I do th

Defeated, you

quit.

Someone is calling your name, soft and familiar and persistent.

—Gordy. Gordy. Where are you?

You try to object, to protest, but this voice is in you and you are compelled—or, it is more apt to say, you are propelled—out of your apartment, through door, over balcony, carried like a recalcitrant child up the slope of the vault toward the great confining seal. It isn't that you're forced to; it's worse—you *want* to. You remain in control but the voice is calling you and you come. You don't intend to open the seal. You won't. But you do it joyfully. You open it larger than you intended. It's not even that you want to; you *need* to. You're barely aware of your movements until you pass through the door, where you find yourself still standing, fully present, upon the wild and waste of the endless beach and the wave stretching up without termination.

—Gordy.

–Here I am.

—What are you doing?

–What has to be done.

—You resist the task set to you.

–You asked me to heal. True healing needs justice.

A minute sound comes from everywhere at once, a susurration frustrated or else amused.

—Observe.

The entire wave—the entire ocean—rolls into an immense ball; it hovers before you in the void left behind, which is true void: not blankness, not inky sky, but antithetical spirit-quailing not-ness. The oceanic sphere shrinks to the size of a grapefruit and hangs inches before your eyes. Intricate patterns dance on its surface, and then it splits open and melts until it is a river encircling your head, flowing counter-clockwise.

Droplets leap from the rapids. Before rejoining the water from which they issue, they turn into bottle-nosed fish resembling dolphins. They cavort in the now-roiling water, and with each leap, the fish split like cells into halves and thirds, with each division becoming some new specie, with familiar morphology as if sprung from familiar genus and phylum, yet without holding to existing forms; they are new creations unto themselves, things never before seen or thought of. Land springs from water and soon there crawl new beasts whose physiologies accommodate to gravity and air and earth and you are in it and among it even as you watch it all around; you are individual and observer, creator and created, and you feel and know you are the activator here, this is being done through you, throughout your consciousness—not your power, but your contribution nonetheless, as things resembling baboons chase things resembling butterflies (whose shining wings are spun of the most delicate stained glass) through trees that resemble palms but for their pine-needles, you think *did I help bring this into being was it my hand too, seen in this...?*

And then, with a wrenching, it flows out of you and away, and the dooming wave has returned to its place before you, monstrous and beautiful in equal measures, promising the full weight of death, offering the entrancement of its impossible expanse. If you scan the line of the beach back to the curve of the sky you can get a sense of its scope; even where the beach has disappeared to a vanishing point it hovers, bulging the horizon; even at the point where it passes from sight it dwarfs the prospect of beach, ocean, all. You can't tell how fast it's moving. It may be here in an instant; it may not arrive in your lifetime.

—Now you have seen. Which do you choose?

–I…don't understand.

—Your task lies incomplete.

–You told me to heal. I healed.

—Look around you. You know better. Heal and warn. If you do not warn him, he and all he calls his own will be destroyed.

–Yes. Destroyed. I was about to start with him. I can get to all he owns later if you like.

Another infinitesimal sound susurrates throughout everything.

—Even after all you have learned, you still misunderstand? Look around you, learn and listen. Should he fail to turn from his path, he and all he calls his own will be destroyed.

–I *know*. I've been waiting for your wave. It's taking its sweet time.

—If it comes it will come. You must deliver the warning. Give the sign I gave you.

–The sign? What sign?

—You call it a ticket. Give it to him.

–Give him the…

—You call it a ticket. Give it to him. It will be warning enough.

It settles upon you in sedimentary layers, the import of what has been commanded, the reality of the command, the ramifications upon ramifications, the injustice of your fate. You allow yourself to imagine it for a moment, what Morris would do with the ticket. Imagine justice's oncoming wave halted forever. Imagine a monument to the tamed wave, remade in Morris's image: a silver wall reaching to the sky, tray upon tray, the human warehouse underground no more, a silverfish sardine wall of oubliettes, holding half the world's population, a prison so immense it is visible from space. The Assizement administered globally.

This is impossible. You have been asked the impossible.

—Give him the ticket? Give *him*?

—Yes. That, and no harm.

–Are you *insane?*

—You have only to look around you to know him.

It's a nightmare. It's is an abomination. You've been commanded to bring it about, and you will be compelled to enact it. No, you have been *summoned* to enact it, in the same way you were summoned here, and with terrible certainty you know you will answer that summons in the same way you answered this one: transported by an awful inescapable joy, without meaning to do it, intending not to, and then doing it all the same.

No. No. No you say and no you think and no and no and no. You summon the remainder of your will in resistance as the voice again speaks throughout your being:

—Go, and I go with you. You are in me, and I in you. I will not forsake.

–Go, and fuck yourself.

The door is still behind you and you pass through it, leaving behind door and beach, wave and the insane voice who through you called it all into being. What you see as you pass through is unexpected: a crowd. You speed your perception, petrifying time. In front, Jane and Sterling—your father. Crouched around them, cloaked in scarlet, trustees with rifles pointed at you. Behind them, also in scarlet, stand others with swords drawn. Among these you see Morris. Him. You must kill him if you are able.

You create a host of tiny vermiform parasites, each equipped at one end with a microscopically small chitinous spike, which is used to burrow through the body of the host, piercing a winding course through flesh and vein, sinew and bone, until the worms reach their real sustenance, the heart. As they go, they secrete from their skin a unique blend of enzyme and protein, which paralyzes the surrounding tissue while exciting the adjacent nerve endings. He won't be able to move, only feel. He'll feel it all, like fire and ice, their slow progress through him. They move a centimeter each month. They are far too small and far too numerous to extract; they multiply far too quickly to eradicate. You place thousands and thousands of them on Morris, covering every millimeter of the palms of his hands and the soles of his feet. This is your intention, but you find you are unable to enact it. The parasites are created, they need now only placement. You can bestow them upon any ready host in the world save one.

With horror, you understand you have left the voice, but the voice has not left you.

—No harm.

You scream.

It has no objection, the voice, that you might leave someone to be devoured by parasites. It has no objection that you have introduced such a plague into the world. It objects only that you might do it to *him*, the worst person in the world, the one man who might possibly deserve it.

You foul the guns of your adversaries. It's the simplest matter in the world to convert the firing pins to cheese. They pull the trigger without effect, glance at one another with rising fear.

Morris observes this new development, unperturbedly analyzing. To his remaining men, armed with swords, he says: Well?

The men look at each other.

Kill him. He has no power over me.

Somehow he knows—how? Has he been told in the same way you have been told?

—Give it to him. Complete the task.

The voice came from within. It resonates in your bones and your tissue; your cells thrum in sympathy with it. There is no physical pain, but each moment of resistance imparts the sensation of peeling the self away and emerging raw into the world. When the voice ceases, the sensation fades by degrees, but the command is in you. The command is in you. You will not resist it long. The effort it requires to do so splits your head. You scream. Even now the wave hangs before your eyes, even now you stand on the beach. You must escape. The voice compels on the level of existence itself; soon you will perform the unimaginable part it demands of you. Worst is how it compels but does not coerce. The command is in you, but the command is not you. Even now it only presents its will—a will so vast it would seem to leave no room for choice, but here is the terror: Space has been left for choice nonetheless, but within a band so narrow, a container so small, you know you cannot long remain in it. Soon you will give Morris the ticket, and, in doing, doom yourself, and all the world, long before any cleansing wave will come and save it. The need for escape is irreducible within you now; some place must be found, some crevice in which to hide from the atrocity you are commanded to commit. The ticket rides in an inner pocket near your breast. Once this power had opened new prospects of peace, prosperity, and comfort, but now you feel its fangs, and its terrible potential for doom sags from you like a gorged tick. This warrant you carry is transferable, it was intended for transference. What it can be used for. . .

—Never. I will never I will never.

Morris's men have found, in their fear of him, enough courage to overcome their fear of you; they approach. You convert their swords to flowers. You create an inescapable wall of wind, pushing them against the cavern wall, but slowly, gently, harmlessly, which allows you to push Morris as well. Pinned like specimens. Against it they can struggle but not prevail.

Two remain beside you, your father and your lover. They look at you in grateful wonder; they think you've won. You want to go to them and explain, but you are carrying something awful—a world-destroyer, a doomsday bomb with the fuse run out, the capsule carrying the unkillable virus, a poison pill potent enough to foul the oceans. You want to say things to them—to her in particular—but you have to go now before the voice sounds throughout you again. You mustn't look at her as you go—those eyes will kill you—but of course you do look. You die one last time. A boy at the circus, hiding beneath the bleachers. You remember. You always have. Without pause you begin to run, through the breach and down the great slope, back into the vault.

Gordy-Gord, where are you going?

Your father. He's pacing with you. You run faster.

Don't you leave, boy, don't you leave me again.

Faster.

Gordon, don't you leave me.

You feel fingers on your shoulder as you begin moving faster than a man can run, faster than a locomotive, faster than a speeding bullet, able to leap across the length of the vault in a single bound and you burrow into the far wall without slowing, pushing molecules aside, carving a path deep into rock, melting it in front of you at vaporizing temperatures and leaving behind you the cauterized perfect glassy "O" of your passing, ten feet in diameter; fusing shale and sandstone, siltstone, quartz, into smooth shiny rounded walls, re-crystallizing deeper igneous layers of granite into heat-buffed glass. You aim deep, deep, deeper, passing in seconds through millennia of millennia, from Paleozoic to Mesozoic to Cenozoic, then flatten out and accelerate in no particular direction. Distance is all that matters. Miles a second. But still the command is in you.

Gordy! Help me! Help!

You turn your attention behind. Sterling, caught up in your backscatter and carried along. You have created a zone around you, protection from the heat you are creating, and he is in it, but where you are going, he cannot come—I'm sorry, Dad. I'm sorry. I have to leave you all behind now. Your father, a distant man but kind. You know him now; you always did. You had a life together once. He would read to you at night after Mommy...what happened to Mommy? Why did you deny those memories? You will find someplace safe for him at least; someplace to hide, heavily populated, out of the way. There is no time for goodbye. The command is in you and you will soon obey it. You push back up, shearing through the strata. You punch up and up and up, until you are a mere dozen feet below the surface. You straighten course for a few miles, leaving beneath the city a tunnel long and straight and cauterized white, and then when you are beneath the heart of a city you send your father out and up and into the air, you send a piece of your consciousness with him for a time—soaring over a wedge of city, a neighborhood resembling a gray slice of pizza, a neighborhood dominated by an immense cathedral—while you continue on digging a long straight tunnel below. Protecting Sterling from the heat and the scattering flecks of plasma and magma and pyroclast expelled along with him, you float him down to the sidewalk, keeping with him for a few minutes after he touches. Aware of the conflagration you have started when you ejected Dad in fiery parabola—ah! the cathedral's caught fire—you create a rainstorm to quench it, and then you lose track of it all as you blast away faster and faster and faster. Below the ocean now. You imagine you can sense the infinite weight of water pressing down. Infinite? Nothing like it. The entire Atlantic would be drowned in the coming wave—and may that wave come soon. Behind you one continent recedes; ahead, another grows larger. And still the voice reaching out to you:

—Gordy, Gordy. Where are you going?

—As far as I can get.

The voice is in you and the command is in you. You cast out your awareness to the limits, but nowhere in the universe can you escape it. But now in desperation, seeking some far land, some territory unknown, you press your awareness into cracks previously unglimpsed, which strangely, unbelievably, open into possibility. It's like a new way of seeing and hearing. All about you other frequencies sing, higher and lower, and in this awareness, a great shimmering appears over your senses, as if you are observing the threads that allow you in small ways to make the great marionette of reality dance. Each moment and each place is entirely mutable, possessing infinite qualities: now simple, now complex, suffused at the atomic level not only with potential for energy but potential for potential. Anything can be anything else. Every point in this universe is a new diegetic portal to every other. Not just holes torn in space, but in possibility itself.

You pick a point on the course ahead of you, focus as sharply as possible upon it for this one task, this one final escape. The point you have picked grows, you widen it, dilating it, you imagine it into being from out of the strands of potential, a transparent disc between this place and that one. Crafting it in your mind into a membrane both solid and permeable, you race toward it and then you are upon it and without slowing you

pass through it.

You are in the same place. You are in a different place.

You are still tunneling below the sea, still approaching a great mass of land. Adjusting your course, you speed toward the largest nearby city. You are generating incredible heat, and, resolved to be more cautious of property and humanity than you were on your previous eruption, you surface in steam and water and then splash back down again, treading in the chop of the sea, bobbing in a harbor, alone, your appearance marked only by waking gulls. Against the chalk smudges of midnight blue and city glow, shipping cranes point their dormant arms in all directions. Later, when you have found a ladder on the sea wall and hauled yourself out, you sit on the embankment and let yourself slowly dry in the night air. This city is…you seek the knowledge, and then you have it. Brasschaat, in the tiny coastal nation of Färland. It will be as good a place as any to hide yourself, but first you list for yourself the steps you must take. It is crucial you don't forget anything, for when you have enacted the last step, you won't know to fix it—you won't even know you can. The ticket cannot be destroyed, and it's too dangerous to discard. It needs to be hidden somewhere on your person, and so you hide it well enough you are confident even you will never find it. But in the hiding of it, you make use of it, and the voice surfaces:

—Gordy, Gordy. Where are you?

You hold perfectly still. To empty your thoughts, you stare in wild wonder at a pebble.

—You are choosing a more difficult path.

Even here the command has found you. Even here. As you make your way into town, you list your steps carefully. When the time comes you must execute them quickly and without error. You will need to be fast and precise if you are to escape. The voice is in you still but the tidal pull has weakened; still, you fear it will soon come back in strength. In your flight you have discovered new threads of infinite possibility, and you have traced the logical chain that follows thereupon: If you, possessed of this ticket, can find these new folds of reality, then Morris, possessed of it, could find them as well, and, in finding them, would desire to own them. More even than the universe is at stake, then. It is time to be gone, erased. It is time to be swallowed up and brought to the bottom of the sea. It is time to escape. You wish it had never come to you, this burden, but to give it to another is unthinkable—how could another be trusted with it? The excruciating truth is, it would be better to be back in the oubliette. It would be better to never have escaped. Yes, even that would be better.

There is a part of the town already awake—or, more likely, it has not yet gone to sleep; you can hear their music and shouts. Desirous of human presence, you make your way toward it, an apparent red-light district. Arriving, you find listless working women standing behind windows, or outside, slouched against walls, smoking at the end or at the beginning of their shifts. Bright signs shout from the windows as you pass by; some advertise beer, others spirits, others sex, others the names of the establishments where you can get one or all of them. From a nearby tavern you catch a scrap of lyric that strikes you as fitting

…nobody's ever taught you how to live out on the street, and now you're gonna have to get used to it…

so you enter. You request a beer, a pen, and a scrap of paper. The bartender brings you a Duvel in a bottle, fat and squat and white. You take it to a darker corner table and sip at it, taking some last seconds to prepare. It is time. You know your steps. It will only take a few seconds. You can feel the ticket in its hiding place, its power still available.

First. The note, which you write to yourself quickly, in precise block letters.

Next. You'll need to be able to communicate. At first you consider giving yourself only French, but then you remember Dutch would also be useful, and then you realize making limits is foolish, so you give yourself Language, locking it deep, preserving it against the coming deluge of your last step.

—Gordy.

The voice arrives at once, like the pressure of the deep, pressing at you on every square inch, compressing you down, crumpling you. But you will not listen, you are buried, you are in the heart of the sea.

Next. You will need to eat. You give yourself a bag of cash, enough to live on for a few months, providing you're not lavish. After consideration, you have deemed a greater amount to be dangerous to carry, and banks would make you visible in ways you don't want. It will be better not to have much to live on, to have to work to create something new.

—Gordy, where are you?

The command is in you. Suffuses you. Engulfing waters threaten you.

…after he took from you everything he could steal…

Next. You will need to live. Here comes the most difficult step. The most precise one; the one you have worried at and shaped to what you hope is perfection. You don't want to be seen, and yet you will find times when it is important or useful to be seen. Only when you want to be seen should you be, and then only by those you trust, and only for as long as they give you reason to trust them. And—crucially—by those who don't take notice of you anyway—the anonymous visible invisibility of the shopper to the cashier, the taxi driver to the fare—this partial visibility should be yours.

You make it so, and to those around you, though they don't realize it, you begin to flicker.

—Gordy.

You bite your cheeks against the rising scream. Even now you have only to wish it and you can be back, standing before Morris. You can obey the command and release it from yourself. The temptation is so strong. It won't be your fault. It will be *Its*—The Voice's. What could you have done? How could you have resisted?

But then you think of the atrocity of it: Morris holding the ticket.

Finally, the last and easiest step, the one you have been waiting for. You think of the wicked white fountain, concentrate upon that black tenebrous water pouring from turtlemouth, that amnesiac cherub piss. Your white bottle of beer squats before you like a fat abbot, waiting to deliver to you either judgment or absolution; you pass your hand over it and now it holds something darker than beer. Your fate was sealed long before you were presented with any card. It has always been both bird and spade for you. You drink it down to the dregs and

A bag rests on a table. A note perches beside the bag, bequeathing you your name, a brief reassurance, and the contents of the bag. You look into the bag and see the money. You sit for a long time. You notice everything as if it were new and there is no judgment in it, no value in one thing greater or lesser than the other. The light of a newly risen sun passing through the window is a revelation to you, but no less so than the ring of water remaining on the table from your empty bottle, or the table itself, or each breath you take. You read the note twice more, fold it, and put it into the bag. There is nothing in you now, nor any knowledge within you that there should be anything in you. Unknown to the world and to yourself, with no more secrets to conceal, you rise and make your way out the door and into the day.

PART III - **THE REVISIONARIES**

A saint does not dissolve the chaos;

if he did the world would have changed long ago.

I do not think that a saint dissolves the chaos even for himself,

for there is something arrogant and warlike in the notion

of a man setting the universe in order.

It is a kind of balance that is his glory.

He rides the drifts like an escaped ski.

His course is a caress of the hill.

His track is a drawing of the snow in a moment

of its particular arrangement with wind and rock.

Something in him so loves the world that he gives

himself to the laws of gravity and chance.

—LEONARD COHEN, Beautiful Losers

a u t h o r

Once again: There have been changes, and not for the better.

Still, you think, eying the newest stack, it's better to be the author. When you're the author you control it. All of it, almost. Most of it, at least. Some of it, anyway. You can play any game you want.

You smoke and stare at the pages.

It was easier before, you think. Still, it's better to be the author.

It's wonderful.

It's only gotten worse.

Since Gordy went to Färland, it's been worst of all. You think—I must have caused it. Who else? You're punishing yourself for something—but what? What crime have I committed? I never intended harm. All I want is to break down the barriers keeping me from myself. Is it best to be the author? After all, to perfect oneself, one may deal only with oneself, and with oneself one may have plain dealings. Even with characters there can be a certain understanding. But to perfect interpretation... How do you overcome an audience? You can never trust those god-damned readers.

Perhaps the donut shop will have made a difference. It will have—it has to have. Nothing else has.

There was the time when you still lived the lie, trapped without even knowing it. Back in there, on the other side of the door—it was so much easier then!

Yes, easier—but not better.

Back on the other side of the door, the day you dispatched your father, the day you unsealed the old cavern beneath the fountain, the day you descended those cold granite steps, found the doorway. So small, so ordinary, that door—how strange it must have appeared to old Isaac, that ancient ancestor, that closest cousin, separated farthest in time but nearest in spirit. You allowed yourself another cigarette, collecting yourself for the task. At last you had reached out and grasped the knob, and it had turned; the door gave easily and you passed out of the cavern into the next place. There was no flash of light, no luminous epiphany, no angels singing, only the act of stepping from one place into another. But wait—there had been something, you remember it now; there'd come, for a fraction of a moment, a sense of doubling and redoubling, a stabbing pain behind the eyes, a rush of too much information, as if an excess of water were passing too quickly through narrow pipes. The room held too much detail, a higher resolution than you had ever experienced or considered. Every mote of dust playing in the sun, every scuff upon the floor and the grain of the wood of the boards, the lack of border between one thing and another... all passed over you like an ocean wave, nearly capsizing your consciousness, and then receded, subsided.

When it had passed, the room in which you found yourself was recognizable as an artist's studio, or perhaps an architect's. In one corner of the room a drafting table presided, its surface lit comprehensively by two powerful lamps on adjustable stems. On the walls, a mob of framed art and keepsakes. Lower down, along the length of the far wall, a low huddle of heavy steel cabinets provided a surface for a desultory repository: stacks of paper, assorted action figures and other toys, cereal boxes, wine bottles, dirty dishes, bric-a-brac. Checking the cabinets, you found, maintained as precisely and specifically as the stacks atop were haphazard, an array of individual paper sleeves, each of which contained a single page of original art—comic book art, by the look of it, with *Cat's Crib* scrawled in an upper corner along with an issue and page number. So: not an architect's drafting table, but one belonging to an artist... of sorts. A comic-book artist. An author.

Your door—looking behind you—yes, it was still there, half-open and you could see the cavern beyond. Good. You judged it safe to reconnoiter further.

The size and appointment of the house testified to the author's success, and a brief investigation in the kitchen turned up recent mail, which provided his name: Landrude Markson, of Knoxville TN. Returning to the studio, you reviewed the trays holding the archives of the author's work, the walls festooned with praise and awards, the shelves holding the collected published work to date in nine evenly sized volumes. You smoked and read, recognizing the feel of the world therein, but not your part of it. Nothing of Pigeon Forge, only some silly place, a parody of a city, some garish approximation of a slum called "Loony Island." A ridiculous story. Daniel "Donk" Donkmien? Bailey and Boyd Ligneclaire? Unrecognizable characters, in an unrecognizable place, with adventures as meaningless as they were puerile. Fools yowling absurd catchphrases. You read faster, impatient to finally find yourself in the narrative—Yes, here you are at last. The most recent pages taking the form of a flashback; the history in Tennessee of the Love clan, as explained to Donk, Boyd, and Bailey by a skittery, jittery, stammering inmate of the nearby mental institute, once a well-spoken college professor, now an escapee from your oubliettes. In the most recent pages the inmate described your recent encounter with your father, specific enough to give you a sense of nausea, or vertigo—Your recent past on a page, a doubling not of vision, but of memory.

You hadn't yet been the author, you still inhabited the lie, your life as a mere character; you hadn't yet learned anything else about this "Landrude"—but in that moment you knew, with unassailable certainty, this was your great enemy. Whatever place this was you'd found behind the door, whatever power allowed the author to maintain ownership of it, you immediately claimed them as your own rightful property—yours, and stolen from you. This author, who had wrongfully claimed both place and position, would need the correction of an oubliette.

You prepared to read on, but were interrupted by the sound of an arrival—key in door. You went slow and cautious, but ready, your hand in your inner jacket. You had seen him then—the author. Enemy. Creator. An older fellow with a broad lined face and more salt than pepper in his mane. Powder blue suit. He had some artwork in his hand and was studying it as if it confused him.

So, you said in a loud clear voice, you're the one.

The author leapt, startled, almost comically so. You regarded each other for a while.

You look just like me, he said at last. This surprised you, but you'd learned not to let surprise tell on your face. Yes, you'd said. I warrant on the other side, you'll look just like me. Then you said: Better make yourself ready, and started for him and he was terrified then and he said wait and he said wait wait wait, just like your father had said earlier, but you hadn't waited for your father nor would you wait for him and once you'd put the fountain water in him you watched the terror in his face go to nothing at all.

Plenty of time now to deal with him at leisure. You left him unconscious on the floor and explored the residence. Making use of the bathroom, you observed the mirror and saw without surprise that the author had spoken truly. In this place you were an older fellow, with a broad lined face and more salt than pepper in his mane.

To your reflection you whispered: You look just like me. Unsurprising—given the strange nature of this place, this lack of demarcation—that you wouldn't have the same appearance on this side of the door as on the other... but why this specific appearance? Then it came to you: You haven't changed. This is what you look like on this side of the door. You didn't change to look like him. He looks like you. He is the lesser; you are the greater. It was your lesson to yourself of your rightful place, of you calling yourself to the higher level. Proof of your singularity.

When you returned to the spot in the book and took up reading, you quickly found yourself. But... flipping from page to page... this was nonsense. Offensive. He's made some sort of mole-cat of you, tunneling to prisons and taking control of the prisoners, your plot slowly uncovered by the intrepid heroes, whose clear narrative task is the defeat and expulsion from Loony Island of this new threat, this monster, this...

I'm the *villain*? you snarled at the author's unconscious form. I'm the... I'm...

You mastered the urge to kick the prone figure. Instead you glared—No. I won't smash your skull in. Wouldn't do to act too *villainous*, now, would it? You fool. No wonder you're a failed strain. Just wait; you'll see what I can do.

It's a sign of how much you've grown that you can now admit; it was fear that held you back. No—not fear, but prudence. His existence suggested strange entanglements best approached cautiously. You didn't know what might happen if he died.

In truth, you still don't.

Later, you found his notebook, and saw his plans for your upcoming dispatch, and your rage overpowered you—in the end, you drop a fucking *safe* on me?—but by then, you'd already done what you did. Dragged him through the door into the side you'd left behind, back into the cavern, flopped him like a spud upon the clay. Flipped him over and studied the face. Yes, it was as you suspected. You look just like me, you murmured to the prone abducted figure. You look like me if I will it, and so I do so will, and so you obey.

It all made so much sense to you. This was the lesson to yourself you'd been awaiting: your ascension to a higher plane, the replacement of a failed vessel with one more suitable, the replacement of a perverse and misguided understanding with one more complete and fitting. On the edges of your vision you detected a strange phenomenon; from one instant to the next, you seemed to be, variously, in a closet the size of a mine shaft, in a room the size of a kitchen, in a cavern the size of a cathedral, and the size of a stadium, and the size of a planet. Your first hints of those readers and their endless variations of interpretation. You shook yourself—it didn't matter—and returned your attention to the figure on the cave floor. Write me as a villain? A *minor* villain? No matter; I'll correct all wrong impressions. I'll make your readers see the world true, and I'll make you feel it. You be me for a while. Try my struggle for perfection and see how it suits you. And I can do it—I hold the controls. What I say is will be. I'm the author. You're the villain. Have my memories. Feel my pain. Know my struggle. It's not a usurpation. It's claiming what's mine by right.

Returning to his—*your*—house, you closed the door behind you, leaving the author, now Morris, behind forever, forever—or so you thought.

You went to his—*your*—closet, saw the seven identical hanging suits of powder blue, tailor-made to fit the author.

They fit perfectly.

It's better to be the author.

You sit and smoke and stare at the pages. These revisions. What's making them? Soon, you know, you must read them—and what horrors will you discover this time? Sometimes there's not much, but sometimes. . .

Last time, for example.

Last time, healing Julius, Boyd completely disappeared.

Three months following the great riot, the circus came to Loony Island.

This was strange in itself. Folks buzzed up and down Transept. What mad fool would bring a circus—a *circus*—to Loony Island?

That wasn't the strangest part. The strangest part was this: Once it had arrived, before the show could even begin, it disappeared entirely. One moment it was there, the next, all in a flash, it was gone. Not a sign left of it, not a tent, not a rope, not a single ball off a clown's blouse, not a scrap of straw. This came as quite a shock to almost everyone, but there was something about this mysterious disappearance that made shock difficult to express; some self-negating quality that made the vanishing not an event within the stories of their lives, but rather a void—something remembered, but impossible to countenance, gone so fast it immediately became difficult to credit that it had ever existed; though remembered by the mind, some instinct beneath the mind, which the more spiritual nature might perhaps describe as the soul, questioned whether it was something taboo, something never to mention, something to treat as if it had ever been there. The circusgoers were disappointed, but there was no hint of a riot over tickets unrefunded. They dispersed quickly, as if suspecting the disappearance was more a reversion to proper form, as if such fancies as a circus had never been for such people as they.

Additionally, there were in the Island at least two direct witnesses to the event who were quickly provided with even greater distractions. Before they'd had time to process what they'd seen, Father Julius and Gordy had been given much deeper things to think about than a vanished circus.

Roughly three months after the Loony Riot. Nearly ninety days. Eighty-seven days, to be precise. Sometimes ambiguity is important. Sometimes nothing will do but precision.

Here's what happened.

—Boyd Ligneclaire, *Subject to Infinite Change*

A T T I C

These days, the dreams are easier than the waking. In waking, there is only the hospital room, and Nettles, and the occasional nurse, and visitors. In dreams, Bailey wanders the Attic.

It begins in the same place each time. Bailey opens her eyes to find she has somehow returned after long absence to the home of her childhood. Awake in the dim of dawn, risen as usual before her brother from their communal huddle on the mattress on the floor in the corner. So strange, she thinks, to have forgotten that she remains young and whole, and that she has a brother. (His name is...Boy? What an odd name.) Every time she finds herself in this place, she thinks *remember this when you wake* but she keeps forgetting. If she could just remember after she wakes back up, she'd be so much happier. Why does she forget? She'll be sure to remember this time.

Sunrise sneaks between buildings and vertical blinds to paint long shadows on the wall. Everything the sun illuminates is as she remembers it. Here on the baseboard, she sees a boot-scuff, into whose obscure shape she as a child once imagined the silhouette of a woman in flight. Here is a chunk of wood splintered out of the doorframe between the living room (where their mattress lies) and the sick darkness of the sole bedroom. Behind the blinds hangs a tiny unadorned concrete balcony; she can open the glass sliding door and go sit there if she wants. She is about to do this when she notices another door beside the slider.

So strange, to have lived so many years in this tiny two-room Domino City apartment and never noticed a door there. It's a normal door. Nothing unusual about it. But...how is it she's never opened it before? Never even thought about it? She opens it now, revealing rough wooden steps leading up to a landing. The landing appears to open, on the right hand, upon a brightly lit area, which, though yet out of sight, gives the impression of spaciousness.

Of course, Bailey thinks—it's the Attic.

Naturally she remembers the Attic. How could she forget it, just because she's never been there before? So strange, to have had this Attic all along and never visited.

When she reaches the top of the stairs she catches her breath; the Attic is vast. Roof beams high on the wall on one side curve like ribs down to meet the gleaming wooden floor. At intervals between the beams, dormer windows set into the roof let in bright shafts of day—the sun must be directly above—in which motes dance and play and chase one another. The Attic is filled with tables and cabinets and trunks and boxes. Upon the tables she finds marvelous assortments: There are cages, some with real birds, some holding what appear to be intricately crafted avian robots whose every movement and twirrup perfectly mimics life; there are tools, antique but well-kept; there are toys, made of wood and made of tin—drummers, animals, a working miniature carousel; there is a table filled with variegated vases, another bristling with timepieces, another stacked with Russian nesting dolls, all un-nested and arranged beside one another with identical stupid hopeful expressions; there's still another with books in impossible stacks climbing halfway to the ceiling; another and yet another and yet still another, table and table and table piled, and looming here and there among them, resting on the floor, are shapes covered in canvas, some of which might be bicycles, some of which might be wardrobes.

Though they're familiar, she's never seen these things before. Why did she bring them up here? Why then did she forget them? She drifts slowly among them, until she reaches the far end. Here she discovers another door, which she opens to find three sets of flagstone stairways, the middle of which leads upward and straight ahead. The ones on either side lead downward and curve away. She's never been here, and is delighted to be back again. Of course—*this* place! She chooses the upward staircase, which leads to a deep dungeon, far underground, windowless and well-lit by the sun. Massive gray brick walls make up the corridor, which seems to have no termination; on either side are doors made of bars, like those found in a prison cell. On a whim she opens one and sees there is a garden within. No, not a garden—a greenhouse. An arboretum. It's the greenhouse as it could have been, before Yale found it abandoned. It is filled with banana and frangipani trees, and with monkeys and butterflies. The monkeys play and chatter and try without success to catch the butterflies. They eat the bananas and throw them into the broad-leafed foliage underneath and pick at each other's fur for snacks. Bailey moves beneath the canopy on a pebbled path. Occasionally she passes an abandoned sculpture pushing up through the undergrowth. Above, she can see the greenhouse roof, and through it the sky set against the cityscape's purple and aquamarine arabesque steeples crowding far above, like the legs of a concubine's pantaloons, like the frosted tops of weightless cupcakes—if only, Bailey thinks, we could have found the greenhouse when it was still like this. When it was whole and safe, on the ground floor, in some other city.

In time she comes upon the great tree in the arboretum's center. Embedded in its trunk is a door, which opens onto a hall of paintings. Here is a field of rippling wheat, a house on one side of the horizon, a jury of storm clouds congregated on the other. Here is a girl floating on her back in a stream, viewed between the overarching boughs of trees, her sun hat undisturbed. Here is a desert. Here is an ocean. Here is a wedding party. Here is a canyon. Here are the rooftops of Budapest at dawn. Here is a table, and upon the table a vase, and in the vase a profusion of flowers, and on a flower, an aphid. Here is an interconnected series of circles of various colors. Here are black stripes on white canvas. Here is a bullfight. Here are peasants gathered around a table. Here is a woman, rendered in sharp geometric shapes, perched on the edge of a bathtub. Here is a man seated in a confessional, unaware of the emptiness on the other side; the priest has abdicated. Here is a meadow suggested entirely by particolored points of paint.

Finally, she comes to a piece she does not want to leave. Viewed from an alleyway, a courtyard within a great city of domed buildings. The sky is lavender, festooned with blue clouds. The painting is rendered in sure lines, thin and even and precise, demarcating each object one from the other. Each cobblestone is a distinct thing, each brick. The colors are also cleanly separated, one from another, but vivid, creating an effect simultaneously real and hallucinatory. The picture's frame is long and wide as a doorway, hung close to the floor. It almost seems you could step into it. Bailey steps into it, and, upon examining herself, discovers she has now taken on the same style as the work into which she has entered. She thinks: Now I remember. All boundaries are permeable.

She never sees anyone else in the Attic; it is hers, and she walks in it alone. Never the same journey twice—though rooms sometimes repeat—but it always ends in the same place: a small room, dominated by a bed. In the corner a woman sits, holding a book. Beside the bed, machines stand guard, emitting beeps at intervals to substantiate their alertness. Lying in the bed is a thing. It is gaunt and nearly hairless, this thing, its eyes sunk deep into its skull, lids closed. This is not the room she wanted. Bailey turns to leave, but to her horror she has somehow found the room with no doors, and the thing is drawing her closer. It lies motionless, yet it emits malign gravity. She scrambles to resist, but her legs will not move, tries to grab hold of something—anything—to avoid the pull, but her arms remain by her sides. (Of course—she can't move. How strange to have forgotten it.) She is as helpless and boneless as a rag doll as it pulls her. It is emitting an odd mechanical keening. She is near now, near. It turns her to face it, and she sees it is a head. Either it has grown or she has shrunk as she is drawn into it. She can see the death-skull contours of it, the tiny hairs growing from its scalp. Its eyes are closed. She is small now and sinking down toward the Thing, slowly, slowly. Then, just as Bailey thinks she will land on the lid, the eye opens and it is black. It is black and she is sinking toward it. She is sinking and it is black and it is all around her now and Bailey is in the blackness and thinks *so there was a door in this room, after all*

and then she wakes with a mouth like sandpaper. Her body gone.

Nettles' eyes lift from her book. "Back with us?"

Bailey says nothing. There seems little point in speaking.

"Want to get up now?"

"I'm not getting up today."

"Doctor's orders. You're getting in the chair, and you don't get to decide about it. What you get to decide about is now or later."

"Later, then." Bailey sighs, then glances at the flask with the steel nozzle. Nettles, attentive as always, raises it to Bailey's lips. Nettles intuitively understands what Daniel hasn't grasped even after a month: For her, a certain type of glance represents the same gesture as an arm extended, finger pointing might for another…but it has to be a certain type of glance. You have to think not just about gesture but intuit intent. Daniel hasn't managed the trick. They've already had one massive fight about it. That was a month ago, just after it happened. Right? Yes—a glance at the calendar—a month. Today, the clock says it is just after six in the morning. Ninety minutes from now, she will receive her breakfast, which Nettles will feed to her. Eggs scrambled, orange juice, drugs à la paper cup. One hundred and eighty minutes from now, one of the doctors will slide in, read some chicken guts typed out on a sheet of paper, murmur a few thin pronouncements, and evaporate for the day. Three hundred and sixty minutes from now, her lunch will arrive, along with more pills. Seven hundred and twenty minutes from now will come her dinner, and the sleeping pills, and finally she will find the Attic again. Somewhere between now and thirty-one million, five hundred thirty-six thousand minutes from now, she expects her body to finally stop pushing oxygen and blood to her head and all this mess will finish at last. Her body (the doctors assert with crisp buoyant assurance) is—spinal injury aside—relatively healthy, recovering nicely, so there's no reason not to hope, with proper medical care, she can't live a perfectly normal span. Although (they further aver with sober shades of admonition), given her condition, they will have to be vigilant against the usual complications…

Given the tone the doctors use when they talk about "complications," she imagines them as squat beasts with the short-bristled hair of a boar and the gaping mouths of anglerfish, lurking in dark places, waiting to strike. Maybe, Bailey considers, you have a matter of months before a complication swims out from between two seaweed trees and gets you. Or maybe there are none coming, and you've got decades of this to go. Daniel's purchased devices for her she can use to read endless books, or else watch hours and hours of film or television, stand-up comedy, documentary, but thus far she can't focus on any of it. She sees little point. She used to be able at any moment see every way she might die. Now she can't find a single plausible path.

Daniel still visits. She wishes he wouldn't. It's so clearly out of duty, so clearly a function of his need for something else. He comes empty and uses her to once again fill himself with the thirst for vengeance. He'd been there when she awoke, and what had been the first thing he'd told her? Nothing to do with her prognosis or her condition, no expressions of sorrow or of relief, no news about the condition of her shop after the riot; no, he'd told her about the culmination of his revenge with Ralph. It's done. He'd told her with declining gusto, the disappointment in his eyes increasingly evident as he went on; he'd expected her to be ready to celebrate with him. Or no— that wasn't it. He'd expected to *be* celebrated. Later, it occurred to her—it was for this he was waiting for me to wake up. To tell me his triumph. To feel it through me. But their plans for Ralph now seem like something in a book unread since childhood, and she disappointed him with her reaction. Even more remote to her are Daniel's pronouncements about Morris, the man who left her in this state. No matter; Daniel has energy enough for them both. Morris is all he can think of—getting Morris. He's like a Mad Lib, a find-and-replace, the same old sentences with Ralph taken out and Morris set in his place. She sees Daniel clearly at last: a creature built only for secret revenge, someone who has carved within himself concealed channels and hidden reservoirs optimized against corrosion, able to hold endless quantities of vengeance's thick and bitter syrup. What would such a man do if he allowed it to drain from himself? Would he slowly turn brittle and hollow, like an abandoned seed shell? Would he fly around the room, sputtering angrily until flaccid, like a punctured balloon? He'd finish up empty either way. You're lucky Morris came along and did this to me, love. You'd have been at such a loss without this fresh outrage to dig your toes into.

She's his fuel now, much as Yale had been. He'll enact his vengeance in her memory—this is what Bailey believes he means, though he never quite says it. He's keeping the donut shop open, getting one of his more trustworthy loonies to run it—Garf, she thinks he said—but he's doing that in memory of her, too. And it doesn't matter to her either way, really, about the donut shop. She has a different pride of ownership now. Donk may not consider her alive, but Bailey knows better. The problem with Donk is, he thinks that since she won't return to what she was before her injury, she's a nothing, a not, an un-person, an object of pity, a button sewed to a curtain. He doesn't understand that she's become something else, in some ways diminished, but in other ways *more*. She lives, but not here. She resides in the Attic, adding room after room as she slumbers, while Daniel, in waking life, erects story atop story, building up his army of loonies, raising up his monument to reprisal. The strangest thing is how much he now sounds like that stammering weirdo Tennessee, who delivered Father Julius to them on a stretcher. According to Donk, the loony ran off shortly thereafter and hasn't been seen since; yet another little-known soul gone missing during the madness of the Loony Riot. Tennessee is a subject of annoyance for Donk; apparently Julius thinks Tennessee's got answers, and the priest is all in a fluster to find him—he won't stop bugging Donk about it. All the same, Tennessee's influence shows up in Donk's speeches to her when they're alone; it's all this toff about tickets of power, and Pigeon Forge, and doors. Caves and fountains.

Julius also visits. Until he found a use for himself by making himself a conduit for the news back in the Island, Julius's visits used to be uncomfortable. Not his fault, really, but it's a small room; they had no place to fit all the guilt he dragged in with him. He looked at her as if she were ketchup he'd just spattered across a pristine white carpet. He appeared unsure of what to do with his hands. They grasped air, seemingly searching for some way to put her back together. During his first few visits, Julius was so unceasing in his remorse that Bailey began to think she'd have to ask him to stop coming, and then *she'd* have been the one with the guilt. He's the one paying for this swank hospital, same as he once did for Nettles, saving her from choosing between the swift eradication of her own bankroll or the bedlam of the county's ICU. A new Neon acolyte named Gordy—allegedly Father Julius's flickering man—comes along with the priest most days. But he doesn't "flicker" anymore; Bailey's able to see him just fine. According to Julius he's visible to the Neon Brothers and Sisters, and to Donk, but completely invisible to most others, which one supposes is how he can walk the streets safely. She remembers the invisible form under the sheet the night of the riot. That had been the damnedest thing. If it was an illusion it was an accomplished one; if a hallucination, it had been shared.

"If he's not flickering for you," Julius had told her, "it's because he trusts you."

Trust or no, Gordy seems almost shy in her presence. He treats her almost like a celebrity. "Donk told me what you did for us," Gordy had said to her when they'd met. She murmured something about not being a hero, but he insisted, and really, she lacked the energy to quibble. She hadn't "done it" for him, or even for Julius. If she'd "done it" for anybody it had been for herself, to prevent Daniel from turning them both into something foul. And she didn't even "do it" for those noble reasons, because she hadn't meant to "do it" at all—because, after all, what was "it"? Nothing but letting her guard down. She had meant to turn the little prick away, and had been adequately armed for the task, but he sliced her right in the spine. Her condition wasn't the result of some brave and noble sacrifice; it was the price of momentary stupidity. But if there's a point in explaining all this, it escapes her.

The morning progresses. Breakfast comes. Nettles feeds her, then returns to her book.

Nettles understands the value of silence without it having to be explained to her. After all, there would once upon a time for her have been a soporifically beeping hospital room, a part of her body gone; Nettles, too, has once upon a time been forced to learn new ways in which to point. In her company Bailey feels understanding and presence and little else. It's a bearable thing, and there are few bearable things remaining. In ways none of the rest can possibly apprehend, Nettles understands. Scratches her nose, distracts her from the pains and itches and heat and cold emanating from her phantom body by tickling her still-sensitive scalp, keeping silent except as needed, save for the regular crisp turning of a page, or the snoring from her chair.

Nettles had been there already when Bailey first woke up, but she hadn't thought much of this at first; they'd all been there: Julius, Daniel (with a couple of loonies guarding the door for him in a hyperbolic pantomime of attentiveness), several of Julius's congregation, including Nettles, whose face Bailey vaguely knew. It wasn't until later, after the rest had departed, that it became clear Nettles intended to stay. She pinched a chair and dragged it over to the bed.

"I'm going to keep this short," she said. "It's going to be hard for you now. I wanted to quit when I was in a situation sort of like this—" displaying her interrupted fingers—"and I didn't lose nearly so much as what you have. Hell, I *did* quit. I quit all the time. Pretty much every day, and for weeks together sometimes. But Julius came and sat with me. He was my spare tire. Whenever I quit, he didn't quit, so there was always somebody trying. Anyway, that's the deal. I'm going to stick by you. Quit whenever you want; I won't. You won't have to entertain me. You won't have to talk to me. I'm just going to be here. You're not going to always like me for it, but I'm your spare tire. And I've got more tread on me than you know. Got it?"

True to her word, Nettles rarely leaves. It's a comfort—usually. Right now, though, Nettles is pestering. Apparently it's past time for her body to be pressganged into some physical therapy exercise and some hours in a seated posture.

"I'm not doing it today. Please."

Nettles just gives a grim smile. "Come on, kiddo. You know better than that."

Bailey shrugs. Or—and this is the oddest part of waking life now—her brain goes to shrug. She makes her brain do the "shrug" thing, but no shrug is forthcoming. She wants to explain—to Donk, to Julius, to the cascade of nurses and orderlies and doctors, even to Nettles sometimes—how impossible it is for her now to keep these things straight. How much she lives elsewhere. How all of this has become for her a sort of toll, the price of admission paid to access the wonder of the Attic. She's passed through a painting and into something far greater than anything she'd known before her injury. Nowadays, when she's awake, she makes her brain do the "regret" thing, the "sorry" thing, and nothing happens. As for the motions, so with the emotions. Her brain does them, but they will not come.

"Must have forgotten," is what she mutters.

With some assistance from Nettles, the nurses drag Bailey into the chair, so she sits and waits until the time when she's not compelled to sit in the chair anymore. Chair-time drags on, second after impervious second. Orderlies occasionally shift her position to prevent bedsores—this is the great medical bugaboo, bedsores. Then lunch passes like a street sign on a desert road. The orderlies bathe her with sponges. They massage her fundament to prevent blockage. They inspect her closely for bedsores and are pleased to find none. Everybody except for Nettles praises her for this with tones of exaggerated cheer, as if she is an exceptionally well-behaved toddler, newly toilet-trained. The nurse informs her that soon she will be eligible for home care. Bailey takes this news in with a total lack of enthusiasm or interest, and sees Nettles note this apathy with a sharp and knowing eye.

In time, the day ends and sleep finds her.

In the Attic, she finds rooms with flowers growing from floor, walls, ceiling. In the Attic, she finds a high-ceilinged trampoline room filled with hamsterlike creatures. The hamsters shoot up high when you bounce, then deploy their furry parachute tummy-pouches, making wee chuckling noises as they descend. In the Attic, there is a room, which has a room in it, which has a room in it, which has a room in it, which has a room in it, which has a room in it, which has a room in it, and each room without holds so much of the room within that nothing is left of any of it but a thin hallway and the door to the next room. In the final nested room, she finds an enormous cylindrical aquarium reaching up five stories, and a spiral staircase, which you can climb to reach a series of observation decks, set at intervals, until you arrive at a domed roof. In the roof is a door, which opens onto a balcony overlooking a cathedral nave. A huge glass window depicts a rock spewing water, and a prophet striking the rock with his staff. The sun rises beyond, illuminating the glass. Climbing down from the balcony, she discovers the altar, which lifts on hinges like a trapdoor, revealing a slow ramp leading down into the round, glass-bottomed carriage of a dirigible thousands of feet above the earth. It occurs to her she has managed to unshackle herself from the physical; her mind is now, piece by piece, giving her a tour of every-thing that is, was, will be, or might be. At the end of each night, she wheels around at last to the final inevitable room: the room with the Thing in the bed. But now the Thing's hair is growing back. Now the Thing is still thin but not so frightfully thin as before, eyes somewhat less sunken. What month is it? They told her but she forgot. She'll ask again. Might they have found some bedsores? Is this the dreaded and hoped-for complication? In any case, the nurses look concerned. Doctors arrive. It's not her problem; she drifts back.

In waking she has clearer and clearer memories of the Attic. She muses as deeply as she can, allowing the daytime routine to pass by quickly through haze of remembrance. Some days she discovers herself in the Attic, un-sure if a day has passed in between, unsure if this is a new visitation or the memory of an old one. She finds it is no longer necessary to respond to the

orderlies, or nurses, or to other visitors. For the increasingly worried Nettles,
to whom she feels some small debt of gratitude, she still reluctantly surfaces
on occasion. Daniel still has his specific and creative and boring plans of revenge—something about eyelids this time. Happily, she doesn't have to solve
it or even remember it exists until the next time Daniel comes visiting, at
which point the mystery will surface once again, as unattainable and illogical
as one found in a recurring dream.

Even the waking hours have gone funny. Right now, for example. Right
now she thinks she sees a strange and vivid man in the shadows, wearing a
tailored suit of powder blue, smoking and watching her. Nettles is gone for
some reason. No, not for *some* reason—there's a reason. Nettles told it to her,
but she had been thinking about the Attic and doesn't remember. Oh yes—
there's a circus in town. Daniel was talking about it. A circus in the Island,
imagine that. Announced just last week, practically no advance notice, no
lead time. Tickets free to all Island residents. Apparently, it's all the buzz. But
no—Nettles isn't attending the circus. She told you that. What did she say?
She's gone to the Neon Chapel for something. Yarn and needles? No, it's to
do with Julius; he's called her back; he's got something to say to the brothers
and sisters. She turns to ask the smoking man if he knows, but he's gone, too.
Bailey returns to contemplation of the previous night's Attic sojourn, and, in
contemplating, drifts back into it without noticing. In her wandering she finds
herself passing from a room shaped like an inverted ziggurat into a leaking
room. Water pours down the walls in runnels, and she chastises herself for
not having patched the roof, which she'd known needed repair—Now look,
the plaster is coming apart, and you just painted. In the corner of the leaking room is a chair. In the chair sits a wan gray young fellow, the first person
she's encountered in all her wandering. He's dressed like a greaser—denim
jeans and leather jacket, impressive pompadour. He's sitting in the chair and
knitting a poem about sardines. She looks to see how he's doing it, the trick
of using the needles to turn yarn into ink on the page, reads:

> Yon sardine incommodious and crampéd home
> Composed of nothing more (nor less) than tin.
> With twenty fish all told caught up within
> Sunk far beneath the sea in deepest black

Six fathoms straining sight, murk'd dark as sin.
Deep buried 'neath the ocean's silt and loam;
Doomed to this fate, with no hope to atone;
For tin was sealed tight, nor ridge nor crack
Would let them pry with tail or lip or fin
Nor could they budge, mewed back to back to back.
"And so," said one, "as we shall never roam
(Nor teeth shall e'er with mercy pierce our skin,
To end our days blockaded in this grave)
With neither hope of death nor life to save
But to eternal prison now a slave
Encircled twenty strong in tinnéd cave
I know a trick which ought to make us brave
For there are stories hid within our stack
Thus I suggest, though we begin to rave
Perhaps each one of us, though knight or knave
Produce a tale which shall with words engrave
And play within our minds beneath these waves
For each of us, methinks, contains a tome"

He smiles. Bailey, look at the rhyme scheme. *Wheatgrass Tea* won't know what hit them.

Who are you?

I'm Boyd. I'm your brother.

You're not. Yale's my brother, but he's dead.

Yale's not your brother, I am. I used to be.

You used to be what?

I used to *be*. I'm not anymore. Nevertheless, I can still write.

I don't follow.

You *should* follow.

What should I follow?

Follow me. I'll show you where to set your feet.

You're not making sense.

For the first time, Boyd looks flustered. He shakes his hands in front of his face, stares at them as if he wishes he could see more eloquent answers written there. He says: There's an author. And then there's *another*. They're fighting each other for it.

It?

Oh…*everything*. They're writing, they're rewriting. But one of them is doing it all wrong. But I'm out of it now; I'm *not*, but I was. I can see both threads, knit them together, write it down and choose what it means. You have to read it. I put it all into Father Ex for you. Father Julius made a way for me to send it. Read it; it'll tell you. Follow what I give you to the letter, until it's time to stop following, and you'll find me again. You'll need to run.

I can't run, she explains with exaggerated patience. I'm hurt. The walls are no longer leaking. Either the plaster has fallen down completely or they have entered a new room without passing through a door. Now they are in a vast room, painted white, but covered from top to bottom with tiny individually numbered dots, a few of which, she can see, have been connected by some kid with a shaky hand.

You'll have to run, he repeats. You'll have to jump, and trust your luck.

Bailey shakes her head, exasperated. Running gives me bedsores. If I try to run, I'll die.

But within her she can feel what's happening now on the walls—millions of dots are being connected with straight precise lines. As the lines connect, they turn bright. As the bright lines form shapes they fall away, revealing windows into the inevitable final room, where the Thing lies. It is there, lying in the bed, but moving—yes, *moving*—it is slowly sitting up. A figure is standing in the doorway. She turns to Boyd, who knits faster and faster the faster he falls. What's happening? she asks him.

The last of the dots connect, the last of the lines shines out bright. The final panel falls away. Now it is only her and Boyd and the figure at the door and the Thing in the bed, which is moving. Which is moving.

You'll have to run, he says. Follow what you find out from Father Ex. Follow it to the letter. Find me again.

Bailey sits straight up in her bed. A shaking spectacled skeletal figure is standing in the doorway, holding a book and a thick sheaf of papers. "We have to get out of here," he says, and she realizes he's the missing loony Father Julius is looking for, the one they call Tennessee.

She waves her arms. "Hey—I can *move*."

"OK. That's good," Tennessee says, glancing over his shoulder.

"I can move *everything*."

"We have to get away."

"What's happened to me?" she gasps. "What's happened? What's— "

"Look, we have to run," Tennessee says.

"Why are you here?"

Tennessee hands her the top paper from his stack, as if it offers some sort of explanation. "It came from Father Ex. I just came from the Neon. Gordy's gone. Julius told me to come get you." He lifts one sandaled foot up onto the hospital bed and looks at her as he expects her to comment on it. When she doesn't, he continues, "Julius wants you to have these pages. But also, he wants us to scram out of here while we still can."

Still marveling at her motile limbs, Bailey takes the page. It's gibberish; something about a circus disappearing, and precision and eighty-seven days. It promises to tell how it happened—whatever "it" is. She turns the paper over, but there's nothing more.

"What is this supposed to mean?"

Tennessee leaps in panicked impatience. "Read on the way. We have to go right now. It's all fallen apart. There's *still* bad trouble after me."

GORDY READS: **FOREHEAD**

Here is part of what Gordy read from Julius's diary, the day after the circus disappeared, the day he and the priest left Loony Island. Beams through the window lent brilliance to the particulate stew maundering through the air. Gordy barely breathed, scanning the pages, taking in the priest's final secrets, all too aware which secrets of his own were even then being disclosed. Reading himself into the history of another, feeling the past become the present, he slipped from *was* and *happened* into *is* and *happens*, and feels, in the moment, he has the power to bring the world along with him.

x x x

My father was a man with far too delicate a mind. I should get this out of the way: He had what he believed to be an aquiline forehead. Most people with aquiline features tend toward noses, but my father had what he believed to be an aquiline forehead. What do I mean by that: "an aquiline forehead"? I haven't the slightest clue. I wish I had. I had to reassemble all this from my memory, and from reading his diaries years later—if you want to call them "diaries." He'd unfurled five rolls of single-ply toilet paper, filled them with tiny letters: meticulous, ledger-straight, perfectly legible. Then he'd rolled them back up onto their cardboard spools and stored them on a shelf behind the crockery, left them hidden and waiting like lost texts to be chanced upon by some passing shepherd boy. Who inevitably turned out to be me, making inventory of personal effects after my mother died. Capital letters. Blue ink. Not one rip. Think about that. I do. It's some sort of testament to the futility of human diligence. On rolls of toilet paper I reconstructed my father. By the time I was born, he'd been shunned from polite society for his oddities, and deposed from control of the family business. I suspect the angle of his social decline increased following his decision to wear a hat furnished with side-mirrors—this to catch people laughing behind his back. My father's lack of gainful employment had no effect on our lives. The family wealth, passed through the generations, had already grown from a sardine to a whale—an entity of its own, immune even to years of inept stewardship of my father. He spent his time in the basement, performing what he called "experiments." These secretive projects, he alleged, were designed to restore him to social life, but in truth he performed scrimshaw upon his own sanity in a tiny, sparsely furnished room with mirrored walls, lit by candles. Not to say he was inactive. No, my father worked down there. My father built. He produced.

Not that I knew this then. A quiet child, I would wait, curious as a ferret, at the top of the basement stairs, as near as I dared come. I stared at the closed and locked oak door at the bottom, until one day my father, noticing me, sidled up, and whispered promises of a day when he would call upon me, and only me, to assist him. By the time he wandered away, my heart was filled with a child's pride and loyalty; in that moment, I determined I would do anything for this man, anything at all.

Yet time did what time always does; it slid the gilt off the lily. The days passed into weeks shuffled into years, yet the door never opened; my father ignored me as ever before. I began to wonder if it was a test. Wouldn't a real son, faithful and obedient, walk boldly down the staircase, knock on the door with confidence, and offer up his service? As I carried on my daily vigil at the top of the stairs, was my father enduring a similar wait, growing increasingly impatient with his laggard son? But what if it was a test of the other sort? If I knocked, would my father instead be disappointed with my impatience? So the agonizing months dragged by.

Finally, on my twelfth birthday, I crept down the stairs.

m o u n t a i n

In early days, you determined it was wise to stay on the author's side of the door as much as possible. Before leaving the author unconscious on the clay, you'd seen the horrible thing that floated over his shoulder. A thing that enfolded dimensions. A tiny speck, it seemed, but the longer you stared at it, the larger you could perceive it to be. You had no idea where it came from, but you innately sensed the immense destructive power of it—and, you suspected, all his to command.

Wisest to keep away.

You stare at the pages. If only it could have stayed the way it had been at the start, before Gordy appeared and started cocking everything up.

It was so clear, this lesson you were giving yourself. As above, so below. Just as you had been required to perfect yourself before being allowed to ascend to this sphere; so here, on the author's side, another perfection would be required, another portal identified, another sacrifice slain, if you wished to be permitted access from this sphere to the next. . . which implied a series of higher spheres. You'd never before imagined more than one ascension might be required, but you didn't quail. The perfection required of you was obvious—the perfection of the story from which you'd ascended—and then the door would open for you to the next place.

Leaving the unconscious figure on the cavern side, returning to the author's side, you'd become aware of your hunger, and a craving for cigarettes. Luckily, his mail had told you already that he lived in Knoxville. You knew Knoxville.

But it was Knoxville *and* it wasn't. There was so much more *stuff* in it, so much finer detail, a specificity and yet a messiness and a muchness to the reality to which you hadn't yet learned to acclimate yourself. And, as you passed out of your residential area and into a commercially zoned district, you could see the details were off, here and there. Familiar things in the wrong places, unfamiliar things in settings you thought you knew well. You stumbled and stared, aware you were making a spectacle of yourself. Wary of unwanted attention, you walked quickly, seeking the first likely convenience store, which you reached at the first major intersection. The proprietor was there alone; he had a potbelly and a walrus moustache. Got your usual, he said, fetching already the cigars from a box under the counter. You'd made a face and shaken your head, pointed (not yet daring to test similarity of voice) to a random brand—it didn't matter which, you didn't recognize any of the names. The man reached for the cigarettes, but he looked at you curiously, and you made vague apologetic motions in the direction of your throat, which he hoped would convey a sense of some temporary vocal inconvenience, paid, and retreated. Back at the house, the refrigerator held nothing more nourishing than condiments, but this paucity posed no mystery and no problem. An archeology of takeout discards in the trash, with plenty of menus on the counter advertising delivery. You found the phone and placed the order, then smoked yourself calm until the food arrived.

Satiated, you returned your attention to the study, beginning with the memen-tos on the wall—So. This author is some sort of famous in this place, which means that, in a way, so am I. This world knows my exploits. You'd found this confirmation unsurprising, but accepted it, the approval of an aesthete finding an expected thing in its proper location.

Except you weren't famous, really, you remembered with mounting rage. You'd read the story already with the author unconscious on the floor; book after book, eyes casting over the pages, following the thread, like one scanning through someone else's photo album for images of oneself. Nothing of you—it was all this Loony Island nonsense, Donk and Boyd and Bailey and loonies. You didn't come in until the end.

You'd searched the archival cabinets, starting at the far end where a blue la-bel, neatly hand-lettered, proclaimed ISSUE 1, Pg. 1. Removed the page, read it, returned it to its translucent pouch, and selected the next. Comic-book pages. You compared it to the published books on the shelf; a match. So: original art in the cab-inets, the finished product on the shelf. Reading through his—your—contracts with publishers, and various correspondence with colleagues and fans, the picture took hold: monthly issues, drawn and written by you; each year's worth of issue repre-senting a story arc, each arc of twelve collected in trade paperback, and ten trades on the shelf. After that, there were the three most recent issues, as yet uncollected. and then the issue that hadn't been completed yet, the one he'd been working on when you interrupted him, the final page of which was still tacked up to his drafting table.

You didn't show up until this latest story line. As the fucking *villain*.

You searched on. In a drawer of the drafting table you found your prizes: a sheaf of notebooks and loose papers, scraps of sketches held on by paper clips, newspaper articles, all bound together in a large folder—the author's notebook. Here you discovered the larger story sketched out, future threads begun, followed, lost, rediscovered. Teasing out the information you wanted proved difficult; the narrative was incomplete. The author maintained only a scattershot organization for his folder, or else it followed some logic you could not detect. As you found references to the "Morris" portion of the story, you extracted them from the notebook and set them on the table. When you'd made a full survey, you brought the pile—a small pile—back to the chair and sifted through. The picture got worse the more it came into focus, and worst of all when at the bottom of the drawer you discovered the thick binders of pages, and the horror of a title page.

L O V E ' S   F O U N T A I N
A Novel
By Landrude Markson

You read it deep into the night, a record of your earliest ancestor carrying forward to the tale of your own exploits. It wasn't a novel. It was a *failed* novel, an *abandoned* novel, tailed off into discursion. You'd seen the author's betrayal then, plain and clear. He was making of you nothing more than salvage, picking pieces of you for use, inserted into his other work, infinitely more puerile and therefore far more palatable to the readers, the proles, the philistines who wanted nothing more than their funnybooks. But at least the author would understand your superiority, would intuit that in you, at last, these so-called heroes of his had, at last, met an adversary that was their better.

When in the author's notes you discovered the details of your planned demise, the rage took you. You screamed and howled and pounded the walls with baboon rage. Not just a demise—a grotesquerie of a death, an insult, a bit of slapstick, a joke.

The artist has them drop a safe on you. A *fucking safe*.

But you would fix it.

Thus the first game began, the game of "climb the mountain." Perfect the sphere below so that you might rise to the one above. You thought of the artist—drugged with fountain water, drained of any knowledge of himself, dragged into his own work and abandoned there—and smiled, almost magnanimous. Ah, you murmured, you poor demoted bastard—I'll gift you the old place. I'll let you have the perfect lower world, before I climb higher. With whom, after all, would I replace you?

It would be simple. Your mind was ordered, perfected. You knew exactly how the world needed to be arranged. Now you simply had to do it.

There were problems.

First came the problem of drawing. You had presumed the artistic ability would now be yours, since it belonged to the one you'd replaced. Even now it's perverse to think a lesser version of you should possess some skill you don't. Your first task was to complete the next installment, and you thought to use that opportunity to integrate "Morris" into the story as seamlessly as possible, but your every line went askew. Once you'd rubbed the eraser through the paper, you tore it in anger from the easel. The second attempt proved more disastrous; there was no way to get the borders right. Even the concept of straight lines conspired against you—and time ran short. You had a deadline, responsibilities—so your management claimed. Finally, seized less by inspiration than panic, you tacked up a new blank sheet. Using a mint tin as a template, you traced in the center a small rectangle, and in the middle of the rectangle, using as reference a previously drawn panel, sketched a service-able duplication of an opening eye. After long contemplation, you began to write. A deep breath—make him disappear to himself completely.

Below the panel, you painstakingly lettered:

When Morris emerges to himself again, he is on the hard clay floor. His head feels as though it has been stuffed with soft packing for transship-ment. His mouth feels raw. He rises to his hands and knees, aware of the damage he has done to his clothing; luckily there are replacements in the car back at the rendezvous point. The flashlight is still on. Retrieving it, he looks around; the door remains closed. Nothing else has changed. Nothing has changed. He looks for a long time at the thing behind him, but nothing has changed, so this means nothing has changed. Here is the bag of tools, and nothing has changed. Here is the flashlight, and the batteries are still powering it and nothing has changed. Here are the stairs leading up into the light of day, and that is the same as well, and nothing has changed. Everything is fine, and everything is fine, and everything is fine and nothing has changed. He still has all his memories, he knows who he is and why he is here and what it is he intends to do, and the thing behind him is still there behind him, and so nothing has changed. The thing to remember is that nothing has changed, and for this reason it logically follows that nothing has changed.

Then you stepped back from your work and reckoned with it. A single drawn panel, the large block of text. It looked different from the ones the author had completed before you'd taken his place, but taken as a final page, you judged this could pass as an artistic flourish.

You'd hidden your enemy. Next you hid yourself. Given strict instructions that all future communications were to be funneled only through your agent—Rupert Paddington, a short but robust round man with a big physical voice. Still capitulated to a valued client, yes, but occasionally strident, increasingly raised in volume as you offered various diffident excuses for your failure to meet deadline—writer's block, ennui, sickness—at last you'd invented a injury, unbearable pain in your drawing hand. Relief, however, proved fleeting; this was a monthly publication. In four weeks, another twenty-four pages would come due. So Juanita Neato entered the picture: an eager and talented young artist ready for a chance, recruited by Paddington for her skill and her discretion. You agreed to meet at a nearby café.

And, Paddington had claimed she was a fan. If you'd known how unendingly treacherous that would make her, you'd never have taken the meeting.

"Julius!"

The priest turned. Gordy hadn't followed him; instead he stood almost in a stupor, gazing at the latest advertisement adorning the windows of Ralph's General & Specific. An identical copy of the thing was pasted up on each pane, including the recently replaced one.

It was a poster. Not the kind of crude one-toned fluorescent garish sheet with sans-serif black text that typically plastered the windows at Ralph's, no, but a triumph of art deco, an advertisement for a show, a really big show, an invitation. Gordy remembered moustaches, a striped suit and top hat, an improbable dancing capering jigging round man exhorting, a circus years ago.

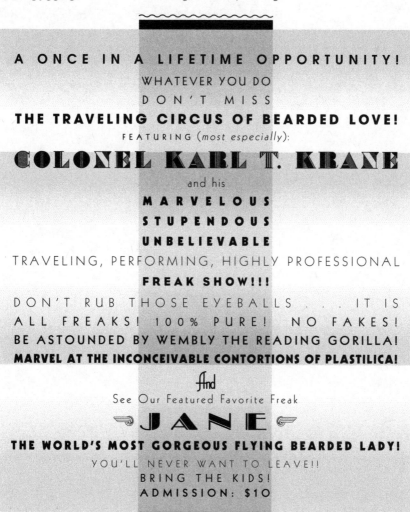

A ONCE IN A LIFETIME OPPORTUNITY!
WHATEVER YOU DO
DON'T MISS
THE TRAVELING CIRCUS OF BEARDED LOVE!
FEATURING (*most especially*):

COLONEL KARL T. KRANE

and his

MARVELOUS
STUPENDOUS
UNBELIEVABLE

TRAVELING, PERFORMING, HIGHLY PROFESSIONAL
FREAK SHOW!!!
DON'T RUB THOSE EYEBALLS . . . IT IS
ALL FREAKS! 100% PURE! NO FAKES!
BE ASTOUNDED BY WEMBLY THE READING GORILLA!
MARVEL AT THE INCONCEIVABLE CONTORTIONS OF PLASTILICA!

And

See Our Featured Favorite Freak

JANE

THE WORLD'S MOST GORGEOUS FLYING BEARDED LADY!
YOU'LL NEVER WANT TO LEAVE!!
BRING THE KIDS!
ADMISSION: $10

And there, below all this, slender and graceful: a woman on a trapeze, with dark hair shot with honey, with almond eyes, a lustrous beard darting from her chin on an oblique trajectory as she floated from one trapeze bar to the next. She was magnificent. She was Jane. His precious bearded lady.

"Oh mercy," Gordy whispered. Fingers on her illustrated face.

"We're late," Julius said, trying and failing to hide his impatience.

"Look," Gordy said, pointing. "There's a schedule. She's coming here. She's coming here."

—Boyd Ligneclaire, *Subject to Infinite Change*

L I E

Each day, Donk knows, he will worry over the lies he's told. Lies of omission, lies of commission, the fine variegations of who he's going to be to each person, strings of lies, each interaction presenting another necessary untruth slid onto his chain, a bead to fret and worry over, the better to remember it, the better to keep it—You walked the narrow path for Ralph; you'll walk a narrower one for Morris.

Donk, natty in his suit, strides the street with his retinue of loonies following, passing Ralph's food emporium, cutting across the lot; he's flagrantly skipping office hours, and the scared and resentful eyes of the old guard watch him from the windows of grocery and donut shop as he goes. But let them smolder. A new game started a week ago, and they're only now beginning to realize they aren't players in it anymore…He approaches the Wales, this time with no need of bowling ball to knock; he's expected. A cardinal waits at the door to bring him down into the tunnels. He leaves his loonies outside, no doubt they'll prance around in their bathrobes, turn cartwheels, harass citizens—in short, blend perfectly into the new madness now descended upon Loony Island.

On the Island streets these past few summer days, paranoia's baked and risen like yeast. More was released during the riot than a mere multitude of inexplicably kinetic insane people; insanity itself was unleashed, chaos incarnate, loose and unfettered and poured out upon a place already representing the very bottom, the worst, the poorest, the most crime-infested; riddled with varied addictions, stinking of desperation and gummed with the sour crust of schemes doomed to fail and schemes already failed, a hustling nonelect already shunned and reviled. But before, there'd been balm in degradation, an order, a context, and within that context, small alcoves of contentment. Even the Domino City shut-ins and the Checkertown impoverished needed look no farther than the Wales for a reassuring sign of someone occupying a position even lower than they. And there they were: loonies. Filling the giant green cracker-box without even their minds to hold onto. Any of them could look at a loony and think: *Sure I'm hurting, sure I'm broke, but hey. I still got my freedom, and I still got my mind.*

But this was before the Loony Riot, which smeared heretofore indelible lines of demarcation, set loose the stored potential madness of the Island, harnessed it, gave it purpose. Society had assayed them all against the loonies, and its scales had weighed them equally. It was too late to undo the psychological damage by the time the police had arrived with their gas and truncheons and rubber bullets. The bluebirds smashed loony heads, chased them off the streets, threw them in the drunk tank for the evening, but by then, even the unheppest cats had gotten good and hep about what the score really was. The loonies hadn't been released; the boundaries of their confinement had simply been expanded to include the Island. Loony Island didn't contain the loony bin. The Island was the loony bin. Even the neighborhood's colloquial name seems dispositive: Whose island is this? Why, it's the Loony Island, of course. The city's leadership had clearly come to consider the asylum walls redundant, and so allowed them to become permeable, allowed society's least valued out, surrounded as they were on all sides by an exactly equal measure of worthlessness. All of this hit folks hard. The general tide of opinion trended toward resignation; a degeneration among the degenerates, a subtle death.

Many for the first time noticed the architectural similarity between the Joan A. Wales Psychiatric Institute and the tenements in which they themselves lived: Domino Town, huddled beside the Wales, popped up nearby, clustered like toadstools, smaller clones of the parental fungus, some freakish urban housing parthenogenesis, the architecture of the buildings themselves testifying to the sameness of their residents. Had the loonies not grown such an inexplicable collective pride in their bathrobes, those former badges of their madness, which they wore like justices their robes or priests their vestments, they would have quickly and easily been able to insinuate themselves into the protean mass, sly as geese among ganders. If anything, the bathrobe of a loony created a mark of distinction, an election to a relevance the rest now found unattainable. Bathrobes everywhere were transformed from shameful brand to badge of pride. The loonies weren't burdened with the indignity of forced equality with those previously considered subordinate; rather, they experienced the thrill of the subordinate promoted.

Moreover, Donk knows, they possess another advantage over the rest, which can be considered "advantage" only within the specific context of Loony Island: None of them remembers a thing prior to the night of their first freedom. A new development—they'd been loonies before, but not amnesiacs. Rather than dragging the ever-accumulating iron links of their past behind them, they've clipped the chain and run free, sans manacles. This provides them with a momentous drive, an impetus to which even their daily amphetamine doses can't compare. The loonies have forced themselves, bodily and psychologically, into the Island's hubbub and humdrum, but without compromise of their own notions of themselves. Donk accepts all this without judgment. He doesn't give a sandy turd about the mental anguish brought on by sudden collective forced recognition of social imbalances. If anything, the disequilibrium affords some advantage: time enough to adjust quicker than the rest, and to act (of course, always) with superior information.

Morris has, on a number of occasions, hinted he knows something about the loony amnesia, but he hasn't explained it to Donk, who, well aware (thanks to Tennessee) of the reason, ignores the hints and does not ask, mystifying his new boss, or else impressing him with his rectitude. Donk enjoys creating the mystery. Morris—who obviously intends for Donk to remain in the dark about loony amnesia and all things Pigeon Forge—isn't aware of the monologues of Tennessee, and in all likelihood isn't even aware Tennessee still exists. But even if Donk hadn't lucked into Tennessee, he might still not have asked. The loonies' collective amnesia would have been a curiosity to him in that case, but it would have been an unsolvable one. Donk has risen as he has by distinguishing well between solvable and unsolvable curiosities. Better when facing an unsolvable curiosity to simply pretend you already have it solved. Knowing things without having to be told them may be the only way to impress Morris. And you'll have to impress him, Donk thinks, following the cardinal down the tunnel, if you want to stay out of one of those oubliettes.

He's heard hints of the muttering around the block; they're all gossiping:

What the hell? Donk's working with the cardinals?...did Ralph give the OK? because if he didn't then Donk'll have his paw caught in the jar pretty soon, and serves him righ...

All this backbiting custard dries up quickly inside the grocery, however—nobody wants to get sideways of Donk in any way, so he's yet to be questioned directly about any of his actions—which demonstrates yet another shift. In the past, he'd been accorded the respect of his position, but the respect had required the position. The respect flowed from Ralph, who bestowed it upon Donk, who wore it imperfectly, like a sweater knit for a larger man. Now, though...there's something new in his eyes nobody wants to see, something in his smile and easy tones which make cats sweat and stammer. Before, he had been considered a great acquirer, a master strategist, an opportunist, a climber, an amazing survivor, certainly somebody to admire or at least to respect, but not somebody you'd fear if it were just you and he and a couple of lead pipes and an empty alley. But now he is feared—and Donk knows they're right to fear. Back in the Fridge, after Tennessee finally came to his discursive finale, Donk had spent another hour in the dark, hands curled and relaxed, curled the heat out of himself and relaxed the coldness in, until finally his hands had relaxed without curling, and the cold calm had filled him and stayed in him. It was in him as he left to attend to his duties for Morris. It is in him still.

The gangs recognize coldness, so the gangs lend him this new respect, and as he's working with the loonies and the cardinals—either with Ralph's blessing or without Ralph's reprisal—they've started drawing wild conclusions: There's no Ralph anymore, some loony cartel's forming, some hidden conductor behind it all, some deformed wizard hiding behind the curtain, some malevolent doctor hiding deep within the bowels of the Wales. Some were beginning to believe this wizard might be none other than Donk. Or— or!—Donk is Ralph, and has been all along...

He's no longer being referred to as "Donk," but as "the Coyote."

The Coyote. Donk smiles—*I like that.*

The cardinal leads him into the long tunnel. The silver eye at the end of the passage grows large, revealing itself once again as a seeming vault door as they approach it and then move past it into the anteroom. The oubliette is here, gleaming steel lid open. A dozen other cardinals are here, including both little Andrews. Morris is here, his leg plastered and jutting. Ralph is here, dressed already in an oubliette harness, his arms tied roughly behind him at the wrists and elbows with white nylon zips. A rubber ball is in his mouth. One eye swelled shut and blood in his hair—naturally Ralph did not come quietly. Ralph's eyes go wide and shocked to see his lieutenant captured, then wider as he understands.

"Hey boss. How's the leg?" Donk asks Morris. Bringing this up might be a mistake, but anything you say to Morris might be a mistake, so what the hell. The cold and the calm are still in him. His hands are relaxed.

"It's fucking broken and won't fucking ever heal right and I'll be in this fucking cast for weeks and the fucking doctors claim I'll walk with a fucking limp the rest of my fucking life," Morris says. Donk says nothing; to speak would risk revealing his amusement. The affectless calm façade Morris projects is starting to show some cracks. Morris's injury pleases Donk more than anything else in the world; since the moment he saw Bailey hit the pavement, the thought of harm coming to Morris is the purest pleasure he can experience. He tilts his head toward Ralph inquiringly. Morris grunts, then says: "It's your show."

The room is perfectly white. The cardinals smear up against the walls like sheets of blood. Ralph's a filthy puddle staining the floor, straining uselessly but diligently against his bonds. Donk can see his jaws working at the ball, as if he intends to take a defiant bite through the hardened rubber apple. He's making angry hoglike noises. Donk squats down; it's novel to get such a close look. They've communicated so long by proxy and note and conference call, so rarely face-to-face, and even then always in dim rooms. Stiff orange hair covers Ralph's body but it's fading from the top of his head. He's fatter than Donk remembers him, but still powerful at the neck, the shoulders, the arms. He came up mean, did Ralph. A big kid, thick-necked, fists like kettle bells, feral and shrewd and with wily eyes. These are the arms, Donk thinks. These are the arms that threw Yale off the HQ roof. And now he's here. The moment he's worked for is here, yet it still feels like any other moment. Soon, he knows, he will feel it. The culmination of it.

Donk steps forward and loosens the strap under the ear, releasing ball from mouth. He thinks about Yale, but now the coldness is in him and he feels no anger. He thinks of the children of the greenhouse. His first friends, their disappearances uninvestigated, perhaps even unreported. He thinks of Yale. His hands are relaxed. The room is perfectly white. "What I do with my enemies," Donk says, "is I put them in an oubliette."

"This suppose to be a joke, boy?" Ralph glares at him with the one good eye. He strains and splatters sputum. His voice the accumulation of ten thousand retired cigars.

"A resignation. I've quit. You lose."

"You're crazy. You think you'll skate on this? When the gangs hear?"

"And who's telling them? You're *here*. Which means your bodyguards are all dead. And the gangs hear from you through *me*."

Ralph licks his lips, turns his attention to Morris. "This is about money? Fine. I've got money. More'n this one does. All you want."

"Spaghetti-shit for your money," Morris remarks, studying the ceiling.

Donk leans in close and whispers. Gives the message he's kept close over years and years and years, a truth long kept refrigerated, preserved to impart in the instant of victory...but he's tired, this hate is old and dried, gone fallow, it all feels like the mechanized preordination of a music box: key wound, gears turning, a tinny tinkling revelation of vengeance. The moment comes and the moment goes, and the coldness is still in him and his hands still relaxed as the cardinals take hold of Ralph and hook him into the box Ralph screaming *crazy you're crazy, children, what children, what the hell are you—*

and the lid snicks closed forever.

It is done. It is over. Accomplished. It doesn't feel like anything.

"So that's one for you," Morris says. "Now it's time to do a few for me."

"He didn't remember the children," Donk mutters. He hadn't meant to say it aloud.

"Nobody remembers anything," Morris says. "It's the condition of the day. Forgetful. People only remember what happens when they're truly paying attention. Let me tell you a few things I think *you'll* remember."

Something shifts and the clustering cardinals are paying undue attention to him. They are only modestly closer, their weapons still sheathed, yet the air is electric with alertness and possibility. Donk stands at parade rest, thinks, so here it is—You knew you'd have to play a big hand today. His hands relaxed, and the coldness in him proclaims—You can do this and you will. It's not that you know how to say exactly what he wants to hear. It's not even the things that you know and he doesn't. It's that he doesn't suspect you know it. That's how you'll convince him. You're holding all the cards, and Tennessee is the trump.

Morris wheels his electric cart around, pointing his bleached driftwood of a leg at Donk.

"Are you listening closely?" Morris asks.

"I'm listening."

"Two days ago, I was chasing a man."

"Gordy."

Morris spits it back at him. "*Gordy.* He disappeared outside *your* place of business."

"That's the word."

"That's the truth. Listen, 'Coyote,' or whatever it is you're calling yourself now," Morris wheels himself a bit closer. "You provide information. It's your entire purpose. Bring me some information now, and I don't mean about how to capture some third-rate crime boss. I want good clear intelligence—now—about Gordy and where to find him."

"You know," Donk remarks, "I seem to recall two weeks ago I told you exactly where and how to find him, and I was completely right. Wasn't I?"

Morris, shaking his head slow, voice measured: "You're displaying a lot less consternation than I'd like to see from somebody who's failed me this badly."

"You'd like me to apologize?"

"I'd like to see you more consterned. I'd like you nonplussed. You're far too plussed."

"I'm a calm guy. You don't want a calm guy working for you?"

"You don't seem like a calm guy to me. To me you seem like the cat with the cream. You seem like the guy who figured out what I need and stole it."

"So. How do I convince you otherwise?"

"I'd feel better if I was sure you were motivated to find that hard-to-see prickhole last seen right next to your headquarters."

"I'll find him."

"That's right, *Coyote*. You'll find him, because here's the deal: I will have Gordy in my custody within the next two days, or you're going in one of those boxes. I've got one here specially for you."

Hands relaxed, Donk lets the moment build, allows it to seem as if this were something unexpected he needs to digest. Then he says:

"You'll give me three months."

Morris is so startled by the effrontery he laughs, once, a single surprised bark. He looks around at his redbird lieutenants as if providing them a share of his own amusement.

"I will?"

"Probably."

"Because…?"

"Because I know what specifically to look for."

"And that is?"

"It might be a little rectangle. It might be shiny. It might be green. I'm being circumspect for your benefit here."

In the silence that follows, something long and poisonous uncoils. It's a serpent Donk knows he's unleashed, which he now must ride. Morris says: "Everybody except for the Andrews, take a walk." When they've gone and it's only them and the little guys, he says. "All right. You have my attention."

"So it seems."

"This had best be good, or you go in the box today. What does Gordy have that I want?"

Donk says. "I expect he has a number of things you want to take from him, including a pound or two of his flesh. But I'm talking about that little green lottery ticket he boosted from you back in Pigeon Forge. From behind your door. Under that fountain of yours. The one whose prize is control over everything in the universe."

The Andrews eyeball each other, the first reaction he's ever seen from them. Morris says nothing for a while but neither does he look away. Donk's hands are relaxed.

"Go get the others," Morris says at last. As the Andrews go, he says what Donk has been expecting and dreading:

"And make the oubliette ready."

His hands relaxed, Donk keeps his face empty. This is the final negotia- tion—I've got you, prick. I've got you and you won't even know I've got you, not even after I've done it.

Morris says: "You've got some terribly classified information, my friend."

"It's what I do. It's what I've always done."

"You realize you're not leaving here?"

"Sounds like," Donk remarks. "But I'm still thinking you'll give me that three months, before you show me a shovel or a bird"—thinking *oh, that one hit all right* as Morris's eyes go briefly wide—Yes, Morris, how *did* I know about the bird and the spade?

"Everything you know," Morris says. "And how you know it."

Donk begins to explain it, all of it, from door to vault. He's cut off before he's halfway.

"How."

"Because I came to realize something true. Which led to knowledge."

"What knowledge?"

"You exist. I don't. Neither does anyone else, only you. These things I know—fountain, ticket, the rest—I think I know them because you know them. I know them because...it sounds silly to say out loud...because I'm a part of you."

"And what part of me are you?"

"I think I'm your lesson to yourself about this place."

From deep in Morris's throat a tiny surprised sound escapes. Neither of them says anything for a while. From his pocket Morris removes a cigar; with deliberate and ceremonial anticipation unwraps, clips, and lights. He folds the cellophane wrapper precisely. Only the slightest shake of the wrapper as he returns it to an inner pocket betrays him. Languorously, he emits a wreath of smoke. "You know everything I know?"

"Not everything," Donk says, immediately. "I think it's whatever you want me to know. Or what a deeper part of you requires me to know. I'm speculating."

"But you know things that I know."

"And other things besides. I may be how you're choosing to inform yourself. I definitely know more about what's going on in Loony Island than you do."

"Then where is Gordy?"

"That much I don't know—yet."

"And you think I'm giving you months to find him?"

"I think it would be a good idea."

"Instead of the box? I'm sure you do."

"Not for my own sake. I want to find the ticket, because I want you to have it. It's yours. None of us can be whole until you have it. I won't stop until you have it or you dispose of me."

"I might dispose of you in five minutes." But Donk can see Morris warring with himself, caught between hope and suspicion.

"If that's what you want, I don't see how it could be wrong."

"You're so deferential now. You weren't so polite earlier."

"I'm your lesson to yourself. Have your lessons to yourself typically been polite?"

"And you don't care what I do to you?"

"You'll eventually get the ticket without me, and then I'll be a part of you, like everybody else. What I do until then isn't of much bother to me one way or another."

Morris, looking keenly at him: "I *almost* believe you."

"You'll believe me in time if you don't believe me today. You'll believe me because I'm a tool you've given yourself."

Beetle-browed, Morris tries on a variety of grimaces. "I still think you're bluffing."

Donk shrugs. "Put me in the box. See how I react."

And so Morris does.

The cardinals come back in with the box and Donk surprises them. He puts on the harness and other accoutrements himself. Folds his suit coat, trousers, shirt. Sets his tie neatly atop the pile. Neither eager nor lagging, businesslike he dresses himself in the harness as if it were just another suit; he latches it to himself where he can reach as if adjusting a tie clip. The cardinals eye each other nervously; they've never seen this one before. He waits patiently as they affix him inside the box, latching and strapping, connecting, his face indifferent. He bides his time and just when they are about to shut him in, in cold crisp tones he says it. "Oh yes, there's something else you could use to catch him: Gordy is still looking for a bearded lady."

His hands are relaxed relaxed relaxed as the lid closes and the lights come on.

"You weren't bluffing after all," Morris says.

Donk can't see much; even the white anteroom looks dark after the brutal banks of fluorescent glare on each side bounding off the mirrors. He can, however, see Morris's eyes at the crack, calm but curious, flitting around to various points on Donk's face, as if reassessing him piecemeal, reconstructing him into something more than he had been previously. Donk bites back the scream of relief. It's over. He's still hooked into the box, but he's come through the narrowest place, shot the rapid, won the big hand. The rest of this will be nothing but pantomime and posture, Morris assuring himself he's still the man in charge, but Donk, about to be released and elevated, knows it's only a matter of time now.

"What do you know about Jane?" Morris asks.

Donk smiles. "Well, *now* I know her name. I know that Gordy's looking for her. She'd draw him out, if we knew where she was."

"She's…elsewhere."

"Can you trust me enough to share where?"

"Down this tunnel. End of the line."

"Can you get her?"

He nods. "Tunnel CATs."

"Tunnel…*cats*?"

"Channel Automated Transports. My researchers developed them. You've seen them. The entrance to the living capsule looks like a safe door. They can carry me safely through, but it takes a week. It's…a far land."

"Worth the trip. Go get her. She'll draw Gordy out."

Morris, musing almost to himself: "She's been gone quite some time. She…stopped being useful, but…there was a time she belonged to a circus I own."

"Then bring the circus and put her in it. Set it up right in Ralph's parking lot if you want. You have the circus, bring the lady. We'll advertise it everywhere. I'll plaster Ralph's store with posters. If he's here, he'll come out." Donk finds he's warming to the plan even as he makes it. It's genius, really—because it'll work. It *will* bring Gordy out of hiding, and it'll keep him here in the meanwhile. "Give this Jane something to do ahead of the show, some dance or something. Make her easy for somebody who wants to find her to find her. Tell her to give a shout if he shows, and have your people watching just in case she doesn't."

"You know for a fact Gordy's still hanging around here."

"No. But I do think it's alarmingly likely."

"Likely, why?"

"It's a fantastic place to hide, Loony Island. There's no end to places in it where nobody would go or would want to go. And there's this: It would be unexpected. The right-under-your-nose thing. Also, his only known friend is here."

"The priest."

"*He's* easy to find. I bet the dummy's already back at his chapel. I'm serious, he's that thick. Even getting shot doesn't run him off, so I doubt his tussle with you will do it. Want me to have some guys go kill him?"

Morris takes a long time pretending to consider this. Even harnessed, trapped, even entirely at the mercy of the one whom he wished most harm, Donk takes pleasure in making him try to order violence against Julius. In experimentation with the priest, it's become clear Gordy's prohibition between them remains: No Harm. Julius had found himself unable even to form violent thoughts against Morris; attempting to do so, he'd reported, was an unpleasant experience.

"No," Morris says at last.

"At least I could have him snatched and brought back here. Torture him until he coughs up what he knows." This is pushing it; but for Julius's sake, Donk needs to make the boss say it in front of all his guys, so they hear it. Surely Morris's pride hasn't allowed him to admit to his minions that an outside force shackled his will to some restriction. Donk tries to imagine how badly Morris wants to order Julius's destruction, how hard he's fighting to give that word. The anguish it's causing him. How he'll even be forced, if pushed on the subject, to order Julius protected, if only to reassert himself. At last, in strained tones, Morris says. "No. Watch him. If we grab him, it might scare off that little bastard Gordy for good."

"It's your call, boss, but even if he's not a lead, he's a loose end. We can snip it…"

Morris snarls, "Are you deaf? I said we leave the priest alone."

Donk thinks: So passes that particular danger. Julius, three times denied, will stay safe from this crowing cock.

"You're a bothersome fellow, Coyote."

"I've heard that before."

"You may be a true lesson for me. I'm going to give you three months to find him." Morris says this as though it's an idea he's originated. "I've had false lessons before who were as convincing as you. If you're one of those, you'll fail, and I'll put you back where you are now."

To the others, he snaps: "Well? Get him out of there."

It's dark when Donk returns to the Fridge. He starts some coffee, looks around as it percolates. There ought to be somebody here to tell that the long path is now walked, that Yale is now revenged, that Ralph has gotten his. He can tell Julius or Gordy, but it won't mean the same to them. He can tell Bailey, if she wakes up, but for now there's nobody. He has the strangest feeling, there used to be, ought to be someboyd here to tell. "Done," Donk whispers. He holds the coffee cup to his forehead, feeling the warmth. He repeats it: "Done."

Five minutes. They'd left him in the box five minutes—a bad eternity… but he'd been right in the end. His hands had still been relaxed when at last the case opened, though in another five minutes they wouldn't have been. He could feel the scream building in him like a slow promise of coming vomit. Within the hour it would have been tearing from him. Nothing but your eyes staring back into your eyes. Your body immobile. Walled in. Donk checks his watch; Ralph has now been in his own box for seven hours. There's a hell, Donk tells himself. Ralph is there. You went and found it, picked it out for him. You even sampled it for yourself to be sure. Our plan is done, better than we ever hoped.

It feels like nothing. Thinking back on the aging heavyset Ralph, blood-caked and struggling on the floor…he may as well have been a different person than that green-suited snake slithering up the fire escape to the greenhouse. Ralph hadn't remembered doing it. He'd forgotten killing all those kids, as easy as a cook disposing of stale biscuits, remembering it years later no more than the cook would remember the biscuits. If he doesn't remember doing it, he may as well have been a different person. To suffer but never know why he's suffering...

In time he realizes the problem: He's had to empty himself of Ralph to fill himself with Morris. That's the only problem. It's good to have completed the job with Ralph, even if it tastes like sand and air. It will be different when it's Morris. When it's Morris, revenge's consummation will feel like he always dreamed it would feel. But for Morris, oubliettes are too easy; they seem a kindness in comparison to the impossible horrors Donk has devised. For Morris, he has suffering planned that will require a new power. His coffee needs a stiffener, so he gets the booze. Drinks half the coffee, fills it back with the other stuff. Remembering oubliette walls. Jesus. The coldness is in him, but all the same...the haunted look in Gordy's face makes more sense now ...the guy spent years in there. And Tennessee, too. Jesus. Oubliettes. And hundreds of people still caged up like that; not monsters like Ralph, but ordinary people who did nothing but cross the wrong guy...

Donk, suffused with outrage on their behalf, pours some more dark liquid into the mug, refills the rest with coffee—not only for Bailey, then. For Gordy. For Tennessee. For all of them. All of them, whether flying through the air to their earthy doom or latched into boxes, or the whores forced by cruel men onto their backs while their kids spend long days alone staring at the same four walls day after day, *tub-tub-tub-tub*; for panes of greenhouse glass smashed forever, for the cold and sick lying on the streets, unattended and cooking unique madness beneath their coverings of filth and rag. You want to be the maker of the whole world, boss? Fine. I'll try you for the whole world's suffering. I'll make you feel it all, once I get that ticket. I'll find it for you, all right. I'll find it. For you.

He pours some more coffee, his hands so relaxed so calm they shake.

The coffee is gone, and so is the booze. Donk is calm now. Very calm, much calmer than before. He is the very calmest of all times. Totally calmery. His hands are so relaxed he could throw the ball into the cup *tub-tub-tub-tub-*

tub a thousand times in a row if he needed to but Yale and Bailey aren't on the other side of the door to help him anymore if he loses his ball Bailey fell her eyes going wide and there was hardly any blood but she fell like meat, now he has no pot to throw into or a window to throw out of, all he has is the lies he's told. The room moves but only a little. In time he stands with exceeding steadiness. Selects a bottle of fine port, then stops himself—you fool, you've left your guests waiting too long, they'll want to celebrate. He walks to the room he once shared with Bailey, rolls back the rug, revealing the door to a panic room set into the floor of the Fridge. Yes, Ralph commissioned a panic room within a panic room; no wonder he was so hard to capture. Donk stomps on the floor in the sequence he and the priest have agreed upon. The trapdoor lifts up, revealing Julius's hairy head.

"Well?"

Donk is mindful not to slur. "It's taken care of. It was just like I said. He wants you dead, you can see it on his face. But he couldn't say it, and he certainly couldn't admit he couldn't say it—not in front of his guys. I got him to demand nobody hurts you."

"Thank fucking God. I'm going stir-crazy down here, sniffing Gordy's farts."

From below, out of sight (though no longer invisible to them), another voice, less hearty, says: "If it's a question of farts, I'm pretty sure I'm not the offending party."

"Come on out, have a drink. You can go back to the Neon in the morning if you want."

Halfway out, Julius stops.

"Thank you, Daniel."

"No worries," Donk says, but unfortunately the priest is in a mood for sincerity.

"No. Honestly. I have to confess, I was beginning to mistrust you. But you truly...I...there are no words."

"Forget it. Easy to do. Schmuck loves me. Got him eating out of my hand."

"And Tennessee?"

Donk shakes his head. "I *told* him to stay with me, but he wouldn't listen.

He ran off. Either he's skipped town like he said he would, or the redbirds got him."

"Please try to find him. I need to talk to him. He was telling me something important, but I kept drifting in and out. At the very least I owe him my thanks."

"Hell. Now you're safe again, you can look for him."

Later, all the lights off, bottle emptied, guests passed out, the priest's snores threatening the structural integrity of the walls, and Donk sits, blinking. It's all he can do. The room spins. He thinks: The mistake was the port. That's not right you fool, you got it reversed, it's wackbird. He blinks. The room moves. He blinks and waits. The room moves. He blinks. He's forgotten the thing that happened to him. He's drowned it in the blinking spin, the safe port of Blink the harbor of Spin, which exports coffee mixed with gold. Any storm in a port. No. Wrong. How does it go? "Andy stort in a porm?" Perfect. Blink. Spin. I wish I could forget being in the box. What I wouldn't give for a fountain. Splinkbin.

From time to time, Gordy sits up on the couch, emits a terrified, terrifying scream, then collapses back down again. The moom rooves.

Later, the room has stopped moving somewhat and he's remembered being in the box again. He considers more booze to counter it, but he knows he needs to think in more structured ways. With effort he makes his mind once more into compartments—anyway the memory of being in the box will always be there, and you can't keep drowning it. You have three months to make moves if you don't want the thing that happened to happen again forever, so you're going to have to learn to live with it. His hands curl and relax. It's going to be tricky. Julius is going back to the Neon Chapel, which is fine. Gordy wants to go off looking for his precious bearded lady (remember Coyote, remember: They don't know that you know about the fountain ticket bearded lady) which is *not* fine. Keeping Gordy hidden here in the Fridge isn't an option, unfortunately, unless you want to use force, and using force against Gordy is too unpredictable. There needs to be a way to keep him in the Island. Julius will be useful there; he seems to hold some sway over the kid—but that won't be enough.

That's where the circus comes in.

Promise the kid his circus, the return of his precious bearded lady Jane, and he'll wait. And Morris will have to gift you a couple valuable weeks to maneuver without his eyes on you when he goes to fetch her. Only Gordy can't be allowed to wander far, that's the main thing, at least not until he coughs up the ticket. The ticket is key. Donk's not sure he believes it works the way Tennessee said, but he's seen enough flouting of natural laws—Gordy's flickering being first among those—to believe there is *something* that gives power. Also, the prohibition of harm between Julius and Morris is a mystery, but it is real for both of them. Yes. The ticket, whatever it is, will give you the power you need to give Morris the punishment he's earned.

The room hardly moves now. Donk reads for a time, then rises and leaves the room, walks briskly to Domino City, keys himself into the most decrepit of the six dominoes, the one most given over to ruin. He jogs up the stairs—the elevator's been busted so long nobody can remember if it ever worked—to the fifth floor, which is the foulest floor of the foulest building. Nobody comes here unless they've got nowhere else. The smell hits you like a wave. Bums and drifters passed out—some seem dead—filth piled in the hallway, half the lights punched out. He goes to this one now, the one at the end, the only other door still opening onto a room Donk keeps. About this room even Bailey knew nothing. It's small and sparsely furnished, a single room containing only a television, a kitchenette, a cot in the corner, and Tennessee on the cot. Tennessee stirs when the door opens.

"What's the story, captain?"

"Morris has the cardinals all still out sweeping for you. All day and night. Morris says he's not going to rest until he finds you. They've got posters up with your face on it."

Tennessee moans and sinks his head into his hands, fingers in hair.

"I need to know where Gordy's keeping the ticket. Hoping you have a clue."

Looking up, hopeful: "Gordy-Gord? You've found him?"

"Negative. Both he and Julius are still missing. But if—when—I find them, we'll need to be able to locate the ticket, and quick, if we're going to stop Morris."

Tennessee rolls back onto the cot. "Your guess is as good as good as my my mine. Back in the day he just kept it in his pocket." This probably isn't helpful, but Donk knows he can't complain to Tennessee; it would lead only to questions better unasked. Every day, he knows, he'll worry over the lies he's told. Keeping each one properly discrete.

"Are you sure there's nowhere else it might be? Nothing you remember?"

"Nothing," Tennessee says. "Nothing comes to mind. I wish Gordy was here with us."

"I *told* them to stay with me," Donk says. "But they wouldn't listen. They ran off and I don't know where. It's just you and me against the world. I've been out and about. Let me tell you the lie of the land."

GORDY READS: **GUILLOTINE**

"Rule Ten!" Father proclaimed. "The most important one. Ready?"

"Yes."

The old man drew in.

"Rule Ten," he said. "Don't ever trust those darned rabbits."

Returning to the table, he rescued the bottle and drank deeply. I saw his mirrored headgear resting like a paperweight on top of the largest stack of documents. It was the sight of the headgear, I think, that finally caused me to break.

"Rabbits!" I shouted.

"Shhh!" My father seemed suddenly unsure. He sidled up to me, draped an arm around my shoulder, guided me to a chair by the table. "Let me explain." He leaned in conspiratorially. The candlelight played on one side of his face, while on the other the gloom made canyons of each crease and groove.

"The rabbits are invisible." he whispered. "But they're there. You'll see. They hide in the corners of all my mirrors"—here he pointed to the mirrors covering every inch of laboratory wall—"and come at me at the very worst times. They gang up on me and pull me down and nibble at my energy. Judging. I thought they wouldn't be able to get at me down here, but they finally found me. Now it's worse. Now I know there's nowhere else to go. But I didn't give up." He puffed up with ridiculous pride. "I'm taking the fight to them." He leapt to the shape beside the table. It was tall and blocky and covered by a sheet, which he soon had lying in a puddle on the flagstones. I looked at the revealed object, no more enlightened than I had been before.

It was a guillotine.

As guillotines go, it was a beauty, reflected to regressive infinity in the lab's wall mirrors. The frame appeared to be made of cherry wood, varnished and lacquered to radiance. The blade was ice-blue stainless steel; pinpoints of candlelight danced from its surface. It had one feature unusual to guillotines: the gap meant for the head lay higher than usual, as if designed for a standing victim. My father beamed with lunatic pride.

"What are you going to do with. . . ?"

"My forehead." My father's tone suggested the guillotine's purpose was self-evident.

"Your. . . ?"

"I've got it all planned out. Look!" He scrambled to the table and rooted through the largest stack of papers. The hat and side mirrors, resting atop it, began to slip, and the old man caught the rig, placing it absently on his head, making him look like a deranged moose. He retrieved a handful of documents covered with stains and geometric figures and trigonometric equations, and waved them in my face.

"It's all in this report," he announced, surveying himself once again in the mirrors. "The angles, blade weight and sharpness, my cranial curvature, cauterization, everything. It's all planned out to the most minor detail. Except how to make the damn thing drop. It all depends on absolute stillness. But I have it rigged. A rope with pulleys. Frictionless. No movement to the important components. But I need to hold absolutely still. Somebody else needs to hold the rope and drop it for me."

His fevered eyes rested, at last, upon me.

Something brittle within me began to splinter and crack. In that moment, my childhood arithmetic was finally solved, and came to nothing. I was amazed, I was tired, I was sad, most of all, I was surprised—not only by what I'd found, but because I realized I no longer cared if I were allowed to stay. I saw myself clearly at last: a sad boy, taking moments, glances, a single conversation, and pasting these together to craft a story he could tell himself, some fine tale transforming him into a figure of consequence. A new story became brutally clear: I was not the faithful son. I was not even something so interesting as a madman's apprentice. I was nothing but a boy who had spent his childhood hoping to become the madman's apprentice, an aspiring Igor. I was the boy beneath even the madman's consideration. The idea that he had been waiting for me to come to him? Ridiculous. And here lay the awful truth: Part of me still wanted to join him, and, in so doing, receive my meaning.

I ran.

p i t

The line on display in her portfolio was clean and steady; even so, Juanita Neato's hands shook at the first meeting.

Sir, can I, can I just say, what an honor it is to meet you. Your book, it's...there's so much, I mean, I feel like I just get lost in it. I've been reading this since I was a kid.

You smiled then, because she was *still* a kid. The only hitch: Neato was such an enthusiast—a fan—she'd balked when she heard your plans for the book.

But...they're your main characters.

Trust me.

They're coming back...aren't they? Tell me they're coming back.

You smiled: Just trust me.

You wrote the script in a blood fever and sent it by express courier. Neato in her zeal returned the pages a week ahead of schedule. You looked them over, chuckling—Why, these are perfect. Donk and Boyd and Bailey dead, vaporized, dropped into an enormous mechanized blender with blades the size of swords. Reading the pages became the culmination of each month, and therein lay the hollowness of it, the emptiness; to achieve ultimate victory but to experience it only in two dimensions. Your subjects, kingdom, fountain...all of these lay on the other side of the study door. The temptation of the study door remained ever-present—back there, you could be anything, do anything, really see it. You reminded yourself: There's a higher plane. As you perfect the lower story— each month providing fresher and higher triumphs for the one you replace—your power will grow in this place, until once again you rise.

But signs of this power remained elusive on the artist's side, which was given to mundanity: groceries and bills and emails, fan mail (diminishing), long hours alone. Meanwhile (as Rupert Paddington informed you with in- creasingly resigned despondency) your publishers grew impatient with what they called the "Morris Tangent." Worried by the lost readership and (more to the point) lost revenue, they demanded a triumphant return of the heroes—even as Juanita Neato grew presumptuous. In the margins she began scribbling commentary: alternative story ideas, frantic notes, angry messages. She delivered issue 136 with her own signature inked on each page. You'd been forced to meet with her then.

I think I'm being used. And not even for good cause.

You're being paid. And it's the best cause I can imagine.

You're ruining one of comics' greatest works. It's time to change it back.

Or else…what?

Or else nothing.

Not a very strong bargaining position.

No. Or else, *nothing*. Nothing more. Not another line or dot. I won't be a part of it.

Then you're fired.

Then I talk about who's been drawing the book uncredited for the last year.

The baboon rage had risen then, a desire to remove her from existence, to make her not be. You'd been on the verge of snarling something hateful, but then, all at once, you understood the nature of your error. It's always this way when you finally understand your lessons to yourself. You wondered at how you'd missed it—how ridiculous. You can't even kill her if you want to, here on this side. There would be actual consequences. See how neutered you've become? Never mind your inability to mold reality here; think how reality imposes upon you. You have to follow laws. This isn't a mountain. It was never a mountain. Think where the power lies.

You made yourself soft then—You're right. No. You're right.

I—What?

There's been a lot of pressure. You displayed the hand you claimed was your drawing hand, for which you'd claimed injury. It's…been difficult. To not be able to draw. To lose the ability all at once. But…I owe you an apology. An apology, and more. I just…I think that's why I killed the characters off. To see somebody else drawing them…you see?

I…yes. I'm sorry. I can't imagine—

No, *I'm* sorry. I've been so focused on myself. Look. Here's what I think we should do. We'll bring Donkeyface and Boyd and Bailey back. And we'll get your name on the book.

Don't kid me.

You want me to call Universe Comics right now and tell them?

They'd go for it?

They don't have a choice. I created the book on my own, and I kept ownership of the characters. They don't own me. They're distribution partners.

I...don't know what to say.

You laughed as easily as you could manage. Well, you say "It's about god-dam time."

She laughed, but she did repeat it, and she sounded as if she meant it, too.

Actually, you should come to my studio. We'll be more aligned then, as we work.

No. *Way.*

We can start right now if you like.

You got a surprise dragging Neato unconscious through the door. "Morris" was still lying there, exactly where you left him. So you learned: The door always opens upon the same moment—though from there you can jump to any moment. By focusing your mind, you can be anywhere, be anything, do anything. Think it and it is—Why hadn't you seen it before? This cavern side isn't the lower tier at all, it's the higher. You weren't climbing a mountain to reach the prize; no, you descended into a pit to retrieve it. It's so obvious. Consider how upside-down in character it is, how perverse in design, how inconceivably contrary to nature, for your author to be such a failed thing as he manifestly was. Consider how much less power you have on the artist's side, how much less influence you possess, how much less *you* you are. Here you preside, plenipotentiary in rightful dominion, your territory the map and your map the territory. Here you can be the clouds, you can make the sky the mountains. Turn the streets to rubber, the trees to steel, the people from cats to dogs to monkeys and back again. Here you can separate the land from the water. "Say" and "is" are at last conjoined, exactly as you knew they must be, for here, all is as you say it is.

Neato lay on the clay beside the author as you pondered her—It won't do to leave you here. You can't belong to the story. I need to erase you and build you another life, then do it again, then again. Backstories onioned all the way in so you'll never be found. Living on the far side of the country from the story, amnesia piled on amnesia, hidden from a reader's prying eyes. Not a Juanita, no, nothing so distinctive.

You'll be a plain Jane.

Returning to the artist's side, everything remained as before, except…

There it was. A new stack of paper, inches thick, on the table. The first revision you ever created.

You'd known, certain past supposition, your journey had generated them. Remember your sense of triumph in that moment? Letting yourself believe it was better than you'd hoped, that you'd be able to make the book without an artist as imperfect interfering intermediary, that you could make it over there, on the other side, with nothing but your will to make the changes, while the pages wrote themselves. Your mind your tool; reality your craft.

Before reading, though, you concentrated on the clean-up. Rubbing every surface with a cloth to erase traces of Neato, the thought met you— Rupert Paddington. They might trace her back to you through him. He won't be suspicious…except…over the past year it was Paddington who'd passed along each of her notes to you, and yours to her. If Paddington read them, he'd have picked up on the increasingly adversarial tone…or—or!—if she had spoken to him about you… after all, he arranged for her employment… How did he find her? Were they friends? Relatives? Lovers? By sunrise, convinced you'd wiped away every trace of her, you dialed Paddington.

Rupert, you told the phone. Call me back. I think we should drop Universe and go back to self-publishing. I'm sick of their constraints. They need us more than we need them.

Paddington took the bait; he arrived a little after noon in a stampede of agitation. A short man, almost perfectly round, with an amazing curlicued mustache. He paced inside the study, his voice rising and falling in a minister's cadence, red-faced, puffing, canNOT beLIEVE you're even conSIDering this course of ACTion, you'll be KILLing your REVenue STREAM, Land, Landlandland LAND have you conSIDered the impliCAtions…

Carnival barker, you thought, making careful note of anything Paddington touched. You're nothing but a little round carnival barker. I know the place for you, right beside your whatever-she-was-to-you. You brought Neato's effects through the door with him. Anticipation for the pages heavy on your mind until you returned. Was the stack thicker than before? You couldn't be sure, but you thought so. Breathless, you rushed to the table.

This is how the first man taught himself fear of the first rattlesnake: hungry for meat, he reached out his hand and grabbed it.

Thought Morris:

Is the thief still in the Island? Does he still carry the ticket? The Coyote—Donk—he claims to know these things. Claims. Still, his advice moved you to action. Jane proved apt bait once; she may prove apt yet again. The CAT rumbles easily through the tunnel, the thief carved it for his impossible escape to a far land—but not far enough to escape you. A magnificent invention, the CAT, constructed to your exact specifications. Cone shaped; seen from behind it resembles a vault door. Fast; it can make the trip in a week. It is on the incline—you're near. They call my people the cardinals—is this an echo of the sign of the bird? Consider it longer, and further meaning will come. These tunnels—you are in them now—were carved in such a moment of meaning. Are they an echo of the sign of the spade? Ponder it. The thief uses your stolen treasure to escape. Later, meeting with engineers, poring over blueprints of prototypes for the CAT, you realize you have no thought remaining for your door in the cavern. That wooden rectangle, subject of long obsession, is replaced by another rectangle, smaller, greener, glimpsed only for a moment in the hands of a wrongful owner, drawn from beyond your door. Why would you care any longer for the door? Who pines after a looted vault? All your thoughts are for the ticket now. It will be yours. . . but your reaching just pushes it further away.

When he fled he chose not to bring Jane and her daughter. It surprised you; it still does. What prevented him from doing so? This lesson is clear. Those two are baggage so treacherous even the enemy you created for yourself leaves them behind. They also, in their own way, are you, and so you are loath to destroy them, but seeing the danger they posed you wisely stored them safe away. But you held the woman only a day before you. . . what? Relented? Reconsidered? Ungrateful in any case. Restored to her rooms but she no longer tended your sheep, not even with a lamb of her own interred. Scribbled gibberish on the wall. Then to Brasschaat for a time, where she served her purpose and was ruined. You've kept her here, on the far end of these tunnels, the thief dug them but you have bested them, you travel through them in the CAT as you please. The thief escaped, thanks to the priest.

The priest Julius must be punish

    must be

    the priest must be

    must

    Never mind the priest. The priest is nothing, a distraction. You must think of the thief, and his ticket, and the lady he seeks, the lady he bearded. She can draw out thief and ticket—so claims the Coyote—but she will need convincing.

              —Boyd Ligneclaire, *Subject to Infinite Change*

A S K

Her room has a large picture window overlooking a back street, an offshoot of a secondary tributary, itself an offshoot from Brasschaat's modest red-light district. Cobbles glisten in streetlight, and across the road Jane can see the houses on the opposite side huddled together, mirrors of the house in which she stands, two stories tall with peaked false fronts. Narrow alleys skulk between these houses, some of them only a few inches... but some you could stand in. You can see right into this window from those alleys, Jane thinks. Which is, of course, why Morris chose this place for you to perform, and for peeping Gordy to see. First Morris sent you to love Gordy. Then Morris sent you to love others. Then he arranged for Gordy to see you. All part of the trap, the plan.

He is outside now—Morris.

Her beard is combed and washed and she arranges it like armor against him: broad like a plate of steel, with gold threading through. She wears a golden robe brocaded with brown and red and green. Beneath the robe hides the outfit of her trade, two black strips of lace and silk and velvet, like ribbons on a very expensive gift. He's out there, waiting for her to go to him. She sits perfectly still and imagines becoming only a picture of herself. Her breathing slows until it is imperceptible. She hasn't seen him since that day. Years. Who knows how long ago it was for him? Slower time here than there. Or—is it faster? Yes, faster here. No, it's faster there. She's not certain on the point, but that seems right. Which means now, in this moment, here, a clock's hands turn more ponderously than the same clock's hands would there—yet it all feels the same. This moment, here, the interval between the second hand's ticking... how much time would it be—over there—for a young girl growing old in a mirrored coffin?

Finch. A finger on her nose.

Time no longer seems an ally. She decides she will go out and teach him that his demand is a request. She passes through the series of beaded curtains into the anteroom. He's arranged himself in the middle of it, clearly pleased he's won their waiting game. Beyond him, in the windows, the less specialized girls, too new or too unpopular to have built an enduring clientele, pose naked, and he's positioned between—accidentally, she presumes—creating the illusion of angel and devil perched on his shoulders, but faced away from him, dancing in desultory fashion in hopes of capturing some better soul to guide. Yes, she decides, looking at him: Time moves faster there. He's aged. Nevertheless, he looks fit despite crutch and crow's feet. He's clad in unadorned black, hair cropped close, poised despite the cast encasing his leg from shin to thigh. He knows how to make his face do the things they need to do to appear normal to the unobservant, but if you watch the eyes you'll know the truth about him; they've gone even more distant.

He grins. "So, it's true. Oddly, it suits you. I was expecting you to look something like Tolstoy. But this is *almost* elegant. It's even pretty, in a way."

She says nothing. It is possible to become the picture of yourself rather than yourself. It is possible to become stillness. He continues, blithely, "Färland must agree with you, anyway." He's making a show. Picking up various *objets d'art* from the shelves, examining them with a pretended connoisseur's eye—a ridiculous attempt at nonchalance. As if he would ever return to collect her out of exile unless his lemonade had gone badly sour back home. "You're not scribbling on the walls anymore like a loon."

"What do you need?"

He jerks his head doorward. "You're coming back with me."

"He's gotten away from you again, has he?" She doesn't attempt to hide her smile.

"He got lucky."

"It seems he broke your leg. Poor Morris."

"An open manhole! He got *lucky!*" He throws the thing he happens to be holding—a Swiss singing-bird music box. It strikes the wall with a velvet-dampened thud, leaving a small hole in the wallpaper.

"Yes, he got lucky. Didn't he. Won the lottery."

That gets him. If you know to watch the eyes you'd see the rage was there already but now that she's mentioned the ticket, rage has mastery. He's shouting, but this doesn't matter in the least. She's learned the trick every woman learns about men; they can't choose your presence for you. Become stillness if you must, or if you want to. Let the fool blow a petty little storm—this fool, who thinks he's got you in hand. But what good is a grip without leverage? What good the handful when you've mistaken what it is you hold? This was Gordy's error, too. Men think they hold the handle of some empty pitcher they can pour themselves into, some unmarred book into which they can write something fine about themselves, some diamond mirror into which they can gaze, which will reflect only excellence, which will tell them they are the fairest of all.

"Oh God, this is love." Gordy had gushed this at her in Brasschaat, again and again. "Love at last," he pronounced, the day after they'd met. Or "met," rather. It was the same nonsense over again. Them at dinner, him talking to himself at her, amnesiac, unaware, thinking they'd only just met, while she feigned attentiveness and played a game—can I get through the night speaking less than twenty words? Will he notice if I do? Then, later, them in bed as Morris commanded, him nuzzling into her as if she could become his lover and his lost childhood both. Abandoner, walked away from his promises and even the obligation to remember them or be troubled by them. Too deliberately ignorant of his past wrongs to dangle hope anymore of a universe of justice, to tantalize with some story of a mythic cleansing wave. If he'd known the trick of looking at her eyes he'd have seen the truth of her. He'd have seen scorn almost like pity. And, with perfect irony, it was her eyes he complimented the most. "I looked at your eyes and died," he said. The exact words he'd used before. Her eyes. He looked at them and died, failing to see how they brimmed with his death. He loved to look at them but he couldn't read them, failed even to understand they were something that could be read, and so in her eyes he saw nothing but what he hoped to see, which was his own illiterate reflection. In the long quiet moments waiting for Morris to activate his plan, during the first early days as Brasschaat bait, she would muse over whether she still pitied Gordy, or if she only wanted to hurt him for how careless he had been with the faith she'd imparted. It made you want to spit on him, the way he'd speak of love between them, as if it were a thing he was at liberty to claim, as if this supposed love were some quality within himself he had developed, or an acquisition he had wisely made.

And her little bird was caged and gone—she's caged even now. She'd known even then Morris would never release her, never heal her, not even once he had the ticket. Her first priority had been harming Morris, but he kept his distance, sent his orders mostly by proxy. She patiently waited for the opportunity to harm him as badly as she could manage, but if, in the meanwhile, he wanted to utilize her to harm this feckless, capricious boy . . . so be it. So she waited, and when Morris turned her out, she did that, and when at last he told her all was ready, she went to Gordy, and held him, and let him have his way, and after, when he would burrow against her, she would stroke his hair lazily and murmur in his ear "Yes, love at last, this is love at last." Filling himself back up with himself.

As Morris had been fond of saying, it's not as if she had a choice.

He's still saying it—it's his line. He's finished screaming now; he's moved on to cajoling. "Look, love," he's saying. "Be reasonable. It's not as if you have a choice."

She smiles. He's so wrong. She didn't know it last time but she knows it now. He still thinks he's holding her, but he's broken the pitcher; he's holding nothing now but the handle.

"I have several choices."

"Oh *do* you?" He's amused.

One finger. "I could help you."

"You *will* help me."

"Give me a reason."

"You've forgotten your daughter?"

"You're not so stupid as to believe you can still use *our* daughter on me. We both know your promises are lies. What do you think is left of her mind by now anyway? After *years*?"

He's trying not to seethe. "I can put you in an oubliette."

Two fingers. "If those are the only choices, I choose that one."

"You've seen what it does to people."

"I'm good at being alone."

"I could just kill you."

Three. "Your best offer yet."

"You're bluffing." And now he's looking at her like she's the crazy one—

how rich. Him, the man who buys and sells people, warehouses them when they annoy, moves them around like commodities, who abandons his own daughter to torture, who pimps out his own wife and leaves her behind in a far land, who believes the universe emitted from his brain.

"I could kill Finch."

Four fingers. The thumb left over to shove into his eye if he gives her a chance. "A mercy, not a threat. Poor Morris. You've already done the worst. Now all you have is second worst. But at least you've said your daughter's name."

So now he sees she has choices. He's shifting subtly, a slight transfer of weight; the leg is troubling him. The crutch pad is probably kindling fire in his armpit at this point. He doesn't want to sit, she knows—it would acknowledge weakness—but the discomfort might grow too much. He may sit yet. A small thing, but a victory nonetheless. These are the stakes now—I'm going to wear you down. I'm going to make you take a seat. I'm going to make you acknowledge your stinking flesh in front of me. She goes away into her mind, and waits.

"You don't even know what I'm asking you to do," he sulks.

"You want me to be the bait again. I'm the only carrot he'll bite on."

"Yes, but you don't know how. I'm sending you back to the show."

"The circus?"

"Think about it, Janey. You could fly again."

Despite herself, she does think about it. The trapeze. The leap, the catch. The moment between rising and falling, alone among multitudes, so close to the striped canvas tent top you can see the weft, all alone for a split second before gravity calls you back home. The implosion of breath from the crowd as you miss the bar, the pantomimed horror of the clowns. The single organism they all become in their relief as your feet find the hidden line of the tightrope. Chuffing along in a train compartment on the way to the next show, watching the world create itself for you outside your window. She catches him catching her considering it.

"I always loved to watch you fly."

Yes. To fly again…the leap, the catch. The catch? Of course—there's always a catch. "Nobody wants to see a bearded lady on the trapeze."

"You're kidding," he says. "*Everybody* would want to see it. It's never been seen before. The freak show melded with the big show. You'd dance as a freak, then you'd fly like a dream. A double-show. Think of the pitch. Think of the posters."

When the beard first sprouted it grew in all at once, Jane still straddling the man Morris had chosen, whose head had, moments before, exploded into spaghetti, Gordy seething at the door, saying things at her. She never once responded; it didn't matter. This was part of Morris's plan, too. He didn't want to hear her and she no longer cared to be heard. The hour had come, the moment for which she had been brought here, the fisherman preparing the net even as the fish closed its jaws around the bait. Who considers the bait, already impaled? Why should even the worm concern itself with the worm? Gordy whispered at her, Gordy screamed. In between he cried and raged, paced, threw furniture. The man still beneath her dead and she sat frozen waiting for her own end. Morris hoped the shock of this event would revert Gordy to something more manageable, safer to grab. He'd told her, outright—he hoped to make Gordy do something with it, something terrible enough Gordy would never want to use it again, not against anybody. Something to make him afraid to say words that come true, think thoughts that unfold into reality before him, too frightened of his power to use it, no matter what Morris might next do to him. And Gordy had killed a man, the man Morris had arranged for him to catch her with, he'd spaghettied his head into literal spaghetti, and she sat astraddle, waiting for him to do the same or worse, yes soon Gordy would do the terrible whatever-it-might-be to her, his own true love. This had been her leap, a leap to save her little bird, but the "catch" required her destruction, and this catch, like so many previous catches, depended on the whim of a clown. Jane hoped after she had been destroyed, Morris would honor their agreement—free their daughter, heal her body, mend her mind…but she knew well that if, after she was gone, Morris chose to betray, he would forgive himself the treachery and credit his forgiveness of himself as forgiveness from her. In the room Gordy had raged and wept like a child. But she had already learned the trick of not being there; she went away as he said things at her, I thought you loved me, he said, and I thought you were different, and you were the best thing in my life, and I looked in your eyes and I died, and why did you never *tell* me.

"Sometimes when I say things they happen," he cried. "One time I turned a dog into a cat. One time I made a surly bartender float inches over the ground. He was ignoring me, but not after I made him float. I'm a dangerous man. You should have been more careful with my heart."

"Do you know how to make a bartender float?" he screamed. "It's easy. Vanilla ice cream, seventeen pounds of it. Add four gallons of Duvel. Garnish with a single bartender." He laughed and screamed and cried.

"Oh God," he said. "Oh God oh God oh God now I've killed a man because of you."

Because of you. She knows this line; it's the mantra of men—Have you ever known a man who worshipped at a different altar? Morris blames you for his failing with the door, and for the female offspring you produced, the end of his great continuance. He blames your treachery for his failing with the ticket. Holds your baby hostage to make a whore of you, and your reward is to be given the blame for the whoring as well, to be condemned as a slattern by a man who has the power of a god but lacks the fortitude even to allow himself to remember how he had been the engine of your compromise. You're forced by men into the shapes chosen by them and then, once you're contorted to their specifications, they demand you defend your unnatural position to them.

The stray thought came as she, present but not present, observed Gordy's rage: They fall in love with us so they can blame us; they sense instinctively they will be disappointed in life, know they will fail, but can't bear the thought they may have to locate the source and cause of failure within themselves—*their* weakness, *their* errors, *their* choices—and so they find another and imagine her as a beautiful crystal container. In their minds they make it perfect, flawless—not because it truly is flawless, but because secretly they know it is not. They prepare it for disappointment, for failure, so when the time comes they will in their rage have something other than themselves to smash. They store their blame in us like they store their seed, draw fault from us like offspring. Here was this boy, this forgetful boy, glaring at her with hatred for the sake of the faceless man he had murdered, prepared to enact revenge on her for his lack of control over himself.

And then he did it. He didn't kill her. Didn't even harm her. Instead he attacked the portion of her he thought was most important. The beard was full grown to her navel even before he'd left the room.

Lately it's strange, to think Gordy would have considered what he had done to her such a terrible thing, such a punishment. More proof—if she had needed any—that to him she had only ever been a body. He'd thought to kill the female in her, mock her beauty, but after a week in the darkness, thinking, she opted to zig against his zag. So this is what I am, she thought. This has been given me. Then I will be it, and I will be wonderful. The moustache curled unmanageably, so she waxed it. The beard she tended and nurtured, shampooed and combed. Likewise she looked at the place she'd been abandoned to and decided this intended fate would be something she took rather than something he gave. Men stopped wanting her, at least for a time, and then she loved the beard as her protection from unwanted attentions. Then the fetishists found out about her, and she was never alone again, but even so she found she loved the thing: her shield, her blade, her power, her completion, her familiar, her follicular apotheosis. The fetishists were johns as before, still buying clean trim with filthy lucre, but now there came into the equation a new factor, changing the outcome. She was a quantity so unknown, so rare, that when they paid for her, she found *she* owned *them*. They obeyed. Before, she had kept alone, venturing only when and where Morris commanded, whether to "happen" across Gordy's path, or to "meet" him, or to give him all the attention he thought love had purchased for him. But after the beard, she strode the streets in a red dress and sunglasses, full-figured, long-legged, beard sometimes braided, sometimes unfettered, sometimes brocaded with beads, fanned out like a peacock's tail. She bought art for her rooms, and fresh bread from the open market, which she ate each day with cheese, sitting on a bench overlooking the ocean. She fed the crumbs to the little birds, and then the grief would arrive in brief stabs, but her own bird was too far gone now, past her reach. Rather than attempting to heal the wound she accepted its inability to heal, allowed the pain, let tears send black runnels down her cheeks, and when the tears had passed, she wiped them, checked herself in her mirror and walked on. The wound, like the beard, was a part of her now, so she determined to be magnificently wounded, and let men fear the wound and magnificence both.

But that was after. Immediately after Gordy departed, she, in the shock of transformation, not yet grown into acceptance, tried desperately to shave it—a futile exercise. The follicles oozed out more beard as soon as the hairs were sliced, the side shaved first grew out inches a minute, tickling as it went, restored to full length before she could lather the other side. There was a length the thing wanted to be: a preordained beard. The rest of the night she sat and waited for Morris, but Morris never returned. She, having caught her fish, no longer had further use, other than as another one of his earners here on a side street off a little-used tributary of the main strip of the Brass-chaat red-light, where she presided as the strange and powerful queen.

Now look at him—Morris. He's back, offering her a return to the mad-ness, the chase for the ticket and the man who holds it, spade and bird, circus and train, leap and catch. To want to return to such a thing would be an unexpected act, like leaping through the air without the safety of a net, or embracing the femininity of a beard. She feels the pull of the circus, the trapeze…and of the ticket. It's out there, she thinks. The ticket—even if you don't trust this bastard to keep his word—is out there. And just because he hasn't managed to find it doesn't mean you might not succeed where he's failed. Who better to cozen it from Gordy than you? If you can kill him with your eyes, you can rob him with your fingers. And—how strange you've never thought of it before—you yourself have never made an attempt on Morris's mysterious door. Something is back there, and if even half of what Gordy said is true, it has more than a few answers.

"What you don't seem to understand," Jane tells Morris, "Is that I like it here."

"I don't believe it." Listen to him. He watched her make a life in a room built off a prison cave, but he can't imagine what she could find here in an ancient continental seaport town. She knows why—it's because this is where he sends people for whom he has little use. Every time he finds a new crop to traffic, a new influx of the weaker strain arrives; fresh meat. Weaklings. Sem-blants. Too puny to hold their selves, he blanks them and turns them out, ships them here or farther inland to whore. How could she find any measure of value in a place that holds no value for him?

"As much as I can 'like' anywhere, I like it," she says. "I'm valued here. The life I lead is strange, but it's mine."

"He feels sorry for what he did, you know. Gordy. He wants to heal you of your beard."

Heal. Of course, it's that. Polish the mirror so she can reflect him better. Even now Gordy would make himself the hero of her story, make of her the mechanism of his redemption. And Morris is the same, save only that he seeks no redemption, for he thinks he is redemption itself.

"You think you have such control, don't you?"

"I've proved it."

"But your feet are clay. And one of your legs." With great pleasure, she sees how angry this makes him. He's fidgeting on his crutch, worse than ever before. He'll sit soon.

"Big talk, little Judas. But you still dance on my string."

"At least now we understand each other."

"So you'll come?"

"And at least now you're asking me."

"But you will?" And, as he at last takes a seat, it finally sounds like a question.

"You'd bring Finch out. You'd let me see her."

He smiles. "That's... negotiable."

It's as if she sees, from a great height, her life spread before her like a river branching, rebranching, deltaing into the ocean, chasing away across the country into river stream creek tributary lake. Before her lies a great branch. She can remain here in this quiet estuary, beauty eroding, money saved up, alone with pen and paper and memories, a great madame in a little-considered city of a little-considered country, visited still by one or two old men who remember her greatness and think of her fondly, coming now to her as if returned to the battlefields and schoolhouses of their youths. This has a deep appeal: to rest, faded, old, a folded newspaper in an unopened drawer. The other path widens, quickens; it leads to the rapids and rocks, where chance will bounce and joust and dash and break.

The quiet depths of this Brasschaat estuary call to her. But out in those rapids, somewhere, caught beneath a rock, heart still fluttering, Finch lies—her little bird. And there is this, too: In those waters will be found other canoes alongside, paddled by the thoughtless or the careless or the wicked. In the rapids, much is left to chance—but not chance for her alone. Others are riding in that white water, among rock and current, little understanding how flimsy their pathetic little punts are. Rushing down the neck of those rapids, she may find a door, a fountain, a ticket, power...perhaps she can locate her lost bird, gather her up, heal her, bring her at last to somewhere quiet and possible. And if she cannot...well, then, at least there will be, one last time, the leap and the catch, the susurrations of the crowds—and, before drowning, she might at least hope to find a firm place to stand and tip the canoes of these foolish careless men, teach the art of swimming to those who have for so long floated, unaware of their ease. She can feel it now, currents drawing her in, the bobbing of a boat in waters growing slowly rougher, genuflecting up, down, like the sure flight of a bird, like the slow nodding of a beard.

GORDY READS: **CATHEDRAL**

I ran toward the city, from the future into the past—or so I imagined, watching declining numbers on mailboxes. 3042. Mansions gave way to domestic shaded streets gave way to pleasant sunbaked avenues. I felt the wind on my face. My bones and joints ached. My little-used muscles screamed, yet I willed myself on. 2665. Now I ran through another neighborhood, where the trees lay evenly spaced and did not cluster to protect from common sight the low houses made of brick and tall ones covered in siding. 2018. An assembly of boys playing wiffle ball in a corner lot watched me pass with curiosity as I shed cumbersome school-issue coat and tie without breaking stride and hurled them away. 1754. My chest burned and the stitch in my side agonized as the houses became smaller and shabbier. 1490. Dingy high-rise apartments loomed. Dirty houses with sagging porches and shaggy, mangy yards. Tall buildings separated by dank graffitied alleyways. 1128. Factories sequestered behind tall chain-link fences topped with concertina wire, abandoned construction sites ringed with plank fences. 712. My feet were molten. 476. My head pounded. Now the street spread out, wide and littered, nearly deserted. At every intersection a bureaucracy of crosswalks and streetlights attempted to block me, but I ran through WALK and DON'T WALK both the same, only marginally aware—my store of will was all but depleted—that I climbed a strange switchback up a mild hill. Streetlights now activated as I ran beneath them, and in my holy exhaustion I hallucinated them as glowing lonely star-fruit each hanging pendulous from the tip of a spindly sprouting finger of a subterranean giant. In the growing darkness, an irregularity of elevation between the regular plates of the sidewalk loomed unseen in a puddle of shadow, and when I, exhausted, tripped on it, I went impressively airborne, then landed hard on shoulder and head. My pain was immense, but my fatigue even greater. I had fallen beside an alleyway, and I fell asleep even as I pulled myself, wounds yet untended, into it.

When I woke hours later, the first thing I saw was the cathedral. It lay directly across the street from my hiding place. The stone face of the tower climbed before me, its summit capped with a steel cross. Huge doors rose, echoing the shape of the arches within which they were set, pointing up the tower toward a huge, round, stained-glass window, black now in the dimness. A green spire climbed in cascades from the far side, rising above even the tower.

Distracting me from this spectacle was the pain. Seven dwarves inside my skull swung ball-peen hammers as if their next seven meals depended upon finding some gem hidden behind my left eye. My cheek felt hot, as though branded; my legs were driftwood. My throat was a raw core of thirst, giving way to the empty howl of my belly. Standing resulted in iron-band cramping of both legs and lower back, but after a few moments upright this torture subsided, and I managed to limp forward on tenderized feet. Wide stairs fronted the cathedral, leading to the huge iron doors. There's no way, I thought as I began my climb, but I mounted the stairs with increasing speed, with muscles newly torn, yet beneath the pain newly strengthened. The first door I tried was locked, as expected, but the second one slid open weightless on oiled hinges. The interior lay dark and undefined, but air pushed out of it like the breath of a living thing, warm, and full of complicated and unfamiliar scents. I slipped into the gloom, which was cavernous and palely lit by candles set on stands at regular intervals. I found myself at the termination point of a long, carpeted aisle lined with symmetrical rows of identical benches. Though the nave's vaulted ceilings were lost to darkness, walls stood on each side, lined with tall spears of dark glass. Ahead, far ahead, stretched the altar rail, and beyond the rail the altar, glowing as if lit from above. Eerie silence blanketed the basilica's vastness.

I was alone there. So I believed.

s t a c k

Now you—smoking your pack empty, working up the nerve to read—eyeball the latest revisions, the ones you just made in the donut shop, talking to Julius and his troublesome ward. You tell yourself: These will be better. They *have* to be. You still shudder to think of the first ones. What you found in that first stack wasn't your triumph, and it wasn't proof you could generate the book on the other side using simply your will freed from constraints of craft. Nothing of the kind.

Original artwork, yes. Crafted by your action beyond the door, yes. But nothing remained of the pages you'd written with Neato. You read the last year's worth; in them Donk, Boyd, and Bailey remained alive—not so much brought back to life as never killed. And more was revised than just the issues you had authored and Neato had drawn. Bad enough if it were only that, but… as you flipped deeper down, numb-fingered, you found pages from earlier times, from all the way back, even a page from issue #1… and… filled with malign presentiments, you went to the cabinets to compare these pages to the original art: yes, exact matches. The published paperbacks were the same. The book had been utterly, historically, changed. And, even worse…

"Who the hell is this 'Gordy?'" you'd asked the empty room.

On the night of the circus, it was Gordy who led the way and Julius who trailed. Julius smiled to see his young friend so enthusiastic, but still the priest kept wary. He'd tried to convince Gordy to avoid it, but there was no dissuading him; the kid admitted the danger was likely real, yet worth risking for the chance to see Jane again. "It's just something I have to do," Gordy said. Julius had switched his strategy, turning to Donk for help. "I don't know what it is, but it's got to be some kind of trap," Julius told him. "Morris used this lady to catch Gordy before—and even if Gordy can't remember it, he's gotten in trouble with a circus very much like this one before, according to Tennessee."

Donk had agreed, and appointed a retinue of loonies as bodyguards, which he decided to lead. They walked in formation around Gordy as they all made their way toward the circus, and Julius, who couldn't help but worry about *something*, noted how easy the ring of bodyguards would make it for somebody who hadn't yet learned the trick of seeing the flickering man to deduce his location. Finally, admonishing himself for perseverating over things that couldn't be helped, he determined to put it out of his mind.

The circus wasn't far; the event organizers put it in the Island's largest empty area; the unaccountably large parking lot at Barney's Suds & Bowling. Perhaps in the days when the factories boomed it had reached capacity, but that was long ago; now it lay empty, filled with grass and weeds, awaiting a use that most assumed would never come. Now it had found a purpose at last, however temporary. The blue and white stripes of the circus could be seen lifting above some of the lower buildings. Their entourage rounded the corner. From a distance, Julius and Gordy could see the round bouncing barker, could hear his call: *COME on STEP right up SEE the see*. . . and there it was, lights and amazing—the Circus of Bearded Love.

—Boyd Ligneclaire, *Subject to Infinite Change*

S T O P S

But Gordy's story isn't lining up—*that's* the problem. Gordy can't remember any of the story Tennessee told, which ended with Gordy escaping the Pigeon Forge dungeons. Perversely, Gordy remembers everything after that point. It's as though Tennessee and Gordy comprise two halves of a single book. It would be reasonable to assume, wouldn't it, that between the two halves, a single coherent narrative might be stitched? But, no, they seem written by different authors who never compared notes, who kept no story bible for continuity. Gordy's never even *heard* of Pigeon Forge. Laws, laws, he don't know nothing about no oubliettes, and no fountain, and no door, neither. For Gordy, there's only a hard start with nothing before it: a pub in Brasschaat in early morning, a wad of cash, a note in his own hand, an empty cup. Imagine living like that. No knowledge of previous life—nothing. Julius knows the curiosity would drive him insane, but not so with Gordy. There's the first day he can remember, followed by a career as a red-light drunk—Gordy's stories are all vague, lurid, and boring—and then, following some momentous unpleasantness with his lady, but for no reason he can think of, he was kidnapped and brought here. "And that's it," Gordy says. "You've got the whole sad tale."

"So Pigeon Forge might have come before?"

"*Anything* might have come before," Gordy says blandly, infuriatingly incurious. Liberation has been good for him. He's taken his place in the Neon Chapel, and while he's considered oddly by the brothers and sisters, who still remember how he flickered for them in the early weeks, he's well liked. Eyes bright, bounce in the gait. He's even getting physically stronger after months of running—literally *running*—daily errands with Julius. The haunted, terrified, hollow-eyed kid Julius met in the Wales is not on display; he's been replaced by a Gordy who's disarmingly uncomplicated, almost light-hearted—during the day, that is.

At night, the screaming comes.

"It doesn't bother you, not knowing what came before?"

"It used to, a little. I look forward now. It's healthier."

"What about God?"

"God?" Look at him. He's already staring at the table. This is how you bring the scared kid back out of the blithe one. This is how you get the once-flickering man to flicker again.

"Back in the Wales, you told me God speaks to you."

"Ah."

"So? When he talks…what does…God…say?"

Is there the slightest of hesitations? Gordy says: "I don't remember."

"Is that why you scream at night?"

"You all tell me I scream. I don't remember."

"Seems likely, though. If it's so bad."

"Anything's possible."

It goes in circles like this forever if you force it. Julius can press him for details but he'll slowly close off, become less and less friendly. Sentences become single words; words become grunts. Press far enough, he'll start to blink out again, and Julius has to stop or risk losing him. Julius finds it infuriating— not even an itch you can't scratch, but one you can't even acknowledge as an itch. If only Tennessee were here this would be simpler. Then they could collaborate, the two of them, thread the one tale to the other, pull the weave tight to create a whole. There are other discrepancies beside the question of Pigeon Forge between Gordy's tale and Tennessee's. For example: According to Gordy there's no ticket at all, and to his knowledge there never has been. Also, many of the characters from Tennessee's telling are present in Gordy's, but modified nearly out of recognition. The woman Jane, for example. In Gordy's tale she isn't an acrobat, and she has no daughter. And Morris is no scion of Appalachian wealth, he's a mysterious Färland brothel owner. "And nobody called him 'Morris,' anyway," Gordy had told him. "I didn't hear the name 'Morris' until he brought me back to Loony Island. Everyone in Brasschaat calls him 'Mo' Love.'"

"Your dad says he always went by 'Morris,'" Julius remarked.

"Pretty strange you can tell me my past and name my father."

"Stranger still that you can't," Julius had said, but gently. There's so much Gordy doesn't know about what he doesn't know. They've had a lot of talk about the ticket—there's never been a sense Gordy is withholding anything about his power or whatever it might be. It's not a dangerous topic in the same way God is, nor a casually impenetrable one like his past; in fact, Gordy seems genuinely curious about it. Down in the panic room beneath Donk's floorboards, there'd been plenty of time to debrief, and Gordy had not failed to disclose. By the light of a single bulb they reviewed experience and perspective. Yes, there are strange occurrences, inexplicable events. Yes, he's sure he was the instigator of those events—in fact, when the inexplicable has happened (he mournfully agrees) they spring from him, from the explicit well of his desire, from the precise words of his mouth. The only exception is his partial visibility, which has, as far back as he can remember, been a perpetual state of his being.

"The invisibility," Gordy said, warming to the topic. "The other drunks were the first to notice it. My first day in Brasschaat I levitated a surly bartender. I'd forgotten. I thought he was ignoring me, but he just couldn't see me. That's when I first knew I could do strange things." He spoke of his friends, his odd jobs, his days given to drink and nights to dissolution, until he met her—*her*. Jane the lissome beauty, his one true love.

"It ended badly," Gordy said, sadly. "I have regrets."

"I imagine most abductees regret being abducted."

"I don't mean what Morris did to me after. I mean what I did to her then. God, how much longer until the circus comes? I need to make it right." This is the other thing: The kid's obsessed. Until the posters started showing up for the circus, Julius was worried someday he'd wake to find Gordy gone, pulled up stakes and wandering in search of his precious bearded lady Jane. Since he saw the posters over at Ralph's, Gordy seems content to stay put. For what it's worth, Donk forbids leaving—it's far too dangerous, he says. The exits are watched. On the day they'd returned to the Neon, Donk had drawn Julius aside. "They can't see him," he said. "At least there's that. They suspect he's here but they don't know it. Remember, I got Morris to order them to leave you alone. If they find him and he's not with you, it'll be a lot easier for them to get him. Keep him here, with you, close and safe."

Still Gordy persists; he's got to find her, fix her, redeem himself for unforgivable acts, the nature of which he's reluctant to disclose, though, unlike de-murrals regarding God and the past, he's not claiming convenient amnesia.

"It's just so shameful," Gordy says, softly, and he's not doing the partially visible thing, he's not withdrawn; he simply looks ashamed. "I didn't know who I was. I didn't know where I'd come from. I just knew I was hiding. There was a friend of a friend, who knew one of the big mucky-mucks over in the red-light district, and he got me a job sweeping up one of the big guy's establishments—the cathouses, you know. And the big guy was Mo'. That was my life. I'd sweep so I could drink."

"Lonely life."

"But then she came and saved me. I looked at her eyes and I died. Love at first sight, and love forever. That's what I thought. Weeks or months of joy, bliss, perfection. But then...I saw her at one of *his* houses...she was...*with* somebody else...I saw them...I did bad things then...I wanted to destroy that beautiful face. Do you know what I decided to do? I decided to turn her head into spaghetti."

"What?"

"I was *so* angry. That's just what rose to my mind. She was perfect. I wanted her random. At the last moment, I did it to the man she was with instead. I..." Gordy pauses, on the verge of saying something he can't bring himself to say. "I don't even know his name. And then I gave her the beard."

"You gave her the beard...as a *compromise?*"

"I can't explain it. It seemed right to me then. It seems so stupid now. I spent all my time in the Wales just thinking about it. I'm so ashamed. I could have done anything in that moment. I could have helped her escape. Instead I . . . did what I did, then I left her there."

"That's another thing. These strange things you sometimes do...why don't you do them all the time? Is it like a genie? You only get three wishes or something?"

Gordy starts to flicker. "I don't know. Sometimes I do it. I don't like it when I do. It hurts."

"Hurts *how?*"

"I don't know," Gordy says, immediately.

"And you can't remember any ticket."

"Wish I could," Gordy says, and rises. Julius follows him out of Bailey's Donuts, annoyed. Having disclosed his shame, Gordy said this last bit with the same blank and cheerful equanimity he gives all his other statements around his amnesia; perfectly agreeable, but never sounding even a little bit as if he wishes he could remember anything before his time in Färland.

"Although," Gordy says more seriously, as they make their way back toward the Neon, "Mo' certainly was looking for *something*. It's clear to me he was behind all of it. He was using poor Jane. He was using us all. He arranged for me to meet her, arranged me to catch her—so he could catch me, you see. Catatonic with what I'd done. After he caught me and brought me to the Wales, he searched every inch of me. Sent me through scanners. Poked every hole, prodded every mole. Drugged me. Questions every day. I think I was due for some surgery right before I gave them the slip."

"How *did* you give them the slip?"

Gordy shrugs. "I do stuff sometimes. Like with you and Morris, down in the tunnels. Or making a bartender float. The restraints they had on me just fell off. I think I did it somehow."

"Why the hell did you stay in the Wales?"

"I didn't know where to go. And…by then it was the only place they weren't searching."

"Maybe Morris knows about the ticket even though you don't."

"Or maybe this 'Tennessee' spun him the same yarn as he spun me," Gordy replied. "He was a loony, you say?"

"No more than you were."

"That's not a particular recommendation for his sanity."

"I wish he was here," Julius says. If Jane is Gordy's constant refrain, this is Julius's: If only Tennessee were here. Julius missed patches of Tennessee's tale, much to his regret; laid out on a billiard table burning with fever, caught in the fugue state of exhaustion and injury, he'd drifted in and out. He suspects this is why the narratives won't join. The first day following their escape both he and Gordy verged on catatonia. By the time they woke, Tennessee had fled already, terrified out of his wits. Donk claims he made such a fuss he'd feared customers would overhear, so he had no choice but to let him split.

Julius knows Donk was loath to let Gordy out of his sight, though he can't guess the motive. Protectiveness, caution, concern, it must be that— What else? To even now suspect Donk of unsavory motives feels stubborn and uncharitable. You ought to tell him Tennessee's story, Julius admonishes himself, or at least the part you know. He stood to advance himself considerably by giving you up, and yet he hid you. Even the fact Donk is now working for Morris testifies to his trustworthiness in a way…it's not common knowledge, he didn't have anything to gain in disclosing it, everybody still thinks Ralph is around pulling the strings. Donk's running a dangerous game, and because of your paranoia (or is it greed?), he's running it without knowledge of ticket or fountain.

But Julius has thus far kept quiet. Their regular meetings have attenuated, their interactions reduced to daily wordless status reports at Ralph's checkout lane, something Donk insists upon as a safety procedure. Donk's even set him up with the same sort of individualized codification as he gives his gangsters. Every purchase tells a story—though Donk made the rules far simpler for the priest than he does for the criminals. It's a simple color code, allowing Julius to buy different things but say the same thing. He buys pears, asparagus, broccoli—anything green—to give the green light: Nothing to report. Yellow means something to report, but not pressing or particularly sensitive. Red means a hot tip or a problem; a request for a meeting, today. And then there's oranges, the worst-case, the particular emergency involving the children's room.

There's a ruthlessness in Donk, something never previously on display. One night, back when Julius and Gordy were still his below-the-floorboards boarders, Donk had let himself become imprudently drunk, and had said with chilling nonchalance: "The thing is to not let it be over too quickly with Morris. That's a mistake I won't make. I need to peel him away slowly. One layer at a time. I'll take it all from him. When I finally have him, at the end, I'll make him eat his own eyes."

"He doesn't care about anything else now," Bailey wheezed, not long ago, when Julius and Gordy came calling. "Nothing but getting Morris."

"He cares about you, at least. Nettles tells me he visits."

"Caring about me makes him keep wanting to hurt him," Bailey said absently.

Julius spent some more time doing what he came to do: telling Bailey the news from Loony Island, bringing her some connection to the life she'd left, but as always, before he'd finished, he had the distinct sense she was somewhere else. At least Nettles listens attentively. Nettles feels a keen affinity for Bailey, as she does for all of Loony Island's damaged and mangled. It's Nettles who had pointed out to Julius—when he'd complained about the mysterious Deep Man: the meanness of such a deity, the bite of his cruelty, the teeth of the universe—how it was the women who usually got chewed hardest. "This God of yours," Nettles said. "He must have gone through a divorce. You men may suffer, but we get maimed. That's my observation."

Waiting in line at Ralph's to purchase a sack of cucumbers, Julius shakes his head, remembering this exchange—That's the real problem with the Deep Man, his mysterious stranger—"God," if you like. Not to say he strikes you as an implausible God, exactly, but rather that, if you were to at last decide to believe in a God, he seems so grotesquely plausible. Look at the Island, a community cut off from the main. Look at the weak huddling behind flimsy doors, breaking their backs to earn a starving wage, dependent on an ever-shrinking pittance of public assistance, living in constant fear of the strong. Look at the strong, whose morality considers nothing but the extent to which they can dominate another, and the depraved means by which others might dominate them. And look outside the Island—what of *them*? The allegedly more enlightened and privileged world outside the walls purposefully demarcating Loony Island from the rest—does this other world, with desperation less immediate, truly differentiate itself in matters of caprice and savagery? The weak owned by the strong, wherever you look. Dog eats dog eats dog eats cat eats cat eats cat eats mouse eats mouse eats mouse, not because dog is hungry for dog, or cat for mouse, but because each is hungry only for the eating. Keep the useful busy, shunt those with lesser or no worth to the margins, where their suffering need not offend you, their sin of existence need not trouble you. Stuff yourself full and then stuff yourself more. Spare a glance as you drive past: Look at it, the filth, the depredation down there, the feculence of rat eating rat eating rat, chuckle ruefully to yourself *who would choose to live like that* and make it home for dinner, in time for a plate-ful of dog. If a painting is the reflection, not of the subject, but of the artist, what sort of God, then, would be reflected by such a reality as this? Distant in suffering. Capricious when present. Insouciant in his ownership of power and authority, ruthless in its application. It's not that you're anymore afraid God doesn't exist. Now you're afraid he does.

Meanwhile, Julius thinks, you keep playing at belief, at ministry. Keep giving your friends the sense you've got some plan for it all. Friends? Follow-ers. You're not comfortable with the label, but that's because you know what a rotten faker you truly are. But followers is what they are—and not by acci-dent, either. You led them to it. Can you deny it? Look at the symbolism you surround yourself with. A desire for disciples has to be assumed even by the most casual observer, along with further presumptions. What astute observ-er—Donk, say—would fail to suspect you of some manufactured Messianic complex, of foolish pantomime and empty pageantry, as if you were a Civil War reenactor who didn't believe there actually had been a Civil War? Or one of those adults who walk around dressed up like their favorite superhero: God Man here to save the day, braver than a gangster with a handgun, more powerful than institutionalized poverty, able to mime faith in a single prayer.

Julius returns to the Neon with the cucumbers in hand and Gordy in tow. They can smell the fragrance of barbecue from blocks away, but Julius is still deep in thought, because now the God question has gone and gotten muddy again—That's the real source of your concern, of this creeping, growing, rapacious need to acquire some sort of divine actualization. You're using Gordy to acquire it. Before, you were driven only by a desire to prove God's existence to yourself, to know God beyond question of unknowing; but now there is a need to prove to yourself, not only the existence of God, but of the *right kind* of God. It's a clawing, greedy, desperate, terrible need—push-ing and constantly grasping after the same ticket Morris pursues, not for its power, but as some sort of divine certification—a justification of the Word you foolishly followed without believing it existed; a conduit to some voice in prayer other than your own, the nagging itching sense of sanctimonious duplicity, a man who knows he is only talking to himself about himself.

x x x

Before they could reach the circus, there appeared a man wearing a suit of powder blue. He didn't step from out of the throng, or from behind a tree or a building. He *appeared*.

Poit

He looked behind himself, saw the circus. Then back forward, saw Gordy and Julius having nearly reached it.

"Nope!" he screamed.

Poof! went the circus.

The man folded up in halves, and again, and again and again, until he was gone. It was the damnedest thing. In the view his absence provided, not a sign of the circus remained. Not even a smell of the circus. Julius and Gordy could only stare across the street at a couple hundred confused circusgoers in a totally empty lot, who in turn could only stare at one another.

It was Julius who finally broke the silence. "That was the guy I was telling you about," he said, voice quavering. "Says he's God."

—Boyd Ligneclaire, *Subject to Infinite Change*

x x x

As the day of the circus grows close—it's only days away—Julius starts to feel increasingly nervous—and not just about the event being a potential trap. Donk says he can handle security, and Julius has decided to trust Donk on that matter. No, it's more a question of what happens after. Once Gordy's met with his precious lady Jane, will he stay in the Island, or will he move on with her? And—be honest, Julius—when he moves on, he'll take it with him. A conduit to God, whether a ticket or something else. And what will you do then?

Julius has no desire to let Gordy out of his sight; the prize was hard fought for and dearly won, and Julius didn't want to lose it (*him*, not *it*, him, him, him)—and, happily, Gordy, meanwhile, is, for now, equally reluctant to separate himself from his protector, though (Julius smiles) small separations are difficult to avoid, as long as the priest insists (and he does) on running everywhere he goes. Gordy inevitably begins to redface and hufflepuff only a few minutes into the morning jog, compelling Julius to slow his pace in accommodation of his less-conditioned wingman, and even—a desecration—to take occasional rests. He kneels in posture of prayer during these as a sort of penance, as he waits for Gordy to catch back up. On the first day, during one of these interruptions, Gordy, between heaves, observed: "There are these inventions called 'cars.' There are taxis, limousines, subway trains, trolleys, busses..."

"First month running's a bitch. You'll toughen up."

"You've had years of practice, though," Gordy whined. "My God, you run in denim. You've gotta have inner thighs like an armadillo's ass."

Julius rolled his eyes. The entire trip is only a whisker over twelve miles. "Every cat in this city is such a fucking baby."

"Isn't your toe broken?"

"It was only sprained. And it healed." In truth a considerable twinge yet remains, but Julius believes firmly in the restorative properties of heavy use. "Come on. Break's over. Day's wasting." And Julius had been right; the first month was the hardest. The second month was merely terrible, and now, in the third, Gordy isn't convinced anymore he's about to die.

The idea is to run all the way out to the farthest point and then run back, catching each appointment as you go. Julius, still a man of routine, has seven stops. Stop one is a meeting at the home of Dave Waverly, who rode out the Loony Riot inside his locked car. "I've still got controlling interest," Julius told Gordy, "But Dave's got power of attorney." Of all of Julius's friends, the Slantworthy proxy had, understandably, been most concerned by the priest's temporary disappearance following the riot, and most relieved by his return. Gordy, Julius noted without surprise, warmed to him immediately—visibility has never been a problem between Gordy and Dave. This is actually annoying; Dave still won't believe that Gordy ever flickered, and still considers Julius's claims that he did as a topic best never breached. But the two have become friendly—maybe even friends. Once, Dave surprised the hell out of Julius, said to Gordy: "I used to watch the sunrise with your priestly buddy, you know. We had the best view in the city. Ask him about it sometime." To Julius's knowledge, this was the first time Dave Waverly has spoken about the days of the cathedral. When Gordy asked, Julius demurred. "That story isn't too sad for Dave, I guess, but it's too sad for me," he said, consciously echoing Gordy. "I wrote it down. Maybe I'll let you read it someday." Gordy, who may have been thinking of his own sad story involving the bearded lady, had mercifully not questioned further.

Their second stop is the hospital. Julius feels overwhelmed each day with guilt and helplessness. "I don't know what to do or say," he usually says, to which Nettles replies, almost as liturgy, "There's nothing to do or say, Jules. Let it be." The usual procession of doctors and nurses and orderlies ghost their way through the room. Whoever else is keeping company, whatever they do or say, Bailey stares and blinks but doesn't quite watch, propped in her bed or—with greater frequency as the weeks go on—propped up in her chair. "The doctor says she'll be able to leave for home soon," Nettles proudly reports. Some days Bailey responds, but before each utterance there's always a long pause, as if her words are being conveyed from a vast distance, using ancient technology. Julius prays over her, and they move on.

"I wish you could have known her before," Julius usually tells Gordy.

"Me, too," Gordy usually replies. There doesn't seem to be any other appropriate response.

After the hospital they run back to Loony Island. Julius can see it in his mind's eye: a lumbering slab of hair and denim trotting with the impatient bearing of a racehorse held in check, followed either by—depending on the observer—nothing at all, or a flickering shadow, or a smaller, younger man, wheezing, stumbling, halting, racing to catch up again, a terrier trailing a bulldog. Putting pavement behind them slab after slab as the overpass looms ever closer and, beyond it, the larger higher slabs rise up; Domino City, holding masses, bearing names unknown by the multitudes driving past: The Deuce and HQ, Florida and Presto, the Hammer, the Penthouse, each with its own character entirely indistinguishable from outside observance; closer and closer they come, the priest and his ghost running through the tunnel leading under the highway, drawing themselves nearer to the headstones around which they will spend much of their day.

"The worst thing," Gordy moans, "is that when we get there, there's the stairs to climb."

Julius grins. "But the best thing is, after all those stairs, the running doesn't seem so bad."

They make their way through each building, visiting shut-ins. The list is extensive, and memorized. Weeks pass before they repeat a visit. "There were only a few in the beginning," Julius had explained, the first day. "But those few knew about others, and the others know about more. If I have time left over, sometimes I go and knock on doors and see who's in there."

"Knocking on random doors around here seems dangerous."

"Can be. But the list grows."

Shut-ins—Domino City cultivates them, the old and the young, the abandoned. The elderly, abandoned, their bodies too broken for work, their children escaping the Island but lacking the strength to bring others along, or else failing to extricate themselves but leaving their elders behind all the same, either joined with the gangs or used by them, or rolled by the cops for the sin of existing unprofitably, made into profitable prisoners. The young, abandoned by their parents, either out of necessity—turning seven keys in seven locks, creeping toward the day's labor to earn enough to purchase the day's scraps—or to meet the body's need, pushing the plunger, emptying the bottle, sinking once more into daily stupor. It's these to whom Julius and Gordy appear. On spiral notebooks Julius marks building, room, and any other more pressing requirements... *six, 1778, broken oven; three, 619, bedbugs; five, 112, windowpanes smashed, need fortified*...To some children, he'll whisper the location of a hidden children's room, a description of the door, instructions on the precise way to knock upon it to be received by Daisy Coyote. Some—mostly the elderly—ask him to pray for them, and this he does with only the slightest hesitation. He listens, and nods, and murmurs.

Up and down the stairs. They run into occasional packs of gangsters, who, recognizing Julius, allow them to pass unmolested. Occasionally there'll be a catcall, a brief grab, a young Zoot showing off in front of his elders, making a show of blocking the hall. Julius ignores them as he moves past, and Gordy, unseen, slides by as well.

Fourth stop is the craps game. Julius always plays a hundred, ten tens from petty cash, winning more than he loses, to the annoyance of The House, the blind lady who runs the game. As they play, The House dishes: the temperature of the street, high-pressure and low-pressure zones, where the lightning of good or bad fortune struck today. Her perspective is more valuable in some ways than Donk's, because she's less apt to draw conclusions. Nowhere are the tongues of degenerates looser than at the craps ring, and what The House hears, she trades to Julius for nothing more than his company. The gossip, the trends, new slang, all fall from her lips without agenda or strategy, a profound and trivial reflection of what's going on. Lately, The House claims, the gangs are nervous. Nervous and getting nervouser. The more authority and prestige a faction enjoyed before the great elevation of the Loonies, the more they chafe now. The cardinals are rarely seen anymore, appearing only occasionally to issue cryptic orders on the Coyote's authority, while various of the loonies appear to be out doing much the same inexplicable work that had once been the office of the redbirds, wandering the neighborhood swinging broomsticks or mop handles or even their own arms at nothing but air. It's unnatural, the street cats say. Loonies being given authority? Orders coming from the cardinals? Nobody's received word from Ralph about these changes, but then nobody ever did receive word from Ralph except through Donk—the Coyote, that is. Meanwhile, the Coyote's gone silent. The goddam loonies have his ear now. Among the now nearly mutinous gangs, desire for power and influence are starting to supersede their fear of Ralph—though, as the fear of Ralph drains from their chalice, it's being refilled anew with fear of the Coyote. There are rumors of disappearances, not only of random soldiers, but of major guys.

"Sylvester has gone missing," The House says, gravely. "Nobody seen him, nobody know where he gone to."

"Who's Sylvester?" Gordy asked.

"One of the top guys," Julius replied, worried. "He knew Ralph back in the day. Some people claim the two of them were still in touch."

"All I'm saying," The House says, "I'm worried it's going to turn into another riot."

After a while, Julius scoops his winnings and they jog down the line.

"You took that blind lady's money," Gordy wheezed, the first day.

"She'd be pretty pissed off if I hadn't," Julius called back to him. "I won it."

"She's *blind*."

"You try to leave winnings behind out of pity sometime. See what happens."

Fifth stop is Ralph's. Donk's there but it's not the same. These days Donk is in the full flower of growing influence. He's the Coyote now, and the Coyote is as taciturn as he is feared, so their meetings now transpire in grunting silence, and their only communications are Julius's purchases. Gordy can buy what he likes—only, to be on the safe side, nothing orange.

"Is all this really necessary?"

"Donk thinks it's necessary. Donk's usually right."

This conversation takes place at Bailey's Donuts, the sixth stop. There's no significance or purpose to this stop beyond enjoyment of donuts. It's being run by an orange-haired loony, a cat Donk's befriended named Garf. It's not the same, Julius thinks, without Bailey here. Still, Garf must be an apt enough manager; the pastries are as delicious as always. They get a baker's dozen; Julius wolfs three, while Gordy savors one.

"This is how I can run all day and not get thin," Julius says. He says it every day.

Julius brings any remaining donuts in the box for later at the Neon Chapel, which is the seventh and final stop.

Gordy's screaming starts a few hours later. Out of the secret dark and silent fabric of slumber it comes knifing through, a wall of sonic misery, then another, then another, inevitable and unstoppable, never failing to arrive until a minute after you've finally—though you wasted half the night waiting for it, dreading being awakened by it yet again—dropped off into sleep. Scream after scream after scream, the same as it had been in the tunnel, the same as it's been every night since. Terrified. Horrified. Wordless. Hopeless. It doesn't seem like a body could remain whole after delivering a scream like that, but still they come, regular as waves, again, again, again. On Gordy's first day the entire Neon Order had rushed to their new member's cell to see what sort of beast had broken in and who it was killing. They'd found Julius already there, holding Gordy, who was stiff-limbed and wide-eyed and catatonic.

"It's fine," Julius announced as they arrived. "Or at least it's normal. I'd hoped it would stop once we left Donk's hidey-hole. It lasts fifteen minutes at most."

Julius lied; it usually lasts a half-hour at least. It isn't a seizure. Nor is it a vision. It's a series of nerve-rattling dark soul-screams. Always the last one the loudest, rising in pitch and volume until, with as little warning at the end as at the beginning, it ceases.

That had been on the first day, though; days have stacked up now. If they were bricks they'd have made a wall: months of weeks, weeks of days, seven stops at a time. Awaken, run. Dave, Bailey, Projects, Craps, Ralph's, Donuts, Barbecue, scream, scream, scream, SCREEEEEEEAM, sleep, repeat. As the weeks have progressed, as they continue their routine unmolested by cardinals, undetected by loonies, Julius realizes he's searching less urgently on the rounds for Tennessee; meanwhile, Gordy has gone more than a day without talking about the upcoming circus. Perhaps, Julius thinks, there's no doom hanging over us after all, no creeping beast swimming up behind us; perhaps this is all there will be: strangeness melting into familiarity, all these changes slowly becoming normal; not better, but comfortable, expected. Certainly, there's no sign of a ticket. Julius finds it's a relief in a way— Ever since meeting Gordy, you've mistrusted your motives, perhaps rightly so. You've felt a hunger for it within you shouldn't trust. And jealousy—yes, jealousy, too. God talks to *him*? Why to him and never once to you?

When do I get my chance at God? All your life that's been your question. Ask another: Should I *want* one?

x x x

After the confused crowd had meekly dispersed, after Julius (relieved) and Gordy (crushed by disappointment) had left for the Neon Chapel, Donk stood in the empty parking lot, alone except for Morris's two tiny lieutenants, who stood at a distance. A lone flyer done in the style of the promotional posters floated by, carried by a momentary gust: The Flying Bearded Lady.

"I'm totally fucked," Donk muttered.

"That's certainly how it looks to us," said one of the Andrews with what sounded like satisfaction. "Just a few days remaining on your deadline."

Donk grimaced. He hadn't seen them there. The fact his voice could carry testified to how completely his plan had just vanished into nothing. It's the guy Julius told you about. The man in powder blue. But *how*?

He decided: No. You won't figure out how, so how doesn't matter. Figure out what's next instead. At least there's no question anymore that a ticket with world-bending powers might exist. You just have to hope Gordy has one. The man in powder blue certainly has one, or something like.

Donk stalked off, deciding not to waste time giving the Andrews the satisfaction of an answer. Let them report back to Morris you think you're doomed— you're not. This just means you'll have to do it the hard way is all. Invite the priest and his friend over for a doctored drink and give them a thorough search when the sedative takes hold.

Hopefully that turns the ticket up. If not, you'll have to get rougher.

—Boyd Ligneclaire, *Subject to Infinite Change*

x x x

Maybe there never was a ticket, Julius muses. Maybe it was always the Deep Man, acting behind the scenes on behalf of Gordy.

Maybe it would be better if that's all it was.

Certainly, it would be better if the Deep Man stayed away.

Julius now thinks of the ticket—if such a thing even truly existed—as an icon, some metaphor or another: a microphone, or an old club-shaped telephone receiver, to seize and scream into, demanding answers at last from one who could no longer pretend not to hear, a way of making oneself known at last. *Gordy doesn't want to talk anymore, bubba. You're talking to me, now. And I have a thing or two I want to say...*

Julius grimaces. Challenging God. Therein lies a thicket of existential perils—especially after last night's vanishing act. Better, maybe, that no ticket has manifested nor seems likely to. Better, maybe, to focus on routine, regularity, forget about flickering and tickering and divinity and doubt. At least Donk appears to have moved on from his tough-guy act; he was friendly yesterday at the grocery, almost effusive. Invited Julius and Gordy by his place— the first such invitation in months—to talk over the inexplicable events of last night. When they arrived, Donk had been loose and relaxed and casually abusive in their old fraternal way. "I don't have any news," he said. "I just thought maybe we'd play some cards and drink some bourbon and I make fun of you for being ugly."

He'd also made fun of Julius's theories about the Deep Man and God.

"Give me a rest with the God trip. Everything we've seen is explainable. We just don't have the explanations."

"A circus just *vanished*. Explain that."

Donk gesticulated vaguely. "There's weird shit in the universe. Things we don't understand. Listen to what the scientists are figuring out these days. Strange particles, dark matter, spooky quantum *action*."

"What's 'spooky quantum action'?"

"Am I a particle theorist? I read it in the newspaper. It's *quantum action*. It's *spooky*. My point is, weird shit you don't understand doesn't equal God. It just equals you don't understand, because it's weird shit. Even smart people haven't figured it out yet, and *you* are not a smart people. *You* are an idiot."

A good conversation. Like old times. The day after the circus. Just a day before the end.

Later, when Gordy and Julius woke in the deep of night from what they assumed was a bourbon haze, they stumbled home, entirely unaware of how thoroughly they'd been searched.

GORDY READS: **WINDOW**

The ways of need amuse me even today. Satisfaction of one need brings not peace, but simply the awareness of the next, a coffle of human demands constantly promoted, one after the other, to eminence. When I was running, my need was rest. Once I was rested, my need was warmth. Once warm, I was hungry. Once full, thirsty. Quenched, the injuries I had performed upon my outraged body presented themselves again to me, and I found I needed rest once more. Outside was the cold, and so I was led by my chain of need, brought to heel like a trained dog, up the spiral staircase behind the altar, seeking some manger for a bed. High above, the domed ceiling, its base ringed with small lamps, illuminated both the valanced (and newly desecrated) altar below, and the frescoes of angels above, in soft lambency. I entered upon a narrow balcony, which rose sharply upward behind me in four terraces, each supporting a row of choral pews made of dark varnished wood and padded with red velvet cushions. The balcony itself described a semicircle huddled against the back of the apse, exempt from the lighting encapsulating the rest of the dome.

I lowered myself into a pew on the front row near the center of the arc, hunched forward like a child at a matinee, my hands and chin resting on the balustrade.

I now faced directly back the way I had come. Below, on the wall opposite, the doors through which I had come were visible. Directly above them, peering at me like a giant's extinguished eye, the opaque glass circle dominated. I closed my eyes, lost in weariness and a growing awareness that soon, despite cold and fatigue, I'd have to move on. Faintly, a choir singing from unseen speakers floated down to me. I sighed again, but relaxed, content, allowing myself to live in the animal now. It was pleasant here, and calm. Long years of ceremony had embedded itself in this place, speaking of depth, promising meaning. But I, cuddled into my new cynicism, remembered my father's "laboratory," and congratulated myself on having pierced the illusion. Belief itself was for fools. I allowed myself to luxuriate in my suffering, melancholic and noble, realizations that pained me, but even in the pain, provided grips to which I could cling. These at least would not change. A painful but constant wisdom had, at great cost, been attained.

I opened my eyes.

I had seen stained-glass windows before.

I hadn't seen anything like this.

It could not have been more than a minute since I had closed my eyes with the window darkened by night, but now the giant's eye had come alive with vibrant light pulsing from delicate, multihued slivers connected by a frame of nearly invisible webbing. A prophet, staff in hand, stood beside a rock gushing water. In detail the artist had not spared pain or labor; the prophet's gray and tangled beard, the folds of his robe, his eyes glinting defiance, his staff raised high, needles of the inhospitable rock, ripples in the stream, white spray of foam leaping from the new-lanced freshet to the lofty upper periphery of the window's circular frame, while below the trickle spread to a creek at the prophet's feet, flourishing to a river as it swept downward and past the window's scope. The glass, so recently impenetrable, now disclosed itself, blue and white and gold and crimson, in its translucence creating a strange doubling effect. You could focus on the artist's vision, or you could shift your gaze, and there, around the image and through it, the prospect beyond emerged: a ragged horizon, jutting sunlight, buildings looming like great trunks on either side, the city captured in color. Near the center, directly above and to the right of the prophet's head, like bishops parting for a new pontiff, the skyline gave way, and for a scant length of horizon, the sunrise pierced through the concrete forest, scraped the roof of the building directly across the cathedral, and shone like a diamond in its setting. Whether by propitious accident or design, the tip of the prophet's staff glowed with divine power as its end made a perfect confluence with the heart of this morning jewel. The nave, now revealed in detail, lay blanketed in diaphanous light refracting from every facet; it bathed me, cleansed me like a benediction, washed me in peace. The altar rails cast long shadows stretching beneath my perch and away out of sight. The slender sentinel windows lining the nave now woke from their slumber and glowed, not from morning light without, but from the ineffable beauty filling the space within.

"It's a fine thing," came a voice from behind me. "I never miss it."

I screamed and jumped. A miracle I didn't go flying over the balustrade.

Behind me, previously hidden but now revealed in morning light, sat a short, round priest. Her hair, black flecked with gray, retreated with precision into a high bun. A cable-knit sweater hung around her black dress. Thick glasses clung to her nose, and her eyes smiled. Her feet rested upon the back of the pew ahead of her. At a remove from her, but in the same pew, sat a filthy man, obviously homeless.

"Don't be afraid," she said.

I stared at her stupidly.

"I'm Father Bernadette," she said, "and this gent is my good friend Dave."

"My friends call me 'Wavy Dave,'" said Dave. "You can call me that."

Then, as I continued staring, Bernadette continued: "And, unless we are experiencing an extraordinary coincidence, you have a different name...?"

"Julius," I mumbled.

"Julius," she said. "Welcome, Julius."

There was a presence about her that encouraged trust. Pointing down to the mess below, I made my first confession. "I ate the communion wafers."

She smiled, kindly. "We saw. You also drank a little bit of the wine, though you didn't seem to like it." When I said nothing, she continued: "They aren't much good, though—as crackers, I mean. You must have been hungry."

"Yes," I agreed. I realized I still was.

"David and his companions were hungry once," she said, as if that settled things. She stretched, and indicated the window. "You're missing it."

I looked back to the wondrous eye holding prophet, rock, stream, city, sky, rising sun.

master

After the shock of the first revision, you decided not to go behind the door again. Interpretation had been the main trouble. Those god-damned readers, you can't trust them.

You stare at the newest stack, the donut-shop stack. Soon you'll have to read. But it's best to approach these things deliberately. You select another cigarette. The pack is nearly empty. Soon.

So the new game had begun: the game of the master, played with the same goal as the first—perfect the story—but to a different purpose. No longer sanctifying a world below to prove yourself worthy to move upward to yet another sphere, but rather sanitizing the one below, to make it a worthy enough vessel for your ascended self to live comfortably within. The first thing was to stop all this nonsense of interpretation, this silly-string movement, this horrid spooky action. You'd devote all new issues of *Cat's Crib* to spell out your intentions in exact language, no drawings, just plain words on the page. Each detail described, from the path of a bird crossing the sky to exactitude of facial expression, posture, gesture, the thoughts governing each action, authorial intent conveyed with inescapable specificity, down to the mite, the mote, the minim, the indivisible particle—you knew you'd need to start from the beginning, explain the book until every reader understood how to read it properly, and to keep at it until they couldn't read it any other way.

The first issue you wrote in this new style came in at seventy pages of text, single-spaced—clearly this wouldn't do. You made the type smaller. Smaller. *Smaller.* Six-point? No. That's not quite it yet, get it down to 24 pages ... perfect, a 5.5 will do the trick. As a sop to your partners at Universe Comics and the expectation of the form, you included pictures with the text: reproductions from previous books, stylized to suggest new, better meanings. The barbarians still complained, but you'd made careful study of all contracts and agreements, remained unconcerned: You owned the rights to these characters, you'd use them as you pleased. Don't like it? Feel free to break our contract. Which is what Universe did, citing "artistic choices purposefully designed to sabotage the viability of the work," along with some vague threats about further legal action based on onerous fine print . . . your lawyer droned on and on, but it was all such a bore—They had no soul; those philistine bean-counters couldn't understand the life of the mind. You were doing the best work of your career. Nor were the suits at Universe the only unsophisticated sensibilities; subscriptions fell to ten percent of peak. No matter, you counted the loss as gain. Those who remained were the only real readers; the ones willing to read properly. You sold original artwork to keep afloat, and explained carefully to your concerned accountants about the singularity of artistic expression.

But there was no explaining Gordy, the kid sprung up unbidden out of those first revised pages, the ones you created by disappearing Neato; no explaining the kid with sure feet and perfect spatial awareness, who could run along telephone lines, leap from ledge to ledge along the Domino City windows, who always arrived whenever the day needed saving; the kid who would, according to the final pages in the revised stack, be the one to drop the safe upon the helpless head of Morris—the same unacceptable ending. No, there was no explaining Gordy, though the lesson he provided was a recognizable one. When you had been a character within the work, you'd known Gordys, hadn't you? Semblants who refused to fall into their places and had the power to resist the doom they'd earned for their disobedience. No, there's no explaining a Gordy. With a Gordy, there's only one thing to do: Get rid of him. Not the bird for Gordy, but the spade. You knew you'd have to risk the door again. You'd have to risk generating pages.

You entered, jaunted to Gordy's first appearance, issue 27, a flashback, Gordy still just a little kid bombing down the streets of Pigeon Forge, on his way to his meeting with destiny—You sonofabitch. What you do to me, I do to you.

Hey, kid.

Gordy stopped and startled when he saw you. Unsurprising; unless you consciously exercised your authority to modify your appearance, everybody on this side gets spooked by the sight of you.

Who are you, mister?

Look out for the safe, kid.

The. . . safe? What sa—

Too late. It landed on him, full force, a big square gray number the size of a

Buick, ending the question unasked, smashing the boy into a mush of red-bone slurry-paste.

That one, kid. That one.

So much for Gordy. You returned to the door and passed through, already anticipating the pages awaiting you. Hopefully the revision wouldn't be too bad.

It had been worse than "too bad." It was unfair. The new stack stood thicker, a foot high, practically the entire run of the book. Flipping to issue 27, you saw Gordy still alive, saved from the safe by a chance tumble into an open manhole. But that wasn't all; this new recapitulation had swallowed all your meticulous 5.5. point text-work; a year's work gone, replaced with more panel art, and… turning to the final page… No!…again, the safe about to drop on the head of poor abused Morris.

Without pause you popped back through the door—I can't kill you? Fine, friend. I'll bury you. You can dodge a safe, but you can't dodge an oubliette.

C A T S

Julius halts so abruptly, Gordy runs SMACK into his broad back. "Come on. We're getting the donuts first," Julius says. This is unusual, but Gordy meekly complies, still stunned about the lost circus, the lost chance with Jane. But . . . wait, Julius appears to have noticed something specific in the donut shop. He's beelining for the place, a bloodhound with a scent.

"Quick," Julius commands. "Before he disappears again."

"He" who? Gordy wonders, still slightly dizzy—Somebody disappearing? I'll sue, nobody disappears around here except me, other than (stomach rumbling) a couple of those glazed donuts, I'll make them disappear. Donuts...or is it doughnuts—Gordy realizes that the spelling he envisions when he thinks the word is now confused—but here, above the door, in shiny mirrored letters, is the now-familiar sign: BAILEY'S DOUGHNUTS: U and G and H are there as though they'd always been. Was it not the other way?

"What's the difference between a 'donut' and a 'doughnut,' anyway?" Gordy asks, realizing even as he says it how this sounds, then chases after Julius, who is already inside. At the counter, Julius acts as if the two of them have tacitly agreed to a secret crime. "Don't say anything," he whispers, side-mouth. "I'll do the talking. I've dealt with him before. Just follow my lead."

"What are you talking about?"

"You don't *see* him?" But even as Julius says this Gordy does see him, whoever he is. It's the guy from last night. Healer of priests. Vanisher of circuses. He's sitting in the corner booth, head wreathed in smoke. There is something about him. He's got the powder-blue suit on still, but that isn't it. He's what you might consider handsome, but only blandly so; it's gone a bit to seed. But...there is *some*thing about him. He is looking right at them both, and smiling, a smile that invites—but only so far. Offers secrets—but only to a point. He clearly has been waiting for them. There is some*thing* about him. A fellow you can't miss for long. He is...he is...there is something about him…"Just be ready to follow me," Julius jaw-clenches. "This guy is danger-ous. He killed five cardinals without blinking."

Gordy, appetite decamped, gets his doughnut plain. Julius gets his usu-al—strawberry fritter, and an extra dozen. The man makes the timeless ges-ture: Won't you join me? Wordlessly, Julius and Gordy obey. Gordy sits, bites, chews, waiting for the man to say something. Julius sits glaring in a hostile posture. The man smokes, poised, as if waiting for his time to speak. "Hello, my muddlers, my meddlers," he says at last. He speaks breezily, though to Gordy the tone seems contrived. There's a tension in him; this is a forced conviviality. "My flies in the ointment. The wrenches the monkey swallowed. My complications. My complicators. Julius and Gordy, and me makes three. Together at last."

"What did you do with the circus?" Gordy demands.

The man smiles, inhales, exhales smoke everywhere. "Call me… Landrude."

"I guess 'God' is more the last name, then," Julius growls, and Gordy spies a flash of annoyance; the priest's deflation of his grand revelation didn't sit well with this mystery man.

"I apologize for the misapprehension. I'm *not* God, exactly." Landrude finishes his cigarette, lights another on the butt before stubbing it out. "That's part of what I'm here to talk to you fellows about—that, and more practical matters. There's danger, and it's growing by the hour. We're close to a great inflection. I bought us some time with the circus, but not much."

Gordy shudders. He's convincing, this guy. There's something about him. He holds himself apart; his gestures slow, testing, as if feeling his way through a dim room in which objects remain indistinct, or walking through swamp, surveying the earth at every step for signs of quicksand. He's… deliberate. That's the word: deliberate. Each movement rigorously precise, each word exact. This makes him hard to disbelieve.*

---

* The gambit of imprisoning Gordy in an oubliette was your first attempt at more subtle manipulation: jumping through the timeline; pushing from the shadows, wreathed in smoke; nudging Gordy this way and that; getting Gordy's dad down Pigeon Forge way for his research; getting young Gordy to the circus; making sure the trustees would catch him, manipulating Morris without telling Morris directly (you knew the dangers of approaching

Julius, apparently less impressed: "We should believe you why, exactly?"

"Well, Julius. Not to brag or anything, but I *did* save your life."

"You put me in a position to lose it. Sent me out to lose it again, which I nearly did."

Landrude takes a moment; a man gathering his patience. "All right, then. Remember the rabbits, Julius? Remember 'those darned rabbits,' peeking from the mirrors? Remember their pink eyes?" Gordy's baffled by this, but immediately surmises this remark was intended not for him, but for Julius. The priest is staring at Landrude in horrified wonder.

"But enough question-and-answer." Landrude brightens again. "Let's make ourselves a nice quiet place, shall we? What I have to tell you is information of a highly classified sort. It's unusual for such as me to interact so directly with such as you." At this, a silence immediately drops upon them, and Gordy realizes they are alone. Outside the windows, a pearly white indistinctness creeps, which is not quite fog, not quite smoke, not quite frost.

Gordy breaks the silence. "What just happened?" Landrude shakes his head. His demeanor is changing, becoming less cocksure. "I'm sorry, friends. I don't want to be rude, and I'll try not to impose more than I must. But... I'm going to need you two to not talk, just for a little while, until I say you

Morris), getting Gordy into the circus (even appearing to him directly; giving him a ticket of sorts for admission), making sure he'd be seen, captured, processed, interred.

It had gone perfectly. It had been a disaster. Returning to the artist's side, you read the new pages through a crimson scrim of fury—after all that work, Gordy escaped. Of course. And of *course* he still managed to meet up with Bailey, Boyd, and Donk, and of *course* they still joined forces against Morris. The pages *still* ended the same way as always: the safe hurtling downward, about to strike, suspended through comic-book magic only inches above Morris's head. But... now the former Juanita Neato, Jane Sim, was part of the story— and she'd brought the former Rupert Paddington along, the unmistakable Colonel Karl T. Krane, ringmaster of her circus. Two more submerged bubbles rising, unbidden, to the top. You hadn't hesitated then; anger devoured deliberation and you were through the door and back into the interpretive mess before you understood what you intended.

can. Once I've explained, I hope you'll understand why I have to take these measures. I'm going to have to stay longer than this when I'm done; I've a lot of work to do. It's much different for me here than it is for you."*

Gordy shoots Julius a frightened glance, but he says nothing, and the priest says nothing to him. They don't talk. *Can* they? Gordy's not sure. It's slippery now, the distinction between *can not* and *do not*. Meanwhile, Julius doesn't appear even to be trying. He's staring at the pearly gray-white nothing and looking angry—pissy, even—like a disillusioned little boy.

"First things first." Landrude claps his hands. "We need to talk about what you need to do. However, I recognize first you'll need convincing, so before we talk about actions, we need to talk about what you are, about your very natures and purposes. But even that won't make any sense, unless I first explain what I am, and how I relate to you. Which means we need to begin by talking about the three big things. The three big things are space and duration and possibility, in that order. Please bear with me. I promise, this will be on the test. I'm going to tell you about everything. I'll ease you into it—and myself too, I suppose. I find myself, strangely enough, at your mercy. Supplicant. I don't know how you're going to react, see, to what I'm about to say.

* Over time, you had learned hard lessons about seeing the world through the interpretation of comics readers. Objects didn't move from one place to another in a coherent way. A bird, for example, didn't traverse the sky in a line; it would start in a single place, held perfectly still, perfectly clear, for a moment—then, a moment later, it would be discernible in another place, once again perfectly exact and fixed in its spot. Those two moments were not a problem; it was the in-between that struck at your sanity like a million microscopic strychnine-soaked knitting needles. The bird flew from exact moment to exact moment in all possible ways simultaneously, all the different ways all the different readers might imagine, an utterly crazy bird-spaghetti—the bird would fly straight as an arrow, and it would fly juddering and it would fly jerking, and it would bend this way, and that way, and it would swoop to the ground and soar back up in a parabola, performing a flick-tailed jaunty loop-the-loop—before all birds distilled themselves back down to the single bird, a few hundred feet farther on. Between one comics panel to the next, a profusion of madness, and on either side, oases of sane perception—and this was just one bird. Now imagine a flock. Imagine a crowd of people. Imagine all the movement in the world. A chain of moments frozen in exactitude and perfection, threaded to one another by progressions of infinite possibility, motile madnesses of infinite extrapolation. This was interpretation, back in the days before Färland.

After Färland, it got worse.

"The first three dimensions are composed of space, exist in space, and define space. For all practical purposes, they *are* space. Think of a point in the universe. Any point at all. An infinite selection. Each point as small as imagination can make it. You could fill a single neutrino with a trillion trillion points. Forget angels and their sock-hops on pinheads. Julius, Gordy, look at this: We're at the infinite already, and we haven't even touched a dimension yet. We're not even at dimension one. Dimension one is nothing more or less than a connection between any two points. A line. Length has gotten involved. Does length seem simple to you? It is. There's nowhere to go with length but forward, and, once you reach the terminus, nothing left to do but turn around and go back again. It's the simplest possible tunnel. All of life reduced to nothing more than a movement from one dead end to another. But then again…it isn't all that simple, is it? The points are infinite. So think of the possible connections you can make. An infinite of infinites? Yes. Ouch, says my brain. Ouch, says yours.

"Next, we have dimension two, where one length joins another length and the two of them tussle over which of them gets to be width. They weave their merry war between and betwixt, and hash things out on a plane of their conflicting desires. But finally, we are starting to see the order of specificity emerge from infinity's chaos. What would you make of a connect-the-dots game if it were all dots and no space, a game that asked you to connect all dots to all others? You and I would refuse to play, if you and I weren't madmen (an open question, I know.) So: This isn't any collection of lengths, infinitely available. This is a cluster of associated lengths, located proximally. *Proximity*, you see, is the basis. That's how organization comes to all this pointillistic mush. Even though any one dot or line *might* connect to any other, once we've made the beast with two dimensions, we look around to find, with blessed relief, that not all connections have been consummated. Some choices have been made. This plane is *here*. Therefore, definitively, it isn't *there*. Thank God, says my brain. Thank God, says yours. Thus, a move into dimensional complexity, is, paradoxically, also a simplification.

"But wait. Here comes dimension three, carrying depth in its suitcases. Planes join planes, and some of them, luckily enough, will agree to become you. Third-dimensional living. A world of buildings and lobsters and galaxies and flatulence, and a few other things. You see? I don't need to explain dimension three to you. It's where you keep your stuff. Length, width, and depth, nothing more, nothing less. In short, everything. And, since you'll never guess what shape your wisest wizards of science think everything has taken, I'll tell you: At present, the wizards believe the universe is torus-shaped. Can you believe it? The universe...is a doughnut.

"So, the first dimensional set is space. Everything. But 'everything' is only the beginning.

"The next dimensional set contains (and is composed of and also defines) duration and possibility. Ah, duration. Simply put: time. I think you'll agree we are at a point in it. Yes? But now we have a problem, because I did say 'point,' again, didn't I? A point in time? But how thin can you slice time? Ask Achilles and his tortoise, they'll tell you. Slice it as thin as you like, for imagination is your knife. A trillionth of a second filleted into a quadrillion equal portions.

"The fourth dimension is a line connecting one point in the third dimension—which, let's not forget, is *everything*—to another. Just another tunnel, you see, but a tunnel precisely as large as the universe. As large as the entire universe, and as small. A movement through the slices, connecting the start to the finish, for the duration of single lepton's spin, or a fruit fly's first wing-flicker, or from the Big Bang to the final collapse, and anything in between. Infinite possibilities of connections. But not for you. Poor fellows, you can only pass through your sadly brief section of this tunnel in one direction, and your points are chosen for you. Predetermined. Birth to death, every last one of you. Nothing before, nothing beyond. And only forward, only ever forward. But that's a statement of how *you* experience time. All that time is always there all the time, whether you can see it or not.

"Which brings us, my comrades, to my first hint to you about me. For me, time is a little different than it is for you. To explain, I'll give you a picture."

From beneath the table Landrude produces a large knapsack. He rummages, emerging at last with a large, well-thumbed, paperback edition of *Moby-Dick*. "So," he says, "here is an apt picture of a passage through time. Each page a slice, you could say, though not a perfectly equivalent slice. In a book, we might jump forward a day in one page, or linger for another fifty pages on a single moment, then in the space of a paragraph leap like gods a century or more forward or backward. Melville doesn't do this (thank you, Melville); he's mainly a linear fellow, which gives him a straightforwardness useful to this example." Landrude raises the book in one hand like a high priest with an offering, then, with one long finger of the opposite hand opens the book in dramatic flourish to the final page. He makes a show of investigating the contents. "Rum luck. Ahab is dead, and so is Queequeg. The Pequod is destroyed, and all the crew but Ishmael are sunk down to the sea floor and drowned. Sorry for ruining the book if you haven't yet gotten to it, but it ends badly if you aren't a white whale or an Ishmael." With equally dexterous and casual movement, Landrude flops the pages in a mass to the beginning. "Oh, look. Ahab alive. Queequeg alive. Pequod not yet set out upon the high seas."

He flips to the beginning. To the end. Flip. Flip. Flip. Flip. "Everybody's alive. Dead. Alive. Dead. Alive. Dead, and Ishmael saved in a coffin." Flip. "And now Queequeg is building the coffin." Flip. "And now he hasn't yet built it."

Landrude closes the book and sets it gently onto the table. "And that," he says, "Is what your time is for me. Your time isn't past and present and future for me. It just is. It's there already, fixed, waiting to move between, as easily as you flip pages of a book. Exactly that easily, if you must know. If you weren't constrained third-dimensional proles (no offense), you could visit *when*ever you wanted, when*ever* you wanted, if you take my meaning.*

---

* But this was before Färland, and besides you'd grown practiced at traversing the interpretive stew, leaping within the work from one moment of stillness to another, moving quickly to the boy in the same time you "killed" him with the safe, near the very start, meandering down the street, about to join the narrative, to cock up the story forever. You materialized behind, grabbed Gordy by the hair and one arm and then you sped, leaping through time, across space, to the cavern, to the door—the kid struggling like a ferret, all wire-whip sinew. You cuffed him quiet and opened the door—I can't kill you out of the story. I can't keep you in a box. Now we do this. I can dump you anywhere at all in this world. You've no identity on the author side. You'll never find your way back to the door.

Mister, please. Wait. Don't. Don't, mister. Please.

Too late for that, kid.

But when you came through the other side, you held air. The boy's shouts cut off in

"'But hold on a second,' you may be wishing you could say (and I'll let you speak again soon, I promise); 'Sure, my past is inaccessible. But my future is still open to possibility. Free will, sir. Free will.' And you're right, insofar as 'free will' goes. Choices are being made, and *some* of them are even being made by you. Let's go back to space. In space, an infinity of points are crafted by proximity into everything, crafted—wittingly? unwittingly? by choice?—into something both more structurally complex yet—merely by dint of being *this* rather than an infinity of opposing *thats*—more simple. As with space, so with time. You choose paths leading to one series of possibilities and probabilities, and these choices cut you off forever from other sets of less proximal possibilities and probabilities. Thus you pass through the tunnel of your life, only experiencing one path of the many possible paths you might have known. Free will is the tool by which people create the universe, or—to be more precise—how they choose the part of the universe their perceptions inhabit, moment by moment, from a ceaseless selection of other ones. This is why we should talk about doughnuts. May I?"

Landrude reaches past Julius's plate, which holds his lone uneaten pastry, and snatches the priest's box of doughnut extras. With another deft flick of Landrude's fingers the box-top nods obediently open, revealing doughnutty goodness within. "So," Landrude says with gusto. "Here we have some *choices*. Father Julius, creating (or choosing) a tiny portion of the universe with doughnuts. I see you've gone with the baker's dozen—bully for you! We could be sitting in a universe where this box only contained twelve, but here we have something prime. Thirteen little doughy dabs of delight, lined in three rows, glazed, sprinkled, frosted, frittered.

"Think, Julius. Think of all the different ways the doughnuts in this box could be arranged. Of other doughnut varieties, which have been, for any variety of different reasons (including but not limited to unavailability), unchosen. Consider the universe where there is no box on this table, because you decided not to continue your tradition today. Or you discontinued the

mid-utterance. You cast about the apartment, searching, hoping Gordy had wrested free and was now hiding in a closet, in the shower, under the table… but you knew better. The kid hadn't broken free; he'd disappeared. On the table another tall stack of pages waited. You couldn't make yourself look; you set a giant red dictionary atop it to avoid the sight of it.

tradition a week ago. Or never took it up. Think of the universe (however improbable) in which you never developed the taste for doughnuts. Let's stop before we arrive at the world in which there was never a demand for doughnuts and thus no doughnut store ever opened its doughnut doors. I think you'll start to injure your poor mind, in much the same way as I may have injured mine, contemplating only the variables of a single box of doughnuts, chosen by one man of many, on one day of many. Yet again, infinite points connected to infinite points. Ouch, says my brain, and yours too, I presume.

"Now you have begun to pass into the fifth dimension. When one line of *possibility* meets another and begins to battle out which of them is truly real. A foolish battle. Both of them are real. All that *can* be, *is*. We cling to our free will as if it was some great power, but it's the weakest possible power. The branches that lie behind, never chosen, or never even accessible to you—they still exist, every bit as real as the branches that lie before, made real merely by their possibility for realness. Potential reality is reality. And we all sense it, don't we?—and don't we mourn?—the ache of the inaccessible branches, the vast expanse of possibilities unchosen and un-choosable, universes of reality unselectable and unselected?

"Apply this to things you *can't* choose; to the movements of planets, of stars, of galaxies. Apply it to atoms, to particles. Everything that exists, in all its possibility, from the beginning of time to the end. And—can you imagine it?—time is a cycle. The bang leads to collapse leads to bang again. The beginning is the end. The snake eats its tail. The shape of time's pastry, which is all space moving through all time across all possibility is...you know it already, don't you? *Everything* is a doughnut. Everything that is and was and will be and could be. Welcome to the sixth dimension. The person who lives here can choose anything in the universe. Any possibility. Any *thing*, at *any* time. The person who can dance the sixth-step can be anywhere, move any when, change reality with a word, choosing it simply by saying it. As easily as you third-steppers walk through a door from one room to another, as easily as a fourth-stepper can move from page to page through time, so a sixth-stepper moves through *possibility*. A sixth-stepper *says* it, and so it *is*. Not because we make it from what was not, but because we *see* it, and go there." Landrude leans back and stretches, taking a posture of summation. "And that's who I am. That's where I live. The Author. Of what? Why…" Landrude makes a minuscule grimace, then gestures all-encompassingly. "Of *this*. And of *you*, of course. So, yes, I'm God, if you like—but only as far as *you're* concerned." After a moment he says, "You can talk again, if you want."

Julius stands in one abrupt motion. "I'm leaving. Give me my doughnuts."

"Really? No questions? No further context required?"

"If you're God," Julius says, "then you're a shit one. Whatever it is I try to worship, it's not you. Even if It's not real, and you are real, It's still better than you."

Landrude stands, reaches in his slow, deliberate way across the table, rests one hand on Julius's shoulder. Julius regards it with distaste. "I apologize. I admit I've possibly struck the wrong tone—but it is important you hear me out."

"To you, maybe."

"Not just me." Hushed, eyes wide. "To *every*body."

"Tough cheese." Julius picks up his doughnuts, looks out at the pearly graywhite nothing. "I dislike this view. Put it back right, or I'll pound you until I see something out the window that looks as good or better. We're going."

Something regretful, even apologetic, passes over Landrude's face, but there is a diamond sharpness in his eyes. "Why do you think your father said he had an aquiline forehead?" he asks.

"How…" Julius shutters a tight smile as he realizes. "Right. Of course you know."

Landrude shaking his head: "More, I made it. In fact, I added that detail recently."

"Horse *shit*. That's from when I was—"

"From when you were twelve. Thirty-four years ago. I added it yesterday. You need to stop thinking in terms of cause and effect. My effects *create* causes. Up and down time's line."

"I…am…leaving." Julius growls thickly. He's breathing hard, as if he's a dray horse pulling an overladen cart.

"Julius sat back down," Landrude says.

Julius sits back down. Landrude sits with him.

"Julius realized he had not eaten his doughnut yet," Landrude says. "Hunger seized him with sudden ferocity."

Julius eyes the doughnut on the plate. Glares at Landrude, then back to the plate.

"Julius found he was helpless to resist the pangs," Landrude says, and now his words seem to echo through something infinitesimally more real than space. "They were like live rats chewing in his belly. His stubborn pride insisted he not eat, but finally the compulsion within him became too great, and he gave in."

With furious deliberation, Julius begins chewing air. He is gripping the table. He's not weeping, but he is visibly fighting tears.

"Julius hated the stranger," Landrude says. "He hated him for his control, his advantage, the carelessness with which he carried his ability to manipulate Julius's actions and even his thoughts. But Julius hated the stranger most of all because, even though the stranger had taken away all reason for him to believe in the God he sought without cease, and whom he worshipped without belief, still the stranger would not or could not take away from him the *hunger* for belief in that God. Julius realized the stranger had built within him an inescapable hunger, untouchable by reason, for knowledge of the divine."

"Oh, you bastard," Julius creaks, reaching for a doughnut. He is weeping openly. "You dirty bastard." He chews on his fritter, hatred and horror playing on his face. Gordy can see the priest's near hand clutching the table, the small tendons of the wrist standing out against the skin.

"But at least you got to pick *which* doughnut," Landrude murmurs. "But back to business. I am a writer and an artist, yes? My work is an extended graphic novel called *Cat's Crib*, and it is—or at least it was—considered one of the apotheoses of the form. Inspiring in scope. Startling in tonal range. Dazzling for its technical proficiency. Admirable for its longevity. And yet, even so, most of polite society *will* insist on distilling my contributions to creative endeavor to the diminutive phrase 'He makes comics.' Don't sympathize, I'm quite used to it."

"I wasn't going to sympathize."

Landrude's stare blisters with mordancy. "Yes. I know. And nobody, it seems, ever will. Oh well."

He claps once, loudly. "So! Now we see where *I* fit. I made this world, which we can call *Cat's Crib*. I am the guy who can choose from all available versions of *Cat's Crib*. Not that other versions don't still exist. There's still a version out there, for example, as real as this one, and identical in all other ways to it, in which our good Father here is still, out of spite and stubbornness, suffering intense hunger while resisting his natural biological urge to eat. I simply have chosen, on the behalf of literally everybody, not to occupy it. You're welcome, everybody. That's what I am, and I don't doubt that (however you may feel about it), what I am matters. Now, my friends, now we need to talk about what *you* are, and why *that* matters. Which leads me to the following question: Does it ever strike you as the least bit odd, that you and everybody you know are all anthropomorphic cartoon cats?"

"Never mind," Landrude says. "It was a stupid question. After all, I don't find my own state of being strange. But I did hope stating it that baldly would ease my problems. No good. Even after spelling it out, they still aren't sure."

"They?"

"I'll explain everything eventually, I promise. We won't leave until I do."

"Thank God for that," Julius says, his voice hollow as a toilet-paper tube, dry as a hobo's elbow.

Landrude returns to his recitation: "In the beginning, was *Cat's Crib*. And Landrude said, 'Let the narrative be set in 'Loony Island,' and there the Island was, and the Island was funky, and a little bit dangerous, but in a goofy, heightened sort of way, and the readers saw that it was very good. And then Landrude said, 'Let there be Donk, and Boyd, and Bailey, and let them be our heroes, and so they were, and the readers saw that it was very good. *Cat's Crib* was a hit, feted in the comics journals and even (ever so occasionally) in mainstream media sources, not enough perhaps to be optioned for film, but nevertheless to the increasing satisfaction of both Landrude's ego and his bank account.

"But then, it happened. Without warning, everything changed." Landrude pantomimes an explosion with his fingers. "By which I mean to say...*everything*. One fine morning, I woke up, came down to work, and the page on my easel was different. I don't mean a line here or there different, or a panel changed—*totally* different. The drawings literally weren't the pictures I remembered drawing. The pictures weren't telling the story I'd written.*

---

* When at last you came to the moment of surrender, you made yourself drunk enough to face it, and then removed the dictionary and read.

It worked, you'd thought. I've done it.

Gordy had gone missing from the story—completely gone. Wait... no. For some reason he still appears early in the story—Why would he still come into the story?—still escapes from the oubliette, for some reason... What was this?... goes behind the door—*my* door? You read quickly, then again, slower, then again, again, again—I don't like that. I don't like it. I don't like not seeing what happens with Gordy behind the door. And, and, and, what the hell is this *ticket*, anyway? The ticket was just a thing you'd found in an inner pocket of one of your suits; you gave it to him so he could enter the circus, but.... it's been transformed into some sort of object of power? And it's a power like *your* power. Realizing you were no longer sodden enough to continue, you drank deeply from the bottle, then set about the important work of deciding none of it mattered.

Worse, what was happening in those pages wouldn't make any sense in the context of the story that had come before. But even this wasn't the worst of it. I found the worst of it that evening, returning to a back-issue to reference a plot point. This is when I saw it clearly: Everything had changed. Do you understand? Even the stuff I had already published. The new pages did fit the story; but the story itself had become unrecognizable to me. Sure, most of the main characters were still there, and many of the story elements, and some of the same plotlines, but jumbled—the entire thing was different. It wasn't the book I remember writing. Worst of all: I was the only person who remembered it the way it had been. Nobody had ever read the story I remembered writing. They had read and enjoyed this other story, parallel to my story, but it was all wrong. The details, wrong. The themes, shifted. The back story, altered. Years of work gone, replaced with something else...or, worse—and I had to consider this—what if this was the way it had always been, and I was crazy? I had only my memory of the way it used to read— the way it was supposed to read. Nothing else in the world had changed, only this. It wasn't impossible to imagine I was..." Landrude's voice weakens, trails off. He stares for a while, drifting. When he looks up, his eyes are moist with recollection. "So, you see, I can appreciate your position," he says to Julius. "I understand why you hate me for what I am. For what I just did to you, have been doing to you, will do to you. I've experienced it, too."

"But I know this much: Along with the changes came new characters. Two new characters, to be specific. Morris is one. A character who had begun only as an afterthought, who was never going to be more than a

After an hour, you decided it didn't matter—you had what you wanted. Gordy's gone from the book. He tunnels through the rock and disappears, never to be seen again. He never comes back.

Nor was this the only piece of good news. There was no longer a safe dangling over Morris's head to conclude matters, either— and look at the final page. There, inch-deep, the cream that rose to the top, sat once again a hundred pages of your text-work, explanations to a recalcitrant readership, exacting descriptions of what it all means. The tiny typeface of your exegesis restored... you'd wept with relief. Here was the only part of the story that truly mattered. It was the real story, your true work. This pile would be the final stack of pages you'd ever generate. It was accomplished.

A month later the legal action began.

minor recurring villain, a temporary number-two bad guy, who I was going to bump off in the next issue. Now, he's the main antagonist. "And you—" here he jabs a finger at Gordy—"You were the other one. You'd become the new hero of *Cat's Crib*. The main character. And I'd never even seen you before. You had your ticket, and your powers, and you were helping Donk, Boyd, and Bailey defeat Morris and his Brotherhood of Solipsist Assassins."

"Who is *Boyd?*" asks Julius.

Landrude, on the verge of some explanation, shakes his head. "Never mind. You, Gordy—you and Morris—brought all this in your wake, or else it brought you. But there's no doubt you were the primary new elements. I trace all the changes back to you."

"I couldn't have done any of that," Gordy splutters, even as, within the deeper bulwarks of his consciousness, he feels some precariously balanced boulders begin to shift. "I've only been here a few months. I never fought with—"

"You have to change your thinking about time," Landrude twirls a doughnut on his finger, then flips it to the table, and, returning the finger to the hole, begins, without taking his eyes from Gordy, to spin it slowly. "You're only looking at what you're doing now, and what you've done in the past now. But from my perspective, your current situation is only one of many I've seen. What you are and have been now can be wildly different from what you used to have been in the pasts, or what you used to 'are' in the presents, or what you used to 'going-to-be' in the futures. And it's not like I haven't created your future for you. You've done many things you never did, and have already done many things you haven't done yet. Remember, I've seen the most recent finished page; it takes place at a moment chronologically beyond this moment we're experiencing now. I'm just trying to put my story back right. I remember. I visit. I alter. I nudge to try to get it back on track. Every time I visit, it changes again, every time I return, I find a new story pressed between covers, new original art in my archives, with me the only one to notice the difference. With me to read it all over again to learn once again what my story has become. To hunt for clues as to how to restore it back to what I remember. And to wonder—What if things have changed that even *I* don't remember anymore?"

Gordy finds he has nothing to say.

"I think it's time to talk about the next set of dimensions." Landrude becomes deliberate again. "These are the dimensions of the Everythings. If the sixth dimension is the sum of all possibility across all existing space and all existing time, then the sixth dimension is, simply, the Everything of everything. All that is and all that ever *could* be. So, how, you ask—or you do if I say you do—how do you go beyond Everything? Eh? How do you pull *that* trick off? In fact, it's the simplest thing. Imagine a realm where some—or all—of the most foundational rules governing the universe are...different. Where those originating points, infinite before even approaching the first dimension, began assembling themselves according to some scheme other than *proximity*. Where space isn't even space, where time isn't even time. Where time is made of magnetism. Where magnetism is made of lettuce.

"I can see I'm failing to capture it. Try this: Think of a more closely associated Everything to our Everything, where time and space still operate in roughly similar fashion, but in which passage down time's tunnel isn't marked by a progression from hand-drawn panel to hand-drawn panel, but rather by words on a page, bricks of paragraph, tributaries of dialogue, letter by letter, word by word. In other words, imagine a comic book and then imagine a novel. Imagine a line connecting the one Everything to the other. The seventh dimension would be that line between our Everything and another Everything. A closed system of only two Everythings. Another tunnel, but from your perspective and mine, inexpressibly large and complex. Now imagine the eighth dimension, a planar assembly of such linear connections, associated one to the other by roughly parallel understandings of time, space, and possibility. Imagine the ninth dimension—the ninth! ay yi yi, the ninth!—the full collection of all Everythings across all their collective spaces (or whatever the various Everythings use as space) and all their collective times (whatever 'time' might mean for each) and all their collective possibilities—*possibilities*, guys!—every single possible shift of every single possible supersub-particular element of every sub-particle, all existing, always. Imagine it. Imagine all the Everythings. You can't. You can't even imagine a single Everything, much less all the Everythings. Can you even imagine imagining it? I can't. But that's what your ticket does, Gordy. Wherever the thing came from, for whatever reason you've brought it, that's what it has done, at least in some small part that is what it has allowed." Landrude thrusts his arm once again within the womb of his red rucksack, rummages, draws out a large book, paperback, its white cover empty save for the title and the single image, centrally placed, of a glass, shaped like a bell, filled with a dozen perfect ounces of golden Trappist beer. A FAR LAND, the cover proclaims.

"Before I was a successful comic-book creator," Landrude says, looking slightly abashed, "I was an *unsuccessful* novelist. This thing is the only work I ever got published. It's not bad. It sold about twenty copies. It's about my misspent youth in the worse neighborhoods of Belgium—or, as I have it, Färland; it's a *roman à clef* with even the names of countries and cities changed to protect reputations. As good as it was that you ran away from Morris, as glad as I am that you kept the bastard from the power he seeks," Landrude says, shaking the book. "When you ran, this is where you ran—into the next book over on my bookshelf. And boy-howdy, buddy, did you ever goof everything up when you did."

Julius sits on the checkerboard-tile floor. "You know what? I'm sick of gods who make simple things impossible. Gordy can play your game if he wants, but what I'm going to do is, I'm going to lie here with my head under this table until you cut this shit and go away forever."

Landrude rubs his forehead. "Let me ask you something, my fine friar friend. Does gravity exist?" Julius lies back, head under the adjacent table, staring at the gum-encrusted underbelly, keeping pointedly silent. Landrude, however, is undeterred. "I mean to say, do you and your friends and everybody go flying off the planet, or do you stay on *terra firma*? I'm guessing it's the latter. Do you know how gravity works? Where it comes from? I don't. As best I can tell, even the biggest brains in my Everything argue about it. And how about the sky? Or how about the entire country of China? Do they speak Mandarin in China? Of course they do. Do I speak Mandarin? No, I do not. How much of my story—your world—takes place in China? None of it does. And yet, your world has China in it, full of Chinese people speaking Mandarin. How? And, why? Better still, let's get back to 'doughnuts.' Or even further back to 'donuts.' This one," Landrude makes a selection from the box. "I suppose you'd agree it exists. I suppose it's made of atoms.

Would you agree? Do you know how atoms are bound together? I mean, exactly how? I don't. But I suppose these atoms are bound by the same natural contracts instructing all atoms to hold together. Now consider the Crab Nebula, my poor petulant padre. Does it exist? You've never visited, I know, but you've heard of it, I'm sure—do you assume it exists? How about you, Gordy—what does your experience tell you? Do the stars exist? Do they form Orion's Belt? The Big Dipper? The Milky Way? Other galaxies too numerous to count? *Do* they? Or let me ask you another question. Do you breathe? You know: in, out, oxygen to the blood through the lungs? Does your heart beat, pumping that blood throughout your body?"

Landrude pauses waiting on truculent Julius's acknowledgment. Gordy finally gives a perfunctory nod on the priest's behalf. "Splendid. Do you know what's interesting about all these things? I never wrote them into existence. Never once did I write, 'Oh, and by the way, there are stars that form the Big Dipper,' not once did I mention, 'Oh, and by the way, throughout this scene, the sky still continues to exist, and it is blue, and also there is China (where Mandarin is spoken, you know), and gravity, which is probably caused by dark matter, and atoms continue to bond one to the other, held together by their unending electrochemical confluences.' Nary a time did I write, 'Oh, and by the way, Gordy's heart continued to beat all the way through this scene here.' And yet it does. Isn't. That. Fascinating?

"So now, I think, it's finally time to explain interpretation and assumption. It's another dimension—last dimension, I promise—number ten. It doesn't sit atop the ninth, like the ninth does over the eighth, and so on down the line. It sits tucked between all of them. The tenth dimension is the observance by audiences of the other dimensions. Interpretation. Assumption. You *do*, and thus you swim through the channels of possibility. I *say*, and so it will be, and thus I dig the larger grooves in reality from which you cannot stray. But them? The audiences? They see whatever they will see, and decide what it *means*, and we are all at their mercy. It's not me who keeps this whole assumed universal and biological apparatus going, and I assure you, it's not you, either. It's *them*. You choose realities into being out of a limited selection. I speak them into being out of a far wider one. *But they observe it into being.* They assume their own universe into yours.

The stars and the sky and China and the very breath in your lungs are all in your world because *they* assume they are. And, as their understanding of their own universe changes, so your universe will change, automatically, with new assumptions and interpretations. So much more is unspoken in the totality of a universe than is spoken. This is their control over me, and over you. Over us all. Ours are the weaker powers; theirs are the stronger.

"Observers. Readers, if you like, since that's what they are in your case. The tenth dimension, situated in any Everything that might have access to my creation and to you, providing all possible interpretations throughout all possibilities across all time and all space of all the Everythings.

"It's always been hard on my mind, being here." With distaste, he prods *A Far Land*. "Now it's nearly impossible. Just sitting here is a serious chore. A comic book is an unusually stable place when it comes to interpretation; it's all visual, you see. Everybody saw you as cats. You were cats. Your surroundings I drew as background, and so everybody saw it that specific way. But then, Gordy, you made your escape—into a *completely different Everything*, into a goddam *novel*—and you scrambled all the eggs.* You made connections

---

* You'd rushed back to the stack and flipped through in a panic. You found them all easily enough; you'd been so blind, so singularly focused upon Gordy's absence, that you'd missed them. Infractions galore against intellectual property and common propriety, revised throughout the pages, the characters of other entities put to the most unauthorized uses imaginable. Mostly you'd find them in the background, inconspicuous but fully recognizable, their inclusion all the more egregious for their routinely unsavory crudeness, their aggressive pointlessness, their total lack of contribution to the plot—you couldn't even argue satirical use. Here your troubles truly began. The back catalogue now offered itself up to the world's legal mechanisms, enticingly actionable, a chum tray for attorneys, and every shark come to take a meaty bite out of you attracted the attention of three more. Amazed they'd never noticed before, but there's no real statute of limitations here, so better late than never... the cowards wouldn't even come themselves, sending instead unctuous functionaries. You couldn't jab them with amnesia and hide them behind the door, they weren't specific enough; these messengers, backed by sentient but non-tactile formless incorporation, bearing perfect blocks of text detailing your sins against them, listing their claims upon everything you owned. Court-ordered injunctions blockading profit from the sale of any of the remaining contested original artwork. The only way to make money now was through detestable appearances, signings, glad-handing—horrible work. You began dreaming of returning to the cavern side—I had it better when I was Morris. I could switch places back again. Or—or!— what if I took the ticket for myself?... Yes. Yes! My God, it's so obvious!

between two Everythings, each with its own set of foundational rules—and I seriously doubt this was the only connection between Everythings you made. You punctured the seal of your Everything; all other Everythings—and *audiences* of other Everythings—came rushing in.

"It's them who make it awful for me in here. Don't you understand? Because I control everything in this Everything, *I have to see it all, all at once.* And, now that you—" pointing at Gordy—"punctured the seal around your Everything, I have observers observing you as comic book, and as novel, *and* as movie, *and*… You see? Some formats I can only guess at. You're being observed across infinite Everythings, and I have to see it all. Can you imagine it? Perceiving reality properly in such an interpretational stew is… horrific. It requires all my concentration."

Beneath the table, Gordy feels his seat shake; Julius's left foot tapping against his bench in impatient staccato. Landrude, ignoring, continues. "That's why I need the two of you so badly," he says, his eyes moist, pretenses of grandeur released, the desperation that has all along been threatening to emerge from him thrown now to the fore.

A doughnut bounces off Landrude's forehead, leaving behind a glistening sugary residue. Julius, sitting, is already holding another in throwing position. "Then why don't you fix this 'goof,' shithead? You're so powerful. So mighty. *You* stop Morris. Stop his heart. Bury him under a mountain. Send a pack of jackal-frogs to eat him. Turn him into swamp water. Take Gordy's ticket for yourself if you need it safe."

Landrude looks mordantly at the priest, blows smoke in his face. "I *have*

But no. The ticket wouldn't let you touch it. It defied you, tantalized, squirted from your grasp like a soapy sardine. And still more pages for your efforts. Within your heart, the notion took root and grew: *I'm punishing myself for something…*

In time, logic suggested a corrective. What had caused these woes? Gordy leaving. If so, then what might reverse them, but Gordy (as distasteful as this prospect might seem) returning? If the ending with the safe returned, you'd just have to find another way of dealing with it; that's all. Anything to avoid this constant stream of papers served, this constant demand upon your depleting wealth and your dissipating reputation. You'd followed Gordy down the tunnel, found him in *A Far Land*, then returned and set yourself to the work. You gifted "Morris" the technology to travel a trans-Atlantic tunnel—his "Tunnel CAT,"—and then watched as he did the hard work of extraditing Gordy back to his original text.

tried. I can't do anything with the ticket. It won't let me touch it. And killing Morris is no good. Cause and effect are hard to predict. I don't create the pages—they're waiting for me when I return. And they've always gone wrong."

"I would very much like to go now," Julius says, with a calm approaching panic.

Landrude ignores this. "There's not much to it, guys; it's a simple game. Gordy, you and your ticket are the only things in this Everything that come from some place beyond me, the only things *I can't write*. You've been injected into a narrative that pushes, no matter how hard I try to fight it, toward a reality in which Gordy gives Morris the ticket. Logically speaking, it follows there must be some horrifically powerful force that wants Morris to have it."

"I have no ticket." Gordy peeps. He wants to scream it, but he's too tired.

"You do. You need to remember."

"I can't remember *anything*."

"Don't be a fool. You can. You do. Every night. Then you scream. Then you make yourself forget again, *using the ticket*, which you absolutely do have somewhere on you."

"I knew it!" Julius, exultant despite himself, smacks the floor triumphantly.

"Then where the hell is it?" Gordy shouts. "Where have I hidden it?"

The look Landrude bestows upon Gordy is slow and sad, and terribly weary. "That," he says, "is one of the few things I do not know." He leans forward over the table. "There's not much time. It's going to happen tomorrow. And it's up to you and Julius to stop him."

"Then I just won't give it to him."

"Ah, but I've already seen it," Landrude says, sadly. "You *do*. The final panel.* He's an inch from taking it from you."

---

* The bad news was, Gordy's return didn't end your legal woes.

There was worse news. The last page of the revised stack no longer depicted the ending with the safe.

In its place, something horrible: Gordy, ticket-empowered, giving that ticket—that authorial fiat—back to "Morris."

What, you wondered, might happen to "Morris," if he received it? What might he realize?

"And what happens…" Gordy asks, though he knows the bad answer. He can see it rushing at him. He knows it; it's been chasing him all along, it's followed him wheresoever he's hidden from it, it wakes him at night screaming, it makes him coffee in the morning, it passes by him repeatedly throughout the day like a multitude of strangers "…what happens if…if I—if I *do* give Morris…" "What happens *then*," Landrude says, with merciless finality, "is why I'm risking sanity to be here today. Imagine a million pages of exacting six-point text, block after block after page after page, free of breaks, free of dialogue, every last detail nailed down. No, imagine a billion pages of it. All possibilities close; your story ends as badly as you could possibly imagine—and I'll have a book nobody wants to read, about a megalomaniac who always had control over everything and always will. And *that's* why we need to talk about who you are, and why you matter."

"What do we need to do?" Gordy asks, envying Julius his place on the floor. Lying down looks like the best possible option. This isn't fair, he tells himself. You're not important. You don't even want to be important. What sort of demon thought you could be trusted with stakes this high?

Landrude leans in to him. "The game is 'keep away.' That's why I vanished the circus, which in all honesty, you must have realized was a trap. In doing so, I prevented a bad ending. But that just revised the pages a different way; you still give him the ticket at the end."

"But where did you send it?" Gordy says.

Landrude rolls his eyes. "Just off to their next stop down the road. A favor. I saved them the expense of transshipment. But stay away from the *circus*—honestly, are you even *listening*? The game is 'keep away.' Gordy, you're the ball. Julius, you're the protector, the champion.* You're the character I

What might he remember? And what revenge might he desire?

You'd give anything, anything at all, to bring back the ending with the safe.

* The only thing that mattered anymore was preventing this terrible, impossible, unacceptable ending.

Now came the time of desperation and experiment, calculated but no less blind for the calculation, and all failed. The time wasted creating and maintaining Julius—My God, how many times did Julius fail? Stabbed, shot, fallen down a manhole. Since you made Julius up from scratch and interpolated him yourself, he never resisted your manipulations like the others, but so fragile he was, so inept. It was comical how not-up-to-the-task the bastard was. He kept dying and having to be saved, and really what's the point, then, if ever and anon invented for it. I'll be honest with you: You've been utter shit at it. Each time you've tried to save Gordy—including dozens of attempts nobody except me remembers any more—you've failed. But each time you've failed, I've started again, and given you another tool to make you more likely to succeed. Here's an example you might find meaningful: In a recent recapitulation, you lacked the stamina needed to catch Morris pushing a stretcher down a long hallway. He got away, you were left wheezing, exhausted, trapped in the tunnel. Not long after you were caught and killed, the top of your head sliced off like a late summer watermelon. So, I made a change. I gave you a motivation, buried deep in your past, which made you run every day. A mad father, with a strange pathology and a guillotine. I gave you a place to which to run—a cathedral. The motivation I gave you for running also furnished you with an unusual version of faith, or at least a desire for faith, so I amplified it. It's been very useful for increasing your interest in Gordy, and thus in keeping Gordy safe these months. So take courage—you've failed each time, but each time you've gotten better at it. More importantly, you're the only one I have such control over anymore. Do you understand, you stubborn fucker?" Landrude gently nudges the silent priest's leg. "You don't recapitulate. You stay unchanged from my intent. So, the game is, stick close to Gordy. Help him remember the ticket. Keep it away from Morris. You, Gordy, have to do something new and unexpected. You have to do something more than 'unexpected,' you have to do something *unexpectable*—some possibility I can't seem to find—and you can't do that, Gordy, if you can't remember."

"Something 'unexpectable' like what?" Julius asks. As Landrude has delivered this last monologue, the priest has, despite himself, drawn back into a seated position. He's obviously struggling with revelations greater than a person should be expected to digest; he looks like a dog who has been taught, for the first time, knowledge of its own mortality.

Very casually, Landrude shrugs. "Give the ticket to somebody else? Use

you're required to pop back through the door, manufacture another set of revisions, just to read how he's once again lost both the plot and his own life? And even this last time, after Julius *finally* got away from Morris alive, at the cost of Boyd's complete banishment and Bailey's broken body, *still* the final page showed Gordy giving Morris the ticket. You waited until morning to read the new stack, to see that even in success, even in success, Julius had failed. You lay on the floor and screamed.

it against Morris yourself? I don't know. If I could tell you, it wouldn't be unexpectable."

"All right," says Julius. His voice sounds like the last straggling gasp of a drowning swimmer. "And is there anything else?""

"I feel I've convinced you," Landrude replies, after consideration. "At least I've convinced you of who I am, and who you are, and why it is important. It'll have to do. So now, I have to wait. I don't know what you're going to do with your new information, but I hope you choose to play the game. And Gordy, at the risk of belaboring the point, you need to remember. Try the confessional.* Everything—and I'm speaking literally now—Everything depends on you."

"And is there anything *else*?"

Landrude sighs. "No, Julius. No, there's nothing else. That's all there is." Inside, without a rush of wind or a pop or any other announcement, the customers and cooks of Bailey's Doughnuts return, slackfaced and chewing: hustle and fry, murmur and call. Out the windows, the pearly mist is gone, Loony Island restored. Julius rises and dusts himself off. He and Gordy stumble away, mutely, leaving the man in the powder-blue suit behind.

"Julius. You forgot your doughnuts." Julius leaves without acknowledgment. Jingle of the bell on the door. "Interesting," says the man in the powder-blue suit. He selects one—frosted, no sprinkles—and begins to eat.

---

* Once you'd finished screaming, you prepared yourself for the next visit. Devoted an entire week to writing exactly what you intended to say and how you intended to say it, the truths you intended to impart, the ones you intended to elide, then committed it to memory. You'd have to pretend to be other than you are, lean into their illusion that they and others exist, pretend you had their interests at heart. You'd need to go into the story, deeper into it, more fully integrated with it, than ever before. Still and ever your thoughts returned to Gordy's unseen visit behind your door. The craving spread like disease, to know what was hidden from your vision—What did you learn, Gordy, when you grasped knob, turned, opened, entered? The stacks of revisions never show it, but you didn't go to the same place I do. What did you see? Who empowered the ticket I gave you? And why? Maybe I can get you to tell, and I can listen. Ah! Now that would be a prize worth divulging secrets to receive.

When at last you felt yourself ready, you went in—Last chance, you bastards. Last chance. No more subtlety. I'm going in deeper than ever before. All the way *inside* your narrative, buried within it until I rise out of it to consume it. I'll explain it all to you in plain language, everything you need to know; if that doesn't do the trick, I'm done with you for good.

✗ ✗ ✗

Outside, they stumble away from the doughnut shop like recent witnesses to hard murders. Only when the shop is long out of sight does Gordy finally speak.

"Do you believe him?"

"I don't give a warm fucking fart either way,"

They trudge on. Gordy says, "I'm leaving tomorrow morning."

"I know. I'm coming with you."

"I know."

Back at the Chapel, when they once again feel themselves unobserved, near Julius's cell, they argue.

"Hell no, I'm not taking your fucking confession. I didn't feel qualified before. I damn sure don't feel qualified now."

"If you're going out on the run with me, you should know what I've done—what I'm capable of."

"I don't know what *I'm* capable of. I don't even know what I'll *be* tomorrow. All I have are my convictions, and even those...do what Landrude told you. Use Father Ex if you need to. There's a memory card in it you can take with you to replay it for me someday. Someday I'll listen, if the reason is right."

"The reason is you're my friend. My only friend. Take my confession."

"Sorry, buddy. When you leave, I'll go with you. It's what I'm *made* for, isn't it? But I'll never do another priestly thing in my life. It's done. I'm not a real priest. I'm not even real. Use Father Ex."

✗ ✗ ✗

Later, shaking with screams, sequestered within Father Ex-Position, Gordy lets great waves of memory crash into him. Most of all, he remembers the voices screaming out from the oubliettes as he opened them—that most of all. The voices of those he left behind.

C O M M A N D

The confessional is dim and still, suffused with odors of cut wood and incense and lacquer. A padded bench rests against the back wall; you face the door as you sit. A hook-and-eye latch on the door provides privacy from intrusion, which calls up images—perhaps apt (given the parallel themes of unburdening), or even intentional (given Julius's natural irreverence)—of a latrine. A lattice to the left suggests a priest listening on the other side, but the space is empty; nobody presides there but Father Ex, recording mutely and erasing each day, hearing and absolving, no presence to him save a slight mechanized whir, and even this is artifice; the booth long ago converted to digital. That distinct *whir*, added years ago by Father Julius, emits from a tiny speaker, an ersatz suggestion of analog equipment, produced (ironically enough) digitally, a suggested sense of the physical to preside over your repentance—creak of wheel, click of gear, recording dumbly, blindly, twenty-four hours' worth, the tail end overwriting itself, second by second, absolving, expunging. Fitting I should remember it all here, Gordy thinks. Me and you, Father Ex, we erase ourselves every day.

It had been easy, in the end, as Landrude had suggested. He'd remembered, like lights switching on—not a single bulb filling a room, but rather a series of lights switching on in a massive space, each light a spotlight on one portion, but scattering illumination over the whole. In this way, the first few memories restored the rest. Remembering before Färland. Remembering cavern, circus, bird, spade, freaks and clowns and trapeze artists . . . oubliette and cavern and ticket and door and sanctuary... Jane, the acrobat, then the caretaker, still smooth-faced then, with the eyes that make you die—her girl, with a bird's name. Remembering anger. Remembering running. Remembering the tunnel. Remembering even the nightly remembering. Remembering making yourself forget. Roughing in the details around the reasons until at last the final light goes on.

Someone is calling a familiar name, soft and persistent.

—Gordy.

—Gordy.

—Gordy.

Remembering: Of course. This is what happens each night: the command.

You call it a ticket. Give it to him. With each call, Gordy feels the order is imprinted anew in his flesh, written into his mind, wrapped tightly in amino helix and secreted into the smallest nests of his being. The naming of him is the naming of his command. With each call a scream tears from his deepest innards. The ticket must be given. It must. Unavoidable. Inexorable. Each night it has come, this furious squall of memory, the divine command to doom the world, to give all power to he who has proven himself least worthy of any. And then, relief—remembering the great hope of the coming wave. Gordy sees it looming, allows himself to believe it's grown closer—soon it will come and wash Morris out of the world, him and all his poisonous tribe: his fountain and influence, gone, his empire of traffic in flesh, done, his pointillist reduction of philosophy, washed and destroyed, crushed beneath an everything of water, rightfully gone and rightfully forgotten.

The temptation is in Gordy to make himself forget. And he will; he does that every night, too. He's located the seat of his power: green, rectangular, flat, shiny, still miraculously whole. He remembers where it's hidden. As he is named, commanded, damned

—Gordy

and as he screams into the horror of it and the pain of resisting, the knowledge rises up—You can use it for another night, silence the command, forget, sink once more into the anesthesia of amnesia. You can't long resist the command, you know you won't long resist it, if Landrude is to be believed, you will give it...The soft and familiar and persistent naming comes with decreasing frequency now, but each time it arrives the intensity compounds. Either expunge its memory another night to live another day, or else obey; there exists no other option. And you could obey. That's the great temptation. Lift the veil you've given yourself, announce your presence in the sky with fire, bring the bastard running for his prize and simply let him have it.

As his naming pulses into him once again

—Gordy

ripping another scream from his bowels through his lungs, out his ears, he considers it, letting himself imagine the peace: of submission, of letting Morris win. The villain wields it at last, triumphant, and then what will come will come, but at least for me, Gordy thinks, there will be peace...It comes to him—Landrude was right. Of *course*, I eventually give Morris the ticket. How could I do otherwise? How could anyone, let alone a poor weakling like myself, resist this storm forever?

You should end yourself, Gordy thinks. Unmake yourself, and it with you. Escape again, but not into your usual selective amnesia. Escape into not-being. Into never-having-been. I can order it and it'll be done. Gone. Deeper than rest. More tranquil even than oblivion. More peaceful even than death. What, then, would save Morris from the coming wave? You should do it, Gordy thinks. You should do it. Take the peace for yourself but deny him the prize. I'll do it. I will. I will.

As the minutes pass, Gordy finds he has not done it. It's been long enough for him to dare hope he has outlasted the command when

—Gordy

a vision of the wave springs up before him again, endless, of volume unimaginable, poised to destroy his enemy but never reaching the terminus, while every cell thrums with the horrible command. Gordy screams resistance until his eyeballs cluster into a single globular entity, then clack together like billiard balls on either side of his head; parts of his body fall off and reassemble into distortions of form: his jaw to his lap, his tongue unfurled like a party favor, every hair electrified, spine contorted, he's being unmade, reformed into something unruly and cartoonish, reconstituted, forced into caricatures of torment. When he arrives on the opposite shore of this universe of pain, he finds he has bloodied the back of his head against the wall.

Somebody is knocking timidly *tap-tap-tap* on the door. Julius, playing the mother hen. The next command may come in twenty minutes, or an hour, but when it comes, Gordy knows, he may damage himself badly, or give in at

last to the command—Better to make yourself forget, put it off another day…
but the end is coming soon. You may not have another day. If Landrude was
right about everything else he's likely right about that…Another knock at the
door. Gordy ignores it—Julius can wait. The priest won't listen to confession,
but he needs to be told. And Father Ex is listening. Let Ex be your memory,
and then you can forget.

Gordy speaks quickly, as calmly as he is able. He's surprised to hear how
calm he sounds to himself, how focused. Time constricts; the next command
is coming: another naming, another torment, another temptation. And, after
that, the next next command. And then the next. And, unless something is
done, one of the *next* commands will be *the* command, the one that cannot be
countermanded, the final edict, the end of the game. The important thing
is to impart to Ex the most salient points, leaping across redundancies and
immateriality. There is a ticket of power. A fountain of obliteration. Prisons of impossible cruelty. An edict to empower the imprisoner. A constraint
against harming him. A promised wave to destroy him. But also, a terrible
command to empower him. Gordy, impressed at how focused he is, how totally calm, how well he's reminding himself on occasion to breathe, speaks in
a voice low and desperate but calm and focused, and his voice arrives from
a far land, serene and ragged and desperate and calm calm calmcalmcalm.
Ticket. Fountain. Prisons. Edict. Constraint. Wave. Command. Landrude
was right;* the game is 'keep away.' But the next command is coming. Julius

---

* You didn't dare risk sifting through a newly revised stack for the answers—those evil revisions had betrayed your best intentions enough times already. Though reality remained a
nearly unbearable interpretive stew, you stayed in the world after leaving the donut shop,
rather than return through the door for the relative calm of the author's side. Moving hours
forward in time, you materialized yourself inside the ever-empty father-confessor side of
the bifurcated confessional, the so-called Father Ex-Position (hadn't it once been called
Monseigneur Ex-Position? When was it demoted? In which revision did that occur? You'd
missed it.) Horribly cramped, you waited, soft and still, for Gordy, yet even in your discomfort you enjoyed the relative interpretive quiescence of the dark space you'd chosen to
unnaturally inhabit. Your patience paid extravagant dividends. Once Gordy faced what he
thought was nothing but empty space, he told it all. What he'd seen behind the door, what
he'd been commanded, why he'd run, the ticket, the wave, the Voice, the command… you
learned so much, and all of it pointed to just one course of action for you to take. Now that
you've returned and read the donut stack, you're more resolved toward that end than ever.

still knocking at the door, and more insistent now, but Gordy is serene, a virtuoso of exposition, a maestro of summary, calm, focused, and weeping and the *tap-tap-tap* of the door soft but persistent just a goddamned minute, Julius, what could be more important than this, I wouldn't have to be so calm if you would take one simple confession, I only need a moment to tell you the game is keep away and Command and Hide and Command and Seek and Command and at last it's all out, saved for posterity provided we extract Father Ex's memory in time, *tap-tap-tap-tap* settle down Julius there's one thing left to say and then I can forget again for another day... The tapping on the door again. Good—time to give the priest his instructions, then go lie down, push delete on your gray matter for another day. Gordy opens the door, and blinks surprise—Julius has changed; he's grotesquely shrunken, emaciated, his beard shaved, his eyes protruding, wearing thick glasses, a knit cap, and the bathrobe of a loony. The apparition smiles, his eyes watering, face crinkled into a road map of delight, and Gordy realizes his error.

"Gordy-Gord," the apparition says, hushed. "It's you. It's really you."

"Hi, Dad," says Gordy, allowing his father's embrace to pull him from Ex's wooden confines. The rest of the cells are dark; the Neon brothers and sisters are either sleeping or listening quietly. His father is weeping. "You remember. You *remember* me." Gordy lets himself be shaken. His father's arms, surprisingly strong for their scrawniness, clutch at him. "Found you at last at last, my boy. Found you at last." He releases Gordy and collapses to the floor, sobbing soundlessly, and Gordy, not knowing what else to do, sits beside him and pats his shoulder. Here's what's left of your dad, Gordy muses. Sterling Shirker, onetime professor, PhD of History, your father—a bag of rags and sticks on the floor. "Tennessee" now. It must have been hard for him; most of what you've been through he's been through, too. Spent as much time as you in the oubliettes, and then when you got out you wouldn't even claim him. Can't even say anymore if it was genuine amnesia or delayed adolescent pique, but unfair, unfair... another soul you've left in your wake. Imagine raising a child by yourself and losing him. Days, weeks, years, the two of you together. The man he'll become revealing himself to you as he grows. Every day the boy unfolds new possibilities, day after day he builds towers of potential. Nobody knows him like you do. To lose that. For that story to end roughly, incomplete, a book torn in half and the back half burned and lost to you forever. Then years later you find it again, but it's written in a strange tongue, an alien alphabet.

Dad weeps and heaves and then shudders and hauls himself from the floor, recovering slowly; they sit side by side, father and son, unsure of each other and made awkward by lost time. Gordy can't think where to begin; there's so much more still to be explained—How to tell this man all that happened, about why you ran from the cavern, about what forced you to leave him behind? How to bridge the moments between? And still in him is the desperate craving in his bones to make himself forget again, before the next command crashes into him.

"I've been looking for you for a *while*, boy," Dad says. He smacks Gordy's back and grins like the loon he is.

"We've been looking for you, too." As he says it, Gordy remembers how excited Julius is going to be. "Where *have* you been?"

Dad makes an ostentatious show of looking around for eavesdroppers. "Donk," he breathes. "He holed me up in a back room. He's been lying to me about everything for months. My new buddy busted me out.* My door locked on the outside, you know, but suddenly, blammo! It falls down. And there he stands."

"Who's this…new buddy?" Gordy asks, suspecting he already knows.

* You were wisely unwilling to leave it to chance that Gordy and Julius would escape Loony Island. They'd clearly mistrusted you to some extent; no reason to suppose your exhortations would be sufficient. Time to enlist Tennessee to your cause, have him provide extra impetus to get out and away. You'd allowed yourself some fun freeing the old fellow. Jumped to the Domino City hallway where Donk was keeping him, asked the hinges and the lock mechanisms to please stop being iron and steel, to become butter instead, and they agreed to do so, and the reinforced steel door fell into the hallway with a mighty CLUD. Tennessee had been most impressed by that; and even more impressed by your warnings of the dangers Donk posed, the extents to which he would go to capture the ticket, the things he would do once he had it.

It had been effective as hell, as the truth frequently is. Apparently, Donk had already been scaring Tennessee plenty with recent pronouncements and threats; the loony had gone tearing ass, bumble-stumbling down the hallway, looking for his lad lost forever. You'd had to call him back to tell him exactly where to find Gordy, so he didn't waste time looking. Why leave anything to chance?

"Well…" Dad screws up his face. "Now we come to the point of it, he never did drop his name. An unusual fellow."

"Powder-blue suit? Chain-smoker?"

Dad is appropriately astonished: "You've seen him?"

"I've seen him," Gordy says. "What did he have to say to you?"

"Not much. He told me not to be scared. He's sort of startling to look at, you know…"

"I do."

"Anyway, he told me where to find you. Told me we had to go. Then he just folded up."

"Folded…?"

Dad nods gratuitously. "Right up. Just folded in halves again and again until he was gone. It was the damnedest thing."

"I've…never seen such a thing." Gordy says, quite honestly.

"And he told me…lots of things. Including, I gotta get you out of town, pronto," Dad says. "But I already knew that. I can add up two and two. You gotta boogie, buddy. Donk is coming for you any day."

"Donk? That's nonsense. If Donk wanted to grab me, he could have done it at any time. He had me hidden away under his floorboards and he let me go without a fuss."

"Listen, boy, I'd be very *very* careful about trusting our buddy Donk. I don't know how he's been presenting to you, but until recently he's been real friendly to me—chummy. Doesn't matter, he's lied to me in every word. Told me Julius was missing and run off. Told me you were long gone and that the heat was on for me. He's been keeping me locked up three months 'for my own safety.' Keeping me around—and I now see keeping me away from you—pumping me for information."

"What sort of information?"

"About your ticket, of course. Where you keep it. Where you might hide it."

"Donk knows about the ticket? Did Julius tell him?"

Dad looks suddenly sheepish. "I told him. Well, no—I told Julius and he overheard. Anyway, he knows. And look, boy—he told Morris he could get it for him, and Morris gave Donk a deadline, which is just about up. Donk was hoping to steal it without harming you. Couple mornings ago, he came to where he had me, drunk and screaming. Told me I hadn't done squat for him. Told me he was done with me. I'd been plan A. Now he goes to plan B. He's gonna bring some guys to snatch you, take the ticket from you, alive if he can. That's what he said to me the other day—'Alive, if I can.' That's when I knew Donk was no friend and that I was in yet another pickle. Not a clue how to get out, either, until my new buddy jailbroke me."

"What does Donk have against me?"

"Nothing. He likes you—you and Father Julius—if you can say he 'likes' anybody anymore. The Father in particular. It's why snatching you was his last choice instead of his first. It's why he's been so patient about it. And, he's not sure what you might do to him with the ticket while he's trying to get it from you. But his big plan was to catch you at the circus; and that plan evaporated—literally, according to Donk. That put him in a bad bind. Morris isn't one to budge. Donk's going to have to deliver or pay for failure, and Donk's affection only goes so far."

"The circus was…?"

"Donk's idea," Dad persists. "Morris owns the circus, but Donk told him to bring it, and to put Jane on those posters. He thought she might draw you out of hiding."

"She nearly did. The circus vanished…"

"Donk says after the Island show she'd go out touring. She's out there, trolling for you."

Gordy rubs his temples. It's all too much. Donk, ready to turn them in to Morris? If true, it's the worst possible news. They've trusted Donk with so much; he's the reason they walk the streets confident of their safety, avoiding only the increasingly rare cardinal and the swinging arms of loonies. But who in the Island doesn't Donk control? If he wants you, he'll get you. But hold on now, wait just a minute…

"If Donk wanted to give me to *Morris* he could do it any time. What's the wait?"

"He wants you for himself. Since Bailey, all he really wants is revenge. He's got extravagant plans for what he'll do to Morris with that ticket once he gets it off *you*."

Gordy, stammering. "But that's just...it's...it's...fine. Actually, it's per-fection." It's as if the great Gordy-an knot has been cut—Why didn't you think of it before? You can abdicate before the next command comes, divest yourself of the ticket entirely and scoot. Donk wants it? Donk can have it. You came out on top by the luck of the draw, or by luck's opposite, by some cosmic happenstance or accident. It could have been anyone; certainly, it doesn't need to be you. In wrath, Donk will erase Morris; no need to wait for divine justice's truant and increasingly tardy wave to do the trick. He laughs. "Donk wants to use the ticket to hurt Morris? Great. I tried. I can't. But if *he* wants to give it a shot..."

Dad shakes his dandelion fluffhead. "Donk isn't the one, son—you haven't heard him go on about what he's going to do when he gets that tick tick ticket."

"I've got to do *something* soon." The fear of the next command is upon him. It may be the one that breaks him. He needs to make himself forget, soon, soon. Dad, who doesn't notice the immediacy of his son's distress, con-tinues: "He's thirsty for it, boy...and I don't think he'll stop with more more Morris...he's been talking about what he'll do to anybody who's wronged anybody...anyone at all. Talking about using that ticket to run the whole city—*all* the cities. He may be as dangerous as Morris."

"Impossible." Gordy, suddenly mindful of the hour and nearby sleeping Neons, whispers, hoping to bring his fulsome father's voice down a touch—a foolish instinct, perhaps, after the hour he spent screaming.

"Well, *I* slept like shit." This is Julius, emerging from his cell, obviously unrested; his head keeps listing to the starboard before coming with a jolt back into sudden alertness. A mug in one paw contains an inky eye of coffee. Surprisingly, Julius takes Tennessee's reappearance onboard with indiffer-ence; whatever other effect Landrude's doughnut-shop speech has had, it's drained him of curiosity for any questions that Tennessee might be able to answer. He's similarly disinterested in the errant loony's urgent new informa-tion about Donk. "We were leaving already anyway," he says. "So, now we're leaving without goodbyes for Donk."

"We've *got* to go right away," Tennessee insists. "It should be today."

Julius falls heavily into one of the sanctuary's plush chairs. "Right, today—but not immediately—I need to talk to my people before I go. They at least deserve a goodbye. And I need to settle some business with Dave Waverly."

"I'm coming with you when you go," Tennessee says.

Julius barely even shrugs.

At Julius's summons, the Neon brothers and sisters gather; they wait for Sister Nettles to arrive from Bailey's bedside. She enters silently, seeming somehow to know Julius's purpose already; her mouth's a fixed line, her eyes focused on a middle distance past the ceiling or beyond the floor. When all the brothers and sisters have come together in the large central room, Julius speaks to them, the first and last homily of this strange gutter priest. As he speaks, Gordy watches their faces go from perk-eared interest to confusion to horror and slack dismay. Julius speaks slowly, distinctly, voice raw and deliberate, measuring each word to avoid choking on emotion.

"I'm going to say some things, and you're going to want questions answered right away. You're going to want to interrupt. Please wait until I'm done. I feel like if I don't say it all right now, right away, I won't be able to say it ever. This is going to be short. It's too hard to make it long. I'm leaving. I'm leaving today. Tonight. I don't expect to come back.

"There, that's the hard part done.

"That's a lie. That's not the hard part done. It's all the hard part. Every part of this is hard.

"I love you all. All of you. I came to Loony Island with the notion that if I came, others would join. A ridiculous notion. No reason to expect others to join me in a mission I couldn't even define for myself. And yet, here you are. Let me say again: I love you. I'm not leaving because I want to be gone. I'm leaving because I see no other choice. You may as well say I've been called by God, though I won't say that. I know leaving without explanation will confuse you and hurt you. But I've decided explaining will confuse and hurt you even more. I leave the matter in your hands. If you disagree with my secrecy, come find me. I have a few errands to run this morning. After, I plan to spend several hours in my room in contemplation. Find me there, and I'll tell you what I know to tell you. If you trust my judgment on the matter, you won't ask. I don't think it'll help you to understand. But if you must know, I'll tell.

"I think most of you know this house rests on the foundation of what used to be a cathedral. In that cathedral was the most beautiful window you've ever seen. I used to wake up early and run into the city every morning to watch the sun rise through it. They told me the name of it was "Sin of Moses." Back then I always took my run at night, and I always ran past this cathedral. But this particular night, I saw…I don't know what. It looked like a meteor, but coming *up*, out of the earth. A fiery tail, arcing way up in the sky and then back down. I saw the glow red in the distance, and kept coming closer until I could tell it was from my…from the cathedral. It was burning when I arrived. The diocese closed up shop a decade before; now it was a rundown haunt, home for vagrants and runaways and people who couldn't even figure out how to get themselves thrown into prison or the Wales. I could hear people in there, screaming exactly the sorts of thing you scream when you're about to burn. I ran around the place, every door heavy and locked tight. Who locked the doors? I wish I could say. If I'd been able to open them, I'd probably have died running through the fire. As it was, I ran around outside like a crazy person. Tried to break through the windows, which were stained glass. Bashed whatever I could find futilely against the tracery to knock it out."

Julius hesitates, seemingly surprised at how vivid it's become in the retelling; the almost sensory memory of smokestink and flame, and Bernadette's old home and Wavy Dave's refuge turning to ash in front of him, and the screams of children and adults. "I felt like…like maybe my destiny was upon me. Like I'd been brought to this place each day for so many years simply to perform this one great act of salvation—but then there came this deafening clap like a bomb from the upper decks as the flames blasted out through the roof and the Sin of Moses came all to pieces, blue and white and gold and crimson tinkling around in shards all around me, and even in some places *into* me, and I despaired. No destiny brought me there, no unseen forces moved, it was nothing but another coincidental cock-up, door and window, frames like granite, and me useless against them. May as well shoulder Everest out of the way. My chest heavy, the air stolen out of me, eyes filled with smoke…

"I couldn't help them. With nothing left to do, I did what I never did before. I fell to my knees. I prayed for divine help for the doomed. I prayed for the help I couldn't bring.

"And, you know, it was the damnedest thing. Help came.

"I felt the first drop maybe a few seconds before the sky dumped half a lake directly on us. The hardest storm I've ever been in. My shoulders sagged, the weight of it. Soon I was in an inch-deep river running down to the drains. I don't know how long it lasted. It couldn't have been more than . . . what? Five minutes? Ten? No more than that. It was enough.

"The onlookers came up to me. They'd seen me drop to my knees. And then the rain. I could see the awe in their eyes, some of them. It was from them the word spread.

Julius pauses for a while, then:

"I didn't pray. I don't know what praying is, really. I wasn't asking for rain. I wasn't asking for anything. It'd all been a puppet show. I didn't pray rain into existence; it simply happened to rain. Eventually in life you win some kind of lottery, I guess; my winnings came in the form of precipitation. I didn't have a thing to do with it, other than being there when it happened. It was still a miracle—almost no lives were lost—but it wasn't *my* miracle.

"*Almost* no lives lost in the fire, I said, but there were lives lost. The church had abandoned the building, but their representative had not. There was a priest still there. She may have been defrocked for refusing reassignment. I never asked, and she never mentioned. Her name was Father Bernadette, and she was my true friend. She was there with them that day. A part of the ceiling collapsed, trapping a child beneath. She crawled under the burning pile to pull the child out. It was hopeless and brave and foolish and heroic and pointless. She was caught under there with the kid. They finally excavated the bodies after the rain extinguished the flames.

"I've been here these years, acting the priest, in her memory. A hopeless cause, I suppose, but whenever it looks hopeless, I think of her. Did she die for nothing? Sometimes I think she did. Sometimes it all strikes me as futile. The result of her heroism wasn't anything like what you would want in a story like this. Often I think it was foolish, a useless death. But other times, I don't think what matters is the result. In those moments, I think all that matters is the hope. Not the hope the world provides us. I think the only hope there is to be had is the hope we make for ourselves, and the only way I know for us to make it is by being fools. I think sometimes that's the only way hope can be made: some utter fool, doing some hopeless foolish thing, with failure very likely, moving, unexpectedly, from the safety of sanity into some hopelessness or other; by being foolish, and moving farther into the foolishness. It's been what I've done thus far. So far, things haven't gotten noticeably better. And yet, some kind of miracle has happened, and, like the miracle of the rain, though I'm credited with it, I had nothing to do with it. I was merely nearby as it happened. It's a simple miracle; nothing from God, no tongue of fire. Only you. You have happened. You have come for a while, and gathered with me, and eaten with me, and without provocation or reward, you have gone about some sort of foolish work. I want to say to you now, with all the sincerity my scabbed up and cynical heart can muster: Thank you. Thank you for letting me be a fool among you. Thank you for being fools around me.

"I've never really believed in God. None of you knew that, at least not from me. I've spent my time here, and some time before that, trying to believe, but I don't. My whole life, it's been like having puzzle pieces the right color but they never fit. Now I have what I sought so long: proof of God. And yet I still don't believe. Before, I wanted to believe but I couldn't for lack of evidence. Now I have evidence, but I don't believe because I don't want to give the son of a bitch the satisfaction. I'm moving on into a new hopelessness. I found an even larger hunk of burning wreckage to crawl underneath. God is real, and he's a monster, apparently, but I'm going to go on believing in a better God anyway, despite a total lack of available evidence—a foolish thing to do. Probably I'll burn, and so will whatever 'child' I crawl in to save. So be it.

"Some of you know I'm worth a lot of money. I suppose now that I've said it, all of you know it. Money's rough and ugly but it's useful. I'm going to put it to use; I'll see to it you can keep on without me. If you choose to stay, the Neon will never be unfunded. If you choose to spread out, you'll have what you need, as long as you only take what is needed.

"You can stay, or you can go. I'd recommend most of you go. There are more hopelessnesses out there—more than can be imagined, I'd guess.

Perhaps it seems dumb to you, the idea that you should leave when there are people here already who count on you and what you do. Maybe it is dumb. There's risk in what I'm suggesting. It's possible that, if most of you go, this place will stop being what it is. It's possible it'll all fall apart. But I think it's equally possible we've begun to stagnate. It's possible there are only so many fools who can cluster together in one place. I think it's possible there are other fools waiting to start here and continue what we've begun, and we're simply in the way; I think it's possible there are potential fools out there elsewhere, waiting for another fool to come and join them. But that's only what I think, and what do I know? Finally, a question I can answer. What do I know? The answer is simple: big fat fucking nothing. So, do as you think is best.

"I ask only this: Take the day and find a place where you can be alone, a place other than here that holds some meaning to you, and think about what you want to do. I'll meet you tonight, and whatever you need to do, whatever you want to do, I'll make sure you have what you need—financially, at least—to do it.

"That's it. That's all. I'll see you tonight."

Father Julius leaves them then, practically fleeing, beckoning to Gordy and Nettles as he passes through the beaded glass curtain to the sanctuary of his cell. Nettles stays where she is. She's looking after Julius now, but Gordy can't tell if it's grief or fury in her eyes. Tennessee follows Gordy uninvited; Julius eyes him for a moment but says nothing. Tennessee looks as if he's been weeping. "That was beautiful," he says again and again, but Julius isn't paying attention. He's barreling around, pulling documents out of his desk drawer, shoving them into a battered leather satchel. Making the maximum possible effort, knocking things over, bending ostentatiously to pick them up, chasing pens under desks, as if through exertion he might ward off the finality of his decisions. At last he stops, facing Gordy, his whiskers quivering, eyes large and moist. He rests one big mitt on Gordy's shoulder.

"Well, buddy," he says. "It's the last goddam day."

Something is building behind Gordy's eyes. It feels like his soul quivering in anticipation. The next command has been too long tardy. He hasn't heard a soft familiar insistent voice speaking his name for hours, but when it arrives, he knows it will impact with momentum accumulated, the power of an earthquake centuries deferred.

The plan is to lock Gordy into the priest's cell for safety. Neither Julius nor Tennessee is willing to trust partial visibility anymore to keep him secure. They riffle through the clichés: better safe than sorry, circle the wagons, bird in the hand. A steel shutter rolls down like a garage door over the entrance to Julius's cell. "Donk may have better hidey-holes than me, but he's not the only one who has them," Julius says. "Had this installed back in the days before Ralph listed me as a protected species." All this precaution seems unnecessary to Gordy—a steel door isn't going to thwart somebody like Donk or Morris—but Julius is determined. "We're going to miss our status report with Donk at Ralph's today," he muses. "That's going to ruffle his feathers. We'll have to be quick after that."

All save Gordy have made their way out of the room. "I'll be back by this afternoon," Julius says. "No later."

"I'll be here waiting," Gordy says, "Obviously."

"You'd better be, boy," Tennessee says. "I'm not losing you again."

Julius tells Gordy: "You should read what I've written. My memoir. You'll find it in the top right shelf. It's all about who I am." He pulls a sick-looking face. "It's my back story. I think I'd like you to know." Then he reaches up for the handle of the shutter. Gordy nods as the door comes down. He hears the locks, one and two and three. The rising sun has made its way through the window, transforming each mote into a gem. He's about to make himself forget when he thinks—Shit! Father Ex's memory! You never told Julius. Remember it when he gets back.

Hoping to stave off the next command, he searches for Julius's diary. In the right-hand drawer he finds it: cream-colored paper, heavy grade, stacked an inch thick. Handwritten both sides. At the top of the first page, he reads: *My father was a man with too delicate a mind...* But reading can't distract forever. At first, he can fool himself into thinking he's subsuming both wave and command from his consciousness, but if anything, there is an opposite effect; the focus of his mind upon the page makes the incipient and unavoidable next command ever more present. He sets the pages aside and closes his eyes but it's no use. It will be here soon. Larger than stars, than galaxies. Filigreed through the infinitesimals—Sorry, Landrude, I can't do it. I have to be like Father Ex to survive. Receive and release. Remove. My mind is too small, it can only hold on to the days. The nights are too hard, they shake me apart.

In the desk the center drawer is empty, but the left one holds a flotsam of office supplies, including pens and notepads, hoping to scrawl himself a note to remember but before he has finished it arrives and

—Gordy

the pen flies through the air and Gordy falls backward, spine strained and reversing, the claw of his hand crumpling the note, every sinew seized in revolt and pulled to extremities. The command is demanding things of his physicality, his actuality, forcing him through portals of being that cannot be comprehended. His tongue the size of a mattress in his head, his skull expanding and contracting, jaw locked, toes extended, eyes like pie plates, eyes like pinheads, eyes everywhere in between. He is invisible. He is omnivisible. He is insignificant. He is everything. He is spread like hot butter across reality's toast, stretched across possibilities of possibilities. Everything hurts. Everything tickles. Excruciating to resist the call of every Thing demanding of him only one task. One task and it will be over. One task and it will be ended. It will be so easy. He has it—the ticket. He remembers where he stowed it, tucked away flat beneath the skin on the roof of his mouth, the impossible object maintaining its impossible physical cohesion in an impossible location.

Gordy reaches into his mouth and feels along its roof until he finds the ridge hiding there. With the sharpness of his fingernail he tears the skin along the ridge. He pulls back one clean flap of skin and begins worrying at the foreign object lying flat against the soft palate beneath. There's no blood and no pain. He wrestles it out, impossibly whole, green and twinkling—LUCKY 21—the papery gem grappled from his gob, sprung after long secluded years from its mangled mouthy setting. He can use it to find anybody at all. He sees them now: Julius, walking away from the Neon Chapel with Nettles, neither of them daring to look at the other, while Dad trails behind at a distance.* Julius straining against the urge to look back at the home he

---

* You were about to finally return to the artist's side then, when it occurred to you: Donk might decide to grab them before they can leave the Island. Better to leave him a distraction, keep him occupied during these crucial hours. A final stroke of genius: appearing to

intends to abandon; the other Neons at farther distances in various places…

…and Jane is drifting somewhere between slumber and waking, riding in a sleeper car, the train heading from one performance to the next…

…and Donk is in the Fridge, suit coat off, reading a book and drinking coffee…he's trying to distract himself from an inchoate sense of loneliness, and from the fact that he's due to meet Morris in twelve hours to have a frank discussion about his rapidly impending deadline, and from the fact that right after the unpleasantness of that meeting, he's either going to have to give himself over to a bad fate, or else finally abduct the only friends he has left…

…and Bailey is lying in her bed, dreaming of a room tall as a skyscraper with walls of soft grass and a terraced spiral ramp along the inner wall leading up to a glass-domed ceiling. Turning in slow wheels near the top are bright-colored birds, which might be parrots, or might be hummingbirds the size of parrots…

…and Morris presides in the deposed Wales' director's corner office. I could go to him instantly, Gordy thinks. I could immediately bring him here to me. Give him the ticket. Fulfill the command. He'd kill you then, and everyone would briefly suffer, but at least this would be over. There's such relief in the thought. Stop struggling. Doom the world. Doom the world? It sounds like nonsense. Why concern yourself with the world? The world is already doomed. You can do it, he thinks, again—End it now. As the thought arrives it seems impossible to him he ever would have considered doing otherwise. He *will* obey; it will be so simple and then it will be over forever, and nobody will accuse him of failure or cowardice or complicity or collaboration, because under the awful will of the ticket's new master, none will exist to do the blaming, nor will he exist to receive it. I'll do it, he thinks. I'll do it now and I'll do it and I'll do it now and I'll do it and I'll do it now and I'll do it and I'll do it now and I will do it…

Tennessee one last time as he lagged behind the priest; handing him a sack of oranges. Go, you know where the Fridge is. Leave them there; put a terror in Donk's heart. Send him in a rush to the children's room instead of to the Neon. Buy yourselves a few hours more.

Tennessee, obedient as ever, trotted off.

Then you popped back to the author's side, and there they were waiting. The donut stack. Revisions.

And yes, once again, there had been changes. But not for the better.

The mantra has passed his lips a hundred or a thousand times before he realizes the torment has passed and he, contrary to intention, has not done it. The morning sun still illuminates every mote in the air. There is relief now, but he still feels, deep but rising, the stirrings of yet another call, the *next* next one coming as sure as the earth spins.

And you almost did it, he thinks—Oh God, you almost did it that time. You'll give in next time for sure. That one burned the last of the resistance out of you. You have to make yourself forget. But what about tonight? And the next night? And the next? Running from town to town; each morning Julius explaining to you what it is you're doing, and why? Burning half your consciousness away at the end of each day, becoming vaguer and vaguer, less and less here, more and more nowhere at all, nowhen, nowhy?

Gordy places the ticket on the table. The thought comes—You've never finished playing the actual game. Five silver unmarked choices left, and the ace alone is a winner. A cool refreshing grand could be yours, one thousand simoleons, if you choose right…Seized by a useless whim, Gordy dowses for coins in Julius's clutter drawer. He makes only the barest hesitation before selecting the final pod, and scratches, revealing the red ace. There it is, Gordy thinks—it was there all the time. A winning ticket all the way through. Someday, when this is over, you can claim the prize. You'd pay a thousand times the value to be rid of it. Remember the moment's relief you felt, when you thought you were going to finally give it away. You can't give it to Morris, but if you could give it to somebody better suited…if only you *could* give it to Donk. Or…

Or.

So ridiculous to take the best man in Loony Island away from the place he's needed most. The look on their faces when he told them he was going—and think of all those folks in Domino City, people he helps every day. You don't want it; more important, you shouldn't have it. Unworthy of the responsibility. Unworthy of the devotion. Unworthy of the sacrifice—Julius leaving all this…for what, for *you*? It all works. It all fits together. Donk and Morris can send out the hounds, send them seeking you, send them *away* from Julius and the ticket. You'll be visible again, but let them find you—let them waste their time at the chase. Let them even waste their time in the

catching. Let them waste their time torturing you to discover you don't have
it, if that's what it comes to. The cleansing wave will arrive as sure as the next
command, if not as soon. And, while you run, you can still look for Jane. You
still have the circus's schedule. It'll be a risk, but only a risk for you now. You
won't be able to fix her, but you can point her to the priest, who can restore
her. Better him than you. You've lost the right to be her hero. Take her to a
man worthy of the title, a man who can tell God "No" and mean it. Sitting,
Gordy reads the last of the diary of Father Julius. When he's finished, Gordy
thinks—Yes, he's the one. If you weren't sure before, you can be now. He's
the one. There is something stuck to the back of the diary's last page. Turning it, he sees a note, once crumpled, smoothed back and taped flat, written
in tiny meticulous letters, the sort of obsessively precise handwriting that
might be found on hidden scrolls of toilet paper.

Julius–

I'm trying it today; with you or without. I don't care. I don't care. I can't
stand the rabbits anymore.

I'm downstairs. Help me.

—Dad

A note. You had been writing a note; you ought to finish it. The ticket is
still on the table. Gordy rearranges Julius's memoir, moves the ticket atop it.
He writes for a while, contemplating, stopping, starting, striking. When he's
done, he writes it again, a clean copy. It's important this be done properly,
this momentous transference.

It will be necessary to use it one last time. He could go out the door—it
unlocks from inside—but leaving the ticket in a locked room seems wisest,
and traipsing visible through Loony Island seems risky. Better the locked-
room mystery. Better to spirit yourself out of town in a single jaunt, leaving
it where only the man with the key can find it.

Last trick I'll ever play with you, you bastard, Gordy thinks. Too bad I
can't get the thousand bucks out of you before I leave.

Then he touches the ticket and he is gone.

Nothing in the physical realm will ever be as real as its imagined counterpart, for imagination is the realm of the ideal form. Not because imaginary things are singular and immutable, but rather because they are endlessly variable. The ideal form is not one thing; it is many.

—*Unknown*

S A N D A L S

Julius stands in his empty cell, holding Gordy's note and staring at the ticket on his table, deep in thought. The ticket isn't God, is what you need to keep telling yourself. Remember that if nothing else. It isn't God and it doesn't lead there, either. No pathway to the divine. It's another yellow door at the bottom of another set of stairs. Or it *is* a pathway to God, but God is no longer to be trusted. As a boy you stood at the top of the basement stairway, reading and unreading and reading again a note in your father's meticulous handwriting, balling it into your fist flattening it out again to read it once more, wondering what awaited you down there in your father's laboratory at the bottom of those steps cold and granite and wide leading down to that brightly painted yellow door. And why would steps in a modern domicile be granite? *Were* the steps granite? It's how you remember them. When in Landrude's creation of you did he add those details—door of yellow, granite stairs? Are they the most recent additions, or were they the first things? *Were* they the first things? Were you in the beginning nothing but a boy atop steps leading to a door, a fiddlestick of creative lint imbued by your creator with enough static charge to accrue other details? Or did the boy come later? The values and beliefs and memories most important to you, the things you'd list to define what makes you into yourself, did he add them as an afterthought? You didn't want the ticket safe from Morris because you seek God. You seek God because *Landrude* wanted the ticket safe. And there it is, the ticket itself, left behind specifically for you. You have only to take it. It's no pathway to God (unless it is) but it's some sort of answer.

Don't take it. Leave it there.*

* blank

You've read it. You sit and smoke, trying to stay philosophical through a scrim of rage. So there it is. The donut stack's revealed. The rattlesnake's bitten. You've read it, and what were you expecting, really?

Well, 'Landrude,' since you *asked*. . .

What a joke—acting as if you have a choice. You'll take it if he decides to make you take it, but maybe he'll let you choose which hand picks it up. You need to decide quickly. The brothers and sisters will be here soon, and they'll want to talk before you go.

No. Decide later. First do what you came here to do.

Julius leaves his room, moves from cell to cell, bathed in glow of neon and beer sign and pinball machine. A glow of late-fading evening light scatters across the floor from the west windows. From his battered satchel he draws sealed envelopes and places one on each bed; his final divestment, hastily drawn up and notarized by Dave Waverly, witnessed by Nettles. He stops, head down, and then with a disgusted grunt turns, gathers the envelopes again. Sits on his bed and rests his hairy head in his hands.

—Fool. Continuing with your plan. You're not leaving with Gordy anymore; he's gone already. You need to make a new plan. He wasn't captured, there's a note. Which could have been forged. But the ticket—nobody who would take him would leave it behind. Once there was a boy who would run from his house into the city each morning to watch the sunrise, running, running, growing powerful legs, huge lungs, and an incidental but useful desire for the divine. It was all for that chase in the tunnel, and only for that. Landrude gave you the physical means to run Morris down, and while doing so stumbled into a motive. He provided you with something you'd want to chase, then burnished it for maximum enticement. You weren't chasing for Gordy; you were after bigger answers. Did Bernadette die in smoke and fire to increase your yearning? Or was she not even there at first? Was she, like you, added after the fact, inserted as a contrived magnification to your fictional motivations? Imagine it, all this time you made yourself a fraud, posing as a priest. On some level you must have known you're a pretender, a recent insert into another's story. Not in the matter of vocation but in the matter of your very existence. Once upon a time there was a boy who ran into the city each day to see the sunrise, but more recently than that, there never was a boy and never had been. Window and sun and sunrise, the priest and the boy and the vagabond, years and years ago, and only yesterday, and never. Focus. Focus. Gordy isn't captured. He's out there, wandering. The note says he's going to find the bearded lady Jane, right the wrongs he's brought into the world. The note says his confession is there in Father Ex, all the information you'll need. And what do you do? Stay? Follow him? In what direction? North? West? Färland? Into some other fiction?

And what do you do with the ticket? Do you pick it up? Leave it? It's too dangerous to leave, too dangerous to take. He gave it to me but I really don't want it. I want it more than anything.* After the sunrise each morning Bernadette would take us to breakfast around the corner, you and Wavy Dave, the vagabond, a man of filth and rags running from something nameless and unspeakable, his pores suffused with filth. Over eggs and ketchup one morning, she explained to us the meaning of the Sin of Moses. The prophet commanded to speak to the rock and thus bring forth water, but instead he disobeyed, broke the letter of the law, opted instead to strike it with his staff. The miracle still transpired, but old Moses found himself dinged with divine demerits, cursed, punished for his insubordination, forced at the end of his obedient life to stand outside looking in, slowly dying while his people lurched into their Promised Land, pots on their heads and swords in their hands. It seemed like nonsense then and it still seems like nonsense. A technicality, a game of "Simon Says." Each time previously, whenever poor Moses had been told to do the God-magic, he'd been told to use his magic God-staff; it strikes you as unfair to gig him for succumbing to habit. Moses above all must have been a tactile man, said Bernadette—just like you, Jules. And even more, it had worked! The water had come! One way or another, the water still came busting forth from the stone, the long thirst of his people still quenched. You wanted to argue the point with God, but he was absent, so you argued with Bernadette. Now look. Here, on the table, lies your chance to face off with the deity and demand explanation for his rough desert justice, the desertion of his prophet, of poor Moses, the only man who would speak to him back in the early days when he was nothing but a bush on fire.

Oh yes, by all means seek answers. Because the last time you sought answers, it worked so well, didn't it? A note on the table from your father, then, wavering for hours at the top of the steps, then creeping down them for the first time in years. You could see as you descended farther into the gloom the

---

*... there had been the chance that Gordy'd destroy himself. Just take himself and the ticket off the board forever. That would have been perfect...

yellow paint hanging from the door in tatters. Drawn slowly downward, as if pulled beyond any will of your own you went, brought to remembrance of the guillotine, compelled to prevent rash and suicidal action if possible, but beyond that motivated by a compulsion only to see, to bear witness to your father's folly if nothing else could be done. In your mind your father was both things—still alive and already dead. The old conundrum posed by that smart cat Schrödinger, Schrödinger and his half-alive (or was it half-dead?) little bunny rabbit, huddled unobserved in his lockbox, Schrödinger was a sharp one, sharp blade, hot flame, the forehead aquiline, never trust those goddam rabbits, oh Jesus, please help. Focus. Bernadette's occasional refrain over the years, *someday you'll need to reckon with your father, you'll decide or he will, but someday you will have to reckon with him.* And she was right. Right about you, about your father, about what Dave Waverly could become if he were given the opportunity. Unquestionably wrong about the structural integrity of a collapsed flaming wall, wrong on the question "Will I burn?" Wrong about that last decision. So seldom are last decisions good ones. Once upon a time there was a boy who ran. But before he was a boy, he was a man. The boy got added in later, maybe, and what does it matter, anyway? Time digs a tunnel backward and forward. You'd see it yourself, were the tunnel wide enough to allow you a backward glance, but you're constrained in a three-dimensional rabbit-hutch, face held at all times mercilessly forward. This was Landrude's lesson, yes, one of many, along with: "You don't matter," and "None of it matters," and "Maybe in another moment you won't exist and never will have." Here on the table before you lies the power that can (if the stories about it are true) free you from all such constraint. Just the ticket. It's there, wrapped up in two dimensions, ink and paper. You've done it to me, Gordy. You've caught me. They'll chase you, but you've left it to me. A wiser man than I would use it to find you, Gordy-Gord, drag you back to your duty. But I won't do that, no, not me. The best thing Gordy ever did was to use it sparingly, almost never. Never would have been better than almost never.* There's enough cooks stirring this soup, enough fools eager

---

*...or, there'd been the chance Gordy'd have just given it to Donk. Donk would have done things to Morris that would have ended everything. You know that much now. And that's something gained. You learned something you hadn't yet known.

to make decisions, to try to name things into the shapes they deem proper. Enough. Focus. The thing to do is to decide what the thing to do is.

Julius takes Gordy's letter and places it in an empty steel wastebasket. With a wooden match he lights it—They'll be looking for you, buddy. I reckon if you're off to do what you say you are, you'll find them before they find you, but let's not make it any easier for them. Whatever I decide to do, there doesn't need to be any evidence of where you've gone or why.

Here's a thought: You could keep it, unused. Your safe-deposit box is only a train ride away. Yes. Row after row of tiny silver steel shelves, how apropos. Or you could stash it after you'd used it, only one time, you could use it to demand of God...

No. The ticket isn't God. There's no hope of that. No path.

But dammit it's a path to *something*. Give me the answers, you omniscient bastard you, you won't fool me. I'm expert at seeing the laboratories of madmen for what they are. Your father was insane, you knew it, you told yourself that with each step down. The man is insane, loony, nutso; whatever he does or did or will do, there's no stopping it, no reasoning with it. It isn't your fault. What could you do?*

But what *did* you do? is what Father Bernadette's voice is always insisting, and you wanted to hurry but you couldn't. Remember? Each step weighed with the burden of your years-long grudge, each step gravid with the knowledge that it is too late, that there is no help, that the deed is done, consummated for the worst, each step propelled by the knowledge that you might yet save him, if you hurry. Wavering between competing disbeliefs.

Once there was a boy who breathed. The boy breathed. He breathed in and then out and then he breathed quite deeply indeed and then all at

---

*... or there'd been the chance Julius would get it and use it for something worthwhile. Do what Gordy didn't have the will or the balls to do and destroy Morris. Or maybe the priest would go further; wind time's thread back up, restore the whole story to the way it had been. Or challenge that Voice that empowered it in the first place, that entity, that whatever the hell it is that is messing with your story. But you didn't know about the Voice when you started; you just learned about that, from Gordy's confession. Another gain from your gambit.

once, as if on a dare, he opened the door wide and in that moment, in the room's center, he saw his father's head affixed directly into the guillotine's padded opening, fitted perfectly, to the micron, after years of calculation, to the exacting angle required to remove his hated aquiline protrusion and nothing else besides, and his hand white-gloved holding the rope, the release of which was to have been the office of the son, his hand shaking with the strain, poised in the moment immediately before the deed, before the dropping of it, before accepting the weight of it, the acetylene torch nearby to crackle-sizzle cauterize, you can see all at once: You have not come too late, but almost too late, so close, and you can tell from the shaking he's been standing there a long time, accumulating his will, the self-discipline to accept the blow, and that he can't hold on too much longer. Hand, rope, father, forehead, son, torch, and gleaming heavy blade all refracted again and again and again into an illusion of infinity by the mirrors covering the laboratory walls—but infinity itself is an illusion of infinity. Mirrors reflect space, but they don't reflect time, they don't reflect possibility. What possibility? A possibility in which his father's arm was not shaking, or in which his father's brain's chemistry had not behaved like a bad drunk, vomiting madness into itself. A possibility in which the boy had been more decisive, less begrudging, more imaginative, and had arrived sooner. You could have chosen any of those for me, you bastard Landrude. You're listening or reading along even if God isn't and what's the difference anyway? You could have chosen them for me if they all exist, but that wouldn't have assisted you in the work you needed me to do. That wouldn't have made me into the shape you needed. Did you orchestrate this? Is that why this ticket is here, because you want me to have it? If not, how else and by whom? What am I meant to become, if not your guillotine slicing off unruly and unwanted portions from your story for you? Fix everything broken? That would be my intent. The cathedral unburnt, Bernadette alive, loonies healed of the chemical morass contorting their perceptions, prisoners in Pigeon Forge (and elsewhere? certainly elsewhere by now) by the hundreds or thousands restored, never interred, never damaged. That's what you expect of me. Hope of me. And *then* what? Do you imagine I'm foolish enough to believe that would be the end of it? To believe I'd find no more pain to solve? No, after that the temptation would be too much; I'd break into time's pocket-watch and start meddling with the gears. As if I could fix anything. What have I ever done that didn't turn to muddle? What goodness has happened around me that hasn't been a pure accident, falling ass-backward for a few minutes into pockets of grace? It all depends on absolute stillness, your father said—perhaps he was right about that. A different game, one of total surrender. Only when you, unresisting, let the wind carry you, only when you take no notice where it will place you, can you fly. Once there was a man who dared believe he could take all the pain and brokenness and madness and wrongness and filth, take it all into himself and pass it through himself and in so doing distill it into something more purposeful, ordered, sensible, a purer potion, but the truth you've learned, you poor dumb old fart, is that all you can hope to do is let it pass through you, like light through a window, a joining *with* reality's muddle, with effects you'll never see, a beautiful hopeful mess and a foolish squander, to do that and nothing else, and then to let that be enough. Once there was a man who dared believe, but years earlier, the boy had been a man, and an author decided to create the boy that made sense of the man. Yes, it all depends on absolute stillness. But the rope, which is frictionless, absolutely frictionless, which is not even connected to the guillotine's body because even the slightest tiny movement at the crucial moment will... *that's why I need you to hold the rope*, and once upon a time there was a boy who breathed and then breathed and then breathed deeply like a diver preparing to grasp pearls and then opened the door and No no no nonononohnonono thousands of copies of the boy Julius lunge forward in endless reflection, but too late, too late, the hand of the father has already lost its grip, the head of the father already shifted to view this newcomer to see his last sight, the long-awaited son and the blade is hot and sharp and it is very heavy as it glides down without hitch or hangnail ponderously but falling so fast and the rich arterial blood jettisons, and before the boy has even entered the room the old man's face, sliced clean and entire, has splucked onto the flagstones while the body falls backward, heavily, *thunt*, and does the boy see (before he retreats), there, in the corners of the mirrors, within the periphery, reflected here and there and everywhere, does he, or does he not, see the large white rabbits huddled, smiling two-toothed smiles, staring with devouring pink eyes?

Oh, yes. He is sure he does.

It all depends on absolute stillness. To hold it but do nothing with it. To hell with you, you bastard. I'll take it, but I'm not playing your game. I'll choose a different one.

Swiftly, without further thought, Julius takes hold of the ticket. He stands wearing a faraway look, and then he is no longer there, nor is the ticket, nor is the ticket, nor is the ticket, no nor is the ticket the ticket ticket ticket.

If anyone had been there to see it, they'd have seen the priest standing holding something small and paper, shiny and green, and then the priest would have vanished, and in the place the ticket had been, hanging for only a fraction of an instant, an equal quantity of water, no more than a table-spoon's worth, which, obedient to gravity, fell, very briefly dampening the floor between a pair of blond leather sandals, one pair among nine exactly like it; ten pairs of sandals, lined in a row. The water seeps through cracks and fissures and, after a brief passage of time, evaporates. The sandals remain. The sandals are not happy, nor are they sad. It goes beyond that. The sandals rest in the wholeness of a form both chosen by him and chosen for him. They are Julius and they are not. So much more has been transmuted; the alchemy goes so deep, much deeper then flesh and bone to leather and Velcro and rubber. There is peace now and completeness, a sense, not of selecting, but of continually being *selected*. He keeps thinking to move his arms, but he cannot. This makes him want to giggle. What do you call a priest with no arms and no legs lying on the floor? His thoughts drift as he waits for the next thing to happen. Bailey…I saw you. Before I went, I saw. I hope I gave you what you need. And Boyd…oh yes. I saw you, Boyd, and I saw where you are; saw what you'd written; I adjusted Father Ex for your position. Not just a receiver anymore but a transmitter. Adding sixth-dimensional laser printers to a confessional is the simplest thing when you can see all the threads. And Gordy…I saw you, too. I saw you *everywhere* you are. You'll have to return to yourself now, you'll have no choice now that I took the ticket off the table. I did what Landrude wanted and swallowed that ticket right out of the world…not that he'll like the way I did it, in the end. No, I don't think he'll like it at all…You poor bastard, Landrude. Ah yes, Landrude. I see you now.* Do you have even less of an idea than the

* At least you got to hear what happened to Gordy when he got behind your door, right from the horse's mouth. A tight fit for you, holding perfectly still cramped up in Father Ex's innerworkings, listening carefully. So. That's what the thing behind Morris's shoulder is: a destroying wave. It's tied to him. He can call it any time he wants, destroy everything, everything. And, if someone—Donk, say—were to kill him, it would come all by itself. Gordy may not know that, but you know it instinctively. That would be the answer—total destruction—really it's the only answer. You've tried everything else.

rest of us? I think so. And you weren't expecting this one, were you? For a moment I moved through all possibility, and I bet you weren't expecting me to choose this doughnut. Sandals, of all things. Nothing can stay the same now. All those competing narratives, the one below from Boyd and the one above the one Landrude knows about, the one he's in now and even all the ones he hasn't guessed; all will inevitably split then inevitably converge into something new. You did say you wanted something unexpectable, Landrude. Sandals. To see your face . . . You think I'd change back if I could. You'll spend the rest of your life chasing my tail if only I had a tail still to chase. You don't realize, I can change back any time I choose. I am as I always was. Once there was a very young boy who watched with amazement the pictures in silhouette, at the lady who turned into the crone, at the crone who turned back into the lady, at the vase that became the face that became the vase that became the face. All done without movement, without changing. Crone and lady and face and vase. Again, and back again. Both and neither. Have you always been sandals? Are you even still a priest? Were you ever a priest? Are you even now ten pairs of sandals? Yes and yes and yes and yes. No and no, no and no. It had not been a new voice you'd heard, when you took hold of it. No, and it had not been old, either. Bernadette tried to explain it to you. It's more complete than ever it was before, but still no clearer. Such a beautiful confusion to rest in, such confusing beauty. You had it all along. The doubt was the faith, and the faith was the doubt. You wouldn't extract the one from the other even if you could. That was the temptation the ticket set to you—yes, and to Gordy, too. You would worry about Gordy but worry is gone. Gordy will be all right, or if not, Gordy will be Gordy, and if that will not be enough, it will, at least, *be*.

x x x

Five minutes later, Tennessee arrives, huffing and puffing. He crosses to the row of sandals and spends a silent moment contemplating them. Selecting a pair, he solemnly unbuckles them, puts his feet within, slowly buckles them, as something like awareness dawns on his face. He mourns then, weeping silently for his missing boy gone forever and now gone yet again, then rises with a new resolve. Moving assuredly—as if carrying out instructions only he can hear—he recovers from the floor Father Julius's battered satchel, and empties it of the envelopes, placing one on the bed of each brother and sister of the Neon Order. He ends in the cell of Father Julius, from which he collects the diary. He next moves to Father Ex, expertly removes a panel from the back, fiddles in the guts, and extracts a memory card. He notices with some surprise the tray that has appeared at the back—or had it always been there?—the printer's tray holding a thick sheaf of paper, upon which are written unusual things. He studies these briefly with growing consternation, then shoves them into his satchel. Then he departs, and for a time the Neon Chapel is empty and still once more. Soon after, one by one, they return in silence and depart in silence, the brothers and sisters of the Neon Order. Each of them collects from the battered leather case an envelope bearing their name, and, before moving on to some new hopelessness (except for Sister Nettles, who comes last of all, who sits again in her old place and does not leave), exchanges their old shoes for the sandals meant for them, their last keepsake from the priest around whom they had gathered, and from whom they now spread out and away, that priest who was rough and coarse and turbulent and doubting, who had gone away, leaving little behind but rumor, who some still argue had been no priest at all.*

---

* Yes, total destruction. When you're the author you can play any game you want. You've played the game of the mountain, of the pit, of the master. You've tried everything. You've tried emissaries, and they've all failed you, scorned you, cast you off. Reading this latest revision had been torture. You'd lifted the bulk, glanced at the bottommost page—*oh God, it even begins wrong*—then flipped a hundred pages up, where it was even worse, and carried implications both baffling and terrifying. Hands trembling, you continued to flip upward, investigating the modifications both subtle and substantive, until you reached the accursed sandals. You stared at them for a while, and then, at last, with an air of resignation, studied the new top page. Different location, same ending. Even with the ticket *gone*, somehow Gordy still gives it away. Well, that's it, you'd thought, when you'd been able again to think. Gordy fails, Boyd fails. Now Julius fails. Only one left to try—the one who would gladly destroy it all in exchange for vengeance. You decide—You're being punished for something

undeniable. Everything you try fails through some inexplicable chance. Each time you reach, it's taken away. Every ball you hit strikes a seagull and falls foul. Every pair of dice you throw gets eaten by a baby. Revisions. And from *who*?

You know what it is. It's them. On some level, it's *them*. Goddam readers all the way down. There's only one way to beat them, only one perfect form. You know now the game you've always been playing is the game of the blank. The only way to defeat interpretation? Give the audience nothing to interpret. You've tried the pencil. Now you use the eraser. Morris can do it—destroy everything. *Everything*. Donk will make him.

A worse idea comes to him: All that time you spent as Morris, only to discover you were written by another

Yes, but you took his place. Ascended. You *are* Landrude Markson.

Answering yourself—Yes, but... what if someone *else*, even now, is writing you?

—Jordan Yunus, *Subject to Infinite Change*

Dogs
think
everybody
is
a
dogs.

⁓BENJAMIN HERRING COLMERY IV

Sometime in the afternoon of that day, a newly freed Tennessee entered Ralph's General & Specific, and, for reasons known not even to himself, purchased a large sack of oranges, which he left propped at the entrance of the Fridge.

—Boyd Ligneclaire, *Subject to Infinite Change*

There are some who believe there is no coincidence, who hold that everything happens for a reason. There are others who hold that all is coincidence. Both notions are correct, to a point. It is correct to say there is a reason for everything that happens—not because everything happens for a reason, but because everything happens. Everything, real and unreal, possible and impossible, likely and unlikely—all of it happens. Hence, there is no coincidence. Even hence-er, everything is coincidence. This is the universe's greatest secret, and its most terrible offense.

And the second is like it: No art ever came about but it was an act of collaboration. No creation without observance. No observance without creation.

—Jordan Yunus, *Subject to Infinite Change*

Decapitation is a funny thing. We—collectively, that is—worry about it precisely the right amount, which is to say: not at all. If you take into consideration the totality of all life and all death, decapitation is a rounding error. Statistically, decapitation doesn't happen. And, unlike many other statistical improbabilities, our species is preoccupied with it very little, to the extent that those of us who do worry about it exist in such small numbers, we actually don't worry about it, collectively speaking. It's for the best; we really needn't bother. It's worth noting: Unconcern isn't humanity's usual posture toward statistically unlikely things.

However, what does not exist in the collective can exist in the individual. Example: Marie Antoinette. Don't tell her decapitation doesn't happen. Or, again: Julius. Julius, as one might expect, thinks about decapitation frequently. But then, Julius is a special case, when it comes to decapitation. Gordy thinks of decapitation, though he doesn't worry about it; he just thinks about it. Jane has considered it, but not as frequently as Gordy has. Bailey never thinks about it, nor does Donk. Andrew and Andrew, the tiny twin bodyguards, will eventually be decapitated in a way that does not happen, statistically speaking, even when set against the tiny statistically insignificant sample size of human decapitations throughout history. Until that moment, however, the thought of decapitation hadn't once crossed the minds of the Andrews.

Were they surprised? You'd better believe it!

Their days as Morris's bodyguards will have already expired by then, so no one will be able to accurately say: "Useless bodyguards. Fat lot of good they turned out to be."

—Boyd Ligneclaire, *Subject to Infinite Change*

"It's a book," Bailey announces from the back seat. "But that's not the crazy part."

"It's a what, now?"

"It's just that the pages were reversed. The title page was on the bottom of the stack." She holds up the page in question for him to see: *Subject to Infinite Change*, by Boyd Ligneclaire.

Tennessee's at the wheel. Bailey boosted the car for them, but she wouldn't drive. The novelty of her restored body posed too much distraction; she worried she'd run them into a ditch. Mile by mile, they put road between themselves and Loony Island, and Morris, and Donk. Tennessee in the driver's seat, reciting again and again his litany of fountain and cavern and flight, of the boy who had been his and was now lost to him a third time, and how some clearly dangerous man has clearly acquired Gordy's power, because Gordy's disappeared, and Julius has . . . well, look at him. Bailey's stretched out in the back, hearing but not listening, rediscovering the groovable feast of her movable meat, wiggling her toes in wonder, watching the play of her fingers in front of her face. Two refugees, crawling up the blacktop toward anywhere.

These are the things Tennessee brought with him in his satchel:

–Some snacks;

–A change of clothes, including a decrepit T-shirt, whose HELLO MY NAME IS sticker remained remarkably well-preserved;

–Father Julius Slantworthy's handwritten memoir;

–A memory card, holding Father Ex-Position's most recent twenty-four hours of audio;

–A thick sheaf of pages, which had been filling the OUT tray of Father Ex's laser printer—and herein lay the surprise: Father Ex hadn't had a laser printer before, much less an OUT tray. A mystery indeed, though greater mysteries remain.

For example, there remains the great mystery of Tennessee's beautiful new sandals, which are, somehow, Julius, and which had, once afoot, informed Tennessee how he might make the extraction from Ex's guts, and which had not failed to point out to him the mysterious stack in the mysterious OUT tray, and which had, moreover, compelled him to seek out Bailey, a near stranger, from her hospital room. Though they've barely met, Bailey's known to Tennessee. Her injury at Morris's hands, and the subsequent vengeance he's therefore earned, has, over the months of Tennessee's sequestration, been Donk's nearly constant refrain, and Donk has been Tennessee's sole companion—but they'd never been formally introduced. Indeed, they still haven't been; between his fear of Donk and grief over the boy lost yet again, and her dazed wonderment at her strange restoration (and perhaps, though she hasn't yet admitted it to herself, at her subterranean but well-founded premonitions regarding the Attic), they've existed in separate trances. Even now, as morning and noon have gone and the sun crawls toward the western horizon, as Bailey turns her attention away from her fingers and toes, she's landed it not on her strange companion, but on the sheaf of papers in his satchel. Head propped against one door, feet on the opposite window, reading, reading. Tennessee wonders—Why did Julius want you to find her? He hasn't said.

Another mystery: There remains some confusion over the fate of Gordy's ticket.

For his part, Tennessee maintains that Donk probably has it, or Morris. "Somebody sure changed Julius into sandals," he whispers in dazed awe. "Now tell me, how could *that* be done without magic?" And whether Morris has the ticket's power or Donk does barely matters, claims Tennessee, because both are dangerous as demons, both are intent on harm and damage and vengeance, and besides, if it's Donk, he's going to be particularly livid at Tennessee, who escaped from his secret room and drew him off their scent with a sack of oranges.

For her part, Bailey has never heard of any ticket.

The Sandals Julius remain silent on the topic of the ticket, and on all other topics, too. Another mystery, at least for Tennessee, who insists the Sandals Julius speak to him: They gave many helpful and detailed instructions back in the Neon, but haven't broken their silence since. "It's not something others hear," Tennessee says. "At least I don't think so. It sounds in my head."

"Voices in your head?"

"It's not like that. And besides, the instructions were accurate."

Anyway, there also remains the puzzle of the sheaf of paper, whose nature Bailey appears to have identified, even if the method whereby it came into being remains a total

disaster. But after the wave, what will be left but the empty page? A beautiful white empty space, full of nothing at all. Nothing to thwart you, nothing to restrain you, nothing (most important) for any goddam readers to interpret.

The game of the eraser will need some help to get started. You dare hope you might do it all in one last trip. Steeling yourself for the assault of interpretation, you pass through the door, come into the dank gray cavern, always the same place. Always the same time, too—look, there's the author just where you left him, still unconscious, not yet woken up to take on the role you gave him. Down in the dim, the spooky action of interpretation proves more manageable; there is, at least, an iconic simplicity to a dark cave, granite steps, a door. But this is the wrong time and the wrong place. You move on, years forward, hundreds of miles, find Daniel "Donk" Coyote at the very apex of his rage. "What

—Jordan Yunus, *Subject to Infinite Change*

XXX

I'd advise you, is avoid trusting overmuch to patterns, the sandals told Sister Nettles. You've chosen a brave and a fine course but a difficult one. The longer you remain, the more you'll discover every pattern either breaks down or repeats. Eventually, every expected form will confound you. In this place there's a great

—Boyd Ligneclaire, *Subject to Infinite Change*

XXX

mystery. "Anyway, it's a book." Bailey repeated. "A novel. It's about what happened. And it's about us."

"Us?" Tennessee's finger wiggles in the air between the two of them.

"Not just you and me—*all* of us. Me, Daniel, Julius, you, even Gordy. It's everything that happened. But even that's not the crazy part. The author has my last name—which is unusual, but not crazy. The crazy part is, I dreamed about him, right before I…got better. Right before you showed up. In the dream, he said he was my brother, and he said…" Bailey pauses.

"He said he'd left pages in Father Ex for me. Which he apparently has." To this, Tennessee finds himself uncharacteristically at a loss for words. Rain starts to spackle the windshield.

"How far along are you in this book, anyway?"

Bailey hasn't heard. "It's not just about us, either. It's got these wild digressions; listen to this bit about decapitation." The clouds release as she starts, haltingly at first, then with gaining confidence and amazement, to read. How does he know this, she wonders; how does he know so much about what happened? Tonight. I'll look for him tonight, in the Attic, this dream brother. If I find him again, I'll ask.

When they reach a city, they stop for supplies. Food, clothes and sneakers to replace the hospital gown, a backpack, some toiletries. Bailey cuts up her cards to the accounts shared with Donk—not Daniel anymore. Donk he's chosen and Donk he'll remain—or "the Coyote," if that's what he prefers. Despite Tennessee's dire warnings, Bailey refuses to believe Donk poses a personal threat to her, no matter how far he pursues his obsessions. Even so, she has no inclination to return. The night of the Loony Riot, he made his choice. For years they've each been all the other had, an entire universe to each other, their love the only warmth they could count on, but he's withdrawn himself from that warmth, and he's done it for nothing more satisfying than chilled vengeance. He'll say it's justice, a principled stand against the cruelty of the world, but push aside that cart of bullshit, Bailey. Look at him, willing to steal a hospital full of the mentally ill, wipe their minds, dope them hyper, use them for his own ends. No, it's nothing of justice anymore, whatever he tells himself. He'll pursue the vengeance on his own behalf, now you're healed, and he'll pursue it to whatever grim ends he chooses. Even if you hadn't been injured, it would have been over for the two of you. There's grief in it, but the grief doesn't change the truth; he's made himself into something too cold, too hard and sharp, to ever share what you once were. Ignoring the truth of the loss can only lead to a tragedy even greater than the loss. Let him have the money and the revenge; give up your half of the funds in exchange for a clean break and consider it a bargain. Nevertheless, money won't be an issue in the near term. Ever a manager, Bailey's been a thrifty spender and a trusty saver. From her plump personal account, she withdraws as much cash as she judges they'll need, stacks the cash in Tennessee's satchel. "We'll hit every bank we pass in the state until we've got all the dough," she says, twangingly sidemouthed, mimic of a classic movie bank-robber. With the cash they purchase a nondescript used economy car and abandon the hot ride in a heavily populated parking lot in a nearby mall. Though Bailey provides him no budget, she notes with approval that Tennessee buys little—just the equipment necessary to extract audio files from a memory card, a device to play it, some cheap earbuds. At the same office-supply box store where these were procured, Bailey gets a hefty binder and has holes drilled into Boyd's manuscript so it fits. On a whim, she has a copy made— or no, not a whim, she corrects, it's just that apparently more's been restored to you than your body. You see the possibilities again, and there's too many ways this book might be destroyed, the sole copy gone and gone forever. Imagine a fire. Imagine a flood. Imagine the car window rolled down unexpectedly as you sleep, the wind of velocity sweeping pages out and down the highway. Better to have a backup. They choose a motel outside town and pay cash for a room with two queens, and use some of the change to have pizzas delivered. "Everything cash," Tennessee says, smiling. "Starting to understand why Father Julius wanted me to bring you."

Bailey shakes her head—talking sandals is a level of crazy best contemplated at some other time, perhaps never—and reaches for the binder. The idea is to read for hours, but the day's been too much and in the middle of a discursive passage about apes she drifts into what

✕ ✕ ✕

seems to be the problem, good buddy?"

"Who the fuck *are* you?" Donk screams, pointing his rifle right at you. He's recognized you, and of course he's pissed. To his mind, you just disappeared his circus—his big scheme—and left him holding the bag.

You smile and light a cigarette. No movement required; you just tell a cigarette to exist in your mouth, then you tell it to be lit. And so there is cigarette, and so it is lit, and you see that it is good. You judge this a useful way to go—with Julius you always approach cautiously and hidden, but Julius goes in for the whole God jive. Donk, he'll respond better to a direct show of power. Thank God it's an empty room. Even so, the dimensions lurch wildly from something like a large closet to a space the size of a warehouse. The walls are painted a thousand colors, they're a hundred varieties of brick. The floor is carpeted and it's bare. Donk looks like a million different people.

Donk, of course, has a multitude of problems, a constellation of complications. That's why he's got the rifle, which really isn't his style. Think of all his problems. Start with the sack of oranges, which he's still got with him—look—tossed in the corner of the room. Donk found those citric globes propped up against the doorway to the Fridge, and to him, in that context, they could only be a message from Julius, and from Julius, oranges could by mutual agreement only mean the compromise of their secret: the children's room, a truly safe place, where food and toys and warmth and a comfortable bed can be found, built beneath-ground, the only entrance a hidden spot surrounded by a scrim of high grass, tucked between two of the projects of Domino City. Only when Donk rushed immediately to the secret door did he realize how utterly he'd been had. He's never visited the children's room; Julius had arranged the whole thing: contractors, payment, bribes, decorating, staffing, all. The idea's always been to have complete arm's-length separation, remembering all too well the danger Yale put everyone in. Gangs are as aware today as they were during Ralph's rise of the extent to which abandoned children can be used as spies and soldiers; to be caught gathering them all in one place, as Yale had done with his greenhouse, can only ever be seen as an act of war—and Morris wouldn't have paused, had he discovered Donk's children's room, from treating those unlucky kids the same way Ralph treated Yale's.

So here's Donk, getting the oranges and immediately rushing, certain beyond certainty he'll find the whole place tossed, a charnel house of murdered kids... barging in only to find everything peaceful, fine... and he knew he'd been tricked, watched, tracked to the spot, his greatest secret exposed. So now Donk's sitting in Domino City by a window in building 2, top floor, an unoccupied room he's secured for himself with clear sightlines, vest on but jacket off, hair mussed though he doesn't know it, watching the entrance through a rifle scope, waiting to see who it is who's tricked him into revealing the door, and what they intend to do with the knowledge. While he waits, he's already brooding over everything else—Someone's got the drop on him, that much is clear. Nobody knows what oranges mean but Julius. Which means Julius has betrayed him... but under what duress? And who else is giving him up? He sent his loonies out and they've brought nothing but bad news. Tennessee's escaped, door off the hinges. Bailey's gone from her hospital bed. Julius missing, and most of the Neon brothers and sisters gone. Donk can only conclude this means Morris has everyone captured. *And* his deadline with Morris is tomorrow, and no Gordy to be found. There's no better interpretation; the new boss has decided he's failed and is getting ready to collect on Donk, hard, and he'll take everyone Donk loves first, just to make it sting more...

You think: I could tell him it's simpler than that. That the oranges were nothing but a feint, just Tennessee acting on my instructions, buying some time for those meddlesome muddlers I wanted safely out of town. But I won't do that—goodness, no. I want Donk as angry as I can get him.

You've waited too long to give an answer; Donk fires. The bullet clips your cigarette, extinguishing it; passes into your right cheek and out through the back of your skull.

You smile and heal yourself slow enough so Donk sees it; you want him impressed—yes, a direct show of power will be just the thing.

"Who are you?" Donk asks, without lowering the rifle. "How did you take it from Gordy?"

Ah, you think. He sees your power, he thinks you have the ticket. He's still obsessed with the thing. A logical conclusion. Still, he sees your power and doesn't quail. Most people are scared just seeing you, but not him. Even when he's seen he can't hurt you, he stays focused on the task before him. It's an impressive display of will and nerves. You need someone who will punish Morris to the breaking point; he appears to be an apt tool for the job. Just wait until you've

—Jordan Yunus, *Subject to Infinite Change*

xxx

observed these behaviors across wide ranges of related species. For example: Apes hate little people. Science hasn't done enough to study this. There's a certain logic to it. Think of the pecking order. Think of living in an ape community, surrounded by jungle. Jungle on all sides—on all sides jungle! And in that jungle, the Things creep. Them. The Things. You, with your body of hair and sinew, without language, without words, lack even the rudiments of comprehension's gruel. All you know is the jungle is out there, pressing all around, deep and dark and hidden, jungle forever and forever jungle. You can smell The Things in there, the unseen Things; you might hear them move but you don't see them, until—with first a rustle and then, immediately thereupon, a horrendous screal of fang or coil or claw or spur—there bursts from the foliage like Satan's dogs a dread beast, releasing massive deathly energy after long stealth to grab you if you are unlucky, or one of your cohorts if they are unlucky, to pull you into the darkness that surrounds and murder you loudly within earshot of the rest, eat warm bananacurry yoghurt from your intestines while you still live. Then there are the other ape tribes, competition for your territory and resources. They're worse than the Things, because they leave nothing behind. If some other group wants your plenty and sees weakness in you, they'll be all around you in an instant, grabbing you with powerful rough hands and smashing you against the rocks, teeth at your neck, clever strong fingers in your eyes. Every male and every child killed and eaten. Learn the smell of your tribe. Any ape from outside is a presumed advance scout and must be dealt with immediately.

So you learn to sleep in the trees. You forage on the ground in packs, you and your coterie of hairballs, picking and chewing each other's curdling fleas. You stick close to your fellows, forgiving them their farts, for only when you cling together like dingleberries can you hope to live even one day more. The largest of you, the meanest, the strongest, he is your best friend. Not despite the fact that he is cruel to you, not despite the fact that he can (and does) hold you down and abuse you, screw your girlfriend while you watch, bully you, torment you, dominate you and at every turn remind you of that domination, not despite all this, but because of it. In the life of the jungle, bigness isn't just good, it is goodness itself. If you are one of the whales in your midst, so much the better. All the best of the difficult ape life will be yours. But if you are small, then you, dependent on whales, love the brute for throwing his weight around. He'll keep you from getting eaten alive, you see. But your love for him in no way mitigates your seething hatred of him—how could it? Outrages committed against you are outrages still. You remember each bite, each shove, each cuckolding, each time your food was snatched from you with a snarl—and not only you. Did you think you were the first weak ape? Oh no, you fool, genetics had its way with you long before any bully did; you are the product of a weaker strain. Centuries of generational submissive memories are packed into your poor cranium, highly pressurized, providing you each night with angry orgasmic dreams of chasing, of catching, choking, biting, screwing, killing. . . this pure naked compressed rage must inevitably find an outlet. It can't go to your actual tormenter, distiller of your ire. Not only would this be suicidal, but it wouldn't even occur to you. You don't want to attack your tormenter. You love him. He's the strength of your tribe. He's your protection against The Things. He's better than a bad death out there.

No, your anger goes to the smaller ape. The one you yourself can hold down, torment, cuckold, terrorize. The one who holds the food you can snatch. The one who, in turn, loves you with rigid devotion, all the while making his own daily microscopic deposits into his own storehouses of shame and hate. The smallest ape is a dangerous ape. Everybody knows it. Abused by all, abuser of none. Nothing but a powder keg. The rest of the tribe tolerates but does not trust him. He goes around, futilely showing his teeth at all times in gratuitous show of submission. Someday his mind will snap from the abuse and he'll attack, and then he'll have to be destroyed. It's only a matter of time. The second-smallest ape dreads, without realizing it, this day of unwanted demotion.

Now: Apply ape logic to small people. You see? Remember, an ape can't tell a person from an ape. Apes think everybody is an ape.

What then, in the eyes of an ape, is a little person? Why, to ape perception, a little person is the smallest ape there is. Smaller than has ever been imagined. He must represent eons of pent-up violence. Distrusted, hated, feared, abused. And from an outside tribe! In the presence of any small person, any ape will convert into a frenzied murder-salad. Any ape, any small person. And what if a small person should be unlucky enough to encounter the one ape whose spleen has found no vent, who has never had a target for his slow years of violent urges? What if some unlucky small person should chance upon. . . the smallest ape? This clearly observable phenomenon

—Boyd Ligneclaire, *Subject to Infinite Change*

x x x

can only be described as a disturbing disappointment: sleep but no Attic.

In the morning, Bailey, beginning to find the familiarity of her body, takes a shift at the wheel. She drives the longest roads they can find, and the most circuitous, and the farthest from the main. Tennessee pops in the ear-buds and listens, eyes closed, while the tires eat horizon. His eyes pop. "It's Gordy-Gord talking, all right!" he exclaims. "Like Julius promised." Then he's gone, listening to the confession of his son gone forever, learning to the whys and wherefores of Gordy's great abdication, information Tennessee has long sought, and sought almost as fervently as he has his abdicating lad. Bailey relishes the silence; she needs the time to ponder her missing Attic, and the strange visitation she'd received from a stranger who said he was her brother. So much else strange has happened, what if it's true? What if you have a sibling, lost to you on some other plane, some other room you only managed in all your exploration to discover once? And what was it he'd told you? To run. Yes. Run and you'll find me, Boyd had said. You'll have to jump, and trust your luck, he'd said. I was; now I'm not, he'd said. If you find me, I can be. Bailey looks out the window, seeing but not seeing the passing sameness of flatland, fixated on her reflection thrown weakly by the glass, which suggests a ghost hovering just inches outside, traveling alongside on a parallel course.

In the evening they stop some miles outside Iowa's capital city, selecting their motel for its remoteness, but near enough to see the city's modest sky-line from the front porch, as well as the roadside distance marker: RACCOON RIVER 12 MILES "Once upon a time, a long time ago, everything *changed* for me," Tennessee remarks, studying the sign. "I think this town was called something different back then." The next morning, Bailey clutches her knees to her chest, weeping noiselessly so she won't have to explain to her compan-ion why she mourns. It's even worse now. When she sleeps, she now knows the Attic will not be there. Her dreams are worse than empty, they're full of nothing. She walks endless hallways of doors but when she tries the doors the entrances have been bricked. She's been restored. She's been banished. But she suspects she knows what she needs to do. "You'll have to run," Boyd had told her. Fine, Boyd, whoever you are. You want me to run? I'll run.

Bailey laces up her sneakers, heads out down the long flat straightness, between the heights of cornstalk. Running out into this perverse sameness to reclaim her infinity of variance, running until she's sun-baked, heaving herself back in time to fall asleep under the shower until woken by the water going cold, hauling herself aching and road-battered to the bed, too exhausted to remember sleeping, waking to find herself unchanged, the Attic still missing. Forcing herself back out in the morning to start again; letting the realities of motion, of pain, of balance, of dominion over her limbs, settle their physical benedictions wearily upon her.

Six days of this. For the first two days, Tennessee remains with her, seemingly unconcerned that they'd chosen to stop driving, seemingly incurious about his companion's strange new routine, sitting on the low concrete slab that serves the motel as a porch, back to the wall, sandals stretched out, letting the sun shine on his face, listening unceasingly to his son's voice.

On the third morning, Tennessee packs his luggage: the envelope, a single plastic grocery bag containing a change of underwear, a toothbrush, the device, and the earbuds. "I found my hopelessness," he says. "Oh," says Bailey. Not until evening, when she returns to find Tennessee gone, does it occur to her: She'd never thought to ask what he meant, or where he was going. He's taken the car and a single stack of twenties from the satchel. Bailey finds herself unconcerned by the theft, even unclear about whether or not it was theft. Had she offered? She can't remember.

Tennessee's departure throws something ineffable but vital, previously balanced, out of skew. The world becomes drab but surreal, unfamiliar, as if illustrated by a vivid and tainted mind. Stranded in an island of corn in an unfamiliar land, each morning she puts the distant modest skyline of Raccoon River to her back and lets it melt away from her, step by step, sun on her left side until it beats down from above. Then she stops, turns and watches the skyline creep back toward her once more, sun crawling down toward the horizon, the sun always on the left; before long, the left side of her body perpetually feels several degrees warmer than the right. On the sixth day she can barely move from her bed and dares hope—in vain—this may be enough to open the Attic. But on the seventh day, rising from a sixth night dreaming of hallways and bricked doorways, she awakens to a new revelation.

Bailey puts the satchel with cash and manuscripts—the original from Father Ex and the copy she made not long after—into her backpack and stands on the motel stoop, watching the sun light the dawn sky. Everything grows sharp and clear for her; the world again becomes exact, comprehensible. The thought rises—I'm still in the Attic, or else this is the real Attic and I never considered it. Imagine: This is the room with all the corn. There are other rooms to find everywhere. It's like Boyd said, you have to run. Run, and it will all reveal itself to you as it comes to meet you. The beauty of it makes her want to weep, and so she does. Two low concrete steps and off the motel porch, weeping and blissful, Bailey runs, but when she reaches the road the wind pushes her out of her usual course. Rather than struggle against it, she surrenders, puts her back to the wind and her face to the skyline, and watches the city of Raccoon River slowly rise up to meet her.

Her suspicion proves correct: Raccoon River is another room. It's the room that has Raccoon River in it. A collection of high buildings that would not have overwhelmed Loony Island's modest towers, spaced wide apart from one another, gaps in a child's mouth, stones across a pond, a city at once urban and rural. They watch her beneficently, the buildings, as she passes in and out and among them, as she slows to a more observant pace, to a trot, to a walk, to a stroll, coming to rest at last in a greensward filled with sculptures. It is, Bailey sees, a smaller room nested within the greater room of Raccoon River. The room with the sculptures, within the room holding Raccoon River, which is itself contained within the room with all the endless gossiping corn. She wanders, captured by this new perspective, thinking— This changes everything. The paths leading to harm and doom are endless, so what advantage is gained in blockading against one or another of them? Choose one of the endless safer paths, and where do you find yourself eventually but in danger, beset once again on all sides by no fewer possibilities of harm and doom than before? But here is the room with statues on the lawn, a reality far worthier of contemplation than any catastrophic possibility. Here is the rangy skeleton of a horse described by driftwood. The sinister and contemplating statue of a rabbit posed in a parody of Rodin. The iron statue of a long coat standing with no visible wearer to support it. The blasted white tree. The steel girders, painted saffron, arranged at jutting angles. The two fat pawns, one black and the other white. The spider with impossibly long spindle-legs. An array of intriguingly shaped obelisks. White monkey bars nested in white monkey bars nested in white monkey bars.

Near the center of the display, a large hollow child crouches, its knees drawn against its chest. The child is twenty feet tall from rump to head, pure white in the places it exists—though these places are few, as the hollow child is primarily comprised of empty space. Its shape a hint, suggested rather than insisted upon, rounded at the borders of his existence but muddled by the jagged internal shapes of his sparsely spaced remains, as if it's been artfully filigreed from paper and then expanded from a denser state, as if its cells have abandoned their structural bonds, and, caught in the act of dispersing like smoke or cloud, have been frozen before the final dissolution. You can see right through the hollow child to the sky and clouds and buildings beyond. As a result of its distention, it seems, from a distance, to be made of arbitrary shapes, spaghetti and tendril, but as Bailey nears, she realizes it's composed of an assortment of alphabetical figures interlocked and artfully arranged. This is the largest statue in the park. There are gaps at the base, allowing entrance and egress. In the center of the interior space a man sits in a posture mirroring that of the hollow child. He looks up as she enters. They stare at each other in amazement.

"What are you doing here?" the man asks.

"What are you doing here?" she returns.

Gordy smiles, shows a pamphlet—a bearded lady flying through the air. On the schedule, a listing for Raccoon River. "I'm chasing a circus," he said. "And I think I've finally

x x x

solved all his other problems, too.

"There's no ticket. I don't need any object to do what I do," you say.

Donk fires again, again, again. It goes the same as before. You watch him accept the fact that you can take his bullets unharmed—and, again, it's impressive, watching Donk receive the new information, almost immediately accept it, and adapt. He shrugs, tosses the rifle *clatter* to the ground.

"All right. And what do you do, exactly?"

You walk over to the rifle, heft it. "'Whatever I want' is what I do." You balance it upright on your palm, barrel down. With your other palm you reach up to the stock.

"I can do anything." You press down and the rifle softens, collapses into your hands and you roll it like clay into a sphere. "Anything—except for one little thing."

You wait for Donk to ask about one little thing. Donk keeps quiet and watches you. My God, you think, I have complete advantage—is he putting me off *my* balance?

"Except for one little thing," you repeat awkwardly, "There's a man I can't go near, but I think you can. More, I think you want to. Hurting him might be the only thing you want."

"Morris?"

"Morris."

"And what makes him so special that you can't go near him, if you're King-Hot-Shit-I-Do-Whatever-I-Want?"

"Call it… the universe's preference," you say, still rolling, rolling the clay sphere that had been a rifle, rolling it smaller and smaller in your hands, thinking with the slightest defensiveness—Of course I *can*. But when he dies, or he calls it, then the wave comes. And the wave is like the ticket—it comes from other levels, from heights I've yet to attain. How fast might it come? Faster than I can escape? It's certainly possible. And why risk it, when I have one such as this to do my work for me? "And…" a dramatic pause for effect "The universe's preferences are *my* preferences."

"That's sort of nonsense, but have it your way," Donk says. He loosens his necktie. "What's your game with me?"

"You sought Gordy for the power he holds. You want to harm Morris. I know why."

"I want *justice* for Morris. He deserves it."

"Indeed he does. All you have to give and more. So tell me."

"Tell you… what?"

"Tell me what you'd have done with Gordy's ticket if you'd gotten it. Convince me you'll do it right."

And so Donk does. His plans for Morris, describing it in lingering detail. Bit by bit, piece by piece, moment by moment, pain by pain. When he's done, you pause and regard him. Extraordinary. His inventiveness may even surpass your own. The clay sphere between your palms is tiny. You harden it into a diamond. You give the diamond a setting. You give the setting a chain. You say:

"And then, the amulet had All Power. And it was so."

Then you toss it to him. When he's put it on, you disappear, folding in half, then half again, then again, reducing to nothing. It's the damnedest thing. But before you go, you can see Donk has become aware of his new limitless abilities, that he has

—Jordan Yunus, *Subject to Infinite Change*

x x x

understood. That's all I ever wanted: to understand.

Tennessee shut off Gordy's confession and sat in the quiet. Nothing but the wall of a motel at his back and the stillness; no wind. The corn standing in the sun made low crackling sounds as it warmed, and the man who had been Sterling Shirker pondered his son's words: command and door and edict and wave and voice. And think of Julius's beautiful words, his last and only sermon, about fools and hopelessness. No wonder it moved you so; after all, your boy's found a hopelessness bigger than the world. That's why he ran. He's out there, somewhere. He's playing out the line for us, as far as he can take it. Disobeying the command. Waiting until that wave finally comes and takes Morris and this whole Pigeon Forge mess away. You should take on a hopelessness of your own. It feels right, with Gordy taking on such a massive hopelessness, that his father should take up one of his own. So what hopelessness could you choose?

You could go back to the Neon—no end to hopelessness in Loony Island. Julius has informed you that Nettles stayed behind; you could go help her. Or you could head out over the sea, find one of those desert lands you hear about on television, those kids with the spindly arms and bloated bellies and teeth escaping from their faces. If ever there was a hopelessness, that would qualify. Or, do the near thing instead of the far thing, wander over into the nearest town, into Raccoon River, find some hopelessness there. No doubt one would present itself. Here's a tempting one—go and find Gordy, join him in his own hopelessness. The boy could use another set of eyes, another pair of hands. Or go buy a giant map and play a game of "pin-the-tail." Go where my pin stuck. Or go itinerant; walk the land, hopping from trouble to trouble as I found it, like a hero from a TV show.

But you know where already, said the Sandals Julius. *Sterling, haven't you realized yet?*

There was no sense of searching for a disembodied voice. Never any question it was the sandals talking. Tennessee didn't even open his eyes. It was as if he'd been waiting the whole time to hear from them.

Tell me then, Tennessee answered back. Where's my hopelessness. *Well, Sterling*, they asked, *where do you never want to go again?* and he answered, with growing excitement and horror and joy, Why, you know where I'm never going back to. As if I haven't told everybody a thousand times. *Well then*, said the Sandals Julius, *you have your answer*. Don't you.

There must be something else, Tennessee said, there must. But the Sandals Julius lapsed into silence. The corn crackled in the sun.

It's funny, Sterling thought, but since I put these sandals on, I haven't stammered even once. Maybe I'm not "Tennessee" any more.

—Boyd Ligneclaire, *Subject to Infinite Change*

Artists, a word to you now—whispered in your ear: Your art is not about you. To be more precise, it is not about you alone. It is about you no more (and no less) than it is about every other consciousness encountering it.

—Unknown

begun already to suspect what he's capable of.

Within an hour, it's no longer anything so uncertain as suspicion; it's certainty, and Donk is gone. For whatever it's worth, he's the Coyote now. Not just what they call him anymore but what he thinks of himself. He's spent the hour in the unfurnished Domino City room, testing the limits of the abilities the stranger gave him. There don't seem to be any meaningful ones.

This room is the one. The very One. Ever a man of compartments, Donk long ago secured for himself an unoccupied room in every tower of Domino City to use, as needed, for surveillance (or, for example, in the case of Tennessee, for storage), and in this tower, he selected this specific room precisely for the sentimental weight of it. As a boy he sat here—right here—hour upon creeping hour throwing a rubber ball *tub tub tub tub* into a cup. The Coyote thinks of the ball and cup, and they appear on the floor. He spends long minutes holding them, these long-gone artifacts of childhood.

Using his mind, he opens and closes, locks and unlocks, the apartment's front door.

He gives himself muscles of comical proportions, shredding his suit. He deflates himself again, restores his suit back around him as he does.

He floats himself a foot above the floor.

There's a shell casing on the floor. He turns it into a potato. He turns the potato into a ferret. He turns the ferret into mist. He turns the mist into a fine filigree of platinum.

He could turn the platinum into a rifle to replace the one that became his amulet, but he has no need anymore of a rifle. The rifle was only ever a tool.

He goes to the window. It's open; it's the one he'd been watching from, surveying the entrance to the children's room in a panic through his rifle scope. A laughable worry now. The Coyote gives himself ultraviolet and infrared senses—Look, there the children are, subterranean, safe. They'll keep safe forever now, he thinks. I'll see to it.

Out the window spreads a cloudy sky. He pushes the clouds away. He turns the sky purple. He turns the sky yellow. He turns the sky black. He turns the sky back the way it was. Here and there, he hears the sudden screams of those attentive souls who had been, at that moment, watching out their own windows, who without warning had seen this inexplicable atmospheric display.

He casts his awareness out, guided by unerring instinct, locates his friends—
amazed to discover how far they've scattered without his knowledge—how? When
was Bailey healed? It's a miracle, but miracles, it seems, are thick on the ground
these days. He's briefly shocked into anger and something like fear to see how
apparently loose was his grasp upon this puzzle's moving pieces, but then he remembers that it no longer matters; that grasp has become infinite, so let them run.
Gordy's chasing the vanished circus, sleeping on a bus out of Elk River traveling to
Buckeye. He locates Tennessee and Bailey driving circuitous roads toward nothing,
running from Morris, but also... ah. They're running from you. They fear you; they
think you're a hard man, consumed only by thoughts of vengeance. They've misunderstood you badly. You'll teach them a better lesson in time; at least they're clear
and safe. He can't find Julius. This is unfortunate, and suggests that perhaps Morris
has ended the life of at least one of his comrades. So be it: one crime more to make
the bastard answer to.

The Coyote thinks—Pragmatism won't be necessary any more, nor secrets.
These were never anything but tools. There won't be any more lies to keep track
of, there'll be no more compartments. These were your cruder tools, your defenses
against power, but now you have the power to make obsolete any need for defense; it will be all plain dealing from here, and nothing but dealing plain.

The Coyote returns to his home, pours a drink, picks up his book, then quickly
sets it down again. Thinks—reading isn't necessary anymore. Reading was only ever
a tool. To know a book, now, you simply have to think about knowing it and you
know it. He steps out his window, rises high, higher, higher, hovers over the city. Tells
himself: Neither is a home necessary. Home, too, was only ever a tool. Now you can
be all the tools you ever needed. Descending slowly back down to the roof where
the twisted remains of the greenhouse stands, he begins to understand the new
forms he'll need to mold for himself.

The Coyote thinks—Consider the weight a place can take on. How many children disappeared that day? Perhaps a dozen. He threw Yale off this roof, Ralph did.
You and Bailey watched him fall, and then you ran. You never saw what happened
to the kids, but you always had your suspicions. Let's keep the math simple. An
average weight of a hundred pounds. Twelve hundred pounds of life. For each day
gone by between then and now, this is the weight of unpaid wrong that lands upon
that roof. Visit it; you'll feel it. The greenhouse isn't gone; you just wouldn't know it

had ever been a greenhouse. Scattering of glass shards, twisting metal framework rusted out and rain-riven, monkey bars for a malicious gnome. This is where you'll start your new republic, the centerpoint of a new reality. The weight of the place expunged at last—no, not expunged, but rather fully invested, converted, redeemed.

They've understood you so poorly—your enemies *and* your friends. The bricks of cash you stored, the prestige you gained, whatever small influence you managed to accrue—all meant to be spent in restoration. You never thought you'd gain such a power as this, but it will be spent wisely and well. A fully restored greenhouse atop HQ, and all the children invited from their hidden secret room. The gangs purged, their slaves freed, their quarreling silenced, the narcotic spike pulled from the social arm. Do they truly think you never intended to finish your quest? Did they think you'd be satisfied once you'd sent Ralph to a fitting and deserved end? As if Ralph were the start and the finish of the problem. As if even the five gangs were. What of the police, who failed to make even a cursory investigation of the sad end of what were, to them, nothing more than a dozen public nuisances? What of the city's entire population, whose practiced disinterest was so complete it gave license to the authorities for their apathy—who with tasteful aversion and willful blindnesses, were the source and the wellspring of that apathy? No, Loony Island is only the beginning of your work on the world, even as the greenhouse will be only the beginning of your work on Loony Island. From the greenhouse, from the Island, it will spread—a quickly growing sphere of order, restoration, peace, and safety, cresting out from you in rapidly expanding concentric circumferences…

But first: Morris. You'll make him pay a slow debt, then you'll block his tunnels and empty his oubliettes, then heal his prisoners, bring them back to themselves, return meaning to their lives. Once you've finished with Morris, you'll go to Bailey, and make her understand. She'll apologize when she understands… but first, there must be a reckoning, some unspecified time for her, of reflection and penance. For her to have understood you so badly, to have healed herself and used her good fortune to run from you… There must be some form of redeeming punishment.

But—it occurs to him—you can allow yourself the fun of one last deception. Your deadline is tomorrow, and you haven't found Gordy. Morris will send for you. Be subordinate Donk another day. He'll find you easily; you'll be

—Jordan Yunus, *Subject to Infinite Change*

all over the country. And who'll replace them? Sister Nettles gazed around the emptiness of the Neon Chapel; without any of the brothers and sisters to share it, the space, once charming and cozy, felt garish and vast. Wanting to glare at Julius the way she was accustomed whenever he was being annoying, but most annoying of all, Julius had left, his only goodbye his sermon.

Brother Tennessee, having only recently arrived, had done nothing. At least his absence left no gap. But the rest. . .

Father Julius, of course, had scoured the city, locating need, folks hungry, things broken, noting it, bringing the list to his proxy for funds

And Dave Waverly, the secret proxy with reserves of moxie, he'd released the funds.

Sister Biscuit Trudy had hauled sacks of fresh-baked rolls to those Julius found.

And Jack and Brock, they'd fixed what needed fixing.

Sister Mishkin, she'd done the baking, then followed Trudy, carrying the excess sacks.

Brother Pretty Trudy, himself only recently escaped from a hard life selling ass, had brought medical and emotional aide to all the pretty girls and pretty boys, and those not so pretty, and those aged out and discarded, all those who had found their young bodies bought them first attention and flattery but then rough treatment and bad use.

And Sister Winnie had tutored in the secret room Donk kept for abandoned children, the only other entrusted with knowledge of that location.

Now none of them did any of that—but still, the expectation would remain, just as she had. She thought about leaving. She wondered why she hadn't yet. She decided to leave.

She stayed. She tended her garden.

Weeks passed. On Sunday mornings, meat arrived for the weekly barbecue. The Slantworthy Trust in perpetuity. She tried to send it back, but it was already sold, so she had it stuffed in the rapidly filling freezer.

"How on earth, Jules," she asked the emptiness, "could you leave all this to me alone?"

No answer, of course. Julius had left, just as he said he would.

She tried not to think of the sandals.

There had been two pairs left when she'd arrived the night Father Julius had gone. One had her name embossed in the leather of upper sole, and the address of the Neon Chapel. The other had Gordy's name embossed, that and a Knoxville address. Yesterday she looked it up; it's a motel. What on earth. She didn't want Gordy's pair, so she mailed them to the motel.

She didn't want the other pair, either, even if they did carry her name. Determined not to wear them, ever. They bothered her. Something about them; a feeling she had about them. An instinct she'd had, a foolish one, that she'd had the moment she saw them there on the floor. *Who are those sandals?* she'd wondered. Not "what" but "who."

A foolish notion. She wouldn't entertain it. They could sit there in the middle of the floor forever, as far as she was concerned.

Nettles brought them with her to the garden, too piqued to putter. Left the sandals on the grass at the garden's edge. She attacked the earth with the trowel, pulled the early shoots of weeds out of the turned soil with the meticulous care that her shortened digits required of her.

The sandals warmed in the sun. Beautiful construction. Handmade crafts-manship, by the look.

She moved down the rows, gathering cucumbers, eggplant, tomatoes. And who's going to deliver these, she thought angrily.

In the sun, the sandals positively glowed.

There was no reason to put them on.

No reason in the world.

Sandals are inappropriate footwear for gardening.

She put them on. There was some difficulty with the buckles but she managed it with the dexterity she'd learned knifing at the sardine sluice, knitting at the Neon.

That was a foolish thing to do, she thought. Why'd you do such a foolish thing?

Not alone, said a voice. She heard it in her head.

Nettles stood and walked away, as fast as her feet could carry her, back

toward the Neon. I'm not answering that, she told herself. I'm not. I'm not.
No no no.

Not alone, the sandals said, again. *They're all wearing me, too. They're*

—Boyd Ligneclaire, *Subject to Infinite Change*

x x x

easy to find. The cardinals come to collect Donk in the morning, at Ralph's,
during office hours. He doesn't argue, just deflates a bit, tries to look defeated
and frightened as he trots meekly in their company, guarded behind and before, tries not to smile or show his anticipation. He can feel the amulet under
his shirt. As expected, they bring him down into the tunnel, to the all-white
antechamber. Still disconcerting to be in that long white sameness, even now
that he knows the secret of the tunnels' carving; it was good ol' Gordy with
his godlike power. The now-familiar round steel door rises up; not a safe
after all but the entrance to the strange Tunnel CAT, the bullet-shaped tank
Morris uses to traverse the tunnels. Soon, Donk knows, Morris plans to ride
the Pigeon Force–facing one, head back to the home office for his little bird-
and-spade ceremony. And yes, Morris is waiting in the antechamber, crutch
in armpit. Soon his leg will be as healed as it can be, and he'll discard the
crutch, but he'll always limp. He knows it enrages Morris; to be forced to
carry a permanent defect, this diminishment, this constant reminder of his
failure to control his reality. It's delicious to anticipate how much worse it's
going to get for him, how many more intolerable indignities he'll be forced
to endure.

In the center of the room, an oubliette waits. There's a gang of cardinals
in the room with them; the muscle. They'll be tasked with forcing him into
the box. The little ones are there—the Andrews. Morris looks expectantly
at the man he still thinks still works for him. Donk pauses to savor the moment—with Ralph it was over too quickly. This time you'll let it last, perhaps
forever. He's momentarily confused—*hang on a minute, you wanted to do this
for Bailey's sake, and Bailey's healed*—but then he pushes it aside. Even if the
effects weren't permanent, he still hurt her. And were you doing this for Bailey alone? Not at all. Think of yourself. Look at that thing, that box. It's for
you. It's here he'd entomb you. He'd torture you there forever. He means to.

Think of those he's done it to, the hundreds who even now scream in their oubliettes. Think of those he's shipped off around the world. Think of those in his prisons. He steals months and years, steals memories, converts them into cash and credit. Think of how he's profited from them all. And Julius, your poor priestly chum. What has he done to Julius? Something unimaginable, no doubt. No, with Morris there can be only plain dealing, and you'll deal with him plain.

"I gave you all the time you asked for," Morris says. A glance over his shoulder.

"Yep," Donk says, and sees his enemy's eyes narrow, enraged at the effrontery of one who refuses to be cowed. The smoke from his cigar smells like shit. Donk tells the cigar to stop burning, and it winks out.

"And have you succeeded?"

"Can't say I have."

"I can't say you have either," Morris snaps. He tries to draw on his extinguished cigar, examines it, finds it dormant. "No Gordy." He produces a lighter. Donk—just toying with him now—tells the lighter to have no fluid, and so it is empty. "No goddamn Gordy..." trying without success to produce flame...still trying without success "...and all this time..." he gives up, curses, throws cigar and lighter against the wall. "All this time goddamn wasted!"

"Quite true. I've wasted your time. I wasted it."

"No use complaining to me that you meant well."

"I agree. But you see, I *didn't* mean well."

Morris stares at him, dumbly shocked. Donk continues: "Julius is— *was*—a good friend. I wanted to protect him, and help him, and I did that. I did it by wasting your time."

Morris opens his mouth and closes it. Donk's never seen Morris flustered before. He likes it. But enough ruse; time to begin. Donk says: "I've got a better idea. Why don't *I* tell you what's going to happen to *you*, instead?"

Donk snaps his fingers—an unnecessary fillip, but he wants to make sure the point is unmissable—and the oubliette turns into an equal volume of eggs, dozens and dozens and dozens, cartoned in molded blue foam, stacked by the gross, shrink-wrapped on new pine pallets. The cardinals all cram back up against the wall in shock and religious awe.

He watches the awareness crash onto his enemy's face; first by bits, then all at once, Yes. Now he finally knows.

"Give it to me. Give it to me right now." Morris commands.

"There's no ticket anymore, *boss*," Donk says, spitting the last word. "Maybe there never was. There's only me." At a sign from Morris, half the assassins step forward; they fall to the ground as a synchronized corporate entity, each of their hearts converted, within their chests, mid-beat, into a single white rose; their suddenly untethered arterial tubework filling their chests with lifeblood as they lie silently twitching on the scarlet carpet. Donk sees the little ones, Andrew and Andrew, ever calmer than their fellows, exchange meaningful glances.

Now. Show this shit of the world who you really are.

"You're going to give it to me," Morris says again, quiet and firm, as though the saying will, by confidence, make it so. The effect is muddled somewhat by two glances he gives over his shoulder. The Coyote says nothing, but smiles.

"I am Continuity. It is *mine*. Give it to me."

The Coyote smiles wider, amazed—The more failure this man absorbs, the larger his certainty in himself grows. A spongiform prophet, filled like a tick, feasting on delusion. Look at his eyes, burning. Look at the zeal. And listen—he's not done. "You're denying reality itself. Taking what isn't yours. Save yourself."

"I want all of you to hear this," the Coyote tells the echoing room. "What's going to happen to this man next is, I'm going to take him. I'm going to replace his eyelids with sandpaper. Then I'm going to bring him back to you. That's who you follow now."

Morris says: "You can be a sign to me of cooperation or you can be a sign of rebellion. Give it to me now, or I won't protect you from the consequences."

You have to hand it to the man for pluck, the Coyote thinks—he truly believes he is all there is. That you are *not*, and neither are the trees, nor the mountains, nor the sun, nor anything else, either. The Coyote steps closer to his prey, who doesn't fall back. You'll regret not running, the Coyote thinks. It wouldn't make any difference if you had, but you'll still regret not at least trying. Come here, old son. I'll show you how real I can be.

Later, when he's carried Morris out of the tunnels, flown him far above the clouds, the Coyote reminds him: You won't know when I'll come. Might be in the morning, or a minute before midnight. You'll never know when. But it will happen every week. And it will never stop. When he returns Morris gently back to his room and streaks up up and away, soaring once again into the clouds, he has taken the first thing. He's enhanced his own hearing, so he can still for a long time hear the

× × ×

two smallest of Morris's bodyguards—longest serving, most trusted—glance meaningfully at one another, then at their unfortunate leader, then instruct their subordinates to fetch the abandoned wheelchair, to wheel him quickly toward a place where something—salve, saline, soothing drops—might be procured for a person in Morris's entirely unique situation. Morris doesn't notice—he's holding his eyes open with exceeding caution, propping them with his fingers against any chance sandpaper blink—but in those glances can be read the slow and ominous blossoming of doubt in soil that has never before produced such a flower. He holds very still and unblinking, but presently he must blink, and when he blinks he

—Jordan Yunus, *Subject to Infinite Change*

× × ×

screams.

The Coyote's hands curled and relaxed. He found himself calmly birthing new revelations to himself. There will be no reason for the innocent to fear you, he told himself, but for the guilty. . . children disappeared on a bright sunny morning have, over time, accrued a mass greater than can be borne. Given suitable mass, any material collected in one place will collapse into infinite conflagration, self-generating, self-sustaining, a fusion with fuel enough to burn a trillion years. It can be terrible to consider, but think of the applications. The sun can burn, yes, but the sun gives light and warmth, growth and life. The vengeance you brought Ralph, the vengeance you'll bring to Morris—that was only the start.

The weight of children, taking on greater speed and inertia, reaching critical mass as they go, faster, faster. They've never stopped gaining momentum. The structures that failed to bring order to their lives, or justice to their deaths—I'll knock down every last one of them and build them back better. Children still alive today will be able to observe and learn the art of virtue. They'll learn to fear harming one another, by observing my punishment of those who have broken that great law. Vengeance upon all, on behalf of all. Which of them hasn't deserved it? Even justice was ever only a tool. The world doesn't need justice anymore. Now it has me.

—Boyd Ligneclaire, *Subject to Infinite Change*

It is wise, therefore, to begin with art. Yes, and to end there, too. Don't trouble yourself with the artist; art is sufficient comprehension of the artist, and the only comprehension available to you, the only one ever intended for you. The substance of the artist, the presence of the artist, the knowledge of the artist, is the art.

—*Unknown*

caught it."

But he hadn't caught the circus, and he still hasn't; he'd merely found it. Bailey knows the difference between finding a thing and actually catching it, actually having it—pride of ownership, you might call it. It's been over a month now since she realized the world is just a room in her Attic, but she still feels the loss of the mindspace. More than once she's thought, despairing: My whole life I'll be chasing it, and finding it. And then, with joy: I'll be chasing it forever. But there's no rush anymore. There is only seeking and finding, and then, someday, the end. Or—who knows?—not the end. Perhaps death is another room. For the last weeks, there's been Gordy, and the road, and a string of motels, and laying low. It's what they have. Someday there will need to be more, but for now it's enough.

x x x

The Circus of Bearded Love had arrived in Raccoon River two days after their chance reunion. By then they'd fallen together, Gordy and Bailey, into their present arrangement. They'd left the sculpture park to find a place to eat and try to piece together what they knew about what had happened back on the Island; Gordy explained his end of things; it seemed around the time Bailey had been lying in a hospital bed wiggling her toes in amazement, Gordy'd been materializing way out in Elk River, Washington, in yet another park, lying flat on his back in the predawn dew of a tulip bed. Clothes on his back and nothing more. And normal for the first time since boyhood—*normal*. Fully visible with nary a flicker, memory restored…and other things, too, but those he'd only explain later. The Voice was gone, for one, its dreadful command dormant at last. Now he can wait for the wave to come and wash away Gordy's enemy, his pursuer, his anxiety for himself and the world. What will it be like when it arrives, this wave? The mechanics of the thing confuse her. Will it be precise or indiscriminate? Will it flood the basin of Pigeon Forge to the treeline of the Smokies, washing it all away, both the evil and the innocent, or will it be prehensile in its judgment, selecting only offenders for a watery grave? When will it actually, finally, finally, finally arrive—and how can we be sure it ever will, given the apparent relativistic speeds involved? What if Morris isn't in town when it hits? How will it reach him if its source is a doorway below ground? She suspects Gordy doesn't know. The closest he has come to explaining is to say, "It's bigger than that." That's one thing that hasn't changed, he claims: the wave. It's still there, a part of his vision, something seen but not yet realized.

He hadn't been disoriented in the Elk River tulip bed, despite the seeming randomness of his new location. "That part was clear right away," Gordy had explained, "the circus was still there." Except *it* wasn't there, exactly, only the ghost of it, the remaining pieces not yet packed up from the previous night; the rides half-deconstructed, detritus of the carnival, two laggard tents. Still, what little remained Gordy recognized from its recent but brief appearance in Loony Island, and from boyhood. And he found a prize, balled up beside a nearby overflowing trash bin.

"It's a modified tour schedule—one without Loony Island listed," Gordy said, wolfing food—obviously famished, the poor guy had been living rough. He'd nearly wept with joy when he saw Bailey's stacks on stacks of crispy cash. He produced the schedule, slid it over the table to her, where she noted the tour's final destination: Pigeon Forge, TN. "Cities and dates. After that, the hard thing was just getting where I needed to be." Destitute, he'd had to panhandle for the bus ticket to Buckeye, Colorado. "Nobody who heard my shuck and jive really thought they were paying for an actual bus ticket," Gordy sighed, "I guess they never will." Gordy, having never learned the trick of approaching strangers in ingratiating fashion, proved as bad a bum as he'd been in Brasschaat. "It took me days to raise enough," he mourned. "The bus I caught wasn't scheduled to get me there in time to do anything but catch the tail end of the closing night. And that was before the traffic jam." A jackknifing semi struck another semi, which spun out, jumped the median, and landed upside-down on the oncoming side. All four lanes backed up for hours. For a second time, Gordy arrived to the phantom of a circus, and was forced to shake his ass for spare change yet again. "I was more practiced at it, and I lucked into a tender soul who dropped me a ten-spot. And here I am," he concluded.

So that was Gordy explained. Bailey, for her part, did what she could do to bring sense to what he'd left behind in Loony Island. Realizing just how strange her story would sound, she made a muddle. "Julius is sandals,

I guess? Your dad said so. He thinks either Donk or Morris did it to him, but this book seems to suggest otherwise." Slowly, haltingly, even ashamedly, she explained Boyd to him. "Anyway, the book came out of Father Ex, according to your dad. And he's missing again, too—your dad. He stole my car." But by then Gordy was waving his arms, begging for mercy; the follow-up questions were piling up too fast to remember. Once they'd picked through all the strands, Gordy became more philosophical. "I think the ticket's gone. If it still were around, I think I'd know."

"The book I told you about agrees. I skipped ahead; it says Julius got it and then he disappeared and so did the ticket."

"When I saw you healed, I presumed it was Julius's doing."

"I still don't know how, and I'm not trying to understand. It's enough that it happened."

"Maybe it was Julius," Gordy mused, picking at the final crumbs on his plate.

"Sure. And maybe Julius really is ten pairs of sandals or whatever."

"Anything's possible," Gordy said, with deliberate sincerity. He'd already explained to her about Landrude and the doughnut shop and the alleged *Cat's Crib*. None of it made sense to Bailey, but then again, much that made no sense had proved true in recent days. Gordy returned to the schedule. "This says she's part of the freak show *and* the circus—Jane. She dances, then she's on the trapeze."

"We'll go to both."

"Are you coming along?"

"I've got nothing else to do."

"They'll be watching for me there. For me specifically. It's going to be dangerous."

Bailey nodded, pride of ownership returning. "That's why I'm

x x x

in the corner of the tent waiting for her—God, had it only been yesterday when he first set eyes on her? No. It had not. He'd first set eyes on her years ago, a boy at the circus. And then again, years later, in the cavern of oubliettes, he'd seen her again for the first time. And then later in Färland, he once again had set eyes on her for the first time. Each time, he'd died, caught in amber, pressed against the timeless perfection of instantaneous love. This meeting to come had to him the dramatic feel of a last breathless encounter, as though they were ancient lovers chosen by destiny, doomed by fate to this cycle of near and far, attraction and separation. This notion appealed to Gordy's romantic nature, and he soon found himself in an elegiac frame of mind. Would this meeting, too, be the first time? Would he still see with new eyes? Would this be another gorgeous and crushing death?

They'd opted to disguise him, or rather Bailey, cautious and canny, had decided. Nothing fancy—a disguise that calls attention to itself is worse than none—just a scarf, some thick-rimmed glasses with non-prescription lenses, and a quickly administered close-cropped haircut that made Gordy rub his hand absently over the bristles. Posing as a couple, arm-in-arm, just a couple of carefree kids, off to see the see—and what a see! Morris had invested heavily in the freak show since the last visit. Krane is barking the names of the big stars: Wembly, the Card-Playing Gorilla, Eddie the Eyeball, the Chuckleheads, as well as the assortment of other distractions and attractions: the inextricably conjoined, Leatherskin, Potato-Face, Shirley Tattoo, three-leggers, crab-handers, Donny Two-Dick, Hottentots, half-ladies, Germans, baby-grandfathers; there's a pig-boy, a monkey-girl, a salamander-man, an ostrich-woman—to say nothing of the displays, offshoots within the main tent where long shelves hid, dimly lit, holding deformity and relic most novel: tumors shaped like former presidents, history's most famous formaldehyded penises, shrunken heads, Sigmund Freud's cigar, Hitler's moustache trimmer, Lincoln's last shit, mummified Aborigines, a stuffed dodo, even an array of the most perfectly preserved pickled punks, packed into beakers and jars and sometimes even nestled jowl to jowl like sardines. And there, at the end of the row, the painted sign:

JANE THE DANCING BEARDED LADY

The light dimmed, and the sounds of a sitar snaked the air. The show was going to begin. Gordy and Bailey made their way in, selected seats as near to the front as they could manage. Gordy sat in a welter of anticipation…

The curtains lifted. Gordy died.

She danced obscured by a translucent scrim, backlit, only the shape of her form visible. Such lissome movements, the dance flowing from one shape to another, tantalizing, seeming even to shape the parabolic chords of the sitar playing on the speaker, while in turn being shaped by them. She moved, and the sinew of the music supported, supplanted, surprised, she made herself supplicant to it, then suddenly she surpassed it, moved in time until she seemed almost out of time. And then—no warning—the thin barrier lifted and the graceful promise of silhouette lay fulfilled, as they saw in flesh things previously guessed at in shadow.

The beard; her chosen shield, her chosen armor, her chosen sword.

Yes, chosen.

Gordy died, but a different death this time. I haven't known anything, he thought. I haven't known anything at all.

Then the curtain dropped and the crowd, groaning their disapproval at the sudden lacuna, stood, stretched, quickly dispersed. But Gordy crept to the stage and lifted the curtain leading to the

x x x

small dressing room. The room, a chamber adjacent to the dance's stage, itself a chamber within the room that has been set aside for her act within the freak show, which in turn is contained within one section of the outer ring of the larger tent, which is itself a roped-off portion of the fair. Here, in her dressing room, Jane is as "within" as she can be, the smallest matryoshka. She's alone except for her attendant—the two are weaving her beard. Jane's attendant is the circus freak show's other bearded lady, the one who was here first. She's shy, the poor girl, but that's for the best, since as a result of shyness she welcomes her displacement. If her temperament were otherwise, she might be inclined to compete to keep her position and rank, and there truly is no competition. Krane had been so delighted to have his rare flying bird returned to him, he'd immediately drawn up a new marketing campaign featuring her, made subtle changes even to the name of the circus itself. She's found victory, has Jane's attendant, the first bearded lady, simply in not desiring the fight. Now her hands work through Jane's beard—shaped for the dance—making it into a less obtrusive shape for the coming acrobatics. She works quickly on the left side, while Jane, already wearing her green spangled body sleeve, attends to the right. It's faster when they work together, and speed is called for—less than an hour remains before the flying bearded lady needs to appear on the platform...from behind, an unexpected voice makes the attendant squeak and jump.

"Hello? Excuse me?"

The globe lights in rows on either side of the mirror obscure their reflection, but she recognizes the voice. Gordy. Abandoner. He's got someone with him. She lets her fingers work, makes him speak first. It's possible to become stillness itself.

"You dance beautifully." Gordy says, voice thick. He is, as always, an idiot. An idiot as always, and—again, as always—a lucky bastard. Morris's goons were thick as marmalade for weeks, crawling all over the circus, swinging wooden swords, watching for Gordy to rise to the bearded bait, but a week ago there must have been some emergency back at the home offices; suddenly most of them were called away, leaving only a skeleton crew as rearguard. These men, though watchful and dangerous, haven't nabbed him, and she understands why: They haven't recognized him. They've never seen his face, have they? They're looking for flickers and shimmers, but he's disguised now in full visibility. Morris set the trap but he never considered...then she realizes—he's counting on you to turn Gordy in. He knows you'll want to, and you do want to—you'll tip any canoe, including his, that comes into grappling range. All you have to do is call for the guards, and they'll have it.

You may as well do it.

You may well.

"It's dangerous for you here," she says.

When Gordy smiles, he looks weary and sad. "We'd worked that out, yes." A nod toward his companion, a pretty cat with wary eyes, wearing a simple suit of black. Her head, recently shaved, now grows around her head almost in a helmet, lending her a martial aspect that belies her slight size.

"Morris's men are here. They're bound to catch you if you stay long."

"We'd better not stay long, then," the pretty cat says in clipped tones. Jane, suddenly much more interested in this young woman than she is in her unworthy former lover, watches her in the mirror; she stands by the pinned tent-flap entrance on the balls of her feet, calm and very present. Her hands clasped behind her back, likely near some concealed weapon. Jane knows her type from living around Morris's semblants and trustees: always prepared for a fight, always expecting one. How oddly practical of Gordy to have picked up a bodyguard.

"I could call and the guards would be here in a second," Jane says. "In fact, that's exactly what I'm instructed to do."

Gordy and the bodyguard share a nervous glance.

"Can you help me think of a reason not to? If they catch you, I'll be well rewarded."

"I didn't think you'd be the type to be swayed by reward."

"But people change all the time, don't they? You should know—you change them." He stiffens at this but says nothing, so she continues: "And perhaps I've been offered a reward that entices me."

She saw it come to him then—the understanding. "Finch. Your reward is Finch."

Jane said nothing; her silence would have to be answer enough for him to puzzle it out. Yes, Finch. Always Finch. It's been Finch guiding me even before she was born. Finch when I tried to warn you under the bleachers. Finch when I tended to you in your oubliette. Finch when I treated with you in the caverns to overthrow Morris. And for Finch I offered myself as sacrifice to you in Färland. And Finch now. I get to see her whenever the circus ends its tour in Pigeon Forge. Morris has not lied in that, at least. They bring her up. We sit by the fountain. She doesn't know me. I weep. She tries to be kind to this weeping stranger. It's the most awful thing in the world; it's all I have. Yes, you Abandoner, you living void, you hole empty even of yourself, yes, it's Finch, who you left behind, who you never thought to return to save, yes, it's Finch, and if I deliver you to them then Morris says he'll give her back to me for good, and of course he's lying about that, but what else do I have but that?

"He really did it to her, didn't he?" Gordy's face undergoes a fascinating sequence of realizations; no less painful than he deserves: Yes, since you abandoned us in the Vault; yes, that moment in Färland; yes, in your righteous rage you hid knowledge from yourself of your unintended consequences; yes, and as you enacted your righteous punishment too; yes, you drowned yourself to escape the storm you brought and then gave no thought of who else might have been washed overboard to be swallowed by the sea. Gordy sits heavily and puts his head in his hands. She observes him in the mirror, her first clear look at him since Färland. He's aged—how strange to think he would age, nothing left of the boy in him. Nothing dramatic to the shift: a slight tracery of lines on the forehead, prominence of nose, a slight diminishment of the density of his new-cropped hair. She's always thought him such a boy, even though he was full-grown back in the cavern days. Even later, in Färland, being with him always carried with it a suggestion of the perverse. Now there's a care about him, a wariness, a weariness, as if something essential and destructive has at great price been drawn out of him and expunged. Look at him. At last he's coming to terms with what he's done, and what's been done because of him, but still he's making it—realization, grief, supplication—all just another part of his story. He's here to save you from whatever it is he imagines you need saving from. He'll patch it up, put things to rights, be the champion, the protector. He'll recede the beard he bestowed upon you, he'll erase that long-ago-deemed punishment without considering how you've reshaped yourself to fit it, without a thought to the underlying suppositions made when he furnished you with it. He'll take it in the same way he gave it, without asking, and as a part of his great hero's journey. His redemption. His reconciliation. He thinks he's come to set things back to rights. He doesn't understand he's just asking you to be compliant with him as he restores you back to a more comfortable place within his narrative. And then he'll expect thanks and praise—yes, that will be your role. To thank him for smoothing your face once again, for restoring and putting right, never considering that for you to accept such a gift would be to accept his framing of it as punishment, which is something you've never done. No, you've never accepted a punishment—he sprouted shame on you and you bearded yourself with a shield of beauty and power. And now that he knows about Finch, he'd do the same with her. Bring her up out of the oubliettes, yes—but only as one of his great heroic works. Gordy the powerful, the wise. Gordy the good. But Gordy the abandoner? No, never that. It couldn't be that. No, here's what he'll do: bring her back up, restore her mind if he can, wind the string back onto the spool into the exact original shape—machine-precise, factory new—re-encase it in its packaging and set it back on its shelf. He'd erase his own part in it, blot out his own original sin so he can go on being his own protagonist. But first, Gordy, be sure to spend a little time on your cross, make sure to pierce your own side—but not too deep—and then you'll forgive us, all of us you've harmed, for we knew not what we did in doubting your innate goodness. Put on the hair shirt. Blubber before the bearded lady, so when you enact your gallantry, she'll be sure to thank you properly. Jane watches him, his head in his hands weeping, and imagines what he might do if he let himself see, as clearly as she does, how he plays his own part for himself.

"No," Gordy said, looking up, at last. "I can't think of a single reason you shouldn't call. Go ahead. Call them. I won't fight it."

She turns to face him. For a long time, she stares.

"You're not going to call them." Gordy's bodyguard says; not as threat, merely as observation. And of course—damn it—this is correct. There's no hope in trusting to Morris for reward, any more than in trusting Gordy to put things back as they were. Disruption is the only remaining hope. Disruption and destruction, and Gordy may someday yet create some of that—who better to do so?

"Why are you here?" she asks, thinking—You'd better not say it. If you say those words, I really will call the guards. What good is "sorry"? What is "sorry" but another burden you're asking me to hold for you?

He sags. Everything about his aspect indicates surrender. "No idea. Not anymore. I'm just here."

She makes a slight ironic sound. "You know why."

"I used to know. I suppose now I'm here to tell you some things."

"No. You're here to decide what I want, and then to do it. Use that ticket of yours. Take something else away."

Gordy turns his palms up. "There is no ticket. I gave it to somebody I trusted. Now it seems it may be completely gone."

"I can't believe it." But even saying it, she understands: This solves the mystery of his diminishment. He gave it up. She supposes this news should bring something like despair—Hadn't getting it been your whole plan? Apparently not; apparently, on deeper levels, you'd never believed in its existence, or at least you'd never believed it would be your path.

"He's not lying to you," the bodyguard says, in a way that amuses Jane. Some interest, some protectiveness, extending beyond the professional. Ah, yes—you're the new one, or you're about to be. And how is he with you? Has he started trying yet to absorb you? Does he cling to you like he clung to me, like you're the life raft, like you're the last unbroken rope? What will it be like for you, honey, when you don't meet those hopes? What happens when you don't make yourself porous enough to draw as much of him into you as he expects, when you're insufficiently buoyant and he sinks, when you're not tied to an anchor stable enough to hold his weight, when he falls? What will he do then? Blame physics for its properties, or himself for his position? No—when you fail to hold him, he'll expect you to hold the blame. But now it's become confused—he's given it up; he can't do to you what he did to me. He'll need to find other tools now. How did he give it up? Why?

Gordy climbs down from his chair and sits on his heels. Eyes on the sawdust. "I know my danger, and I'm here anyway. That's all the proof I've got. I came as soon as I found out where you were. Once I thought I'd come to heal you, but that's done." He speaks as someone realizing the truth even in the midst of saying it. "Now... I think... I've just come to give you the power to decide what to do with me, and the chance to decide what that is."

So, Jane realizes, he can still surprise you after all. She turns back to the mirror, returns her attention to the braiding. "If you have things to tell me, you have five minutes. I can't be late for the trapeze."

"I want you to know that I've wronged you."

"Oh really? Thank you. Thank you for that *information*."

"I mean I want you to know that I know it. I intended some of what I did to you. I never intended for...for Finch, but my intentions don't matter. I had my reasons for some of it, and some of them were even good, but my reasons don't matter. If I had it to do over again, I'd do it differently, and that doesn't matter, either. It's happened, and it's happened to you and your little girl, and that's what matters."

"And you just... *needed* me...to *know* that."

"I had this thought, that you needed me to tell you I knew. That's probably all wrong, I don't know. I'm an idiot, just like you said. That's all I should have said: I'm an idiot. I did my best, except—" he looks meaningfully at her beard "—except when I did my worst. I've learned how terrible the result can be when an idiot does his best."

"And yet here you are. Still trying your very best."

"I gave up my power, but I haven't given up trying. I don't know how to do that."

"So you run away. Again."

"I suppose so. I've been running since I was a boy. It's all I know to do."

They sat in the silence of spoken truths. Later, as the implications of what he'd told her seeped into her histories and recolored them, she would hate him for taking away simpler perspectives and replacing them with swampwater. Now she would have to understand his actions; not to condone—never that—but to see the whys and wherefores, to remember the complexities, to know why a scared man would act without regard for the fate of those he'd led to believe in him. And even the atrocity of Färland. This is what he thrust back upon her: the first memory of him. A boy hiding, spying on the Assizement, peeking between the slats, taking in spade and bird and fountain, the sight of which can make you crazy with fear. That had been him, not yet Abandoner, only a teenaged boy gone tharn from the wonder of the darkwater white fountain, a day later trapped in an oubliette, staring for a decade at nothing but his own simultaneous growth and desiccation in relentless light and mirror. And even after all that, he'd had compassion in him. He'd tried—hadn't he?—in his failed way, to heal. Yes, later he'd given himself over to corruption, run away from responsibility, pumped himself full of the pustulent lessons of the red light in Brasschaat, stuffed himself like a tick with a boy's sense of romance and a pimp's sense of ass. He'd given himself a licentious license, but even in his self-degradation there was still much of that boy left in him. She hates him so much more now that he's forced one charitable memory of himself past her armor. Oh, he did an evil thing to her in Raccoon River, eviler by far than the scorn and the beard in Färland: He'd made himself understandable. Now, when she thinks of him, she still sees what she'd seen before—Abandoner, blamer of the innocent, punisher of the scapegoat, shirker of duties, fool of the world—but now when she thinks of him, she sees—can't help but see—Finch herself. The night after Raccoon River, sleepless on the sleeper car as it plunged through darkness to the next show, she thought— If only you had said something terrible like "I'm sorry." Then I could keep despising you.

But all that came later.

Now she says: "You wanted me to hear you. I've heard you."

If he'd hoped for more out of her, he didn't reveal himself. He looked at her with what she took for gratitude.

"I want you to go, now."

Quickly Gordy rises. At the door, he pauses.

"Sometimes even when an idiot does his worst, the result is still beautiful," he said. "Or maybe that's taking too much credit. Maybe your beauty is simply stronger than my stupidity. In any case—your beard...it's beautiful." Then he leaves. But the bodyguard

x x x

Bailey—peeking out the tent flap to ensure Gordy hadn't strayed—tarried, seemingly on the verge of confession.

Jane said: "Well? Do you have something you want to ask me?"

"As a matter of fact, I have something to give you. I think I just found out I have a brother I never knew about."

"I see," Jane said, though she didn't.

"It's not the usual situation for those sorts of things," Bailey said.

Jane waited.

"He's a writer."

Jane waited.

"I have his book here. . . " Rummaging through her backpack.

"I don't read much these days."

"I haven't read most of it yet, either."

"Then keep it."

"This is a spare. I think you need to have it."

Jane smiled. "And why is that?"

"Because," Bailey said, producing it at last. "He dedicated it to you."

"I don't understand."

"I didn't, either, until today. But it's got to be you. See for yourself."

She opened the book—really just pages in a binder. On the back of the title page, she found it:

For the flying bearded lady. The door's always open

Studying the title page, she said: "I don't understand. I don't know this Boyd Legging-clear."

"I don't know him, either. But still I think he's. . . real."

"And if I read, what will I find in this book your maybe-brother maybe-dedicated to me?"

"I don't know." Bailey seemed suddenly younger, the bodyguard no longer. Bashful. Embarrassed. Her words came out in a tumble. "The things in this book really happened. Or at least my parts in them did. In any case, I think you should have it." Jane studied the cover. On her way out, Bailey paused at the portal. "I don't understand why you're here. Doing *his* dirty work. You're amazing. You could go anywhere else."

Jane smiled, terribly weary, terribly sad. "Sweetie, I could give you the same speech. All I know is I'm

xxx

going with you." And so she had. Bailey returns to reading Boyd's book, but keeps catching herself strayed from the page, drifting, thinking back on their strange circus interview, the singular woman who had given it to them. Bailey thinks—Silly girl. You left the bearded lady's presence as obsessed with her as Gordy ever was.

When the scrim had dropped, Jane had seen Gordy immediately. She'd been expecting him—she must have been, she knew she was meant as Gordy bait—but Bailey still marked her shock, caught between the abstraction of expecting something someday and the reality of the expected moment suddenly arrived: a widening of those almond eyes, a visible start, mouth slightly agape. She'd recovered; likely the rest of the crowd presumed the startle on her face was a dramatic flourish, part of the act and nothing more. They'd all been wearing their own various expressions of awe or revulsion or entrancement, and might easily have assumed she'd been making brief satirical commentary on their own flustered faces. Then, afterward, her eyes had been cast first to Gordy, then to her, and then back, and then that beautiful beard had risen and fallen in a gesture too subtle, too enigmatic, for Bailey to discern if it represented true approbation or the parody of it. *Yes it matters, and you'd better figure it out*, her eyes had seemed to say, dancingly.

So here you are, Bailey thinks. Exchanged a single Iowa motel room for a series of identical ones across the country. Exchanged as companion a weird old loony for his even weirder son. And yes, there's Gordy, sitting on the floor on a pallet he's made of cushions, back against the foot of the motel room's lone bed, reading the other material Tennessee had brought along: Julius's memoir. He's being a gentleman, he never even asked who'd get the bed, just made that pallet and made himself comfortable. He's even cute . . . Bailey, curious, peeks a prospective toe out from beneath the coverlet and—the room is small enough to allow it—tickles Gordy's ear. Gordy barely registers; after a minute he swats at it, without looking over, as if it were no more than a fly—which may be, Bailey realizes, what he thought it was. There's no further acknowledgment.

I suppose it's just another dreamless night, she thinks with resignation. Tragically, the Attic remains absent without leave. She can reassure herself all she wants by way of regained physical control and sensation—wiggling fingers and toes, jogging the streets, lifting food to lips, stretching, standing, sitting, maybe sometimes sex…all these are fantastic, but the loss of the Attic still leaves her emotionally rawboned.

"*This* is interesting," Bailey murmurs, later. Half-serious, but she senses opportunity, too. Gordy hasn't moved. Bailey toe-nudges him again in the ear. "We're famous. Boyd wrote about our visit to your bearded friend."

"What?"

"I'll read it if you like," Bailey half-teases. She pokes Gordy again with one stockinged toe. "According to Boyd, you found her dance *very…* stimulating."

"It's only a book," Gordy mumbles. "Doesn't mean it happened that way." Bailey smiles playfully. Something about the book is nagging at her, but it's ignorable, a slow leak. And…does Gordy at last seem to be coming out of himself? Why, yes he does. Time to try for a bit of fun. "But the shadow part was real," she says, poking again. "And she was lovely. A girl could get jealous…"

Gordy finally registers. He glances her way, sidelong, and tosses his pages on the floor. His smile, still mostly quizzical, now has its own playful glint. "Could a girl, now?"

"A girl might already have."

"And what might a girl do about it?"

"Come on over here," Bailey says, "And a girl might show you."

✗✗✗

Later, with Gordy asleep on top of the coverlet, Bailey fishes the flashlight out of her duffle and creeps back to the book. There's a problem. Until now, Boyd's book had been an accurate account, fictionalized, to be sure, but generally accurate: a Boydish chronicle of all that's happened—but this passage of beard and shadows has a new and concerning quality, the implications of which have only recently begun to dawn on her. She whispers into the dark. "It's not just about what *happened*. It's about what's *happening*. Everything that happened to us *after* I

✗✗✗

took flight on the trapeze, after the leap and catch and roar of the crowd, Jane retires to her sleeper car and begins to read Boyd's book; obligingly at first, but with growing absorption, until by the end for her there is no sleeper car, no hoot of train, no racket of track, no moon outside, only words and page and page and page and page. The book does indeed describe things that happened, things that the author couldn't have known. Jane never concerns herself with questions of how. It *is*; "how" is an irrelevance. She finishes at break of dawn and falls immediately into turbulent sleep. That night, a secretly furious Colonel Krane expresses his regrets to the disappointed crowd on behalf of the flying bearded lady, who has unexpectedly taken ill. Jane keeps to her dressing room, cross-legged, book in lap, making notations, filled at last with something like hope, waiting, anticipatory, for the day the Coyote might begin to perform his good vengeance upon Morris, thinking back on the book's dedication—Yes, this is why news of the ticket's destruction didn't bother you; it was never your target. There's a leap available with a much better hope of a catch: Boyd's reminded you, whoever he is. The door's always open for the flying bearded lady, he claims. You'll be in Pigeon Forge soon enough, Jane. It's time to find out if what Boyd

x x x

says is even true?" The Sandals Julius said nothing in reply to this for a long time—hours—and Sister Nettles began to wonder if she'd offended him. Or them. Or. . . oh, balls. Now you're worried about offending footwear. And you'd promised yourself you wouldn't even answer when he talks.

This is no business, Nettles decided, for someone who deals in the tactile. Father Julius used to be a kindred spirit in focusing on the physical over the metaphysical, or so she'd thought. And still there remained the work of the Neon Chapel to do, and only her left behind to do it.

You haven't offended me in the least, said the Sandals Julius. *I'd be happy to tell you what's happening with the others. They're wearing me the same as you are. We're all still together.*

Nettles wandered the empty cavern of the Neon, futilely straightening, rearranging chairs that needed no rearranging, repeating to herself the advice she gave herself constantly, and which she constantly ignored: Don't answer your shoes. Do not answer your shoes. Do not.

The sandals said: *Tennessee is back in his home state, for example.*

Sister Nettles couldn't help herself. "After all the times he said he wouldn't go? What on earth?"

I'll help him, Nettles, the sandals said. *Don't worry. I'll help.*

—Boyd Ligneclaire, *Subject to Infinite Change*

The physical laws of the universe are indifferent to your struggle. Certainly, they make no special dispensation for your desires or needs. Still, it would be an error to presume the indifference of the universe's laws represent the universe's indifference. The briefest glance at a great painting belies the notion.

—*Unknown*

He might have returned to Pigeon Forge any number of ways: by car, train, private jet—but after the Coyote's betrayal, the CAT seems safest. There's been precious little sense of safety in the weeks since the Coyote revealed himself. They've rigged up a system for him, and he lies on his back and submits himself to it as the CAT rumbles uphill, just minutes away from its destination. It's a simple contraption, really; some clamps to hold his sandpaper lids, a tank of soltion hooked up to a drip. Every ten seconds precisely, another moistening drop obscures his vision. Traversing the tunnel in the CAT's guts, Morris, enclosed on all sides, feels at last unfindable, unharmable. Finally he's been left free to consider what he'll do when he finally puts his hands on the ticket.

What shall we do with the Coyote? Your trust was falsely placed, but now that you know him to be dishonest, he is more knowable and you trust him more, you've learned the handle by which to grip him. He will come, drawn to you, and you will have prepared for him... something. He thinks himself greater than you, but he's drawn to you just like anything else. All things are drawn to you: The signs of your Allness are so clear. And the thing behind you is still behind you. In much the same way, the circus will soon return to Pigeon Forge to join you. Soon you will see Jane again, still beautiful, ruined as she may be. A greater attraction now she's been bearded than ever before, so Krane claims.

The CAT halts; you've arrived.

Look, the Andrews have been made alert to your approach. Sent ahead to prepare the ceremony on the Pigeon Forge side, they attend you as you emerge from the CAT's vaultlike back hatch, but you wave them off and make your way with the cane. You've practiced and are quicker with it now. They share a sour look, which they imagine you didn't see. They still doubt you, the Andrews; sensitive they are, able to detect disloyalty in the quiver of a whisker—oversensitive to it, and without doubt jealous. Closely, closely, they watch status and position. There are rumors about them and there are truths. You remember when they were three—triplets standing before you beneath the circus tent, child-sized but fierce, caught up by Krane's freak show for the Assizement, the troika exuding unnerving calm in the pen amidst the rest of the chattel, who rattled the bars begging and fearful or else stood catatonic staring at the sawdust. Throughout the ceremony you had a growing awareness of them, watching and waiting, listening to the liturgy, the presentation of bird and spade, of water and box. When they were called forward the middle one interrupted you, strong-voiced: There is no need to remake us; and you: There is, you must be made perfect, and he: We are perfect already, we will prove it to you, and then without hesitation the two behind him twisted with impossible quickness, loosed the grips of the guards and snatched the guards' weapons—not the swords but the quick long knives hidden deeper in the folds of ceremonial red—spun about and without hesitation plunged the lovely blades deep into their brother, their third, their spokesman, who smiled and said: Now you see, and fell, quietly dying, as his brothers threw the pilfered bloody knives with expert precision juddering into far-away beams, then bowed to you their obeisance. The puzzle of the Andrews, the one who died and the two who lived. You ponder it frequently; every day you sift the memory, searching for clues. When did they decide? How did they choose among them the sacrifice? The one who died went willingly. There was no sense of betrayal when he saw the handles sprouting from his body. Yet still, alone among all the thousands to ever pass through the Assizement, only the Andrews never saw spade nor bird. They alone selected their own baptism. The unnerving intensity of their devotion, the sacrificial nature of their arrival, unexpected and unexpectable. As a result you are never entirely comfortable in their presence. These tiny pieces of yourself, lessons you gave yourself about the power of will, about the unpredictable nature of what you choose to bring forth into the world. Reflections of your own fierceness. Reflections of your own ruthlessness. Most others among the trustees avoid the Andrews, fearful of offending them by failing to tell one from the other. Any fool can detect the difference merely by noticing behavior. In truth they couldn't be less alike. Andrew is typically taciturn, watchful, waiting, offering nothing not directly asked of him, while Andrew, on the other hand, speaks without cease when given cause. He is at it now, brisk and assiduous: updates on the circus; how many runaways collected according to Krane's report; when the circus is expected to arrive; preparations for the ceremony; dossier of the unworthy, blue tickets already delivered; quarterly earnings from the prisons, revenues down over-all though the new facilities in Missouri are a bright spot and lobbying efforts for stiffer mandatory penalties are sprouting results, new bills coming to the floor after the recess to help drive future revenues, less inmate turnover and more opportunities for resident extensions, requiring gaudy government contracts to build new facilities necessary to hold new inmates, whose habits are not yet being punished with requisite severity... also the sex trade: New infusions to the red-light districts in EU are showing a fast uptick, expansion to ASEAN is on track with Thailand set to open in quarter two next year... You feign attentiveness—if your interest flags, Andrew will take offense and then of course Andrew will also be offended on his brother's behalf—but your leg aches from long hours in the CAT, and your eyes yearn for the comfort of the drops. You seek and in short order find home and bed, the skylight directly above, and you gaze out into a clear night sky, stars and constellations wheeling high above, unreachable for now, their cold light traveling for aeons before the birth of civilization or even species to meet you here, now, the stars a bleak stark lesson to yourself of the distances you have yet to attain. All of this you call your own. You will soon have Gordy in hand, you'll take back the power he stole, and then you will know each star through each moment of its existence, balls of gas forty thousand times the size of this planet, each particle, each photon, for hundreds of millions of years, all of it you will call your own. All of it is yours it springs from you and yet you have distanced yourself from it locked it hidden it behind a door, spirited it away in the hands of a thief, but you will have it, you will possess it control it understand it break free of this so-called matter and this so-called time, restore all things to the rightful ways and the rightful places, unmake all who resist. The thing behind you is still behind you. All things you call your own and you own all things, all things you call your own, you own all things you see and all you see you call your

× × ×

best available path, in his slow and deliberate way: down a foothill, along a ridge of trees, down a long two-lane road; a sign declares PIGEON FORGE 3 MILES. Sterling Shirker follows it. Stumbles down the main strip in early morning light. Finds a bench and sits himself down, tired down to his liver and kidneys, not knowing whether to laugh or cry—You've only just realized, old man, how forehead-slapping stupid you are. You haven't got the slightest idea where this damn fountain is. Gordy found it, sure, but they'd captured you and brought you to it blindfolded.

Just stay here I guess, Sterling thinks, it's as good a place as any other. Either they'll pick me up or they won't.

But you know how to get them to take you there.

The old man groans. "Yes sir," he says. "Yes, I suppose I do know."

Sterling reaches into his satchel, draws out the toothpaste-striped robe of a Wales loony.

He's wearing it when the morning crowds begin to arrive. Sterling stands on the bench, starts to speak in a loud voice, proclaiming it all, the old litany: fountain and ticket, bird and spade and cavern and door and oubliette by the row.

It doesn't take long.

They come in the guise of police, but Sterling never doubts he's going beneath the fountain, and there it is again: the door at the top of the ledge, the long slope opening up onto the cavern, the high wall of oubliettes. He's held there at swordpoint until Morris arrives. The two of them stare at each other, two old beat up tom-raccoons negotiating over a trashcan lid. Morris looks a mess. His eyes are a bloodshot wonder. He glances over his shoulder unceasingly, almost manically.

"So you've returned to me," Morris says. "Did you decide you deserved your punishment and come back to get it, or have you gone the rest of the way crazy?"

"Oh, I've been crazy a long time," Sterling answers, truthfully enough. "Gone so crazy I looped back round again to sane a couple times. I guess I got tired of talking crazy and wanted to start doing crazy."

That puts an atmosphere in the room. Morris's lieutenants' hands creep toward sword pommels. They think you're strapped with a bomb or gun, Sterling realizes, and laughs. He can't help it; it just bursts from him.

"And what crazy thing are you planning to do?" Morris asks, real quiet and real soft.

"There was a woman used to live here," Sterling says. "She took care of the people in your prison. You let her do that, so I assume you saw some value in it once upon a time."

It's Morris's turn to laugh. "You've . . . what? Come to apply for her *job*?"

Sterling salutes, bathrobe arm flapping. "No, captain, no sir. I'm not asking permission to do it; nothing like that. I'm just going to do it until somebody stops me."

In the moments that follow, Sterling has no idea what Morris might be thinking, but under that owlish gaze, he feels as if he's being watched and measured by something mechanical and precise. At the end of this scrutiny, Morris looks at his guards and barks: "Well? Show him to his room." It's a nice enough place, despite being at the far corner of a prison cavern. Bedroom. Living room. Kitchenette. The only real complaint I can think of, he thinks, is that every inch of the walls is covered in writing: *I did not run away with the circus, the circus ran away with me.*

"Wondering if I might ask for some paint," Sterling says, without much hope of

x x x

a meaningful role. Under the fountain in Pigeon Forge, caring for prisoners. It was tricky for the first few weeks, but now he's got the hang of it.

"What about Biscuit Trudy?" Nettles asked, as much for distraction from her present task as out of curiosity. The meat had arrived as it did every week. She'd woken with no intention of doing anything other than tend her garden and read, like every other day since Julius had apparently become . . . but today, the deep freeze couldn't hold any more, and Nettles simply couldn't countenance the waste. Nothing left to do but to try her best; haul the heavy steamers out to the front yard and get started. Nettles could see it was going to be an absolute bitch, and no Brother Brock to man the tongs—and even if you figure that one out, who's going to make his secret sauce? Nettles cursed and muttered. You wanted me to find a hopelessness, Jules? Here's a hopelessness: the Neons without its members.

Biscuit Trudy's made her way to Florida.

"And what's she doing there?"

What she's always done. Only she's doing it there.

"And where's Jack?"

Still heading west. Walking. His preference, obviously.

"Be better if he headed back east," Nettles snarled, wrestling the first steamer onto the lawn. "I'm going to need the recipe for his sauce in about an hour."

I'll ask him, the Sandals Julius said.

"I . . . what?"

We're all together now. I'll ask him for

his perfect and complete order. As night falls, the Coyote finds beauty in the metropolis. The precise lines of the skyscrapers, arranged in regiments like sentinels of order and justice, assure him of human intentionality and regulation. Ferries patrol the harbor, displaying to their cargo of tourists and commuters the ranks of skyscrapers set against the dusk autumn sky—their unbending majesty, their testament to the ingenuity of engineering, to technical exactitude, to imagination and toil, to their own illusions of permanence. He's surprised how easy it's been, maintaining order in a territory so glutted with humanity, but perhaps, he muses, this should not be surprising; these people have been optimized for order. They know each train route, they've memorized the times of arrival and departure, they have an almost genetic sense of the grid of streets, and their own specific rules of engagement with body and machine. Here, in the metropolis, they've even shaped and ordered the horizon.

The Coyote rests in his perfect control.

He need only think of a skill apt to his need to possess it; each day he gifts himself with new abilities. At first, he swooped down from the air to stop a crime in its moment of execution, but this soon proved tedious—far more efficient to hover above it all at a remove, raining justice down upon each perpetrator. His laser eyes produce most of the desired effects in the pettier cases: sudden loss of a hand or head or leg for the purse-snatcher, the carjacker, the rapist. His ice-breath freezes the arsonist solid, freezes even the stream of gas leading from floor to red plastic jerrycan. His hearing can catch the quieter thefts—graft, corruption, vice, bribery—in their various inceptions, and he whispers warnings with his super-targeted whispering power, fomenting a paranoia in the white-collared overworld, aborting misappropriation, terminating usury, strangling fraud in the crib of intention. Occasionally, he descends from the clouds to put the fear of himself into some still-saucy kingpin, pimp, or drug lord, some uncowed banker, financier, or broker, who still believes him nothing but rumor. They know him well by now, but soon they will know him better. They recognize the stylized crimson C he wears on his powerful chest and on his cape, the diamond amulet he's removed from the chain and embedded into his forehead. In the minds of the evildoers awareness of him has grown. They whisper about him now: the Coyote. With his super-hearing, he hears this. He is everywhere, and everything. He cannot be evaded, nor bought, nor is he neutered by legal tricks. Pleading doesn't work. There remains only one successful strategy, they think, which is to wait for the Coyote to go away. How amusing—compliance isn't even considered. Poor fools. It's so simple, really it is. Obey. Be quiet. Harm none. At times, briefly, he feels sorry for them, little big men still clinging to their filthy engines of misery—foolish like children, covering their eyes, thinking you can't see them if they can't see you; foolish like babies crying about the filth they've created for themselves to lie in; foolish like dogs ashamed of an infraction they barely understand and remember only vaguely—almost innocent in their misunderstanding of how the world has already changed. Life won't go on as it has. That was the old order. Man's inhumanity can breed itself out, now that he is here to teach them justice.

But now the hour has come, and there is a weekly promise to be kept. There is one in particular—Morris—who requires a more attentive justice, whose worst impulses require a slower extermination. Today you'll take his feet, replace them with something new and inappropriate. This will seem to him a punishment, but the day will come, when you have taken every original part of him, when you will begin to replace even the replacements, exchanging them again with something yet worse, and then he will long for the return of the lesser torment. Over the years you will make an example of him to pierce the dullest awareness—the suffering due to any who ever again dare cause the suffering of another being.

Over the city rolls a reverberating cannonade of exploding air, a flash like lightning, and then the Coyote is gone—miles away already, flying, faster than sound, fast almost as thought, over the mountains toward

x x x

Pigeon Forge that morning, the train having stopped in Knoxville the previous night. She'd come in with the rest of the circus people—Jane the Flying Bearded Lady. Later she came to the cavern to visit her daughter's creche, saw you at work on the scaffold. No, Sterling thinks: not *the* scaffold. *Her* scaffold. After all this time, for her to see the oubliettes have another caretaker. The confusion on her hirsute face, to see you, vaguely familiar from years before, fulfilling her old office, living in her suite. You'd taken the scaffold downward and she'd leaned in, smiled as if you were an old chum, gone in for a hug. "I'm here to tip canoes," she whispered. "Get me behind that door if you can." There hadn't been time for more talk; she'd been well-guard-ed—but not as well-guarded as Morris's door. How, wonders Sterling, does she expect you to help her do *that*?

Now they've taken the girl Finch out of her shelf and gotten her present-able to meet her mother. Finch waits patiently until it's time for her to climb the stairs, take her turn out in the sun beside the fountain, keep a promised appointment with a mother she can't remember. Sterling, not knowing what else to do, has brought her back to his apartment, which used to be her apart-ment, of course. The place smells of fresh paint, a pleasant eggshell matte, which Sterling laid on himself over the course of his first day, rolling it over *I did not run away with the circus* and *the circus ran away with me*, until he came to the last uncovered iteration, at the center of one wall, which he couldn't bring himself to paint over. She's reached her full growth down there in the awful bright, has Finch. She doesn't remember that time either, for the moment they took her out screaming they dosed her again with the fountain water. Now she's friendly, alert, and completely blank. Sterling, not knowing what else to do, serves her tea, and tells her of his time on Loony Island. "They cut all the loonies loose," he explains. "They never told us why. And if they told any of the loonies why, no loony ever told me. Which wouldn't be

x x x

unbearable, Jane thinks. It's absolutely unbearable.

The girl with no memory sits on a bench, facing the turtle's stone eyes and yawning mouth. From the turtle's massive back the fountain's bleached, cherub-encrusted extremity launches, rising above white basin and black water. The turtle screams stone anguish against the unfairness of its burden. The girl is placid, indif-ferent, as if she were waiting for a bus.

At a slight remove stand two tiny men dressed all in red. On the topmost of the stairs leading into the cavern beneath the fountain stands the new caretaker—a skinny, skittery-looking man wearing a bathrobe and pajamas and sandals. Jane sits beside her girl, occasionally touching her lightly upon her nose with a single finger. "Finch," she says between sobs, "Finch. Finch." But it isn't Finch—that's the cruelty. It's not her. Finch is gone. This is the girl with no memory. "I'm sorry," says the girl, presently. "I don't know a 'Finch.' Is that my name? I don't remember." Jane thinks of the hours Finch spent, reading books, filling her life with stories, the years they spent together making their own story—all washed out of her now. The girl turns to the bearded lady. "It's funny, don't you know? I don't remember anything at all before this. But I get the sense this is a magical place. So quiet. So still. *Have I been here before?*"

No prisoner save Finch has this routine. Each day they disinter her from her oubliette for her communion of obliterating water, the cleansing of her memory. Each day she is wiped fresh. Morris told Jane this on the return trip from Brasschaat. To him, it is a mercy. "You know better than I, dear," he'd said. "What they're like down there. You wouldn't want to meet her if she were like that." Each day, she is tortured with internment in the oubliette, but without the memory of the previous days, months, years preceding it. Each day begins anew without the horrific realization. Morris credits this to himself as an absolution, as he does these visits, which comprise the main part of her negotiated payment in exchange for compliance— and, to her surprise, Morris has not yet reneged. He gave her three visits, one a day, before she headed out with the circus for the dance and the stage and the leap and the catch. Yesterday was the fourth. Today makes a fifth. After the Assizement will come a final visit, and then she will go back on the road with the circus once more. She feels the coming wrench of departure, a different grief than the grief of presence.

"Yes," Jane murmurs. "You've been here before."

The girl takes this fact in without appearing to ascribe any value to it. "What a lovely beard you have. Did you braid it yourself?"

"You did," Jane says. "Yesterday. I taught you how."

"I don't remember."

"I know, I know, I know, I know."

"Will you teach me again today?"

"Yes."

"Why are you crying?" Finch asks, but they're interrupted by Morris, risen from his morning meditations below ground.

"We're close now," he says. He's stubbornly made his way up the steps unassisted, crutches shoved into armpits, eyes propped wide, and the... other alteration. "These are all lessons of my coming ascendance."

Jane glares at him, then away. From what source does his unaccountable belief in himself spring? She's heard the whisperings. Yesterday the Coyote found Morris in his home, turned his feet into something difficult to look at. The Andrews share a glance whose significance Jane can read: blossoming apostasy of two of Morris's truest believers, for if this can happen—if this can be done to him—if these outrages can be permitted to be committed against him... then what is he, really? Explanations for past setbacks no longer align with the plumbline of received doctrine; when this sort of thing happens, future setbacks seem increasingly likely. It's a question of worthiness, along lines of proof Morris himself has established within their orthodoxy. Now they're unsure of his inevitability, unsure of his promised coming apotheosis. It seems everybody except Morris is meant for power. But Morris persists: "Possession of power is working its way toward us. Possession running from the hands of those farthest from me to the hands of those closest. Soon it will be in my hands."

"That poor man," says the girl.

"That's no 'poor man,'" Jane says.

"Who is he?"

"He's the man who keeps you in prison."

"Am I in prison?" asks the girl. She wonders this with the same polite interest as she wonders anything else.

"Yes, dear. You are."

"Will I get out?"

As soon as I can manage, Jane thinks. Her fingers curl around those of her daughter and she squeezes—As soon as I can manage. And if I can't manage, I'll try to tip it all over.

"Yes, dear. You will get out," Morris says, clumbering over the grass. "Your release, sweet girl, is a certainty. They all will get out. All of them. All imprisoned, both those below here and those who crawl the earth out there"—he waves his cane—" all of them are imprisoned. The mercy I have given those below is revelation: They know they are prisoners. The rest have no conception. But they too will be set free. I will set all the captives free. I will draw all men to mys—"

They see it in a flash and it is done—the flying figure of the Coyote striking like a bolt from the blue sky, straight downward, as if he had fallen from a cloud with ankles connected to a tether gauged to exact precisions of length and elasticity, hands reaching open, grasping closed, pulling Morris back up with him again.

Keeping him there, twenty feet up, suspended, holding Morris close in his embrace, close, close as love, close as pain. He is whispering something to him.

"No fair," Morris screams. "No fair. No fair." And then he isn't screaming words at all.

The Andrews look up in astonishment, observing the new harsh forms their lord has been instructed to inhabit, observing that he has no choice but to obey. Hearing the wordless chuckling screams. They leave their posts, move together to a spot beneath the floating atrocity, and look at each other with fresh understanding and new resolve. From beneath the fountain, the other red-clad guards race up, investigating this unexpected commotion, and they too see, in the sky, their leader's woeful wordless tale.

"That man can fly!" the girl says, surprised at last. She's risen from her seat, looking up, hands shading her eyes against the sun. Jane is enjoying watching events foretold in Boyd's book come true when she feels a hand on her shoulder. The old guy, the new caretaker, come from the open stairway to meet her. "If you want to get behind that door," he whispers, "I don't think you'll get a better chance."

Jane runs for the stairs.

Everything that's happened to us *after* I got my hands on this ridiculous book has *happened*, too, exactly the way it says. Which means…beneath the covers, Bailey gazes up from the flashlight-lit pages in wild wonder. It's not just what's happened, or what's happening. It's what's *going to happen*. It's as if it's all coming together…As Gordy snores insensible and sated beside her above the duvet, Bailey, no longer feeling the tug of slumber, reads on through the wordless chuckling screams. "No fair," screamed Morris. "No fair. No fair."

"Oh but a week is so long to wait," laughed the Coyote. "The rule has changed. It's every day now."

—Boyd Ligneclaire, *Subject to Infinite Change*

fair, no fucking fair.

You smoke and read the latest revisions. It's *so* unfair.

All that work enduring the nightmare of interpretation, setting everything up just so, and now *Jane* goes behind the door to cock things up? You course through the revision, the doughnut stack, back and forth, reading its woeful report. Even Donk, the mighty Coyote himself, vested with all power, fails you. The problem with a comic is, what it shows you, it shows you unmistakably—pictures on a page—but what it leaves out is just as unmistakably out, lost, and unguessable. Example: Here, on this page...close to the end...You flip to the page...yes, here: Julius takes the ticket. The priest turns to sandals, and the ticket turns to water. It's gone. It's *gone.*

How then—*how*—do you account for this unexplained and inexplicable final page?

You decide to brave the interpretation. Once more through the door, dear friend. Go to Morris yourself, face to face, and push him to the breaking point your-self. You'll have to risk his wave. No choice but that your work be done on the other side; it's the only way you can see behind the panels, the only way to know.

—Jordan Yunus, *Subject to Infinite Change*

How redundant, to lard a book with epigraphs and quotations. Every book you read is itself already a quotation.

—*Unknown*

Sterling brought her back below the fountain again, back to the apartments, thinking only to keep her safe from the chaos above: the howls of tortured Morris, returned from the sky, set down by the Coyote upon the fountain lawn, a civil war that his followers have been fomenting now broken out around him, a schism not between loyalists and traitors, it seemed, but between various tribes of apostates, deciding the final fate of their defeated boss, determining among them the new order of dominance and dominion. It was only a matter of hollering when he scuttled her below-ground, but it looked apt to turn to blood any minute.

The girl remained friendly, alert, and completely blank. What the hell am I supposed to do now, Sterling wondered, heating tea for no reason other than to have a thing to do. I've already told her my story. I suppose I could tell her about my experience of

x x x

reading until dawn lit the room and she could rest the fading flashlight batteries. It's all here, all in the book, captured not with exacting fidelity, true, embellished in ways, yes—but certainly correct in a general sense, certainly rendered in more detail than might be expected from even a first-rate parlor diviner. No, never-known brother Boyd's prognostications go beyond the talents of the corner mystic; as soothsayer, his sayings are sooth from surface to sump. Page to page to page to page, curiosity curdling to fear, fear fulminating to dread, Bailey flips forward. And—can it be?—here at the end who is it, anyway

x x x

wearing the Sandals Julius? What's it *like*? Oh, my. Nobody's ever asked me that before. You're in good company, in not asking me, is what I'm saying. But there's something so polite in the way you don't ask—so, since you haven't asked me so nicely, I'll tell you. Wearing the Sandals Julius. Well. It's an interesting sensation. They're real nicely padded, for one thing. Cushiony. Like walking on clouds or on the surface tension of water, or deep-pile carpet. But still supportive in the arch. You get a real nice balance there. You can't usually run in sandals, but you can run in these better than tennies. I think there's something in the soles. Then there's the uppers. Look at this. Just feast your eyes. Blond leather, connected to the lowers by what looks to me (I'm no expert, now) like hand-stitching, tight loops, very sturdy. Look at the pattern of the stitchwork. Look at the etching on the buckles. Look at the tang—see there at the tip of it, where it's crimped back just a bit for maximum hold to the buckle? See the way the uppers are serged into the soles? Tucked in. That's craftsmanship. This isn't some slipshod slipper-shoe, these aren't the cardboard foot-bags they gave us in the Wales, this footwear's been constructed with intention and purpose. They don't talk as much as you might want—considering who they are, I mean—but you can't deny the craftsmanship. And they don't wear out. At first I wondered, but at this point it's damn near undeniable. Take a look. Not a scuff, not anywhere, no wear on the tread, not a single stray thread or popped stitch, nothing—and after the miles I put on them, too. That used car I borrowed from Bailey didn't last all the way to Pigeon Forge. Some people may have cars last the whole trip, but not me—I promise you I'll never have that good of luck. Threw a rod right through the engine block in the western tip of Tennessee over the Kentucky border. I had to hoof it.

"Here's the tea, sweetheart. Careful, it's still too hot. Just blow on it a bit and take it easy.

"So. What I'm telling you is, to get here, I walked the length of Tennessee, most of it—walked when I wasn't running. It's odd. I've never been one to run, and if ever there's been a trip a fellow might want to consider dawdling on, this would have been it. All the same I kind of felt the running itch as I went; a sort of feeling there was something ahead that might be better seen to sooner than later. So, I'd get into a kind of a trot, and then I'd get into a sort of a gallop. Then I'd walk when I got tired or the hills got too steep. And so when I say I find it singular—noteworthy—that these sandals haven't taken on a bit of wear, that's what I'm talking about. Was there precipitation? Does a bear shit in the rain? It poured on me most of a day. That sort of thing is hard on leather sandals, or at least that would be my expectation, but have a look—not a stain, not a blot. And, as far as I can tell, there never will be one. And I'll tell you another thing, which is harder to prove. These sandals are as lucky as I am unlucky. I can see by your silence you're confused. I'll explain to you what I mean, and I agree explanations are in order. When you make a claim to have lucky sandals (not 'lucky' sandals, in the sense of a preference or a superstition, you know: 'I always wear my lucky sandals on game day,' but, in a more literal sense: 'These sandals are, as a part of their nature, lucky, filled with luck and exuding luck and providing luck to their wearer'), well, any fool will tell you, that's a claim you have to back up with explanations and evidence.

"By way of explanation, a question: Are you clumsy? No, I can tell looking at you you're not. You're more like my boy, he could run a fence-rail the long way, post-to-post, and never slip or slurry. You met him years ago, but I daresay you don't remember. Don't get offended at the question, now. I'm not asking out of a sense of superiority, only it'd be easier for you to empathize with me if you were clumsy. You have to understand me, it's a particular type of luck I'm speaking of here. Not the sort of luck that will win me the lottery someday. Not even the sort of luck that can keep my car from a breakdown. It's all to do with finding the next step. Clumsy versus adroit is our dialectic. Me, I am an irredeemable stumble-crumb. Trip over my own feet. Over the feet of others. Over small creatures and their leashes. It's a documented fact I've fallen off a curb on more than one occasion. I'm a terror in a public park, a menace in a library, and it's an inescapable fact: Since putting on Sandals Julius, I haven't fallen or even tripped—and not for lack of opportunity or increase in my own nimbleness or grace, neither. A good piece of my statewide stroll was cross-country work, you understand. The backwoods around here aren't above throwing up a tree root or a shrub in the grass for you to stumble over, and the Smokies have no end of scrub and steepness to scramble up, loose stones and shale waiting to turn under a fellow's ankle, hidden holes, sudden drops camouflaged by scrims of weeds, and on and on and on. Given my particular lack of aptitudes, I should have broken a leg and died out there. But these sandals, they always find a firmness in a slough, a flatness in the midst of a skid. They miss the hole. They masticate the miles without misadventure. They never skip a step. I bet they could safely dance a minefield. I can tell you with authority they can cross a field larded with cowflop and never catch a squish. They're the reason I'm here with you, in more ways than one. Without them I couldn't have made it here all in one piece. Without them, I'd have never come in the first place.

"Hush. Hush. Did you hear that? Are they coming? I thought I heard somebody knocking.

"No, it's passed. We might dare hope they've forgotten us in the commotion. They're scared. Look what's being done to their great leader. Something's falling apart, and they know it. Hopefully your mama can find something behind that door. Maybe she'll bring us a

x x x

hint of memory. Finch, perched on a chair she doesn't recognize as having once been her own, doesn't feel from this loquacious stranger any expectation that she should speak, and therefore she does not speak. She sips tea and listens, restful in silence. She likes to hear his voice. She likes the way it goes. Occasionally she takes note of the words and their meanings, and sometimes she drifts, enjoying the music and the rhythm of his sounds. Then she tries to experience and enjoy each individual sound of each word, as if each articulation were its own distinct presentation; each glottal, plosive, fricative, and glide encased in velvet, placed behind glass, attributes and contexts authoritatively delineated by handsome placards. All modes of listening are equally pleasurable to her, as is shifting from the one to the other.

In time the words halt. She opens her eyes and sees that the kindly bearded woman from before has come again, whose name is Mother. When they were beneath the sky, she was sorrowful. Now she looks different; her eyes have gone wide and urgent. Sterling has gone to her. This is interesting. Finch keeps her eyes open and decides to do the listening where you follow the meanings of words.

"What did you see?"

"Everything. There isn't much time."

"Did you see a. . . a wave?"

"Yes. Oh, yes."

"Is it close?"

The woman makes an indistinct and impatient noise. "It's the wrong question. We've been thinking about that wave all wrong. We've been thinking about *everything* all wrong. We have to find Morris. He'll need our help. And we have to find—"

"But Gordy said we're waiting on the wave. Is it coming soon?"

"*Wrong question.* It might be here any second. It might never come. We need to find Gordy. Do you know where he is?"

"Even better. I know his motivations." The man rummages in a bureau drawer, procures from a travel-battered rucksack a large brown envelope, unopened, as

527

well as a device and a set of earbuds. "Now that we've got a bit of time to ourselves, I've got something you really ought to

x x x

know better than that. Page to page to page to page, curiosity curdling to fear, fear fulminating to dread, Bailey flips forward… Yes, just now, as she'd been reading, the Ex-Position pages had shimmered, flexed, *changed*. Most of it was… yes, mostly the same, but now it's got more at the end… but this ending…

The crowd fell into a deadly hush. The two lay together on the ground, one atop the other, broken past repair. Ah, Jane, the thing that had been Morris thought. My only confidant, my constant betrayer. It's good of you to be with me at the end. You've given me this at least. You've let me catch sight of my last intention. As Morris watched he saw the wave lurch forward to take all—everything. It's right over his shoulder, the wave, sardine-sized no more; it's the size now of a gorilla charging. Soon it will be the size of a train, of a mountain, of a planet. Soon it will extinguish sun and stars. Soon it will be the size of the everything, and then there will be the nothing, and, in the nothing, only a oneness. Only Morris could see it but he knew soon everybody would see, and all the nations of the world will mourn as they see it forever—but forever will be no more than the flit of a pigeon's wings, for this wave is large enough to destroy even time itself. . .

Hang on, Jane begged. Her final breaths, she spent on him. Don't. Hold it back.

It's too late, Janey, Morris said. He felt so calm and so free. Aware Jane couldn't understand the sounds his empty mouth made; they weren't even words. He said them anyway, and looking into those beautiful almond eyes as the light went out of them forever, he thought: She did understand. It's the last thing she ever did. She knew. I've called it already. It's done. It's done it's done it's done.

THE END

Done? Bailey thinks, closing the binder. Done already? Done forever?

"The hell it is," she mutters to herself, getting out of bed. "Nothing's done."

✗✗✗

As soon as you do it to Morris, you return quickly to the door, fearing the oncoming wave. In moments, you find yourself back in the study on the author's side. Lying on the table, thicker than ever before, the expected stack of pages. Come, wave, come, you think, almost beg, nearly pray.

Then, reading: This ending… it's *perfect*.

He calls it. It comes.

No safe dropping.

No Gordy giving Morris any ticket.

You want to weep with joy and relief. Showing yourself to Morris worked—and you'd been so frightened to do so. Still, you waited until the moment was right to get this ending. It's perfect.

But… wait… no. This is the game of the blank. The ending's perfect but the story's still there. *There's still a story*.

Why isn't the story gone?

✗✗✗

"Gordy, wake up. Wake *up*." Gordy's gone, out cold, lost in platinum unconsciousness; he requires a rougher jostle. "We have to go right now. We have to get to Pigeon Forge."

"Blmmmph?" Gordy inquires.

"Boyd's story just changed. Something's terrible is going to happen. Jane needs us, soon."

Gordy, still pushing sleep from his mind: "Did she… call to tell you that or something?"

But Bailey is already up and packing.

It may seem brave to abrogate this notion, to face squarely the inevitable realization: There is no pattern to be found in the universe, no sense, no meaning, only dust. Yet if we are braver still, we may come through this realization to a further realization. Of course there is meaning, of course there is pattern, of course there is sense. We created it ourselves: first by imagining it, and then by naming it. And, in naming, causing others to imagine it, too.

—Unknown

Nettles finds that once you've accepted your old friend has somehow become your talking sandals, accepting their pronouncements is a less complicated matter. She finds herself in possession of a great and sudden belief, and a terrible dread. "But if... if *everything's* going to end, Jules... shouldn't we go there, too?"

The sandals keep quiet so long she thinks they may have embraced sandal-ness and given up talking completely. Just when she's stopped listening for an answer, they speak. *Whether it ends or not is their business,* they say. *Our business is what happens after. We have*

xxx

a knife, but he hasn't used it yet. Here, in the straw in the main-tent freak show in the Circus of Bearded Love, chained to a stake near Wembly's gorilla cage, sits the greatest freak the world has ever known. Most freaks are born to it, but not this one—he's a recruit, a novice, a greenhorn. Even so, he's a main attraction. There'll be a hush when he's displayed, a great intake of breath, an understanding that in this freak, a culmination has been attained. Here at last is the Ur-freak, a freak who keeps enfreakening.

He calls himself Goop-Goop. He doesn't know what else to call himself. It's what the hateful sign above him says. The sign is wooden, and hand-painted, and hung too high to reach, to tear down and smash to bits. It reads: THIS IS GOOP-GOOP OF PIGEON FORGE, FREAK OF THE FREAKS. Below this, a hasty scrawl: *Beware! Danger! Keep Your Distance!* A desultory ring of paint around Goop-Goop's stake demarcates the zone of peril, Goop-Goop's range of motion. It's a wiser precaution than they know, Goop-Goop thinks; they're unaware of his knife. Colonel Karl T. Krane, author of this message, visits regularly, overweeningly proud of this new addition to his freak show. "They're going to go nuts for you, my lad," Krane propounded this morning with false avuncularity, smacking Goop-Goop on one cheek, his preposterous moustache taking the liberty, it seemed, of twirling itself, his patois slipping momentarily into his carny-barker shuck and jive: "THEY will be AB-so-LUTE-ly AWE. STRUCK. for you." Goop-Goop muses upon Krane, who has betrayed him, as did all others. He thought of using the knife on Krane, but Krane isn't anything more than a messenger, a barker. He'll save the knife for the Coyote. Fat old Krane breaks away from his barking at the tent entrance every ten minutes or so to peep over, his expressive face full of naked hope for the moment of revelation—What is the next modification going to be? The Coyote's come every day, just as he promised. He hasn't arrived yet.

Occasionally, Goop-Goop sneaks a glance over his shoulder. The wave is still there, a comfort to him. The proof he's always had; this at least cannot be taken away. But everything else is gone, gone. He lists the things the Coyote has

x x x

taken Finch and Sterling away from Jane. The Andrews have promised both will be processed in the Assizement. Already they've been sent to the cages. It seems to Jane natural it would be the Andrews, truest of believers, to fill the void of leadership Morris has left behind, naturally they'll continue the traditions for which they have such zeal. They haven't stopped believing in Morris's vision, they've only stopped believing in Morris specifically. Now they have a new god, one who floats down from the sky and daily proves his worthiness by seizing their old god and unmaking him. The Andrews have taken to looking skyward for him. It's on the Coyote's behalf they will continue the old ways, bird and spade, fountain and cavern. Besides, there's no stopping this ceremony; the tickets were delivered already, days ago, to every Pigeon Forge resident. Blue if you've been chosen for the Assizement, green if you're invited to the show, a distraction as those left behind are collected: carnival and circus, freaks and fun, the flight of the acrobats, the caper of the clowns, the roar of the lion, the dance of the bearded lady.

But today there will be no dance, the crowd will leave disappointed. Jane has neglected to tell Krane, or the Andrews, or anyone else. It's her decision; one they won't like, but by the time they know, it will be too late to correct. There's no time to dance, not with Gordy's confession to listen to. The confession was Sterling's first gift. His second gift was a promise of hope, the only hope remaining.

It feels like a year ago. It hasn't even been a day.

"We need Gordy. And we need him immediately. Gordy's been given a command he needs to fulfill. Gordy's the only chance."

Sterling's eyes widened. "The ticket's gone," he whispered. "Julius turned it to water. It's gone."

She shakes her head. "The ticket's beside the point. The ticket only matters because your idiot son thinks it matters. Gordy can be miracle enough. But he has to get here soon."

"Gordy *is* coming!" Sterling had yelped, with almost comic relief. "In fact, Gordy's on his way here as fast as he can get." This had been Sterling's gift of hope, though Jane had to admit he'd tarnished the gift significantly by the next thing he said, which was this: "My sandals told me so."

She'd wanted to ask him more, but that's when the Andrews had burst into the caretaker's apartment and captured them. "I'll keep her safe," Sterling shouted as he and Finch were bustled away—another promise of hope, though an empty one. Nor would there be any safety, not if Gordy didn't arrive. Braiding her beard for the trapeze, Jane filled her ears with Gordy's voice and waited for him to come. It has to be soon, she thought. It has to be soon. If it's not soon, it won't matter.

Jane listened, then rewound and listened again. How typical. Naturally, Gordy had seen everything behind the door. Just as naturally—for Gordy at least—seeing had not brought understanding. Gordy had been

x x x

stolen from him. First, the eyelids, replaced by a chitinous substance resembling fingernails; forcing him into a terrible, careful, never-ending awareness of his blinks. It's easier to simply keep the lids closed, opening them only at need.

Then, a week later—last week—Goop-Goop lost his feet. Legs neatly replaced from the knees down, the shins tapering grotesquely into prehensile pink boneless worm-squid nubbins.

Next the Coyote played his terrible trick. He'd vowed to come once a week, but he'd lied. After the legs, he returned the very next day, duded up as a caped superhero, his diamond of power set in his forehead, and changed Goop-Goop's tongue. It belongs to some rougher beast, this tongue. The only order it can give is *Goop*. Along with the tongue, he lost his authority. The Coyote made his modifications in the bright of day, right where all

Goop-Goop's followers could see, then set him down once more on the grass. Goop-Goop had crawled for his crutches, but the Andrews moved faster, knocking his props away, pinning him with prods as he rolled legless and mewled wordless on the turf, making for the first time the hated *goooop* noise—guttural, epiglottal, the baboon of rage within him finally given full throat. Meanwhile his lieutenants fought each other for dominance, and the Andrews prevailed.

The next day, the Coyote took Goop-Goop's name.

He wishes he could remember it—his own name. No other memories have yet been stripped from him, but his name is...is...no. It's empty there. He remembers the moment it went, but he can't remember what it was, only that it's now gone. He lost his teeth next. They still work somewhat; the sand is dense and hard, making a shred of the unfortunate tissue of the inner lip. Then the hair, turned to a horrendous tin filament you can *feel* extrude from the scalp with the excruciating slowness of hair's growth. Losing his name is more maddening than any of the physical disfigurements. To search within your mind and not find it. To be compelled, for lack of a suitable alternative, to take the name bequeathed by the lout Krane.

Goop-Goop grinds his teeth, bringing a fine dusting of sand to his tiny, inarticulate, salamander tongue, and he stops, mindful; he can't allow his teeth to disintegrate, he needs to parcel out their use now, just as he needs to ration his blinks to spare his eyes as long as possible. This is the cruelty and the genius of the Coyote: He doesn't take away, he transmutes. If you simply remove something, then it is gone and you can begin to learn to live with the lack, but if you replace something correct with something unsuitable, a torturous maintenance and constant consideration of your predicament becomes necessary. So it is with the name: Goop-Goop's learned you can't not name yourself, there must be some signifier, some placeholder. But worse than the maddening itch of the misplaced name is the terrible notion that a piece of one's internal furniture might be removed. The time may come, Goop-Goop knows, when he will remember only that he once occupied a better state and a more commodious form, but not what that state or form might have been. Even the idea of Continuity will someday be stripped away. Why, might he even take away the—a quick glance over his shoulder—no;

it's still there—the wave.

The stake that holds him is a thick wooden tent peg, a four-footer used for the big top, driven deep into the ground and affixed to a heavy buried concrete slab. A series of chains are merged by welds to a heavier chain, which is wrapped around the stake, and the smaller chains are themselves welded to the iron collar and shackles around his neck and wrists. Carefully, Goop-Goop closes his eyes—Yes, these are your dividends. You've got nothing else, except for

xxx

the flight in. If you want an indicator of what sort of a froth Bailey's been in since reading the end of Boyd's book, Gordy thinks, look no further. For the sake of speed, she was willing to buy an airline ticket, which means she was willing to appear on the grid—and Boyd's book has taught her things about Donk's new powers and cruelties that have made subtle living less a preference and more an obsession. It was the late flight into Nashville, then a rental to another motel in Knoxville for a rest ahead of the circus, both of them judging it wisest to roost at a reasonable remove from Pigeon Forge proper.

The wave is coming, according to the book. Morris is being tortured past endurance—Donk's been up to this horrific work. Gordy doesn't see the trouble with that. "That wave is *exactly* what I've been waiting for," he'd sputtered, "and now you want us to go and be there when it...?" But no, Gordy, stop it, you've followed this line of reasoning, and it only leads to another squabble. If we're going to do the unimaginably stupid thing, it's better to do it quickly and silently, and then be gone.

And, it must be admitted, the book also has it set down that Jane will die; a fate Gordy would gladly risk himself to prevent. It must be further admitted, the book has proved... unnervingly predictive, enough so that basing your actions on its prognostications no longer seems entirely insane.

The idea is to sneak to see Jane, and get her clear. It makes sense to find her in any case; she's the only person who might not attack them. Also, Gordy does have to admit that Jane, with her insider's knowledge of Pigeon Forge's subterranean politics, is likely to be authoritative regarding the question of whether Morris really is being replaced piecemeal by a hyper-powered Donk, and what to make of that. And Jane will be in town, if the circus schedule's still accurate. Gordy knows exactly

how to find her, as long as Morris is still using the circus as cover for his fountain she-
nanigans. Crumb's 'Mazing is still open; it stands to reason the maze will still contain
the secret entrance, and Gordy can still remember the trick.

"There's a gross coffee machine in the gross lobby." Bailey emerges from the
bathroom dressed in her customary black. She's ripping a flimsy motel towel into
strips. "Want some gross coffee?"

Gordy smiles. "I'll live without."

Bailey's got a heavy-duty flashlight she intends to use as a baton, her preferred
weapon. Now she works the strips of towel into a makeshift holster. "Think we'll find
our way in?" she asks, absently.

"One way or another," Gordy answers, truthfully. No doubt if they can't sneak
in, they'll be captured and brought in.

Bailey takes the meaning. "Stay behind," she says. "Tell me how I can get in; I
can take it from there. You're not wrong; it's dangerous. But it's more dangerous
for you."

Gordy looks at her, and feels a rush of emotion; here's someone whose instinct
is always to run toward the danger, never away from. Not because she loves danger, but because she refuses to dismiss the way it reaches for others. He shrugs,
says: "We've come this far already. Let's go put our minds at ease if we can."

And that's it, in the end, isn't it, Gordy realizes, as Bailey leaves for the coffee.
That's the whole mission: putting a single lovely mind at ease. It's insane, but it's
enough. Gordy can find peace in it, if not logic—and anyway, there's not much logic in anything, is there? What do you expect from the world? Salvation? Justice?
Sanity? This course may doom us, but the risk is our own. If it leads to a world ruled
by Morris, so be it; those are global concerns. I'm finished shouldering the burden
of a world that allows someone like Morris to rise. Worse, a world that insists on the
success of its Morrises. He and this world are hand and glove, so perfectly matched,
it's difficult to know if it created him or he created it. He works the way the world
does: Give the useful enough slack in their reins to let them imagine they run free,
take the useless and make a use of them, herd them together and make money from
the consumption of their bodies, profit from their poon, lucre from their labor, or
(if they are especially incompatible) interest from their incarceration. If you're killed,
then the world will end—for you at least. Let such a world end. Or, let Morris rise to
take control of it, so we may at least be honest about how we are dominated. For

those of us on the margins, there won't be much difference either way. Meanwhile, if there's a scrap of comfort to be found, let's make a try for it. If there's a chance for a modicum of hope, pursue it. Where can you find even the hint of sanity or clarity in a world like this, hold it. Wrestle what you can away from the world, dodge and scrape and pull a scrap to sustain you from between those eternally grinding teeth that exist only to consume, for whom you are nothing more than a catholic particle of the fuel allowing them to continue their grind. Here is a hint, a scrap, a chance: to settle Bailey's mind about this apparently existential danger rising up in Pigeon Forge, and maybe find her never-was brother. It's not logical, but Julius is (if Boyd is to be believed) many pairs of sandals, and you were only partially visible for years, and somewhere nearby hundreds or thousands linger in mirrored boxes, screaming their lives away at their own images, so screw logic or sanity or justice or certainly salvation—none of that foofaraw for you. Here is love, Gordy-Gord, riding alongside, somehow discovered, unlooked-for, invested in you without any wheedling or clinging or wishing. It might be love for the first time, friend, and you don't just stroll past love. Nor does love stroll by every day. Nor, perhaps, does it always last. Perhaps sometimes love is nothing but a momentary ray of sun, the most precious gold there is. How foolish not to bask in it, while it shines.

"Gordy...?" It's Bailey, in the doorway, holding a cup of coffee and wearing a trepidatious expression. "Look at this." She brings a large brown envelope into view.

"What is it?"

"Mail. For you. Somehow somebody's found us."

She tosses it to Gordy. The return address is a familiar one—the Neon. Sister Nettles.

"What is it?"

Bailey gives him the fish eyes until Gordy realizes there's really only one way to get the answer; he opens the envelope, extracts the sandals.

Sandals. Gordy whispers it: "Are these...?"

"What else could they be?" Bailey asks. "Or should I say 'who?'"

"What do I do?"

Bailey looks at him like he's the imbecile he supposes he is. "Well, Gordy," she says. "I think what you do is, you put them on your feet. And then maybe you'll get

xxx

the inexplicably restored loyalty of the bearded lady.

Jane's recent transformation is the one pleasant lesson Goop-Goop's mind has provided him throughout this ordeal: a restoration, at the precise moment all others have fallen away, of his greatest disciple from pure apostasy and opposition to accommodation and renewal of allegiance. She's arrived each day—she's here now—with cool water and a sponge. A comb, a razor. Some food. Drops for the eyes. Her expression inscrutable, but in these actions, he divines an impending return of his singularity—She understands that harm was never your intent. All these people, projections of your distracted mind; they harm themselves, they've spilled from your wire's plastic jacket like wayward filaments. When was the original sin, the breach of the casing? When did they escape your perfect Oneness? It must have been some time in the deep past, before Isaac, even before memory. All you've ever done has been to tease them all back into their original configurations and seal the breach. It was your great work, as the world's only consciousness, to trace each of them to their source, to reconnect the links, to restore the connections. No wonder, thinks Goop-Goop, your entrepreneurial mind gravitated toward prisons: some way of holding people and keeping them properly ordered, so perfect unity might be reached—What, then, is the lesson of this present suffering? Is this the end of your being, or some other beginning? Jane has cast her lot with you. Is it possible she represents the part of yourself that holds the deeper consciousness? She may have an understanding of you greater than your own. This seems to be one of only two possible conclusions. The other is that both you and she have gone mad—a distinct possibility. "Hold the wave," she says. "Please. Don't call it."

The water from the sponge is blessedly cool. But wait, she's gone—When did she go? His eyes were shut; he hadn't noticed.

Goop-Goop realizes—Jane isn't insane, she's a prophet. She even has a prophet's beard. More has been revealed to her than to any other. She knows about the wave. He's never told any other about the wave—the great certifier of his position—of this he is sure. But she knows. It's always there, in the periphery of his vision, over his shoulder, kissing his awareness. Never in his recollection has it been absent. Through his life he's tried not to think of it if he can help it; accessible to him at any moment, the ability to call it and end the entire struggle, wash it all away until nothing is left but a great blankness and himself—unless it were only the blankness left; unless he would be the blankness, or the blankness would be him. It's there for him, the relief of a criminal about to surrender, the haven of the fox who lies down at last to await the baying hounds. He could call it now, a trillion trillion tons of cresting water, and end this. Bring an end to this pain in a great cleansing deluge. Each day, as another thing is taken from him, he contemplates it. If he's honest, he's been thinking of it more than he likes. Lately it calls to him powerfully, and, more frequently, he returns the call.

Goop-Goop spares himself a peek around the tent before shielding his vision once more beneath the jaundiced translucence of fingernail lids. He allows the world to become a thing captured in glimpses.

He can hear telling sounds of early arrivals to the circus. It's all these others, thinks Goop-Goop—all *their* fault. Why can't they see that any power—all power—must be given to you? Why won't any of them understand it? This pain all stems from their universal stubbornness. But look here—their stubbornness is your stubbornness, for they all came from your mind. This realization is good; it simplifies. No need to waste any time on mercy even for yourself. This, then, is your lesson: to reach your apotheosis, it has become necessary to divest yourself of those things that are not truly you. Even your name. Even that. Strip away all illusion until only the essential character remains. Nothing but undistilled self. The Coyote is the tool for this perfection, and your punishment for the stubbornness of your consciousness, as well— yes, punishment. Even you have failed to entirely become yourself.

For a moment, Goop-Goop entertains the notion that Continuity, having been offered no fit offspring from him into which to house itself, has passed from him and moved to another…but who? A vengeful hypersteroidal sky-god in cape and spandex? A pair of midgets? It's an atrocity either way. An aberration. A mockery. Why even consider it? Since the onset of his torments, so many strange and false notions have been pressing their noses against his window. It's maddening—Continuity passed down to the Andrews? To Donk? No. Whatever lesson this is, it isn't that. It's a hard lesson you've given yourself, but the difficulty prefigures great significance, so you must resolve to learn it well. A test of your own faith in yourself. No. This, too, is nonsense. Or perhaps it isn't? It's all become so unbearably muddled. Goop-Goop throws back his head and brays a single howling

GooooooooooooooooooooooooooooooOOOOO$_p$

Half a minute it stretches, gaining in volume as it moves from sorrow to rage. The gorilla Wembly doesn't even attempt an echo of it, but merely looks up from his solitaire game and blinks. Goop-Goop allows himself another glimpse at the fairgoers who've wandered over to the freak show, meandering among the mutants, walking with the confident posture of the overlooked elect, the passed-over chosen people, the unmarked elite. Do they know of the others, even now being corralled into cages behind the big top curtain? Yes, they do. On some level, they know it. And I know they know it—why else would I have arranged matters this way? The perfection of it. The unlucky chosen paying the price for inherent inadequacies or purposeful rebellions. The well-pleased compliant masses, distracted by nonsense. Oh, they know what's behind the curtain. Never once has a Pigeon Forge circus commenced without friends and neighbors, husbands and wives, parents and children divided, some on one side and some on the other; never once has Krane announced the clowns and the lion tamer, tumblers or bumblers or jugglers or elephants, without each of them fitting themselves for a suit of well-tailored ignorance. If the curtain weren't there to hide the view, they would raise one. What, after all, is more important than the comfort? And what is more comfortable than ignorance?

Another glimpse; the crowd has swelled. Across the room—at a far remove from Wembly to avoid the natural bigotry of apes toward little men— Andrew and Andrew, the Fighting Midgets (not too proud to take their usual part in the freak show, even now that they run the show) enact their choreographed combat. There's also a sizable crowd now around Goop-Goop himself, but despite his novelty and the extremity of his deformations—or as a result of them—a distance is kept. The gawkers and looky-loos debate whether the chains are indeed necessary for their safety or are merely an effective bit of showmanship, but none of them ever come within grappling range to test the proposition. Jane's dance begins in ten minutes, and, as this is announced over the loudspeakers, Goop-Goop sees many of the crowd peel away from the other freaks, hopeful for a seat.

Another glimpse; Goop-Goop sees that only one of his onlookers remains— an unnaturally vivid man in a powder-blue suit, his face wreathed in

x x x

smoke and waited for the creature Goop-Goop to become aware of him. Landrude didn't mind; he appreciated having time to acclimate himself to this side of the door. It was best to be slow and deliberate. What he couldn't do was stabilize how the ape looked. Blink. Six hundred pounds of bruising muscle. Blink. Four hundred pounds of sad wastrel mangy depredation. Playing solitaire, as was his wont, but now the cards have disappeared; somebody's forgotten that's what Wembly does—how does one forget that? It's his whole act. It made Landrude mad—Are you readers not paying any attention at all, or are you just ignorant of gorilla physiology? Haven't you ever been to a zoo? I wrote it all for you. Four paragraphs describing the ape: the shape, the size. Why won't they see it that way?

Morris, meanwhile, was a mess, interpretation or no. Donk had proved most creative. Landrude watched, confounded by the arrival of Jane Sim, who ministered to his pustules, moistened his eyeballs, spoke gentle and soothing words—another sign of how disgraced this world had become, how in need of eradication. There's no reason for mercy from Jane Sim, it wasn't even in character for her, it made no sense. Think of what he's done to you, Juanita. There's no call to show any kindness whatsoever, it's barbaric, it's objectionable... Finally, when she had gone, Landrude emerged and slowly made his surroundings aware of him. Presently the creature noticed him and froze, startled. Landrude spoke:

You look terrible.

GoooooooooooooOOOOOOP!

You don't look "just like me," anymore. Not at all.

GOOP! Goop! GOOP! Goop!

Landrude murmured: This won't do. I'm going to give you yourself back. Remember what you once were. Remember it all.

Goop-Goop shimmered, warped, changed. In his place, chained to the stake, a man on the taller side, a man in middle life with a full head of upswept salted hair, rangy features tamed somewhat by a well-scrubbed look and a recently developing belly; portrait of the once-starving artist in the comfortable repose of satisfactory success, wearing a filthy suit whose color might once have been powder blue.

The smoking man who had once been something other than Landrude moved closer; I want to see it happen, he thought. I want to see him understand. Do you see? he whispered to the chained figure. Do you see that you are the fallen strain, and I am the ascended? Never call me usurper. Never suggest I stole yourself from you. Your only remaining power is the eraser, but after you've used it, I will create.

Now do you see?

Imagine you could speed time to view the passage of millennia in a matter of minutes, so you could see the slow degrees by which a river claims a mountain: carving it, taking it by bits and then, in an instant of release, taking it all. It was like this with the prisoner's face, which fell by pieces into despair and then abruptly crashed, as he experienced for the first time the horrors inflicted upon him, stolen from his world and inserted unnaturally within another, the blasphemy of squid feet and sand teeth and painful screw hair, of what was yet to be visited, of his long abandonment, and—worse—of how cruel he had been made to become, what he in false persona had inflicted upon his own creations. . . He howled, then wailed. Author once again, he fell boneless like meat to the ground and shuddered, each memory now reinterpreted away from him into something false. It's done now, Landrude thought. He's finally understood.

Why, the chained author moans, why, why did you, why—as if he didn't know. Even in his utter defeat, even now, still he clings to his folly, his false ignorance of any crime? It fills Landrude with the old fury he'd had, back when he was Morris. You made me a minor character, Landrude screamed. You wrote me as a villain. Nothing of my motives. You never let them see me. And then you dropped a fucking safe on my head.

Coming back in close, Landrude said: Now I'm going to put you back the way you were. First your body. Then, memories. You'll be Morris again, my friend. You'll be Morris. Do you see? You won't remember my visit. But the despair I'll let you'll keep. The knowledge of how wrong you are, how utterly beaten—that is your keepsake forever and ever, until the day you decide to end all this. Until that day.

As soon as he'd done it, Landrude returned quickly to the door, fearing the oncoming wave. In moments, he found himself in the study. Lying on the table, thicker than ever before, was the expected stack of pages. Come, wave, come, he thought, almost begged, nearly prayed. Then, reading—This ending. . . it's perfect. But wait. . . no. . . there's still a story. Why isn't the story gone? Landrude wanted to

x x x

rest his haggard head for a moment, and Goop-Goop's mind wanders out of conscious thought. Then it comes, from nowhere, unlike anything ever before experienced: a dark plunge into icy soul blackness. Unexpected, un-called-for, a despair darker than any he has ever known comes washing over him; there is no end to the pit, no end to the falling. There is no questioning, only a certainty—You've failed. You must see that. No door opens for you, no ticket comes to you, always you are passed over, always you are thwarted. The lesson you're teaching yourself is this: You are nothing. There is some other from whom reality springs. You aren't the center. You're not even a point on the map. You thought yourself the fulcrum, but you're not even a figment. You are beyond zero, un-nothing, failure's failure, ah *God!*—

He almost calls it then. It's still there, but he can't take comfort in it— The wave isn't a sign of your power. All it represents is your ability to end your sad struggle in the damp fizzle of a dud squib. It's not the failsafe; it's the only move remaining. He almost calls it. He's about to do it, but then, in the crowd, he sees. . . Gordy. *Gordy?*

Yes, there he is, Goop-Goop tells himself—Gordy beyond doubt, despite impossibility. You've spent too much time studying that face to mistake it for any other—it is him: the man you pursued around the worlds. Gordy, the Flickering Man flickering no more; Gordy, back from the dead; Gordy on a mission, accompanied by a pretty cat who seems vaguely familiar. She carries herself with a certain slow ease and perfect control; only her eyes are quick. Gordy, less quick, more foolish, though, isn't reading any warning signs; he's charting a meandering course that looks likely to cross into the white circle of DANGER. Goop-Goop reaches into his hiding place and brings knife to hand—Gordy. I'll never kill you enough, boy. Come here.

The flippers that had been his feet are bad for balance but they are powerful, and the suckers on the underside provide sufficient traction even in the straw. Goop-Goop lunges, but the pretty cat has seen, reached out with both paws, grabbed his knife-hand on the downswing and pulled, leaping with the force of her own action and then landing with full weight on his back. She never releases the arm, either—it's pulled behind him in untenable repose. The knife skitters under the straw and Goop-Goop howls in a turbulence of frustrated vengeance and torsion of aggrieved tendons, and GOOP-GOOP GOOOP GOOP GOOOOOOP goes his rage and GOOOP goes his impotence and GOOOOOOOP goes his pain and frustration and sorrow. The whole crowd turns toward the chaos.

"I've still got it," she says, with a certain pride of ownership. Goop-Goop can hear them perfectly well; the tent is hushed, stunned by this display.

"We're drawing a crowd," Gordy says, nervously. It's true. Goop-Goop rages; though his mind is now cold and precise, he cannot stop his horrid fishwife of a tongue from releasing a stentorian metronomic *goop*ing. Confused, Wembly quakes; he's attuned to the brume of animal rage filling the tent, susceptible to it, and his handlers hastily drape his cage with a decorative tarpaulin in hopes of staving off the ape's empathy-wrath. Cage or no, gorilla strength mixed with gorilla rage is frightening, like malign industrial machinery knocked off its tracks.

Quickly, efficiently, the pretty cat releases him and steps clear, and the two retreat to Jane's tent. The crowd returns to other distractions, makes their way circusward, climbing to their seats in the swaying bleachers. All the freaks return to their acts—no, not quite *all*. The fighting Andrews, all the way across the tent, safely clear of the midget-hating rage of Wembly... they're making their way over. Have they recognized Gordy? It's possible; Andrew and Andrew have ever been among the most observant...yes, here they come. They sneak to Jane's tent and stand by the portal, one at each side, waiting for Gordy and his bodyguard to emerge. They can afford to wait; the tent backs up against the big scrim of the big top; the portal by which they stand is the only way in or out of the sub-tent holding Jane's act.

Goop-Goop pulls himself from the straw, enraged, runs the chains again, and again they pass the test he sets to them—pulling him back, making him *goop* idiotically at the tent roof, which in turn compels Wembly to answer with confused chuffs from beneath his tarpaulin. The Andrews turn and favor Goop-Goop with a scornful glower, which he returns—*Gordy's mine, you bastards*. They move farther in, toward Jane's inner sanctum, passing out of Goop-Goop's sight, then one of them re-emerges and runs off, no doubt for reinforcements. Goop-Goop can see the knife, but it's well out of reach. The stake has a three-inch diameter, buried four feet into a plug of concrete. A fine dust coats the inside of his poor shredded mouth. His teeth are made of compacted composite grit plugged into soft pink gums like a set of rotary bits, extraordinarily abrasive and mercilessly hard. If used, they will slowly disappear...but they can be used.

Goop-Goop lies recumbent beside the stake, inspecting it closely. How interesting, this stake. How interesting. There's a fine dusting on his tongue. He spits, and moves closer, closer, discovering...Yes! Just barely!...he can fit his mouth around its girth. Goop-Goop goes to work, his teeth lessening. Dust fills his mouth, making him pause at intervals to spit. The same thoughts, but pitched at a new frequency, once placid, now frantic, once proclaimed in assurance of fulfillment, now howled in desperation for survival—Yes. You are the Continuity of all. All of it. The Everything. There is pain and the pain is your teacher—but not all teachers are good. Soon you will take your power back, and your name, too. You will restore all things. And—glancing over shoulder—if you fail this time, you will end all things. A singularity either way.

Goop-Goop's teeth quickly recede as he works, but the stake also is attenuating. Which one, he wonders, tooth or stake, will come first to an end?

There comes a point in one's life when one senses—all at once—the profound instability of everything once believed stable and secure, a moment when one understands how the universe's architecture sways and creaks, ever on the verge of collapse. In this moment, one becomes dangerous and unpredictable. Imagine, then, the advent of that unlikely yet inevitable alignment, when every living person shares this epiphany simultaneously.

—Unknown

hand on her shoulder. The old guy, the new caretaker, come from the open stairway to meet her. "If you want to get behind that door," he whispered, "I don't think you'll get a better chance."

Jane ran for the stairs. What

xxx

I'd advise you, is avoid trusting overmuch to patterns, Julius tells Sister Nettles. You've chosen a brave and a fine course but a difficult one. The longer you remain, the more you'll discover that every pattern breaks down or repeats. Eventually, every expected form will confound

xxx

you should know: A dance is nothing like a leap. When you leap, every movement must be in service to the plan. The clowns throw the bars with precision, but they need to know where you'll be. Even the seeming mistakes must be practiced for weeks and woven into the fabric of the whole. During a leap, Jane's mind needs to become rigid and exacting, her thought must become a single thing, a gear engineered to fit without margin of error into the teeth of another. But in a dance, she waits for the music—whatever the music might be each night—and then moves within the surprise and the sinew of it, her body becoming the trance and flow of the sitar, or perhaps the crystalline percussive insistence of electronica, or else the athletic leaps of jazz trumpet, or the recursive adagios of Spanish guitar, or any of a dozen, a hundred, a thousand other possible forms. Her mind can become many rather than one, it can become the moment, the epiphany, the water that finds its path. Rather than becoming rigid, she melts. The dance is not a leap, because no catch will ever be needed. There is a shimmer in the air, as of heat, but there is no heat. There is only perfection.

But tonight, Jane refuses the dance. On the other side, sensed by her but unseen, the audience begins to gather. Ears full of Gordy's confession, she returns to the

xxx

stairs. What it was like to run for the stairs, trusting to the distraction of the guards, was this: a leap without a plan for a catch. The caretaker was correct, Jane saw; this was indeed their awaited moment. Normally the stairs would be guarded by two trustees, but they had abandoned their posts, distracted like the rest by the horrified sounds coming from directly above them.

The steps were made of the same material as the rondure of black stone encircling the fountain, and cunningly concealed. Jane was upon them nearly before she spied them, sharply checked her speed to avoid a stumble, and then she was descending, down in the dark, safe and unnoticed, her leap finding the catch yet again, but now on its heels another leap, please god, please let the door open, please let me find the

x x x

manuscript she received from Gordy's bodyguard Bailey, the one whose dedication assured her the door would open for her. Mae stays quiet; helps her braid her beard. She takes the left side while Jane takes the right. Mae is a skillful braider. Each night Jane secretly races her to finish her side of the beard first, and each night she loses. Tonight, the race isn't even close; Jane's distracted by the mutter of Gordy's confession, by Boyd's book, by her anticipation of Gordy's prophesied arrival. Jane laughs. Of *course* Gordy's coming—after all, a lunatic's sandals said so.

He'd better arrive soon if he's going to arrive, Jane thinks. There's precious little time left. His recorded voice is in her ears, and she thinks—You knew, you son of a bitch. Back in the cavern while you were running things, you knew. You weren't lying about the wave being real but you were lying about what it was—to me and to yourself. Think how much trouble I'd have saved if you hadn't made me pity you. Think how much trouble we'd save now if I'd called the guards to have you killed. Then we'd be completely doomed and I wouldn't have to waste time worrying.

Jane braids the beard and listens to Gordy's voice and reads in the manuscript the report of her own doom. Sterling says Gordy will be here soon. Everything depends on him coming, but she can think of no reason to hope she'll

x x x

find the door open please let it open for me and then she was past the stairs and there it was; the simple door affixed in the clay, looking less like a relic and more like the sort of standardized mass-production item you'd buy at the nearest home improvement center. Here Morris spent long hours in ancestral echo, holding vigil, trying to unlock it with his mind, or to make it vanish, or to transport himself to the other side. Here Gordy had stood, hand on knob, turned, opened, entered, discovered. Jane could see the doorknob. She reached for it, time

s t r e t c h i n g

out in taffy of adrenaline, rubbery fear and elastic hope, anticipation of capture, expectation of discovery—then snapping back, jumping her forward from eternity to instant. She would never reach the door; she had reached it already. There was nobody to stop her. Hand met knob, knob gave way to query of rotation. Latch clicked, hinge creaked.

She entered, and then

x x x

Jane finds herself in a strange place. It would perhaps be more accurate to say: 'Janes find herselves in strange places.' If this paradox troubles you, take comfort in knowing that Jane was similarly troubled.

Perhaps it will help if I describe what Jane saw.

x x x

and then Jane saw the endless beach, and the infinity of its ocean gathered up into a crushing tidal wrath, suspended against the field of stars—unless it was so monstrously large that it encompassed the stars, submerging them.

And she saw the study, and the desperate struggle of the two men who occupied it.

And she saw the small room at the end of a short hall, and, in it, someone familiar.

And the voice said:

x x x

be successful. Everything's gone upside-down after the door. One of the secret cruelties of life is its tendency to deliver your desire to you only once it has devised the means by which it might withhold your enjoyment of receipt. The Coyote's torturous transformations of Morris came daily, with each change compounding Morris's just and delicious misery—that is how she saw it at first. But this had been before she'd been past the door and learned deeper and crueler truths. Jane yearns for the simplicity of the earlier perspective, but she doesn't have Gordy's knack for self-deception; there can be no return for her to the Eden of her previous ignorance. She knows too well how each of the Coyote's modifications pushes matters excruciatingly closer to the

x x x

voice, who says:

—Watch them well.

Jane watches the identical men in their struggle. Watches the one overcome the other. Watches what the victor does after. What he does to the woman named Juanita Neato, and to the round man named Paddington, and to others.

—Do you see?

"Yes."

—And now the boy.

She watches the boy stand and struggle and split into multiple copies of himself, each holding the slim green scrap of paper. Watches one copy go, watches one stay.

—And now the wave.

Jane gazes at the wave. The blasphemy of its size.

"Gordy made it."

—Yes, from him and of him; but also from those who contend: the author and his usurper. Tell Gordy it will soon come, if he does not do that which has been laid upon him. When it comes, all he calls his own will be destroyed with him.

"That's what we've been hoping for," Jane said, weeping: unfair, unfair.

—The hope is a false one. You know the reason now. He must do that which has been laid upon him.

"Gordy can't obey you anymore," Jane said, despairing. "He doesn't have it. He gave it up, and now it's gone."

—Look again. Look at the one who stayed; who stands on the

XXX

brink. The Coyote provides Morris a torture more perfect than any she might have devised; the ruin of the body, combined with—far worse—the denial of his spirit's great conviction. He's spent his life believing all things spring from him; now, every day, the Coyote teaches him the lie of that belief. She sees the signs of Morris's resolve weakening, evidence of load-bearing pillars of his internal cosmology beginning to crumple—things he says, rawness in his voice, a desperation in his brutalized eyes she'd never seen before. She should be drunk on the pleasure of it, but instead of a glutton she is a tantalus, strung taut, reaching for succor but unable to grasp it. All she can think when she watches him is: *Will the next one be the one to finally collapse him? How much longer can he hold?* The Coyote doesn't understand what he's doing; it's desperately important to stop him, but she can't think of any way to reach him. He keeps no timetable, his arrivals have no forewarnings, his movements are faster than thought, his visits are brief and filled only with the incoherent ululations of his victim. And, even if a message could be delivered, would the Coyote stop? She thinks not; he's as blind to any possibility outside his own beliefs as is Morris. For the Coyote, as with Morris, the universe is a graspable thing, a realm of study he believes he's apprehended perfectly and entirely.

If the Coyote can't be stopped, all that remains—unless Gordy truly is on his way—is the desperate, useless task: Provide what comfort can be provided; plug the dam of Morris's suffering and try, from restricted vantage, to reach the other leaks that spring up daily. Sterling's offered his assistance, but in truth there are none better suited to the task than she, who has known Morris longest and best. Her servitude, more than any other, can be for him a bulwark against despair. He'll see it as a lesson to himself, encouraging him into subhuman acts of persistence and endurance. This is the cruelty of the universe, she thinks: to hope for revenge, and watch another enact it; to see the enactment, but be compelled to prevent it; to come to the man who took away what is yours, even your selfhood, who used you however he chose, who took from you your bird, who replaced a mother's constant flow of simultaneous goodbye and hello with an inescapable series of goodbyes.

This now is the man you must comfort. She had hoped there might be found behind the door some trick or tool or knowledge to further throw him into hazard, but the trick was on her. Behind the door she found, not a tool to sever him from her, but rather knowledge of a great and unforgivable inter-connectedness. Jane knows Gordy hasn't understood the full truth of it; that much is clear from the flawed understanding he delivers in his confession. How can anyone be so surprisingly right and yet so entirely wrong? Again, the terrible wickedness of the universe, that it can lend such great under-standing, and for that privilege enforce such a perversely high interest, this usurious empathy. How unfair, after hoping so many years for this man's bad end, to be made to look upon even him and feel for him such depths of pity. That she should look upon that hateful face and see in it her daughter's, and her own—even an hour ago, when she last visited him. "Shush, shush," she said, as the creature scrabbled at the ground with its approximation of feet and mewled. "Shush, shush. Shush shush." Slowly the creature soothed. Slowly the sponge moved from face to bucket, from bucket to face, the water darkening with filth removed. Pity, like suffering, like mercy, all draws from a common pool.

She's braided her beard for the trapeze with time to spare. Jane sits alone in the dim of a single candle and prepares herself. There's been some sort of disturbance outside, in addition to the occasional agonized "Goop" and the gorilla's miserable echolalia. It's drawing nearer; she can now hear some indistinct voices, and, louder, angrier, some shouting, including some impas-sioned screeching from the Morris-thing. It's been quiet for a minute now. He hears their approaching familiar voices. Gordy and Bailey.

So. Sterling was right. A second meeting, and then whatever happens next. We're all spinning down the neck of this funnel; everything narrows from here, attenuates and distills into singularity. In the final quiet moment before they come in, Jane, who has been beyond the door and returned, sits in this infinite handful of remaining seconds, hand upon the dog-eared man-uscript, and prepares herself for flight.

x x x

When they'd visited her in Raccoon River, she'd never looked at them: back turned, purposefully detached, purposefully remote, snatches of reflected eye contact, head wreathed by the halo of globular lights. Now she swings to face them as they enter, leaning forward, as if she expects something from them.

Gordy grins weakly at Jane, begins the speech he rehearsed on the way: "I suppose you're wondering why we're—"

Jane interrupts: "Shut up. We don't have much time. We may only have minutes. And—" premonitory finger to Gordy's already-opening mouth—"no questions. If you have a question that doesn't get answered by what I say, it means your question is stupid and the answer doesn't matter. You have to obey the command you were given. The Coyote is torturing Morris past despair. I assume you saw him out there."

"Saw...who?"

"So-called Morris. What's left of him. These days they call him 'Goop-Goop.'"

"That was *Morris?*"

"He's holding on by his fingertips, but the wave's coming. We don't have much time if we're going to *stop* it."

Gordy laughs. "I don't want to stop it. I've been waiting for it to come for years."

"I know you have, you idiot. That's why we're in this mess."

"You've got this all wrong." Gordy hopes he sounds patient, not pedantic: "The wave is going to destroy him. It'll bring an end to all this. We're just here to save you first."

"You've read Boyd's book," Bailey says gently. "You'''' you *die* at the end of it."

"The book only goes so far, and it can change. I've been on the other side of the door."

Gordy stupidly repeats: "The door?"

"It's not a place inside time. I saw what you saw. I heard what you heard."

"Then you know the choice I have is no choice at all." But then Gordy realizes. It's so clear what he's up against: a mother's love—Of *course.* You've been too calculating, he admonishes himself, thinking of it as a mercy—the wave flooding out the prisoners along with their jailors, killing them. A grim mercy to be sure, but an end at least to suffering—an unfortunate but unavoidable cost—but for Jane, it would be something else entirely. Her only daughter...of *course.* You haven't rehearsed for it, but you know your part. Here's a chance to do one fine thing before the end. A sacrifice, no doubt, but a worthy one. You ought to have known it; there was never a good end in this for you. It's better this way. Look at Jane, the poor thing, sick with worry. She's been carrying all this weight alone. Gordy smiles sadly at her. "Don't worry," he says. "Before it comes, I'll get Finch to safety." He rises and steps around Bailey, takes Jane's shoulder in what he hopes is a friendly and reassuring grip. "I promise you, I'm not leaving until we get Finch out of the oubliette first. I'll get her safe or die trying."

She looks up at him hatefully. "Oh, you unbelievable asshole... 'Safe?' There's no 'safe' if the wave comes."

"Hey—" he's pleased with himself, that he can still be magnanimous in the face of her understandable but misplaced anger. "It's all right. I understand."

She brandishes a listening device and earbuds. "I know everything you understand. I know how you think of it. But I was there when you got the ticket—I watched. You understand? I was there. I heard what the voice said to you. 'He and all he calls his own will be destroyed.' "Think of Morris. You know him. Listen to the actual words. It will destroy him, this wave. It will destroy him *and all he calls his own*."

"Oh," says Bailey, sinking to the ground. "Oh." Gordy gives her a quizzical look. She seems to have understood something—but what? Is it some sort of her concern for her missing Attic? Does this somehow make her mistrust the book's hope of a long-lost (or is it never-had) brother floating to the top of the narrative when all is finished? Or is it only that Bailey, who shoots every angle, realizes the devastation to Pigeon Forge, the tragedy, the death of the prisoners, population, tourists, all? Yes, it must be that. Bailey hasn't had as much time as you to consider this quandary, she can't know how fathomlessly impossible it all is to stop, she hasn't yet comprehended the immensity of the gears of this horrendous machine. Against this, a single Appalachian town is a tragic but needful sacrifice. He turns back to Jane.

"Look, if I could save all of Pigeon Forge, I would. If I could save all the prisoners, I would. I tried and failed. It's too big. But we might save Finch if we—"

Jane grabs him then, pulls him close, snarling: "Listen. To the words. All he calls his own. All he calls his own. All he calls his own."

"Oh," Gordy says, then: "Oh."

It's dawning on him: Not all I call his own, but all he calls his own. What did Landrude say, back at the doughnut shop? Imagine an Everything of Everythings. Can you? Can you even imagine imagining it?

There's a kind of falling that feels like flying.

Gordy feels he's being swallowed up by some mythic subterranean beast—All this time spent walking on dry land, he thinks, but it wasn't ever land at all, it was only the face of the beast, who waited, patient as Moses, for you to meander close enough to its mouth, until it could open up and eat you without effort, let you tumble down, down, all the way down, into pitch-black digestive realization . . . A dream logic is taking hold—You've returned to Pigeon Forge, to the circus, and Bailey is here, and Jane. Around here somewhere are your dad and Finch, according to Boyd's book. Morris is a nightmare freak, and Donk did it to him. Julius is here, and there, and everywhere: He's sandals, at least in part he's the sandals you're wearing now, he's spreading through the country like yeast being worked into dough. Stories are converging, overlapping, buzz of feedback from competing realities. You thought you were in your own story, and now you're in somebody else's. How do you climb back into your own?

"Oh," Gordy says. He wishes he could argue. Instead he says: "Oh."

"Oh," he says. He sits down next to Bailey on the floor. There is grass here; Jane has cut away the canvas flooring in a rectangle; apparently, she dances with her feet on the turf. He hadn't noticed before. How interesting. It's all so worthless now. The world destroyed, or the world saved. No, not the world—more. Much more. Larger than the scope of imagination.

Somehow in his distraction he hears the sandals speak.

Hello, buddy, the sandals say.

"Hello, Julius," Gordy mumbles.

How are things?

"They've been better," Gordy says. It's hard to breathe. Oceans. Land. Species. Stars. Galaxies. All he calls his own. And more. Morris's claims upon reality are omnivorous, extending not only across the totality of the present but also into the past. Not only the past but also the future. Not just what is, but all possibilities that might be or could have been. Morris has seen Färland, so Morris will have claimed that as his own.

The old familiar thought arises—Let it come, then. What kind of universe is it you would save, which would elevate such a creature as Morris, which would enforce such grotesque mercy upon one so little deserving, which would stack the deck, rig the dice to make a winner of the worst before the first throw? What

God would make sport of his creatures and bolster the worst delusions of its own cruelest creation? Submersion is preferable—isn't it? To be carried away, to allow the swirl of flotsam over billions of millennia to find some more suitable order. Better to throw existence itself to that uncertain fate than to defer such richly deserved punishment.

Gordy reaches out and takes Bailey's hand. Lost in her own shock of discovery, she numbly accepts it. From far away, he can hear Jane: "Don't tell me you didn't see what I saw. You knew all along what the wave was. Who made it. Who could call it."

"I thought. . . . I thought I had called it by myself. The Voice told me to."

"You're just like him. You think it all springs from you. But how can you; you saw the two of them, like I did."

"I didn't see anybody but myself."

"They were right there. Did you at least turn to look around you?"

"I . . ."

"How typical. How very you."

"I looked out at the ocean."

"Yes, that's right. I remember; that's exactly what you were doing. You never saw them, or me, or any of the rest you'd have seen if you just looked around. You didn't even see Morris and Landrude. Unbelievable. You're the least curious cat I've ever known."

"I just—"

"Never mind. You made it wrong, but you can make it right. You have to do what you should have done from the start. The Coyote is coming soon. Whatever he'll do to Morris next won't be nice. He's disturbingly creative."

"The Coyote," Bailey moans. "Oh God, Daniel. Oh God."

"You've got to hurry. Use the ticket since you still seem to need it. Use it to take the Coyote's power away—it's in his diamond whatsit on his forehead. Then, give it to Morris. I've tended to him as best I can, but he's near the end. He'll die soon, or he'll give up and call it. Either way, the wave will come, and if it does, who can stop it then?"

Gordy sighs. "What does it matter, though? You're forgetting, I don't have it. I gave it away. Now it's gone. There's nothing I can do about it."

Jane sets her hands on her head and rubs her temples. She breathes in once, slowly and deeply, then out. Finally, she says, "You're going to make me take you by the hand and walk you every step."

"I don't understand."

"Yes you *do*, you chickenshit. You let yourself not understand just as much as you need to, so when it all finally ends, when you simultaneously get your sweet oblivion, and Morris gets his punishment, you can still say to the rest of us: 'But I didn't know.' Won't we just *have* to forgive you, then? Too bad you won't have any excuse soon—I'm telling you all of your own secrets. Why do you think you take so easily to invisibility? Why do you suppose you keep hearing the Voice, seeing the wave, even after you returned from the other side?"

"You're not making sense." But the dread is rising now. Gordy can feel a cork, long ago inserted deep and sealed against the hazard of poison bottled within, about to be wrested out of the neck.

"You know the trick you always used to play, back under the fountain, in the vault you made of the oubliette prisons—back when you played at being god, taking care of all the freed prisoners? The here and there trick, where there'd be multiple versions of you? You'd use it to visit us all simultaneously."

"I hope your plan doesn't rest on me doing anything like that again."

"You're still playing it, dummy. You never stopped."

He holds out empty hands. "Impossible. No ticket."

"You have it. You don't need it, but you can't not have it."

"I don't!"

"Not *here*. But I've seen; in *there*, you still have it."

"There? Where is th—"

But then the tent fills with the scarlet tunics of cardinals. Time has run out.

x x x

His teeth ended before the wooden stake did. In time, he realized he was merely bloodying his gums on the splinters. Goop-Goop allowed himself a count to ten, breathing heavily, in the dust, then put his hands on the post. He'd ground it down significantly; perhaps his arms could complete the job his teeth had sacrificed themselves to begin. He pulled, dimly aware of the red cloud of adjuncts and trustees gathering outside Jane's inner tent, then entering it. The Andrews were taking no chances; they'd mustered the full force. You can't possibly break through them, Goop-Goop told himself—there's so many of them and there's only one of you. You'll need to create a distraction. Immediately, the answer came. Ah yes, Goop-Goop thought, this won't be a problem at all; you've always been able to find the most useful available beasts. This is your lesson to yourself. But now this inner voice was unsteady, desperate, no longer in possession of its own convictions, nothing remaining in the words but the saying—and the striving of hands on post, hoping without expectation to hear creak and snap and splinter of wood.

He pulled, and screamed. He screamed, and pushed. Within his cage, from beneath his tarpaulin, Wembly returned his pain, howl for howl. Scream away, friend, Goop-Goop thought. Fill yourself up with my rage. I owned this circus once. I know where to find your key.

X X X

The dressing-room tent is crowded now with ceremonial red. Gordy still hasn't risen, nor has Bailey—though standing is no longer a matter of choice for them. At the directive of the Andrews, they've been tied up, back to back.

"Let them go," Jane insists. "Or I'm not flying the trapeze."

The Andrew on his right beckons with one hand: Bring it in.

A skinny old man is led into the room, fresh blood spilled down his nose onto his shirt. Behind him walks a young woman Gordy knows he's seen before. "That poor man was hungry," the young woman says, pointing back the way she's come. "He was eating wood."

"I fought them as much as I could." Sterling Shirker gasps. "I'm sorry."

"Don't be. It was inevitable," Jane says. She sounds like an unskilled actor, speaking memorized lines by rote. "They learned that one from Morris, too. There's always somebody willing to pull the dirtiest trick."

Suddenly the old man notices Gordy; without preamble he leaps, and Gordy is hauled into his embrace. "Gordy-Gord," Dad chokes. "All we get is moments, boy. All we get is scraps."

Gordy lacks the will even to answer. He can feel the shakes of his daddy sobbing, and then they pull him away. He can't bring himself to speak. All he wants is to disappear, to not be, to un-become. If I had the ticket, he thinks, I could make us all so small they couldn't see us anymore. If I had it, I could fade us all away and let them gnaw on each other for a change.

Every member of this patchwork outlaw band has an overeager cardinal's sword-point at the ready, warning against sudden movement or aggressive action, while every spare blade is directed at Finch's neck. The Andrews return their quizzical carrion-bird gaze to Jane. It's clear what is intended: The show must go on. There will be an Assizement, bird and spade, and also a circus; the Andrews will see to it that all is done as it must be. It's as if Morris has crafted tiny clockworks of his own will to carry forth his edicts in his absence. If ever Morris had a Continuity, he has found it in them, the Andrews, a self-broken triumvirate.

"Put your swords down, you win," Jane says.

The cardinals crowd around her. They take her by the arms to compel her outward. They've forced Gordy and Bailey to their feet. Jane is nearly to the exit now. She digs in her heels to resist them, and, twisting suddenly, she falls from their hands and lands right on the rope-conjoined couple, knocking them all to the grass in a clutch and tangle. In the moments before they regain her to pull her up and away, she whispers: "The here-and-there trick. *You never stopped playing it.* You've been playing it ever since you opened that door. I saw you in there. You're *still* there, Gordy. Behind the door. *You never left.*" Then they have her again, and she says, louder, so they can still hear her even as she disappears from sight and is carried away: "You still have it, back there. I saw you holding it. I saw you. You never left. I saw you..."

Gordy disappears. It's the second-damnedest thing. The first-damnedest thing is that, by the time he disappears, nobody takes notice. The gorilla has attacked.

x x x

Into the dressing room bursts a howling hairy pandemonium, tearing down the privacy flap and stomping it flat. It screams, swinging long black arms scythelike in the cramped space, upsetting trustee and adjunct, knocking red-clad attackers and prisoners alike to the ground. Espying the brace of little people near its knees, it doubles-redoubles-trebles the yawp of its red-eyed rage, and, without pause or presentiment, takes the head of an Andrew into each of its purposeful paws. There is in Wembly's simian screams the frustration of decades of captivity, of the cage, of years gone flaccid playing solitaire with a filthy deck missing the four of hearts, all now distilled and focused upon new objects of aggression and hate, focused with inerrant primordial instinct upon the smallest apes he can find. He raises them like clubs and swings them; with these tiny cudgels he demolishes furniture, wrecks mirror, dressing table, desk, lamp, and then, still howling his song of righted wrongs, still swinging bone-broken midgets like bats, bursts through the opposite canvas divider and passes out of sight. They hear him howl as he goes, and then the tumultuous ejaculations of the crowd as he lurches, presumably, into full sight of the circus beneath the lights of the three rings.

For a moment they all abide in the silence and the detritus of the ape's passing. Former foes lay united, dazed and wounded equals in the devastation that had come and gone. Jane scrambles back into the tent and makes her way to Finch.

"Are you all right, baby?" She searches for a wound to tend.

"That monster was angry." The young woman, unhurt, confused but untroubled at this desperate pawing, says. "It hated those small men."

"Goooooooooop!"

Into the space that had been a dressing room lurches a thing that had been a man: tin nails for hair, eyes a bloodshot roadmap, legs attenuating to grotesque pink flipper-flaps. Attempting to speak, it reveals a mouth bloody of gum and empty of tooth, a void lined with fresh sawdust. "Goop," it says, searching the floor. "Goop-Goop Goop gah Goop-Goop gally gall Goop. Goop-Goopy Goop gow." The stunned and surviving cardinals attempt to obey as best they can, while Bailey scans the tent for Gordy. Where he'd been, there remains only a tangle of ropes.

"The gorilla must have him," Bailey mourns. "It'll tear him apart."

"No it doesn't," Sterling replies. "He's elsewhere."

After another minute's attempt at communication, Goop-Goop throws up its hands in frustration and commences drawing with its finger in the dust on one of the shattered mirror's larger shards. Trustees and adjuncts, worshipful once more, crowd around to observe the creature's efforts, the better to divine from him some sign or instruction.

"Come on," Bailey says, struggling out of her newly loosened bonds. "While they're distracted."

Sterling demurs. "We're going to need to stay close to Morris now, you and me. He'll need whatever help we can give him. Donk's coming soon."

"But. . ." Bailey points at the creature in the center of the knot of redbirds. "That's Morris, isn't it? He's dangerous."

"He's even more dangerous if Donk gets him again," Sterling whispers. "Even one more time. Jane told you, I expect. We got to stick to him like butter on rice, keep him from going even one more toe over the line." Any question of escape has, in any event, become moot; the trustees have recovered well enough to secure their prisoners. Somebody produces a notepad and a pencil for the *goop*ing thing; it now furiously scribbles its directives.

"But. . . Morris is insane," Bailey protests. "He thinks it all came from him. That all of us sprang from his mind. He thinks he created everything."

"That's the problem," Sterling says. "Didn't Jane tell you? That's the exact problem. He isn't Morris, not really. And he did create everything. He *did*."

✕✕✕

Perhaps it would be helpful if I explain what the Gordys saw.

Gordy stood on an endless beach. Behind him, the door: same as it ever was.

Gordy stood in the tiny room. In many ways the only chamber onto which this door has ever opened. Four square gray walls. Nothing to report.

Gordy stood in the room where two identical men contend. Did I see this before, he wonders? Was this here last time? Did I force myself to forget? Did I simply fail to turn and see it? He watches their struggle unfold, watches the sea rise into a wave as the loser makes one last desperate act.

Oh, God, Gordy thinks. I think that I know what I haven't known yet.

Gordy stood on the endless beach, clutching a shining green ticket in his hand. The wave no closer now than ever before. Thrumming throughout his being, he heard the Voice:

—I desire mercy, not sacrifice

–Damn you. Do your own dirty work, why don't you? Damn you for giving me this thing.

—Who told you I gave it to you?

–I. . .

—He has called it. It is Time.

xxx

Suddenly, immediately, at a speed immeasurable, the wave lurches forward. It will arrive in minutes or seconds. Possibly it has arrived already to devastate all he calls his own.

Gordy has the ticket in his hand. He leaps for the door.

Story is entirely subject to authors.
But authors are entirely subject to readers.
And readers are subject to infinite change.

          —Unknown

At night, he finds beauty in the metropolis.

Downriver a prison lurks, one of thousands across the planet, teeming with degraded men and women. Most of them, the Coyote knows, are guilty and deserving of their state. Still, the day will come when those walls can be destroyed. No good comes of those places. The Coyote hangs in the sky, listening to the city wail and murmur and thrum.—You'll do more than free their bodies from the degradation of cruelty; you'll free their minds. An untended river cuts an unruly path, but it can be channeled. So, too, with the mind. Your control over your super-telepathy power is crude, but you'll learn the mastery of it. When the time is right, you'll open their minds and punish their bad impulses until their rivers run straight. Each man and woman will become as precise as architecture. In time, the people will obey because they won't remember any other state but obedience, but first, they will obey because you will teach them this new truth: The only other option is to burn. Now they're ruled by fear, but you'll harness their fear, use it, turn it to better ends. Soon their fear will set them free.

But now the hour has come, and there is a daily promise to be kept. There is one who requires a more attentive justice, whose worst impulses require a slower extermination. Today you'll take his skin, and replace it with something new and inappropriate. This will seem to him a punishment, but the day will come when you have taken every original portion of him, when you will begin to replace even the replacements, exchanging them again with something yet worse, and then he will long for the return of the older, lesser torment. Over the years you will make an example of him to pierce the dullest awareness—the suffering due to any who ever again dare cause the suffering of another being.

Over the city rolls a reverberating cannonade of exploding air, a flash like lightning, and then the Coyote is gone, flying toward Pigeon Forge.

x x x

Three spotlights light the three rings. Somewhere in the dark beyond, the crowd knows, the tumblers and clowns wait to entertain; to leap and fall and catch, to thrill them to breathlessness and draw them to their feet. The tapestry is hung from the tent roof, and on the other side, the entertainers await their cues. Somewhere there, behind the tapestry, readying themselves, backstage, are the...Here the line of thought fades into imprecision and distraction. Something's happening back there, though—something exciting and preparatory.

Beneath the tent roof, overpopulated bleachers toss and roil in a welter of anticipation, fear, and hope. Vaguely aware of the Assizement, yet at the same time purposely unaware, the crowd is already given to giddiness and a rather specific form of denial. The men, women, and children filling these rickety bleachers are all local employees of Love Forgeworks—an amalgamated corporate empire of various concerns: amusement parks, food manufacturing, military contracting, metalworking, prison management and supply—though this connection is not a thing talked about. There's a vague understanding that the home offices of Love Forgeworks are located in Pigeon Forge, that everyone who works in any part of Pigeon Forge draws their checks from this parent company. Ask any member of this crowd, they'll tell you: *Oh, I've been living and working here a long time, since, since...oh, always, really.* How long you've been here is not a thing that's talked about. On occasion—back on the cul-de-sac, back in the apartments, back in the trailer park, back at the motel that rents by the month—the concept of the before-time will drift into the conversation, only to dissipate, unreleased, into a suddenly charged atmosphere. The past? I don't ever think about that, what *did* happen before, anyway, I came here from, from...why, I swear (here a wry chuckle), I swear I've been here my whole life. How funny, you'd think I'd travel more, but I suppose that's just how it goes. But it's a good life. Food on the table. Heat in the register. Clean water in the tap. A little extra to spend on the nicer things. And the circus is coming—how exciting! Every six months a private circus, who gets that? Not everybody, I'll tell you. We're lucky. It's not a bad life...

The tickets arrive in the mail a few days before, green and green and green and green and green and green and green and green and...blue. The blue tickets are backstage passes. The blue tickets aren't discussed. There's a tacit and catholic lack of interest regarding the blue tickets and their recipients, and the reason, or lack of reason, for having received one. There's a counterfeited jealousy, overenthusiastic congratulations offered the beneficiary, unacknowledged relief at having been spared receipt. Some people get blue tickets, and they get to go backstage, that's all—how fun, how lucky, to see the circus from *inside* the circus! Yes, we'll see those folks again. Lord, what a thing to say. I don't know why I said that. They've been chosen for a special privilege, land's sakes. Lord, I must be tired. More coffee?

But today there begins to edge into the already-nervous hum a new energy, a concern, an idea of some crossbeam gone, however incrementally, out of skew on the treadle. Colonel Krane stands center-stage, top-hatted, his tuxedo striped in vermilion and pink, but for whatever reason he isn't bellowing the commencement into his microphone. Instead he stands, awkward in silence, looking off into the dark as if expectant for some inexplicably delayed signal. The idea grows: Something's gone awry. The circus always begins promptly, always. Something has gone fishy backstage. Backstage—this brings to mind thoughts of the blue tickets, but those thoughts are squelched before they lead to other thoughts, which are better not to have, and best not to share.

Just then, a roar goes up—but not from the spectators. It begins from somewhere out in the darkness, as if from an adjacent room: an animal howl, followed by angry and fearful shouts, shrieks, scuffle, tumble, clatter-bang-crash—and then Colonel Krane hops in comic terror and scampers out of the limelight. Immediately, this vacated space is filled by an immense nightmare of black hair and white fang, a naked beast with an immense pointed skull, bare chest, tiny eyes. When it screams, they can see the teeth, sharp and white. In each paw it clutches a stuffed rag doll, child-sized, dressed all in scarlet. Raising its hideous face to the heavens, it screams confusion or triumph; then, with its long arms, it swings the mannequins round once, round twice, round thrice, until the dolls' bodies pop off of their heads and fly out, sailing into the dim hidden corners of the tent, emitting two red streamers projecting behind themselves as they fly, as if each is being propelled outward by its own crimson tail. Still howling, still clutching the doll heads, the beast rushes out of the blinding light, into the dark, unseen for a matter of seconds until it tears a hole in the tent wall, admitting a freshet of night air, and then it is gone, its protestations diminishing as it flees.

The breathless crowd sits mute in shock. Then, as a single entity, they begin to applaud, hoot, stomp, and howl in tumultuous approbation of this new distraction, this bold and daring opening act. The Circus of Bearded Love has begun.

x x x

Bailey's in the wrong room. She's not sure how she fell into it, but this is the room with nightmare in it. In this room Gordy has either been murdered by a gorilla (if correlation can occasionally be buddies with causation) or else (if Sterling is to be trusted) has disappeared completely.

This is the room in which Morris was right all along, if Jane is to be believed. Where his death dooms the world, and so does any eventuality that fails to end with his triumph. Jane has also disappeared completely, in a way—she was ordered to the platform by the salamander-tongued thing that is Morris, to twist and jump and fly, and, with one last desperate look at her daughter, compelled by weaponry, she went. Look at Morris. Daniel did that to him—your Daniel. This is Pigeon Forge, and Pigeon Forge is the room in which Daniel has become some grotesque god of vengeance. This is a bad room—the worst room.

This is the room with the fountain in it.

The fountain, white as a gorilla's tooth but deadlier, looms beside the cage. It makes a high and wheedling sound in your brain, a sound of hardness destroying hardness in seven synchronal but discordant squeals, of toenails on the chalkboard of perception, of a diamond lath cutting steel. Looking at it makes you feel as if you want to vomit but lack a stomach from which to do so. Looking at it is like looking at a paradox of blasphemy, as if it were simultaneously three mutually exclusive concepts of evil.

This is the room with the cage in it, and Bailey is in the cage.

This is the room with the stage in it, and the thing is on the stage.

The thing. Morris. Earlier this year, this thing had been the cat who had, with a flick of his arm, set her head free of her body. He's making himself understood by way of pantomime and scrawl; somebody's procured a chalkboard for him. On the chalkboard, Morris has commanded them to bring the guns, all the guns. This is the room where Morris has amazed everybody, overthrowing a coup by the Andrews that had heretofore been presumed successful. He is ascendant once more, and his remaining servants huddle around his grotesquerie, wearing red ceremonial garb.

They're scrupulous and attentive and dazed and terrified. One trustee has made her way forward, advancing while bowing, presenting to him a velvet-lined box. From the box, he removes two placards carved from dark wood, one bearing the image of a shovel and another the image of a bird. With ostentatious deliberation, he selects the image of the bird, and, borrowing a nearby sword, with slow and ceremonious strokes, hacks it to bits.

The man in the corner of the cage moans. He's a tall cardinal, this man in the corner—or a former cardinal, to be accurate. It seems the man in the corner has been deemed more collaborative in the coup than the rest. The man in the corner's costume is gone to tatters, his face and body pulped by his fellows, who, each relieved not to have themselves been elected scapegoat, punished him with zeal before caging him. "That's bad," the man in the corner mumbles through broken teeth, indicating the destruction of the placard. "That's really bad. *Nobody* gets the bird?" Bailey has no idea what this means, nor does she ask. What do details matter? She can read clearly enough the sign of a man prepared to wield the spade: This is the room where everybody dies. For a season, Bailey tells herself, you even let yourself think you'd found your Attic—you believed the world was full of rooms, each as fascinating as the next—but that was a lie, too. Where are you now, Boyd? None of this was in your book.

The cardinals have brought the guns. They've made a circle around their leader, and they watch the tent roof. "The Coyote always comes from the sky," Sterling murmurs. Bailey, tired of listening, decides the tall redbird has the right idea—solitude—and hutches up in the far corner. She thought if she fought long enough and hard enough she could keep them all safe, get them all free, but it was a lie. You can ignore a lie if you live with it long enough, but the lie led to this room, which, like all other rooms in the world, lies. This is the room with death in it, and so are all the rest of them, all of them hiding death within; despite all other enticements and wonder, underneath is only death and death and death. This whole wide world is the room where all those years ago we should have simply let Ralph kill us with the rest of the kids, end the pain before it could get started. Now Yale's dead, and soon you will be. Daniel's not dead; not dead, but something worse. Soon he'll be shot dead by the waiting redbirds, or else he'll survive to become something even graver than a corpse. Daniel got everything he wanted, which is the worst thing he could ever have gotten.

But—Bailey can't stop herself wondering—what if there's still something in him left to save? He's not dead, not yet. Just look for a chance, one chance. There was a time when we were young and hungry and alone. There was a time when all we had was each other, and that was real. Two pieces of flotsam lashed to each other in the wide ocean, forehead to forehead, hands on each other's ears. I'd have died if not for him. He'd have died if not for me. We don't owe each other anything and never have; it's past anything like debt. We are what we are to each other, and that's all; we're the original lost children, we're survival itself. And what if—what if, in fighting for him, you might find some new possibility, one where there is and always was a brother? What if somehow you can run through rooms until you find Boyd, lost and writing to you from the never-was? What was it he told you, back in the Attic?

You'll have to run, Boyd had said. You'll have to jump, and trust your luck.

Bailey sneers at herself—Stop it. You're done fighting. This is the room with death. Maybe there will even be a wave, if crazy bearded Jane's right. The end of the world—wouldn't that be nice? To let it happen and then everything will be done and over, and you can stop thinking about it?

Sterling has picked his way over to her, careful not to step on any of the huddled prisoners. He's removed his sandals and dangles one from each thumb. "Got a feeling you ought to put these on," he says, tossing them onto the sawdust beside her. "I'm going back to tend to Finch." Obediently, with nothing better to do, Bailey exchanges shoes for sandals, watches Sterling retreat once more to the far side of the cage near the door. Next door, on the other side of the partitioning tapestry, she can hear the great roar of the crowd, thrilling to the trapeze. The next room over is the one with the circus in it.

Hi, there, the Sandals Julius say. *There's going to be a scuffle soon. We might dare to hope that in the commotion they'll forget to close the door to our cage.*

x x x

In the aftermath of the beast's rampage, the ovation swells and carries, it fills the tent and holds them, suspends them, lifts them, exalts them. A new thing has happened, something wholly unanticipated, something never previously conceived; this is why they celebrate. Not just for the distraction of it, not just for the spectacle, not even for the violence, but for the novelty, the originality, the innovation. It's a harbinger of change, an indication that—for the first time—there may be some hope, some possibility, of a different outcome than the one they've so long unconsciously prepared themselves to accept. They applaud the very idea of change, hoping without fully allowing themselves to know why they hope; they rejoice and clap and jubilate, triumphant as if they, having witnessed innovation, have also been the cause; they celebrate what they have seen until it feels as if they celebrate themselves.

Then, just as the extended plateau of their tumult has begun to seem awkward, two of the spotlights blink out. Music builds as the remaining center light rises, rises, rises, finding at last the bearded lady atop the platform in her bright-green singlet. She is utterly alone. Deaf to their acknowledgment. Blind to their entreaties. Like a high priestess of flight, she raises her hands in ceremonial flourish, and, as the music reaches crescendo, she leaps into the air.

× × ×

Most folk in the cage huddle on the floor or lean on the bars, as if their fate and numinous fear of the fountain has robbed them of strength sufficient to hold their own weight. Finch stands near the cage door, watching the thing that had been Morris with a concerned expression. Sterling Shirker hurries back to keep watch beside her. He's eyeing the semblants and trustees, watchful and nervous—You hoped to finally protect your boy, but Gordy's like water, you can't hold onto him more than a second or two. If you can't watch over your own child, you may as well look after another's. Look at them, prowling, guns pointed skyward, watching for the Coyote. Nervous as unshorn spring sheep. Dangerous as winter wolves. They don't know who to side with no more. They don't know what to do. Gordy never attacked with his power, he only defended—his big trick was to run away. But what to do with the Coyote? The cardinals have learned the toady's game; befriend the meanest dog in the yard and ride his mangy back. They'd take the Coyote's part if he'd have them, but he won't mess with them. They took up with the Andrews when they could, but now their old boss is back. They're clinging to him the best they can, but what do they do when he loses? What do they do when the Coyote finally gets bored with Morris and switches his blood for lighter fluid, then flicks his Bic? Then who will the Coyote fix his attention to? They know who; it'll be *them*. Or—here's a worse thought—what if Morris somehow, someway, beyond any hope and any sense, wins this battle? Is he apt to forget his servants didn't take his part during his torment, when he was tied up like an animal, being rearranged piece by piece? No. The Coyote might spare them, however thin the chance may be, but Morris never will. He's using them now only because they'll let themselves be used. They're all dead men and they won't let themselves know it.

"That man is scared," Finch says. She's pointing at Morris, who is strutting about on the stage, using an axe as a makeshift cane. He's got a revolver and he's fervidly scanning the tent roof, waiting for the Coyote to come bursting through. For now, he seems content to wait for his tormentor, but he'll soon begin the proceedings, for reasons of continuity and decorum if nothing else. Sterling puts a hand on her shoulder, but the gesture feels foolish, and he withdraws it.

"Yep," Sterling says. "He's scared all right. He's the biggest scaredy-cat in this joint. But then, we all ought to be scared right about now."

"I'm not scared," Finch says.

Yes, thinks Sterling, you aren't scared; that's my problem. You're your mama's girl. I best stick close. From the front side of the tent, he hears the exaltations of the crowd, lately on the decrease, reach new heights of enthusiasm. Jane must have started flying over on the other side, catching and tossing and catching herself, bearding gravity in its lair; Jane Sim, defender of prisoners, artist of the page and the stage and the wire. The bravest girl in the world.

Sterling is glad of Finch, who provides some focus for his fear—I reckon if Jane's girl weren't here to protect, I'd pick someone at random. It's fool's work. We're trapped in this cage. Protect her, how? With yourself? To save somebody's life for how long? A minute extra? Useless. Fool's work, but I'm just the fool for the job. Wish I hadn't given my sandals away. What made me do it? Some impulse. Idiot thing to do; now I'm all alone.

Morris has for now stopped ruminating over the danger from above. He's turned his livid, chitin-lidded eyeballs to the cage. With the hand holding the chalk he jabs emphatically at Finch, and then, for good measure, he scrumbles to the board and scrawls:

THE GIRL FIRST.

Sterling sighs for Jane's sake—It's like you figured. He's going to go for the throat. A final lesson about crossing the boss. No thought to the mercy Jane showed you in your pain now that you've crawled back to power. Certainly no thought for the fact that this is your own daughter. Jane returns from sky-dancing for the yahoos and finds her bird already crushed. Then the rest of us. Then he'll empty out the oubliettes and shear his sheep. He's done trying to cajole us; now he only wants to end us.

Two cardinals step forward, weapons at the ready. One of them has the cage key. All the others have plastered themselves against the back of the cage, as if they hadn't read the instructions, but the girl doesn't fluster or flinch. She watches them come, not unafraid but calm and still, as curious as any bird. Sterling chuckles at her bravery in spite of it all—She's her mama's child all day long. As they swing the door out, he slips smoothly in front of Finch.

The trustee puts his gun muzzle an inch from Sterling's nose; Sterling goes cross-eyed for a moment in an attempt to track it. Not such a bad way to go if that's going to be it. Nice and fast and then it's done. Sterling spreads his arms out and grabs the bars on either side of the door.

"Not the girl first, captain. Me first."

The trustee looks dumbly back at the board, points to the instruction written there.

"The *girl* first," he says, dumbly comic in his confusion.

"No, cousin. *Me* first."

"Girl first," the other trustee snaps.

"Step aside," says the first trustee in a schoolmarmish wheedle.

"There's no moving me," Sterling says, more confident—If they were going to shoot they'd have shot already. No way these two want to get on Morris's worse side, breaking the protocol of the ceremony with freelance killing. "Me first. Him next. You next-next. You next-est of all." They don't like this. His babble is incomprehensible to them, but they know some sort of fun is being made. The first trustee makes a quick stab with his gun, popping Sterling in the nose with the muzzle. There's a burst of pain, a rush of blood, but his hands on the bars steady him and he finds he can manage through it. Sterling says, loudly, so all of them can hear:

"I'm going up there *first*, and you'd better believe you all are going to be next. Boys, your best move is to take off those fancy red jimmy-jams and walk away, quick as you can." He looks at Morris, a nightmare goulash clustercake: his mouth toothless, his matted beard a glut of gore. "If ever a man got on the losing end of a tangle, it's that boy right there. And you're betting on him? He got his ass wrapped in a tamale and handed to him in a paper bag every round of this fight. You want be wearing his uniform when the Coyote comes?"

Morris has made his way from the platform during this speech, as quick as his foot-flails and gamy leg will allow. It's hard to read his expression; Sterling assumes it's fury, but with his eyelids altered, he's going to look furious no matter what. As Morris shoulders between his trustees, Sterling smiles—Ah, Jane. I've learned a trick or two from you, lady. I ain't scared of this chicken-buzzard any more, either.

He steps from the cage to meet whatever's coming. "Howdy, captain. We never did finish our old conversat—" But Morris has put his right fist on his own left shoulder, and then, swift as a diving swallow, has passed it across his chest; now he points at the sawdust. Somehow he's holding a short sword, or else it's a long knife, how interesting, what *is* the difference, where do you draw the distinction, when does a knife become a sword? What a funny thought. There is a burning and a pulling. A smell of burning whiskers, a smell of fresh sardines, a smell of peaches, a smell he can't place that puts him in mind of his childhood. There is a deep and growing pain lower down his midsection. How interesting. Sterling smiles at Morris, because he can see they are finally thinking the same thing about his weapon's categorization: knife or sword, or swife or or, nord? You see, Morris? You see it too, it's funny, yes? Yes.

There is a tremble in the ground, a premonitory subterranean approach of something large. He looks downward for its source.

His belly is smiling, too—smiling wide and friendly. Everybody's in on the joke.

Oh, Sterling thinks. I get it now.

His belly is smiling, and his belly's smile sticks its gray-gut tongue out at him.

Gordy-Gord.

Ah, Gordy-Gordy-Gord. Ah Finch. Children, I didn't have too much help to give you, did I. Hope it was enough. Probably it wasn't even close.

Ah. Here we go then.

The subterranean rumble grows and then there's a nearby explosion upward. Quite a lot of shouting, and what sounds like firecrackers. Sterling intends to turn his head to take a gander, but it's too much right now, he'll look at the commotion tomorrow—Remember, tomorrow you should turn your head to the left to see the. . .

the

xxx

Jane's audience has become a mass, a collective, an undifferentiated tissue of apprehension and sensation. There is the ever-moving spotlight upon her, and a flood of lumens bathes each of the clowns on their poles who throw and catch the bars for her, but the largest spotlight is trained on the ground, to show beyond conjecture there is no net. None but the long-timers have seen the act—it's been years since Jane has performed to this crowd—thus they are unmindful of the high wire suspended below, able to convince themselves there is nothing but the leap and the catch, flip and somersault, jack-knife, spin, one-handed grab, and if any one catch should go awry, there will be nothing but the fall.

They are with her now; almost they think they *are* her. They lift with her, they soar. Jane flies, so they fly. No more thought to the worry of the day, fear of the week, terror of the year. Here it is, a moment of perfection, a reality past their own, which can transport them from the thought of what is being done to them in their midst. After will come the usual distractions: animal trainers, the forced hilarity of clowns, and a few other oddments—unicyclists, tumblers, the strong men in their gray sweatsuits, jugglers, prestidigitators—but this is the real show, restored as it used to be, as it always again will be. The opening masterpiece, the transport of the flying lady...

Suddenly, without preamble, like a magician's trick, like a guillotine blade, the backing tapestry falls, and the circus confronts them with its innerworkings, without mask or prevarication, spilling its evil guts for the audience, who, rapt already, find it impossible to dissemble any longer away from it. They see the cage, and all of their own meticulously unremembered sons or daughters or husbands or wives—lucky recipients of backstage passes—packed within. They see the stage. They see the armed trustees dressed in scarlet, pointing their weapons in chaos, bewilderment, indecision. Beside the cage, there's a hole in the ground. Beside the hole, an older fellow kneels in a growing puddle of blood. He smiles at them like a child with a drawing, and, with a flourish of his arms—ta-da!—he reveals the spill of his belly. Still and staring, he crouches in the quickly reddening straw as the crowd, still a single entity, falls into a hush. But their sudden quiet is not for the disemboweled man, nor for the cage of prisoners, nor for the red-clothed army and their guns. All of this they see, but barely. Their attention is terrified into diligence by two other spectacles.

First, there is the fountain, the evil white fang, the cherubs pissing dark-water into the abyss of the basin, the turtle's eternal alabaster stare. They've known about it so long and so deeply they've forgotten how much of themselves it has become necessary to spend in order to deny their knowledge to themselves. Now here it is, and no expenditure of the soul will put it off. Face to face they are with its claim upon them all, its radiating malignancy, quelling them into fear, hurling them into submission.

Then there is the floating man. He's a wonder to behold. Seconds ago, he burst like a rocket from the ground, emerging from a spot close to the gut-spilled man, and dropped the curtain with well-aimed eye lasers. A cluster of men in scarlet seem to be shooting him, but that can't be right, because they have no weapons—are they janitors? They hold brooms and mops pointed at the floating man in pantomime of gunplay, like children aping the posture of soldiers in war movies. The floating man hovers over all this scene, nearly to the top of the tent's ceiling, duded out in a cape, a diamond on his forehead, his muscles poured into a skintight outfit of blue and red. In one strapping arm he holds a creature—Why, it's that Goop-Goop fellow, the freak, what's he doing up there?...

x x x

It's so strange, thinks Sterling, because now the crowd is all around. They've dropped the curtain. You've been given the spotlight, have you? Well that's fine. They aren't applauding, but they're interesting. No, not interesting—*interested*. Interest, Ed. Now you have their attention, Ed. Yes. His belly has a joke to tell, goodness look at it grin. It would be good to lie down somewhere. Right here would be good. Steady as you go. You don't want your belly to tell its joke too fast. It's sort of a dirty joke, but this is a hip crowd, they can take it; nevertheless, you have to time it right. First one knee. There we go. Now the next. Let's settle onto our side. Steady as she goes—whoops! Well, there's the joke told, and you flubbed it. They're not laughing. Just a sort of shocked silence. At least it's made an impression on them. You could hear a pin drop, if you had a pin, and a dropper to put it in.

I never meant to come back to Tennessee ever again. I promised myself every day I wouldn't. Now look.

x x x

Do you see?" the floating man announces. His voice, super-magnified, fills the tent. With his free hand he indicates the fountain, the cage. "Do you understand?" He shakes the freak. "Citizens of Pigeon Forge, I say to you now: This is the man responsible for your pain. He's stolen your selves away from you." The floating man holds the freak out to them, arm's length, a display piece. Goop-Goop is writhing now, twisting and warding, anticipating some terrible and fast-approaching development: a child about to be spanked, a dog foreseeing a kick.

"You see what I've done to him already, on your behalf. Citizens, since I find you all gathered together, I wanted you to see what happens to him next!"

Below the floating man, the show goes on. The bearded lady, all but forgotten, still flies, flips, swings, grabs at every last chance presented her. Do any in the crowd understand? Is even one of them still watching the lady? If they are watching her, are they *watching* her? Not her actions, but her intent? Are they watching what she's watching? Do they even for a moment consider her hopes, her plans? It seems unlikely. It's too much to ask of a crowd already distracted past comprehension.

Still the lady skips past gravity with a wink and a flip, flies agile around their awareness, eschews pretensions of grandeur by locating grandeur itself, an Icarus who discovers the sun, then boldly flies straight at the center of its dazzling eye.

x x x

They tell her it looks effortless from the stands. From there, they don't hear the grunts, creak of rope, slap of hand on bar, labor of breath. From a safe distance, she looks like a feather on the breeze. Here, up close, where she can hear herself, she is as real as any carcass on any butcher's block. From the stands, a spectator might be fooled into thinking the acrobat is an angel, someone who has transcended physical law, but the acrobat on the trapeze knows she is only certain associated pounds of solid meat and bone, subject to gravity's original sin, not defeating gravity but wrestling against it, pulling gravity's bleeding fees from its jaws with her bare hands. For all flesh, falling is the natural state. Every catch takes its own toll upon the tendons and ligaments. Every leap pushes you down. Even as you rise, what you feel most is not the lift, but the hand of God pushing against you, gently but remorselessly slowing you, slowing you, stopping you, forcing you down.

It's glorious. She tries to lose herself into it: leap, catch, spin, flip, the inertia and inevitability, the knowledge and the skill. Best to enjoy it. It is certainly her final flight, whatever comes: Succeed or fail, sacrifice or wave.

The Coyote has come. She didn't see where from, but he's there now, floating directly above, addressing the crowd. He's got Morris in one hand by the scruff of his shirt, shaking him like a naughty pup. He's about to deliver some new deserved atrocity. He's so certain of his correctness, the Coyote, so taken with his self-perceived moral authority. Having targeted the worst person he's ever met, he's bestowed license upon himself to bestow the worst punishments ever yet devised. Puffed with power, he wallows in the justification with which he's gifted himself, and imagines he's coating himself with righteousness rather than a different ordure— But you're nothing but a new Morris, asshole, another dummy who thinks because you've put his hand on a bit of power it's a sign you deserve to wield it. Worse, you think you are the power. You think you know what you're doing. You don't have the slightest idea. You'd do well to learn the trapeze. The trapeze would teach you necessary lessons about what must happen to everything that goes up. It would teach you not to be so proud of your rise. It would teach you that you are not justice, cannot bring justice, it would teach you there is no justice, only physics. When you're in the air, the solid ground is all the justice God will ever deliver. Here's the great blindness, the great ignorance, what none of these little men or prospective gods understand: We're all in the air, all taking any catch we can find. You'll feel every catch, pay every toll, just to stay in the air. How cruel, how cruel, how cruel—but that's the inescapable condition, Coyote. Would you cut the strings to each bar and attach them to your fingers, as if your hands had the strength to support all our weight, as if you weren't falling, too?

There isn't much time now. There's precious little hope in Gordy—all he's ever done is run. Even if he understood your meaning, there's not much hope in his return. Even if he does return, you can't be sure it will have the effect you intend. There's no reason to trust in your version of the metaphysics; it's up to you, and you only. You'll need luck. Morris can't possibly sustain himself against another replacement of his physical being, even though he's probably telling himself otherwise. He's puffed himself with false confidence, like he always has before. His cosmology is a rubber ball: compact, self-contained, impenetrable. Every setback for him has only ever been an opportunity to rebound. She knows him. Suffering is no teacher of his; he's learned nothing from it. The fool. Even now she's forced to chance herself for him. No more rubber left in his ball, not another rebound left in him. The Coyote is going to do something to him, then return him to his stake and tether. Whatever comes next will certainly be the end, the tipping point, the event horizon of despair. He'll call the wave, and in so doing he won't think he's risking anyone but himself. He thinks because he's invented all of us, that means we're not real.

It will come soon; the Coyote won't be content much longer with presenting him to the audience. You're going to have to snatch Morris from him before he does it. And what then? Where will you run? It doesn't matter; these questions are too far ahead to answer; they are catches after the one immediately before you, and you'll seek them when you need.

Jane knows exactly how high she can leap. She knows it to the inch. The Coyote's lowering slowly, sinking almost into range. The diamond on his head holds his power. If she can reach him, perhaps she can snatch it away. Just fly a little lower. Just a little lower. Just a little lower.

But then, without warning, everyone is falling.

x x x

Sterling Shirker blinked. Then he blinked.
He didn't blink again.

I remember. . . oh, everything. Everything.
   I.
   Gordy-Gord. Gordy. Is that you?
   I remember you
   I remember our last
   Our last breakfast

Is that you, coming up the fountain steps.

Gordy-Gord.

I almost think I see you.

x x x

The floating man dangles the struggling freak, then brings him near, whispers cruel instructions to him, and it happens: The freak's skin blurs and shimmers and *changes*, and an involuntary sympathetic moan goes out from the crowd. Then, improbably, the diamond on the floating man's forehead bursts into a spray of water, and he changes, too: Muscles deflate, chest collapses, coif loses its perfect forehead curl—and gravity, long denied its due, once again exerts its claim. He and his captive fall, but the crowd has only eyes for his captive, the Goop-Goop, that most unfortunate thing. *It* has happened to him, the bad thing, the worst thing ever to happen to anybody. If ever this audience has felt pity, they feel it now for this awful translucent thing.

The Goop-Goop begins its descent to the earth, and the crowd knows its fatal landing will be the only mercy it will ever receive in life. They scream in unison, rise to their feet, and, as they rise, there is something audible beneath their scream, deeper, darker, vibrating far beneath their feet and coming on impossibly fast, rushing toward them with the speed of rage. The Goop-Goop has only begun to fall, but what can stop the fall? They could look away, but their curiosity or duty won't allow it. They are the witnesses; it all will happen and they will see it, not because they want to but because they are meant to. They've become the eyes of the world, the memory of the universe, a jury without a verdict to deliver. Then they gasp—the flying lady has swung vertical on her bar, let go at the absolute apex, and, releasing, launched straight upward to catch the poor falling thing, to gather him up, catch him tight by the crook of her knees beneath his armpits, her beard caught in the spotlight like a wreath of flame, a holy hirsute halo. For less than a fraction of a second before they're both carried downward, the two of them are emblazoned into eternity by her audacity. A stunt beyond any she's yet shown them—but to what purpose? She has no handle, nothing to grasp, she's connected to nothing but him. What possible catch could there be after such a heedless leap?

Forgive the crowd a slight lapse of attention. During these impossibly fraught moments, none of them has marked the slight figure climbing swiftly up the ladder, wearing sandals, scrambling up the rungs to gain the high wire.

x x x

Goop-Goop thought—Even now, you're calm. That's good: These are decisions that should be reached rationally, not emotionally. We'd been watching the air for him. We should have been watching the ground. The Coyote used that old tunneling trick of the original burrower, Gordy. Burst from the straw and earth, he scattered your men. Their bullets bounced off him until he converted their guns to brooms. He has you now. He's lowered the tapestry, exposed the Assizement. They all see you. Every pair of eyes on you. It was Sterling Shirker, he distracted you in the crucial moment—isn't it always the way? Every pattern broken, each expectation confounded, every victory impregnated with defeat. Now this idiot has the power you sought so long. He shakes you and pontificates. It's a failed world; there's no good in it. You've given it your best, you've given it all you had. To it, you sacrificed your leg, feet, teeth, tongue, name, more. Methodically, you've created systems to help your unruly parts find themselves, but it's a failed world, one you now have no choice but to regret creating. In a way, the Coyote is the kindest part of you; through him, you are teaching yourself the futility of continuance; through him, you are finally giving yourself permission to release it. You are calm now, done with fighting, and that is enough. You can relax into the relief of surrender, knowing that soon, seconds from now, you will end it all.

There it is, over your shoulder—the wave. Your proof to yourself that you are what you say you are. Frequently you'd catch others noticing your peculiar affect, your tendency for the over-the-shoulder glance. None of them ever guessed what you were looking at, for none could see it. It's a tiny thing, so small, a wave the size of a pickled fish, but in truth, it's small only if you don't look at it. It's when you look at it direct, take it in, that it unfolds and unfolds and unfolds, and you realize you're seeing it inverted, looking down the wrong end of the telescope. It isn't small; rather it's the totality of everything else that exists that is small: planets, even galaxies, even systems of galaxies, all are dwarfed by the wave perched over your shoulder. Ah. This was your lesson you gave yourself, about the midgets, so much larger than their stature, so much more destructive than initially imagined. So many lessons! It all connects when you think about it. As wicked as the universe has been, as uncooperative, as painful, still what a shame to wipe it clean. . . The Coyote is done speechifying. He draws you near and whispers, and you feel your skin go into something else. The pain is beyond horror, but still you are calm—it's good, it's right. You want to kiss the Coyote, for making it so easy for you. The crowd howls in revulsion and pity, as if they were your missing tongue—which is what they are. If only you could comfort them, hold, caress, soothe—no, hush-hush, hush-hush-hush, it will be over soon. Soon you will see my sign coming, and then you all will mourn, and then it will be over. All it takes is a thought.

Come. Come, wave, come.

Yes. In an instant it's already twice as large as it was the moment before. Ah. The atmosphere is pregnant with the coming momentum. Everybody in creation will see my sign coming. All the nations of the world will mourn. Suddenly falling—I see your plan, Coyote, dropping me, thinking to kill me before it reaches us, and to thereby escape it. Fool, it's all the same effect—my death would have brought it on as easily as my thought did. I can remain calm, but— What's this? The descent intercepted before it's begun, Jane, coming flying up from below to catch you. She's taken hold; feel the tightness in the axes of your axillae, feel the momentum of her upward thrust trying to halt your fall—but then gravity reasserts its authority upon you both. Here comes the earth, and—no!—a gut-surging loop, then another. . . and you've been halted somehow. Caught up in the high-wire line. It's a whole tangle up there, a moaning shudder of torn tendon and dislocation. Jane has you still, you dangle beneath. Ah, Jane. My only confidant, my constant betrayer. It's good of you to be with me at the end. You've given me this at least. You've let me catch sight of my last intention, to see the wave as it takes us all. It's right over my shoulder, the wave, sardine-sized no more; it's the size now of a gorilla charging. Soon it will be the size of a train, of a mountain, of a planet. Soon it will extinguish sun and stars. Soon it will be the size of the everything, and then there will be the nothing, and, in the nothing, only a oneness. Only I can see it now, but soon everybody will see it, and at last they will know. They'll see it forever, and forever will be no more than the flit of a pigeon's wings, for it will destroy even time itself. . . .

Hang on, Jane begged. You hang on. Don't do it. Hold it back.

It's too late, Janey, Morris said. He felt so calm and so free. Aware Jane couldn't understand the sounds his empty mouth made; they weren't even words. He said them anyway, and wishing he could see those beautiful almond eyes one last time, he thought: She does understand. She knows. I've called it already. It's done. It's done it's done it's done.

—Boyd Ligneclaire, *Subject to Infinite Change*

x x x

All at once they see her, a slight figure, running, top-speed, down the tight-rope. The long-timers know about the tightrope—stretched from flet to flet, the high-wire, always incorporated into the trapeze finale. But this lady... she carries no pole to counterbalance. She doesn't even go barefoot, as any tightrope-walker knows to do, the better to sense every vibration of the line, the better to grip with the toes—but she makes no concession to balance, shod in soles of rubber and strap of leather, running the thread, pell-mell and heedless, gatling-kneed and holler-betsy, never missing a step. You don't know what you're seeing as you see it, it would be impossible to understand, it's all-at-once, it's too much, you're a part of it now. Only afterward, when you talk about it, will you piece together these events, and you'll wonder, all of you together, what could conspire to create such a singular confluence of action. Everybody is falling now—the man in the cape, the bearded lady, the freak she holds by her legs—save only this one, this last hope, this impossi-ble sprinter. The caped man has deflated somehow, lost his muscles and his flight. The ruin of a man, the creature, the Goop-Goop...is he smiling as he heads toward his inevitable skin-sack explosion? The bearded acrobat has him, but to reach him she's abandoned all hope of a catch. And the sandaled cat running the tightrope, what does she hope to accomplish? Running the line in sandals, she's already a scofflaw of physics, is she going to attempt... a catch?—No! —Yes! The fool!

She's skated on the line two or three yards, *slid* on it, feet sideways, bury-ing the line between foot and sandal sole, then leapt, and in leaping, she's *spun*, she's tangled the twanging tightrope into her sandal straps, eaten up

all the slack it's been given to accommodate an acrobat's surprise landing. . .
reaching out her arms to the plummeting bodies like a supplicant mother
who doesn't know which half of her severed baby she should beg Solomon
to first return to her, she's, she's—oh no she is NOT, she's going for *both* of
them?....The bearded lady knows how to make the catch, hand on forearm—success!—but the other one, with the C on the chest...he hadn't been
expecting to fall and has no control—no! she's missed his grasping hand by
an inch...the crowd's groan goes from defeat to exhilaration as they see it:
nnnooooooooooooooooooooooooOOOOOO

OOOOOOOOOOOOOOOAAAAAYEESSSSSsss!!
SHE HAS HIM BY HIS CAPE BY HIS CAPE BY HIS GOD-THUMPING
CAPE! The momentum swings them all the way looping around, 360°, as
they come at last to rest, still swinging, groaning and torn, hanging from the
tightrope, sandals and line in an unfixable tangle, the sandaled savior inverted, feet caught in the line, the no-longer-floating man dangling by his cape,
bearded lady beside him, and, suspended from the bearded lady's legs, the
chuckling freak show.

It's all happened. There's been no time to process it. All they can do is
stand on swaying bleachers, cheeks wet, and stomp, clap, pound, scream:
What have we just *seen*? But they cut their own enthusiasm short—something
is amiss. There is a thrum, an edge, a subterranean current, a pre-emetic
sense of rushing and ineluctable doom. It settles upon them all, a barometric
warning, known if not felt, like the foreboding of dogs before a tornado. A
sudden understanding of mortality, usually visited only singly, only at night,
now comes to them all collectively. They're weeping, but they don't know
why. The living hang yet suspended from the ropes, while below, the kneeling
man with the opened belly gently falls, almost in portions, onto his side, and
lies, still and peaceful, in his pile of guts and blood and straw.

From granite steps cunningly cut into the black stones ringing the fountain—they hadn't even noticed the steps before—a figure has risen, holding
something small and green and gleaming.

x x x

Listen: You are Gordy.

You stand for a moment, taking it all in.

There is a man lying unpeacefully on the ground, his unblinking face turned to you.

I've failed you again, old man, you think—haven't I? At least I finally know you. I can give that much to you, even though you can't receive it any more. I'm sorry, Daddy. I was given a promise the wicked would perish if they weren't warned. I did my best to not warn them, but I misunderstood the promise; it was crueler than that. I ran as long as I could. I can't run anymore. The wave's coming—can you see it yet? There's always a final move the losing king must take before the winner can declare his checkmate. A formality, you understand. I see you do—you've already fallen onto your side. Time for me to fall onto mine.

The crowd is full of silent weeping women and men and children. You want to explain to them: It's not my fault, there was a promise of justice if the wicked weren't empowered. That's what I thought, but it's not that way. There's only a promise to let the wicked play with all of you, again and again. I'm sorry.

There are others, men mostly, wearing scarlet, clustered in the area near the cage. They're holding brooms and mops as if they were guns. Seeing you, they swing them around to cover you—Somebody's done a switcheroo on you, boys, and you've not realized it yet.

In the corner of the tent, you see two tiny decapitated bodies. A funny thing.

In the center of the tent, hanging like laundry, you see them: loved ones, hated ones. The one you need is the lowest-hanging fruit. He's a shambles, a wreck, a chuckling skinless organ bag, a marvel of pain. You're grateful—At least you made him sing for his supper, Donk. At least you made him suffer.

There's no reason to hesitate. Look how large the wave has grown; there can't be more than a few moments left. You walk the air, rising on invisible steps, until you face him, eye to bloodshot eye. For a moment you daydream one last time about letting it come—the wave and the simple end—but you reject the false promise of oblivion. It wouldn't be simple, you now know nothing is ever simple. He's making noises at you, Gooping japes as if he thinks he can talk. His eyes a feast of madness. Beneath this unholy ground is dug his cavern. Hundreds—thousands—of the most cruelly imprisoned beings time and man have yet devised. All at his hand. And this is God's favored one. So be it.

It's is in your hand. Trembling, you thrust it onto Morris's forehead—Take it, you bastard. Take the full measure. Take it. Let God talk to you for a while and see if you like it. You deal with it now if you can. Run all you want and see where it gets you.

Divested of power, praying for oblivion, you fall.

x x x

Listen: You are Landrude. You've been Morris, then Goop-Goop. At last again you are Landrude.

It's on your forehead, crawling into your mind. You wanted it. Why did you want it? It's shredding into you, tearing away false contexts and replacing them with true, destroying your I-Am. It's all rolling at you, cascading through you, every action you've taken wearing this wrong self, every sin you've committed crashing into you, memories of what you've done.

Crashing through like waves.

The wave. It's still coming.

A voice speaks, soft and persistent.

—There's little time now.

You know what to do. You have the ability now to do it. It's so easy, in a way. It doesn't matter what it will do to you. First, there are smaller remedies you can enact. Most of you hanging together on this line are badly injured. Torn connective tissue in shoulder wrist elbow and knee, distended pelvis; poor Jane's spine has been badly twisted. All this is easily healed; gently, you reknit them, lowering them back, along with yourself, to the level earth, as you go restoring the parts of yourself the Coyote took: skin, hair, teeth, feet, eyes.

The fountain stairs await. Racing, you feel the rage of the surging wave growing all the closer. All your work, all your dreams, visions, so close to extinction—but never mind your own concerns—think of all of *them*, those in the spotlight and those on the margins, real to you at last as they've never been—it's *them* to whom you are everlastingly accountable. They hang in the balance. You are the most important person in this universe, the key, the linchpin. You know what this means now; it means you don't matter at all. It's not fair, you want to say, I didn't know, I was replaced. I called the wave because *he* wanted me to—the usurper—don't you see how he orchestrated it all? He wants the blank canvas to draw on, not me. All my grasping was only a blind seeking, casting about for home. I was both wrong and not wrong.

But who did, or who knew, or why, or even guilt or innocence, are unimportant. I'm sorry, you might want to say, but your sorrow doesn't matter. There isn't time. The wave once called cannot be stopped. The only thing to do is to make yourself large enough to meet it. You throw open the door—using your power restored, you throw open *all* the doors—and there it is, filling everything, no more beach, nothing else, rushing at speeds unseen since the first velocities. You say it anyway, even though it doesn't matter—I'm sorry—and then you bring it all into yourself, let it finally crest and crash into you and throughout you. You've swallowed the wave, and it's swallowed you. You've contained it, you're lost in it. You're caught up in and among it now, it's filled you up until nothing else is left, you're swimming in it along with all the other everythings, the infinities of possibilities all enmeshed together with one another, the fullness upon which you have drawn, from which you always did draw, without which you never could have begun, without whom you could never now effect this great and needed convergence, drawing all things into yourself, making all things new.

Oh, you think. That's right. Everything old is new again. Everything new is old.

Oh, you think—*that's* right. All of you. Readers, all the way down. You're all at the center, too. You've all been here all along.

x x x

Oh, says the man in the powder-blue suit, reading the final page. But I

x x x

Once, long ago, Daniel Coyote found Bailey Ligneclaire and hid her, just in time, from an approaching monster named Ralph, as Yale flew over the side of the building on the way to meet the earth. Bailey thinks: You saved me that day, Daniel. You and me, the ones from the beginning. You saved me that day, and abandoned me on another. This is the room where we settle up and leave the ledger balanced. We'll never be what we were, but we can bury the old debts here under the tent, and then when they pack the tent away, they can take the debt with them. You were right, Boyd. I had to run. I had to jump, and trust my luck. Even then I almost didn't make it.

It all went out of me at once, Daniel thinks. All power, gone. Now how did that happen, how, how. Bailey is saying something to him but he can't hear. He's over-aware of his slack superhero pajamas. He feels foolish; this spandex was meant to cover a much more powerful frame. They sit together, Daniel and Bailey, side by side, somehow not dead. Crawling toward each other, they lie together in their customary strange and intimate posture, forehead-to-forehead, uncertain of the needed reckoning of any future, holding only the moment; clutching each other's ears, sharing a wordless communion. Still there seems to be someone missing. There are two; there should be three.

My God, Bailey realizes: I can remember Boyd again.

x x x

Oh, says the man in the powder-blue suit, reading the final page. But I

x x x

From far below, rushing up the underground fountain stairs comes the howling sound of a newly freed multitude. Soon the tent is filled with the exonerated, mingling with the erstwhile circus audience. All around the three rings, many long thought missing are being found. The first to reach the top step is a gray cat dressed in denim and leather, a third wheel looking for his tricycle. He's got a book under one thin arm, and by the way he's holding it you can tell he regards it with a certain pride of ownership, as if he wrote it himself under significant pressure, a narrative wrested from literature's broad sky at great personal risk.

x x x

Oh, says the man in the powder-blue suit, reading the final page. But I

x x x

Rupert Paddington stumbles about the tent, caught betwixt and between;

there's himself and there's Colonel Karl T. Krane. Who has he been? And, whoever that is, why should he stay? He's seen at least one of his freaks hopping about without deformity, rubbing his suddenly unblemished forehead and grinning—it's probably happened with the rest, too. There's been a universal healing. It would be AX-io-MAT-ic to say the circus has run its course. It's been such a strange dream, but the time has come to wake... and he knows how. He has a compass's dumb but unerring sense of a door nearby, which he suspects will lead him home...

✕✕✕

Oh, says the man in the powder-blue suit, reading the final page. But I

✕✕✕

Gordy lies on the straw, looking up. Not dead after all. Something's broken his fall, or healed him—No matter. Soon it will all be destroyed, and you can stop thinking about it. There's so much excitement in the world. Nothing to do with you; you've discharged your duty. You can hear all the noise, so many people milling around. It's all happening, but why bother to look? Suddenly he sees something pierce the striped canvas tent roof, producing a glimpse of the starry night sky. Something large has fallen to earth. The sky, Gordy thinks. I could leave here and look at the sky. That would be nice. He rises and stumbles through the crowd, exiting the tent through the hole torn in the canvas by the fleeing gorilla.

✕✕✕

Oh, says the man in the powder-blue suit, reading the final page. But I

✕✕✕

The last fellow to stumble up the fountain steps has a face they all recognize and fear. They know him as Morris, but *is* he Morris? He holds an uncertainty in his expression they've never seen before, which makes him seem oddly unfamiliar. He holds a tiny ticket of green and sits by himself in one corner of the tent. The rest, unsure of him, keep their distance. Suddenly, for no discernable reason, an enormous safe falls like a meteor from the sky, ripping the tent roof, hitting the ground with a massive *thump* audible even over the din of the gathered crowd; its impact splatters the lonely familiar

man in spludding mud, leaving a crater whose diameter began only inches from his feet.

x x x

Oh, says the man in the powder-blue suit, reading the final page. But I

x x x

Of all the prisoners, Finch comes first out of the cage, stepping past the kindly dead man who fell on his side. She's sad about him, but now there's something else to which she must attend. The main acrobat is over there, the pretty lady with the beard, the one they call Jane. She's lifting one leg, then another, flexing her newly re-knit spine in wonder. There, among the milling crowd, they face each other. Once there had been a girl, and a woman, and nobody else in all the world.

Now Finch reaches out, and with her finger gently brushes her mother's nose.

"Mama?" she asks.

As they watch each other, hardly daring to embrace, the fountain's never-ending supply of dark water springs out, for the first time, clean and clear, and many people discover things once forgotten are now remembered.

Oh yes, Juanita Neato thinks. I'll stay. Yes, I'll stay.

x x x

Oh, says the man in the powder-blue suit, reading the final page. But I

x x x

You should go to the door, Sandals Julius says. They're waiting out there, afraid to knock.

"Who's out there?" Sister Nettles asks.

They've seen you working to make the barbecue for them.

"They who, Jules?"

Go and see.

Muttering, Sister Nettles rises, crosses the empty floor of the Neon Chapel to the door, which she opens, and she's astounded by the collection of gathered loonies and gangsters, civilians of Checkertown and denizens of Domino City, the lost and the losing, the helpless and the dangerous and the deadly and the hurt. They're waiting on the porch and spread across the lawn, captured by the sight of a fingerless lady who still somehow intends to try to work the barbecue tongs. They've come, hoping some good work might be set before them, waiting expectantly for her to speak.

x x x

Oh, says the man in the powder-blue suit, reading the final page. But I

x x x

Three days later, it was more of a stupor than a meltdown Gordy finally pulled himself out of.

o h

Come, wave, come, you think. It's the game of the blank. Let's have it. Then, following three breaths—deep, fast, preparatory—you look, finally, at the new pages.

"Oh," you say. "But I

You disappear. It's the damnedest thing. There's a feeling of falling that's almost like flying; falling not down but into. The page you'd been holding drifts, seesaw, through the air, coming to rest softly on the floor.

—Jordan Yunus, *Subject to Infinite Change*

B L U E

Gordy sat in a field. The field lay atop a crest of a high foothill; farther on, behind him, the green mountains reached for the sky. Below, he could see the town of Pigeon Forge, still unaccountably undrowned, untouched by fire from above, unpunished. So, Gordy thought, Morris wins after all—everything you tried, everything you did, everything you risked; it really was all for nothing. There truly will be no final accounting.

It would be better if you were dead.

x x x

After his three-day swoon, he'd found himself in a different field than this one, lower down, beside the circus staging area and the fountain. The circus had been packed away but the fountain remained. The morning dew had grown on the grass and soaked his clothes. Gordy kept still, hidden in the deep grass, trying to once again pass out of knowledge of himself, but catatonia, or even sleep, proved elusive. At last, bored, he'd risen in late morning and made his way through the hip-high grass to the treeline on the horizon, his back to the fountain as it receded and dwindled until distance at last claimed it. The treeline was a narrow strip of spruce, demarcating the field he'd crossed from another identical field beyond. If you follow this treeline, Gordy thought, you'll find a ridge. Follow the ridge, you'll reach the mountains eventually. He couldn't think of a single reason not to do so.

He'd climbed about an hour upward and the strip of woods had widened out into forest when he happened upon the gorilla. Startled, Gordy froze. The ape sat with his back against a huge tree in contemplative posture. After long minutes, it swung its immense conical wedge of a head toward Gordy and fixed its tiny eyes upon him. They remained still for a long silent time, Gordy afraid to move, the gorilla watchful but unconcerned, inert, breaking his pose only occasionally to rub his giant back against the tree. At last, Wembly snorted his derision, turned, and crashed away through the brush, heading lower down. Gordy heard him going for a long time after he'd lost sight of him in the trees. He went more cautiously then, aware of every woodland sound, at once frightened of, and sympathetic toward, the displaced ape, another creature caught up in events beyond his understanding, wandering from nowhere toward nothing.

In time, the woods thinned again to a narrow band and finally attenuated entirely, and Gordy again found himself wading through grass. Guided by his ears, he found a waterfall feeding a pool. He drank deeply, then stripped and bathed and laid himself out to dry. Rested, he followed the water upstream until at last he came to a level field, from which he realized Pigeon Forge could be seen. As good a place as any to watch the end of the world.

So: Gordy sat in the field, but the world failed to end. It would be better if I were dead, Gordy thought again. Night came, and with it the cold, and still he could see the lights of Pigeon Forge below: spangle and flash and ditz of light, never to be extinguished. There's the world for you, Gordy decided; the mean get meaner, the cruel old show will go on and on. After a while, without lying down, he slept, and dreamed he was the gorilla, and that his back itched. He went to scratch it against the tree, but there was no respite; either there was no tree there behind him, or else his back was somewhere else, somewhere beneath the roof of his mouth. He was awake for a long time before he realized he wasn't a gorilla, and the realization did not improve his mood. The sun came on and the sky grew bright and dazzling blue—not a cloud in it from end to end. This is what I needed, Gordy thought. Something uncomplicated. Something perfect. He looked out into the sky.

Beautiful day, Julius said.

"If you say so," Gordy muttered, annoyed to be returned from monochrome reverie and blue oblivion.

Look around you. You wouldn't say lovely?

"What's the point, though?"

There rarely is one. *Only* one, I mean.

"You sound like that crackpot. Landrude."

Oh, yes, Julius said, sounding merry—I remember him. He took himself even more seriously than he expected us to. I wouldn't worry about him. He's somewhere safe.

"Who's worried about *him*? Morris has all the power he ever wanted."

Morris is only partially his name. He's also named—

"I don't care about his name. He's alive and my dad isn't. Thousands of others aren't. Who knows what he's done to the rest of them, and who could count all the years he stole from them? It all goes on like before. *He* goes on like before—but now with total control—doesn't he?"

Well...why not just...you know...*ask* him? Julius said.

"What?"

See for yourself.

Gordy looked up; Morris stood some distance away, holding something in his hand. It was...Gordy squinted...a book. They eyed each other in silence, and Gordy was reminded powerfully of his encounter with the gorilla the day before.

Finally, Morris called out: "Can I join you?"

"Do I have a choice?"

Morris started saying something, but stopped. Finally he said, "Yes, of course you have a choice. You always have a choice. So?"

"Free country," Gordy said. "As they say."

Morris came up and sat a few feet away. He took a long time; he limped ponderously.

"You missed a spot," Gordy sneered.

"I don't follow." Gordy realized he'd never heard Morris speak in a quiet moment. His voice held a deep and abiding sadness.

"When you were healing everyone up. You're still limping around."

"I..." Morris paused. He shook his head. "I decided to keep that one. I came by it a bit more honestly than the others."

"Oh? Well, I'm real *proud* of you."

Morris said nothing.

"What a big man you are. Up on the cross for your sins. Walking around, free and clear. You should be going to one of your prisons."

"That's one of the options being considered. I'll accept whatever they decide."

"They?"

"All of them. They're still down there, talking over…everything."

"Just talking about what to do to you?"

"There's a lot to discuss. It seems there was a nearly universal awareness of the coming wave, and what it meant, and of some…other realizations about the nature of reality," Morris says. "Many are already making themselves forget what they knew in the moment, but many aren't. People are gathering at specific points of interest—here in Pigeon Forge, back at Loony Island—finally looking to places they've long ignored for answers."

Nothing was said for a long time. That was fine with Gordy. They could sit without talking forever, as far as Gordy was concerned. However long Morris could sit quietly, Gordy decided, that long plus one minute more was how long he, Gordy, could sit quietly. Gordy decided there was nothing he'd like better than to sit here, in this place, and never say another word. He'd listen to the crickets. Gordy listened to the crickets.

"I suppose this is your chance to tell me you're rehabilitated," Gordy said. "Tell me how much you've learned. How much you've grown."

"I don't know what I've learned," Morris said. "I'm still not even sure of what I am."

"You're still Morris. That's all I need to know."

"That's more than I know," Morris said. "But it's the name I've decided to keep. It's the appearance I've decided to keep. These people have the right to deal with the face that harmed them, however they see fit."

"Fun riddle."

"It hasn't been much fun so far."

"Boo-hoo," Gordy said flatly. "So you're here to—what? Say 'I'm sorry' for all the torture and murder and enslavement and whatnot?"

"There's nothing I can say or do to answer to all that."

Gordy stood up and walked a little way away. "What do you want from me, then? What did you hike all the way out here looking for? Absolution? Piss off. You've got your power. You've got your empire back. You've got everything you ever wanted. You change or get destroyed—that was the deal. I guess you changed."

"I certainly have awareness I didn't have before. I hope I'm something other than I was."

"Well. I didn't *want* you to change. You don't deserve to change."

"I can't disagree with that," Morris said. He stared at the grass. Gordy wanted to rush him then, punch him, scratch, gouge, bash, anything to get him to take some sort of posture that could be contended with, fought against, beaten, destroyed. "Well...*great*. So, if you have something to say, say it. Then, go. Scamper. Bug off. Leave."

"I came to bring you something, actually. We cut it out of the safe that fell from the sky. It was the only thing we found in there." Morris held out the book, and Gordy, after a slow suspicious moment, took it, and read the cover:

SUBJECT TO INFINITE CHANGE
A Novel
By JORDAN YUNUS

Morris said: "A few of us read it. We decided you should have it. And... it was decided I was probably the best one to bring it to you, considering."

With deliberate incuriosity, Gordy tossed the book beside him. "Thanks. Are we done?"

Morris looked at him meaningfully. "I wanted you to know," he said. "That *I've* decided I'm staying."

"Staying?"

"Yes. I'm not going back."

"Back?"

"Yes." Then, sensing more needed to be said, he added: "Back behind the door? I've abdicated, I suppose. I'm done trying to craft it. It's better to let everybody craft this story themselves. I'd rather see what they do with it, to be honest. On the other side, as an author again, I think I'd just make a mess. The group gathering around Pigeon Forge is looking to Jane right now for leadership." At her name, Morris looks down, remembering a particular shame. "Or...I called her 'Jane.' She's a good choice for leadership—you might say she's a good *draw*."

"You're making no sense."

Morris looked at him searchingly, then wide-eyed. At last he whistled and said: "Jane's right. You really still don't know, do you?"

"Better still, I don't even care. *Now* are we done?"

Morris put his hand on Gordy's shoulder. No, thought Gordy. Apparently not.

"What I'm saying is, *I'm* not going back. That's my choice, you understand—just mine. It doesn't have to be…anybody else's. But *I'm* staying."

"Sure you're staying. You with your ticket."

"What, *that?* I don't have it anymore." Morris laughed. "Happier to be rid of it. I gave it to a nice lady with whom I believe you are well acquainted. She's sharing it with Jane for now, but I think she'll be using it soon enough. She said she had some exploring to do. 'Other Attics to discover,' is how I think she put it. But look—" he raised his feet, each in turn. "She gave me this nifty pair of sandals. They're how I found you." As he said this, for the first time, Morris seemed free of the sadness. Gordy tried, without success, to say something. After a while, Morris said, awkwardly: "That's it, then. I'll leave you to it." He walked away and Gordy was alone again.

Gordy sat in the field. After a while the sandals said: So let me get this straight. You're *angry* with how this turned out?

"He doesn't deserve to end up that way. He deserves what Donk gave him."

And for that, you'd condemn all those animals—and many people, too?

"It's the pointlessness of it, Jules. The whole thing was rigged. A big setup. If the story was always on rails heading toward a specific station at a specific time, why not just do it? Why the production? And why *me?* Why force me to have to be the one?"

You're not seeing it, the sandals said, because you don't want to see. Landrude wasn't completely lying to us, you know—about the doughnuts, the possibilities, the choice. And it wasn't ever about the ticket, you know. Not really.

"Then what was it about, *really?*"

Landrude was right about interpretation—and wrong. He only saw them affecting physical manifestations. But we readers, and we creations: We don't just decide how it looks. We decide what it *means.*

"But why even make it a choice? Why make me the middle man in some moralizing transfiguring partially visible comic book freak-show nonsense?"

Sandals Julius spoke then, peaceful and quiet.

Don't you know? they said. They said, Jordan, haven't you realized it yet?

Feeling himself possessed of some unstoppable momentum, perched on the lip of a precipice, annoyed at the sudden precariousness of his position, Gordy looked up once again into the unvarying simplicity of the sky. He stared up into all that endless blue. He stared until it surrounded him on all sides, until he felt he was falling straight up into it.

—A. R. MOXON, THE REVISIONARIES

ACKNOWLEDGMENTS

It couldn't have happened otherwise, and it couldn't have happened without these people:

Early readers, who provided the encouragement and perspective every writer desires and needs. You were my rocket fuel: Sue Brooks, Charity Kilbourn, Paul Loukides, Karen Moore, Beth Raese, Peter Sobanski, Scott Taylor, Mary Vanderploeg, Emily Vietor, Martin Vietor, Brad Willis, Walter Wolf, Hal Wyss, the entire WPBT, and most especially the artist and musician Juanito Moore, the most frequent reader, who crafted the comics page featuring cats you'll find between these covers.

Family: my wonderful wife, Linda, and my three wonderful daughters, who are the reason (along with coffee) that I get up early each morning, and who give me the support and love and joy that makes the writing I do (and everything else I do) worth it; my parents, Ruth and Roger—I love you.

Kind friends; professionals in the publishing world who offered their valuable time to guide and advise me well before there was ever a book deal: Kerry Cullen, Benjamin Dreyer, John Hartness, Brooks Sherman, and Suz Brockmann.

My excellent agent, Sam Morgan, who shepherded a trembly-legged new writer (that'd be me) through a strange and wonderful and occasionally disorienting process. Sam rules. Thank you for ruling, Sam.

All the good people at Melville House who brought their formidable skills to this project, including but by no means limited to: Dennis Johnson and Valerie Merians, who decided to give my book a home; my editor, Michael Barron, who took a first-timer's ambitious and weirdly shaped sword swing, and gave the blade an edge and a direction even while it was in motion (Michael, you're a magician and I thank you); Melville's extraordinarily patient and encouraging production director Susan Rella; also: Stuart Calderwood, Stephanie DeLuca, Marina Drukman, Archie Ferguson, Beste Miray Doğan, Alex Primiani, Michael Seidlinger, Amelia Stymacks,

Tim McCall, and Simon Reichley. You made my book real. I'm forever in your debt.

Finally, my very good friend, Ben Colmery, who 20 years ago took a writing prompt I'd given him, about a man who was surprised to learn he was a pair of sandals, and returned a weird little story about a meeting of friends in a grocery that moves to a donut shop—but only after avoiding the interruptions of an annoying fellow who won't stop talking about all the reasons he will never return to Pigeon Forge, Tennessee. For years, we expanded the idea further and further, and made it weirder, and weirder, and weirder, and wondered what it all might mean. Well Ben, it sure has changed since those years, but this is what I think we meant. Hope you like it.